THE BOOKS OF EL

THE BOOKS OF EL

***

ELOAH
Book One

ELOHIM
Book Two

EL
Book Three

ELOAH · ELOHIM · EL

THE BOOKS OF EL

AT THE DAWN OF THE EARTH, THE MASTERS OF
THE UNIVERSE WALKED THE PLANET.
NOW A PORTAL OPENS TO THEIR LONG-LOST WORLD....

JEFF NESBIT

BroadStreet
PUBLISHING

The Books of El

Broadstreet Publishing
2745 Chicory Road
Racine, WI 53403
Broadstreetpublishing.com

Published in partnership with **OakTara Publishers, www.oaktara.com**

Cover design by Yvonne Parks at www.pearcreative.ca
Cover and interior design © 2014 by OakTara Publishers
Cover image © iStockphoto.com/Duncan Walker/Selahattin Bayram
Author photo © Jeff Nesbit

Copyright © 2014, Jeff Nesbit; © 2008, Jeff Nesbit (*The Magician's World Trilogy*).
All rights reserved.

All rights reserved. No part of this publication may be reproduced, stored in a retrieval system, or transmitted in any form or by any means without the prior written permission of the publisher. The only exception is brief quotations in professional reviews.

ISBN-13: 978-1-4245-9903-5 ▪ ISBN-10: 1-4245-9903-2
eISBN-13: 978-1-4245-9902-8 ▪ eISBN-10: 1-4245-9902-4

The Books of El is a work of fiction. References to real people, events, establishments, organizations, or locales are intended only to provide a sense of authenticity and are used fictitiously. All other characters, incidents, and dialogue are drawn from the author's imagination. The perspective, opinions, and worldview represented by this book are those of the author and are not intended to be a reflection or endorsement of the publishers' views.

Printed in the U.S.A.

ELOAH
Book One

***

PROLOGUE

Araqiel had never seen anyone with a mind such as Laura's, not in the immense span of time he'd watched for someone like her. And to find her here, near the Wiccan forge. It was extraordinary. She had the ability, and the other two in the trinity were close at hand.

For Laura, the concept of God was a manifestation of the human race's intellectual frailty, and Satan was nothing more than an ancient myth.

Araqiel's eyes flashed mischievously as he watched Laura's mastery. A strange smile flickered across his face.

"You are my magician—may you also someday be our *Eloah*," he said quietly. "Discover what others before you have failed to unearth. Forge a path again for the *bene elohim,* and deliver them from this place of desolation."

1

***

WATCHING

You could feel the pressure. It cascaded off the walls, careened around the room, and settled uneasily on every shoulder. One of the students repeatedly tapped the end of his nicely sharpened, number-two pencil on his desk as they passed out the test.

The hall monitors had spread the desks apart to make sure no one cheated. Not that it would have mattered anyway. It was hardly the kind of test on which you could cheat. Either you understood organic chemistry or you didn't.

And it soon became apparent that the kid with the nicely sharpened, number-two pencil didn't understand organic. He'd prayed to understand it. He'd sweated to understand it. He'd pulled three all-nighters in a row to come to grips with it.

All to no avail. He was a complete, utter failure. His $500 hand-held calculator, a present from his parents this past Christmas, could handle derivatives, logarithms, and compute the distance to the sun within six decimal places, but it was worthless to him now. His graph paper, bound in an expensive leather folder, mocked him as he struggled to pull answers from the mist of his confused mind. The lines blurred, despite his best efforts to concentrate.

He tapped his pencil again absent-mindedly. Oblivious to everything around him, he began to mutter. Then he stepped up the cadence of his tapping. The tapping grew louder and then louder still…

"Shut up!" a male voice roared from the back of the room.

"Yeah, if you can't hack it, you know where the door is," said someone else.

Laura smiled to herself. The test was a breeze. They'd probably use hers to set the grading curve. She looked over at the pencil-tapper, who would undoubtedly bring up the bottom of the curve, with disgust. He had no right to sit in this classroom. Who did he think he was, anyway? He'd change his major—to something harmless like political science or maybe sociology—by the end of his freshman year. She was certain of that.

Except for an occasional nervous cough, the class settled into an uneasy silence. The pencil-tapper stopped muttering and started to shake his legs nervously instead. Then he ran his hands through his hair.

At last, he could stand it no longer. With tears streaming down his face, he leaped from his desk, toppling it in the opposite direction. He crumpled his test paper, flung it toward the nearest hall monitor, and smashed his expensive calculator against the wall as he fled the room.

Laura felt no pity as she watched him leave. None whatsoever. He was better off. Obviously, he wasn't tough enough or intelligent enough. He'd buckled under the pressure, something she would never do.

Fifteen minutes later, with a supreme, satisfied air of confidence radiating in every direction, she handed in her test. She hadn't even bothered to look it over much after she'd finished. She'd known the stuff cold. She always did.

Only one person watched her exit—a hall monitor who'd kept his eyes riveted in her direction during much of the test. Well over six feet tall, with blond hair and blue eyes, he had a powerful, imposing, athletic build and a guileless face. It wasn't the first time he had watched her prowess and almost regal bearing, nor would it be the last. He'd been to the ancient places, many times, in almost every corner of the learned world. Always watching those with the gift, with the potential. Like Laura.

He had never seen anyone with a mind such as Laura's, though, not in the immense span of time he'd watched for someone like her. To find her here, in such a place, near the Wiccan forge, was extraordinary. She had the ability. And the other corners of the trinity were close at hand, finally.

Laura was unique and single-minded in her pursuit. She was an agnostic, believing in nothing but her own quest for ultimate knowledge—in what she alone might be able to understand and master. No higher principalities or powers even seemed possible to her. To Laura, the concept of God was a manifestation of the human race's intellectual frailty, and Satan was but an ancient myth.

No one paid any attention to the watcher. His job, one he had relentlessly and tirelessly pursued for a very long time, was to observe. He was dressed casually, in the style of most of the grad students who populated Duke's campus. You could tell right off he wasn't one of the undergraduates. He was much more serious than that. But now his eyes flashed mischievously. A strange smile flickered.

"You are my magician. May you also someday be our *Eloah*," he said quietly. "Discover what others before you have failed to unearth. Forge a path again for the *bene elohim,* and deliver them from this place of desolation."

2

***

THE PRIEST

"How's your thesis coming along these days, Jon? Perhaps I can help you with your bibliography?" Dr. Logan tossed the question out casually, in between sips of tea.

"Oh, I'm in great shape," Jon said breezily. "I'm satisfied with my bibliography. Just need to work on some of the philosophical underpinnings, that's all."

Dr. Logan smiled benignly, precisely as a good college processor should—teeth not too prominent, eyes fawning yet commanding, jaw set squarely. But Jon knew better. He'd seen that intense, yet patient, manner tried under too many circumstances to fall for it this time.

He doesn't care in the slightest about my pretentious thesis, Jon thought bitterly. *It's a good thing I don't need him. He's not on my advisory panel, and I've already suffered through his intolerable Eastern religion classes. What an outrageous bore! Who gives a flying gazebo about the shift in western literature toward transcendental Buddhism? Or the overarching theme of Shiva in the never-ending cycle of war?*

So he can stuff his bibliographies, Jon thought smugly. *The last thing I need is his interference. I'm not like the rest of his idiot graduate students who do his dirty work and watch helplessly as he reaps the professional and literary harvest.*

"That's nice, Jon." Dr. Logan lightly dabbed his mouth with a napkin. "Please let me know if I can be of any assistance. Really, I do mean it."

"Thank you, sir, I appreciate your offer. I'll keep it in mind," Jon answered brightly.

Carefully, so he wouldn't be noticed, Jon's eyes flitted around the cafeteria, hoping to spot someone who could rescue him from this ghastly predicament. Under normal circumstances, Jon was an artful master at avoiding direct confrontations with people he detested. Call it intuition or luck; he had a knack for easing his way past trouble spots. Rarely, if ever, had he encountered a situation he couldn't handle, either by deception or stealth.

But today was obviously an unfortunate exception. Too much of a good thing the night before, and his brain was tired from the ordeal. Why, oh why, had he stayed up until three in the morning discussing Plato's Cave with those undergrads who'd stopped by? *I can't even remember what we decided,* he thought wistfully.

Still suffering under a buzzing headache from the night before, slurping down coffee to ease the pain, he'd never seen Dr. Logan slip up on him in the din of the cafeteria.

"By the way," Dr. Logan began again, looking intently into Jon's bloodshot eyes, "have you thought about your future plans? After graduation?"

"Not really," Jon lied. "After all, it's a good year or so away. I don't see how I can possibly wrap up my thesis for at least two more semesters."

"I see," said Dr. Logan.

Actually, Jon had thought of nothing else for almost three years. He had his entire life mapped out. Duke's Divinity School wasn't Harvard or Yale, but Jon was here by choice. He could have gone to Yale's Divinity School. He was that gifted. But he liked what he had at Duke. He was perfectly content, right where he was in life. With a doctorate in religion from Duke, he could pretty much name his tune at any given university around the country.

If he was lucky, Duke would even offer him an associate professorship. Then he wouldn't be forced to give up his highly lucrative "hobby." He could suffer by on the meager wages afforded college professors while continuing to pull in scads of money from his second, very secret, profession.

Several years ago, trying to support a steady diet of cocaine on a graduate student stipend, Jon had stumbled across a little-known fact of life. You can make more money selling a little inspiration powder to your friends on campus than you can earn in almost any profession. The beauty of it was that, except for the hair-raising necessity of buying the initial load of cocaine from the shady wholesalers in downtown Durham, North Carolina, there was very little actual risk. Jon lived by just two credos: never give anything away free and sell only to tried-and-true friends.

With the steady income from his "hobby," Jon could indulge wholeheartedly in the aimlessness of graduate school. It was a way of life he could not easily renounce.

Jon could afford to wander carelessly through the fruits of the world with no thought for tomorrow. For tomorrow would bring only more friends to his doorstep, eager to step magically through the doors only cocaine could open.

With an inaudible sigh of relief, Jon spotted one of his grad school classmates— an imposing, blond-haired, blue-eyed behemoth who almost seemed too large for the classroom—and waved his hand high in recognition. Jon scoured his memory for the student's name. It was a strange name, something like Araqiel. Other kids just called him Eric, if Jon remembered correctly. Did he know him from the History of Calvinism? Augustine's City of God? *No,* Jon thought, *it's neither of those. It's another class, one I'm taking this semester because I've only met him recently.*

Then it came to him. Eric was auditing Jon's advanced New Testament course, the one required of every doctoral student in the divinity school. Jon argued against the divinity of Jesus incessantly in this class, insisting that Jesus was not the son of God—or, to be precise, a son of man who was also God's divine son.

For there was a difference. Unlike the unwashed masses, Jon knew that the phrase "son of God" in the Bible usually referred to an angel or demon. That was, most likely, why Jesus always referred to himself as the son of man—to emphasize that he was a man, not an angel. It was Jesus' followers who believed that he was God's human son, who came to Earth to redeem human souls.

But Jon wanted nothing of that. Jesus was an interesting philosopher, perhaps one of the best. But he was not God's son, not by any stretch of the imagination, Jon believed. Invariably, when Jon argued this position, he was alone in this class. Except with Eric. While Eric largely spent his time simply watching Jon's antics, Jon could always rely on Eric to serve as his "amen chorus" on this issue.

Eric did seem like a passive sort, though. Not the type to actually take sides or do anything proactive. *No matter*, Jon considered. *He'll have to do for now.*

"Oh, I'm glad I bumped into you," Jon called out blithely when Eric was within earshot. "Can I borrow your notes from our last class? I couldn't make it."

Eric gave Jon a curious look, as if he somehow knew Jon was lying, for whatever reason. But the expression was swiftly replaced by a broad smile. "Sure." Araqiel handed Jon his notebook.

"Oh, thank you," Jon said with more enthusiasm than was needed, "but why don't I come copy these right now so you can have your notebook back?"

Blessedly, Eric continued to smile and simply look to Dr. Logan for his approval.

"Quite all right with me," Dr. Logan said beneficently. "I'm just enjoying a spot of tea."

"Great." Jon fairly leaped from his seat in his eagerness to flee. Once again, Lady Luck shone brilliantly in his corner of the world.

They found the nearest Xerox machine and, to keep appearances, Jon dutifully copied the notes from the previous class. His rescuer was strangely silent, answering Jon's questions in a cursory fashion.

Well, that's no skin off my nose, Jon thought as he handed the notes back. *We're like two ships passing in the night. Don't dent my prow, and I won't ram your hull.*

They each said a quick good-bye. Jon hurried around the nearest corner and promptly dropped the copied notes into the first available trash can.

Araqiel followed silently in Jon's wake, watching his every move intently.

"Until we meet again, my wayward priest," Araqiel said as Jon disappeared into a throng of students. "The *bene elohim* are calling. Minister to them well."

3

* * *

WARRIOR

*N*ow *is the test. Here is where it all pays off. I'm stronger than he is. I know I am. I have to be. One push here and it's all over...*

They rose in the crowded gym as one, stomping their feet and clapping their hands in rhythm. Like the spectators of ancient Rome, they could smell the blood, taste it, savor it. Defeat—and victory, of course—was only a moment away.

Most of the crowd had been there before. They'd seen the show dozens of times. Watching Samson work an opponent over was a study in exquisite physical torture. He rarely pinned anyone in the first round, or in the second for that matter.

No, Samson knew the physical and mental limits of his opponents as surely as he knew his own. He toyed with his foes as a cat would play with a wounded bird. He worked the crowd to a fever pitch and, at its zenith, slammed his opponent to the mat with a display of power and grace that always took the crowd's breath away. That was how the world saw Samson, possibly the greatest wrestler in Duke's storied athletic history.

Samson, of course, wasn't his real name. The son of Armenian immigrants who fled to America after the turn of the century to escape certain death at the hands of the Turks, Samson had been christened Armand Rothian. Later, when his prowess as a wrestler began to take shape in high school, he stumbled across the story of Samson in the Bible and promptly latched onto it.

Samson wasn't a religious person. In fact, he disdained religion as something for the weak of mind, body, and spirit. But he liked the myth of Samson so adopted his name.

Now, at Duke, only his closest friends knew his real name and his origin. To the world, he was just Samson, complete with long, dark brown hair he let grow wild. To most of the student body, he was a walking legend. To his professors, he was a troublemaker who rarely showed up for class.

And to himself, he was a seething cauldron of troubled, unbridled anger. He lived his parents' tragedy every waking moment of his life. Someday, he vowed, someday he would have his revenge. If not on the Turks with the blood still on their hands, then on their descendants. The world had forgotten the slaughter of more than a million Armenians, but Samson had not.

On the mat, he was free. He ceased to be a prisoner of his passion. On the mat, he turned his driving obsession into something useful. Only there could he transform the endless hours of practice and inner anguish into a tangible asset.

Tonight was no different. He'd intimidated his opponent from the first moment they'd faced each other during the weigh-in. It was hard not to be intimidated by Samson. Unlike most wrestlers, he'd realized long ago the folly of losing weight to drop down in class. It sapped your strength and your willpower.

Instead, Samson had lifted weights and run until he was a virtual tower of strength and stamina. Many of his opponents were taller, but none were stronger. And it was a rare person indeed who could match Samson's inner drive, his obsession to dominate his environment. As a result, Samson manhandled his opponents.

The first two periods had gone exactly according to form. He'd racked up more than enough points to coast to an easy win, while pushing his opponent to the edge of exhaustion. And then, halfway through the final round, Samson began to draw from his inner passion as he always did at this point in the match.

Here it is, he thought. *All mine. He'll give it up soon. He can't last much longer. Not much longer. His arms are tired. There's no strength left. He's just hanging on, hoping I won't stick it to him. But he's wrong.*

"SAM-SON! SAM-SON!" the crowd chanted in unison, their feet pounding the bleachers so hard the entire structure shuddered. Almost if they could read his mind, they could see him closing in for the kill.

It was over in seconds. Samson, in a mock gesture of impatience, released his opponent and let him stagger to his feet. And then, quick as a cat, he reached up and grabbed his opponent's head and right arm, pinning both under his own right arm. With a savage jerk, he pulled the head across his body and slammed his weary opponent to the mat.

"One, two, three," shouted the referee, spread-eagled on the mat to make sure his foe's shoulders were pinned flat. Satisfied, the referee slammed his right palm down with a resounding crack to end the match. A deafening roar lifted through the rafters as Samson leaped to his feet, his hands thrust high in victory.

A lone spectator—a strapping, blond-haired, blue-eyed grad assistant who equaled Samson's physical presence—kept his composure in the din as he watched the drama unfold. He was proud of his find. Samson was the last, absolutely essential part needed. It had been so long. They had all watched, and waited, for someone such as Samson to emerge in the same place, at the same time, as the others.

"My lord, you are magnificent. One of the mighty men of old," Araqiel said.

His words were lost in the madness of the moment.

4

***

JUST A FRAME OF MIND

The party is called a kegger. It's a weekly ritual. Most fraternities at Duke had at least one or two a year, and each frat had its own unique style.

The rich, preppie Betas ended theirs by throwing a color TV off the roof. The Phi Delts, the football team transplanted from the locker room to a foul-smelling haven of lust and avarice squarely in the middle of campus, liked to end theirs by setting one of the campus cop's pants legs on fire when he showed up to bring the party to a halt. The ATOs, who dressed and partied just right, invited only the crème de la crème of the female population, so naturally their parties were always quite well-attended.

Jon hadn't been to a kegger in years. He detested the things almost as much as he detested fraternities. As far as he was concerned, a fraternity was nothing more than a mass of discombobulated humanity groping for a sense of community. But he'd consented, grudgingly, to stop by one tonight. One of his best clients, a dear friend and a cocaine cowboy from way back, had invited a group of his old high school buddies to Duke for the weekend. Naturally, they'd need a little entertainment, and Jon, as always, was the logical choice as master of ceremonies.

He peered through the smoke-filled room, already littered with empty beer cans and half-smoked cigarettes, trying to find his friend. Reluctantly, he worked his way through the crowded space, glancing in all directions to make sure he wasn't missing some hidden corner.

A young girl, obviously a freshman, stepped squarely on the arch of Jon's left foot as she staggered past in a drunken, giggling stupor. Jon sighed indignantly and continued his trek across the barren wasteland of human frivolity. *Too bad I didn't take a few snorts before coming.* But, as always, business came before pleasure. It certainly wouldn't do to consummate a deal without a clear head.

Jon cased the entire room, but still no luck. *Maybe they wandered upstairs. At least the air's better than in here.*

Leaving the stale confines of the common room, Jon turned right down the nearest hallway, muttering darkly to himself.

12

He passed up the first stairwell he came to, where a couple sprawled in an unflattering position, then thought better of it. *Why should I let these dolts run my life?* Turning on his heels, he marched back to the stairs and cleared his throat. "Excuse me, please," he said loudly.

The intertwined couple parted for the briefest of moments, just long enough for Jon to slip through, before collapsing into each other's arms again. *Oh, the perils of college life....*

Once he'd reached the second floor, he realized the utter folly of his quest. Every room in these infernal dormitories looked the same. *You could wander for days in here and the landscape would never change.*

Off in the distance, down the hall to his left, Jon could hear shouts of drunken encouragement. Shrugging, he headed in that direction. He had no immediate plans anyway. Yet his curiosity grew as he drew near. The comments, drunken though they might be, were intriguing nevertheless.

"Throw the bird!" came one shout.

"No, you idiot, he'll eat it!" came another.

"So, big deal. It's worth a try!"

"You're both wrong," shouted a third voice. "That bird's finished. He won't help here."

"Yeah, that's right," said the first voice.

"Okay, so throw the axe!"

"And what if it doesn't work?"

"You got a better idea?"

"No, but you're a moron," shouted the first voice. "The axe only kills those slimy dwarfs."

"So maybe it kills dragons, too," said the second voice.

"Fat chance."

"Come on, it's worth a shot," urged the second voice. "Throw the thing."

There was a moment of silence, followed immediately by a staccato, violent outburst.

"Now look what you did, you toad!" shouted an unintelligible voice. "You gave our axe to the dragon!"

"How was I supposed to know he'd do that?" answered the second voice.

"Everybody knows you can't kill a dragon with a puny axe."

Jon wasn't prepared for what he stumbled into. He figured he'd seen nearly everything during his travels hither and yon, but this was a first.

Not only were more people crammed into one tiny dorm room than he'd thought was possible, but the object of their fascination astounded him. Sitting calmly at a desk, with inebriated coeds pressing in on all sides, was the blond-haired grad student, Araqiel, who'd given Jon his notes earlier in the day. Propped up on the desk in front of him was a 19-inch computer screen. Some sort of game was in full swing on the screen, and everyone in the room was into it. Araqiel seemed to be in charge of the show and took commands from all sides.

Whenever the crowd reached a consensus, he'd quickly type in the command, which would immediately be followed either by bellows of outrage or shouts of triumph.

Jon worked his way around the fringes of the crowded room to a better vantage point. *What's so fascinating about this?*

"All right, *now* what are we supposed to do?" said the first voice, which Jon now identified with a short, overweight, disheveled upperclassman who perched on the computer table with a mug of beer in one hand and a stubby cigar in the other.

"Give me a break," said the first voice, a gangly, freckle-faced kid with buck teeth, straight-legged jeans, and a beer-stained Hawaiian shirt. "You're the genius. You get us out of here."

"I'm not leaving without that axe," said Stubby.

"All right. Go get it then," said Buck Teeth.

A moment of silence as the blond-haired student typed in a few words—Jon was still too far away to see what exactly was transpiring—and Stubby let out another monstrous roar. "You moron! We can't get the axe back from the dragon."

"Then let's get out of here," said Buck Teeth.

"Yeah, we've got the gold and the jewelry," said a fourth voice, which belonged to a clean-cut, pimple-faced preppy who wore his brand-name collar turned up. "Let's high-tail it back to the water tower."

"And just how are we supposed to get out of here?" said Stubby.

"The way we came in," said Preppy.

Stubby waved his mug of beer high. "Anybody here remember the way back?" He was met by a chorus of blank stares and sheepish grins. "See, we're all lost. No choice but to go on. Tallyho," he said and took a big gulp of beer.

Jon was definitely confused. Obviously, they were playing a game, using the computer as a tool. But what sort of game? He slipped between two girls who'd lost interest and had decided to compare eye shadow instead. He bypassed a kid in a frat beanie who was obviously debating whether he was going to throw up or not.

Ducking under the arm of a basketball player, or someone masquerading as one, Jon finally positioned himself where he could see the screen of the computer. The game, he soon discovered, was fairly simple and straightforward. It was a pretty fancy version of a medieval Dungeons & Dragons game, with the latest accelerated graphics and 360-degree view control. The 3-D characters were so real they almost jumped off the screen.

The adventurers were exploring an underground cavern replete with monsters, unusual dangers, and treasures galore. To conquer each new predicament required a smattering of problem-solving logic, intuition, and just plain luck.

The problems seemed simple enough, but they clearly had this crowd stumped. When the computerized, 3-D adventurers finally "died" at the hands of one of the slimy underground dwarfs, the wayward adventurers had accumulated only a fraction of the points possible in the game.

His curiosity piqued, Jon decided to stick around after the game broke up and the spectators drifted out of the dorm room. He grabbed a seat next to the blond-haired grad student, obviously the progenitor of the night's festivities. Jon felt a little awkward. Even sitting down, Araqiel towered over Jon.

"I find this fascinating." Araqiel swiveled slightly to meet Jon's curious gaze. He typed in a couple end commands before turning the machine off. "It's the very first Zork. Someone added graphics to go along with the text. Interesting, isn't it?"

"I guess so…Araqiel. But what is it, exactly?"

"It's a game, Jon. And you can just call me Eric. Everyone does."

"Okay, Eric." Jon frowned. "But what I meant was…what kind of game?"

"It's pure fantasy." A funny smile played across Eric's face. "It lets you escape to a place where the dangers aren't real and the rewards are pure illusion."

"Everything is pure illusion. Nothing is real," Jon said wryly.

"You're a gnostic, I see."

"No. Just a cynical mystic…"

"…who doesn't believe in himself." Eric finished Jon's sentence.

"Maybe." Jon shrugged. "What's there to believe in?"

"Your soul, the gods, salvation, immortality, the battle between good and evil…"

Jon was beginning to like this blue-eyed innocent. *Rare indeed is the person who has a taste for philosophical warfare.* "An illusion, nothing more. As fruitless as the search for a Holy Grail," Jon said firmly.

"What of the world's major religions?"

"Grand, hero-worshiping delusions, founded on ancient myths."

"The human spirit?"

"No such thing. Something we've cooked up to keep ourselves from going mad at the thought of our own demise."

"Love?"

"An emotion."

"Evil?"

"The natural state of humankind."

"Hell?"

"A frame of mind."

"Heaven?"

"A literary construct."

Eric broke into a broad, radiant smile. "All right, I give in. You're the expert on religion, not me. But, tell me, if you don't believe in anything, why choose religion as a profession?"

"Why not? What else, besides politics, offers such a wide variety of thought and argument?" *Brother, would my religion profs drop dead if they knew what I was really like*, Jon thought grimly.

"Oh, I can think of a few things," Eric said. "Take science. It's unlocking doors to worlds we never knew existed before. Take the new theory of holographic physics, for instance, that seems to show we're all just 3D projections of a 2D world."

"I know, I know," Jon said confidently. "Like C.S. Lewis and some others, you probably believe in transcendent realities that superimpose themselves on this world. If we only imagine or look hard enough, we'll stumble onto greater realities. That's as old as Plato, and no one's ever proven it yet."

"Haven't they?"

"Not to my knowledge," Jon answered.

"Perhaps you haven't asked the right questions." Eric arched his eyebrows.

Jon stared hard at him. "Maybe you're right. Then again, maybe you're not. And there's no judge in sight."

"I suppose you *are* right." Eric sighed. "But it's a shame."

"What is?"

"That your theory of reality prevents you from searching for deeper truths or even wondering if, just perhaps, the world we see with our own eyes isn't what it seems. Inherently believing a Holy Grail doesn't exist naturally precludes the possibility you might jump on a horse to gallop off on a magnificent quest, doesn't it?"

"I suppose so," Jon said wistfully. "But I'm usually game for anything. I suppose you could say I'll try anything once—even believing in something that doesn't exist."

"Nice philosophy. Arrogant, but utilitarian."

"Just practical," Jon said. He *was* arrogant, but with good reason. No one had ever challenged his spiritual prowess, and he doubted anyone ever would.

"I think I can." Eric smiled.

"What? You can what?"

"Challenge you."

"But I didn't…"

"You didn't have to," Eric said quickly. "It's written all over your face. You're begging for a new challenge, something you can sink your teeth into."

"Maybe," Jon said cautiously.

"Well, I think I can give it to you. If you give me a chance."

"What do I have to do?" Jon narrowed his eyes suspiciously.

"Play a game," Eric said simply.

"A what?"

"A game. Like the one you saw tonight."

"A *fantasy* game?" Jon asked skeptically.

"Yes, but you'll quickly see there's more to it than that. If you have *imagination*."

"Don't worry. I'm not lacking in that department," Jon said hotly.

"Then you'll play? You'll take part?" Eric asked with a bemused half-smile.

He's mocking me, Jon thought, *and there's nothing I can do about it. Except beat him at his own game.* "Sure, why not?" Jon found himself saying. "What do I have to do?"

"Not a thing," Eric said confidently. "I'll take care of the details. Just show up with a clear head when I call."

"And when will that be?"

"Soon, very soon." He laughed easily. "Before you know it, in fact."

5

***

LAURA'S BANE

The date was over almost as soon as it had begun, at least as far as Laura was concerned. In fact, she'd come close to walking. She'd done it before and doubtless she'd do it again.

Oh, how she hated the little boys at Duke. That's what they were, after all. Just little boys, pretenders to the throne of manhood. One day, yes, they would be grown up—doctors, lawyers, certified public accountants, sociologists, and who knew what else. But not now, not at Duke, while they were college sophomores and juniors. Now they were drunken louts with foul mouths and more arms than an octopus.

This night had been worse than most, though, if that was possible. Laura grimaced as she thought about how sweet he'd been in biology class, borrowing her notes and asking her out with a poem at the top when he returned them. She'd almost hoped it would be different this time. Almost hoped.

It had begun fine—dinner at Mario's, a serenade at their table, and then an early movie. But it degenerated fast…a casual hand slipped across her knees, an ensuing arm wrestle, and angry stares at the characters flickering on the screen. It was obvious the guy could barely control his rage in the theater. It didn't take him long to unload when they were out in the open air, walking through the main quad to a frat party.

"What's your problem?" he said with a sneer.

"No problem," Laura snapped.

"Sure." He laughed sarcastically. "Then why'd you get all bent out of shape over a harmless little touch?"

"Harmless?"

"It's not like I was trying to rape you," he protested.

"Really? And what do you call it?"

"Oh, brother, you're a hard case."

"Not really."

"Give me a break. I mean, what are you anyway? Some kind of nun?"

Laura stopped dead in her tracks. She pivoted slowly to face him, wondering if she shouldn't give him a *real* piece of her mind. But, no, that wouldn't do either of them any good. "Are you always this rude to your dates?" she said quietly.

He paused in mid-retort. "No, I'm not," he said instead. "But I usually don't get the door slammed in my face quite so hard either."

He was fishing for an apology. She wasn't about to give him the satisfaction.

"Who gave you the right to come knocking like that in the first place?"

"What in the...?"

"Oh, never mind," she said sharply, turning away from her date. "It's pointless."

"What is?" he asked, following after her quickly.

"You. This date. This school. Relationships in general."

"You left out life and the universe, I think," he said breezily.

That made Laura laugh. All right, maybe she *was* a hard case. Too demanding. Maybe she asked more of the opposite sex than they were willing to give. But she had a right to ask, didn't she? A right to look? And if she came up empty, well....

"Look," Laura said with the sweetest voice she could possibly muster, "why don't we call a truce for now? See how things go from here on out?"

"Fine by me," he said with a shrug.

But he'd given up already. The hunt had ended. Laura could tell because she'd had plenty of practice. *You can't stick pins in their little-boy ego like that, deflate their balloon so easily*, she warned herself.

He tried again later on, of course, almost because it was expected. More than once. At the frat party, he tried other methods. But there were no sudden moves this time. No, now it was more subtle. A light touch, a casual brush. Laura almost smiled as she watched him slowly try to work his way through her defenses.

The worst part of the night, though, wasn't the physical pressure. She could handle that easily. It was the intellectual mauling she was forced to endure at the hands of this mindless twit.

The guy never shut up about himself. Laura barely managed to get a word in edgewise the entire night. He was well on his way to medical school, he planned to be a millionaire through investments by the time he was 35, he had a stock brokerage firm picked out, he'd visited half a dozen medical schools already, he sailed on weekends, he ran five miles each morning to keep in shape, he had one of the largest CD collections on campus, he...

Laura closed her mind to the steady stream of self-absorbed drivel several hours before the evening had ended. It was her only hope of salvaging some peace of mind. But the guy never even noticed her eyes had glazed over. He just droned on.

At the door to her room, he gave it one last valiant try, sliding his hand down her backside as he pulled her close for an embrace and a kiss. Because he'd been such a jerk, Laura gave him a viciously aggressive French kiss he wouldn't forget for a while, then yanked away in a rush, said good night quickly, and stepped through her door.

She could picture him panting outside her door, wondering stupidly what he'd done wrong, why he wasn't inside her room. *Serves the jerk right,* she thought smugly. *He'll figure it out someday.*

But as she collapsed on her bed, bone tired from fending off the guy's advances all night and weary from the mind-numbing, one-sided conversation, Laura succumbed to the depression that had trailed her like a shadow in recent weeks.

Since one of her only friends—a very sweet but troubled girl who had been as unlucky in love as anyone Laura had ever known—had ended her life by walking off the top of the chapel that towered over campus, Laura had been unable to shake the sadness that closed in around her when she was alone. Nights like these made it worse, much worse.

Jennifer had been abused badly by a hometown sweetheart—an unwanted abortion, a couple beatings and, when he visited the campus occasionally, some of the worst shouting and shrieking matches imaginable. Jen's only solace had been a church of Wicca nearby. Jen talked incessantly about how the Wiccan religious movement had been founded in North Carolina, of all places. She said she'd found women who didn't judge her and helped her understand the meanings of the natural world. Laura thought the entire thing was absurd but said nothing and just listened.

The boyfriend had introduced Jen to all manner of strange things and even stranger places. Laura wasn't entirely sure what all Jen had been into. But Laura never dreamed, not for a moment, that it would lead to suicide. Still, in the back of her mind, she wondered if maybe she'd overlooked something. A clue. Perhaps she could have stopped Jen in time, talked her into seeing someone…

"No!" she said loudly, the word sounding strange in the empty room. "It wasn't my fault, and I'm not sitting in here another minute." She bolted from the bed, threw on a sweater, and fled the room without a thought for where she was going. Anywhere. It didn't matter.

The bright, full moon and the brilliant, starry night startled Laura as she hurried out into the darkness. Funny she hadn't noticed it before. A soft breeze lightly tossed her black hair around her slight shoulders. It was a wonderful night for just walking.

Unconsciously, Laura headed across campus toward some of the lighted walkways that crisscrossed much of the Duke forest. There were dozens of such walkways at every corner of the campus because the school owned most or all of the forest surrounding the Gothic campus grounds. The walkways were, generally speaking, safe even in the dead of night. It had been some time since someone had reported a rape on campus so Laura didn't give much thought to the possibility.

That's why she didn't notice the leaves rustling in her wake or the occasional shadow that flitted across the walkway 30 or so yards behind her. She didn't hear the snap of a heavy twig or the labored breathing. It never broke her consciousness.

Laura was too full of the evening—too absorbed and lightheaded with the fragrance of the night air and the musky scent of the fallen leaves in the forest—to notice the dark shape as it stepped onto the path at a point where the towering trees of the forest blocked the light of the moon and the stars.

Her pursuer, a greedy smile plastered on his face, followed Laura, picking up the pace with every step. He knew a shriek here, at this place along the pathway, wouldn't be heard. He couldn't believe his luck. The voices had told him she would be here, in this place, and that he could have her. The voices had been right. She was here, as promised. The place was perfect—more than a mile to the nearest building, too far for his quarry to outrun him. It had been a long wait for such an opportunity.

Laura finally felt the pursuit in some corner of her mind. She swiveled in sudden fear as a cold shiver of warning swept through her. She had just enough time to catch the man's leering face bearing down on her. A shriek rose in her throat.

But the cry of terror never came. Laura's pursuer halted dead in his tracks. Uncontrolled anger contorted his face. She stared with wide-eyed horror as the man stood only a few yards away, trembling fitfully, clenching and unclenching his hands.

Laura had no idea why the man had stopped so suddenly. But she hadn't seen what her pursuer had: Araqiel, the tall, physically imposing hall monitor who'd watched Laura take her exam stepped sprightly from a deep pocket of shadow along the path not 10 yards on the other side of her.

Laura never heard Eric move up silently beside her. She was too frightened by the ghastly creature seething with barely contained violence to notice anything else. She jumped terribly when the hall monitor placed a gentle hand on her shoulder.

"Laura, how are you?" he said, never taking his eyes off the pursuer for an instant.

It was easy to see what was running through the pursuer's mind. He was obviously weighing the possibility of charging both of them. But there was something about Eric that gave even this foul creature pause.

So as Laura was turning in renewed fear to see who had joined her along the path, the pursuer had already realized the folly of such a course. Better to wait for an easier opportunity, as he'd done for weeks on end. The voices hadn't told him of this second one. That had been a surprise.

"I'm okay," Laura said in a weak voice as her pursuer took a hesitant, shuffling step backwards.

"Good." Eric's eyes remained riveted on the retreating pursuer, urging him silently to retreat back into the darkness and the night.

"But...but do I know you?" Laura finally tore her gaze from the creature retreating into the shadows who had almost changed her life forever.

"No, not really." Araqiel only turned to face Laura once he was certain it was safe to do so. "But we had a mutual friend, I think. Jennifer?"

"You knew Jen?" Laura asked, incredulous. "You were a friend of hers?"

"Yes, I knew her briefly. Enough to know she was moving toward a very tragic end," Eric said with regret. "And she talked of you often."

"I never knew," Laura whispered. "Not for a moment, not that…"

"I understand." He reassured her with a touch on the shoulder. "No one can ever really know about something like that."

"But I feel so guilty, like I failed," Laura said, not even pausing to wonder why she was unburdening herself to an almost total stranger.

"Don't." He tugged lightly on her sweatshirt to turn her back in the direction she'd been heading. "You didn't fail her. There's no way you could have known."

"But you said…?"

"That I knew she was in trouble. Yes, I knew that. But there was nothing either of us could do," he said compassionately. "You were her friend. You listened to her, as a friend will. That's as much as anyone can do."

"I don't know…I still feel awful about everything. Like someone yanked the foundation out from under me."

"The pain will ease with time, especially if you talk about it. And I'd like to listen. There's a lot about Jen I didn't know. Maybe you can help me understand as well." He took her arm gently and led her back down the path.

They talked through the night, most of it on Laura's end. Eric listened patiently, asking a probing question every so often. Laura had never felt so comfortable with anyone. Suddenly several shattered pieces of her mind had fallen into place. Laura had been blessed with a complete photographic memory that allowed her total recall, but she'd never talked about it outside her family, never let on that her prowess in the classroom was more an unearned gift than anything else. She'd always wondered if it would carry her through in a complex intellectual arena like college, where rote memory often isn't enough, where intuition can be the crucial element to success.

Eric watched and listened with a knowing smile. They talked of her hopes and dreams, her bewilderment during her first several days in college, her exciting realization that she could, in fact, handle the workload, the eventual knowledge that she could more than cope, that she could actually *master* her environment with ease.

Laura watched the sun come up over the horizon through an open window with profound sadness. How she wished their conversation could have lasted forever.

But Eric assured her they would get together soon and talk again. Strangers when they met, they parted as more than that. Laura had at last found a friend who would listen. Without making demands.

The irony was that she had no way of knowing that the happenstance meeting, though a beginning to her, was the end of a very long search for Araqiel and others.

6

***

STRENGTH AND HONOR

He would crush the upstart. If you let it happen once, it would happen again.

Samson's blood had curdled at the sight of it, someone who dared to approach one of the countless worshipers who trailed in his wake eagerly. Yes, she was a faceless, nameless follower, someone he would vanquish once and discard as carelessly as he had the others.

But, by the gods and heaven, he would not allow anyone—most especially someone whose size and physical presence matched his—to challenge his throne. Not for a moment could he permit such a challenge. It was unthinkable. The fool. How could he not realize whose wrath he was inviting?

Samson walked slowly, deliberately, across the dance floor, jostling the few who had not seen his coming and stepped from his path. Samson did not offer an apology. His eyes never left the corner of the room where the two of them had been absorbed in conversation for nearly half an hour. Samson had only noticed the two of them when a friend pulled Samson away from one of the many girls he'd danced with that night and pointed it out to him.

The gorgeous brunette who had almost wilted when he'd asked her to accompany him to the formal leaned close to whisper something in the young man's ear. He shook his blond hair in return, smiling quickly and reaching out to grab her hand. The hairs on the nape of Samson's neck stood on end.

A small measure of anxiety crept into her eyes as she glanced in Samson's direction. They widened in growing fear as he approached, towering over her.

At least there's that, Samson thought smugly. *She's smart enough to fear my anger.*

But even when he'd closed in on the two of them, when he was only scant feet away, the young man did not look in his direction. The girl was frantically trying to pull away from him, but the young man persisted in talking softly to her.

Only when the girl frantically yanked on his formal, pale blue suit jacket did the young man at last turn to face Samson. And when he turned, strangely, there was no fear. If anything, the young man's eyes glowed with an almost feverish anticipation, as if he'd waited for this moment to present itself.

23

Samson had seen this on occasion before, this lack of fear right before a confrontation. But here, on this dance floor, it was out of place. It made no sense. But there it was—the young man showed no sign of cowering in his presence. Well, Samson would teach him to fear.

"What do you think you're doing?" Samson asked calmly, his arms hanging loosely at his sides.

"Talking with a friend," the young man replied, his words barely audible above the noise of the band in the background.

That almost stopped Samson for a moment. "You're friends?" he asked his date stupidly. "You know each other already?"

"We met tonight," Araqiel said quickly, defiantly, cutting off the girl's answer. "We just met, in fact, a few minutes ago."

Samson took a deep breath. This numbskull was actually baiting him. "Did you mean to tell me…?"

Eric sighed. "Yes, we met tonight, here in this corner. We were discussing—"

"I don't care what you were discussing!" Samson roared, unable to contain his anger for another second. "You don't discuss anything with my date. Not a thing. Understand?"

Eric smiled patiently. "No, I don't believe I do. We were simply talking. Nothing more. I was making a new friend."

"Not on my time you aren't!" Samson bellowed.

"You were occupied elsewhere," Eric answered matter-of-factly.

"Look. You were making a move on my date. Admit it, and we'll let it drop right here," Samson almost hissed.

Despite his baser intentions, the last thing in the world Samson wanted was a direct confrontation with someone inferior to him. Eric may have been his size, but there was no way he was an athlete on campus. Samson would have known him, heard of him. Nothing would be gained by sending this brash young man to the hospital, but he refused to follow Samson's logic.

"I'm not about to admit that. It isn't true." Eric casually leaned back against the wall. The girl, who'd cowered throughout much of the conversation, almost fainted now. "Like I said, we were just talking. There's no harm in that."

To say the least, Samson was perplexed. By now a good dozen of his acquaintances had drifted over to the corner, so he couldn't simply let the incident drop. Something would be settled here, one way or another.

"I'll give you one more chance," he said through clenched teeth. "Admit you were making a move on her and we'll leave it at that."

"Or else?"

"Or else I'll have to call you a liar and a coward."

"You know I'm neither," Eric said coolly.

"Now, how would I know that, when you're sitting here trying to make a fool out of me in front of my friends?" Samson roared. "Most likely, you're both of those and more."

Eric paused, then said slowly, easing his way out of the corner, "I think you've called me a liar and a coward. And I don't appreciate that."

"So?" Samson asked, surprised.

"So I think you'd better take both of those back. If not, I'm afraid we'll have to step outside," Eric answered, his eyes locked on Samson's.

"You've got to be kidding!"

"No, I'm not. I wouldn't joke about my honor."

Samson sighed. There wasn't much he could do now but finish the job. If the guy wanted a funeral, so be it. "Let's go outside, then."

Eric nodded slightly and moved for the door. Nearly half of the dance trailed behind to watch the spectacle.

The moon was full and most of the stars were out, so there would be enough light to see by. Not that it mattered either way to Samson. He could work just as well in close quarters, without light, as he could under these circumstances.

As Samson handed his coat to a friend, he decided not to waste time. He'd come in close, put a clinch on the guy, and squeeze him like a ripe melon until he called it quits. It wouldn't do much for the crowd, but it would have to do here.

But Samson was wrong. Just how wrong he was he would not learn until it was too late.

Before they began, Eric gestured to Samson. "Look," Eric said under his breath, so the crowd of onlookers couldn't hear, "I don't think you understand how grievously you've pierced my honor. Where I come from, to accuse someone of cowardice or lying is tantamount to a death penalty…unless it's proven true."

"And what about it?" Samson said. "Let's just get it over with."

"No!" Eric said sharply. "We will not just get it over with. We'll set the ground rules first. I want more than my honor avenged."

"You're certainly cocky, aren't you?"

Eric smiled coldly, his blue eyes creasing at the corners. "No, I possess understanding. That's as important to true strength as natural ability. But, then, you wouldn't know that, would you?"

Samson's nostrils flared slightly. "You earned yourself a trip to the morgue, my friend," he said softly, dangerously.

"That's more like it," Eric said. "Now I think we understand each other."

"What do you want?" Samson asked, cutting him off.

"Your life."

"What!" Samson whispered.

The crowd began to murmur impatiently.

"You heard me," Eric pressed. "Should I lose, I will forfeit my life to you. I ask yours in return, should I win."

"You're crazy."

"No. I simply come from a different world. And I'm asking you to wage war by my rules."

Samson reeled in confusion. *Fight to the death? That sort of thing disappeared centuries ago.* But the perverse logic of it appealed somewhere in the deep reaches of his mind. Yet, no, such a thing wasn't possible. It wasn't an option. Nevertheless, he could agree to the rules. *Why not?* He was sure to win anyway. And what was it the idiot had said? He would forfeit his life? That meant Samson could claim it, then give it back to him.

"If I win, am I free to choose your fate?" Samson asked slyly.

"You are."

"Thumbs-up or thumbs-down? Like ancient Rome?"

Eric laughed. "Yes, of course. You may command me as you wish."

"Well, you're dumber than you look." Samson stepped back for the start of the fight. *This might be interesting.*

"Perhaps. Then you agree to the rules? You will stand firm by your word?"

"Yeah, sure, if you do," Samson said gleefully.

"I do," Eric agreed solemnly. "Now let us begin." He stepped back lightly, his hands held before him as if he meant to bow in Samson's direction.

They circled for a minute. Samson wanted to make sure the guy didn't know karate or some other martial art. Even so, it wouldn't matter. No man was a match for Samson in close.

Samson quickly realized Eric wasn't about to make the first move. *Okay, I'll force his hand. I'll make him commit himself.* Lunging in on one knee, he swept his right arm wide to grab his challenger's leg. An elementary move, one he'd mastered years ago. Samson meant to grab the leg and force the guy to react.

But Samson came up empty-handed. Where Eric's leg should have been, he found air. A second later, Samson's ears were ringing as Eric darted in like quicksilver and rapped the side of Samson's head with sharp knuckles.

Samson burst to his feet, his anger rising. Eric should not have done that. It was a mistake. *He will pay dearly for that.* Samson moved in slowly for the kill, pressing Eric toward the inside of the crowd ringed around them. Only a step or two closer…

Eric leaped to Samson's left to evade him. Samson moved just as quickly, blocking the dodge. It was a mistake quite a few had made, underestimating Samson's speed.

But Eric, in mid-stride, began to pivot even as he was about to land on his right foot, turning his back to Samson. The reverse pivot was almost completed even as Samson's arms started to enclose him.

Eric's right elbow, flying around as he completed his pivot, caught Samson square in the solar plexus. The blow, had it been a fraction of an inch lower, would have been a killing one. As it was, Samson simply vomited instantly and collapsed in a heap on his face, his last thought one of sheer terror as he drifted off into unconsciousness.

Eric stood over his vanquished opponent with angry, brooding eyes. Kneeling, he felt Samson's pulse. Reassured he was still alive, Eric motioned for some of his friends to help take him inside.

Samson came to moments before the ambulance arrived to find Eric and several others staring down at him. "What happened?" he whispered hoarsely, an unbearable pain rippling through his chest.

"You fainted from the pain," Eric said with an easy smile. "You'll be fine in a few days. Just rest now."

Samson closed his eyes, suddenly remembering the savage blow that had sent him into oblivion. His chest throbbed at the thought. *The bigger they are…*

Then Samson remembered the young man's words before they'd begun. *My life or yours,* he'd said. Had he been serious?

"My life is yours, I think," Samson said with a painful laugh.

"Yes, I know," Eric answered. "I hope to make the most of it."

"There you go again," Samson mumbled as the men in the white coats arrived, gently lifting him onto a stretcher. "I never know what you're talking about."

"You'll learn, my friend, you'll learn," Eric whispered. "As all men have through the ages."

"So it's thumbs-up, then? You have plans for my worthless life?" Samson asked half seriously, half in jest. He peered at the strange young man with unabashed awe as the orderlies carried him toward the waiting ambulance.

"Yes, of course, of course." Eric smiled. "Just be glad I'm not a Roman emperor. Your life is far from worthless."

"If you say so," Samson replied with a crooked grin, tilting his head back on the stretcher to concentrate on the pain.

7

***

TRUE BELIEVERS

The old, white house was spooky. Cobwebs hanging conspicuously in corners, doors that actually creaked as you walked through them, and stairs that sagged under your weight. There was no question about it. The place deserved to be haunted.

Jon had to laugh at the inside joke as he turned onto the street, Druid Hills Road. The house must have been incredible, once. Though long forgotten and neglected, it would still be standing 100 years from now. It seemed to be made of oak throughout and was a little out of place on the isolated street.

Jon walked gingerly through the musty corridor toward the back of the house. Sure, he knew some of the off-campus housing was pretty bad around Duke, but this place should have been condemned years ago. Maybe it had been.

Still, this might be fun after all. It had been awhile since he'd taken a risk on anything. Too bad it was so early in the morning...and a Saturday at that. It had taken three cups of coffee to prop his eyes open.

He had no idea why he was here. Eric had indeed called him, as he'd said he would. One day, after their class together, he simply handed Jon a note, letting him know where and when the game was. A map came with the note.

The Game. It was practically a cult to some. Jon knew a few kids who spent almost every waking minute playing it or thinking about it. It was a diversion, a break from reality. But it was a shame so many of them took it so seriously.

It's just fantasy role-playing, Jon thought as he came to a door at the end of the corridor. *Assume a character, knock around in some caves, ward off a couple monsters, and accumulate your booty. Simple.*

As he opened the door cautiously, though, Jon had a second thought or two. This house was taking matters a little too far, even for him. Who would live in a place like this? Dust everywhere, no running water, no apparent electricity and, therefore, no lights. Even a broken window or two...crazy.

Which explains why Jon was once again completely unprepared for the room he walked into. Or the crowd of people gathered in it.

28

Jon had to squint from the brightness and the shock of the sudden light that flooded his eyes as he entered. The room was rather large, maybe 50 feet in either direction. And clean. That's what caught Jon's attention initially. Unlike the rest of the house, this room could have passed for an ordinary den.

Terrain maps covered each wall, which appeared to be freshly painted. An extremely large, five-sided wooden table was situated in the heart of the room, in the middle of a nicely polished hardwood floor. The table was striking. It looked like it was made of oak. Papers and books were strewn everywhere.

Jon counted 12 kids around the odd-shaped table, all of different hues, shapes, and sizes. He noticed the only girl in the room, sitting shyly next to Eric across the table from the doorway. The girl was quite striking, in an austere way. Perhaps if she combed her hair more regularly, applied a bit of rouge to give her cheeks some color, or banished her stern demeanor, she might even be considered beautiful.

His eye also caught someone else who appeared distinctly uneasy in the room—a hulk of a human specimen with long, flowing hair. There was something about the brute, some kind of charismatic thing.

But while the gears in his mind tried to grind their way out of park, a short, pudgy kid with a face full of pimples, pants about to fall down at any moment, and shirt tails flapping loose, pushed his chair back and meandered over to Jon.

"Hi, I'm Thomas," the kid said with a nervous smile, brushing a mousy brown lock of hair from his eyes. He refused to look at Jon as he spoke, though, opting to gaze back over his shoulder at his comrades instead. "Glad to have you aboard."

"Thanks." Jon glanced furtively around the room. "I wasn't expecting anything like this…"

"I know, isn't it great?" Thomas risked a peek at Jon for one fleeting moment. "This was Eric's idea, to renovate the room like this for the Game."

"Oh? So no one lives here?" Jon relaxed a bit.

"Live here? Are you nuts?" the pudgy kid said incredulously. "This place was condemned years ago."

"So why is all this here, if the place is condemned and no one lives in the house?"

Thomas answered with a shy smile, scuffing his shoe on the wood floor. "Aw, you know what people would think about all this fantasy stuff. They'd think we're weird."

"Yeah, I guess I can see that." Jon could imagine what the reaction would be if this room was transplanted to one of the dormitories.

"We needed a private room. Somewhere we could go, where we knew we wouldn't be interrupted. Eric was the one who found the house." Thomas pointed to the table. "And he also got us this. He teases us that it's made from the ancient oak of Moreh, or possibly the oak of the sorcerer."

"The oak of *what*?" Jon asked.

"You know. Oak." Thomas shot Jon a quizzical look, as if *everyone* knew about the mystical powers of the oak tree. "Legends say that oak trees have their roots in the unseen world of spirit, that they're doorways into that world. Oak trees were the most magical Celtic trees. The word *oak* comes from the Sanskrit word that means 'door.' So oak is sacred. It's a doorway to the Otherworld. The Druids believed you just needed a branch of the oak to get there."

"Fascinating." Jon tried to conceal his amusement at this kid's utter naïveté.

"You know," Thomas continued, oblivious to Jon's disdain, "we all think the oak was the original tree of the knowledge of good and evil, that the acorn was the forbidden fruit and all that. Not the apple. The Bible never actually calls it an apple. But no one really knows for sure. And the fruit of the oak, the acorn, can feed entire families for a year, just from one tree. If you know what you're doing."

"Got it." Jon nodded.

"Isn't it great, though, these maps and stuff?" Unabashed enthusiasm spilled from Thomas's voice. "It makes it all seem real, like this world really exists. That it's not only a fantasy world Eric made up."

"Really?" Jon worked hard not to yawn.

"I mean, look at this." Thomas steered Jon toward the map on the near wall. "These mountains. The contour and the different peaks." He pointed a stubby finger at a pass in one of the mountain ranges. "This is where a storm giant has been spotted. We're just waiting for a winged mount to take us there, so we can explore."

He moved Jon a few feet down the wall and pointed to a large river descending from the mountains and emptying into a large valley below. "See this river? One of these days, we're gonna mount an expedition upstream. There have been rumors of a dwarf hole somewhere along it, hidden deep in the heart of the mountains."

"A dwarf hole?"

"You know," Thomas said, as if any fool in his right mind should know *exactly* what a dwarf hole was. "A pathway to the underground caverns, where the legends say the dwarves fled in a previous age."

Growing more excited, Thomas motioned impatiently for Jon to follow him down the wall. The rest of the room was strangely silent, watching Jon's reactions, testing him. The girl's eyes especially followed him.

"See here?" Thomas jabbed the huge map where someone had neatly illustrated a multiple-level log cabin at the fringes of a vast forest. "That's the wayfarers' lodge. At one time, legend says it was a meeting place for the various races. Before they vanished, that is."

"Vanished?"

"Yeah, left the land for good."

"I'm afraid I don't understand." Jon turned finally to Eric for an explanation.

The pudgy kid, his face blushing red, also looked to Eric for help.

"It's all right, Tom, we'll get it all straightened out," Eric said easily. "I know how easy it is to forget that others can't visualize the land. They don't know the history as you do."

Jon finally took a good look at the others in the room as Eric made the introductions. *I've never seen such an odd assortment*, he thought, nodding slightly to each as Eric moved around the table. *What a miserable lot I've stumbled onto.*

They were all like Thomas—very intense intellectuals bent on learning more of the Game. All looked like they'd spent way too much time holed up inside this house. They had the gaunt, weary appearance of those who've slaved away at books for days on end. *They actually believe this drivel.* Jon was awestruck. It had never occurred to him that anyone would take a mere game so seriously.

But the hulk and the girl did seem out of place here. As did Eric.

The minute he was introduced to Samson, Jon realized where he'd seen the guy before. Of course! The wrestler. The walking legend. The scourge of the opposite sex.

But Laura continued to baffle him, even after they were introduced. He stared at her as she peered back intensely at him.

"Well, that's the band," Eric concluded. "And a good one, too, I should add. We have three magicians of the eighth order, two clerics of the seventh. The others are all fifth or better."

"What are you talking about?" Jon asked. He could tell by their expressions that Laura and Samson were every bit as confused as he was.

"Oh, you'll catch on soon enough," Eric said confidently.

"Yeah, don't worry," Thomas reassured him. "Once you've got a quest under your belt, you'll get the hang of it. Eric's a good dungeon-master. He's sure to pace you well, start you off slowly—"

"No, Thomas." Eric cut him off. "I'm going to try something new with these three."

"Something new?" Thomas's jaw dropped open. The others around the table, Laura and Samson excluded, stared at Eric in equal amazement.

"I plan to move them up to your level tonight," Eric said in a clipped voice.

"Tonight!" Thomas gasped. "You can't. That's not possible."

"No one's ever tried that before," one of the others said.

"They're sure to croak right off," said a third.

"They don't stand a chance," added a fourth.

"They won't know the spells to use. They'll never remember all of them," said another. "It took me weeks to master the spells on the first six levels."

"I have faith in Laura's memory," Eric said firmly.

"B-but," Thomas sputtered, "there's no way they can even recognize lawful evil from chaotic good, or perceive danger quickly enough."

"I trust Jon's intuition completely," Eric replied.

"But how can they survive the melees?" Thomas asked timidly. "How will they recognize the right weapon for the right occasion, or when to duck and run for cover?"

Eric smiled. "Samson has a good feel for combat. He can size up his predicaments quickly."

The room fell silent. They were loyal followers, able players, and devoted to each other. They obviously resented the favoritism Eric, their dungeon-master, was showing the newcomers.

Yet they had no way of realizing the careful game within a game Eric was playing with the three newcomers. They couldn't know what Eric knew—that he had but one chance to draw these three within the circle. If he missed, the search would begin anew in other ancient places, in another part of the world.

"You know we would never question you," Thomas said slowly, speaking for the entire band. "You know the land well. Its dangers, its perils. You know the rivers and the mountains as we know our own minds. But is it wise to let them plunge into grave danger so quickly? Why must they be cast into the maelstrom so soon? Why not let them build up their storehouse, as we have?"

Eric held up a hand and Thomas stopped immediately, obediently. Jon's bewilderment, meanwhile, grew by the moment. They spoke of the land as if it really and truly existed beyond Eric's fertile imagination. Although, Jon had to admit, the map surrounding him on all four sides would allow almost anyone to indulge in make-believe.

"I understand your concerns. And they are warranted," Eric said soothingly. "But I have good reason. These three will make an excellent team. The best I have seen, in ages. Perfect, in fact." Eric stared hard at Thomas. "You must trust me on this."

Thomas couldn't hold the gaze and looked away, toward his friends. "You know we do."

His comrades nodded.

"I have other plans for them," Eric said firmly, eyeing each of the players to still their questions. "Do you understand? They will take another road, different from yours."

"But why?" Thomas squeaked. "They have yet to prove themselves in combat, as we have…"

"Their road will be much harder, much more demanding," Eric said quietly, glancing again around the table.

"But they don't know the land as well as we do," Thomas insisted. "They can't possibly know where to begin, where the greatest treasure is to be found."

"True," Eric answered, "which is why I intend to give them a complete history of the land before they set out."

"Now?" Thomas asked.

"Yes, right now. You have some historical background to go over before your next quest, right? You were considering the dwarf hole?"

"Well, yes," Thomas answered grudgingly.

"And it will take you some time to study the various types of creatures who might have trailed in the dwarves' wake?"

"I guess. We'll need half an hour or so to prepare."

"Then I'll have time to brief these three," Eric said crisply. "All right with the rest of the band?"

They all nodded, albeit reluctantly.

"Good, then that's settled," Eric continued. "It would be better if you pulled your chairs over to the map, where you can see the lay of the land surrounding the dwarf hole as you discuss your strategy. The four of us can meet at the other end where we won't disturb you."

"All right," Thomas said with such utter sadness that Jon almost laughed aloud.

They really do take this stuff seriously. Simply amazing. Jon did let a small chuckle loose as the band, eyes downcast, picked up their chairs and trooped slowly over to the far wall where the contour map revealed the vast mountain range split by a river that appeared to be the size of the Amazon in South America. They looked like they were on their way to a funeral.

Jon didn't see Eric's eyes, though, as he followed the players he'd nurtured across the room. He didn't see the brief moment of exhilaration at what he'd accomplished by bringing this motley group together to complete the circle.

But Laura did. She hadn't taken her eyes off Eric the entire morning, so she sensed his excitement. It made no sense, though. *Why would he befriend such miserable human specimens?* she had asked herself over and over since entering the room. *Why would he throw his lot in with these misfits?* With his quick wit and sharp mind, he could have the world. The very best friends any young man could ask for would come knocking at his door. *What are these simple, naïve, gullible, and believing fools to him?* It was almost enough to force Laura to walk away from him, to give up before the ship had even sailed. She tried to imagine what a double date would be like with one of these cretins.

Samson was strangely at ease in the room. For once, he could relax. No one would dare challenge him here. A bizarre collection of the male species, yes, but not fools. He could crush two or three at one time as he would ants. But he'd given Eric his word—a promise that he'd keep his anger in check in this room. Eric had been adamant that Samson not allow emotion to seize control.

Eric, meanwhile, had moved to a point on the contour map that none of the three had spotted earlier, at the far end of the room from where most of the players gathered around the large, five-sided oak table. A locked second door was nearby.

As the three drew closer, Jon could tell this part of the map was different from the rest. This was no illustration of picturesque mountain ranges or lush valleys. This was of a large city with enormous walls that surrounded the entire place. Jon counted 12 entrances. It was the only city, as far as he could tell from a passing glance, on the entire four walls.

It also had an ominous cast to it. Where the rest of the map appeared round, this appeared square. Where the other illustrations spoke of grandness, this spoke of the mundane and ordinary. Where most of the land appeared wild, this appeared tame. Spires and turrets reached for the sky, yet were protected by the vast walls. Winding, narrow streets intertwined throughout, yet all led eventually to one gate or another.

And in the center, towering above all else, was perhaps the most magnificent house Jon had ever seen. It rose to a monstrous point, a summit of some sort, partially obscured by clouds. The huge building was the largest Jon had seen in a drawing. It rose skyward from a large foundation, narrowed somewhat in the middle, then grew outward again with what seemed to be an endless series of porches and balconies and additions in all directions.

A castle? No, that would hardly do it justice. This house rose above the rest of the city by levels, one more magnificent than the other as they reached toward the heavens. The lower level was surrounded by an empty courtyard marked throughout by upright torches and lanterns. Jon found himself wondering why anyone would need such a huge courtyard.

The second level, which seemed in itself to rise out of the contour map toward Jon like some graphic trick, appeared to be a vast spider's web, branching off in all directions. The third level seemed more frightening than the previous two, with what looked like fireballs and lightning bolts in flight throughout.

The fourth level was a careful illusion, giving the appearance of one thing from one angle and something entirely different from another. Jon rocked side to side in his chair, catching different glimpses of what the fourth level actually was.

The house went on and on like that, with each level entirely different. The only change was that, starting at about the tenth level or so, the porches and balconies spread out horizontally even as the rest of the castle continued to rise toward the heavens. It was quite an architectural and artistic endeavor.

There was no way to tell how many levels there were because, after the thirteenth, the house disappeared into a thick, white cloud.

As Jon gazed at the magnificent city, Eric began, "For now, I'll keep things simple. I won't give you proper names to start. That's not really relevant anyway. The ideas are important here, not what clothes them."

Jon tried not to appear bored. This was all so silly, listening to the history of a make-believe land, staring at a make-believe city. *With make-believe people talking about dwarf holes at the other end of the room. I wonder...*

"Hey, space cadet, why don't you pay attention?" Laura glared in Jon's direction. "As long as you're here, you might as well listen."

"Why are we here anyway?" Jon said defensively. "This is all pretty ridiculous, even for a game."

"You're free to leave," Eric replied quickly.

"Hey, I didn't say anything like that," Jon protested.

"I know, but I want you to know you can leave anytime you want. If you don't find this challenging enough, then go."

Jon studied Eric. *I should just leave this place right now. It's weird. These people are strange. But this is a fascinating map. Whoever put it together is obviously gifted...*

"Why don't you give the guy some room?" Samson growled. "Shut up and listen. You can leave after he's finished."

"What's your problem, bozo?" Jon retorted. "I'll hear the guy out. Don't worry."

Samson began to rise from his chair but, at a glance from Eric, eased his way back quite reluctantly. He sat very still from that point on, his attention constantly directed at Jon, who now squirmed uneasily.

"I only want to give you a general history of the land," Eric continued. "Nothing fancy. You could call it a working history, enough to know what to look for."

Eric stopped then and gazed at the three of them. This was the moment. The crossover. These three would never believe as the others, but they had to believe *enough*. They had to commit enough of their souls in order to make it truly work. The path to freedom for the *bene elohim* was so close now, after all this time.

It was very, very hard to conjure up imagination, Eric knew. *Anyone with any intelligence and the ability to rise in this world through his or her own efforts quickly realizes that anything worthwhile comes with a price tag. It all has to be paid for. Somehow.* And Eric had nothing to give them, really, that they could purchase. Just a fantasy, a sorcerer's tale, something to fuel whatever imagination they'd been blessed with. A good story, perhaps, but nothing they could believe in.

"In the beginning, there were seven races," Eric said slowly, looking each in the eye to make sure they were paying attention. "Men, of course, were the first."

Laura frowned. "I assume you're including women there."

"My humblest apologies," Eric said with a slight nod. "Yes, men and *women*. The human race..."

"That's better," Laura replied, satisfied.

"...was the first," Eric continued. "There is no record of how they arrived in the land. At least, none has ever been discovered. Some have speculated and, of course, there are the legends."

"The legends?" Jon asked.

"That the gods created the land in a great outpouring of magic. And with the help of the human race created the other races. Yet, as I say, there is no record of any such event. No one, not the greatest magician or the most powerful cleric, has yet to approach anything of that magnitude. Most scoff at the legends, choosing to believe instead that the land has always existed and that the races have always—"

"Wait a minute," Jon said viciously. "You created the land, didn't you? We all understand that, right?"

Eric stared at Jon coldly, wondering how to handle his question. This was just the sort of situation he'd hoped to avoid, this questioning of the fundamental basis for the land's existence. "It is true I am the dungeon-master—"

Laura cut him off, directing her anger at Jon. "Look, you pompous, arrogant, egotistical worm. We all know none of this is real. But we're playing a *game*. Okay? Let's hear the rules. Let him set up his hypothesis; then we'll pick it apart. You can manage that, can't you?"

When Jon merely shrugged and settled back in his chair, Eric continued. "Regardless of the land's beginning—or the origin of magic, for that matter—there is one thing that seems relatively certain. Of the seven races, humans can ascend the rungs of power much higher than any of the other six races. Which may explain why the other races have fled the land."

"Fled the land?" Samson asked.

"Yes, I'm getting ahead of myself, but there is hardly a trace of the other races left in the land anymore. A few relics are unearthed every so often that give a hint or two of the past—a broadsword with ancient runes, perhaps forged by dwarves, or a silver-tipped arrowhead crafted by elves centuries ago. One farmer claimed to have discovered a fairy ring in his pasture one evening, but the grass was green and full when the neighbors arrived."

"So who is in the land?" Laura asked, perplexed.

"Yeah, and where did these races go?" Samson added.

"Well, men and women are in the land. As for the races, it is said they have returned to the farthest reaches of the land they were originally given domain, beyond even humankind's long and powerful arm..."

"Huh?" Jon asked.

"Okay," Eric said more slowly. "Let me give you a little history first of the other races. Then I can tell you where most believe they've vanished.

"At one time, all seven races worked hand in hand. They coexisted peacefully, you could say. Each lived where they were most comfortable, but there was always traffic to and from the various parts of the land.

"The elves felt free to leave their forest land to journey to the dwarves' underground forges. The centaurs—half-men and half-horse—frequently waded into the oceans to visit the men and women of the sea. Fairies were regular visitors in the great and vast halls of the giants.

"But all this came to an end, so the legends tell us, when a few of the human race, which had always held sway in the land but never abused its power, began to set themselves apart. These few had ascended beyond even the reach of their own race and no one dared say a word against them. Their power was simply too great.

"What happened was inevitable. At some point, these few decided to focus their power more narrowly and decreed that magic would no longer be free and available to all human beings. These few set up a city—this one here on the map—and decided that only within the walls of this city could magic be learned and practiced.

Eric shook his head. "The consequences of such a decision are equally obvious. Magic disappeared from the land as its basic elements were slowly concentrated in the hands of an elite among the human race. The human masses who weren't quick enough, gifted enough, strong enough, intelligent enough, resourceful enough, or lucky enough were left out.

"Most of the human race turned to the land and its products for their comfort as the magic dried up. Where once they might have conjured up dinner, now they were forced to till the soil for it. Where once they might have spun cloth through magic, now they were forced to spend hours at a handmade loom to spin their clothes. While the powerful played effortlessly behind the walls, the masses toiled for their daily bread outside.

"Gradually, the men and women of the land saw less and less of their brethren who lived behind the walls of the city. The powerful magicians, who had initially made frequent trips to outer reaches of the land, saw no reason to venture outside their fortress and stopped visiting them at all. The masses weren't allowed inside the city. In fact, it's been years since a magician has ventured outside the walls. And it's been 2,000 years or more since one of the common folk have ventured inside."

"But what of the other races, the ones you spoke of earlier? How could they let such a thing happen?" Laura asked.

"What choice did they have? By their very limited nature, the other six races combined could not match the concentrated power of the human magicians. Each race, in its own way, had power of a sort—magic has little or no effect on elves and giants are unusually strong, for instance—but each also lacked the versatility of the human race. Even the greatest of each race could ascend only so high and no higher.

"So, you see, the races were left with no choice. With magic disappearing from the land, with most of the human race becoming servants to those in power within the walls of the city, and with no hope of overthrowing the powerful human magicians, the other races chose to withdraw from the land. They left, each to their own domain. No human has seen a member of the other races for nearly as long as the city has been standing."

"No one?" asked Laura.

"No one. And there's another thing. A rumor, really. No way to prove or disprove it, because none of the other races is around to answer the question."

"Which is?" Jon asked with an edge of impatience.

"That the magicians did something truly horrible, something considered quite impossible, and drove the races away for good. There had always been rumors of races enslaved within the confines of the city—for who knew what purposes—for centuries. And when the races discovered the abomination, they fled and all magic started to fade entirely."

"So magic doesn't work at all now in the land?" Jon asked.

"No, not quite," Eric said quickly. "Magic works—or would work, I should say. But the means of learning it, the means to practice it and hone it to a fine art, are beyond the reach of nearly all the inhabitants of the land. The tools of knowledge, by and large, are within the walls of the city. And, as I said, no magician has ventured outside the walls for quite some time."

"So if some of the men and women in the land were taught magic, if they were given the chance to learn, then they, too, could wield that power?" Laura asked.

"Yes, definitely. But who will teach them? And, even if such a teacher is found, there is the certain risk that those within the city will rise up again to stop it. Their power, most likely, is still very great. Rest assured, they won't take too kindly to a challenge to their power."

"Why hasn't it occurred to the people in the land to just storm the city?" Samson asked. "If there are so many of them, and so few in the city, then they should be able to trample the city."

"Like good Marxists should…," Jon offered, risking yet another withering sidelong glance from Laura.

Eric smiled. "It's all right. Jon's right. That is good, solid Marxist theory. But it won't work against the city, not in the day and age of this land. All the tools of power and knowledge are in the hands of a few. And no amount of sheer, brute strength will change or challenge that fact."

"Why not?" Samson persisted.

"Because, as any of the common folk would tell you, it's impossible to draw near to the city. Only a magician of the thirteenth order, or higher, can even approach it and enter one of the 12 gates. None of the band in this room is even close to approaching that level of magic."

"Huh?" Samson asked.

"The perimeter of the city is protected either by a magic minefield, to put it simply, or by something else entirely. To enter, you must possess the knowledge to repel those powerful spells or know the secret. You see, along with power comes the ability to repel magic as well. They are equal talents, of a sort."

"Do you mean that if you don't have a...a counter spell, if you can't repel the magic spell or whatever it is that guards the city, then you'd be turned into a toad or something if you tried to enter? Or that you'd need to possess some secret knowledge to enter?" Laura asked.

"Exactly."

Jon exhaled. "Well, that hardly seems fair."

"I'm still confused," Samson said, ignoring Jon. "You've told us about these races. But who are they and where did they go?"

Eric nodded. "You're right, and I'm sorry. But you must remember that what is known of the other six races is only speculation. No one really knows if, in fact, they ever existed, if they actually were a part of the land thousands of years ago, or if, as the legends say, they are somehow a creation of the gods and the human race.

"The six, separate from the human race but inextricably linked to it, are these— the elves, the dwarves, the giants, the centaurs, the people of the sea, and the fairies. And there are offshoots or cousins, both good and evil, from each of these races as well as creatures who live near each.

"The nymphs and dryads, for example, are closely aligned to the elves and the forest that is their domain. The orcs, or goblins, are close cousins of the dwarves and dwell in the nether regions with them. Ogres and trolls live in close proximity to the giants. Leprechauns, sprites, pixies, and brownies are very close relatives of the fairies. Unicorns are often found among the centaur tribes. And, naturally, mermen and mermaids often use sea horses as their mounts.

"Each of the six races, according to legend, was given lordship over a part of the land. Humans, on the other hand, were given the freedom to live and prosper in every corner of the land. The elves, for example, ruled the forest lands. The others similarly ruled their own corner of the land—the dwarves, the caverns, and regions below ground; the giants, the mountain ranges; the centaurs, the great plains; the fairies, the air or the sky; and the mermen and mermaids, the sea.

"As I mentioned, the races frequently mingled and visited each other, journeying between cities in each realm. It was even common for one member of a race to apprentice with another—for example, a centaur with an elf, which would explain why centaurs are such excellent shots with a bow and arrow, according to legend.

"At any rate, when a few of the human race forced magic from the land, the races held a war council and decided to go their separate ways rather than challenge the powerful magicians. They reasoned, quite logically, that they would eventually see their own innate magic dry up as well in the blighted land so long as they lived in the shadow of the magicians' city.

"There is also a shadow of a myth about the abomination within the city, which triggered the war council by the races. But there is no record of this, and the oral history says nothing of this event, either.

"What is clear is that the six races reasoned that, while they existed within easy reach of the city, there would always be the threat of reprisal or conquest. So they decided to make it all but impossible for the lords of the city to move against them—or to move with ease against them—and moved their cities and their people to the very heart of their domain, as far from the city as they could manage.

"The elves fled to the deepest, darkest, farthest reaches of the forest. It is said that, even if you knew the way, it would take weeks of travel through unexplored forest to reach the outermost fringes of the elves' kingdom. A powerful magician or two might chance such a journey, but no large contingent would stand a chance of making the journey successfully. And the common folk venture only far enough into the forest now to cut their timber.

"The dwarves moved their cities, it is said, to the very center of the world. They dwell near the molten fires, and it is rumored that the weapons they now forge are of such strength that not even a fire giant could hope to bend one. There are even stories that the dwarves have learned how to bathe and swim in a river of fire that has its roots in the core of the land. Again, it would take an extraordinary magician indeed willing to brave those fires in search of the dwarves.

"The giants journeyed to the other end of the land, to the very top of the highest mountains at the end of the mountain ranges. The giants' kingdom is so cold, it's said, that a common man with no magic would freeze within minutes even if he somehow managed to climb that high. And the air is bitter and devoid of life-giving oxygen as well, so it would be hopeless to think of reaching even the edge of the giants' realm. But, of course, no mortal could hope to make such a journey.

"The mermen and mermaids, they say, have gone to the bottom of the sea. There, hundreds, perhaps thousands of miles below sea level, they have re-established their cities. Yet rumors persist that on rare occasions the people of the sea still venture near the surface to hear of tidings throughout the rest of the land. Because, more so than the other races, they are cut off from the land. And perhaps, for this reason, common folk fear the sea more than any other part of the land. They are afraid of stumbling on the people of the sea during one of these sojourns to the surface.

"The centaur tribes traveled far across the windswept, barren reaches of the land. They now roam at the edges of the Great Plains, where only a few could hope to fly and none could hope to ride. A wayfarer would be hard-pressed to sustain himself as he crossed the plains, where life is sparse and water almost nonexistent.

"The fairies flew for weeks and months on end to the second heaven, as they call it, a place beyond even sight where they can frolic in peace. On a clear day, if you stare very hard up at the sky, you can perhaps catch a wisp of their land. But only a wisp and it will look like just another cloud to you. Even that glimpse is but the beginning of the fairy kingdom."

Eric settled back in his chair, his head resting against the wall and the city outlined on the map. He stared hard at the three extraordinarily gifted individuals but looked most carefully at Laura. She was the key. "There," he said at last, "that is the story of the six races. It is a story told to very young children of the land before they fall asleep at night. It is told around campfires and at parties.

"Yet no one in the land, I think, really believes the story that the races even exist. I doubt if they believe the magic exists in the city anymore, although no one ventures close to it nevertheless. Disbelief is one thing. Foolhardiness is another entirely.

"No, the people of the land believe only that they must harvest their crops this year or die of starvation. They know they must cut the timber or risk freezing in winter. And they know the folly of thinking otherwise. As a consequence, no one talks of magic or the races with any measure of seriousness. They are bedtime stories and campfire tales, nothing more. Something to pass the time."

"Some fantasy land," Jon muttered. "Sounds a lot like our own world."

"In some respects, they are similar," Eric said casually. "But it's not easy to draw parallels. The land cannot change its nature. Only its people can do that."

"So what do we do now?" Jon stifled a yawn.

"You will eventually make your first foray…go on your first quest in the land." Eric glanced over his shoulder toward the others, who were arguing ferociously at the end of the room. "But, for the moment, I want you to study these. They were stolen from the city. They are the first and only books of their kind."

Eric held out three books. Each was a slightly different off-color—either darkish green, light brown, or dark brown. They were odd books, with imperfections on each cover and page. They were clearly very, very old, perhaps hundreds of years old. The binding must have been quite good for the books to have held together so well. He handed one to Jon, another to Samson, and the remaining one to Laura. They were extraordinarily heavy to the touch.

"These are known as *The Books of El,* which taught wisdom to the human race. There is nothing even remotely like them, on this world or any other. Go ahead, open them," Eric said very softly. "Take a look at what's inside."

Jon smiled at the irony. "As in El, the father of humanity, and Eloah, his female companion, who the ancient texts have largely obliterated or forgotten?"

"Derived from that notion," Eric said quietly.

"You mean you got the idea from those myths and legends?"

"More or less."

The three of them, even Samson, gingerly opened their volumes. But Laura, after only a glance at the contents, suddenly looked up at Eric.

"I want to know something," she said with the fierce intensity that had become almost a trademark to her classmates. "What can be done to bring the races back to the land? We know how to bring the magic back—reduce that city to rubble and free the knowledge within its walls. But how can we bring the races back to the land? If they exist, that is."

Eric had to smile. Laura had assumed her role perfectly, as he felt sure she would. She talked as if the land existed. She had for his sake, he was sure, stepped easily into the role of magic initiate, questioning her mentor. He could only hope Samson and Jon would, of their own volition, do the same.

"Well," Eric said, as the other two also looked up, "there is another legend."

"And it is?" Laura asked impatiently.

"That if the best and brightest of the human race, serving as emissaries, made the perilous journey to each of the kingdoms, convinced the races that the common folk and the powerful magicians alike would welcome them back with open arms, then they would return."

"But that's impossible!" Laura scowled. "Those within the city would never give up their monopoly."

"True," Eric said sadly, "which is why the races will never return."

"Is there anything else?" she asked.

"Well…"

"Go on," Laura demanded.

"Those same emissaries, the gifted of the human race, also have the ability and the power to command the races to return," Eric said. "But, to do so, they must also win the hearts and minds of those races."

Laura slumped. "I don't understand."

"Neither do I," Eric said softly.

"Come on!" Jon snorted. "What do you mean, you don't know? You're making up the rules, aren't you? You said yourself that you were the dungeon-master."

Eric chose to sidestep Jon's sarcasm. "All I know and all I can tell you is what the legends handed down in the land, from generation to generation, say about this."

"Would these emissaries be risking anything by going to each of the races?" Laura asked.

"Yes, their lives. Collectively, any given race could snuff out the lives of a few of even the most powerful of the human race. It would be a very real danger," Eric said solemnly. "And if they should violate the laws of the land, they would also be subject to the strictest of penalties."

"I see." Laura opened her book again.

Samson and Jon glanced at each other, shrugged, and turned back to their own books in the set of three.

"I should tell you something about these books," Eric added while the three started to leaf through them. "They are the only books of their kind in existence. If you look carefully, you will see they are bound as no other book on Earth is. The covers were stripped directly from the bark of the tree, and the paper is almost a direct byproduct of that same tree. They cannot be taken to the land, so you must memorize as much as you can right now. You must familiarize yourself with the contents of these books before you journey there."

"That's nice," Jon mumbled. "Like cramming for a test."

"Basically," Eric answered.

"So tell me," Jon asked, "are all three of these alike? Do we all have the same book?"

"No, not at all. Each is vastly different. Yours, for example, contains cleric spells through the seventh level. Beyond that, you must learn as you go along because nothing further exists in writing beyond the walls of the city. Laura's contains magic spells through the ninth level. Likewise, she must also learn beyond that as she goes along. And Samson's contains the various types of weaponry available to sophisticated and powerful fighters, from glaives to tridents, and what is most successful against certain types of opponents."

"Gotcha." Jon stuck his nose back in the book.

"Now, I must warn you again," Eric said. "Learn all you can from these books now. For, as I said, they will be unavailable to you during your sojourn in the land."

"We heard you the first time," Jon retorted. "Although how we're supposed to remember this stuff is beyond me. Creating water, detecting evil, controlling the weather, resisting cold, resurrecting dead people." He leafed through the pages of the massive volume. "It's all pretty spooky."

"Oh, just shut up!" Laura snapped. "I don't want any deadbeats on my team, so you'd better know that book inside and out by the time we set out."

Jon almost told her to stuff it in a hat, then thought better of it. *All right, you cold witch, if that's the way you want to play it, I'll oblige. I'll go along with your little game.* Turning his full attention to the book, he determined to memorize every line if he had to.

"You'll have as much time to learn as your patience will allow you," Eric said to the silent group poring over the strange books. "When you're ready to set out on your first quest, let me know. I'll be with the others. But," he continued, "I'll say it one more time. You'll be alone and on your own in the land. So be prepared."

"The third time's a charm," Jon grumbled.

"There's just one last thing. I must ask you something." An almost chanting intonation pervaded Eric's voice as he spoke. "If you agree to journey to the land, to believe that it exists if only in someone's imagination, then you must pledge also not to act against it. You must pledge, in fact, to act in its behalf. Paths that you forge are permanent. Will you agree to all four of these? To journey there, to believe, to act in the land's behalf, and to make us a path?"

"Yes." Jon sighed without bothering to look up from his tome as Samson and Laura nodded in agreement. "Now will you leave us alone so we can learn this stuff?"

"As you wish," Eric said with a weary smile. "You are now on your own."

An unearthly silence descended on the room as he moved away from the fruits of his study, labor, and watchfulness. The task was finished. The deed, at last, was done.

8

* * *

A YOUNG BOY'S COURAGE

The black crow settled gently to the ground. Preening its black feathers with a practiced ease, the crow studied the man where he lay, only feet away, resting under the branches of a giant oak deep in the heart of the forbidden forest.

The crow's quiet reverie lasted only a moment, though. Suddenly, from several directions at once, the forest came alive with the crackling of branches, shouts and curses, running feet and, at last, the cry of discovery.

The crow, with one last glance at the slumbering giant of a man, took to the air with a screech. It soared high with only two or three strong sweeps of mighty wings that had carried the creature to and fro across the land, delivering its own tidings of news, both good and evil. The bird had disappeared through the treetops by the time the first of the search party arrived.

"There he is!" one of the men shouted to his comrades. "And still asleep."

"Well, I'll be an owl," muttered a second.

"He's every big as she said he was," said a third. "Maybe even bigger."

Slowly, in whispering awe, they gathered around him. More than one of them, no doubt, secretly wondered if maybe he shouldn't plunge a dagger into his heart as he lay. Just to be sure.

"What do we do now?" one of the men asked. "We can't let him come in like this and then leave at his pleasure."

"No, we can't allow that," another grumbled. "That would be the end of it for us. The end at last."

"Maybe he's, you know, a—" said the first.

"No!" said a gruff, scraggly, black-bearded hulk. The man's full, round belly jiggled and rippled as he bellowed the rebuke. "They'd never dare to enter here. We all know they can't risk the consequences."

"Yes, yes, that's true," said the first man, a timid soul as frail and thin as Blackbeard was full of waist. "And we've not seen one in a hundred years or more. Not in a hundred years."

"Oh, shut up, Weasel." Blackbeard glowered. "We all know that. And this man is

45

no more than that—just an ordinary man."

"He looks like…like he could be one of them, though, doesn't he?" A young boy, perhaps 16 at most, said in a hushed voice, peering at the object of their fascination so intensely his eyes seemed ready to pop out of their sockets.

"Oh, get off the log, Mark," growled one of the other men. "He's no more one of *them* than you are."

"And how do you know?" Mark shot back. "If we've not seen one in so long—"

"He's not, I tell you!" Blackbeard roared. "Leave it be. Do you hear me?"

"But…but where did he come from, then?" Mark sputtered. "How did he slip past our sentinels so easily?"

One of the men laughed. "It's a big forest, lad. And it isn't hard to slip through our wretched guard, I daresay."

"It's not *that* big. Somebody would have heard him, or seen him, or something!" Mark shouted, almost in tears.

"All right, then wake him," said Weasel. "You be the one. See for yourself if he's one of them or not. Perhaps he'll take pity on you."

Mark tried to shrink back into the forest, suddenly afraid he might very well be right. But strong hands took hold of him and thrust him back toward the still-slumbering man. These same rough hands continued to push him forward until he was no more than a couple logs' width from the man.

"Well, go on. Do it," the Weasel goaded the boy. "Wake him. Or take your knife to him. We don't much care which. Just be done with it."

Mark hesitated and almost turned to make a run for it. But, no, the cowards would only catch him and bring him back. Never willing to lift a finger for themselves, always complaining, always bickering and quarreling, always preying on the weak and the helpless…

"Go on, lad," one of the men said with a low snarl that told Mark he meant business.

Just do it and get it over with, Mark thought, *before I make matters worse for myself.*

Mark reached out with a trembling hand, terrified but determined to go through with it, to stand firm. Even if he was turned into a toad. Or worse. Prepared for the worst, yet hoping somewhere deep, deep down inside that maybe he was right, Mark let his hand rest on the man's shoulders.

The man's eyes fluttered open, looking first at Mark in utter shock and confusion, then to the knot of gnarled, weather-beaten men surrounding him, then at the dark forest rising all around him, then back to Mark. When the confusion morphed to fierce, boiling anger, Mark stumbled backward, suddenly afraid.

"Where am I?" Samson roared at the top of his lungs, his deep, bass voice echoing through the reaches of the forest. "What in God's name is all this…?"

"Easy, friend," one of the men said. "We mean no harm. And God has no place or name in this forest."

"Harm!" Samson shouted, his voice now only a dull roar and not a full-throated battle cry. "What do you mean 'harm'? Tell me what has happened? Where is the room, those nerds, the map, the book I was reading…?"

"Hold on." Blackbeard spoke authoritatively, if not exactly bravely, from just the other side of a wall of men. "We know nothing of these maps and books you speak of. What we *do* know is that you are trespassing on our property. And that, my friend, is punishable by death. Surely, the entire land knows of our law here."

"Where am I?" Samson growled, his voice dropping nearly an octave in pitch. "Just tell me that."

"Why, man, you're in the Silver Forest, of course," Blackbeard said.

"The Silver Forest?" Samson glared.

"Are you daft?" one of the men, also safely out of Samson's reach, dared to ask. "You've not heard of the Silver Forest?"

"No, of course not," Samson said.

"By the magician's most holy name, how is it possible that he's not heard of the Silver Forest?" another of the men asked.

Samson took a deep breath. His head swam with possibilities, but none made sense. *What's the last thing I can remember?* He furrowed his brow. *Oh, yes, that book. I'd come to the end. There was a picture on the inside of the back cover, a picture of a forest, very much like this one.…*

Samson glanced around again, wildly. Suddenly, it all came back to him. The picture had fascinated him so; it seemed to shimmer on the page, as if it were real.

Then, as if he had suddenly leaped from the top of a very tall mountain, he'd begun to fall. He'd plummeted headlong into the picture he was staring at, hurtling at an ungodly speed, his mind reeling before he blissfully passed out.

And he'd opened his eyes here, to find a young boy staring at him in wide-eyed terror, surrounded on all sides by these gaunt men. *It has something to do with the Game—that game Eric was talking about,* Samson thought as if in a waking dream. *This is all some sort of a game.*

"Well, do we slit his throat or not?" Blackbeard said loudly. "What is the verdict?"

"I say we must," the Weasel replied quickly. "A man who has not heard tales of the Silver Forest cannot be trusted."

"He could be an advance scout. For *them*, you know," added another. "Come here to see if we've grown weaker and smaller in number."

"Yes, yes, perhaps they're planning an attack," the Weasel said. "After all these years of defying them, perhaps the time has come."

"I'm no scout," Samson said scornfully. "And I have no idea who you are or where I am, for that matter."

"Silence!" Blackbeard bellowed. "Say another word without our leave and your fate is sealed."

"Yes, silence," the Weasel hissed in Samson's direction.

"I say he's a spy," Blackbeard continued, looking around at his comrades. "And I say, like all spies who dare to venture into our domain, his sentence must be death."

"Death to the spy!" one man shouted.

"Off with his head!" shouted another.

"Yes, and send it back over the walls as a warning," said a third. "That'll teach 'em to send someone our way again."

"Good plan, good plan," the Weasel said.

"Is it settled, then?" Blackbeard queried his men. "His fate is sealed?" A chorus of "ayes" rang out in the stillness of the forest. "Then seize him, men, and string him up!" Blackbeard shouted feverishly.

Samson, still groggy but aware enough of what was about to befall him, leapt to his feet, planting his back against the oak. They'd not take him easily, of that he would make sure. Slowly, warily, the band closed in around him, none daring to make the first move and risk a broken neck.

"All at once," the Weasel urged the men from behind the ranks. "Rush him. He's strong, yes, but he can't stand up against all of us."

The men looked back and forth at each other, nodding in agreement among themselves. A moment more and they would do as the Weasel suggested: rush the giant of a man all at once and topple him in a torrent of bodies.

"NO!" came a small voice, barely audible above the growing clamor. Mark, elbowing and clawing his way through the men, burst into the clear and stepped defiantly in front of Samson. "This is not the law of the forest and you know it," Mark said to the men.

"Get out of the way, lad," one of the men growled.

"I will not," the boy said. "He deserves a fair hearing."

"A fair hearing?" snorted the Weasel. "A spy who would cut our throats and slip away under the cover of darkness?"

"We don't know if he's a spy or not," the boy managed through clenched teeth. "And, anyway, why would he come here in broad daylight and then fall asleep if he was one?"

"A trick," the Weasel claimed. "That's what it is. Like the rest of his kind, he's trying to pull the wool over our eyes, lull us into sleep."

"He deserves a fair hearing. Before the Council," Mark said adamantly, refusing to step out of the way of the strangely silent man he was defending.

Blackbeard scowled. "You're as daft as he is, boy. What right does a spy have to a hearing before the Council?"

"As much right as you or me, that's what." Mark spit the words right back in his face. "It's the law."

"Hang the law," muttered one of the men. "He's one of them, that's for sure. We don't want none of their tricks here."

"Oh, get off it!" Mark fairly shouted. "You all know they'd never come into the forest. It's not safe for them. They wouldn't risk it."

"Then he works for them," said one of the men.

"That's right, that's right," the Weasel said. "He's on their payroll, come here to see if the forest is still as it was a hundred years ago."

"Well, it is, so what's the worry?" Mark said reasonably, despite his trembling. "What's the harm in waiting? Why not let him speak before the Council?"

The Weasel leaned over and whispered to Blackbeard, who then nodded, his belly rippling and shaking as he did so. A huge grin finally crossed his face.

"The boy's right," Blackbeard said heartily, startling his comrades. "He deserves a fair hearing."

"What's that, eh?" one of the men asked, puzzled like the rest.

"He must have a hearing, you donkey!" Blackbeard said. "If he's a spy, then he'll have some valuable information for us. I'm sure a few hot coals will be enough of a guarantee that he's not hiding anything."

"And if he's not a spy?" Mark asked suspiciously.

"We'll cross that bridge later," Blackbeard replied testily.

"That's not good enough," Mark argued. "I don't think—"

"Look, you little runt," Blackbeard said, "I give you my word that he'll have a hearing before my father and the Council."

Samson, deciding he'd heard enough, placed a gentle hand on Mark's shoulders. "All right," he told Blackbeard, "I'll go peacefully."

"But…," Mark protested, turning to look at Samson for the first time.

"It doesn't seem like I have much choice, now does it?" Samson said to Mark. "They're making the rules here, aren't they?"

"Yes, they are," Mark answered, "but the law of the forest has been around for hundreds of years. They can't just do whatever they want."

"Doesn't appear that way from where I'm standing," Samson added. "Looks to me like they *are* the law in this…what did you call it?"

"The Silver Forest," Mark said quickly. "They call it that, you know, because the legends say that after it rains…"

"That's enough!" Blackbeard rebuked. "Another word out of you, boy, and we'll put you on trial for aiding and comforting the enemy."

"I was only explaining—"

"We all know what you were doing," the Weasel said slyly. "Can't wriggle out of it now."

"The boy isn't part of this." Samson pushed Mark roughly to one side. "You've got a problem, it's with me. You hear?"

"Hey, wait a minute," Mark protested.

"Look, kid, you've done your good deed for the day, but I can take care of myself," Samson said to him. "Now run along to your mother before you get hurt." Samson ignored Mark's pained expression and swiveled toward Blackbeard. "Let's get the show on the road, Ace. Take me to this Council you spoke of. I'm prepared to defend myself."

As Samson strode forward from the tree, eager hands latched onto his bulging muscles. Within a matter of minutes, his hands were trussed and knotted behind his back. A loop of rope was tossed over his head. Two men grabbed it, jerking viciously on it as they led Samson away.

Mark, forgotten as he trailed behind the band of rogues, valiantly fought back the tears of anger and humiliation. No one marked his act of bravery; his courage was now ignored in the rush to judgment back at the camp. It would be a long while before he could find it in his heart to forgive the man whose life he'd surely saved.

9

***

THE MAGIC AWAKENS

The old woman peered up at the bright sun and wiped a glistening bead of sweat from her forehead. "Land sakes, it's hot again today," she muttered. Flipping the bill of her woven-straw hat down low, she bent her back again.

She had tilled the soil this way, by hand, for as long as she could remember. Her entire family had. Yet neither the soil nor the air had ever been so dry before, not in the half century she'd worked the fields. Her two daughters, and their three daughters, were all out that day with the men, pulling their weight. They had no choice. The drought had lasted for months now. Not a drop of rain and hardly even a cloud on the horizon.

What made it worse was the river. So close by, so tantalizing. *By the magician's name, if we only had a tiny portion of that vast, coursing artery,* she thought miserably, *our crops would be all right this year.*

But, no, she must banish any thought of the river. Beyond what they were able to carry back to their home in buckets for drinking water and cooking, the law of the land was firm. They must never touch the water. The river did not belong to them. Only the land did.

Secretly, though she would never admit it aloud, the old woman didn't believe the legends or the strictures. Why should she? In nearly a century, no one had seen or heard from a soul within the city. And the people of the sea, to whom the vast river belonged, what of them? Where were they?

No, she did not believe any of it, least of all the legendary warnings of reprisals from the people of the sea should the common folk ever tamper with the river and the course of nature. "The river is ours, not yours," they'd said before vanishing forever.

So? And what do we do now, when our crops are withering and dying under the constant glare of the sun?

She thought of those living near the forest land. Had the elves returned when a few began to venture into the edge of the forest to cut logs for their homes? Of course not. Had the dwarves returned when several of her neighbors dug deep wells to provide water? Where were the giants, now that some brave, hardy souls had ventured into the foothills to build their homes and establish communities?

The law was a sham. The river should be theirs, not the property of some legendary race that had probably never existed in the first place, she believed with all her heart. Yet, and the old woman was hardly alone in this, she would never lift a hand against the river.

As if it mattered, anyway. Even were she to carry buckets of water from the river to her crops, day and night, it would hardly keep her crops from dying. Only rain could save them now. Best to put the river out of her mind, she reasoned.

The old woman looked up as a hoarse voice called out to her from across the fields. Squinting, she finally recognized her youngest grandson, Nathaniel, barreling toward her as fast as his little legs could carry him.

"Come quick, Grandma, come quick!" he shouted when he was close enough for her to finally hear him clearly. "There's something you gotta see!"

"What is it?" she asked her grandson, who almost collapsed from fatigue when he reached her side. "What's happened?"

"It's…it's a boat," he managed, gasping for air.

"A boat?"

"Yeah, on the river. Drifted into shore." The little boy bobbed his head up and down in excitement. "Just now. Katie saw it first."

"You're sure it's a boat?"

"Yep. Come see it for yourself."

"So where did this boat come from?" the old woman asked, still wondering whether to believe the little boy.

"Don't know," he said with a careless shrug. "Just appeared, Katie said."

"That's what your sister said, that it just appeared and then drifted into shore?"

"Didn't I say that?" Nathaniel pouted. "Now come on before it goes away."

"All right, young man, but this better not be a trick or your bottom's likely to be sore for quite some time," she warned.

"Not a trick, I promise." He pulled on her hand to make her hurry.

By the time the two had reached the banks of the river, the rest of the large family had also gathered there. Nathaniel had been telling the truth. There was a boat alongside the river. It had drifted near the shore, into a thick growth of reeds. The current would soon free it from the reeds, however, and carry it farther downstream.

"Well, has anyone been out there to look inside it yet?" the old woman asked.

They all simply stared at her, waiting for some kind of a matriarchal decree. Not a soul among the thirty or so family members who'd gathered had dared set foot in that river before she'd arrived.

"Just as I thought. A bunch of ninnies," the old woman said scornfully.

Two of her granddaughters giggled. She was always calling everyone a ninny, or a silly willy, or any other name she could think of.

"Okay, let's bring it to shore and have a look. Tom and Jack," she directed two of her sons, "you wade out there and tie a rope to it. We'll all help pull it into shore."

The two broad-shouldered men grabbed the end of a thick rope one of them had remembered to bring from the farmhouse and stepped gingerly into the river. The water was above their waists by the time they were able to reach the bow of the boat and fasten the rope end to it.

It took all of their muscle to pull it ashore. The boat was a good 30 feet long and made out of very heavy wood, most likely oak. The men were breathing heavily by the time it was successfully moored.

"Look at this!" reported Nathaniel, who'd been desperately trying to peek inside the boat as it was being pulled ashore. "There's someone in the boat."

"Oh, she's so pretty," said one of Nathaniel's sisters. "But look how she's dressed. It's strange."

The old woman stared inside the boat. A dark-haired, striking young girl, perhaps in her late teens, was fast asleep at the stern. The rest of the boat was barren. Not a bit of cargo.

"*Strange* is the word for it," the old woman agreed. "The pants are made out of cotton, I'd say. That's my guess. But the stitching is so fine. Must have taken someone months and months to weave such a fine pair of britches."

"But where'd she come from?" one of the men asked. "Nobody's heard tell of a boat on this river, in our lifetime, at least. How about you, Mother? When was the last time you've seen a boat on the river?"

"Never," the old woman snapped. "I've never met a soul brave enough to challenge the people of the sea."

"Aren't no such people," Nathaniel muttered under his breath.

"That's enough!" the old woman rebuked her grandson. She turned to Katie, the little boy's oldest sister. Katie was nearly the same age as the girl in the boat and just as pretty. But where the girl in the boat had dark features and a fierce countenance, even in repose, Katie had the fresh-faced innocence of a girl who had never strayed far from home. "Nathaniel said you saw the boat just appear? Is that true?"

Katie nodded solemnly. "I looked up and it was just there. I didn't actually see it appear or anything. But it wasn't there when I looked down and then it was when I looked up."

"I see," the old woman said.

"There was something else strange, Grandma," Katie added uneasily.

"What was, child?"

"Well, you know we haven't seen any crows around here for a long time, not since Father—"

"You've seen crows?" The old woman cut her eldest grandchild off before she could finish. The return of those ghastly, black-winged devils would finish them for sure. Everyone knew they were the unholy messengers of the gods. They could pick the corn clean in two days' time.

"No, no, Grandma," Katie said quickly. "Not really, not like before. There were only three of them."

"Three crows?"

"Yes, Grandma. I didn't notice them until the boat appeared."

"Tell it to me *exactly* as you saw it, child." Where there were three crows, more were sure to follow. Best be prepared for the worst now.

The girl was pensive for a moment, trying to remember the incidents in the right order. "Like I said," she began slowly, "I looked up and didn't see nothing…"

"Didn't see anything," the old woman said, correcting her grammar out of habit.

"Yeah, anything," Katie continued. "I looked down at my work, and when I looked up again, the boat was sort of out there."

"And then?"

"And then these three crows swooped out of the sky like black arrows," the girl said excitedly. "They came *fast*, like they had to get to that boat in a hurry."

"What happened next?"

"All three of them pulled up hard, like when they come down to get some corn and then fly off again. You could hear their wings from here flapping hard to keep from going into the water. Then they just landed on the boat, right up there." She pointed at the prow of the boat. "They stared down into the boat for a little while until I screamed at them to shoo them away."

"And that's it? They flew away?"

"They sure did, as fast as they could. That's when everybody came, after I screamed at the crows."

A sudden movement in the boat caught everyone's attention. While Katie had been telling her story, Nathaniel had quietly clambered over the edge of the boat and, at that very moment, was attempting to wake the sleeping girl.

"Wake up, wake up," he whispered, gently tugging on her shoulder. "Time to start the day."

Laura's eyes opened slowly, dreamily. Nathaniel leaned over to stare at the creature he'd awakened. As their gaze met, Laura's hand shot to her mouth, stifling a scream. Her eyes were wide with unbridled terror.

Startled, Nathaniel sat back in the boat with a very loud thump. "Why'd you do that?" he pouted from his sitting position. "I just wanted you to wake up 'cause it's time to start the day. We've all been up since Cawka called us and you were still sleeping."

Laura looked at the little boy sitting before her with dark, brooding eyes and, for the life of her, couldn't make a thing of it. "Where am I? and who's Caw…Cawka?" she added in a raspy voice.

"The rooster, silly." Nathaniel sighed. "Don't you know anything at all?"

"No, I guess not," Laura smiled at the little boy who very much resembled her own brother she'd tearfully said good-bye to when she left for college.

"Is this yours?" Nathaniel's natural curiosity took over now.

"Is what mine?" she asked back, her mind still numb from the shock of waking up in a strange place with a little boy staring intensely at her.

"The boat!" Nathaniel exclaimed in thorough exasperation. "What'd you think I meant?"

Laura glanced at her surroundings, something she hadn't bothered to do yet. She felt that familiar throbbing at the back of her head, the pain she always got when she'd studied too long and hard. "No, this isn't mine." She squinted hard to bring the world back into focus. "I don't know who it belongs to."

Just then, the rest of Nathaniel's family peeked over the side of the boat. Silently, they all took their places around the boat, staring at her as if she were some sort of ghost. An eerie chill worked its slow fingers along the nape of Laura's neck.

"Where am I?" she asked again. "And who are all these people?"

Nathan looked up. "Oh, just my brothers and sisters, mom and dad, grandma, my cousins."

"But where am I?" she asked again in hushed horror.

"On our farm," Nathaniel said petulantly. "Boy, are you ever dumb."

"Nathaniel, be nice," his grandmother scolded, breaking the ring of silence around the boat. Laura gazed up at the old woman expectantly. "But the child is right, young miss. This is our farm."

"But I don't understand," Laura said, almost crying despite the hard years of practice she'd put into trying to teach herself *not* to cry in difficult situations.

"What is it you don't understand? Maybe we can help," the old woman asked kindly, patiently. She'd always been a good neighbor, even to those who had never been so nice in return.

"I don't understand what's happened to me, why I'm in this boat with all these people looking at me, how I fell asleep in that room…"

"You just magicked out of the air," Katie said abruptly.

Laura stared hard at the girl. Katie had the kind of scrubbed-clean face that doesn't lie, the plain looks of an honest girl. "What did you say?" Laura asked her directly.

"I said you magicked here." Katie carelessly tossed her long, brown hair over one shoulder. "One minute you weren't here, the next minute you were."

"What the child means to say," the old woman added, "is that it appears magic brought you here from some other part of the land. Not uncommon, though it's been a good number of years since anyone in these parts has seen it happen."

Laura let the old woman's statement sink in slowly, just as she'd taught herself to assimilate lectures in class. Don't dismiss anything yet, work through the hypothesis, let the plain facts speak for themselves. "Do you mean to tell me," she said at last, "that magic works here? Real magic?"

The various members of Nathaniel's family exchanged bemused smiles.

"Even I know the answer to that." Nathaniel shook his head in disbelief. "Where do you live, anyway? In the mountains?"

"Wait a minute," Laura said defensively. "Then magic does work here? And all of you know it?"

"No, not exactly," the old woman said. "But we could, if we knew how. If somebody would teach us, that is."

"Who knows, then, if you don't?" Laura asked aggressively as she always did in class.

"In the city!" Nathaniel practically shouted. "Everybody knows that."

Laura drifted back to something she'd been listening to before…. "The city!" she remembered. "Tell me, is there a city here where only powerful magicians can enter?"

"Yes, of course," the old woman answered, plainly as confused by the questions as Laura was confused about what had happened to her.

"And no one's seen a magician for a very long time?"

"That's right," the old woman said. "I've not seen a one of them in my lifetime."

"And it's been more than a thousand years since the six races vanished?"

"Closer to two thousand, but yes, that's true," the old woman answered.

"Yep, you're dumb, all right," Nathaniel added. "I hear this stuff every night before I go to sleep."

Laura groaned. The throbbing in her head had turned into a jack-hammer. She could feel herself slipping, beginning to faint. She closed her eyes to let the emotions and the reality of what she had heard wash over her for a minute until she could collect her wits.

Nathaniel's family continued to stare in silence, afraid to disturb the striking, young girl with raven-black hair. They all waited for her next move, afraid it might be what all of them had both dreamed about and dreaded all their lives. *Perhaps she was one of them, come from the city and the glorious castle again after all these years*, they thought, almost as one.

Laura set her jaw firmly. "There's one way to settle it. We'll just have to test the hypothesis."

She hopped to her feet, wobbled slightly, and asked for help out of the boat. Now that she'd charted a course of action, she set to it with complete, total determination that left no room at all for fear or despair. Not until she'd answered the fundamental question, the basis for the hypothesis, would she allow another question to enter her mind.

Okay, I need a simple, first-level spell with only a one-word command and an almost elementary material component, something easily at hand. She searched the ground for something to use, simultaneously scouring her memory for one of the dozens of spells she'd almost automatically memorized back in the map room, before she'd somehow fallen asleep and arrived in this nightmare world.

Spotting a dry stick a couple feet away, she hurried over to it, Nathaniel and the rest of the family trailing in her wake. She picked the stick up gingerly, as if the thing in itself could reach out and bite her. *What can I do with a stick? What kind of a spell is this the material component for? Oh, yes, that's right. A fire. I can create a fire if I bury the bottom end of the stick in the ground and say the word.*

Silently, she dropped to one knee and scrubbed at the soft, yielding soil. Within seconds, the stick was in the ground, pointing up at the sky. *All right, here goes.*

"*Pur*," she said softly to the stick, using the precise pronunciation from that strange tome from *The Books of El* she'd been reading before.

As she'd read through the book of spells, Laura had discovered that nearly all of the magical words used to invoke spells were ancient, root words, many of which predated even the very Olde English. This word was like that. It was clearly the root of the word that had eventually become known as *fire* in modern times.

The word seemed to hang in the air for an instant. And then, without ceremony, the stick burst into flame.

The onlookers gasped in fright, their deepest hopes and fears confirmed before their eyes. "She is one of *them*," whispered a middle-aged woman, Nathaniel's aunt. "We are doomed."

As Laura got to her feet and gazed at the crackling fire, her own worst fears confirmed as well, Nathaniel slipped up beside her. "Hey, that was great," he said, bubbling over with unbounded enthusiasm. "Can you teach me how to do that?"

"Sure, kid, no problem," she replied gloomily, a deep despair settling in now that her fantastic hypothesis had borne fruit. "It's easy, once you get the hang of it."

"Teach me now. Right now." Nathaniel impatiently tugged at her shirt sleeve.

"All right." She sighed, her mind slowly blanking out, refusing to take the next logical step as it always had in the past.

Nathaniel raced away from Laura's side, found two sticks nearby, and raced back.

"Here." He pushed one of the sticks into Laura's hand. "Show me how."

Laura knelt wearily to the ground a second time. Nathaniel mimicked her perfectly, bending the same knee and holding his own stick in the same hand. The little boy obviously figured that he had to do everything she was doing *exactly* right or it wouldn't work when he did it.

"Okay," she whispered so only he could hear, "you have to dig a hole in the ground like this." Both of them scooped out the loose soil. "And then you place the stick in it, exactly halfway." Each placed their stick in and filled the hole back up. "And then you say the word."

"The magic word?" Nathaniel whispered back.

"That's right. It has to be pronounced exactly right. If it isn't, then the trick won't work."

"So what's the word?" he asked conspiratorially.

Laura pronounced the word again, with the right tone and inflection. Her own stick caught fire. Nathaniel quickly said the word, too. His stick didn't catch fire.

"You lied." Nathaniel pouted. "Mine didn't work."

"You didn't say it right. Keep trying," Laura told him, adding that the word sounded like *moon*, or *soon*, or *tune*, or any of a hundred other words with long *o* vowels.

On his second try, it worked. Nathaniel whooped for joy as his stick caught fire. Before anyone could restrain him, he raced off to gather more sticks. When he had as many as he could carry, he dropped them to the ground and began to practice, one after another.

Laura watched him for a minute, then said to the boy's grandmother, "Perhaps you could tell me exactly where I am in this land. How close I am to the city, what the rest of the people are like in the world, where this river leads to." *And how I can get back home,* she thought bitterly.

"Yes, of course," the old woman said in awe. "But you must tell me something first. Are you one of them or not?"

The question stumped Laura before she remembered the history of the land Eric had given them. "Oh, I see what you mean. One of the magicians from the city?"

"Yes, that's what I mean." The old woman nodded fearfully.

"Of course not. I haven't come from that cursed city," Laura snapped. "I'm not from this world, but then you wouldn't have any way of knowing that, would you?"

"Then where are you from?" the old woman asked timidly.

"A place I'm sure you've never heard of." Laura sighed. "Very far from here."

"And, please, why are you here?"

"I wish I knew," Laura said with sarcasm. "Believe me, I wish I knew."

10

* * *

THE SONG OF THE MUSES

The fountain had been there from the moment time began, the legends said. It should not have been there, bubbling up from well below the earth to the very top of the mountain overlooking the vast city.

An old couple lived nearby with their nine daughters these days, foraging for their food in the sparse forest lands that dotted the top of the mountain and drinking daily from the waters of the fountain they so jealously guarded.

No one could say how long the happy family had lived there, though a few of the mountain people who'd migrated north from the plains claimed they'd been there since anyone could remember. The family kept to itself. As far as anyone could tell, they never ventured far from the magnificent fountain. Even now, with every creek bed and stream for miles around beginning to dry up, they didn't offer even a drop of their water to their neighbors.

Only one daring soul had ever drunk from that fountain—a young shepherd boy, Lucas, who tended the flocks during the day for half a dozen families. In fact, although he'd never let on to his parents, the boy had drunk from that well on more than one occasion. After all, he was 15 and he was entitled to take such a risk. It was almost expected.

Besides, there wasn't anything all that scary about it. Lucas would wait until dusk, when the flock had been safely herded back, and then he'd slip out and back before dinnertime. No one was ever the wiser, least of all the old couple and their nine daughters who lived in a shanty built into the side of the mountain near the fountain.

At least, that's what Lucas had always assumed. He'd never even seen a light coming from their woeful home. No one had ever challenged him. And the water was so cool and clear, it made his head spin and his mind giddy sometimes. He loved that first taste, when he lifted a handful of water from the clear pool that gathered around the fountain.

The fountain was also on the very best part of the mountain, the spot overlooking the secret, magic city more than a mile below. The shanty was in even a better vantage point—sitting atop the highest part of the mountain—but the fountain was almost good enough. Lucas could see most of the city below from there. And from his infrequent visits to the fountain, Lucas noted that the city appeared to be a very strange place indeed.

At night, the place was almost always pitch-black. However, sometimes a light or two would flicker in different parts of the city. And during the day, he could only catch glimpses of what looked to be a huge beast of some kind strolling along the twisting corridors of the place. Occasionally, he would catch glimpses of smaller folk, but he wasn't sure because it was so far away.

Lucas didn't mind, though, that there didn't seem to be a great deal of activity within the city. It matched his solitary lifestyle. He tended flocks all day, alone, on the mountainside, watching for the wolves as the sheep grazed contentedly. He had no brothers or sisters and his parents were old, so he would sometimes stay out with the sheep until well into the evening. Neighbors were few and far between. And, during his jaunts to the fountain, he never ran into a soul.

Which made tonight's discovery doubly exciting. For, as he slipped up on the shanty and the fountain, his eyes spotted something, or someone, lying off to one side of the fountain pool. In the fading light, it almost looked like a young man, which made no sense to him because the old, white-haired man in the shanty had nine daughters.

Perched in a nearby tree, Lucas realized with a start, was a huge black crow. That was strange. Crows rarely ventured so high up from the plains below, where foraging for food was so much easier. But it was a crow, of that Lucas was almost certain. And the bird's eyes were riveted on the young man reposing beside the fountain.

As Lucas cautiously drew closer, the young man tossed fitfully, turning his head from side to side every few moments and moaning softly as if in pain. Lucas decided then to rush to the fountain and wake the man before he rousted the residents of the shanty nearby.

As he moved swiftly across the ground like a silent thief, his quick ears picked up faint music drifting from somewhere, a sweet chorus of voices singing a song he'd never heard before.

It must be coming from that shanty, he thought, his mind now torn between the sweet music and the task at hand. The music was calling to him, urging Lucas to join them at the mountain's edge....

But, no, I've got to wake this young man first, Lucas thought in sudden anger. *Then perhaps the two of us can explore this mystery together. First things first.*

Lucas wasn't prepared, though, to find someone in such a horrid state of affairs. The young man seemed to suffer from a high fever and hallucinations of some kind, for he called out names and places Lucas had never heard of.

Lucas was almost afraid to touch the young man's ghostly pale face, for he looked deathly ill. The dark, brooding, and glazed eyes with the huge dark circles frightened Lucas a little. The gauntness of his face, the frailness of his shoulders, the disheveled clothes, and the unkempt hair made him appear to be a beggar.

But, no, those were not the eyes of a beggar. They were the eyes of the haunted, who may not even be aware of it yet.

When Lucas finally worked up his courage, he shook the young man gently at first, and then more violently, when he didn't awake from his daze. Frantically, because the music nearby was growing louder by the moment, Lucas dipped one of his hands into the cool, clear fountain pool and, without hesitation, dashed the water in the young man's face.

"What the…?" Jon almost shouted, his eyes blinking furiously. His face was numb with cold from the water. Something sharp, like a splinter, was poking him in the back as well.

"Hush!" Lucas whispered. "Or they'll hear you."

"Who will hear me?" Jon whispered back angrily. "And who are you?"

"A friend," Lucas said. "And if you don't be quiet, I'll leave you here and let you take your chances with *them*."

"Them?"

"The strange family that lives here, on the top of the mountain. Can't you hear that music?" Lucas asked, tugging him to a sitting position as he spoke.

Jon could hear now, too. An incredibly delicious chorus of voices, off in the distance somewhere, but growing louder, or closer, every second. It was, perhaps, one of the most delightful sounds he'd ever heard.

"Yes, I hear it," Jon said thoughtfully. "But what is it?"

Lucas shook his head gravely. His sixth sense—the intuition he'd had since early childhood, the innate knowledge that always told him *exactly* where wolves were lying in ambush—now told him to get out of here. As fast as his legs would carry him. "I don't know. I'm not sure," he said frantically, trying to block the sweet music from reaching his ears. "But we've got to leave this place right now, before whatever it is gets here."

As Lucas gave a vicious last tug, however, Jon groaned loudly and sank back into the grass beside the fountain. "Oh, my head." Jon gasped. He put his hands to his throbbing temples, attempting to push the unexpected pain away. It did no good.

"What's wrong? What happened?" Lucas leaned over Jon as fear grew in his heart. *They* were close now. He could feel it. There wasn't much time.

"Feels like a migraine or something," Jon muttered. "My head is pounding like a loose cannon ball is rolling around inside."

"You don't look too well, either," Lucas added. "But trust me. We must leave."

"Just let me rest a minute. Then we can go." Jon eased his eyes shut and leaned his head back too quickly. It cracked against something hard. He reached back and pulled a piece of wood from behind his head.

"Looks like what's left of an old oak bucket," Lucas said nervously as Jon turned the piece of wood over in his hand. "To drink from the fountain."

"There's a fountain right here?" Jon asked, his curiosity winning out over the fierce, aching head.

Lucas regarded him suspiciously. How could he not know there was a fountain only a foot or two from him? "Reach your hand out. It's right behind you."

Jon did as he was told. His hand plunged into the cool, clear water and he sat bolt upright, forgetting the pain completely now. "That's the ticket," he said with renewed enthusiasm, leaning over the pool, vigorously splashing water in his face.

As Jon lifted one handful of water after another to his mouth thirstily, Lucas listened more keenly to the approaching music. He could almost make out the melody—an eerie, haunting refrain that, at the same time, sounded almost peaceful—but not the lyrics. Whatever it was, it would be on them in moments.

"We can't wait much longer," Lucas almost shouted, grabbing at Jon's arm. "Let's go."

"Just a few more." Jon greedily plunged his hand into the cool water yet another time. "This stuff is so wonderful. It's like nothing I've ever tasted."

"Are you crazy? Can't you hear them coming for us?" Lucas permitted himself to shout. It didn't matter now. He felt sure *they* knew who was drinking from their fountain.

Jon paused to listen. The pain in his head was gone. A lightness, almost a dizziness, had replaced it instead. *The water!* His thoughts spun giddily. *It has done something...altered my mind somehow.*

The music started to enfold its sad, wonderful tendrils around Jon's mind then, urging him to give up the cares of the world, to forget his dark thoughts and his troubles, to yield the sorrow and grief in his soul. *Gladly*, Jon cried silently. *Gladly will I give those over to you.*

"What are you doing?" Lucas screamed at the maniac he'd stumbled on, the music around them both enraging and fascinating him at the same time. "Can't you hear them? They're all around us!"

Yes, I hear them! Jon thought gleefully. *I've waited for this peace for so long. I've waited for just this moment, when I could turn my dark visions and my burning anger at a godless universe over to someone else, someone greater than myself....*

Lucas clapped the surface of the water in the pool, splashing a wave into Jon's placid face. "I'm leaving! Do you hear me?" he yelled into Jon's uncomprehending face. "Are you coming or not?"

When Jon didn't answer or even respond to the sudden move, Lucas leaped to his feet and, heart pounding, raced to the shanty. There were no windows to peek through. He could hear no voices from within.

He glanced around more frantically now, wondering what to do next. He had this absolutely awful feeling that, if he didn't do something quickly, the strange man at the fountain was a lost soul. How he knew that, how he was utterly *certain* of that fact, he couldn't say. But the glassy, unfocused look in his eyes, the way his head was lolling about aimlessly, and his almost total collapse of will were sure signs that the man, whoever he was, had succumbed to the eerie magic of those sweet voices.

Not that they didn't have an effect on Lucas. Oh, they did indeed. They reminded him of sunsets during the summer as he herded the sheep home. They made him think of fresh, hot, spiced goat's milk by a roaring fire at home. They brought to mind the marvelous wool coat his mother had made for him last winter and midnight swims during the heat of summer at a stream near their house.

But Lucas fought those feelings. They were nothing more than pleasant memories, not things or moments of importance beyond that. And he did not want those memories forever, as living things, which is what the voices surrounding him almost seemed to be promising.

"Come with us," they seemed to be saying, "and it will always be sunsets, forever goat's milk by a roaring fire, and eternal midnight swims. Come with us, give us your worries."

But what will you take in return? Lucas cried out to them. *What must we give up for the peace of our soul? No answer was forthcoming, beyond the sweet sounds of the unchanging music.*

So Lucas closed his soul to those promises and searched desperately for a way to shake the young man from his waking dream. There must be something he could do, some way to rescue the man before it was too late. Even now, the music was rising toward a grand finale. The sweeping crescendo would be finished soon. The deed would be done.

Lucas ran back to the fountain, despairing, and started to physically drag Jon away from the water. It was no use at all. Jon was almost comatose by now. His eyes barely showed any sign of life. They were dull, unseeing, uncaring.

But even as Lucas was about to give up all hope, Jon suddenly stiffened with resolve. He rose to his feet clumsily and, like a sleep-walker, headed toward the mountain's edge. Lucas, confused, followed in his wake. They made a strange pair— Jon barely able to put one foot in front of another, moving inexorably onward, and Lucas following warily, not quite sure what was happening.

When they were only feet from the edge, it finally dawned on Lucas what was happening. He'd seen it, felt it, before. The pull at the edge of the mountain was alluring, compelling. It called to you. It took the firmest sort of willpower to stare down the side of a mountain without succumbing to that urge.

Lucas quickly stepped in front of Jon and held him in his place. Jon tried to sidestep the young boy, but Lucas held firm. "Where are you going?" Lucas asked him directly, not really expecting an answer.

"Let me go. I want to be free," Jon mumbled.

"What is it you want to do?" Lucas asked, surprised at the answer.

"Freedom. Peace. I want to fly," Jon said with a dreamy smile, the words barely able to fall from his lips.

"You want to fly? Like a bird?"

Jon's dreamy smile broke into a wide grin. His eyes were almost closed, though. "Yes, fly."

Lucas glanced nervously over one shoulder. The man, a good foot or so taller than him, could easily take the two of them over the mountain's edge if he wanted to. It was very close.

"But that's impossible," Lucas said.

A strange gleam almost worked its way through the dull lifelessness in Jon's eyes, as if he had remembered something amusing. "No, not impossible. Magic word. *Pleu*." Jon tilted his head back and opened his mouth wide, like a drunk waiting for a rain shower to rinse his mouth clean. "*PLEU!*" he shouted to the heavens.

Jon began to force his way past Lucas, and there was nothing the young boy could do to stop him. He didn't want to go over the edge as well, so he stepped to the side, still holding onto Jon's leg, desperately trying to keep him from moving forward. It didn't work. Inch by inch, they came closer to the edge as the music swelled to a feverish pitch.

Then, out of the sky, like a bolt of lightning, came the most elegant and marvelous creature Lucas had ever seen. It streaked toward them, racing across the sky like a light fury.

Lucas stared in stunned disbelief as the creature winged its way closer. There was no mistaking it. The creature was a horse—a huge, winged horse whose shadow dwarfed the two of them as it approached. Each beat of its mighty wings caused the air beneath it to shudder in its wake.

The ground shook terribly as the winged horse landed several feet to the other side of them, away from the mountain's edge. Jon never even blinked. Lucas didn't either, but for a far different reason. He couldn't take his eyes from the glorious creature. The animal looked as if it had been chiseled from marble.

The horse stood there, staring intently at Lucas, before it anxiously pawed the ground with its right hoof, shaking its proud, regal head back and forth. Plainly, it wanted something from the two of them. But what?

Lucas, in renewed desperation, stood and put his shoulder to Jon's belly and heaved with all his strength. Jon, not expecting the assault, took a couple stumbling steps away from the edge, almost losing his balance.

The effort was enough for the winged horse. Sensing that it could now pick up what it had come for—or been called for—the horse took a step forward, bent its front legs, and settled to the ground. The creature's eyes pleaded with Lucas.

"Oh, I get it!" he said excitedly. "You want us to get on your back?"

The creature said nothing, but its intent was obvious.

"It's time to fly," Lucas said directly to Jon. "Let's go."

When Jon tried to mumble something in return, Lucas gave another mighty heave and pushed Jon in the direction of the horse. Jon tripped over one of the creature's wings it had lowered to the ground and fell headlong across its back. Lucas scrambled behind and piled on top, straddling Jon.

The horse didn't hesitate. It rose from its haunches, leaped with a mighty flap of its long wings, and soared out over the mountain's edge. Lucas almost fainted from fright as the land dropped away beneath him. Jon simply groaned.

"We're flying, stranger," Lucas finally managed to whisper when his fear had subsided some and the powerful, compelling music had begun to fade. Jon still didn't answer, though some of his color returned as they flew further from the music and the ghastly mountaintop.

Where they were off to, however, was another question entirely, a question Lucas wasn't sure he wanted the answer to. For, with the earth slowly falling away, the horse was swiftly making its way toward the clouds far, far above.

11

***

HIGH TREASON

Mark slipped up quietly behind the two of them when the band stopped to rest and catch its breath. He'd been practicing the fine and subtle art of stalking, when no one was looking, and it had been an easy matter to move within earshot of the Weasel and Blackbeard.

The boy sometimes fancied that the faint strain of elvish blood that ran through his veins manifested itself when he concentrated on the elvish arts. Maybe just a little, anyway. Why else had he mastered a bow so quickly, or the quick yet soundless effort needed to track someone?

For whatever reason, his skill, or perhaps his inheritance, paid off handsomely this afternoon. Mark was only able to catch the end of their conversation, but it was enough to convince him that the two were planning something horrible. And they meant to use their prisoner as bait.

"You know it is! It's our only chance," Mark heard the Weasel whisper fiercely to Blackbeard. The boy had managed to worm his way along the ground until he was safely concealed by some undergrowth yet still within several feet of the two.

"Yes, you may very well be right." Blackbeard thoughtfully stroked his thick beard. "But perhaps we should wait a bit longer, until we can arrange a hunting accident for my brother. That would make it so much easier...."

"No! You must seize the opportunity now, before your father—curse his senility—hands the crown over to your brother," the Weasel warned. "That would complicate matters greatly. We would be hard-pressed to win as many men to our side."

"But why must we force the issue now?" Blackbeard asked plaintively.

"You know the answer to that as well as I," the Weasel said scornfully. "Your father is a fool. He will never believe that the world has changed. He would never admit there is no longer an enemy."

"I suppose you're right." Blackbeard sighed.

"Of course I'm right. For years now we've known how barren this accursed land is. There are no magicians left, if ever there were any to begin with. The drought is setting man against man, yet your dolt of a father persists in pretending everything is as it always has been even as the threat of starvation looms over our heads."

"A good thing we know differently, isn't it?" Blackbeard leered. "We always bring food back to the tables. Too bad we can't bring some of the wenches back with us."

"'Tis sad but true," the Weasel said diffidently. He didn't much care for the frequent forays, the pillaging that was terrorizing the land for miles around the enchanted forest. But it was a necessary evil. The men had to eat somehow and, well, if they raped and killed some women along the way, so be it.

"Your father will always cling to his misguided beliefs that the forest, the Sanctuary, must be preserved at all costs, as a haven for those seeking sanctuary from the powerful magicians." The words tripped off the Weasel's tongue easily. They should come out easily, after all. They'd been repeated by every man, woman, and child in the forest for centuries. It was the basis for their existence.

No matter that no one had sought the forest's sanctuary for nearly 100 years, or that the food supply was dwindling in the forest, or that the men were almost savage in their desire for entertainment to break the eternal boredom, or that most, if not all, no longer believed the magicians had ever existed....

"Which means we must force him from the throne *now*," the Weasel continued, "before he drives us all completely mad with his insane notions of nobility and preserving this wretched Sanctuary. From what? From ghosts of the past! We must seize the opportunity now, while the momentum is in our favor. And the prisoner is our key."

Blackbeard nodded gravely. The scheme made sense. The time was ripe. His men, who perhaps numbered at least half the haven, were ready to follow him. Yet he was obviously having second thoughts about his decision to give the prisoner a fair hearing before the Council.

For Blackbeard knew, as the Weasel had pointed out, that such a hearing would force the issue of his father's growing senility and inability to realize that the rest of the world was crumbling and decaying while he faithfully abided by laws that no longer held any meaning whatsoever in the world.

If Blackbeard played his cards right, and the prisoner proved as honest and forthright as he appeared, then the scene would play into his hands. The stranger was sure to challenge the very fabric of the haven's existence within the Silver Forest. And that would give Blackbeard the opening he needed.

"Yet what if he passes the crown to my brother in the process?" Blackbeard mused. "What then?"

The Weasel chuckled. "Then we kill two birds—one senile and the other witless and naïve—with the same stone. There's nothing to fear. The plan will work. It is time to end this farce. Your father is no ruler, and neither is your brother."

"Yes, I am the rightful leader of this haven." Blackbeard puffed out his chest grandly. "Who, in the haven's history, has ever led so many successful forays outside the forest?"

It was all Mark could do to contain his anger at the treasonous words. What made the pill all that much harder to swallow was that—and curse the fates for arranging it so—Blackbeard was his uncle. The foul creature was the younger brother of Mark's father. It was a fact Mark bemoaned almost every waking moment.

And now, despite the kindness and generosity Mark's grandfather, the head of the Council and the rightful leader of the haven, had shown him his entire life, it appeared that Blackbeard was about to make a desperate, yet calculated, move for the crown that rightly belonged to Mark's father.

There wasn't an actual crown, of course. Mark's father was no more a prince, and his grandfather no more a king, than any peasant in the land. But for nearly two thousand years, or so he had learned in his early childhood, the leader of the haven within the Silver Forest had been a king of sorts by virtue of his lineage.

For, it was said, one of Mark's ancestors had been an elf. And only elves, or those with elvish blood coursing through them, could hope to rule justly within the forest. So, from the instant the elves had vanished from the land, leaving only faint traces and stories behind, Mark's family had served as stewards in the forest, awaiting the elves' return.

Over the course of several hundred years, as the magicians consolidated their power within the city and decreed this and that across the land, more of the peasantry turned to the Silver Forest as a haven from the tyranny of the magicians. They had nowhere else to turn, now that the races had vanished from the land.

For magic did not work within the forest. Or, rather, it never worked as the users intended. Magic was wild, unpredictable, almost random, within the confines of the forest. The forest obviously still retained something of the elves' mystical ability to withstand even the greatest magicians, although its masters had left it in the hands of peasants centuries ago.

Consequently, the magicians had long since given up any hope of maintaining control over those who lived within the forest. A few, nearly a thousand years ago, had tried to conquer it. But their spells had gone awry. One magician had turned himself into a white stag, and legend said he still roamed the land in that form.

There were other rumors, of heroes and heroines in search of some holy grail who had foundered in the Silver Forest as they searched fruitlessly for a path, and of powerful magicians unfamiliar with the land who likewise could not navigate the Silver Forest. But they were just that—rumors and idle legends to frighten children.

Mark's family had ruled peacefully, and wisely, for decades, moving easily through the phases in the land. Those who lived in the forest hardly noticed when the magicians stopped visiting the land and chose instead to remain within the confines of the magical city they had erected for themselves.

And the stewardship of the forest grew easier as the years progressed. The migration to the forest had leveled off as magic slowly dried up in the land and as the need to hide from the magicians dwindled as well.

In recent years, however, as Blackbeard had hinted, the stewardship had faltered under his grandfather's weary hand. Mark's father did his best to keep the men in line, but he was waging a losing battle. Boredom and empty bellies created widespread discontent.

The food supply within the Silver Forest was thinning out in the face of the severe droughts that had ravaged the land in the past several years. And, unbeknownst to Mark's grandfather, Blackbeard had taken to leading small raiding parties outside the forest at night.

Blackbeard's parties always returned at dawn, their bellies sated on peasant food, their minds filled with carnal memories of the countless women they'd brutally raped during their forays. That, of course, explained why Blackbeard's belly protruded so prominently over his belt when the faithful within the haven counted beans for supper each night.

Mark's father suspected what was happening yet could not prove his fears true and so remained silent. Mark knew, of course. He had followed the raiding parties at a safe distance on more than one occasion and was perfectly aware of what was happening. Yet he said nothing, for he was only a boy and it wasn't his place to snitch, even on a rat like his uncle.

Mark's grandfather, meanwhile, continued to hold Council meetings regularly to discuss ways to conserve what little food they had and new ways to restock their supplies. He acted for all the world like nothing was changing, that the forest would always remain a haven for those who would defy the magicians, that he must hold his stewardship of the forest to his bosom and pass peacefully into death with the sure knowledge that he had done his duty faithfully.

Recently, though, Mark had noticed his grandfather often doted on old hopes, old prophecies—that the elves would return in the land's darkest hour and bring with them a happier time, when magic abounded in the land and the simplest peasant could dine at a feast regularly. His favorite was the oldest legend of all, that of a trinity of champions who find the magicians' key to ultimate knowledge and return the land to its greatest glory.

It was sad the way his grandfather carried on. Mark wasn't sure he really believed that elves had ever existed in the land. In a perverse way, he almost believed as Blackbeard did, that you had to take matters into your own hands because the world was devoid of any surprises. Mark and his uncle were nearly of a like mind on the reality of the world. Where they differed greatly was on what to do with that knowledge.

Curse the legacy of the forest and the fact his family had always maintained a haven within it, Mark felt keenly. The world had changed! There was no need to fear the wrath of the magicians any longer, or hope and pray for the return of the elves. It was time to shape the land without prophecies, without magic, and without old fears. Or so he believed from where he stood.

As he rejoined the band and its prisoner, Mark started to shape his own plan of action. It would do no good to reveal his hand too soon after they'd returned to the haven. Better to wait and see what happened before his grandfather's Council. There would be time to warn his father of Blackbeard's intentions.

12

***

THE LAW OF THE LAND

Laura stared glumly at the table, barely noticing the stares of awe and fear that surrounded her in the kitchen of the old woman's sparse farmhouse. She accepted the lukewarm cup of tea the woman offered her with a stiff nod and a mumbled thanks and turned her mind, reluctantly, to the task at hand.

There was simply no escaping the fact that, somehow, she was no longer in a comfortable world where the laws of science governed with an iron hand. The rules were vastly different here. She caught herself wondering, fleetingly, if perhaps she hadn't died and gone to heaven.

But she let that thought pass by quickly. If that were true, it would become self-evident over time. If not, then she'd better adapt quickly to her surroundings and make the best of a horrid situation.

So, her hypothesis was true. Magic worked here, worked very well, in fact. Ancient words, spoken in the proper context, invoked the magic. Which meant, of course, that virtually anything was possible and even probable.

Yet what could she do with that knowledge? And had she arrived in this world purposeless? Would the gods of this world, if there were any, allow her to move and act freely? Was there any point in invoking the magic anyway?

Actually, there was only one fundamental question. On it turned the only hypothesis worth anything to Laura at this point. Answer it and perhaps she could return to her own world, to her books and her certain future as a physician, the only thing she'd ever wanted out of life.

Why was she here? What was *she* to the gods and magicians? That was what mattered most. Everything else—the magic, the awe these people held for her, her despair—paled in comparison to that question. She must have an answer to it. Laura knew she had no choice.

"Is the tea to your liking?" the old woman asked politely, breaking Laura's self-absorbed mood.

"Yes, it's fine," Laura answered.

"Would you care for some more, perhaps?"

"No, this is fine, thank you."

The old woman looked at her family members, who were seated, stone-faced, in a ragged circle around the beautiful sorceress. They would never say a word, not unless they were spoken to first. She was certain of that.

"Pray tell, child, what is your name?" the old woman asked her abruptly.

Laura looked up from the table, startled. "Laura Brisbane," she answered quickly, the name sounding harsh and unfamiliar in the room.

The old woman nodded somberly. "It is an honor, Laurabrisbane. Now, if I may, we are the humble farm-by-the-fork-in-the-River family. My name is Anna—"

"Farm-by-the-fork-in-the-River?" Laura interrupted. "That's your last name?"

The old woman, Anna, frowned slightly at the question. "Last name? I don't understand. We, each of us, have but one name."

"Your first name is Anna?"

The old woman nodded.

"And what is your last name, then?"

The old woman was thoroughly confused. "I have no last name. I am Anna. Our family lives by the fork in the River. That is how we are known."

"But there surely must be another Anna in this world," Laura said, exasperated. "How will people know one Anna from another?"

The old woman stared at Laura as she would at someone bereft of her senses. "There is no other Anna living on this farm by the River. Surely, everyone in the land knows that."

Laura closed her eyes and took a deep breath. Oh, it would be a very long day. Yes, a very long day indeed. "All right. I believe I understand now. Then my name is just Laura."

"Not Laurabrisbane?"

"No. I also have but one name and it is Laura." *There*, she mused spitefully, *figure that one out.*

"I see," the old woman said thoughtfully. "Then your family must live near a...a brisbane?"

"Yes, something like that," Laura answered, glad to be rid of the situation.

"And, may I assume that you are from another land? For I have never heard of a Brisbane."

"I am from another land," Laura said softly.

"I see," Anna said, afraid yet tempted to ask how it was that she was able to move from one land to another. Magicians were powerful—yes, that must be it—and she'd never seen one in the flesh. But the old woman held her tongue, choosing not to question the young sorceress further. Best not to press her luck. So she moved around the room, introducing each of her family by name.

When she came to her eldest granddaughter, she was in for something of a surprise, though. Katie was almost 18, headstrong, impatient to begin her own family and a woman who knew her own mind already. And yet...

"*Kathryn*, Grandma," her granddaughter said sternly when it was her turn in the round of introductions. "Kathryn is my given name. I'd rather not be called Katie any more. It's a name for children, and I am a child no more."

"Why, yes, that is true, child," the old woman said. "But you never said a word."

"There was no need to. Until today," Kathryn said solemnly. Which was true. She would always be Katie to her family. But to others? That was a matter for her to decide, in her own time. And evidently that time was now.

"Pleased to know you, Kathryn," Laura replied with the barest hint of a smile. Funny how some things never change, even from one world to another. She had been Laurie as a child and had only changed her name after going away to school.

"It is truly my pleasure." Kathryn blushed.

Slowly, cautiously, the family opened up to Laura. Though still profoundly awestruck, they grew less and less reluctant to talk of their world. Laura, always inquisitive, asked an endless stream of questions. She needed facts, answers, information with which to surround her hypothesis. And Anna, Kathryn, and the rest of the family seemed more than willing to supply her with what she needed.

From them, Laura learned the vast farm community had begun to unite as the drought blighted the land and their crops. No one had any solutions, other than to continue to pray for rain, but it helped to have others to commiserate with.

She learned that fierce bands of rogues now roamed the countryside, leaving men, women, and children dead or mutilated in their wake, farms burning, and food storehouses depleted. No one challenged them. There was no central government in the land, save the magic city, and therefore no troops or militia to police the land.

There was talk of forming a government, or something, to unite against the lawless ones who brought terror to the land. The farmers, most of all, talked again and again of the need to unite, for neighbors to link arms, to thumb their noses at the magic city and anyone else who would stop them from protecting their families.

Anna was among those who felt this way. None of the bands had set foot on their lands, but it would only be a matter of time, especially if the drought continued. She feared for the lives and well-being of her family, though not her own. She had lived a full life, if not an especially glamorous or exciting one.

Laura learned that Anna and others steadfastly refused to consider the deep, wide river that flowed alongside their farms as a solution to the drought. It was unthinkable and, besides, they had no way of bringing the water to their farms. It astounded Laura that no one had developed irrigation in the land. It would solve a great many of their problems, at least until the rains finally came. But then, she quickly reasoned, if no one considered the vast river—and others like it flowing down from the mountains—as a source of water, then there would be no impetus to develop the means to divert it. The irony was that Anna and other farmers depended on the river for small things—cooking, drinking, bathing occasionally.

What was strictly taboo and unconscionable, under the unwritten law that had pervaded the land for centuries, was the wholesale use of water from the river. At all costs, so it seemed, they must not tamper with the forces of nature on any kind of a grand scale.

That was plain foolishness, Laura felt. No, it was more than that. It was downright stupid and ignorant to leave that vast resource untouched while families starved across the land. And all because they feared the wrath of the magic city or the people of the sea? Heaven help her, Laura couldn't see the sense in that and told them so.

"Ridiculous!" she said when Anna told her why their crops withered so close to an abundance of water. "It's a simple matter to divert that river onto your lands. Farmers do it all the time."

"Not here!" Anna exclaimed in horror.

"No, I didn't mean here," Laura said crossly. "I meant in my own world. It's called irrigation. It would solve all your problems. All you have to do is—"

"No! I don't want to hear any talk of your sorcery," Anna pleaded, plainly afraid of what might befall her family if she listened to Laura.

"It's not sorcery." Laura scowled, hardly bothering to mask her disgust. "It has nothing to do with magic. It's unbelievably simple. You just build a series of trenches, or ditches, from the river to your crops and build a temporary dam to divert some of the river's flow. Before long, the river will flow along those man-made streams and—"

"No more!" Anna said sharply, the fear now unmistakable in her voice. "Sorcery or not, the river is not ours to use as we please."

Laura stared at the terrified old woman. It was beyond comprehension that she would stubbornly refuse to irrigate her lands, even if it meant watching her own flesh and blood starve.

Perhaps, though, they were all waiting for someone else to take the fateful plunge into the unknown? Perhaps if one successfully diverted the course of the river to irrigate his or her crops, then the rest would follow willingly? In that case…

"But it is mine to use as I please," Laura said brusquely, rising to her feet, her jaw set squarely as she tried to remember the necessary spell for the plan she had in mind.

"What are you going to do?" Anna's eyes were horrified. "Please, I beg you."

"Oh, relax, you won't be held accountable." Laura's eyes flashed. "If they come from the city, you can all point accusing fingers at me—"

There was a sudden knock at the door. Anna turned, startled. It had been ages since anyone had come calling at their farm. She glanced at Laura, wondering what new horror might be around the corner.

"I'll get it." Kathryn rushed to the door.

A smallish woman, dressed in a simple, green cloak, strode inside the instant the door was opened. She asked no one for permission. She didn't bother to remove the cloak that partially obscured her face. She simply scanned the room until she spotted Laura, who was still standing. The two gazed at each other briefly.

"So it's true," the stranger said, more to herself than to anyone in the room.

"What is?" asked Kathryn.

Anna rose from the table. "May I help you?"

The stranger nodded curtly at Anna. "Yes, perhaps. My name is Demeter. I live nearby. I've been meaning to pay a visit for some time now. But when I heard that you had a visitor this day, I decided now was as good a time as any."

Anna regarded her quizzically. "Demeter, you say? You live nearby? I can't say that—"

"Not close by." Demeter brusquely dismissed her. "I'm a distant neighbor, within walking distance." She turned to face Laura. "And you? Where do you hail from?"

Laura didn't say anything right away. She wasn't sure she liked this woman much. She was used to imperious sorts, but it seemed out of place here in this household. "Nearby," she answered finally, with a slight smile.

"Nearby?" The woman drew her hood back slightly for a better look at Laura.

"Nearby," Laura replied firmly. "In a place you've likely not heard of before."

"Oh, you might be surprised. I've been many places in my day. So where did you say you came from?"

"I didn't." Laura walked toward Kathryn, brushed past Demeter, and headed for the door. Swiveling back, she looked directly at Kathryn. "Are you coming with me?"

"Where?" Kathryn asked.

"You'll see. Come, follow me."

Kathryn glanced at her mother, then at the stranger, and finally back to Laura. "Yes, I'm coming." She hurried to catch up to Laura and also brushed past Demeter.

Laura strode out into the brilliant sunlight, with Kathryn hurrying to keep up.

Demeter, Anna, and the rest of the family trailed behind as Laura set off toward the river, each of them filled with a giddy mixture of terror, excitement, and wonder at what the brash young woman intended. They could sense doom hanging over their heads, yet were powerless to stop it.

Laura surveyed the lay of the land as she marched to the river. The crops were laid out in neat rows abutting the river. Good. It made it that much easier. She could do it all with just two words combined in one spell, perhaps, if all went right.

Before she could reach the river's edge, Kathryn suddenly caught up to her. The girl said nothing but simply matched Laura's long, purposeful strides.

Laura gave Kathryn a reassuring smile. "I'm going to irrigate your land, if I can."

"I know."

Laura turned abruptly at the river and marched alongside it, between the river and the crops. Periodically she stopped and dug to divert a tiny stream of the river toward the farmland. Kathryn, watching intently, quickly joined in. The two of them worked their way down the river, digging tiny, little trenches of water no more than a couple feet long, until they'd walked the entire length of the cropland.

Bone weary, Laura gazed at Kathryn. Her face was covered with mud and her shoulders sagged from the colossal effort, yet she looked profoundly happy. She fairly glowed with an inner radiance.

"There are some words—ancient ones, root words from the Olde English—that I am going to say," Laura told her. "Hopefully, they will cause some of the river to flow onto your land and water your crops."

Kathryn simply nodded in mute understanding and stared hard at the older girl, content just to listen and take orders.

"One of the words means 'water.' The other will send that water in a straight line. I'm not completely sure it will work like that, combining two words into one spell, but it's worth a shot because I don't have a spell to irrigate something. Understand?"

Again Kathryn nodded, but Laura could tell she didn't understand. No matter. There would be time to teach her later, to explain that, despite her extraordinary memory, she couldn't remember words that had never existed. She was improvising here with the only words she could remember.

"All right." Laura took a deep, nervous breath. "Here goes nothing." She knelt on the ground, placing her right hand in the river and the other on the ground. "*Wedreg*," she said softly, impelling the water to flow from the river to the land, a vivid picture of what she wanted to happen forming in her mind. "*Wedreg*," she said again, louder this time.

There was a deep, ominous rumble in the earth, almost a cavernous groan. The river churned near shore, as it would in the middle of a storm. It seemed to Laura that the river had a mind of its own, that it was deliberately trying to fight the command, to keep its waters from obeying the spell of the magician.

The river lost its battle, or whatever it was that roiled its waters so, because the water tumbled over the shoreline and into the trenches. Creating its own path, the water flowed in a straight line toward the crops.

Laura glanced in the direction they'd come from. The river was overflowing along the shore at every point where the two girls had dug out the soil. Little streams flowed directly onto the land at every point. The river, despite its protests, was irrigating the land.

"Oh, it worked, it worked!" Kathryn shouted, throwing her arms around Laura in a sisterly hug. "I didn't think it would, but it did. You're marvelous!"

"Just lucky," Laura said, embarrassed by the unexpected embrace. "I didn't really think it would work."

Letting go of Laura, the young girl looked again out over the land. Her family had run out to meet the water as it worked its way through the neat rows of tiny plants. Even Anna. They were out there, digging for all they were worth to turn the streams into trickles crisscrossing every corner of the cropland.

"It's like a dream come true," Kathryn said in a hushed, trembling voice. "The crops were almost gone. Another week or two without rain…"

A raucous, ear-splitting cry interrupted. Both girls whirled around. Nathaniel was hanging out over the edge of the boat Laura had arrived in. It was now drifting slowly down the river, with Nathaniel aboard screaming at the top of his lungs.

"Help me! Help me!" the little boy yelled. "Somebody get me out of here!"

The boat had obviously slipped loose from its mooring. *Nathaniel must have been playing inside it*, Laura figured. She frantically tried to recall a spell to stop the boat or fetch the little boy. But nothing came to her. Her mind was blank, frozen in the panic of the moment.

Kathryn, meanwhile, dove into the water almost without thinking. With powerful strokes, she began to swim toward the boat.

Demeter, Anna, and the rest of the family raced to the water's edge. "You'll need to join her," Demeter urged.

"I know that!" Laura turned back toward the boat.

"Tell my brother," Demeter started to say as Laura dove into the water.

Laura frantically searched her memory for a spell as she swam through the cold water. Both she and Kathryn reached the boat's side simultaneously, in the nick of time, before it drifted into the faster currents toward the middle of the river, which would have soon carried the boat out of their reach. They clambered on board.

Nathaniel collapsed into his sister's arms. "I didn't do anything, Katie, really I didn't," the little boy said in between sobs.

"We know that," his sister assured him.

"I was inside and it started going. All by itself," he said tearfully.

"The question," Laura interrupted, "is what do we do now? This boat is starting to pick up speed, and I can't remember a thing to save my life…."

They glanced toward the shore, where the family had gathered as soon as they heard Nathaniel's cries for help. They were drifting away from view as the boat was pulled into the swift currents.

"Do something," Kathryn pleaded.

"I can't remember anything," Laura said. "My mind's a blank."

"But you just *have* to."

"Why don't we just jump and swim for it? It's not that far to shore."

"NO!" Nathaniel squealed.

"He can't swim," Kathryn said softly. "He hasn't learned yet."

The boat suddenly pitched and rocked, throwing all three of them off their feet. Its nose tipped toward the water, as if a giant hand were pushing it down toward the bottom of the river.

"Do something! The river is pulling us in!" Kathryn shouted.

Panicked not for herself but for the little boy who might never make it to shore alive if the boat went under, Laura tried to still the craziness in her mind, to pull a word from the depths of her memory as she'd done so often in the past....

"Yes, yes, I remember," Laura said triumphantly. There had been a spell near the front of the book that allowed someone to breathe underwater. Laura held onto the side of the boat firmly with one hand and asked Kathryn and Nathaniel to hold on to her hand firmly. "When I say the magic word, we'll be able to breathe underwater. Don't be afraid."

And if it doesn't work, she thought, *I'll still have Nathaniel's hand and I can carry him as I swim to shore.*

"It won't work!" Nathaniel shouted.

"Be quiet," his sister said, suddenly very calm. She had complete and utter faith in Laura.

"*Bhreuwe,*" Laura said once, and then again.

Almost instantly, a faint, shimmering light, like a transparent bubble, surrounded the entire boat. A moment later, they and the boat plunged below the dark waters of the river. Nathaniel, panicked, tried to jump overboard, but Laura held his hand firmly. They'd know in just a second or two if the spell had worked.

"Hey, I can breathe!" Nathaniel exclaimed.

Laura nearly collapsed as an immense wave of relief swept over her.

Yet the worst was still ahead, perhaps. Because, although the three could breathe, someone or something was pulling the boat through the water. It wasn't sinking. It was moving inexorably forward even as it plunged deeper into the heart of the river. And where they were headed was anyone's guess.

13

* * *

OFF TO JUDGMENT

Lucas had never seen the city from such a vantage point before—from the back of a huge, winged horse soaring effortlessly toward the highest clouds a man or a boy can see.

After making sure the befuddled young man was secure in front of him, and after his heart had ceased its wild fluttering, Lucas knew he only had precious minutes to glimpse the endless spires and turrets that rose from the very center of the magic city before he and the buildings disappeared from view as they entered the first tier of clouds.

The city had no name. Or, rather, it did have a name, the legends said, but it was a hidden one, known only to the great and powerful magicians who had built it. For with the knowledge of that name came a certain measure of power, the legends said. Some said it was a key, a password that unlocked a great number of mysteries.

From high atop the mountains, looking out over the land as Lucas had for so many years, he'd never really seen the city in all its glory. Yes, he'd seen the dancing lights and stared endlessly at the three gates visible to him in order to catch any glimpse of the comings and goings of the magicians. But he'd always longed to move closer, to gaze down into the city from a different vantage point, one that would yield more than just a long-range view of the magnificent structures. He longed to be the first to see *them*, to carry the news back to the villages and the towns that *they* still lived after all, that the magic had not fled forever and ever....

Then, like a bolt of lightning, the chance was given him. A winged horse leaped down from the heavens, picked him up and carried him off, bringing him closer to the city than he'd ever been. Lucas made the most of his chance. He strained for all he was worth to gaze at the streets of the city and its centerpiece, the castle with its myriad levels, never once wondering or doubting how it was that he was being given this chance. It was his and his alone. He would seize it and tremble with fear later.

The streets of the city, as he'd always imagined, were intricate and complex, winding off in every direction with no thought or care for order. In fact, the city looked more like a maze than anything else. One of the streets, incredibly, curled in upon itself as a serpent's tail would. A second had so many forks it seemed all but impossible to guess where it would end up. And a third looked like a series of boxes, or squares, each smaller than the one around it, finally ending in what appeared to be a deep, black hole of some kind.

But there was one road—a straight and narrow one with no twists and turns at all—leading from one of the gates directly to the castle at the heart of the city. Lucas scanned the city's perimeter, counting the gates. Yes, there were 12 of them, as the legends said. But from which of those gates did the road lead? How could you tell one from another, for they all looked identical from here?

As the horse neared the clouds, Lucas searched desperately for a clue that would identify the gate. *Wait a minute. The sun! It rises out of the west and sets behind the forestland in the east at night. And I am looking at the sun now as it rises in the morning sky. As the sun casts its first light across the plains, it would first reach...yes! That's it!* Lucas almost shouted. *The sun's first light streams through that gate, the westernmost one. That's how I will know, if ever I have such a need. Just follow the sun.*

In the waning moments left before they soared into the clouds, Lucas turned his attention next to the castle. He peered anxiously from one level to the next, hoping against hope to catch a fleeting glimpse of movement in one of the many windows.

He saw any number of wonders—spiral staircases, windows of exquisite beauty, doors of such size it would take a giant to open them, patios so vast and expansive entire villages could congregate on them, ornate walls with strange and mysterious figures etched across them, domes so huge that he could not imagine what manner of halls they covered—but no signs of life. Not a movement, not a flutter, not a trace.

Lucas was surprised at how broad the top of the castle was. It was especially noticeable from this vantage point. The castle narrowed and then broadened again at the top, with porches and balconies and all manner of additions in its higher reaches.

The city, for all Lucas could see, was a ghost town. How he'd prayed and hoped to spot something or someone through one of those windows! But there was nothing. There were no inhabitants, at least none in plain sight. Perhaps they came out only at night, Lucas reasoned, as the dancing lights seemed to say to his heart.

But just as the horse reached the first, white wisps of the clouds, just as Lucas' vision of the city and its castle was about to be obscured, Lucas saw them—a man and a woman, near the uppermost part of the castle. They pointed at them, or was it a wave? Then the horse sped into the clouds, and Lucas saw no more.

Were they magicians? *They must be,* Lucas reasoned. *Who else? It's only common sense to believe, after all, that the magnificence of the creation must naturally reflect the will and intent of powerful creators.*

When they broke free of the first tier of clouds, Lucas could see nothing for miles in either direction but clear, pale blue sky above, dotted with more clouds higher up and the tops of the clouds they'd just risen through below. His heart sank. Lucas had expected to see the top of the castle, but it was nowhere to be found.

It was then that the second passenger aboard the hectic flight to the heavens chose to finally wake from his stupor. And, predictably, Jon almost fell from the horse. Only Lucas's last-minute grab held him in place.

"Oh my," Jon gasped, almost fainting. "This... can't possibly be happening. I've overdosed. No question about it. Always knew it would catch up to me someday."

"What are you babbling about?" Lucas asked him, not exactly happy about the prospect of trying to keep the two of them from plunging to their death far below.

"Nothing, nothing," Jon muttered, refusing to look down and refusing, at the same time, to look Lucas in the eye. That meant he was forced to simply stare morosely at the horse's powerful flank and the wings that continued with their steady thrum, thrum as they propelled them higher.

"What is this overdose? Is that why you are so sick?" Lucas persisted. He'd always had an uncanny knack of recklessly striking to the core of something quickly. It had made him more enemies than he cared to number.

"No, well, yes, I suppose it has something to do with...this predicament I seem to find myself in." Jon's words were barely audible as the wind carried them away.

Lucas looked out grandly across the land. The clouds were stretching out, seemingly to eternity, below them. It was a breathtaking sight, one Lucas would have liked to carve upon his soul forever.

"I am truly sorry," Lucas said, still gazing at the awesome splendor below him. "You were sleeping fitfully when I found you. I could not awaken you..."

"Sleeping?" Jon asked, confused.

"Yes, by the well, by the home of the nine daughters."

"Well? Nine daughters?"

"Yes, when I finally managed to wake you and you refused to stop gulping madly from the well, with that horrible, or wonderful, music coming closer, you began to walk toward the edge of the mountain like a madman..."

Fuzzy memories filtered into Jon's brain. He remembered waking up, staring at this boy, wondering where he was, that marvelously delicious water, and then...

"The music! I remember!" he cried, almost unseating himself again. "It was like nothing I've heard. Much, much better than Beethoven's Ninth."

Lucas eyed him. "It almost cost you your life."

"Yes, I can see that,' Jon said thoughtfully. "I vaguely remember wandering toward it, wanting to fly with it." Jon looked down, then, as if realizing for the first time exactly where he was. "But...but we are flying!" he sputtered.

"Yes, of course," Lucas stated matter-of-factly. "And just where did you think we were?"

"I had no idea," Jon said, stunned. "I must be dreaming."

"It is no dream."

"Then I must be hallucinating."

"This is real," Lucas said, understanding the intent, if not the actual meaning, of Jon's statement.

Jon gazed out across the land, again trying to collect his wits. "Then I really am sitting on a stupid flying horse that might simply drop us off if its tiny brain suddenly decides—"

A violent tremor rippled through the horse's flank. Both Lucas and Jon, unprepared, listed unevenly to one side. Both came dangerously close to slipping completely off the horse.

"I don't think he likes what you said," Lucas said softly, pulling himself up.

"Horses can't think!" Jon snorted, yanking himself viciously back to a sitting position, pulling mercilessly on the horse's mane in order to do so.

The horse reared its magnificent head, reached around, and nipped Jon on the leg. It happened so quickly, Jon had no time to react.

"I wouldn't be so sure of that," Lucas said, unable to suppress a huge grin.

"Brother, that hurt!" Jon complained bitterly. "I have half a mind to just—"

Lucas cut him off. "I wouldn't, if I were you."

"I don't see why not. The thing just tried to take a bite out of me," Jon retorted.

"He also saved your life."

"Sure. How so?" Jon said smartly.

"I couldn't stop you from walking off the top of that mountain. He showed up in the nick of time, after you shouted out this strange word."

"What strange word?"

Lucas pondered. "I don't remember it, exactly. You said you wanted to fly and then, like you were dreaming or something, you shouted it out."

"And the horse appeared? Just like that?"

"Something like that."

"I see," Jon said thoughtfully. "Very strange."

"No, not really. Stuff like that used to happen all the time, when magic was in the land, at least."

"What's that?" Jon asked, suddenly very alert. "No magic in the land?"

"Not for a hundred years or more, not since…"

"…the powerful magicians stopped venturing outside the magic city."

"Yes, that's right." Lucas furrowed his brow. "Some say they never existed in the first place, but I've always believed—"

"This isn't possible!" Jon exploded.

"What isn't?" Lucas asked patiently.

"That I'm in a land some jerk created in his imagination."

"What are you talking about?"

"Oh, never mind!" Jon snapped, angry, sullen, and thoroughly confused all at once. "We'll just play make-believe until I can figure this out."

"Whatever you say," Lucas said uneasily, vowing to leave this madman to his lunatic rants at the first opportunity.

"Do you have the slightest idea where we're going?" Jon scowled.

"None at all," Lucas answered truthfully.

"All right. So where is this magic city then?"

"Down there." Lucas pointed in the general direction they'd come from.

Jon grunted. "You said something about nine daughters and this wonderful, terrible music near a well a little while ago. Was there an old man and his wife anywhere around?"

"Yes, though no one sees them much."

"Tell me, then. What's the name of the well? It does have a name, doesn't it?"

"Um, it's hippo...something or other."

"Hippocrene?"

"Yes, that's it!"

"Should have known." Jon sighed. "Explains where this...magnificent creature came from."

"It does?"

"Certainly. It's plain, basic mythology. Why, any dunce knows of the nine Muses, their father, Zeus, and the spring that every poet from the dawn of time has heard of. Hippocrene is the legendary spring of inspiration. The name of that mountain—it's Helicon, right?"

"Yes, I think that's what some call it. But we rarely have names for anything, except for ourselves, of course."

"Yes, of course," Jon quipped. "Makes perfect sense. No wonder the music made me lose my head. I'm surprised it didn't affect you as well."

"But it did," Lucas protested. "I was drawn to it, as you were. But I managed to resist somehow, until this creature showed up."

"I see...as they say, all's well that ends well. I wish I'd known, though. I have some questions I'd like to ask the old man."

"The old man?"

"Zeus, you oaf," Jon answered. "While I'm floundering around here in this drug-induced, imaginary pea soup, I might as well make the best of it. None of this is real, but I can give it the old college try, now, can't I?"

Lucas simply stared at Jon. Never had he seen a stranger human being. "Are you trying to say that you...you think you're dreaming all this?"

"Precisely. There's no other realistic probability. Eric must have slipped something in my drink...though I don't remember drinking anything."

"That's very interesting. You're completely mad, you know."

"I've known that for years."

"You aren't dreaming. This is all very real."

"If you insist."

"I'm not insisting. I know what's real and what isn't."

"From your point of view. Not from mine."

"From any point of view!" Lucas said, now angry. "How can you sit there, calmly denying that any of this is real?"

"Quite easily," Jon answered gaily, enjoying himself now that he'd settled on the reality he wanted. "I'm surprising myself at my ability, in fact. This is by far the best mind-trip I've been on. Beats the one I took in those caverns in Kentucky hands-down."

"You've lost your mind." Lucas gritted his teeth to keep from punching Jon in the nose.

"I'll find it again, don't worry."

"I doubt it!" Lucas shouted.

"That, too," Jon said smugly.

"What?"

"Doubt. It's an integral part of this reality. You've got to suspend a good measure before all the pieces begin to fall into place."

Just as Lucas was about to punch Jon in the nose, it became clear they were about to land. In the heat of argument, neither had noticed they'd reached the highest level of clouds, the ones just beyond the sight of someone standing on the ground looking up. They'd drifted up and over the outermost edge in almost the blink of an eye.

But what a place to land! The horse settled easily as it soared to a graceful landing, giving both Lucas and Jon a chance to see the landscape without fear.

Where there should have been only white, colors abounded. Where there should have been only flimsy wisps of cloud, half-solid shapes appeared. Where there should have been randomness, there was purpose.

Where there should have been valleys and empty spaces diving deep to the heart of the clouds, there were soaring peaks of austere whiteness that contrasted sharply with the colors throughout. And it was upon one of these peaks that the horse came to an almost effortless halt, his powerful wings surging with backward circles to bring the three of them to a standstill in the air before dropping the last few feet.

Despite himself, Lucas gasped before they touched down. He'd never actually believed that any of it—despite the colors, despite the appearances—was, in fact, real enough to land upon.

Jon wore a vicious smirk as the horse's hooves touched soundlessly to the top of the peak. He slipped easily from the horse's back, glad to be off the creature and anxious to attack with a vengeance the altered reality he'd set up for himself.

"Oh, I never…," Lucas whispered, still seated atop the horse. "Not in my wildest dreams."

"This *is* your wildest dream, fool," Jon said absentmindedly.

Lucas ignored him. "It's magnificent, glorious. But where are we?"

It was then they noticed the landscape. It shifted continuously before their eyes. Peaks expanded and contracted, rose and fell, almost as if the winds swirling around them were sculpting the landscape. Which, of course, they were. That soon became obvious as well. Jon felt a gust of wind carry past him and, moments later, noticed that the land under his feet bent beneath the force of it.

"I wonder what it's all made of," Lucas asked, more to himself than to Jon, "that wind would shape it so?"

But the winds shaped more than the white peaks. They mixed the colors of the landscape together, creating new colors as they blended one part with another. Lucas watched in absolute fascination as the winds pushed a yellow peak into a bright red lake, turning both into a blazing shade of orange.

"Good thing I don't get seasick," Jon said wryly. "This could get to you after a while."

"How could you live in such a place?" Lucas shook his head.

"You'd need wings, as this creature has," Jon replied confidently. "Obviously, the air would be your home. It's the only constant."

"I suppose you're right." Lucas finally slipped from the horse's back.

As if it had been waiting patiently for the boy to come to his senses and drop to the ground, the horse almost immediately turned to face them. It shook its mane once, back and forth. It pawed the ground several times, all the while directly looking at Jon.

"It wants something," Lucas said quietly.

"I'm perfectly aware of that," Jon retorted.

The horse suddenly folded its wings and fell gracefully to the ground, its long body stretched out across the ever-shifting ground. It was an interesting effect, watching the horse roll slowly as the wind caused the land beneath to shift slowly. His eyes never left Jon's.

"He's waiting," Lucas said again.

"I can see." Jon had a glimmer of an idea of what the creature wanted from him, but he was having trouble remembering. Not an uncommon occurrence.

"Well, do something," Lucas insisted.

"I'm trying to remember…"

"Remember what?"

"The word I need, you idiot," Jon almost shouted. "It was in that stupid book, part of the set of *The Books of El.*"

"What book?"

"Oh, never mind," Jon said with a careless wave. "I've got it now." He paused for dramatic effect, a funny smile betraying his cynicism. "*Spreg.* That should do it."

"I should think so." A crystal clear voice rang through the air. "And it's about time, I might add."

"Who is that?" Lucas's eyes were wide in terror.

"It's the horse, you ninny," Jon said scornfully.

"But…it can't be," Lucas protested.

"Why, of course it can," the voice said again. "Now that this young cleric has finally broken the barrier that separates our minds."

"Do you mean you can read my mind?" Lucas asked aloud. "And I can understand yours?"

"Of course," the voice assured him. "How else could you hear me?"

"I'm glad that's settled," Jon interrupted. "Now I have a few questions."

"They'll have to wait," the voice, which both Jon and Lucas now identified easily with the winged horse, said firmly.

"And why is that?" Jon asked.

"Because your reckoning is at hand," the horse said. "If you survive, which is hardly likely considering the fragmented chaos you pretend to call your mind, then I will answer your questions."

"What reckoning?" Lucas asked nervously.

"Have no fear, my friend," the horse told Lucas. "You have done no wrong. You were simply a witness to your companion's witless decision to cross the forbidden boundary."

"Are you mad?" Jon spewed. "What boundary? What reckoning? And for what?"

"Why, summoning me, of course," the winged horse said indignantly. "Drinking from the sacred spring, challenging the daughters of Zeus, using the air for your own selfish, unconscious wishes. What else?"

"Are you saying I had no right to summon you, which, I might add, I never meant to do and which I claim no responsibility for?"

"Yes," the horse answered simply. "The land is well aware of the law. The air is not to be used either foolishly, unwisely, in haste, for personal gain, profit, selfish desires…"

"What law?" Jon asked.

"The law they gave the land before they left, of course," the horse answered.

"They?" Jon asked.

"The fairies," Lucas answered, suddenly realizing what had happened. "And he is right. You have broken the law, though I hardly see how you could have known."

Jon's eyes sparked. "Try it so I can understand."

Lucas held a hand up, sensing that the horse was about to explain. "I'll do it. It's fairly simple. When the fairies fled the land 2,000 years ago, they left behind strict orders—their law, as he has called it—that men were never to invoke the magic of the air except under extraordinary circumstances. If your life was in grave danger, for instance, you would be within your rights to flee through the air."

"This is crazy," Jon muttered.

"No, it's the law," Lucas continued. "The air, as he said, is not to be used foolishly, for personal gain, whimsically, in jest, or anything like that. Its magic can be used to protect or aid."

"When the fairies left humankind to its rotten, self-centered, way of life—and a wise choice it was, I might add," the horse added, "they left behind their strictures, which your companion has so generously recited to you, as if you needed such a recital."

"Now wait a minute," Jon said quickly. "I never knew of any such laws, so I couldn't possibly have known I was breaking them. And who gives these fairies the right to go around making them, anyway?"

"They have the authority over the air, according to the legends." Lucas spoke softly. "They always have. But since there hasn't been anyone around to break them in 100 years, I can understand how it is you forgot them."

"I didn't forget them!" Jon shouted. "I never knew them in the first place! How many times—"

"Stop shouting," the horse commanded. "We can all hear you just fine. And it does no good to complain to me about it. I didn't make the laws. Your reckoning will be with them. And they'll be along any moment now."

"Oh, great." Jon groaned. "Just what I need. A hearing before the fairy tribunal."

"You should be so lucky," the horse said, unable to keep the mirth out of his thoughts. "A witless fool like you would at least have a chance before a tribunal."

"And what's that supposed to mean?" Jon asked indignantly.

"It means that you don't stand a chance on trial before the fairies, not with your mind in its present state of affairs," the horse answered. "I've never known a man yet who can stand the pace the fairies set during an inquisition."

"I'll match their wits, don't worry," Jon stated grimly. "I've never met a man who can match my pace." Yet, for perhaps the first time in his life, Jon was worried. He actually, heaven forbid, had second thoughts.

14

* * *

ELVEN LIFEBLOOD

S amson allowed the fools to bind him to the base of another oak tree like some animal. He'd considered, for a moment, putting up a titanic struggle for his freedom as they wrapped the length of the rope around the tree, but he ultimately chose to bide his time.

He suffered the humiliation, though, with only one thought in mind. Revenge. He'd never killed a man before, but there were other methods of revenge. A broken leg, perhaps, or a crushed rib cage. They would do nicely.

Samson wondered fleetingly, as he plotted his escape, if these half-crazed wild men were indeed serious about killing him because he'd trespassed on their land. Surely not, he reasoned. Who, in this day and age, would kill for something so trivial?

Such a strange name, though, for their home. *The Silver Forest.* And just where in Allah's name was he, anyway? Why were they so uptight about protecting the forest in the first place?

Curse that idiot, Eric, for drugging him and sending him among these bizarre characters. This was worse than the time his fraternity had stripped him and dropped him off in the middle of nowhere in the dead of winter.

Yet somewhere, deep in the recesses of his angry soul, Samson knew his assumptions weren't true. Yes, Eric was responsible for his current predicament. But, no, it was more serious and complex than simply being drugged and carted off to some hick, backwater stretch of the country.

This wasn't North Carolina. Samson knew that. Where he was, exactly, he couldn't say. Or how he'd gotten here. But there would be time enough later to sort it all out. Right now, he had just one priority, and that was to somehow manage to work his way free of this settlement.

And it was indeed a settlement, the likes of which Samson had not seen before. The houses, if they could be called that, were built entirely from wood. But that wasn't what made the community so unusual. It was that the neighborhoods and streets, or whatever, stretched upwards, not outwards.

There were a few scattered houses along the ground, mostly decayed, rotting hulks that looked more like they'd been thatched together with sticks, brambles, and bushes than anything else. Off the ground, perhaps 20 feet in the air, was another level of houses built among the heavy, lower branches of the trees.

This first level of the tree houses was sturdier than those on the ground, but not by much. The main difference seemed to be that the lower-level tree houses appeared to have solid, wooden planks as their foundation while their walls and roofs were similarly thatched with sticks and brambles.

Higher up, there were more houses, each more magnificent than the homes below them. From Samson's vantage point at the base of one of the trees, the homes at the very top of the massive trees here at the heart of the forest seemed to interlace with the branches of the tree itself, solid planks of wood weaving in and out of the live branches.

Samson was still staring up when a very tiny voice said at his side, "I saw you first."

"What's that?" Samson's deep voice rumbled.

"I found you when you were sleeping," the tiny voice said again.

Startled, Samson glanced down to see a little girl not more than nine or ten. She had the bluest eyes, which were, at this moment, staring intensely at Samson—unafraid, questioning, curious, searching, happy. It made Samson uneasy to be stared at this way, as if he were a specimen being studied.

"Don't look at me like that, little girl," Samson chided. "I'm not some freak."

The little girl didn't bat an eyelash. "I know who you are," she said instead, shaking her blond, almost white, curls as she did so.

"You do, huh?" Samson grunted. "So why don't you tell me?"

She reached up and pulled on his sleeve, urging him to lower his shaggy head. Samson did so, reluctantly. "You're one of *them*," she said softly in his ear.

"One of them?" Samson whispered back.

"You can't fool me. You're from the city. I just know it."

"The city?"

"Don't play dumb." The little girl's blue eyes flashed. "I know a fighter when I see one. And you're one."

"And how do you know that, little girl?" Samson wondered what a fighter was and how she could mistake him for one.

"Because Mark tells me about them all the time. In the stories, before I fall asleep," the little girl said conspiratorially. "They're the strongest, most courageous of all men. They always know the right weapons to use, against even the most evil of creatures…"

"Sounds like someone's been telling you stories." Samson smiled.

"They're not stories!" the little girl whispered fiercely. "They're true. Mark says so. And he said they would come back, just like the elves will."

"So who's this Mark?"

"My brother, silly. Everybody knows that."

"They do?"

"Of course. Because he'll be king some day," she announced with certainty. "And I will be his princess."

"I see," Samson said thoughtfully, although, of course, he didn't see at all.

"But my father must be king first. When grandfather lets him, that is."

Suddenly, Samson put one fleeting thought together with another. "Hold on," he said slowly. "There's a fellow, with a black beard, who spoke of his father and the Council. Is that...?"

"Oh, he's my dumb uncle." The little girl scowled. "After I found you asleep at the tree, I tried to just tell Mark about it. But my uncle heard and, of course, he found you first. He always has men out in the forest."

It was becoming clear now. "What's your name, little girl?"

"Samantha." She smiled radiantly. "What's yours?"

"You can call me Samson."

"Hey, the first part of our names sound the same!"

"So big deal," Samson muttered under his breath, wondering how he could use this little girl's friendship to his own advantage. "Let me ask you something," he said aloud. "Your grandfather—is he the king or something here now?"

Samantha sighed. "For one of *them*, you sure don't know very much. Of course my grandfather is the king. He always has been."

Samson ignored the girl's rebuke. "What's his name? And your father's as well?"

"My grandfather's name is Francis. I never call him that," she answered solemnly. "My father's name is William."

"And this fellow with the black beard, this uncle of yours, is he older or younger than William?"

"I don't know," Samantha answered truthfully. "Does it matter?"

"It could," Samson said, more to himself than to the little girl. "Depends on the game they're playing here."

"Well, anyway, I'm sorry they tied you up like this." Samantha gave him a timid smile. "I told them it was silly, that you could just go whenever you wanted, but my uncle didn't believe me."

"Tell me, Samantha, do you know what they plan to do with me?" He leaned close.

"Oh, sure," she said brightly. "My grandfather is telling the Council to come right now. For the hearing."

In fact, the Council had already been assembled. Even as Samantha finished her sentence, two armed guards dropped to the ground along a rope not more than 20 feet from where Samson had been tied up.

"Will you come peaceably?" one of the guards asked Samson as they approached.

"Certainly," Samson said humbly.

"Better make sure," the second guard grumbled.

"Guess you're right," the first said. "We'll send him up as he is."

Without another word, the guards unhitched the rope from the tree. But they didn't untie Samson. Instead, they led him roughly to a wooden platform surrounded by an elaborate rope and pulley system and ordered him to sit.

No sooner had Samson done so than the platform jerked upward. Startled, Samson glanced over the edge to see that Samantha was following in his wake, scrambling up a rope ladder nearby.

As they rose slowly through the branches of the massive oak trees, Samson was able to see that his first assumption had indeed been correct. The tree houses were more elaborate—the wood more solid, the carpentry more intricate—as they rose. And, also, as they rose, Samson could see that the houses higher up were much larger, often interlocked with four, five, and sometimes six treetops.

"Who lives up here at the top?" Samson asked his captors.

"Why, the lords, of course," the first guard answered, startled by the question.

"And just how does one become a lord?"

"Inheritance, how else?" the second answered.

"So there's no merit involved, then?" Samson asked bluntly.

"Merit?" said the first.

Samson held his temper in check. "Have these lords ever done anything to earn these houses?" he asked through clenched teeth.

The two guards glanced nervously at each other, unsure how to answer the question. The houses had been passed from one lord to his son or sons for as long as anyone could remember. There had never been the need to earn them. Not ever.

"No. It is their right," the first guard finally answered.

"I'll show them their rights," Samson muttered.

"Hold your tongue!" the second guard said.

"It has always been," the first guard said meekly. "It is best, anyway. This is the Sanctuary. We can't afford dissension, not here."

"You're all stark, raving mad." Samson stared directly at the two of them. "So tell me. Who lives in those horrible things on the ground pretending to be houses?"

Again the guards glanced at each other. "Why, the women, of course. The cooks, at least, and the cleaners," the first said.

"The cleaners?"

"To pick up the food scraps or whatever else is thrown down."

"Are you telling me that the women collect the garbage you throw down upon them?" Samson's mouth dropped open in utter amazement.

"Certainly. It must be done," the second guard said.

"Where do the rest of the women live?"

"Most live on the ground. Some live on the first level, a few on the second," the second guard explained.

Samson was too dumbstruck to ask anything further. They were approaching the top, anyway. But he wasn't too stunned by the guards' words to notice the sheer magnificence of the structure they were about to reach.

It appeared to be made out of solid oak. It extended for hundreds and hundreds of feet away from Samson. Its wooden foundation intertwined with the tops of so many trees that Samson soon lost count. Its pointed roof rose above the tree tops, the only structure this high to do so.

Samson wondered how such an architectural masterpiece could ever have been constructed so far from the ground. It must have taken years to haul each log up from the ground. For that matter, it must have taken centuries to build all the homes at the tops of the trees here at the heart of the forest.

The guard escorted Samson through two thick, double doors that had been opened wide. Samson was hardly surprised at the vastness of the hall they entered. What did surprise him, though, was that the hall was almost completely filled. And all of them were men. He scanned the rows and rows of curious onlookers for one female visage and found none.

It was a round hall. Wooden bleachers, upon which sat some of the roughest men Samson had ever seen, ringed the hall. In the very corner was a round table with a large hole in its center. Around the table sat a dozen or so men. And within the circle was a lone, wooden chair.

The guards unceremoniously escorted Samson through an opening in the table and shoved Samson into the chair. They didn't remove his bonds but simply nodded to the men at the table and left.

"Didn't I tell you, Father?" Blackbeard declared almost immediately in the direction of an old, white-haired man. "There can be no question."

"That is for the Council to decide," the old man said solemnly.

Samson gazed intently at the old man, obviously Samantha's grandfather, Francis, and the self-styled king of this bizarre congregation of cutthroats and brigands. Without quite knowing why, Samson suddenly decided to take the offensive. "Before I'm to defend myself before this Council, I must have a few answers," Samson demanded, his eyes riveted on the king's.

Almost immediately grumbles of discontent resounded around the table.

"Very well," the king said slowly, his eyes matching Samson's intensity. "Ask your questions."

"First, is it true that women aren't allowed beyond the second level?" Samson asked, assuming they would know what he intended.

Blackbeard scowled, but before he or anyone else could answer, the king held up his hand. "I will answer his question. No, it is not true. They may roam freely at their will."

"But there are none here," Samson persisted. "And I was told they live below, to fetch your meals and your garbage alike. Is this true or not?"

"The women are not here because sentencing someone to death is a man's job," the king said in all seriousness. "And the women live below because they lack the strength to make the repeated climbs to the top of our sanctuary."

Samson said nothing for a moment. *So*, he thought, *they mean to kill me. And, like feudal lords or barbarians from some dark age long ago, they have no compassion even for those closest to them, those who have obviously carried their children....*

"Who built this hall? And the rest of the houses at the top of the forest as well?" Samson's voice rang loud, strong, and clear throughout the hall.

The king again silenced the room by holding his hand aloft. "They have always been here." He peered hard at Samson to discover the intent behind the strange man's questions.

"I see. The elves built them, then," Samson said simply, cutting to the heart of the matter as he saw it.

"So we've always assumed," the king agreed.

Samson considered his next question carefully. "Is there *anything* in this forest you can lay claim to as your own?" he asked at last.

Violent murmurings swept through the room like the winds of a storm. How dare this creature, who was no doubt one of *them*, ask such a question?

"We are the defenders!" Blackbeard bellowed above the growing din in the hall. "We protect the Sanctuary! We ward off the tyrannical magicians! That defense is what we may call our own!"

Shouts of encouragement and agreement thundered across the hall from virtually every direction.

Samson waited calmly for the storm to subside. "And that gives you the right to live well at the expense of others? To dump your garbage down below while you feast up here in luxury?" he asked quietly, so only those around the table could hear.

"We are not on trial here!" Blackbeard shouted again. "You are! You and all your filthy, corrupt kind."

"Silence, my son," Francis commanded. "We will not have a shouting match. This man deserves a fair hearing, not a tongue-lashing." When Blackbeard, glowering, sat down again, Francis continued. "It is hard work defending this Sanctuary. We afford ourselves luxury here at home, because we must break our backs toiling to protect it from the magicians and the rest of their ilk."

Samson, remembering something the young boy, Mark, had said, something that vaguely brought back other memories, played what he felt was a trump card. "But isn't it true there have been no magicians spotted in the land for a hundred years?"

"It may be," the king spoke slowly, "that it has been some time since—"

"You're all fools!" Samson rose from his chair to address the entire hall. "There are no magicians! There is no need for this so-called Sanctuary! You are living in the past!" Yet even as he shouted these words, Samson knew they would fall on deaf ears.

Every word he'd heard since awakening under that first oak tree—the murmurs he'd picked up from the sentinels, the words of the little girl and her older brother, Mark, the confusion from the two guards who'd escorted him up to this hall—all told Samson one thing. These people, existing in this idyll setting, were living a fantasy. Just whose fantasy it was he couldn't be sure. But they would never listen to his reason. They preferred their own. They would always prefer their own.

"He's right!" called a shrill voice from the doorway of the vast hall. "You know he's right!"

Samson turned to see the young boy, Mark, striding purposefully across the hall toward the table. His lithe, young legs carried him quickly, before any of the guards could halt his approach.

"He has no right to come here," Blackbeard told the king. "Send him away."

"I have a right," the boy answered. "I will serve as this man's counsel."

Gasps of surprise, almost as one, echoed around the hall.

"You? You will be his counsel?" Blackbeard asked, incredulous.

"Is there another in this hall who will represent him?" Mark asked brazenly. No one came forward as he searched the crowd. "Then I am his counsel."

"But...but that can't be," Blackbeard sputtered.

"Of course it can. There is nothing to prevent Mark from representing him," came another voice.

Samson glanced in this new direction. The voice belonged to a man who remarkably resembled Mark. *Well, of course*, Samson realized. *It must be the boy's father.*

"But he's just a boy," Blackbeard protested.

"A man," Mark answered.

"A *young* man," Mark's father, William, said quietly.

"I want a ruling from the Council," Blackbeard demanded. "Thumbs-up, the boy can stay."

Seven hesitant thumbs turned up.

"That's settled," the king said with authority. "The boy stays."

Mark, hardly pausing to take a breath, plunged right in on Samson's behalf. "I meant to stay out of this. I don't even like this man, but he's telling the truth. That's what persuaded me to—"

"I can defend my own hide," Samson insisted, trying to cut the boy off.

"Maybe so," Mark whirled angrily in Samson's direction, "but you're stepping on a thousand toes at once. You'll hang yourself before you even have a chance to defend yourself."

"So who cares?" Samson shrugged. "This place is out of the dark ages. All this Robin Hood stuff went out centuries ago."

Mark turned away from Samson, ignoring him. "This man is not from our world. We must release him immediately or pay a heavy price later."

Again, the crowd gasped in surprise.

"What are you saying, Mark?" the king asked. "Do you mean he's one of *them*, after all?"

"No, I'm not saying that at all," Mark replied impatiently. "I'm saying someone, or something, brought him here from another world. It's happened before, several times, especially in the ancient and legendary times of Arawn. Every child knows some of the names, like Pythagoras, Hiram, Pwyll, others. According to the legends—and you know there isn't a man in this room who knows them better than I do—men have journeyed to our land from other worlds."

"Preposterous!" Blackbeard snorted.

"No, I don't think so." Mark gestured toward Samson. "Look at his clothes. Were they spun on a loom in this world? Does his proud bearing speak of this world? Ask him yourself. Ask him if he's even heard of the magic city, or knows anything of its inner workings."

Samson's head was reeling, his worst fears confirmed. This was the world Eric had described to him, just before…

"Is what the boy says true?" the king asked him.

Samson heard the question through a hazy fog. Was it possible? "I've heard of the magic city before," he managed to say. "In a room, in a house…"

"See?" Blackbeard waved a triumphant hand. "He admits it. He's been sent here by *them*."

"He's admitting nothing of the kind," Mark's father said contemptuously. "He merely said he's heard of the city, not that he's come from it."

"You've heard of the city in another world? Isn't that right?" Mark asked the prisoner in a hushed voice. "Before you were sent here, right?"

"Yes, yes, I suppose it could be true," Samson said in a hoarse whisper. "It hardly seems possible, but, yes."

"We must release him. At once," declared Mark, who was living out one of the many roles he'd played in his mind over and over again when he recited the ancient stories to his sister and others. He pivoted toward his grandfather. "If he's been sent here, it's for a reason. We must not stand in his way."

"You and your stories be cursed!" Blackbeard seethed with unbridled fury. "You're the only one who believes those stories. This man is no more from another world than you or me."

"Wait. He's admitted as much," Mark's father began.

But Blackbeard sensed that his opportunity was slipping away, and at the hands of a mere boy at that. It was now or never. He knew it. So did some in the room.

"This man's origin isn't the question here," Blackbeard said loudly, pushing his chair back from the round table. He glared in his father's direction. "The question is whether you intend to let him off free as you please. Well, do you?"

The unexpected turn of events took the king completely by surprise. What had moments before been a calm, orderly hearing had suddenly turned into a two-fisted brawl.

"He had a right to a hearing," the king began.

"The hearing be cursed as well!" Blackbeard shouted. "What are your intentions? What say you to this man's fate?"

The king stared hard at his crazed son, not quite sure what to make of these turn of events. "I would say to you," Francis began slowly, "that the boy, your nephew, may be right. If this man is indeed from another world…"

"As I thought!" Blackbeard turned now to the crowd. "Your king," he said to his followers and his foes alike, "is about to set the man free. Just like that. He intends to turn him loose, where he can prey upon our women below and wreak havoc in our Sanctuary. I say that's wrong. I say we must protect the Sanctuary at all costs."

A lusty cheer rose from the throats of Blackbeard's followers, most of whom had been forewarned of what their leader intended to do. The trick was turning those on the fence over to their side before the fight ensued.

"No, no, he has it all wrong," the king attempted to shout. "I never meant to free the man, only to hear him out." Most of the crowd never heard their king's words. The cheers were simply too loud for the old man's frail voice.

But not too loud for Blackbeard's bellowing roars. "I say we must have a new king! Now, before he sells our Sanctuary to the enemy!" Blackbeard shouted again. "It is time. At long last, it is time for new leadership, before our blades grow dull and our wits fail us."

As if from nowhere, swords flashed in the crowded hall. The unmistakable shrieking of metal as swords were torn from their scabbards filled the air. Before the king or Mark's father could stop them, the men were upon each other.

Because they had the advantage of surprise, Blackbeard's followers nearly won the battle within seconds. A few of the king's men, though, had wisely carried their own weapons to the hearing and were gamely holding Blackbeard's followers at bay while dozens of men streamed from the hall through the windows to fetch their weapons.

In the confusion, no one noticed Samson leap from his chair and over the round table toward the nearest exit. Only a small hand stopped him at the last instant from fleeing the room.

"You must stop them," Mark pleaded as Samson swiveled to see who had grabbed him. "They'll kill each other."

"No skin off my nose," Samson snapped back. "This isn't my fight, so let go of me. I'm not about to stick around here."

"But you can't escape, not like that," Mark persisted. "And where will you go, anyway? This isn't your world. You have nowhere to go."

That gave Samson pause. In fact, his blood ran quite cold at the boy's matter-of-fact statement. If what he'd said was true, that he was in another world, then he really had nowhere to turn, no reason to flee anywhere. For all he knew, he might be jumping from one hangman's noose into another.

"Anywhere's better than here, kid," Samson said finally.

"I'll make a deal with you." The boy decided to risk everything on this stranger. He had no choice, really. His entire world was crumbling around him. "I'll untie you and help you escape if you agree to help me with something."

"What something? And you'd better make it quick."

The fierce fighting had almost reached them.

"Can't explain it here. There isn't enough time. You'll have to trust me."

Samson eyed Mark carefully but made up his mind. "You've got a deal. Now untie me."

Mark did so, pulling a dullish silver blade from his waist that sliced through the knotted cords as if they were butter. Samson only had a second to marvel at the blade before it was quickly concealed in the folds of the boy's shirt again.

"Let's go." Mark grabbed one of Samson's massive arms and led him through the doorway. "I know a quick way down."

They hurried along the wooden planks outside the vast hall toward a rope ladder half-hidden by a thick growth of leaves and branches. Without pausing, Mark leaped to the ladder and beckoned for Samson to follow.

As they worked their way toward the ground, hand over hand, Samson questioned the boy. "Can you tell me, now, where we're going?"

"To fetch the weapon you'll need."

"What weapon?" Samson asked, laboring heavily to keep up with the nimble boy scampering down the ladder.

"A special one. One I've saved for just this moment," he answered mysteriously.

Swiftly they reached the ground. Beckoning Samson to follow, Mark hurried off. The clangs and shouts of fighting still echoed through the treetops. Mark ducked into a decrepit house and emerged a moment later with a huge axe.

The handle was carved of stout wood and the head was made of some heavy metal. But the edge, which caught Samson's eye almost immediately, gleamed a dull silver. Just as the boy's blade had.

Mark handed the huge axe, which he could barely wield, over to Samson without hesitation. "Here. Now follow me again. We've got to get back to the tree quickly."

As Mark hurried off, Samson ran a careful finger along the edge of the axe. No question about it, this was some kind of silver alloy. The axe would be worth a pretty penny back in his world.

Back in his world. The words slammed into his mind like a tidal wave. He almost reeled from the blow. *Unbelievable. I almost believe it myself.*

"I fashioned it myself," the boy said breathlessly as they hurried along.

"Where did the silver at the edge come from?"

"From the leaves of the trees, after it rains. I tried to tell you before, when we first met."

"Do you mean to say…?"

"Yes, if you know where to look, you can find traces of silver gathered in the water the leaves hold after it rains. My sister, Samantha, discovered it first. She taught me where to look. We're the only ones who know."

Samson laughed so loudly and so hard it startled even himself. "So the clouds have silver linings here in this world, is that it?" he finally managed between guffaws.

"The legends have always said so." Mark was confused but willing to answer the man's questions. "But until Sam knew where to look, no one could ever prove it."

Samson shook his head in wonder. "So what do you want me to do with this axe?"

"Fell the Center Tree," he answered with just a trace of apprehension.

"The Center Tree?"

"The huge oak, the one that braces the hall we came from. You can't miss it. The tree is the largest in the forest."

"But why?"

"To stop the fighting," the boy said simply, refusing to elaborate.

"But I can't fell a huge oak with just a couple strokes," Samson protested.

"You won't have to. You only have to bite deep enough to tap its lifeblood. The tree will take care of the rest."

By this time, they'd reached the tree in question. Samson glanced up. The boy was right. It extended into the heart of the vast hall they'd fled from. But the thing was monstrously huge, perhaps a dozen feet or so in diameter. It would take weeks to fell a tree of this size and he told the boy so.

"You don't have to fell it!" Mark declared angrily. "I told you that. Don't you understand? The trees in this forest are alive. If you cut deeply enough into them, you'll reach the core, the center…"

"…the lifeblood," Samson finished.

"Exactly. The legends say cutting into the lifeblood is strictly forbidden by the elves, that it sets off a chain of events…"

"Then why in heaven's name are we doing this?" Samson roared.

"Because we have no choice!" Mark shouted back. "My father's life, my grandfather's life, the whole Sanctuary is in danger right now."

"Has anyone tried this before?" Samson said, more quietly now.

"No, never."

"No one's ever felled a tree in this entire forest?" he asked again, incredulous.

"No, I said it's forbidden."

"Then where does the wood come from, the wood you've used for some of your homes?"

"We wait for the trees to die, of course," Mark snapped. "We post patrols at the old ones to catch them before they can rot and decay on the ground. It's our only choice."

Samson stared in complete horror at the boy. He'd stepped into an insane asylum. "So what do I do now?" he managed to ask.

"We only have a couple minutes, at best, before someone wins up there. You're going to have to put everything you have into each blow. Perhaps, if we're lucky, you'll hit the lifeblood before it's all over."

"Whatever you say." Samson would follow through on his end of the bargain. The boy had, indeed, helped him escape.

The axe bit deeply into the tree, much deeper than Samson had expected. And, to his surprise, the entire tree seemed to shudder and convulse with the blow. Reluctantly, he pulled the blade free for a second swing.

"You sure about this?" he asked over his shoulder as he swung the heavy axe back.

"We have no other choice," Mark said grimly. "Keep going, no matter what."

Samson's second swing took a huge chip from the side of the tree as the axe bit deep below his first swing. He attacked the tree higher up with his third and followed that with a fourth just below the gap he'd already carved. Within a matter of a minute or so, the sharp blade had widened the gap to nearly a foot on the side of the tree.

"Hurry," Mark urged him. "We don't have much more time." Already, shouts of victory were beginning to ring out from above, only to be answered by curses.

Samson, the sweat now pouring from his brow, put everything he had into his blows. The muscles knotted and bunched across his back from the effort. The tree shuddered under the onslaught, almost beginning to rock and sway as it did so.

Samson could sense it as he drew close to the tree's lifeblood. It wasn't a tangible thing, more like a high, fierce keening that penetrated to the very core of Samson's soul. From the agony on Mark's face, it was obvious he could hear it too.

It took every ounce of courage Samson possessed to continue. With the gravest sense of foreboding he'd ever known, Samson lifted the axe again and again and sank the dull silver edge of the blade deeper even as the wail started to rend his mind.

Then it was done. With one mighty swing, the axe cut through the last remaining shell surrounding the tree's core and plunged into the lifeblood. Samson had only an instant to see his objective—a seething pulp of what seemed to be molten silver.

"It's an inferno," Samson said in awe, still holding the axe handle. There was a monstrous rumble beneath their feet. Samson tried to yank the blade and found he couldn't. The silver core, or whatever it was, refused to release its tormentor.

Then, unbelievably, the blade began to melt before Samson's very eyes. A split second later, the wooden handle turned white-hot. With a scream of pain, Samson let go. The handle burst into flames.

The ground continued to rumble, louder now. Samson watched in disbelief as the metal axe head was swallowed up in the core of the tree. The wooden handle was burned to a crisp almost instantly.

"Now we'll see," Mark said at his side with a look of fury.

The rumble beneath their feet grew. Shouts of outrage from above resounded as the Center Tree rocked violently, tearing at the framework of the vast hall. Samson looked up. Men were abandoning the fight to stream outside.

"All right, it's working. We have to leave here now." Mark yanked at Samson again, to lead him away.

"What's happening?" Samson asked, bewildered.

"The tree is dying," Mark said simply. "It is giving up its place in the earth, so another may follow."

"What!"

"You can watch. Just a little farther."

When they'd reached the spot Mark had been heading for all along, they stopped and turned to watch. It was unlike anything Samson had seen before.

The roots of the tree were alive. They seethed and writhed up through the ground like the coils of a gigantic serpent. The upper part of the tree, meanwhile, was bending and swaying just as violently. Every tree house attached to it was splitting asunder.

"It won't be long now," Mark said.

"How do you know?"

"The legends say so, that's why," Mark answered, tight-lipped.

Mark was right. With a mighty heave, the roots thrust the entire tree from the ground, shattering the hall intertwined at the top. Bits and pieces of the vast hall showered down below.

Once free, the roots moved chaotically along the ground, carrying the tree with them. After what seemed like an eternity, the base of the tree had moved far enough along the ground so the upper portion was forced to fall of its own weight.

The huge oak ripped, clawed, and tore through leaves and branches as it fell. Both it and what was left of the meeting hall hit the ground almost at the same time with a mighty crash.

Mark scoured the ground for bodies. When he didn't spot a single one, he almost collapsed as the terrible relief swept through him. It had worked. The men had escaped. The hall had been destroyed, but the battle had ended. It was over.

Well, not quite over. Like molten lava pouring from a volcano, the silver lifeblood of the felled tree's core began to spill onto the ground. And where it fell, a curious thing happened. The molten silver puddle formed a mirror.

Fascinated, both Mark and Samson drew closer. Standing side by side, they gazed down at the dull mirror, expecting to see their own reflections. What they saw, instead, came as quite a shock.

"That's not me," Mark said. "And it's not you, either."

A dozen men or so, all with blond hair, slim, and smaller than Mark even, looked up at Samson and Mark.

"What is this?" Samson growled. "Who are these people?" From his viewpoint, the men appeared to be standing on a ceiling just below his feet, staring up at the sky. How they managed that, though, was beyond him.

Just then, one of the men also leaned up—or down, depending on your perspective—to get a closer view of Samson and Mark, who naturally recoiled in horror at the strange sight.

Before either could react, another of the men dropped a slim rope into the puddle. The rope went right through the mirror, reared up high over Mark's head and then Samson's, fell loosely around their shoulders, and tightened.

And then, against all reason, the two were yanked headfirst into the silver puddle. In the blink of an eye, they'd vanished through the mirror, their muffled calls for help soon dwindling off into nothingness in the sudden stillness of the forest.

15

* * *

PROTECTORS OF THE SEA

Nathaniel was, perhaps, the bravest little boy the land had ever known. He could have cried or collapsed in his sister's arms. But Nathaniel did none of those. He faced the dark, unknown depths with his eyes wide open in wonder.

And there were wonders to see, as incredible as it seemed to Laura. For, as the heavy wood boat settled lower and lower into the murky depths of the river, soft, eerie, greenish light cast a soft glow in all directions, illuminating some of the strangest formations Laura had ever seen or imagined.

It hardly compared at all to the summer she'd spent in Duke's marine biology lab on the coast of the Carolinas. That had been merely impressive. This was awesome.

She and the others first began to notice the light's subtle presence as they passed the very top of what would have been a vast mountain range above land.

"Oh, look at those!" Kathryn pointed to a school of rainbow-colored fish that were, just then, flowing around the tip of the mountain by the hundreds.

"Yes, I see them," Laura answered. "But how is it that we can *see* them at all?"

Kathryn looked back at the fish with a puzzled frown. "The light from the boat, I guess."

"No, it isn't that. There's another source of light coming from somewhere."

"But…but that's impossible."

"Nothing seems so impossible here," Laura replied with a bemused smile. "But, for the life of me, I can't see where it's coming from. If my guess is right, we're thousands of feet underwater."

"That's about right. There's no way—"

"Oh, you're both so silly," Nathaniel suddenly piped up. He'd been deathly quiet the entire trip, watching the drama unfold. "It's for the people of the sea."

"What is, Nathaniel?" his sister asked.

"The light, of course," he offered impatiently. "It's for them."

Kathryn and Laura shot worried glances at each other. Until now, for some strange reason, they'd been too absorbed in the voyage itself to wonder who, if anyone, had orchestrated it.

Not Nathaniel, though. He'd thought of nothing else but the legendary people of the sea almost from the instant they'd first plunged toward the heart of the river.

"You know, your brother may be right," Laura said. "That would explain the need, though not the origin."

Kathryn, terrified, wasn't ready to accept that conclusion just yet. "But we *can't* be near the ocean, can we? Can we?"

"Yes, I think so." Laura peered hard at the rock formations they were passing. "It's been awhile, but I seem to recall that formations such as these can only be found on an ocean floor."

"Oh no!" Kathryn gasped in abject horror. "Please. Make us go back."

"I've already tried," Laura said quickly. "Awhile ago. It didn't work. Someone else is controlling the boat, someone with power greater than mine, I guess. I didn't want to tell you because I was afraid it would worry you."

Kathryn closed her eyes, trying not to cry in front of her little brother. Nathaniel would never have noticed, though. He was too absorbed with his newfound world.

"Look at that." He pointed toward a fish he'd had his eye on for some time. His high-pitched voice filled a long pause in the conversation. "See? It puffs up real big."

"It's a blowfish. Some people call it a puffer," Laura answered, recalling her marine biology lessons. Kathryn still hadn't opened her eyes yet.

Just then, the boat passed neatly between two twin peaks and emerged into a vast, cavernous opening on the ocean floor, if that was indeed where they were. More mountain peaks loomed ahead of them.

"You know, it's strange how we're drifting right through all these formations without hitting anything," Laura said slowly.

Kathryn looked up, her eyes blazing with conviction. "Don't you see?" she said fiercely. "Don't you understand what you've done? You've broken their law. Now we'll have to answer for it."

Laura considered the young girl thoughtfully, remembering her grandmother's warning. "Well, if anyone's to answer for it, then it's me," she said at last. "Not you or Nathaniel. Neither of you had anything to do with it."

"I helped," Kathryn answered grimly. "You've forgotten that."

Laura said nothing in return. She'd make her own arguments when, or if, the time came. Meanwhile, the scene filled up with dozens of new actors—big fish, schools of little fish, flitting and darting every which way around the boat, which was slowing in its approach toward the ocean floor.

Laura watched in horror as one rather elongated fish—a barracuda, if she wasn't mistaken—caught a tiny fish not far from the bow of the boat and devoured it with just three snaps of its obviously powerful jaw. She glanced at the other two, relieved that neither had seen the predator.

Nathaniel was the first to notice a school of dolphins approaching fast off the starboard side. "They're coming at us!" he shouted gleefully, completely unafraid.

The dolphins, moving so quickly it was almost hard to follow them, arrived at the side of the boat within moments. Laura, despite herself, felt no fear at the sight of these creatures. And with good reason. There were obviously friends. They flowed in, over, and around the boat playfully, their powerful tails propelling them through the water with ease.

Then Laura felt something prickly at the fringes of her mind, a tingling, buzzing sensation she couldn't shake. As the dolphins followed the boat on its inexorable march toward the bottom of the ocean, though, the sensation began to take shape.

The dolphins were trying to speak to her. As strange as this seemed—although, she reasoned, it couldn't be any stranger than anything else that had happened—she accepted it calmly, almost readily. Concentrating, at last she started to make sense of the words, blurry at first.

"Who are you?" Laura was finally able to ask them in a language of the mind that had no real form or grammar to it, only images of what she wanted to convey. It seemed a distant cousin to the formless way in which you conjured up images of magical import.

"*The friends, the friends.*" The answer came back in such a resounding chorus it took her by surprise.

"Friends?" she asked again.

"*The vigils,*" came the answer, filled with such joy and conviction it almost brought tears to Laura's eyes.

"Why are you here?"

"*Protect. Shield. Watch.*"

"From what?"

There was a long silence.

"From what?" Laura persisted. When the silence seemed to stretch into eternity, she decided to try a new tack. "All right, then. Where are we going?"

"*To them, to them,*" their chorus of voices said grandly, filling her mind with such force she almost lost her balance in the boat.

"The people of the sea?"

"*The masters,*" they answered as one.

"What do they want with us?" she asked, afraid of the answer.

"*We don't know.*" Their collective voice filled with questions at the logic of the people they knew only as the gentle guardians of the vast sea, their playpen.

Laura sensed that the dolphins, indeed, had no idea what the people of the sea wanted. *The people of the sea. Then it was true*, she thought, again feeling no fear. *Why? Why should I feel no fear of these people?*

She knew why. Because the dolphins felt no fear, none at all. They felt only awe and wonder, a kind of reverence, toward this mysterious race. And if they had nothing to fear from these masters, as they called them, then why should she?

"Are there many of them, these people of the sea?" she asked.

"*Yes, many.*"

A new, timid voice came from another direction. With a start, Laura realized that it was Kathryn's, though how she knew this, exactly, she couldn't say.

"Will they harm us?" Kathryn asked the dolphins almost shyly.

"*No, no,*" the voice resounded.

"They are friends, then?" Kathryn asked again.

"*Yes, like us.*"

Laura probed Kathryn's mind gently. Kathryn turned hers, not unwillingly, in Laura's direction. "Can you...can you understand me this way?" Laura asked the younger girl.

"Yes, I can," Kathryn answered back with growing courage and conviction. And with it came a sense of excitement, of a kind she had never known before.

"But you couldn't before?"

"The dolphins...I heard them first." Her thoughts faltered a little as she struggled with the strangeness of the conversation. "And then I heard you. I understood from them."

"Are you still afraid?"

"I think so," her small voice came back.

"Did you hear what the dolphins said, that the people of the sea aren't to be feared?"

"Some of it." Kathryn looked directly at Laura. Her eyes belied the deep-rooted fear she had of the race.

"I think we should wait to see what they want before we jump to any conclusions," she said, trying to frame the words with a sense of sureness and firmness. She couldn't be sure how successful she'd been. It was still too new to her.

"I know," Kathryn answered back. "I agree with you, but..."

"I understand." Laura turned her mind back to the dolphins. "How long must we journey before...?"

"*We are here,*" came the answer.

Startled, Laura peered off in the direction they were moving. Caught up in the newness of her strange voice, she hadn't noticed the boat slowing its speed. Or the city, if it could be called that, they had arrived in.

The boat had drifted to the bottom of what, on the land, would have been a lush valley nestled between several mountains. Laura glanced involuntarily around her at the rising peaks that almost totally encircled the valley.

As she gazed at them, it finally dawned on her where the soft, green light was coming from. Of course. Phosphorus rocks. Ten times brighter than any she'd seen in her world, but it was still the same principle. Here, in the valley with so many mountains surrounding them, the boat was bathed in so much of the eerie light they could see for hundreds of feet in any direction.

What convinced Laura they'd come to a city were the caves that dotted the sides of the mountains. Quite obviously, they were homes. Even from the bottom of the ocean floor, Laura could see that the entrances were adorned with some of the most beautiful sea shells she could imagine. And nearly all of the entrances were covered, as well, with absolutely huge clam shells.

Despite her best efforts, and the dolphins' joyous reassurances, a cold knot of fear gnawed at Laura's stomach. What if, after all, they'd been summoned to this strange place only to be sentenced?

A sudden movement at the other end of the boat jerked Laura violently out of her introspection. Laura watched in stunned horror as Nathaniel, who had been incautiously leaning over the railing of the boat for some time now, slipped over the side and literally jumped into the ocean. *He'll be crushed by the weight of the ocean,* Laura thought to herself in a panic, remembering her marine biology lessons. *And he won't be able to breathe.*

None of which came to pass. As if in a dream, the little boy drifted slowly into the watery depths and then turned a blurry face in their direction. "Come on!" his mind shouted impatiently at them. Then he turned and, awkwardly flailing his arms and legs, moved away from the boat.

"He can breathe!" Kathryn exclaimed.

"It would seem so," Laura answered soberly.

Without another word, Kathryn flung herself over the side of the boat, following her little brother. Reluctantly, Laura followed.

Nathaniel was in pure, absolute heaven. He showed no fear of his surroundings, but that was as it should be. What little boy, suddenly confronted with such a vast playground, wouldn't revel in it? He paused, letting one hand drift idly out to the side. Laura could almost hear his squeal of delight as one of the dolphins quickly moved to his side, positioned its hump under the hand, and then sped off with the little boy in tow.

As Nathaniel frolicked with the dolphins, Laura cautiously adjusted to this new world. She found she was not only able to breathe—the water somehow never entered her lungs, although oxygen did—but could open her eyes without the awful, stinging sensation you get when you try to see in saltwater.

In fact, she was concentrating so hard, she never saw the first, timid appearance of one of the people of the sea. And she didn't notice as Kathryn disappeared, following her little brother and the dolphins behind an outcropping of rocks.

A young mermaid, who looked to be no more than 17, opened one of the nearby clam shell doors a fraction. When she saw the visitors were just two girls and a very little boy, she grew more bold and opened the door all of a foot or so.

The young mermaid was striking. Her hair was sea-green. It wrapped and swirled around her in the water, falling well below her waist. The skin on the upper half of her slim body was almost pearly white. It faded very gradually to a polished silver as the bottom half of her torso gradually became scaly and ended with two, large fins.

Laura noticed the young mermaid out of the corner of one eye as she eased her way through the door. Almost without effort, the mermaid moved with the same kind of fluid grace as the dolphins did, with the powerful lower half of her body moving up and down in long, sweeping motions.

Within moments, she'd covered nearly the length of a football field. She stopped short, again with apparent ease, only 20 feet or so from Laura.

"*Who…who are thee?*" A soft, almost bell-like voice gently probed Laura's mind.

Laura had never believed the legends in her own world. Oh, occasionally, during introspective moments at the marine biology lab as she stared through the large plate glass window that looked out upon the shallows of the vast Atlantic Ocean, she'd fantasized. She'd imagine a mermaid swimming casually up to the window for a peek, as the legends in her own world said they did occasionally when ships passed by in the deepest heart of the ocean. Then the mermaid would smile shyly and swim off, never to be seen again.

But she'd never believed, not really. Now, staring intently through the water at the object of those occasional fantasies, she wondered why.

"I…my name is Laura," she answered back, unsure of the meaning behind the mermaid's question.

"*No,*" the young mermaid answered back with a shy smile, the kind Laura had always imagined. "*You are a magician. I can sense it.*"

"Perhaps, yes. By the standards of this world."

"*This world?*" The mermaid was obviously confused.

"I was not born in your land. I have come here by accident."

The mermaid almost seemed to shimmer in the water for a moment, but her fin swirled nervously. "*You are very sad,*" she said at last. "*But why?*"

Laura, wondering how the mermaid had seen the sadness she had never allowed herself to feel, answered, "I fear that I'll never return to my own world. And perhaps, I guess, it saddens me."

"*You have friends there, loved ones you are afraid you will never see again?*"

"Well, no, not really." Laura thought bitterly of Jennifer, perhaps the only real friend she'd ever had. *Poor Jennifer. If only she'd seen this world, seen the magic of it, she'd never have taken her own life.* But, then, perhaps, it was this very magic she was so desperately longing for in her short, tragic life.

"*No friends?*" The mermaid, again, seemed perplexed by the answer.

"I have no time for friends," Laura answered quickly, violently.

The young mermaid swirled away from Laura, her eyes wide in terror. Her fin now twitched nervously. "*I am sorry. I did not mean to anger you.*" The voice made only a very small presence in Laura's mind.

Laura cringed. She hadn't meant to frighten the young mermaid with her own inner turmoil, her almost constant rage at the world. "I only meant I am too busy to have friends," she offered lamely.

"*Too busy?*"

"Yes. I want to be a physician. It takes up nearly all of my time."

The young mermaid was silent for a long moment before speaking. "*A healer? Is that what you mean?*"

"A healer, yes."

"*It is a noble calling.*"

She tried to keep it out of her mind, but it was almost impossible. So she didn't. "Yes, and a lucrative one," she admitted through clenched teeth. "It is a long, hard road with a pot of gold at the end of the rainbow."

As the mermaid reached Laura's mind without words, again, Laura slowly began to sense her presence in this way. It was a strange feeling, this searching for impressions without words.

"*I see,*" the mermaid said. "*Knowledge brings power.*"

"I suppose," Laura answered haughtily, afraid to admit even to herself why she'd always wanted to be a physician. She'd hoped it was simply because she longed to heal the world of its pain. But she was afraid she could never be sure.

"*We share knowledge here,*" the mermaid said simply. "*Some are able to share more than others, but it all belongs to our community here.*"

The thought stunned Laura. Share a pool of knowledge? How could something like that be possible? "Then you have no privacy here?"

The young mermaid smiled shyly, perhaps misinterpreting the intent of Laura's question. "*Oh, no. We may have privacy whenever we like. That's not a problem.*"

Kathryn suddenly appeared by Laura's side. Laura, absorbed in her conversation with the mermaid, had not even bothered to notice that the young girl had gone off in search of her younger brother. Nor had she noticed the growing crowd of mermaids and mermen.

Kathryn spoke softly to Laura's mind, trying to shield her words from the young mermaid nearby. "These are gentle people. But they are angry, Laura."

"Angry?"

"Yes, and afraid. They fear you, Laura. They are afraid of your power."

"But why?" Laura asked bitterly. "Why should they fear me? What have I ever done to them?"

"Not you. Others like you, thousands of years ago."

"But I'm not like them," Laura insisted angrily. "I would never do anything to harm them."

"I know that," Kathryn said gently. "But they don't. They are afraid of the power you hold."

"And just how is it you know all this?" Laura asked, her eyes blazing fiercely at the unfairness of the way she'd already been judged by these people.

"They've spoken to me," Kathryn said simply.

"They don't fear you?"

"No. I am not a magician. I can't harm them, as you can. I have no power."

"That's absurd! You could be a magician just as easily."

"No, not just as easily. It takes a certain understanding of what it is you want to accomplish before the magic may work, as well as a certain understanding of all the words of knowledge. At least, that is what these people have told me."

Laura was thoroughly confused. "That's crazy. You say the words and the magic work. It's that simple."

"It isn't that simple," Kathryn persisted. "It has something to do with the total knowledge you have of something and the way it all fits together in your mind. That's what these people told me. But I don't understand it either."

Their conversation was cut short by the approach of several mermen. They were a stark contrast to the almost fragile young mermaid who had so timidly approached Laura.

The men, who all carried large tridents, were powerful and broad-shouldered. Their sea-green hair flowed loosely around their shoulders. They swam toward Laura with assurance and purpose, their powerful tails thrusting them through the water with staccato bursts.

Laura could almost sense their anger toward her as they approached. It was a subtle thing, mixed with a good measure of fear and awe. It frightened her.

No one had ever feared her, at least not that she'd ever known. Yes, she supposed, her classmates probably feared her intellectual prowess. But this was different. These people feared for their very lives.

Yet, was there any real difference? Laura stood between her classmates and a life they'd always dreamed about. For every action she took at Duke, she cut someone else off from a future. *Well, so what?* she reasoned again as she had for so many years. *I can do the work and they can't. It's that simple.*

"*You must leave this place, magician,*" a voice said.

Laura couldn't immediately identify the author of the statement, so she directed her answer at all three. "I'd like nothing better," she said tersely. "You brought me here against my will. I had nothing whatsoever to do with it."

The three mermen looked at each other in obvious confusion. This was something they hadn't expected. "*You are not telling the truth,*" the spokesman said after a brief consultation, swirling forward slightly from the group to identify himself. "*We have not brought you here.*"

That was about all Laura could take. She had half a mind to turn him into a toad. He was begging for it. But, no, that wouldn't be proper. Or very nice. "Ask her," she said instead, inclining her head in Kathryn's direction.

"*Is what she says true?*" The spokesman looked at Kathryn for confirmation.

Kathryn, holding onto her little brother to keep him from scurrying off again, nodded. "Yes, it is as she says. We were brought here against our wills."

The spokesman swirled back to his companions, brandishing his trident angrily. Laura could sense that these people were unaccustomed to anger of any sort. Realizing this, she took a closer look at the tridents they carried. They were crusted green. They probably hadn't been used in centuries.

The spokesman came forward again, more slowly this time. "*We are gravely sorry. We have wronged you. We beg for your mercy and forgiveness.*"

This turn of events startled Laura. "But why did you accuse me of lying in the first place?" she asked bitterly. "And why did you tell me I had to leave?"

The spokesman, with an expression of grave pain, said, "*The legends speak of your kind. They warn us to have nothing to do with your ilk. Only at our own peril must we have dealings.*"

Laura cut him off. "My kind? My ilk? What kind of utter nonsense is that?"

The young mermaid, who had swum a small distance away at the approach of the mermen, moved forward. "*It is not nonsense,*" she said, her voice edged with softness as it entered Laura's mind. "*There have been others, powerful like you, who have brought great tragedy to our people.*"

Laura bristled. "Like what? Name one of these great tragedies."

The young mermaid gazed directly into Laura's eyes. "*The legends say that, once upon a time, some of our race was enslaved within the city by the old magicians and used against the land. The legends also say that it was once great sport for the magicians to hunt our people. And, although we were never turned into toads, quite a few of us lost our humanity.*"

A cold, uncontrollable chill swept through Laura. The young mermaid must be able to read her innermost thoughts. Why else…?

"*Yes, I can see your private thoughts,*" the young mermaid continued. "*You have not yet learned how to shield your mind. That comes only with time.*"

"Well, stop it!" Laura was beginning to panic. It was an unfamiliar, and extremely uncomfortable, feeling.

"*I am truly sorry,*" the mermaid offered. "*There is nothing we can do. Your thoughts come to me as the light that enters my eyes.*"

Laura struggled to control her mind. "All right," she said tightly. "Then you must know that I have come here against my will. You must know that I mean you no harm and that I am here, in this world, for some unknown reason."

"*Yes, I have known from the moment I met you.*"

"Then why don't they?" Laura glanced at the mermen.

"*Because they have shielded themselves from you. They do not wish to touch you, as I have.*"

The meaning of the mermaid's words slowly dawned on Laura. "Do you mean…that you have opened yourself up to me? And that they have not?"

"*Yes.*"

"And that you could shield yourself from me, as they have?"

"*Yes. I would be unable to see your private thoughts. Or understand you, though, and feel as you feel. See as you see.*"

Laura felt a surge of the old anger. How dare this creature invade her privacy when she didn't have to? "Get out of my mind," she ordered the young mermaid sullenly. "I don't want you muddling around in there without my permission."

"*Is that truly what you wish?*" There was unmistakable sadness to the question.

"Yes, but first answer me one question. When these magicians, the ones you referred to in your legends, hunted you for sport, was there nothing you could do to prevent it? And what did you mean about losing your humanity?"

The young mermaid bowed her head. "*To answer your questions, we were powerless to prevent them from turning us into fish in the shallows of the ocean, where we once lived in close proximity to men. Here, deep at the bottom of the ocean where we dwell in great numbers, they could not hunt us so.*"

"Which is why you live here, I presume?"

"*Yes. We grew tired of the constant slaughter.*"

Laura shuddered. "But why? Why would anyone do such a thing for sport?"

"*Who knows? Perhaps they had grown bored with their power and needed amusement.*"

The mermen spokesman moved forward again. "*Enough of this talk. You must leave this place at once. You remain at your own peril.*"

Laura clenched her teeth. "Gladly. Show me the way and I'll leave."

"*Find your own way back,*" the merman answered.

"That's impossible," Laura shot back. "When the river swallowed the boat, it brought us here of its own accord. We have no way of knowing how to return."

The merman regarded Laura with horror. *"The river swallowed your boat and brought you here?"*

"Yes, that's what I said. If you'd just listened before when I tried to tell you."

"Then you must have violated the covenant of the land. Only that would explain your presence here," the merman said ominously.

Laura looked at Kathryn for help.

Kathryn nodded. "What they say is true. I tried to warn you against invoking magic to turn the river from its natural course, but you insisted."

The merman spokesman groaned aloud. Or at least it seemed so in Laura's mind. *"Then we have no choice. You must remain with us until we can determine from the legends what we must do with you. It has been so long since anyone dared violate the covenant."*

"Wait a minute," Laura protested. "If I'm so all-powerful, as you say, then you can't hold me against my will."

"You have violated the covenant of the land," the young mermaid said solemnly. *"That, only, strips you of your power over us. You have entered our domain because of your actions. And until we have rendered a decision, you could not leave even if you wished to. It has always been thus, the legends say. It is our one protection against the magicians."*

Laura glowered. "You're all mad."

"No. It is our right, under the law," the merman spokesman said. *"Now, please, if you would come with us, we will call a meeting of the elders."*

Laura frantically tried to think of some word, some spell she'd learned. It hardly mattered which one, because any would do to test the truth of what they were saying. When she'd settled on a word, she tried to speak it. And nothing happened. She was unable to utter the ancient word.

"You are bound by the law," the young mermaid spoke softly to Laura. *"Until we have released you, there is nothing you can do to us."*

Laura's will collapsed. "All right, I'll come. Just tell me where the prison is."

"Prison?" the merman said. *"No, there is no need for that. We have none anyway."*

"You can stay with me while the elders meet," the mermaid said gently to Laura, swimming to her side to lead her by the hand.

Laura, clutching the mermaid's offered hand for all she was worth, felt strangely like a lamb being led to the slaughter. Kathryn and Nathaniel followed meekly in their wake, saying nothing.

16

* * *

WRONG, STUPID, AND FOOLISH

Jon was laughing so hard he almost fell off the cloud mountain. Lucas, of course, simply couldn't understand what was so funny.

"The legends say fairies can be cruel and terrible when they're provoked," Lucas protested.

"Oh, give me a break." Tears from the unrestrained laughter rolled down Jon's cheeks. "Who in their right mind would fear a bunch of fairies?"

"I would, for one," Lucas defended. "I wouldn't be sitting there laughing like some fool—"

"Oh, you're the fool," Jon said, his laughter subsiding to a few hearty chuckles.

"We'll see."

A buzzing in the air caught their attention. Faint at first, it soon grew to the point where it sounded like a gale was blowing in from the north. Either that, or a gigantic buzz saw.

Lucas and Jon quickly saw where the strange sound was coming from. A horde of tiny, winged creatures had appeared on the horizon, flying in tight formations as they approached the peak of the cloud mountain. The sound came from the frantic beating of hundreds of tiny wings.

The sound terrified Lucas. It was all he could do to keep from running away from the onrushing horde of tiny beings. Only a word from the winged horse kept him from such a foolish action.

"It is not your fight, boy, remember that," the horse said to him.

"But...but," Lucas sputtered.

"Have no fear," the horse said again. "They're coming for him, not you."

There were literally hundreds of them. As they surrounded the mountaintop, the beating wings obliterating every sound in their path, Jon stopped laughing. He stared in disbelief, realizing for the first time that the horse had been telling the truth. They were fairies. And they had come to get him.

"How utterly bizarre," he said, his voice barely audible above the buzzing. "They're just as all the stories describe them."

The little people were no more than two or three inches tall. Their translucent wings shimmered in the brilliant sunlight. Each was clothed in thin, flimsy, brightly colored garments that fluttered as their wings beat.

It was hard to identify any single individual from where Jon was sitting. They were, as yet, too far away for that. But as they closed in, Jon saw that each was, in fact, unique. One had a beard, another had red hair, a third had a dashing mustache, while a fourth had long, flowing locks.

Suddenly, before Jon could react, a hundred thin, weblike ropes appeared as if from nowhere. They were tossed down toward him almost as one. He did his best to ward them off, swatting at them as if they were gnats or flies.

He managed to sweep several away, but one or two managed to snare an ear. Two or three more finally encircled a hand. Four or five looped over his head while more snared his feet. Within moments, he was trussed up like a pig on his way to the chopping block. The ropes were all pulled tight. Jon found that he couldn't move. It was all he could do to keep his composure at such an indignity.

"Unhand me, you brutes," he managed to say with as much sarcasm as he could muster. "Run along, or I'll tell your mothers you were naughty."

"Oh, be quiet, you twit," said one of the fairies, working hard to loosen the ropes around his neck so he wouldn't choke when they carted him off.

"I'm warning you. Let me go, or I'll do something drastic."

"Be my guest," said another fairy working on Jon's other shoulder.

"Hey, that tickles," Jon said as a third fairy pulled a rope from his nose.

"Sorry, I'll make up for it." Without another word, the fairy reached up and plucked one of his nose hairs.

"Ouch!" Jon squeaked.

"Shall I put it back?" the fairy asked him.

"No, you can have it," Jon said, trying to look down at his chin so he could see the nasty offender.

As the loud buzzing picked up again, he felt himself being swept off the ground. He glanced up at his captors in disbelief. He was being born aloft by the collective efforts of hundreds of fairies. Somehow, it didn't seem possible.

"Tallyho," Jon managed bravely as he was slowly lifted from the ground.

Lucas, who had remained frozen with fear despite the horse's reassuring words, finally returned to his senses. "Where are they taking him?" he asked the horse.

"To the fairy kingdom, of course," the horse answered. "Come along. Climb aboard and I'll take you there. The trial should be great fun."

Lucas hesitated only a moment before clambering aboard the huge, magnificent creature. "Is there anything we can do to help him?"

"Thankfully, no," the horse answered. "The impudent wretch will be defenseless unless he somehow figures out how to acquit himself. We can do nothing more than watch."

As Lucas and the horse flew, keeping a discreet distance between themselves, the fairies, and their ungainly, protesting baggage, the two began to talk.

It seemed the horse had been quite bored for the past two thousand years or so. As the magic dwindled away in the land, fewer and fewer magicians had called upon him for his services. In fact, it had been hundreds of years since anyone had invoked the magic that bound him at all, for noble reasons or otherwise.

Until Jon had broken the code of the air by calling on him for utterly selfish reasons—the horse didn't believe Jon had a prayer in the land of acquitting himself on the charge before the fairies—the horse hadn't even been sure he could respond. He was out of practice. Those within the city had certainly not bothered to call on him for some time.

"My joints creaked, boy," he told Lucas. "I had to step off the cloud and hope for the best."

"You're not serious!" Lucas said, aghast at the thought of a horse blithely walking off the edge of a cloud.

"Well, what choice did I have?" the horse asked indignantly. "I didn't have the old get-up-and-go to lift off gracefully, so I glided into action. I thought it worked quite nicely myself."

"I have to say, you certainly were magnificent when you approached us," Lucas said softly.

"Why thank you…and, boy, what is your name, anyway?"

"Lucas. And what may I call you?"

"Oh, I guess Peg will do fine."

Lucas grew silent, watching the landscape change below them. Unlike the clouds where they'd first landed, which had been largely devoid of anything but color, the fairy kingdom was taking shape.

Now the colors found structures to highlight. Lucas saw amber, honeycombed buildings, bright yellow dewdrop homes, tiny silver domes that seemed to breathe of their own accord as the wind played against them, light blue jet streams winding through the kingdom, white rectangles built atop deep maroon ethereal planes that drifted hither and thither of their own accord….

As before, the landscape shifted and drifted to suit its own fancy. Nothing stayed in any one place for very long. Bubble homes would bump into each other as they floated along and emerge as simply one, larger bubble home. Lucas found himself wondering how they lived inside. A tall building perched atop a cloud mountain would become a long row of rooms strung out along a deep valley.

"Is nothing permanent here?" Lucas asked finally.

Peg sighed. "Nothing. And that's the problem, I'm afraid. Before the rise, before the magicians drove them from the land, it wasn't half bad. The fairies can be amiable sorts, when they want. And when I grew tired of their games and their endless, changing home, I could always saunter over for a visit with the giants or the elves—I always especially liked them—and have a few laughs. But now that I'm forced to dwell up here with them," the horse continued wistfully, "it's grown deadly dull. How I long for the days of peace when the races lived together in the land."

"Well, why don't you come back and live on earth yourself? Why live up here?" Lucas asked. It seemed a fair question.

"No, I am bound to the guardians of the air. I serve at their whim and fancy, until higher authorities and powers have need of my temporary services," Peg answered solemnly. "But none have called in some time."

"Then why don't the fairies come back to the land?" Lucas persisted.

"Are you mad? They would never consider that, not for a moment."

"And why not? Surely they don't fear the magicians any longer. No one's even seen one in nearly three generations."

"So I've heard," Peg said softly. "But don't dismiss what you can't see, or what you haven't seen in quite some time, so easily. You might be surprised."

"How's that?"

"The magicians. Don't assume, simply because you haven't seen them for so long, that they've ceased to exist. They're a powerful lot. I wouldn't write them off so quickly if I were you."

"But the city? There hasn't been much movement in that city for as long as anyone can remember."

"Life can take strange twists, boy, remember that," Peg said mysteriously. "There is life in that city. I can assure you. And, remember, just as I've grown tired of the fairy kingdom, so, I'm certain, did the magicians grow tired and weary of this land they have mastered and conquered. No doubt they've gone off in search of other challenges, other worlds to conquer or corrupt."

"You're making no sense. Other worlds, mysteries, challenges." Lucas scowled. "If you know where the magicians have gone, then just tell me."

"I have no way of knowing where they've gone," Peg answered truthfully. "Not anymore, not since they lost their ability to summon me."

"Lost their ability?"

"Well, yes. They forfeited that right, under the law, when they took the land into their own hands and turned it to their own will with no thought for its fabric or those who dwell in it."

"I see," Lucas said thoughtfully. "Because they'd grown selfish, they couldn't call for you without breaking the law of the land?"

"Something like that, yes."

"But it still doesn't tell me where they've gone. If they still exist at all."

"Oh, they exist all right," Peg said, deadly serious.

"But how can you be so sure?"

"I am a creature of magic." The horse bowed his head even as they flew. "I would know when it has vanished altogether, not merely gone into hibernation or journeyed elsewhere. And the magic is alive, somewhere."

The fairies had begun to slow and descend into the heart of their kingdom. As Peg and Lucas drew closer to the fairy escort and their prisoner, they could hear Jon's raucous protests.

"So you're finally going to put me down? Well, it's about time, you nitwits," Jon said loudly. "I have to sneeze."

There was a commotion before they touched down as several hundred fairies burst from the doorways of halls and rooms in all directions. They buzzed, zoomed, and flitted toward the prisoner like a mob of angry bees protecting their hive.

They had set Jon down in the very center of a vast, golden ring—the only thing Lucas had, as yet, seen in this strange kingdom that didn't shift with the eternal currents of air. There was nothing inside the ring, save the hundreds of fairies who'd arrived for the trial.

"I've never seen so many spectators at an event," Lucas mumbled.

"Spectators?" Peg laughed. "These are the judges."

"What! Every one of them?"

"Every blessed one of them," the horse said.

"So what are the rules of this trial?"

"There aren't any. Now, hush. It's about to begin."

Jon, still bound by the thin ropes, sat very still in the center of the ring, wondering not too idly about what was happening to him. Dozens of fairies circled his head, examining him, occasionally poking his eyes, pulling an earlobe, pinching a cheek, or prodding his proboscis.

At last, the buzzing subsided to a sort of dull hum—that was really about all you could hope for with fairies because they never seemed to stop moving. Within the circle a rather plump fairy with a full, black beard, a crown of some sort perched rakishly on his head, solemnly approached the prisoner.

"I am Dent, the lord, majesty and ruler of this fair kingdom," he began, peering intently into Jon's eyes as he hovered in the air at nose level less than a foot away from his face.

"Not for long with that kind of talk," grumbled a nearby fairy.

"And you stand accused of the highest crime in the land," the king continued, ignoring his detractor.

"Go on. It's not as bad as all that. I can think of worse," said a wisp of a fairy with light, brown hair and a grim, stern demeanor on what would be, for most, a pretty face. On her, the face seemed to be a mask, hiding a sea of turbulence. It was hard to think of this seething dynamo as anything but a ruler, for she also wore a crown, albeit smaller than Dent's.

"Your crime—violating the sanctity of our province for base, selfish reasons—is punishable by death." The king glared at his wife now, rather than the prisoner. "Or a fortnight with Maya, our queen here…whichever we deem to be more terrible punishment."

"Now hold on," Jon managed to interject. "Would you mind explaining to me what it is you think I've done wrong?"

A prim and proper fairy flitted forward. He was garbed in a drab gray robe, pulled tightly around his frail body, his coal black hair parted evenly down the middle and seemingly glued in place. "It's elementary, of course," said the fairy, Rand. "You invoked the magic of the air not for the good of the land but to promote your own self-interests, whatever they are."

"Is that so?" Jon asked. "And just how would you know that?"

"You would not be here otherwise," the king said.

"Yes, when you so brazenly and callously interrupted the natural flow of the elements," Rand spoke, "you must have done so for some crass reason or else the ancient laws would not have forced your winged steed to bring you to us."

"Well, I beg to differ." Jon desperately tried to remember what had happened before he'd come to.

"All in due time," the king said. "First, how do you plead?"

"Not guilty," Jon claimed indignantly.

"No, no," the king pronounced, "we'll have no moral judgments here. The deed has already been done. How do you plead—wrong, stupid, and foolish or right, prudent, and wise?"

"Right, prudent, and wise, I guess," Jon said, confused.

"Will you defend yourself?"

"Yes, I suppose so."

"Are there any witnesses?" the king called out aloud. Dozens of the fairies within the ring glanced over at Lucas who, until this point, had been too absorbed in the proceedings to think much about what was actually happening, so the question took him by surprise.

"Well? If there are any witnesses, would they please mind coming forward?" the king prodded when Lucas didn't respond right away.

"Why, yes sir, that would be me," Lucas mumbled.

"Speak up, boy," Rand said, "so we can all hear you."

"Yes, I was there," Lucas declared.

"Good. Don't leave, then." The king turned brusquely back to Jon. "Now you, defend your actions quickly or we'll just make an end of this and—"

"Hold on, dear," Maya said sweetly. "If you don't mind, I'd like a word or two with the prisoner."

"No time for that," the king blustered.

"Oh, of course there's time." Maya reproved her husband with a look. "We haven't had a trial like this in a hundred years. No need to hurry on so."

"Swift judgment, that's our duty," Rand said.

"And a fair trial," Maya added with a withering glare in Rand's direction. "Now, would you kindly keep your words to yourself for a moment?"

Rand and Dent exchanged glances and shrugged, so Maya continued. "Why are you here?" she asked simply.

"I have no idea," Jon answered truthfully.

"Fair enough," Maya said with a curt nod. "But where have you come from? Are you of this world?"

"No, I've somehow managed to stumble into this one."

"So you are, in fact, from some other world? Not of this land?"

"Yes, I suppose."

The buzzing at this answer grew so loud that Maya was forced to hold a hand up, silencing everyone. "I see," she said when the din had subsided. "So you had no foreknowledge of our laws here?"

"Exactly." Jon nodded vigorously. "So there's no way—"

"I don't see how any of this means a whit or a widdle to these proceedings," Rand interrupted. "Whether he knew of our laws or not is of no consequence. All we must know is whether he violated them or not, simple as that."

"Oh, of course it's important, you twit," Maya said. "If he didn't know the law, then his action was neither wrong nor right. It was simply neutral."

"But it still may have been foolish, stupid, or selfish," said another fairy, a muscular sort dressed only in black skintights. "We can still give him the axe."

"Keep your knife sheathed, Blunt," the queen commanded. "There will be time for that later. If he was selfish, stupid, or foolish, that is."

"Oh, he's one of those, all right," Blunt said with a greedy smile. "Just look at him squirm."

Jon had, in fact, been squirming. He was having a very hard time following the course of the proceedings. As yet, he still hadn't discovered what it was he was trying to defend himself against.

"To the task at hand," Rand said, "we need an explanation of what happened so we can judge for ourselves."

"Witness!" the king bellowed. "Front and center."

Lucas bolted toward the middle of the fairy ring as if he'd been shot out of a cannon. "Here, sir," he mumbled.

"Speak up," the king ordered. "Now, tell us what happened."

"We were on this mountaintop, nearby where we live," Lucas said. "There's this spring I sometimes visit. That's where I found him."

"Found who?" Maya asked. "The defendant?"

"Yes, that's right. Jon was just lying next to it, fast asleep, when I first saw him. I'd been out with the sheep…"

The king frowned. "Get on with the story."

"And I'd come for a drink," Lucas said, hurrying through his story. "Jon was there and when I couldn't wake him, I splashed some water on him. That woke him up all right, but then he started gulping the water down like there was no tomorrow."

"Peg, is that your spring?" Maya shouted out, glancing in the horse's direction.

The horse nodded lazily.

"Then the music began," Lucas continued. "It was more beautiful than anything I've ever heard. A chorus of voices that kept growing louder and louder."

"That would be the nine daughters, right, Peg?" Maya shouted out again in the horse's direction, who again nodded.

"Would you stop that shouting," Dent grumbled to his wife.

"I just want the facts," Maya said. She never paid any attention to her husband.

"Well, you're interrupting the witness," the king argued.

"With good reason," Maya said.

"Anyway," Lucas continued, "when the music was especially loud, Jon began to walk toward the edge of the mountain like he was in some sort of a trance."

"The water from the spring," Maya said, more to herself than to the other judges.

"I couldn't stop him," Lucas reported. "He kept walking toward the edge, like he wanted to just walk right off. That's when he said he wanted to fly."

"Oh, he wanted to fly, is that it?" Rand said with a pleased smile.

"He's finished." Blunt grinned viciously.

"We started talking and this strange look came over his face," Lucas said. "Then he said a word I've never heard before. A moment later, the winged horse, Peg, came thundering down out of the sky to rescue us."

"Rescue you?" Maya asked. "Is that what you said?"

"Yes, I guess I did," Lucas admitted.

"And why is that?" the king demanded. "Were you in danger?"

"No, I mean, yes. Jon seemed to be in danger. I wasn't."

"Care to explain that curious state of affairs?" Rand said.

Lucas sighed. He didn't like answering questions. He never had. "It was simple. The music was drawing him over the edge. He'd have surely plunged to his death if Peg hadn't come along."

"Just as I thought," Maya said, satisfied.

"That'll be enough," Dent ordered Lucas. "You can run along now."

Maya looked sternly at Jon. "You don't remember any of this, do you?"

"Can't say that I do." Jon wasn't altogether sure he liked what he was hearing. He had truly tried to walk over the edge of a mountaintop?

"I don't think there's much left here." Maya addressed her constituency who were, even now, grumbling among themselves over this turn of events. "The boy has done nothing wrong. He was only saving himself when he invoked the magic."

"Ha!" Her husband, the king, wagged a reproachful finger in her direction. "You always take up for the underdog. But it won't work here."

"The king is right," Rand said. "The defendant may, indeed, have been preserving his life with his actions, but it doesn't remove the stain of culpability. The facts would seem to stand for themselves. It was a flagrant, wanton act of selfishness."

"Just so," the king said. "He wanted to fly. Probably always had, ever since he was a little boy. Isn't that right…by the way, do you have a name?"

"Yes, I have a name. It's Jon Arteu," he snapped. "And what does that prove, that I've wanted to fly since I was a little boy?"

"Then you admit it?" Rand arched one eyebrow.

"Why shouldn't I?"

"No reason," Maya said. "It proves nothing."

"Oh, it most certainly does prove something," Dent argued.

"Premeditation," Rand said. "That's what it proves."

"Oh, pish-posh," Maya corrected scornfully. "It proves no such thing. The boy was in trouble. He called on Peg here to get him out of a tight spot. Nothing more, nothing less."

"I didn't know what I was doing," Jon said lamely.

"That's no excuse," the king fired back. "Who among us ever truly knows what he's doing?"

Rand darted to within two or three inches of Jon's nose. "Have you or have you not always wished to fly? Yes or no."

"Like I said, I—"

"Yes or no!" Rand demanded.

"Yes, then!" Jon shouted.

"And you seized the first opportunity to ruthlessly exploit that secret desire, yes or no?"

"I wouldn't exactly put it that way."

"Yes or no?"

"No," Jon emphasized.

"You are a liar," Rand said flatly. "Do you deny you invoked the magic because you wanted to fly?"

Jon recalled a warm, tingling sensation, a burning desire to just fly and rid himself of all his troubles. And he vaguely remembered using a word from that strange book he'd been reading before coming to this world....

"Okay, so I did. Big deal. I'm sorry. I won't do it again," Jon finally said.

"It doesn't erase the fact that what you did was prideful, foolish, and stupid, all in one," Rand said.

"Yes, I'm afraid 'sorry' doesn't cut it, boy," the king said. "If that's the best defense you can muster..."

Lucas decided he'd heard enough. He leaped back into the fray, scattering more than one fairy as he charged back toward the center of the ring. "This is all ridiculous!" he shouted. "I made him do it. I forced him into doing something because he was about to take me over the edge with him."

"Eh, what's that?" the king asked.

"You heard me. I was trying to hold him back, but it wasn't working. The magic was too strong for the both of us. Peg was our only hope. It was all I could do to just get him on the horse so we could escape."

"So you're the guilty party here, then?" Rand asked suspiciously.

"Do you mean to say we have the wrong suspect on trial here?" the king asked.

"String 'em both up by their big toes," Blunt said, "and let the blood rush to their heads. Then they'll tell the truth."

"I am telling the truth!" Lucas yelled. "I made him do it."

The judges morphed into an angry, buzzing mob. This wasn't the way these trials were handled, at least not according to the legends.

Maya seized the advantage. "I want a vote," she said, raising her voice above the din. "I want a vote to release these two. The facts speak for themselves. This one," she pointed at Jon, "didn't know what he was doing or that he was in danger from the Muses." Then she pointed at Lucas. "And this one was merely doing what he felt was best when he prompted his friend to call on Peg. Together, they did the right thing honorably."

"Hold on," the king said. "Those aren't the facts of the matter. They've both done what they shouldn't have, I say."

The queen glared at him. "I've asked for a vote. We've had enough of this drivel."

The judges flitted back and forth across the ring, arguing among themselves now. Maya folded her arms smugly. Dent and Rand scowled. They could sense the tide turning against them.

"Scorekeeper!" the king bellowed when it appeared the judges were ready to vote. A scholarly looking fellow flitted forward, red nectar pen in hand. "All right, let's be quick about it. Kindness, yes, pranks, no."

And before Jon had prepared himself for the vote, the first fairy flew up close and promptly tweaked him, hard, on the nose.

"That's a no," the king said happily.

A second fairy, a shy female, flew forward quickly and patted Jon on the head.

"And a yes." Dent scowled. A faint cheer went up from the ranks of the judges who obviously were supporting Maya.

A third—a young, ragtag muffin of a fairy—burst from the edges of the ring and plowed headlong into Jon's midsection. A lusty cheer, louder than the previous cheer, went up as the second tally against Jon was recorded.

It went on like that for some time. By the end, Jon was so battered, sore, tweaked, pulled, plucked, and prodded it would probably take a week to recover. He most certainly did not approve of the way these people voted.

But, in the end, compassion won out. Maya's supporters were many and, despite any reservations they might have harbored, they weren't about to go against the wishes of their queen. She was their leader, and they trusted her. And, by the count, she had the clear majority.

Jon survived the vote of the fairy judges with some bruises, not because of his stellar defense, but because Lucas had come to his rescue and the queen of the fairies, Maya, had established a record of wise and sound decisions.

He should have been immensely relieved and thankful. He wasn't. What he felt was anger. The stupid horse had been right. He hadn't even defended himself adequately, much less matched wits with these people.

He'd muddled through, yes, but he'd sullied his reputation in the process. At least in his own mind. And, to Jon, that was all that had ever really mattered.

"Final tally," the king said miserably, "is 217 yes and 134 no. The lucky stiff is free to go and do as he pleases."

"Sad state of affairs when we let these humans do as they please," Rand muttered.

Maya wasn't celebrating, though. She wasn't even in the ring when the final vote was announced. She was off to one side, discussing another matter with Peg.

"There's something else going on here, isn't there, Peg?" Maya asked the horse.

"I think that's a fair assumption," the horse answered.

"This boy, or whoever he is, didn't show up by chance. There's a powerful hand behind all this, I'd wager," she said thoughtfully.

"Without a doubt," Peg agreed.

"So what do we do now, though?" she asked the horse, one of the few creatures she trusted.

"Hard to say," the horse answered. "I think we all need to talk to this young man a bit more, find out what he knows."

"And then?"

"And then it may be time the fairies returned to the land, before it's too late. You've let the magicians run amok far too long. Heaven only knows what they've gotten themselves into these days."

The queen frowned. "That won't be easy, you know, convincing some of these lazy louts to give up their carefree life. In fact, it may be impossible."

"That's true," Peg said. "But I think you'll have to try."

The queen sighed. Oh, the hardships of the crown. Sometimes the burden seemed far too heavy, especially since her dear husband, the king, wasn't exactly what you would call a wise ruler. Lovable and kind to those nearest to him, yes, but naïve and foolish when it came to the ways of the principalities and powers.

"I suppose you're right," the queen said. "I have no choice."

Peg brightened visibly. "It'll be nice to see some of my old friends. There are quite a few I haven't seen in centuries."

"Let's hope you get the chance." The queen's expression was grim. "Now let's go rescue that young man from my husband before he loses what little reason and sanity he has left."

17

***

CYTHEREA AND THE DRYAD

Samson was startled, to say the least. Mark was simply overjoyed. It was a dream come true.

They had stumbled on the elves, of course. Unwittingly, they'd triggered the dormant trap door the elves had left behind so long ago, a window that afforded them the opportunity, if they so desired, to keep track of the land they'd left behind.

What neither could have imagined, though, was the welcome they received. No sooner had Samson and Mark arrived in this strange forest than they found themselves swinging upside down from the limb of a heavy tree, their feet snared in trip nooses.

But that wasn't even the half of it, at least not as far as Mark was concerned. The elves had taken but a moment to see who'd sprung their trap. And then, convinced the two were nothing more than bumbling fools, the elves had vanished into the depths of the forest. Without a word.

Mark had only a glimpse of them, perhaps six in all. Though it was hard to tell— he *was* upside down, after all—they were shorter than he'd always imagined, smaller than he was, in fact. All had been dressed in light brown deerskin, their hair a white blond. Long bows were slung over their backs.

They'd also seemed intensely angry. Perhaps they'd expected to snare a wayward magician, or perhaps a pious cleric, and they'd been unable to mask their emotions at finding nothing more than two careless mortals. They obviously thought little of fighters, even one as fearsome as Samson. And justly so, Mark reasoned. The elves were renowned, according to legend, for their ability to defend themselves in combat. Only the dwarves carried themselves as well in a fight.

Samson, meanwhile, was sure he'd heard one of the elves mention to another, before they'd melted away suddenly, something about the punishment fitting the crime and that the dolts would either die hanging upside down or drop back through the rabbit hole they'd fallen through.

Samson had little thought for the stuff of legends at the moment. He couldn't have cared less that he'd just caught a glimpse of a race the land had not seen in centuries. No, Samson's only desire was to figure a way out of his present predicament. The blood rushing to his head was already making him dizzy. If he remained much longer in that position, he would black out. His blood pressure would drop, the blood would cease its endless trek through his body, and that would be that. "Come on," he urged Mark. "We've got to get ourselves out of this."

"But don't you know who they were?" Mark asked, unable to keep the profound awe from his voice.

Samson, beginning to pull himself upright, hand over hand, almost growled. "I don't much care who they were. They weren't very hospitable, leaving us caught like this."

"We broke their law," Mark almost whispered. "They had every right to fill us full of arrows."

"Oh, that would have been great sport." Samson grunted with the effort to pull himself up to where he could unloose the rope around his foot. "Plugging us while we dangled here like turkeys."

"They would never have done such a thing. Not them."

"Look," Samson said, already disgusted with the way Mark was fawning. "Whoever they were, I plan to give them a piece of my mind when I see them next. To leave us stranded here…"

"Oh, you won't ever see them again. Not if they don't want to be seen."

"And why is that?"

"Because…because they're elves," Mark stammered.

"So what?"

"Don't you know who they are? Don't you know what that means?"

"No!" Samson shouted, now impatient as well as disgusted. The rope had knotted around his ankle. It was amazingly strong rope, and it would take a Herculean effort to unloose it. "I don't *care* who they are. All I know is that I plan to teach a few of them a lesson when I get the chance."

"I already told you. They won't give you that chance."

"That's absurd. They're not ghosts."

"Just about, here in their own kingdom. They could follow us for miles and we'd never know they were there."

"I'll worry about that when I get to it. Right now," Samson said through clenched teeth, "we have our hands full. I can't free my foot from this rope."

"That's because it's one of *their* ropes," Mark explained with a glum face. "They hold forever. The knots are permanent, if they want them to be. The more pressure you apply, the tighter they get."

"Forever's a long time," Samson claimed fiercely. "Nobody makes a rope that strong."

"They can." Mark refused to even attempt to free himself. He'd sunk into such despair he didn't much care what happened to him. He could feel himself slipping into the darkness. Before too much longer, he would surely pass out.

Why did they treat me with such contempt? Mark desperately wanted to know. For nearly all his young life, he'd dreamed of such an opportunity. To meet the elves, for whom they'd preserved the Sanctuary! And for what? So the elves could turn up their noses and walk away, leaving him to die an ignominious death hanging upside down from a tree?

Samson broke Mark's reverie. "Shake out of it, boy. You've got to forget about it for now. Try to free yourself. You can sort it all out later."

"I guess you're right." Mark sighed. "No point in just hanging here like a potato sack."

"That's the spirit."

Mark nimbly pulled himself up to the knot at his ankle and examined it with a critical eye. His father, bless his heart, had taught him the fine and ancient art of knotting ropes for just about any purpose. Mark quickly recognized this one as a fairly intricate variation of the running knot. Before he could even wonder at how he'd managed it, he'd applied a little pressure at one place, pulled the loose end in one direction while pushing a strand of cord from another....

"I'm free," he said simply as he slipped his foot out. He glanced at the ground. The silver mirror they'd fallen through had turned into a giant lake beneath them. If he fell, he'd simply go back to where he'd come from. And, with all his heart, Mark did not wish that.

"I thought you said these things hold forever," Samson said with no small measure of scorn, angry the boy had escaped before he had and, apparently, with little difficulty.

"Looks like I was wrong." Climbing hand over hand, Mark quickly pulled himself high enough to give Samson the proper instructions. After some frustrated grumbling, Samson finally slipped free.

"Now what?" Samson held onto the rope with both hands as he surveyed their situation.

"Well, we either climb up these ropes to the tree limbs above, or we drop to the ground and fall back through the silver mirror." Mark glanced up. The nearest tree limb was a *long* way up.

Samson glanced up and then down. "I don't know about you, but I'm not going back." Without another word, he began the slow, arduous hand-over-hand climb up the rope.

Mark quickly followed. "Me, neither. I've waited all my life to meet the elves, and I'm not about to miss the chance now."

It took nearly an hour, but they made it. Mark almost lost his grip twice, but Samson had no problem at all with the climb. Once they'd made it to a tree limb, it was then a simple matter to climb from limb to limb until they were well clear of the silver lake and could head back to the ground safely.

When they were both on the ground, they finally took stock of where they'd arrived. They were nowhere near the Sanctuary, of that Mark was certain. He was familiar with almost every square foot of his home, and this was completely different in virtually every respect.

The largest difference could be summed up quite simply. This forest was *alive*, whereas the Sanctuary now seemed a little tame for a forest. Here, you could sense the pulsing life everywhere you turned. If Mark didn't miss his guess, strange creatures he'd only read about in the legends lurked nearby, perhaps, even at that very moment, waiting to pounce…

"We've got to move from this place," Mark said suddenly, searching frantically for the direction they should take.

"Why?"

"I-I don't know for sure. Just a feeling. There's something very close. I can sense it somehow."

Samson glanced around. The forest seemed especially dense here. "I don't see anything."

Mark, though, had already settled on a direction—the same one the elves had taken when they'd left the two of them hanging from the tree. It seemed logical enough. As if they had much of a choice anyway, here in this strange and terrifying forest.

And it *was* terrifying. Perhaps not to Samson, who didn't know any better, but it most certainly was to Mark the more he listened to the unusual sounds flittering through the thick leaves—raucous, throaty bird calls and, off in the distance, the deep growls of some predatory animal who'd come upon his prey for the day. The faint whispering wind carried other things—the sound of large creatures moving through the forest and the fragrance of exotic plants and flowers, to name a few.

"Come on," Mark said. "We'll try to follow the elves. Perhaps we can pick up their trail."

"Sure." Samson shook his head scornfully. "And just how do we do that?"

"I can track as well as anyone in the Sanctuary. My father taught me."

But tracking the elves proved no easy matter. They left no footprints to speak of…only a twig or two broken in their wake. That forced Mark to look for other telltale signs—a bush brushed back where the elves had passed, a still-green leaf that had fallen unnaturally to the ground, or unusual pockets of stillness in the forest where the elves had scared away the neighbors as they passed through.

Samson followed behind, convinced the boy was mad and perpetrating a hoax. For he saw nothing, heard nothing, and doubted whether Mark knew where he was going at all. But, short of an alternative, Samson would give the boy the benefit of the doubt.

The forest grew stranger and stranger, almost with each step. It was like nothing Mark had ever seen. The undergrowth was unbelievably dense. What the forest needed, ironically, was a good fire to clear away much of it.

But what perplexed Mark most was that he was certain someone, or something, was following them. Or watching them, perhaps, as they wandered aimlessly through the forest. Maddeningly frustrated, he almost caught a glimpse, once.

"Didn't you see that?" he whispered to Samson. There *had* been something. He'd caught something out of the corner of his eye as it disappeared behind a tree.

"No, of course not," Samson said crossly. "What's there to see?"

"Can't you tell? Can't you feel their presence?" Mark asked, for he was convinced there were more than one of whatever it was keeping an eye on them.

"You've lost it, boy. There's nothing here but the birds and us, as they say."

Mark knew Samson was wrong, but he kept quiet. After all, the presence didn't seem unfriendly. Curious, more than anything else. What troubled him more, now, was the gloomy fact that the elves trail grew dimmer with each passing moment. What had been merely unlikely before was now becoming impossible.

Samson saw the young girl first, for Mark had his nose to the elves' trail. She wasn't quite fast enough to slip behind the giant oak. Perhaps she'd lingered too long to catch a glimpse of the wayfarers as they passed through her domain. Or, perhaps, she'd hoped to be seen.

"Wait, come back!" Samson shouted in the still forest, startling both Mark and the birds.

"What did you see?" Mark's head snapped up at Samson's booming voice.

"A girl, I swear it." Samson moved quickly toward the giant oak where he'd seen the girl. "She was peeking out from behind a tree."

A warning bell sounded somewhere in the recesses of Mark's mind, something he couldn't quite recall from the legends of the elves he knew so well. But, whatever it was, it refused to surface, so he followed in Samson's wake, abandoning, most likely, the elves' cold trail for good.

"She was right here," Samson said as he reached the oak. He stood glaring at the tree for a moment and then circled it, looking for any telltale signs that someone had been here.

"I don't doubt you saw something," Mark replied, not wanting to anger his companion, "but are you sure you saw a girl? Out here?"

"Yes, I tell you! Plain as day."

But they found nothing. Mark scoured the area around the tree for any clue that someone had been there recently and came up empty-handed. Whatever Samson had seen, it left nothing in its passing.

Samson banged a heavy hand against the stout bark of the tree. "I *saw* her, I tell you. She was right here, peeking out at me from behind this tree."

Mark, not wishing to anger him further, decided to search the perimeter. Not that he expected to find anything. But it would give Samson some breathing room to compose himself. And perhaps Mark could discover something useful.

Samson, meanwhile, slumped dejectedly at the base of the tree, his head in his hands. He barely acknowledged Mark as the boy started his perimeter search within a radius of 50 feet or so around the thick tree.

As Mark, eyes ceaselessly roving, made his way through the forest, the nagging thought nudged again. It was maddening, really. It touched his consciousness for a flicker of an instant, only to flee before he could catch it. It had something to do with the elves and some of the creatures who had followed the race when they fled the land. According to the legends, there had been all manner of creatures, both good and bad, who made the journey—satyrs, fauns, wood nymphs and…

Too late, Mark remembered what had been nagging at him. He turned in a panic, only to see Samson being led by the hand by a lovely, gentle, young girl. Before Mark could even shout out a warning, the two disappeared through a portal that had magically appeared in the side of the giant oak. It closed behind them in the blink of an eye.

"No!" The agonized shout erupted, unbidden, from Mark's lips. "No!" he said more softly, running to the tree, knowing it was useless, hopeless.

Mark now knew, with a horrible certainty, why the elves had simply left them hanging upside down from the tree. Even if they'd managed to free themselves from the ropes and avoid falling back through the silver portal, the elves knew that this forest would never let them pass through alive.

He would never see Samson again, for Samson had been lured away by a dryad, a tree spirit who took the form of a girl. That's what Mark had been unable to remember in time. They lived near the elves in the giant oaks. In fact, they lived forever within several feet of the trees.

Although they were shy, reclusive creatures by nature, one could occasionally beguile a naïve wayfarer and invite him into her home, the tree. And once inside, that person was almost never seen again. Even those very, very few who were seen again, the legends said, came back years later, profoundly changed by the experience.

Groaning in horror at the turn of events, Mark fell to the ground at the base of the tree, almost in the identical spot Samson had been sitting when the dryad had undoubtedly slipped up on him.

Mark sat there, silent as a stone, his back to the oak, for the better part of an hour, wondering what he could possibly do next. It was hopeless, of course. He could never manage to open the magic portal in the tree through which the two of them had slipped. And he couldn't simply sit here forever, waiting for them to return. Most likely, he would be waiting forever.

But as he sat there, a plan formed. It was a dangerous one, but did he have any choice, out here in the middle of who-knows-where? Mark, still dejected, glanced around him at last, afraid even to hope for what he needed to carry out the plan.

His heart pounding, he spotted what he was looking for—another giant oak, close by. He looked up toward the sky. Yes! Their leaves touched near the top where their upper limbs arched toward each other.

"All right." He sighed with determination. "Let us see what we shall see."

He approached this second oak cautiously, hoping against hope that a second dryad dwelt within. It wasn't likely. Two tree spirits rarely lived near each other. But, if there was any chance at all, he had to take it.

As he drew near the tree, though, he knew the task was futile. After all, just how do you entice one to come out and play?

"Hello, anyone home?" he said uneasily, feeling like a fool as he knocked a cautious fist on the bark of the tree. "Please, I must speak to you if you're there."

Nothing, absolutely nothing, which was precisely what he'd expected. He knocked again anyway. What harm could it possibly do?

"There's no one there, silly," a demure voice said from behind him.

Mark whirled in a panic. There was nothing to see, though. The ethereal voice had seemingly come from nowhere. "Where…where are you? I can't see you."

"Of course you can't, my dear," the sultry voice said again. "You would faint dead away if I let you look at me directly without at least some warning."

"And why is that?"

"Just because," the voice said mysteriously. "Now, I want you to shield your eyes. And when I tell you to, open them ever so slowly."

Mark wasn't about to be fooled. "How can I trust you?"

"You can't," the voice said lightly, "but if you hope to ever see your friend again, you'll have to trust me, now, won't you?"

"Yes…I guess so," he said slowly, deciding all at once to do as the voice had compelled him. He covered his eyes with his hands.

There was a slight rustle of leaves as someone emerged from the shadows of a nearby tree. That much Mark could tell just by listening. "Now, I want you to look at me very slowly, as if you were trying to peer at the sun."

Mark did as he was told. As slowly as he could manage, he removed his hands to peer at the speaker. Involuntarily, he gasped. "You're so…beautiful," he whispered, his throat dry and his heart racing.

"Yes, I know," the creature said shyly.

"I don't think I've ever seen anyone quite like you," Mark said truthfully.

Standing before him, clad only in what appeared to be a patchwork of leaves loosely linked to each other, was by far the prettiest girl he'd ever seen. Her hair was a deep, rich brown, hanging almost down to her knees. Her face seemed to shine like the sun. And her body was, well…perfectly proportioned.

"Have you ever seen the likes of me before?" she asked Mark.

"No, no," he said quickly. "I have never been this way before."

"Have they no woodlands where you come from?" she asked, tilting her head to one side, a gesture that sent Mark's pulse pounding.

"Yes, they do, but…"

"The forest is not alive there." The girl smiled. "Yes, I think I understand now."

"Who are you?" Mark blurted out.

"Do you mean my name?"

"Well, yes, I think so," Mark said, unwilling to admit his ignorance. He wasn't thinking clearly, or he might have realized who, or what, he was talking to.

"I have many names, but Cytherea will do nicely," she answered with a slight bow that sent cold shivers through Mark.

"Pleased to meet you. I'm Mark."

"Why were you knocking on that empty husk of a tree?" she asked abruptly.

Mark glanced over his shoulder at the other oak, where his companion had disappeared. "I was looking for a friend."

"In the tree?" the girl asked, incredulous.

"No! Of course not." Mark flushed. "I was looking for someone, actually, who could help me find this friend…"

"Who has gone away with the tree spirit?"

"That's right."

Cytherea smiled and the earth turned a half degree. Mark was certain of this because he could feel it down to the core of his being. And when the girl took a timid half-step in his direction, it was all Mark could do to keep his knees from buckling.

"Do not be afraid of me," she whispered. "I would never harm such an innocent one as you."

"I'm not that innocent," Mark defended, standing his ground. Half of him wanted to simply rush forward and melt into her arms. The other half screamed at him to flee to the farthest ends of the earth.

Cytherea took another hesitant half-step forward. "Oh, you have much to learn, I think. Much indeed."

"My father says my education is coming along."

"In the ways of females." She moved even closer.

"Oh, that," Mark said stupidly, still managing somehow to look Cytherea in the eye as she continued to move forward with a flowing grace.

"I will teach you."

"Oh, don't bother. My father says it's not that important yet."

"It is of the utmost urgency." Cytherea's eyes glowed with a fervent intensity now. "Let me lead you down that path of knowledge."

"Really, it's very nice of you, but…"

Cytherea was close enough now that Mark could see through and around her patchwork clothing quite clearly. He held his own eyes steady, locking his to hers with a steely glare.

"There is nothing to be afraid of," she said.

"I know that," Mark voiced a bit too loudly.

Cytherea lightly placed a soft, petite hand on his shoulder. Shudders of ecstatic delight coursed through Mark's body. "See what pleasure I bring you," she said with a beguiling smile.

Mark frantically searched his mind for something, anything, to lead him out of this predicament. It wasn't easy. Part of his mind was working frantically in a quite opposite direction, blocking out virtually everything but the sweet caress of the girl's hand and her musky odor that was even now setting off siren bells in his head.

"There is…a friend I must help," he gasped.

"You cannot help him," she answered, reaching out her other hand.

Mark locked his knees in place, absolutely refusing to let them buckle. "I must. I have to," he said resolutely.

"I will show you a way in a little while," Cytherea said, "but first…"

"You know a way?" Mark demanded.

"Yes, of course. We are kindred spirits."

"Then you must show me! Before it is too late," Mark said impatiently, trying to ward off the sultry advances of the nubile young girl.

"Too late?"

"Yes, my friend isn't of this world." Mark tried to seize the advantage. "He won't understand. It could change him forever."

"Perhaps. But there is no dishonor in change." Cytherea said with mischief.

"Oh, please, Cytherea, you must help me," Mark pleaded. A moment or two longer and it would be too late. Not for Samson but for himself. He was on the edge of the precipice, and he knew it.

Cytherea hesitated. The pause was breathtaking, for it gave Mark an opportunity to see a new emotion flit across her flawless features. Even indecision became her.

"You would truly like my help?" she asked him.

"Oh, yes, please. Would you?" A flood of such relief surged through him that his eyelids fluttered.

Before Mark could react, Cytherea suddenly embraced him with a sweet caress. Despite himself, Mark enfolded his own arms around her. There was no stopping it, not now....

But the young girl slipped free of the embrace and quickly turned away, leaving Mark confused, hurt, and angry all at once. Before he could say anything, though, she'd glided over to the oak tree where Samson had disappeared, an event that now seemed ages and ages ago to Mark.

Trailing in her wake, Mark had to wonder what he'd passed up. Or had he? Perhaps he would never know. At any rate, he was wrapped so deep in thought he almost missed Cytherea calling softly to the gentle spirit who inhabited the giant oak and then, when the portal appeared, wriggling quickly through it and disappearing from view.

Cytherea was gone for what seemed a very long time to Mark, who fretted and fumed, walking endless circles around the tree. In fact, she was gone for just a few minutes. It only seemed like an eternity to Mark, who was equally torn between his missed opportunity and worry for Samson's well-being.

As he paced outside the tree, Mark considered the strange, young giant with whom the fates had unexpectedly linked him. In his young life, Mark had only met one other so sullen and angry—his uncle, Blackbeard. Not that Samson and his uncle had much of anything else in common. But they did have that burning sense of outrage at their own particular place in the world. To Mark's way of thinking, it was not only self-centered but destructive to view the world ceaselessly as it related to your own, tiny, inconsequential life.

But what did he know? Perhaps when he was older, his soul, too, would burn with unfulfilled longing and unrequited anger for a better world where he might seize his advantages quickly and easily.

He was on the opposite side of the tree when they emerged, so he only caught a glimpse of the savage joy on Samson's face. The expression faded in the harsh glare of the land he'd returned to, the only remnant a haunting, troubled look in his eyes that could, in an instant, turn to longing and remembrance.

Mark couldn't bring himself to ask Samson what had happened to him in the tree spirit's world. And Samson didn't seem inclined to mention it, so there was an uneasy silence between the two of them when Mark almost stumbled against him as he rounded the base of the tree.

Fortunately, Cytherea broke the sullen atmosphere. "Well, that's that," she said to Mark with a radiant smile. "I've done as you asked. Are you pleased?"

Mark reluctantly pulled his attention away from Samson, who as yet had still said nothing, offered no thanks or even any acknowledgment of the events of the past hour or so. "I am deeply in your debt," he said solemnly to the girl. "If there is anything at all I can do?"

"There is," she answered, a slight catch in her voice.

"Name it."

"Take me with you," she said unexpectedly.

"What!" Mark whispered hoarsely.

"That is my favor." Her eyes pleaded even more than her voice. "Take me from this place."

"But why? I don't understand."

"The time is at hand. That is why," she said mysteriously. "And I need to know the purpose of this stranger. I must know. All of us must."

"The time? The time of what?"

"The time of healing, of returning. The land is changing. Old ways are returning. The elves have sensed it for some time, but I have not believed for a very long time."

"But how can you be so sure?"

Cytherea glanced at Samson, who was still mute, remembering the world of the tree spirit. "*He* is why I'm sure. You are right. He is not of this world."

"I know," Mark said. "But what does that have to do…?"

"He has come for a purpose. There can be no question of that. He has come either to heal the land or to destroy it."

Mark weighed the young girl's words carefully. They made very little sense, at least for now. But on one thing he would likely stake his life. He doubted whether Cytherea could ever lie. Bewitch, yes, but never outright lie.

"All right," he said at last. "It would be an honor if you came with us. But tell me this. Where, exactly, are we going?"

Cytherea smiled, melting Mark's heart again. "I will take you to the elves. And he," she pointed to Samson, "must convince them to return to the land they now scorn and curse with every breath."

18

* * *

THE UNGUARDED WALL

Laura certainly was glad they didn't share knowledge in her own world. She despised herself for thinking that way, but it was only logical. For if they were able to pool their cumulative knowledge, as the people of the sea could, where would be her advantage? There would be none. And what would she have to live for?

"Oh, there is much to live for," the young mermaid, Tara, told her.

"Name one thing," Laura said haughtily. "Knowledge is a yardstick in my world. We measure almost everything by it. That and money."

"Money?"

"Oh, never mind," Laura answered curtly. "You probably don't have any of that down here, either."

"There is love."

"Yes, I suppose." Laura gave a heartfelt, inward sigh. "Not too practical, though. And pretty mushy."

"There is protection," the young mermaid persisted.

"Protection?"

"The people of the sea, by virtue of their great knowledge, are wise and just rulers in their own kingdom," Kathryn chimed in.

"And how do you know that?" Laura asked her traveling companion. For some reason, she had trouble thinking of her as a friend. But, of course, except for Jen, she'd never truly had a friend.

"The legends say…"

"The legends!" Laura burst out. "Those accursed things. Who cares about stories that are probably as old as those hills?"

"I do," Kathryn said softly. "They kept me alive for a long time, when I didn't think I had much to live for."

"Stories? Simple stories gave you hope?"

Kathryn kept her mind silent for a very long time, afraid to voice what had remained buried deep within her heart so very long. And now, when the fondest dream she'd ever carried was so close to being a reality, so near at hand, she was utterly terrified to bring it to the light. "I have always wanted to be a magician," she said at last, turning away so she would not be forced to look at Laura.

"Oh, is that so?" Laura asked. "And just why is that?"

"To heal, as you wish to do in your own world. That is all I've ever longed to do, in every waking moment."

Numb shock descended on Laura. She had the strangest sensation she was looking at her alter ego, but one far superior and more noble. Yet, as always, she refused to yield to defeat. "That's nice. Perhaps I can give you some suggestions."

"That would be wonderful!" Kathryn broke into a broad smile, though it was hard for Laura to see this through the dim, pea-green light of the interior of the cave they'd come to while they waited for the elders' decision on Laura's fate.

Tara glanced back and forth between her two guests—or prisoners, depending on your perspective—with dismay. "*But you could do more than that,*" she told Laura.

"Do more?" Laura asked.

"*Yes, of course,*" Tara said quickly. "*You could share your knowledge with her, if you wished. I could teach you how.*"

"Do you mean just give her everything I know?"

"*Not entirely, no, but something like that. It would only require that you open your mind totally to her. She could learn, or take, what she felt she needed or required...*"

"No!" Laura could not stop the word from screeching forth from her mind. "Not ever."

Kathryn reeled in shock, the water masking the tears that sprang to her eyes.

Tara, also stunned by the reaction, took it more calmly. "*There would be no threat to you,*" she said to Laura. Because she had honored her pledge, their minds were closed to each other except for the simple pathways of communication. She could not understand Laura's violent reaction, but she could guess.

"It's not that," Laura said, wishing with all her heart she could just leave this place, leave Kathryn, forget any of this was happening, shut her mind off to all this soul-searching. How she longed simply to return to her books, where she was safe. No more people, no more dealing with emotions, no more words buffeting her cruelly, no more give-and-take that laid her soul bare for others to see. That's what Laura feared more than anything. That others would see how evil she was, how petty, how single-minded, how obsessed, how thoughtless, how vain, how selfish...

"*We never judge here,*" the young mermaid said.

"Get out of my mind!" Laura said.

"*I am not in it,*" Tara answered gently.

"Then how...?"

"*It is a common fear,*" the mermaid answered, "*one we must contend with when the foundlings are ready to enter into the shared knowledge of our community.*"

Laura seized on the word the mermaid had used. "*Foundlings*, you said. Does that mean your children never know their parents?"

"*We are all their parents,*" Tara said.

"That's pretty bizarre." Laura spoke without thinking.

"*You have changed the subject.*"

"I have not," Laura shot back.

"*If you insist,*" the mermaid said mildly. "*Nevertheless, I will repeat what I said. You have nothing to fear, for we do not judge your actions or your thoughts.*"

"Oh, everybody judges!" Laura snapped. "It's the only common theme of religions where I come from."

"*We do not.*"

"Well, I don't care. I said it before and I'll say it again. I refuse to let anyone go mucking around in my brain."

"*Even when it deprives a friend of a dream she has held for years?*" answered Tara. "*A dream only you may fulfill?*"

The mermaid's words struck to the core of Laura's being. Did she, after all, have the right to guard her privacy so jealously if it meant that made her the enemy, made her someone else's stumbling block? "I just can't," Laura said lamely.

The mermaid inclined her head. "*You can. You have nothing to fear or lose but your pride and your vanity.*"

"I refuse to confess my soul to anyone," Laura interrupted. "When it comes time, if I'm able and willing, I will confess to God. To no one else."

"*As it should be,*" Tara said gently. "*God is here, too, and I ask him for help and guidance often. Everyone in our community does.*"

"And does he judge you here as well?"

"*I think…he asks us to help others learn from the mistakes we make, so we may not make them again. He sees our thoughts all the time, so it is not something we can hide, even if we wanted to. So, no, it is not judging, as you think of it.*"

Laura wouldn't budge. God was one thing. But letting others see her mistakes, misjudgments, slights, petty jealousies, and who knew what else? Simply unthinkable. "I really can't," she said finally.

The mermaid looked at Laura. "*Tell me something, then. You're not of this world, right?*"

"That's true."

"*Then where have you gained your own knowledge? How were you able to step into this world as a full-fledged magician? How is that possible unless someone shared their knowledge with you?*"

"Oh, that's silly," Laura said. "No one shared their knowledge with me. I read it in a book. I learned it myself."

"*I'm not sure I understand. The picture in your mind is of something, some product of the trees that grow in the land, upon which someone who understands the ways of magicians has set their knowledge. Have I described this…this book you spoke of?*"

"More or less."

"*Why,*" Tara said with a smile, "*that is shared knowledge. A different form, yes, but it is still shared. The only difference is that it is selective. It is not as intimate.*"

The thought took Laura by surprise. To her, books were tools for her own pleasure. She never identified them with their authors. In fact, the authors were irrelevant, as far as she'd always been concerned. The only thing that mattered was her ability to take from those books. There was nothing shared about it. She simply gobbled up as much as she possibly could, as fast as she could manage.

"*In a way,*" the mermaid said, "*your mind is like a book. The knowledge has been written upon it. All that remains is for you to…open it so someone else may gaze upon it.*"

"My mind a book?" Laura thought aloud. "How utterly strange."

"*Not so strange,*" the mermaid said. "*The only difference is that you cannot selectively choose which knowledge you wish to share, as I gather you are able to do with these books you spoke of in your own world.*"

The concept was so alien to Laura she hardly knew what to think next. But of one thing she was certain. To open up her mind as the mermaid was suggesting would be to invite disaster. Her life, she felt, would never be the same. Someone else to share her burdens, her guilt, if only for a moment? Never.

"I don't see how it is possible, what you ask," Laura said flatly.

"*It's a simple matter. Simply offer your knowledge. You would sacrifice nothing.*"

"Nothing, except all those things I don't want anyone to know about," Laura said, the thought a mere whisper even in her own mind.

"*True, but where is the harm in giving someone else a picture of your innermost self?*" the mermaid asked blithely.

Where indeed? Laura thought bitterly. *Oh, how horrible, how disgusting, how truly terrible she would seem to Kathryn. I just can't. It would be ghastly to let her see what I am truly like.* Then a new thought occurred. *Where is my pride, my confidence in my own ability? What would be so wrong in letting her know the depths of my knowledge and my learning? No, no, it would not be worth the risk. I could not expose myself in that way.*

"I will open up my mind to you first, if that will help," Kathryn said timidly, interrupting Laura's train of thought.

"What?" Laura asked, confused. "What did you say?"

"I will share my knowledge, what little of it there is, with you first, if that will help," Kathryn repeated.

Laura gasped mentally. "Oh, I couldn't. That wouldn't be right."

"*Of course you can and of course it would be right,*" the mermaid said. "*She has offered. All you need to do is accept.*"

Laura closed her eyes. Had they been above ground, she'd have broken out into a cold sweat. Here, she only shivered as she weighed her decision. *No, no, no, I just can't go through with it, even if it is an opportunity I may never again see in my lifetime.*

"What must I do?" Kathryn said to the mermaid. "Tell me what I must do to open my mind to her in that way. How can I give her what I know?"

Tara smiled faintly. "*It is not a simple matter, but I can lead the way. And the first thing you must know is that you, in truth, cannot give her your knowledge.*"

"I don't understand."

"*Picture yourself, who you are, standing at the edge of your mind, guarding the walls that surround your mind, keeping all others out with a watchful eye. Can you do that?*"

"I-I don't know. Perhaps," Kathryn said.

"*Close your eyes,*" Tara directed. "*That will make it easier.*" Kathryn did so, and the mermaid continued: "*Now, think of your soul, your being, looking out defiantly at the world, jealously guarding the treasure within, the storehouse of knowledge you have accumulated throughout your life. You have never turned around to gaze at the wealth of knowledge yourself, although you occasionally reach behind to pull a morsel or two forward. You are too busy guarding the wall, too busy looking out to make sure no one else comes in.*"

"I think I understand!" Kathryn said, the excitement evident in her thoughts. "That's why it's so hard to gaze deeply into someone else's eyes. You're trying to look in past the wall and they don't want you to."

The mermaid nodded. "*Just so. You catch on quickly. But now comes the hard part. You're standing there, as you always have, guarding, protecting, watching. What you must do now is try to step backward. You must try to force the wall away from you. In a sense, you are leaving the wall unguarded for the first time in your life as you move away and toward the center of your own mind.*"

There was a very long pause. Laura found herself holding her breath. Kathryn, serenity on her face, said at last in a very small voice, "It's growing darker."

"*Yes, it will, for a time,*" Tara murmured. "*But keep pushing the wall away from you, keep moving backwards and inwards. Soon it will grow lighter. And, as you go, imagine yourself pushing all the knowledge you've accumulated forward toward the wall.*"

There was a very long pause this time. Laura began breathing again, but her apprehension was soon replaced by a new feeling—horror. The reason was simple. She knew she couldn't refuse the young girl's offer. She would have to sift through whatever she might find on the other side of this imaginary wall.

"*Kathryn, can you hear me?*" the mermaid probed gently. There was no reply. "*Kathryn? Kathryn?*" she called out again. When there was no answer, she turned to

Laura. *"She has offered herself to you. You may refuse, if you like. But the gate has been left open, the wall is now unguarded."*

"But where is she?" Laura asked.

"She has gone to the very center, the core, of her mind," the mermaid explained. *"She has been there before, occasionally, when she sleeps. But never purposefully, consciously, so that another might enter and sift through her memories."*

Laura's stomach was knotted in fear and repulsion, but she steeled herself with one thought. Could it be any worse than opening someone up during surgery, which her father had done almost every day of his adult life and which she had witnessed on several occasions? Could it be any harder than that?

"You will accept the offer, then?" the mermaid asked her.

"I suppose so," Laura said reluctantly, sighing inwardly. "It would be hard to refuse, but I suppose you already knew that, didn't you?'

"I had high hopes," the mermaid answered truthfully.

"Okay, now what must I do?"

"Your role is far easier. Project your mind out. Search for something, anything, and when you see it, you'll know you've reached the unguarded wall. At that point, simply move forward, keeping whatever you've found in sight."

Laura closed her own eyes to make the concentration easier. She did as she'd been told, which was much easier than she'd expected. Because she'd grown accustomed to communicating with thoughts alone, it was a simple manner to project herself toward the young girl's mind.

Within moments, she'd found something. It was obviously a fragment of a recent memory, for Laura herself was a part of it. Laura saw herself and the little boy, Nathaniel, huddled at one end of the boat as it sank like a stone into the depths of the river.

"I've seen something," she told the mermaid.

"Now, follow that direction. You will soon come upon other memories."

Cautiously, Laura projected herself farther into Kathryn's mind. Almost instantly, she found herself in a deluge of remembered feelings, fleeting glimpses, and recalled incidents.

It almost overwhelmed Laura. But she kept her resolve and began to sift through the memories carefully, afraid to do anything that might harm the young girl.

There were so very, very many of them—thousands upon thousands. But she was quickly able to tell the extremely valuable and meaningful ones from those that were only vague memories or, perhaps, long-forgotten ones.

For the important ones stood out in stark contrast from the others, which were very gray and dingy, frayed at the edges, faint to the inner eye, almost transparent. They almost seemed to disintegrate at a glance from Laura.

The important memories, on the other hand, shouted out in bold colors, vivid outlines, sharp corners. They evoked powerful, emotional responses in Laura. They remained there steadfast, as a rock, when Laura approached them. It almost seemed as if the memories had taken on a life of their own.

Laura chose an especially vivid childhood memory to look at first, of a young man out in the fields at harvest time. With a sense of shock, Laura discovered that she was looking at the memory of a startling realization on the young girl's part—a snapshot of that moment.

It was fairly obvious what had happened, for much the same thing had happened to Laura once upon a time. It was the moment in Kathryn's life when she'd first realized her father was not a god, that he was indeed fallible and human. Laura had discovered it the first time her grandmother had come to visit, watching her father react angrily to his own mother's petty criticisms. She had seen then the child in her father.

Here, Kathryn was obviously standing over her father, who had collapsed on the ground, clutching his leg. Perhaps his calf muscles had cramped in the heat of the noonday sun. She couldn't tell. What she could tell from the memory, though, was the sense of terror Kathryn must have felt as she looked on helplessly, unable to comprehend why her superhuman father had crumbled so.

With sadness, Laura turned her attention to another memory. With a start, she realized it was of a young boy in his early teens, about to kiss a young girl. *Oh my.* Laura smiled. *This is her first kiss, the very first time. How strange. And how sweet that it's such an important memory to her. All of that is such a blur in my own mind.*

Laura almost reeled in shock at the next memory, by far the most vivid the young girl carried with her. It was so much more vivid than all the rest, in fact, that Laura wondered how she'd overlooked it to begin with.

It was of a group of coarse men, gathered around some animal while one of their own grappled with it in the center. No, no, it wasn't an animal. It was…another young girl. They were about to attack her. Of course, that was it. Kathryn must have been hiding. She must have witnessed this hideous thing from the bushes nearby.

Laura was dumbfounded with shock. How utterly helpless Kathryn must have felt, to be forced to sit there and witness such an act and to be able to do nothing about it. *If I'd been there, with the powers I seem to possess now in this world, I'd have done far more than turn these foul creatures into toads. I'd have…*

And then it dawned on Laura, finally. It had taken this shock, this horrid scene to do it, but she'd finally realized why it was so utterly vital, so absolutely necessary that she give Kathryn the tools of magic she'd been given herself.

Here, in this world, the young girl would no longer be helpless, always a victim, always weak, always forced to run in fear from those who dominated her physically.

Laura quickly left Kathryn's mind and turned her attention back to the mermaid.

"I understand," Laura said to her. "I know what I need to do, what I should have been willing to do all along."

"*You will give her the knowledge you possess, then?*" the mermaid asked.

"Yes, I will give her the knowledge, so she may use it as a shield. And as a weapon, when the need arises."

The mermaid stirred. She turned from Laura and beckoned toward the door to her cave. Before Laura could even react, nearly a dozen mermen had swirled through the opening into the room.

"*These are the elders,*" Tara said simply. "*And they have made their decision.*"

"Their decision?"

"*Actually you made it for them. You passed the test. You met the challenge with honor, as I always thought you would, despite your pride and selfishness.*"

Laura started to shake uncontrollably with anger. "Do you mean to tell me that you have put me through all this simply because you wanted to judge me? This is nothing more than a test? You watched me like I was some experiment?" The words charged forth from her mind as fast as she could form them.

"*No,*" one of the elders said. "*There was a genuine need. You must give your knowledge to this young girl, your companion. We knew that from the start. We needed to know whether you would be willing to give it to others. It was necessary to find that out.*"

"So I passed your little test?" Laura replied in a bitter tone.

"*Yes, you passed,*" the mermaid said brightly. "*Your power has been restored. The elders have released their hold on you. Your act, the one that brought you to us, has been forgotten from our community of memory.*"

Laura glanced around the room, at the serious faces on the elders and the almost childlike smile of radiance on Tara's face. *Strange,* she thought. *I never even suspected.*

"*Now,*" one of the elders said, "*it is time for more important matters.*"

"*And just what might those be?*" Laura asked suspiciously.

"*You have agreed to help restore and develop this young girl's mind,*" the elder stated. "*Now we must see how willing you are to restore the land she comes from.*"

Laura frowned. "What does that mean?"

"*It means,*" the elder clarified, "*that it is time the races returned to the land, for we fear the magicians have gone beyond the law of this world, to a lawless place where we cannot reach them. To a place where only you may confront them.*"

19

***

THE MESSENGER GOD

Maya did not have an easy time of it. Not that she'd expected one. But, still, she was their queen and that should have afforded her some dignity.

"Go back to the land? Are you mad?" roared one roly-poly fellow, to whom the idea of work was not only foreign, it was downright repulsive.

"That's right!" Mays shouted. "I said it's time we returned. We've rotted up here in our self-imposed prison long enough."

"But…but this is our *kingdom*," sputtered another, a bland sort who followed orders well enough as long as they didn't keep him from his afternoon nap.

"I'm sorry to say this, Your Highness, but we can't just go traipsing off for no good reason," the ever-reasonable Rand said.

"I've told you already," the queen said with a heavy sigh, "there is a good reason."

"Really, dear." The king frowned. "Return to the land where we're always underfoot, forever dodging those foul, disgusting humans who masquerade as one of the noble races?"

"That's precisely what I mean," Maya continued patiently. The trick to ruling wisely and well was patience. And she needed as much as she could muster with this crowd.

The fairies, as many as Maya could summon away from their play and frolicking, had gathered at the base of what was a rather large mountain at the moment. Soon she would be standing at the corner of a large valley, with the throng of fairies rimmed all around her.

But for now, she stood addressing her subjects from the top of the mountain, along with Dent and his self-appointed advisor, Rand. Already, the gathering had begun to drift. Some at the fringes had already darted off, started to doze, or take up their favorite pastime, dodge.

The latter was a big favorite among the fairies. Dodge was simple. Two fairies would dart through the air at each other, challenging the other to swerve away at the last moment. The net result, more often than not, was a mid-air collision, a sore noggin, and a bent wing or two.

Realizing she was losing her audience, Maya grew desperate. "What would it take to convince you of the gravity of this request, Dent?" she asked her husband.

"Well, now," the king mused, "it would take something extraordinary."

"Yes, something extra special," Rand chipped in.

"Novel and unique," Dent said, with a slight glance of irritation at his advisor.

"So what would qualify as novel and unique?" Maya asked, knowing full well that her husband was stalling for time. He was always stalling for time, especially when she'd asked him to do something like clean up the fairy dust that gathered in the corners of their humble abode or keep the royal children amused.

"Novel and unique, novel and unique," the king repeated, the distant look in his eyes a sure sign that he'd rather be anywhere at this moment than the object of his wife's level gaze. "That would have to be—"

"A covenant!" Rand burst out. "That's what it would have to be. No question about it."

"Of course, a covenant." The king snapped his fingers with delight.

"What sort of covenant?" Maya asked cautiously.

"Yes, what sort would that be?" The king cocked one eyebrow.

"Why, a very simple one," Rand said proudly. "Before we'd risk our necks in the land again, we'd have to know that the other races meant to return as well."

"Of course, of course." The king nodded sagely.

"I mean, after all," Rand continued, "we can't just drop our important work here to go off half-cocked if the other races aren't willing to as well."

The king puffed out his chest. "That's right. If the situation is as grave as you say, then the other races will need to play a part. It can't always be the fairies to come to the rescue, now can it?"

Maya closed her eyes. "Of course not," she murmured.

"So what we need is a covenant," Rand said. "We need a guarantee, a firm indication of support from the other races."

"And who, do you suppose, is going to bring about such a covenant?" the queen asked.

"Why, the two humans." The king pointed to Lucas and Jon off in the distance. Since the verdict, Lucas had passed the time with Peg. Jon had merely sulked.

"Yes, let them do it," grumbled a fairy who was too close to the king and queen to drift away unnoticed.

"That's right, let them take the responsibility," said another, who even now was hovering in the air, eager to take wing toward a rather large game of dodge.

A glance assured Maya that the gathering would dissipate to almost nothing within a matter of moments. The fairies, nearly all of them anyway, were never noted for their attention spans. So she made her decision. And hang the consequences.

"All right," she announced with a loud voice so all could hear. "You will have your covenant. Do you hear me? You will have it, for I will accompany the two humans, as will Peg."

"No, I forbid it!" The king stomped his foot. "It's unthinkable. The fairies would be lost without the able leadership of their queen."

"Oh, that's just silly," Maya said. "I never do anything worthwhile. Mostly I issue edicts that are always ignored."

"Not true," the king replied haughtily. "Your word is respected."

"As long as I don't ask them to do anything." The queen laughed. "Now I'm going, and that's final. I won't hear another word about it."

The king cast a wary glance at Rand. It was obvious what both had on their minds.

"Oh, don't worry," Maya continued. "I wouldn't dream of asking either of you to come along. Besides, you'd just get in the way."

The king gave his wife his sternest gaze. "I resent that. I insist that I come along."

"We could be gone for weeks," Maya said reasonably. "What will the kingdom do without its king?"

"That's a good question, sire," Rand acknowledged.

"Yes, I suppose it wouldn't do for both the king and queen to abdicate the throne, even for a little while," the king said thoughtfully.

"Of course not," Maya reasoned. "The people must have their king."

"And the advisor must remain by his side, vigilant next to the seat of power," Rand said.

"Without question," Maya agreed. "So it's settled? I'll return with the covenant, signed by the rulers of the other kingdoms, and you'll agree to return to the land?"

"Certainly," Dent said. "I'm a man of my word, a man of principle and honor, one who lives by the highest standards…"

But Maya had already turned away to call for Peg and the two humans. The gathering of fairies had almost entirely broken up, most of them taking part in a colossal game of dodge. Already the ground was littered with dozens of fairies nursing injured limbs and wings.

There wasn't much she needed to take with her, so they were off toward the land within minutes, the two humans perched comfortably on Peg's broad back while she rode near one of his ears where she could carry on a private conversation.

Lucas took one last, long look at the fairy kingdom as they left it behind, slipping over the edge of a cloud and heading back toward the land. He was filled with a wistful sense of sadness, knowing he would probably never see it again.

Jon, though, was glad to leave the cursed kingdom. He'd had as much of the frolicking fairies as he could stomach. He was well rid of the little bursts of mayhem.

"Where are we going, exactly?" Lucas finally asked Maya as they neared the second level of clouds.

"I don't know yet." Maya was forced to shout to be heard as they winged their way back to earth.

"Come on," Jon said, unable to shake the lethargy and numbness of brain that still enshrouded his mind. "Do you mean you just zipped off without any idea of what you're doing?"

"I didn't say I had no idea what I'm doing!" Maya snapped. "But I haven't worked out all of the details yet."

Jon sneered. "Well, why don't you let us in on your little secret?"

"I plan to reunite the land," the fairy queen said simply. "I'm going to ask the races to return to the land and live in harmony again."

"You are?" Lucas said.

"I am," Maya stated.

"Fat chance." Jon snorted.

Maya turned at Peg's ear to give Jon a baleful stare. It wasn't an easy task to accomplish, but she managed somehow. "Look, you." She jabbed an accusing finger Jon's direction. "I'm going to do this with or without your help. It would be nice, seeing as how I saved your obviously worthless life, if you chose the former."

"I won't choose either until I know what I'm getting into," Jon answered. "And until my head stops buzzing."

"Buzzing?" Lucas said.

Jon said nothing right away. How do you explain a hangover or withdrawal to someone who's never overloaded his body with spirits? Or the awful feeling of depression, loneliness, anxiety, and general crankiness that always settled around him like a gloomy cloud when he hadn't gotten high? He couldn't.

"I feel lousy," he said simply.

"Sorry to hear that," Maya snipped, "but we don't have time for sympathy. We have a colossal task ahead of us and, perhaps, not much time to finish it."

But before Lucas or Jon could ask her why she felt that way, Peg plunged into the clouds. When they emerged again, it seemed dark and gloomy compared to the ever-present brightness of the fairy kingdom.

The first thing any of them saw, of course, was the castle at the center of the magic city. They stared in awe at its magnificence as they descended. Even Jon shed some of his gloom as he viewed the city for the first time.

Before they neared the ground, though, Lucas's sharp eyes caught sight of something moving rapidly through the air toward the top of the castle. It was too far away to see clearly, but Lucas swore it was a huge, black bird.

"Did any of you see that?" he asked excitedly.

"See what?" Maya asked.

"The black bird, up near the top of the castle," Lucas said, almost bursting.

Jon shook his head. "Nope. Didn't see it. Are you sure you saw something?"

"It was there, I tell you. It circled once and then disappeared through a window."

Maya and Jon glanced at each other. They hadn't seen it but, of course, that didn't necessarily mean it hadn't happened.

"Was it a crow?" Peg asked without missing a steady beat of its wings.

"It could have been," Lucas said. "Yes, probably. Most likely."

"Apollo, then," Peg said simply and continued his flight.

Jon snapped out of his lethargy. Mythology said that Apollo was responsible for the blackness of the crows. Once they'd been white, and the Greeks considered the crows as his. "Apollo's here?" he asked Peg.

"Do you see him before you?" Peg responded.

"No, not like right here, with us," Jon said irritably. "In this world."

"Yes, of course," Peg replied with unmistakable sarcasm. "But you, of all people, should have known that."

Maya decided to change the subject. "Anybody have any bright ideas? What we should do first, I mean?"

"Why don't you try telling us, exactly, what it is you hope to accomplish?" Jon asked, hardly enthusiastic about the prospect of gallivanting all across the land on some glorious quest when his head still felt like someone had stuffed it chock full of cotton candy. Sticky, gooey cotton candy at that.

"Reunite the land. Bring the races back," she said impatiently. "What do you think I meant?"

"But how do you propose to do that?" Jon interjected. "Visit each? Send out invitations? Throw a big party and hope they show up?"

"Why, visit them, of course." Maya's words were heated.

Jon groaned. "You're serious, aren't you? You really intend to visit each one?"

"Well, what choice do I have…," Maya began.

"If I may, Your Highness," said the horse. "I have a suggestion."

"Certainly, Peg," the fairy queen acknowledged. "What is it?"

"Well, seeing as how we have a cleric—sort of—in our midst," Peg said as he settled gracefully into a long glide down, "it seems only reasonable to summon someone who could give us some news of the other races."

"Why, that's an excellent suggestion, Peg!" Maya said gleefully. "It could save us quite a bit of time."

"What's this about a cleric?" Jon asked, a funny feeling in the pit of his stomach.

"That's the dumbest thing I've heard you say yet," Maya said with a curious look in Jon's direction. "Almost as dumb as your question about Apollo."

"And why's that?" Jon asked, miffed.

"Because you're the cleric, of course," Peg stated matter-of-factly.

"I am not," Jon said, indignant. "I have at least another year of school left before I can enter the priesthood."

"You're a cleric already," Maya said. "There's no escaping that fact. You could not have summoned Peg from my kingdom otherwise."

Jon sighed. This world was mad. Or he was. He wasn't sure yet which one was true, but he'd have to sort it out. "So if I'm a cleric, as you say, how can I help?"

"We need to speak with Mercury," Maya said simply.

"You know," Peg noted fondly, "it's been ages since I've seen him. I wonder what he's been up to."

"Causing mischief, no doubt," Maya said.

"Hold on," Jon interrupted. "Do you mean the messenger god?"

"Of course," Maya said. "Who else? There isn't another I can think of who would know more about the tidings of the land."

"So come on." Peg turned to look Jon directly in the eye. "Give him a call."

"And how do I do that?" Jon protested.

Peg gracefully settled to the ground in the middle of a grassy knoll on the side of the mountain. He stomped his front right foot. "The same way you called me, only with a different incantation, of course, you nitwit."

Jon's mind reeled as the horse's words sank in. *Incantations? What is the creature talking about?* "Well, I'll be," Jon suddenly said aloud in wonder, his shoulders sagging with relief as the memory of that room, with those strange kids, and Eric's book flooded in. All those spells and words were real, then.

"Would you do something?" Maya prodded.

"Of course, of course." Jon's thoughts raced furiously now that he had the game figured out. Or, at least, the rules. He had no clear idea yet what the object of the game was. Now what was the word, the one that summoned the messenger god…?

"*Smeit*," Jon said at last, the word emerging from the muddled mist as his memories always did. He had a strange mind. He didn't have a photographic memory; it was more like an associative memory. That's the way one professor had characterized it. Jon remembered things by linking one idea with another until he'd recalled what he needed.

Several moments later, the wind gusted viciously, nearly knocking Jon and Lucas over. Maya had to grab hold of Peg's mane to keep from being blown away.

"He always was one for a big entrance," Peg grumbled.

The messenger god came toward them almost at the speed of thought, seemingly running effortlessly through the air, his winged sandals kicking up great clouds of dust as he neared the earth.

Blinking furiously, Jon stood in absolute awe as the god came to a long, graceful halt, the tiny wings on his low-crowned hat working to slow his descent. He was every bit as magnificent as Jon had always imagined.

As he approached, Jon couldn't help himself. *A god! Just like the myths, and he's right here, in front of me.*

Somewhere in the recesses of Jon's muddled mind, he remembered the old myths, many of which had made their way into modern-day religious beliefs. The gods had never been known to help the human race of their own free will. They spent virtually all of their time in subtle intrigue designed either to trip up one of their own kind or exact revenge on someone for some perceived wrong.

They were never ones to do anything out of good will, or for the sheer joy of something. There was always self-interest involved. Had Jon been thinking a little more clearly, he might have wondered just how he was able to command a god such as Mercury. But those thoughts were quickly replaced by a less noble, but certainly understandable, human reaction—profound awe.

"Why, Peg," the messenger roared with a hearty laugh, "you old plow horse. How goes it?"

The horse cast a dour look at the winged messenger. "Fine as always, oh witless courier to the fickle gods. Let me guess. You and the rest are up to no good—meddling in human affairs at every turn, constantly harassing those less privileged, causing endless intrigue..."

"Now, now." Mercury chuckled. "We'll have none of that. You know I am called the shrewdest and most cunning."

"Certainly not by me," the horse said. "I know you for the thief you are."

"Jealousy doesn't become you," the messenger quipped with a twinkle in his eye.

"Neither does boasting or unfounded pride, but that never stopped you," Peg tossed back.

Mercury, the wings on his helmet still fluttering, gave the horse a good, solid whack on his backside. "That's what I like about you, my friend." He laughed. "You're not one to mince words."

"Likewise," the horse answered with a polite bow of his regal head.

"Now, who has summoned me?" the messenger asked, switching almost instantaneously from his lighthearted banter to a grave demeanor. "I was in the midst of something quite serious."

"It was me," Jon said nervously. "I'm the one. I did it."

Maya interrupted, counseling Jon. "Don't take him so seriously, man. Just state your business, and ask him for news."

"Why, if it isn't the fairy queen herself!" the messenger said with obvious delight. "I didn't see you hiding behind Peg's ear."

"I wasn't hiding." Maya drew herself up to her full three inches.

"As you wish, Maya." The messenger laughed again. "So tell me what this urgent business is."

"We must have news of the land, what has happened in our absence, what the other races are up to, if there is any news of where the magicians have vanished to…"

"Maya, Maya," the messenger said patiently, "surely you don't think I keep track of every coming and going across the land. I can only be in one place at a time, and I have very little interest in the affairs of men, anyway."

"I know that!" Maya thrust her tiny hands defiantly on her hips. "But we must have news and, unless I've missed the mark entirely, you've always kept one eye open even as the other roves mischievously in other directions."

"'Tis true," the messenger agreed wistfully. "I can't help myself. I'm naturally curious, I guess."

"Who isn't above using the knowledge he picks up to his advantage," Peg said scornfully.

"Well, there is that as well," Mercury added with a rueful smile.

"Please," Maya pressed, "do you have some news for us or not?"

"As luck would have it, I do," Mercury said with a wave of his hand. "The races are well, safely tucked away from the magicians."

"As it was when I last visited the land?" Maya asked.

"Precisely, though nearly all have grown impatient with their exile. The giants, especially, have grown weary of their solitude. The dwarves and the elves, as always, would prefer to remain at the outskirts of civilization for all eternity before they would deign to bend a knee to men."

"Of course," Maya said thoughtfully. "The stiff necks. They were always long on courage and boldness but short on common sense and the ability to compromise."

"The centaurs have all but exhausted their storehouse of knowledge. They now travel great distances to gaze on new wonders, if there are, in fact, such wonders."

"And the people of the sea?"

"The last I spoke with Neptune, they were flourishing as always. It's never mattered much to them what the other races did with themselves. Their only concern has always been the mischief of man."

"And what of the magicians?"

Mercury grew silent. "I think that is best answered by others. I have no news of them. But I will tell you this. They have withdrawn from the land and may have vanished entirely. I have not seen one in ages."

"That's not possible!" The fairy queen gasped.

"It is possible. They have hidden themselves. Either that, or they have gone to a place that even the gods cannot go."

"Vanished? Perhaps they've died?" Maya queried.

"No," the messenger said firmly. "You know as well as I that the gods would be aware of such a passing. It has not happened."

"But where have they gone?" Jon blurted out.

"No one seems to know," Mercury said. "In my travels far and wide, I've not heard a word. Not a whisper or a misplaced thought to give me an idea."

"How strange," Peg mumbled. "How very, very strange."

Maya shook her head sadly. "It is worse than I feared. Perhaps we have waited far too long to return."

Mercury turned his gaze to Jon. It was a terrible gaze, one Jon could barely withstand. "There is one other thing, however," the messenger said deliberately. "For the first time in perhaps 2,000 years, there is a new magician in the land."

"A new magician?" Maya asked, incredulous.

"Yes, and she has met with the people of the sea," Mercury said.

"But I thought you said the magicians have vanished?" Peg cocked one eyebrow suspiciously.

"They have," Mercury said solemnly. "She isn't from this world. She's been summoned, or sent, here to this world by others."

"What others?" Peg asked.

"How should I know?" Mercury answered. "I am a messenger, after all."

"But where did she come from? Do you at least know that?" Maya asked.

"Most likely the same place *he* came from." Mercury nodded in Jon's direction.

"Why, of course!" Maya said. "That would make perfect sense."

"Who sent you here?" Mercury asked Jon sternly.

Flustered, Jon answered, "I-I don't have any idea, really. I was visiting someone and it just happened. One minute I was there, the next I was here."

"And how is it you've come to master the clerical spells as only a few throughout the history of the land have? Answer that, priest." The wings on Mercury's helmet rotated faster, kicking up clouds of dust again.

Jon was afraid now. There was no mistake about that. The last thing in the world he wanted was an angry god accusing him of who-knows-what. "I'm almost a priest in my own land," Jon explained quickly. "I've studied religion for years. I've read of every god and great religious thinker in history, almost."

"I see. And that's where you gained your mastery of the clerical spells?"

"No, those came from a spell book someone handed me," Jon clarified. "I thought it was just a harmless game. A silly one."

"Curious indeed," Peg grumbled.

"It is that," the fairy queen said. "So you have no idea who sent you here?"

"None at all. It just happened, while I was reading this book of spells."

"There's something else you should know as well," the messenger continued.

"And what is that?" Maya sighed.

"A great warrior has appeared in the land," Mercury said. "And if I don't miss my guess, Hercules himself would have his hands full with this fighter, although, as yet, he is still green."

"And where is this warrior?" Peg asked.

"On his way to see the elves, though not by choice."

"I see." Maya tapped her forehead. "So three of the races have already been approached."

"So it would seem," Mercury acknowledged.

"What are the odds the magician will succeed in convincing the people of the sea to return to the land?" Maya asked.

"Almost a certainty. She has passed a crucial test they placed in her path and won their allegiance. Neptune says the people of the sea now trust her."

"So they'll return if she asks it of them?"

"Indubitably."

"Good," Maya announced. "And the elves? Will this warrior know to ask them to return?"

"Most likely," the messenger said with a sly smile, "now that he's accompanied by none other than Aphrodite herself."

"So Venus is up to her old tricks again?" Peg snorted.

"Of course." Mercury laughed.

"But will the elves return?" Maya asked nervously.

"It seems unlikely, but it's hard to know for certain," Mercury said. "Perhaps the fighter is resourceful enough. Who can say?"

Maya considered her alternatives. "All right. We need one last favor from you, Mercury."

"And what might that be, fairy queen?"

"Let the magician know somehow that we wish to meet with her, at the lodge, the ancient meeting hall where the races all met regularly in council," Maya said.

"Anything else?"

"Yes, let the fighter know that he must meet us there at the lodge as well, whether he's successful with the elves or not."

"And then?" Mercury asked.

"We must enlist the aid of the other races," Maya said. "They all must return to the land, regardless of past injuries and injustices. I only hope and pray it isn't already too late."

20

***

HIGH STAKES

The two elves were furious, to say the least.

"She has no right, you know," said one as they watched the trio from a safe distance.

"Of course she has the right," his companion retorted. "Might makes right, as they say."

"You know what I mean," the first sentinel said scornfully.

"So what do we do now?" the second voiced in a low whisper, even though the three sojourners were still a good distance away. "I was sure that either the silver lake or the dryad would take care of the problem."

"Yes, until *she* showed up, curse her. What I can't figure is why she's helping them. They *never* help anyone, save themselves. And, even then, others suffer because of their deceit and cunning."

"That's for certain. There's no history of them helping men. And when they do get involved, it's always with their own ends in mind. Always. So they must be up to something, else why is she here?"

"Only they know," replied the first. ""I suppose we have no choice but to make our way back quickly, to warn Fairhaven of their approach."

"You know, of course, that they'll hang us out to dry for our failure."

"So be it," the first said. "There's not much we can do now."

"Then we'd better hurry. The least we can do is give them plenty of warning."

The two elves hustled off.

***

Samson began to emerge from his doldrums as they walked. He had yet to say a word, but his eyes, at least, had lost their dullness. Life was working its way back into them bit by bit.

Mark couldn't see how or why Cytherea knew where she was going. Without hesitation, she'd set off through the woods in almost the opposite direction from which Mark and Samson had come. He didn't dare ask if she knew what she was doing. He had no choice but to trust her. After all, this seemed to be her home, not his. They walked in brisk silence for quite a while. Cytherea seemed preoccupied and Samson, of course, was still lost within himself, so Mark was forced to take a closer look at what they were passing through.

It was very, very different from his home. Not only were the trees much larger, and taller, but the fragrances of the plants overwhelmed his senses. The lushness of the undergrowth amazed him. The darkness of the green moss at the base of the trees astounded him. The teeming life that filled the woods seemed incredible. Mark had grown accustomed to the bareness of the Sanctuary, from which most of the wildlife had fled as the drought grew in intensity and the men charged with guarding it grew careless and thoughtless in their wanton slaughter of almost anything that moved.

At every opportunity, Mark searched desperately for a sign that elves had passed this way. He found not a clue, which only added to his confusion over the certainty with which Cytherea led them through the forest. At last, he could stand it no more.

"Do you know where we're going?" he asked her timidly.

"Of course," she said without breaking stride.

"But what if they don't wish to be found?" Mark persisted.

"They don't wish to be, but it doesn't matter. We'll be there shortly, whether they like it or not."

Samson suddenly came to life. "Would you mind telling me where we're going?" he said in a husky voice.

"Fairhaven," Cytherea said.

"And what's that?" he asked, his voice slightly stronger, more controlled.

"The elves' kingdom. That's what they call it."

"I see," Samson said and grew silent again.

But Mark could barely contain himself. "What if they run from us, as they did before? What if they decide to fill us full of arrows without warning? What if they see us for a moment and then force us to leave…?"

"What if the moon fell into the ocean?" Cytherea laughed. "You ask too many questions. Relax. Enjoy the forest, for you may not have the chance again. The elves will see us. Don't worry about that."

* * *

The elves were well prepared for their arrival. They'd posted a virtual army of archers at the outpost to Fairhaven. It was not their intention, in fact, to let them pass. And had their contempt for humans been slightly stronger, they would have plunged a quiver of arrows into their hearts without a question asked.

But they were, or so they fancied, the noblest of all the races. And they would not sully their reputation with the slaughter of innocents, even two who had so thoughtlessly spilled sylvan lifeblood on the soil.

"Halt!" one of the archers barked when they were within hailing distance of the elven kingdom. "Trespass no further."

"We are not trespassing," Cytherea called out. "We come in peace."

"Hardly," the archer called back. "You will not enter this place."

"But we come with an urgent message," Cytherea said.

"Take another step and we will drop your two friends where they stand," the archer warned coldly.

"And what of me?" Cytherea asked.

"You may go on your way as you please. We have no quarrel with you."

"Those little pipsqueaks," Samson grumbled. "If I get my hands on them…"

"Keep those thoughts to yourself," Cytherea said under her breath. "We have enough problems already."

Mark took a bold step forward. "Do you know who I am?" he called out loudly.

"No, and we don't care," the chief archer said.

"I will lead the Sanctuary one day," Mark announced, "the place we have preserved in your honor for centuries. Now do you know who I am?"

"No, it still means nothing to us," the archer answered.

"You know nothing of the Sanctuary?" Mark asked, incredulous.

"And why should we?" The elf was still concealed. As yet, none of the archers had shown themselves.

"Because it's the place you left for us to guard and protect, the Silver Forest."

A grumble of anger swept through the ranks of the archers. "What of the Silver Forest?" one called out.

"We have preserved it, shielded it from the magicians for centuries," Mark called.

"It needs no protection, for it is elven and, therefore, a thing of beauty and strength," the archer called back.

"Big deal," Samson muttered.

"We have sheltered that strength and that beauty," Mark said diplomatically.

"I told you, trespasser, what was once elven requires no protection. There is no need."

Samson leaned close to Cytherea. "Are all elves this arrogant?" he whispered.

"No," she whispered back with a faint smile. "Some are worse."

A flash of intuition came to Mark. "If the elves need no protection, then why have you shielded yourselves from us? Answer that."

There was a long silence as the elves obviously conferred. "You are nothing to us," the chief archer finally called out. "It is the witch we don't want in our haven."

"The witch?" Samson murmured.

"They mean me," Cytherea said quietly. "They don't want me coming near any of their menfolk."

"But I don't understand," Samson said to her.

"It's a long story," she replied with that smile of hers before turning to Mark. "Tell them the two of you will enter. Without me."

"But..."

"Do it," she emphasized to Samson and Mark. "Only, when you have met with their leader, demand one thing for me, as reward for delivering you from the dryad."

"And what is that?" Samson asked.

"The elves must return to the land. You simply will not take no for an answer."

"We won't?" Samson asked.

"Whatever you must do, then do it," she stated. "That is my request."

"Done," Samson said simply.

"We're coming without her!" Mark called out.

"Just the two of you? The witch stays behind?" the chief archer answered.

"You heard me," Mark said, barely able to mask his irritation and anger. These were anything but the noble, valiant creatures he had always envisioned. Far from it. Mark only hoped the others weren't as petty as these.

"Walk toward us slowly," the elf said. "We want no sudden moves."

"You'd think we were common criminals or something," Samson hissed as they bade farewell to Cytherea.

Mark shrugged. "To them, we are, I suppose."

When they were close enough, a dozen pair of hands grasped the two of them by their lapels and yanked them roughly forward. "Easy does it, friends," Samson growled. He'd about had it with rude welcoming parties.

"There's nothing easy about any of this," one of the elves answered.

Mark finally had his first, good look at them. They weren't as short as he'd first thought as he gazed at them before, upside down. But they weren't all that big either. Four, perhaps four and a half feet tall, they were dwarfed by Samson.

"March," said another elf, obviously the one who'd done most of the negotiating, although it was hard to tell because they all looked like they'd been cut from the same mold: blond hair, bluish eyes that narrowed sharply, pert noses, pointed chins, dark clothes that blended into the natural environment.

They marched in silence, which suited Samson and Mark just fine. It gave Samson time to clear the last of the cobwebs from his head, and there had been more than a few of those, while Mark closely studied Fairhaven.

It was very similar to the Sanctuary, with one vast difference. The trees were much more a part of the community, blending in perfectly with the homes and structures interwoven in the branches. The community seemed to pulsate with the very life of the trees, giving it a sense of tranquility, if nothing else.

As they passed under the limbs of the trees, Mark quickly saw another difference. This community wasn't segregated as theirs was. Females weren't second-class citizens. The obvious proof was that a good third of the vanguard of archers escorting them were female, a fact easy to overlook because their physical features differed only slightly from the males.

"Keep it moving." One of the elves prodded Mark in the small of his back with a heavy stick. "We don't have all day."

Mark kept silent, not wishing to anger these people. But any delusions he still harbored about the elves were vanishing quickly.

As they neared the center of Fairhaven, Samson had a strange sense of déjà vu. Hadn't all of this happened once before? Hadn't he been led by the nose to the center of just such a camp before? Well, he wasn't going to stand for much more of this. Patience had never been one of his virtues. All that held him in check even now was his promise to Cytherea.

A great contingent of the elves had gathered at the base of an absolutely huge oak tree, similar again to the Center Tree that Samson had dispatched with relative ease. They stirred nervously as the prisoners drew close.

One moved forward when they arrived, his eyes flashing, his feet rooted squarely in the earth as if he expected a gale to sweep through, attack, pick him up, and carry him off. He was much like the others, the same slight build and tiny, chiseled features. Yet this one carried himself even more proudly than the others, if that was possible. He exuded an air of confidence Mark had seen in no other creature before, save his unlikely traveling companion, perhaps.

"Why have you come here?" asked this elf, his head cocked slightly as if listening for a distant sound. He faced Samson and completely ignored Mark for the moment.

"To bring you back to the land," Samson said with no hesitation.

Mark groaned to himself as the elves immediately murmurd with anger at his brash statement. This situation called for tact, diplomacy, careful words. Not the heavy-handed club and hammer approach Samson had quickly adopted.

"Then the rumors are true?" the elf asked Samson. "The others are returning to the land?"

"What others?" Samson said blithely.

"The other races, you fool," the elf stated angrily. "We have reports, scant ones, that at least two races, perhaps, are considering whether to return to the land."

"I wouldn't know about that," Samson admitted.

"You wouldn't, eh? I think you're lying. I think you're in league with this new magician they say has suddenly appeared in the land."

"And don't forget about that powerful cleric," another elf called out.

"And the cleric as well," the regal elf echoed. "You're in league with them, aren't you?"

"I have absolutely no idea what you're talking about." Samson still struggled to check his temper.

"Let me tell you something!" the elf fairly shouted in his face. "We're not going. I don't care what peril is facing the land. We're not going, and that's final."

Unprepared for such hostility, Samson turned to Mark for help. It was as if the elves, deep down, were mortally afraid of something.

But Mark had no answers. This was hardly what he'd expected from the most legendary of all the races. *Yet it's worth a try,* Mark reasoned. "Why not?" he asked boldly, stepping forward.

"I'll not deign to answer that," the elf retorted. "And who are you, anyway?"

"My name is Mark. I will someday serve as the guardian of the Silver Forest."

"So? Am I supposed to be impressed?"

"Well, who are you?" Mark snapped.

"Regis, king of the elves," he snapped right back. "I am a direct descendant of the First Ruler, Aubrey."

"What is it with you people?" Samson sneered. "Don't you ever give anyone else besides direct descendants a chance to run the show?"

When Regis stared at him like he was daft, Mark seized the advantage Samson had unwittingly offered him. "As you can see," the boy told Regis, "my friend here has no manners."

"Obviously an uncouth barbarian," Regis said.

"Not quite that. But he has no sense of history. None at all, which explains why he treads so heavily."

"And why is that?" Regis asked dourly, his guard still up.

"He isn't from this world, of course," Mark said simply.

"Not from this world?"

"No. And I suspect the magician and the cleric you mentioned are, like him, from another land. Which, as I'm sure you quickly grasp, means something quite extraordinary is happening. In Aubrey's day, there were sojourns from other worlds. But it has been hundreds, perhaps thousands, of years since that has happened."

"It matters little, if at all, to the elves," Regis interrupted. "I don't give a whit if the land curls up and dies. It will not reach Fairhaven. It's not our concern."

"But it will reach even here!" Mark protested. "If the land dies, it will eventually affect your kingdom here."

"Eventually can be a very long time," Regis said smugly.

"You're a coward," Samson hissed quietly, so only the elf king could hear him.

Regis convulsed with anger. "Did I hear you right?" he almost whispered.

Samson squared his shoulders. "You did. You're terrified of returning to the land, aren't you? Admit it."

"I'll admit nothing of the sort!" Regis snarled. "It's an outrageous statement."

"Come on," Samson prodded softly. "There's nothing to be ashamed of. You're hiding out here, away from the magicians, aren't you? Cowering and trembling with fear out here, where no one can ever possibly reach you."

"Enough!" Regis roared. "Those are vile and treasonous words. They will be answered."

"How?" A leering half-smile played at the corners of Samson's mouth.

"I challenge you to a duel."

"Just the two of us?"

"Certainly," Regis said.

"What are the rules?"

Regis thought for only a moment. "Three contests. One of your choosing, one of mine, and a third upon which both of us must agree."

"Done." Samson nodded. "And the stakes?"

"Your life if you lose," Regis said without blinking an eye.

Samson, likewise, never even hesitated. "As you wish. And your pledge to return your people to the land if you lose," he said firmly.

Regis was obviously a little surprised at the terms Samson offered. "Not my life?"

"No, why would I want something as worthless as that?" Samson said with a light laugh. "So? Do you agree?"

The elf king held his anger in check and simply said, through clenched teeth, "Of course. It is done."

"And when will we decide on the contests?"

"Tomorrow. At first light. That will give you at least one night to mull your foolish decision and make your peace with the gods of your world," Regis said tightly.

Samson said nothing in return, turning instead to the elves surrounding him who still held him captive. Almost as one, each dropped their hands from his side. "I'll need lodging for the night." Samson pivoted back to the elf king. "And a meal."

Regis nodded curtly. "You'll have it."

Mark glanced at Samson and wondered for the first time who it was, exactly, he was looking at. A madman, perhaps...or a hero? He couldn't tell which of those it might be.

21

***

NEW MAGICIANS

The elders were surprised and pleased. It had been a very long time since Amphitrite or any member of her family had blessed them with their grace and presence. Amphitrite had come quietly, with no warning or fanfare. Laura had noticed but chose to wait. There would be time for answers later.

Unlike the other races, the people of the sea feared only the magicians. Amphitrite was welcome, even if she chose to close her mind to them. The people of the sea were the guardians, and they welcomed anyone who provided protection and shelter to those within their domain. Amphitrite had always shown an affinity toward those within their domain.

"*Why have you come?*" the elders asked Amphitrite.

"To observe," she had responded.

"*Observe?*" they had asked her.

Amphitrite, keeping her distance, had simply nodded in Laura's direction. Because the elders were unable to pierce the veil surrounding Amphitrite's mind, they could not discern the nature of her fear or the truth behind her statements. But it was clear that she feared Laura. Which surprised them. For, in all the time they had known the lovely wife of Poseidon, fear had never been an aspect of her countenance.

"I wish to see, for myself," Amphitrite answered.

"*See what?*" the elders had asked her politely.

"The beginning, again."

"*Beginning? Of what?*" they'd asked.

But Amphitrite did not respond. So the elders had turned their attention, reluctantly, back to Laura.

In the end, Laura simply could not refuse, even though such a thing had never before occurred in the land. She decided to let Tara enter her mind, as well, along with Kathryn. It mattered not at all to Laura that Kathryn was a human while Tara was a mermaid. Laura allowed both to share and revel in the power and knowledge she'd always treasured above all else in her former world. There was no refusing it

161

now. This was a far different world, a simpler one at times but a vastly more complex one at others.

It was a strange experience for Laura, learning how to recede to the center of her own mind in order to allow others to sift at will through her memories. She wondered what they might find, what she herself could no longer remember.

And it seemed like such a short time. No sooner had she journeyed to that quietest of all possible places than they summoned her to return. Seemingly within the blink of an eye.

"*It is time, now, to decide what we must do,*" one of the elders said to Laura after her mind had reacquainted itself with the things of the world outside her own mind.

Laura looked at Amphitrite. "Who are you?" Laura asked guardedly.

Amphitrite came no closer but answered, "You know who I am, I think. The others have told you."

"Yes," Laura answered with a thin smile, "they have. But I would still like to hear it from you, especially because you have closed your mind to me and the others here."

Amphitrite smiled. "You learn very quickly. You've already taken on the mantle of leadership, just as I was told."

"You're avoiding my question."

Amphitrite paused. "Your question is not about me, or the nature of the gods," she spoke finally. "Your question is the fundamental essence of this world, the ultimate root of knowledge."

"Yes, that is certainly one question. A very large one, I might add."

"For you, it may be the only question that matters," Amphitrite murmured.

"Perhaps."

"May I make a suggestion?"

"Certainly. We'll decide—Tara, Kathryn, myself, the others—whether to take it or not," Laura answered politely.

Poseidon's wife looked at Laura and then at the elders. "I think you have no choice but to return to the land. The other races are beginning to ponder that question as well, even as we deliberate here."

There was a collective gasp among the elders. Return to the land? Their exile had been so long, the question seemed almost unthinkable.

"*Must we?*" said one elder. "*Why?*"

"Because the land is in peril. Forces are moving. And because the other races are beginning to return."

"The races are returning?" Laura asked sharply.

"Yes, and that is not all," Amphitrite said. "There are others in the land as well."

"Others?"

"Yes, a priest, of sorts, with quite a bit of power and a fighter of the highest magnitude. From all reports, they appear to hail from your own world, Laura."

"My world?" Laura said, startled.

"Yes, and what's more, the priest has returned to the land with the queen of the fairies. And, with any luck, the fighter may convince the elves to return to the land as well, although they can be a stubborn lot."

"*Even at the best of times,*" another elder chimed in.

"*Which leaves the other three races,*" the first elder said.

"Can I make another suggestion?" Amphitrite asked politely.

"Yes, you may," Laura answered. "What is it?"

"That you meet the others—the priest and the fighter I spoke of—at the ancient meeting hall where the races once held council regularly."

"When?"

"As soon as you are able, I would think," Amphitrite said simply.

Laura looked around at the elders. It would be physically impossible for any of them to return to the land. "I can go, and Kathryn, of course. But how would…?"

"You could send a representative," offered Amphitrite.

"*I'll go,*" Tara said quickly.

The elders looked first at each other, then at Laura, and finally at Tara and Kathryn. "*We, the people of the sea, have never walked on the land,*" said the first elder. "*We could only accompany you to the shallow waters, where our presence could be felt.*"

Laura saw it immediately. "I will help Tara. I can allow Tara to walk the land, with me."

"*You would do that?*" the first elder asked, surprised.

"Yes, of course. I have already shared my knowledge with her."

"*But that would make her…like you,*" the first elder said. "*No magician has ever done such a thing.*"

"Then I am like no other magician," Laura replied pleasantly.

"Then it is done," Amphitrite said firmly. "Tara, representing the people of the sea, will join the magician in her quest."

Laura turned to the young mermaid. "Will you come back with me, Tara? Will you use one of the spells you discovered in my mind and forsake your tail for legs for a while?"

It took a little bit for the mermaid to focus her eyes. "*Yes,*" she finally said dreamily. "*If you ask it of me, Laura, I will do it.*"

"Okay. It's settled, then. Tara, Kathryn, Nathaniel, and I will leave for the meeting hall, or whatever you called it. But I do have one last question. I can see that the races must return to the land. But why have you remained in exile for so long in the first place? What is it you fear?"

The elders again looked at each other before the first, the one who'd done most of the speaking thus far, answered. "*You must remember, child, that the magicians have always abused their enormous power. Oh, there have been a few good, decent ones. But they were quashed by the others. It is hard to assume power when no one is willing to teach you. The good ones were forced to learn on their own, and that simply isn't the best way to acquire the sort of power that magicians wield.*"

"I can understand that," Laura said, remembering her own experiences in college. She'd be lost without good teachers.

"*At any rate, they've always managed to find horrible ways to misuse their power.*"

"Like hunting you and changing your shape?"

"*Precisely,*" the elder stated, "*and that is almost mild compared to some of the horrific tales I could tell. The oldest legend of all is the abomination within the city…*"

"Abomination?"

"*Something we cannot understand. Something that changed the fundamental nature of things, for all time.*"

Laura wrinkled her brow. "I don't understand."

"*And we do not, either. You see, they haven't shown their faces in hundreds of years. No mischief, no terrible deeds, nothing at all. And that's what we fear, that their absence for such a long time means they're hatching something truly awful.*"

"Perhaps they're all dead?" Laura offered.

"Oh, no," Amphitrite said with confident assurance. "They are most certainly not dead."

"Then where are they?" Laura demanded.

"We do not know. Not even us."

"Very curious," Laura mused.

"*Return to the meeting hall with all haste, child,*" the elder urged Laura. "*And when the other races have agreed to return to the land, send word to us. We will help in any way we can when, or if, you decide to seek out the magicians.*"

Laura nodded. "I will. Now, I think it's time we were off."

"*Yes, by all means,*" the elder said. "*And may heaven guide your footsteps.*"

22

* * *

PLACES OF THE PAST

Jon hadn't really considered the land until they'd left Mercury and started to make their way to the hall. The land was breathtaking—the vast mountain ranges to the north, the plains to the west, the huge sea that lay to the south, and the abundant forest land to the east.

In the middle, with a little of each mixed in, lived the human race. And right in the middle of *that* lay the magicians' city.

The meeting hall was toward the eastern part of the land, at the fringes of the great forest and within a day's journey from the Silver Forest and other places where the human race had established itself. That's when it occurred to Jon. These were land contours he could see from Peg's back, but what of the rest of the land, beyond what he could see in any direction?

"Oh, it goes on forever and ever," Maya said.

"What do you mean forever?" Jon asked.

"Just what I said. The land extends forever in each direction."

"Do you mean to tell me that if you continued to go west, the plains would go on forever?"

"That's exactly what I'm telling you."

"Well, that's absurd. They must end."

"No. They don't," Maya said firmly, obviously quite sure of her conclusion.

"Maybe no one's ever journeyed far enough to really know with certainty what lies beyond," Jon said.

Maya sighed with exasperation. "Why don't you be the first, then? Just start walking. You'd die of starvation or worse out on the plains. You'd freeze to death in the north. You'd have no water to drink in the salty sea. And it would take you forever to work your way through the forest to the east."

"Then no one's ever been as far as they can go in any of those directions," Jon persisted.

"I suppose, but each of the races has gone far enough to know there isn't much point in going any further."

"How so?"

"The giants, the hardiest of the races, have gone to the point where their toes turn blue from the cold. The centaurs, by far the fleetest in the land, have discovered nothing but barren wasteland far to the west. The people of the sea say the waters grow murky and lifeless the further south you journey. And the elves, likewise, say the forest grows dark and lifeless far to the east."

Jon said nothing for a while, trying to sort out what, if anything, Maya's words meant. The four of them flew toward the east in silence, the sun fading slowly to a dull orange as it set before them.

There was something about this place. He had this vague feeling that he knew it. Or knew of it. Parts of it seemed so familiar to him, as if he'd heard of it, or read it, or perhaps discussed it with someone, somewhere. He knew most of the myths from around the world, from the Greek to the Norse. The Celts were a little tougher, because very little had been written down.

But Jon felt certain there were parts of this world, besides the gods themselves who seemed so intimately familiar, that he had some knowledge of.

Peg began his long descent, a slight downward tilt of his head giving the change of direction away. As yet, Jon couldn't see the hall, but obviously it must be nestled somewhere in the forest that seemed to stretch off in every direction now that they were drawing close to the earth again.

"We're almost there?" Lucas asked, unable to keep the excitement from his voice.

"Almost there," Peg called out over one shoulder.

"I've had dreams about this place," Lucas said timidly. "It's supposed to be a wonderful lodge, with a vast meeting hall and enough bedrooms to hold an army."

"Don't get your hopes up, kid," Maya told him. "Most likely the place has fallen on hard times."

"I don't care," Lucas determined. "This is a place I've wanted to visit for as long as I can remember." He knew the stories. All the great ones had been here to hold council and turn the land away from disasters—Oberon the fairy king, Aubrey the great elf chieftain, and Chiron the centaur, known for both his good nature and his wisdom.

But Maya was probably right. The place hadn't been used for centuries upon centuries. In fact, it might not even be standing. It might have crumbled with decay while the land continued on its merry way into oblivion, with no one there to mark its noble passing.

Lucas was the first to see the famous watchtower extending high above the forest from which a sentinel could always tell who was approaching the hall and at what speed. "There it is!" he shouted, almost knocking Maya from her perch at Peg's right ear.

Lucas was so preoccupied with his search for the watchtower that he never noticed the two black crows that lifted off from a nearby tree as they approached or the four men on horseback waiting at the edge of the forest, who likewise took off at a gallop away from the lodge as Peg made his approach.

"Easy, boy," Peg said calmly as he glided down slowly over a meadow out behind the hall. "I've known where this place was for quite some time."

But Lucas was paying no attention at all to the winged horse, so absorbed was he with his first sight of the legendary meeting hall. It was all he could do to keep his seat until they'd landed. As the horse's hooves strained to touch the green grass of the meadow, his wings slowly circling in reverse to halt their forward movement, Lucas tumbled to the ground, falling head over heels before righting himself and running toward the hall as fast as his legs could carry him.

"A little anxious, wouldn't you say?" Maya said with a wry smile.

"A little," Jon agreed.

"Not that I blame him," Maya added quickly. "I feel some twinges myself coming here. This place holds quite a few legends. They say that Oberon befriended Merlin here."

"Wait a minute," Jon said. "Merlin? The magician?" That familiarity was, again, causing the hairs on the back of Jon's neck to stand on edge.

"Why, yes, one of your most famous, I'd say, if the legends are even remotely close to the truth."

"But he's one of ours," Jon protested.

"One of your what?"

"Legends, of course. We have a few, you know, where I come from and he's one of them."

"Maybe this is another Merlin?"

"I doubt it," Jon said thoughtfully. "So Merlin was here, then. I wonder how many others from my own world have come here that I don't know about?"

"Peg could help you some there," Maya said while the three of them followed Lucas up a slight rise in the meadow toward the hall. "He's got the best memory of anyone I've ever met. And, of course, he was around back then when the legends were nothing more than everyday occurrences."

But Peg said nothing, however, as they walked. Jon was beginning to learn that about the winged horse. He generally spoke when he felt like it. And when he didn't, there wasn't much anyone could do about it. Not even Maya, for whom the horse held an obvious fondness. He kept his own counsel.

Lucas had disappeared into the huge hall, which Jon figured to be a good six or seven stories high. It looked eerily similar to the graphic he'd studied on the wall of the room in that house back in his own world.

But there was one big difference. The graphic in Eric's room had been of a regal, magnificent building. This structure was crumbling and rotting badly. Timbers sagged; doors and shuttered windows seemed ready to fall from their hinges. The whole place listed to one side. What it needed, desperately, was a score of carpenters with valiant hearts.

A whoop of joy shattered the silence, followed by Lucas's shout. "It's still here! After all these years!"

Jon quickened his pace. Without pausing even to think he might be risking his life by entering the badly decaying building, he ducked under a slightly askew archway and hurried down a musty hallway. Fighting to keep from gagging as he parted the cobwebs, he blinked furiously when great dust clouds rose. Emerging in a hall that seemed to stretch above him forever, he halted in wide-eyed wonder.

And in the very center of the hallway was the object of Lucas's shout of joy—a large, round oak table. Lucas continued to walk round and round the thing even as Jon stared at the scene.

"That's what all that ruckus was about?" he called to Lucas. "That dumb table?"

"It isn't dumb," Lucas almost whispered. "It's the Round Table. There are so many legends about this place, about this table. The greatest magicians, the greatest kings and queens…they've all been here, made their decisions here, held counsel here. This is the place. This is the very table."

"So big deal," Jon said irreverently. He never was much on ceremony, history, or relics of the past. "A table's a table."

Lucas ignored him, continuing to run his hands along the smooth edges of the perfectly round table, around which a good three or four dozen people could sit comfortably. As he did so, he raised more dust. The place was thick with it. The table was covered by a good quarter inch of the stuff.

Jon looked around the hall, holding his nose now to keep from sneezing or coughing. The lodge was in complete disrepair. Everywhere he looked in the rapidly fading light he could see the signs. It was obvious no one had been to this place in a very, very long time. Perhaps hundreds of years.

A number of chairs had been reduced to broken shards on the floor, possibly left over from a fight in the hall because it didn't appear to be the work of vandals. And it was amazing the sunlight even filtered through the windows at the top of the hallway, so faded and dirty were they.

The whole, dreary, gloomy, decaying atmosphere saddened Jon terribly. Never had he seen such neglect in what must have been, once upon a time, a place of great magnificence. Who would allow such a thing to happen? Why had no one kept the place from turning into such a nightmare? Where had the guardians and the keepers of the lodge gone?

"Ouch, what a ghastly place," Maya said as she arrived at the hall. "I had no idea it had been ignored for so long. But a good magician could restore the tone and color of the wood. Then it would be a simple matter of sweeping it clean. The dust is absolutely filthy."

"Why don't we sweep it ourselves?" Lucas called out from across the hall where he was still examining the table.

"You're mad," Jon replied. "It would take us a year."

"Well, we can at least get started, can't we?" Lucas was exuberant. "We'll finish as much as we can until the others arrive."

"Peg and I wouldn't be much help," Maya said quickly, averting her eyes from Jon's, "so we'll explore some of the upper rooms. See what we can find. Candles would be nice, don't you think, before it becomes too dark to see?"

"Good idea," Jon said with a sour look. "I think I'll join you."

"No, you won't." Lucas made his way across the floor. "You'll help me find something to sweep away this dust and pitch in."

Jon regarded Lucas with murder in his eyes. Oh, how he hated to clean. Someday he would be rich enough to let some sop maid come in and do all the dirty work, the stuff he really detested. But there was no escaping it now. Lucas had enough energy for three people in this place. Jon simply had no choice. He had to follow in the boy's wake or reveal himself as the lazy lout he truly was. And heaven forbid that anyone should ever discover his true nature.

They could hear the steady *clop-clop* of Peg's hoof beats as he and Maya ascended the stairs to the other rooms. Meanwhile, Jon's luck continued to hold true to form. Lucas found several well-crafted brooms almost immediately in a small closet against one wall.

With gusto, Lucas set in. Jon followed meekly behind. Within minutes, the two had raised great, billowing clouds as they swept the dust before them.

They stopped abruptly, though, when Peg suddenly called out from above them, his deep voice echoing strangely through the empty hall as he beckoned for the two boys to come upstairs quickly.

Jon didn't need to be asked twice. He dropped his broom as if it were on fire and raced upstairs with as much haste as he could muster. He followed Peg's voice until he'd discovered the horse and fairy queen in a room on the third floor of the hall.

"What is it?" Jon asked breathlessly when he'd reached the room.

Maya perched on Peg's shoulder, gazing at something on the far wall. "Can't say for sure, but it's a map of some sort. And it may give us a clue about where the magicians have vanished to."

Jon, with Lucas at his heels, strode briskly across the floor, only vaguely concerned that it might give way.

"I wonder what it's a map of?" Maya asked thoughtfully. "It's not of this world, that's certain."

The map was etched into the smooth, pale face of the wooden wall. It was carefully done. Someone had obviously taken a great deal of time to put the map together, to carve out the outlines.

Jon stared at the map numbly. In any other place, at any other time, he would not have given a map such as this even a second glance. He'd seen such maps a thousand times. But it was precisely because he was looking at such a map in this place, in this world, that he focused on it in a state of shock.

"It's a map of my own world," Jon said in a still, small voice. "That's exactly what it is."

23

***

HEROIC DEEDS

S amson had never slept better, not since the days of his childhood, before he knew the torment and anger of his birthright and his ancestry.

Perhaps, for the first time in his life, he sensed a chance to truly avenge some ancient wrong—the chance to best a king by birthright. It would be a victory for the downtrodden.

No, it wasn't that, for Samson knew, in his heart, that he was no longer part of the downtrodden class. Once, perhaps, long ago, before his family had fled to America. But even they had grown fat and successful in their new lives; almost all trace of the past horrors was now erased from their lives.

The reason for his inward peace may have been far simpler. Samson loved a good match. The more intense, the better. The higher the stakes, the greater the joy. And the stakes in this particular contest could not have been greater.

The evening meal had been sumptuous. Samson suspected Regis had been trying to slow him down and dull his senses with fine food. Well, it may have worked, for Samson gorged himself on the offering. He fell asleep, in fact, by a roaring fire near the center of the elven kingdom, a wine goblet still in hand.

Mark, though, took quite the opposite tack. He asked as many questions as he could think of and then watched carefully and listened closely as the elves responded—reluctantly, at first, but with more abandon as the evening wore on.

By the time the sun made its first appearance the next morning, the young boy had barely snatched an hour or two of sleep. He was so groggy and bleary-eyed, it was all he could do to rouse himself for breakfast.

But the effort had been worth it. He'd learned more in one night, he felt, than he'd learned in a lifetime. The elves were pompous, yes, and arrogant and conceited and more than a little absurd in their narrow view that nothing worthwhile seemed to exist beyond the boundaries of the elven kingdom. But they were, nevertheless, a truly remarkable race.

The stories they told of their ancestors—the legends of the great deeds, past glories, wondrous adventures, enchanting encounters! They were magnificent storytellers, most likely because they'd honed the art during their long years of self-imposed exile deep in the heart of the forest.

Yet what enthralled Mark the most was the ease with which the elves carried themselves physically. There was almost no apparent movement as they made their way through the forest, even when fetching another jug of wine from a hollowed-out tree or putting another log on the fire when it began to dwindle.

Mark knew he could never hope to match the grace with which they glided across the ground, the fluid way they seemed to melt from one point to the next. They were obviously inherited characteristics enhanced by years of practice and effortless play.

Yet what he hoped he could someday match was the nameless bond they seemed to have with the forest and everything that was a part of it. That bond seemed so obvious to Mark, he wondered if the elves even realized it existed.

He first noticed it as he watched them skirt bushes without touching them. Later, it became more distinct as he saw them gather dead branches beneath trees, the way they managed to pluck only the branches from the ground while leaving the living things of the forest intact. That explained the abundance of life that fairly exploded throughout the elven kingdom. There was a wholesomeness to the air that came only from the richness of the plant and animal life that so obviously coexisted in harmony here.

In the meantime, Mark barely thought of the contest in the morning. It didn't seem real, somehow, not in this place of such tranquility. Yet the place was also a mask. It hid something. Mark suspected it was, most likely, an insane fear of the power of the human magicians.

He was startled to see the vigor with which Samson strode to breakfast. He actually seemed to be *enjoying* himself, reveling in the challenge to his own existence that was about to take place. *How strange,* Mark thought, *that he could look forward to such a thing. But of course, Samson must not believe he can possibly lose this contest. Why else would he act as if he didn't have a care in the world?*

Mark had no way of knowing how wrong his assumptions were.

For his part, Samson had no idea what sort of challenge to expect from Regis, the elven king. As yet, he hadn't even decided on a contest, beyond the obvious fact that he must choose something that played to his great strength and wrestling ability. He had a thought for the final contest but would wait until the moment arrived to test it.

Which it did fairly quickly. Regis seemed overly impatient to have the thing begin. He seemed distraught. Most likely he hadn't slept much the night before. And it seemed to anger him when he spotted Samson in such good humor.

Samson chuckled to himself. Long, long ago he'd learned a very simple lesson: There is more than one way to expend your energy. You can waste precious, nervous energy worrying about something before it actually happens, or you can leave the future to itself and save your energy for that moment.

And Samson had learned the folly of worrying yourself silly over something he had no control over, namely the outcome of something that, as yet, had not happened. Which partially explained why he'd slept so well. Through sheer force of will, he'd learned the art of relaxing in the face of enormous pressure.

Regis obviously had not. And why should he, though? How many challenges such as this had he faced in his lifetime? None, most likely. It was an occurrence he could not possibly have prepared himself for, while Samson had learned to come by such challenges naturally.

Regis barely touched his breakfast. Mostly, he spent it staring sullenly at Samson, who again ate with gusto. It was at that moment the elven king realized the contest he must obviously choose. And it gave him some satisfaction to think of the agony it would cause Samson.

The elven king would make the giant of a man run a great distance. *If that doesn't sap his strength and empty his stomach, then nothing will,* Regis considered grimly. *Yes, that will do the trick. And perhaps luck will be on my side and he'll be forced to run the grueling race first, before his contest.*

As Samson watched the elven king assessing him, he realized, too, the contest he must choose. It wouldn't do to choose something that required a great deal of endurance or skill. A wrestling match might be a bad idea.

What if the king put up a good fight and took too much out of Samson? Unlikely, but still a possibility. No, it must be sheer, brute strength. And he had just the thing to humiliate the king—a log throwing contest. Simple but effective. The elf couldn't hope to match his strength.

* * *

"A race?" Samson grimaced, reacting predictably as hundreds of elves gathered around them in the open air at the center of the kingdom for the start of the contest. "That's what you want?"

"That's exactly what I want," the elf king said. "Your choice?"

"A throwing contest," Samson said immediately, a bemused grin barely noticeable. "With a log of my choice."

Regis looked at him bleakly. "That's settled, then. Now for the last contest?"

"To be fair," Samson answered, gazing intently at Regis, "it must be something that combines every skill—speed, strength, endurance, coordination and, of course, intelligence."

"And what contest would include those?" Regis asked suspiciously.

"You have deer in this forest?"

"Yes, of course," Regis said with a frown.

"The first to bring back a stag. That is what I propose," Samson said.

"Using any weapons at hand?" Regis asked, hardly believing his ears. Hunting was second nature to his people. They knew the deer's habits almost as well as they knew their own. And bringing down a stag with a bow was almost child's play.

"No," Samson said firmly. "Using no weapons at all."

"What!" Regis exploded.

"And the stag must be brought back, to this very spot, still alive."

"You're serious?" the elf said, incredulous.

"Completely."

The elf king pondered the proposal. It was, indeed, a fair one. It would require speed and coordination to catch the stag, endurance to track it, strength to manhandle it, and bring it back alive. And, of course, intelligence to know where to look and the best approach to take. It was this last skill that convinced the elf king to accept the challenge, for he knew the forest almost as well as any of his people.

Although it had been some time since he'd joined a hunt—the affairs of the state can be dreadfully tiresome—his skills were considerable and he seriously doubted he'd lost his touch. It would not be easy, but the advantage was still his.

"I accept," Regis said with a solemn nod. "It is a fair and reasonable proposal."

"Thank you," Samson said with equal gravity.

When the two parted to prepare for the contests, Mark hurried to Samson's side. "Are you mad?" he whispered fiercely. "You played right into his hands on that last one. Hunting is almost hereditary with these people."

"It won't be as easy as he imagines it," Samson said with an unconcerned shrug. "He only accepted the challenge because it was familiar to him. It's something he feels comfortable with."

"Then why…?"

"Because, in the end, it will be something vastly different than anything he's ever encountered before," Samson said. "It's one thing to stalk an animal with a weapon of death in your hand and to make the kill from afar. It's quite another thing entirely to corner a wild beast and bring it back alive. I simply don't believe he'll be able to, in the end."

Mark could almost understand that strange logic. But it didn't explain one thing. "And how will you find a stag yourself?"

"I have absolutely no idea," Samson admitted. "That's the one flaw in my plan."

* * *

The first two contests unfolded exactly as both had expected. The only difference, to the elf king's disgust, was that Samson put up only token resistance in the race, barely extending himself to finish it.

Regis was forced to wait for Samson at the finish line for quite some time before the irksome human finally strolled across leisurely, as if he'd been out on an afternoon stroll through the forest.

Boiling with rage, the elf king put every ounce of strength he could muster into the log-throwing contest—only to fall quite short of the mark Samson set for him. It was a valiant, but totally wasted, effort. Samson had tossed the thing almost twice as far as Regis.

So by the start of the fateful third contest, Regis was in such a funk he could barely see straight. Which was precisely where Samson wanted him, of course. It might be some time before the elf king could gather his wits and intelligently figure a way to win the contest.

As the two set off into the forest, the elven people cheering madly for their king, Regis almost immediately spotted the trail of a stag and set off in hot pursuit.

It took him less than half an hour to close in. He could already taste the sweet victory as he cautiously took each step without a sound, an art he'd learned as a child. He spotted the mottled brown of the stag through the bushes. He'd been careful to stay downwind of the animal, so it hadn't spotted him. Nor was it likely to until Regis was close enough to make a good run at it. His mind was still a torrent of angry emotions as he drew ever closer. *Just get it over with. Make it quick.*

The animal's head jerked up at the last moment, only an instant before Regis struck. It could sense something, though it had no idea what. Before the animal could react, however, to this sixth sense, Regis made his move, leaping through the bushes at the animal with as much speed as he could muster.

The stag, instead of bolting, turned immediately on its attacker, lowering its head of antlers as it did so. Regis suddenly found himself confronting not a harmless animal, but a very worthy opponent. An opponent, by the way, that could inflict death quickly.

Too late he realized the folly of his blind charge. Better to have discovered a way to trap the animal and worry about bringing him back later. But Regis had already committed himself and he continued his charge, trying his level best to avoid the antlers.

He almost succeeded. He came within inches of skirting those deadly antlers—though whether he could have held onto the massive beast, subdued it, and then carried it back to the center of the elven kingdom was doubtful at best.

As it was, what might have been never became a question, for the stag's antlers gored Regis in the side as he tried to sidestep them. It wasn't fatal, but it was serious.

The elf king's only saving grace, if there was one, was that the stag didn't finish the job.

The stag stood there for a moment, pawing the ground as Regis writhed before it in agony, but it didn't follow up with another charge. Instead it turned and trotted off slowly in another direction. It was all Regis could do to suppress a groan at both his pain and his abysmal failure.

Samson, meanwhile, was almost at his wit's end. He had about as much chance of finding and tracking a deer as he would trying to scale a sheer mountain cliff with his bare hands. Maybe even less. At least he'd be able to see the mountain. He didn't have the first idea what to even look for here in the forest.

He stumbled on the stag by total accident. The irony of it was that the stag was the same one that, only a short while before, had attacked the elf king. Regis's blood was still on the tips of its antlers, despite the animal's attempts to rub it off against the bark of a tree.

But, of course, Samson had no way of knowing that. He'd been sitting, resting, with his back against a tree on the banks of a stream. And the deer had walked casually up to the water for a drink not more than 20 yards upstream from him.

Samson managed to stifle a gasp when he spotted the animal. Somehow he kept from simply making a mad dash for the creature. No, he swiftly realized, that wouldn't do at all. The thing would sbolt away and that would be that, the end of an opportunity.

What he needed was a diversion, something to draw the deer's attention away from him until he was close enough to pounce. But that was absurd. Any diversion would probably scare the stag away. Unless…

Samson scanned the ground for the tool he needed. The very thing, fortunately, was almost immediately at hand. Cautiously, not making a sound, he pried the medium-sized boulder from the soft, yielding earth. He hefted it in one hand and again measured the distance to the stag.

Satisfied, he glanced up. Again, lady luck had smiled in his direction. There was a breech in the branches overhead, mostly because the trees thinned out near the stream, and he could see patches of light blue sky. Now it was only a matter of hurling the boulder as high and far as he could possibly manage.

The boulder actually landed closer to the stag than Samson had planned. It came crashing to earth only a scant three feet or so on the *other* side of the deer, away from Samson. And just as he'd hoped, the stag bolted away from the crashing noise in terror as fast as its legs could carry it.

Right into Samson's waiting arms. Well, not completely. Samson had to make a desperate lunge at it, his right hand outstretched to grab hold of the antlers as the animal charged past in full flight.

At the last possible moment, his hand closed on the antlers. The powerful stag almost pulled his right arm from its socket, but Samson held firm. The stag's hindquarters whipped around. It staggered slightly to recover its feet, but Samson had already grabbed the antlers with his left hand. Within seconds, he'd bulldogged the creature to the ground.

But now what? Samson's mind shouted in that half-second. It took every ounce of strength he possessed to keep the antlers pinned to the earth. Even now, the deer's powerful legs and cutting hooves were scoring his arms.

Wait a minute. The fireman's carry would do the trick. Yes! He ducked his head under the deer's soft belly and shouldered the animal, his right hand still firmly pinning the antlers to the ground and his left hand now resting on its rump.

With a colossal heave, he hoisted the animal to his shoulders and staggered upright. The animal was kicking furiously, but Samson had the leverage now. It was simply a matter of keeping his feet and making sure the stag couldn't whip its head back and forth. The legs kicked and splayed out in front of him as he walked, but they could no longer be used as weapons against him.

Now, to find his way back to the elven kingdom. Hardly an easy matter, considering he had absolutely no idea which direction to set off in. He had two choices. Either follow the stream or set off at random through the woods. He chose the stream.

It wasn't easy going, not initially, with the animal continuing its frenetic attempt to kick free. But, gradually, the stag opted for a different strategy, one that was almost worse. It would remain still for as long as half a minute and then, in one sudden burst, desperately and violently try to work itself free.

Samson, however, was able to anticipate these bursts of movement before they happened because the animal's muscles tensed beforehand. It didn't make it any easier to hang on, but it allowed him to tighten his grip that fraction of a second beforehand.

And he'd guessed right. The stream did, in fact, lead to a larger stream, which in turn led to the outskirts of the elven kingdom. An hour after he'd first spotted the stag, Samson marched wearily to the corner of the kingdom. Not long after that, in the spot they'd set, a dozen not-so-eager hands reluctantly relieved him of his burden.

The elves simply stared at Samson in unremitting awe. Not one of them had ever expected to see him return, at least not carrying a stag. To be honest, only a few had expected even their own king to return.

Which he hadn't, by the way. Regis still lay out in the forest in a pool of blood, his mind wavering in and out of consciousness from the pain of his wound. It wasn't a mortal one, but it would fast become one if it wasn't tended.

***

Mark had met Cytherea just outside the boundary of the kingdom an hour or so after Samson and Regis had set off. In his own heart, he expected Samson to fail. It was inevitable. So he'd decided to go to Cytherea for counsel.

"I wouldn't be so sure about that," she'd warned him.

"But he's certain to fail!" Mark had protested.

"Don't underestimate your powerful friend. It's been an unconscionably long time since this world has seen a man of such power and resourcefulness."

Only moments after Mark had arrived, though, Cytherea turned the conversation in an entirely new, unexpected direction. Her eyes had lost their bright sheen for a moment, as if listening to some secret voice only she could hear.

"Their king has been hurt," she said almost immediately.

"What?" Mark asked, confused at the sudden shift of direction.

"The elf king, Regis, has been hurt badly. Gored by a stag, I think."

"How do you know?" Mark demanded uneasily.

"Never mind about that. You've got to find him. If he dies, all of this will have been in vain. So go. You can track him, can't you?"

"Well, yes, I suppose," he said, trying desperately to shake the cobwebs from his cluttered mind. Her words made no sense.

"Get moving then." Her eyes implored him to be on his way.

Mark continued to stare stupidly. "You're sure?"

"Yes, I'm sure. And hurry."

"Will I find you here when I'm finished?"

Cytherea smiled. "No." She sighed. "My job is finished here."

Mark was more confused now than before. "But where will you be? When will I see you again?"

"When the time is right," she said coyly. "Now be gone. You may not have much time before the elf king dies."

So Mark set off in search of the elf king, his mind reeling with unanswered questions as he raced back to where he'd last seen Regis enter the forest.

At first, it wasn't easy. Regis had left barely any clues behind. But at the point where the elf king had picked up the trail of the deer, it became almost child's play to follow the trail. For there were two trails, now—the elf king's and the stag's. Within minutes, his sharp ears picked up labored breathing. He found Regis not long after, fallen.

His heart pounding, Mark hurried to the elf king's side. He gasped as he spotted the pool of blood where it had collected beneath Regis.

He inspected the wound quickly. His father had taught him the simplest, most rudimentary mechanics of binding wounds, but this was well beyond his limited knowledge. It was a ghastly wound. The stag's antlers had ripped up one of the king's internal organs as well, though Mark had no idea which one.

Pulling his own shirt over his head, Mark used it first to staunch the blood and then to bind the wound. It didn't do much good, but it might hold for a little while. He wished now he'd had the foresight to bring some of Regis's subjects along with him. Though the king was small, carrying him would be no easy task.

Regis regained consciousness only once on the trek back, long enough to mumble almost incoherent thanks to Mark. He blacked out almost immediately, though, when the pain became too great.

Toward the end, Mark was sure his arms would simply fall off. It felt as if someone had set them on fire with a torch. They were so heavy, so weary. It was all Mark could do just to put one foot before the other as he trudged through the forest, the elf king cradled in his arms.

Dozens of elves pressed in around him almost immediately after he'd arrived, stunned. Some eyed Mark suspiciously, as if the young boy might be responsible for their king's wound, but most quickly grasped what had happened.

Yet not one of the elves so much as said a kind word to Mark for returning their king to them. Instead, the elves seized Regis from him and rushed him to the nearest home to tend to his wound.

Only moments after he'd arrived, Mark suddenly found himself standing quite alone in the growing stillness of the forest. Again, no one had marked his courageous deed. The birds, perhaps, or maybe a stray squirrel, but that was the extent of the recognition. Yet, for a reason Mark couldn't quite comprehend, he didn't care. Not in the least. They could all rot, he figured. He hadn't saved the king's life for them or for any hollow praise they might manage to muster. He'd done it because it was the right, decent, proper thing to do. Simple as that. Nothing more and nothing less.

He made his way slowly to the home where a bevy of healers were, even now, tending to the elf king. A throng of elves pressed against the windows and doorway to the home.

Without a word, they parted to let Mark through. After all, Mark had saved his life. While the elves would, perhaps, never acknowledge the fact, they at least possessed the grace to let Mark discover whether his effort had been for nothing.

Mark was relieved to see color in the king's face. It was quite obvious he would live. In fact, his eyelids fluttered open even as Mark peered down at him.

"I won't forget this," the elf king whispered to him. "You have brought honor to your race."

"I had no choice," Mark said evenly. "I did what I had to."

Regis nodded. He understood the boy's words, perhaps more than Mark could know. Regis had often done what he had to do, rather than what his heart had asked him to do instead. "But how did you know to look for me?"

Mark laughed lightly. "The witch, as you call her. She knew, somehow, that you'd been gored by the stag and that you lay dying in the forest."

Regis returned the smile. "I should have guessed. You know who she is, don't you?"

"Sure." Mark shrugged. "A wood nymph."

The elf king laughed aloud and immediately regretted it as a convulsion of pain swept through his body. "A nymph?" he gasped. "That's who you think she is?"

"Who else?"

"She's a goddess, my friend, none other than Venus herself," Regis said gently. "She can turn any man, or boy, to her fickle will. That's why I didn't want her in my kingdom."

Mark reeled in shock. Venus? A goddess? That would explain, of course, the terrible, terrible compulsion he'd felt when they'd first met.

"I see she's used some of that charm on you," the elf king said through half-closed lids, his voice drifting off at the end.

"No, nothing happened," Mark said quickly. "I resisted, somehow. It's just that it seems so very strange. To think that I almost…"

"I know." Regis's voice was barely audible. "But I suppose she had her way, in the end. The elves will return to the land. I've been told your friend succeeded where I failed."

Mark said nothing for a long while. And when he did, he wasn't even sure the elf king heard him, for his eyes had closed again. "I'm glad. You've been gone too long."

ELOHIM
Book Two
**

PROLOGUE

The land was changing.

The elves were returning. So were the fairies, as well as the people of the sea. A mighty warrior, like the mighty men of old, had returned to the land, along with a powerful cleric. But, more importantly, there were now three magicians in the land, all women.

Old fears were returning—fears of witches who could enslave men's emotions and encircle their lives, of magicians who could control the forces of nature and turn them against the land, and of dark forces with the power to pit neighbor against neighbor, and race against race.

And they feared it would be time, soon, to mobilize against them, before even more magicians could join their ranks and return to the land.

1

***

DRAGONS AREN'T ALL THAT BAD

The word had begun to spread. A few incautious words here, a furtive whisper there, and soon the word raged across the land like a forest fire burning out of control.

Demeter had done her job. After leaving Anna's farm, she'd visited as many nearby farms as possible, spreading the message far and wide about the arrival of new magicians and that these magicians would likely turn their sons and daughters into toads, newts, sheep, goats and who knew what else.

Towns and communities were all hearing the same thing: the magicians had returned. They must have come from the city. The land was in peril.

Blackbeard and his men swept in on the tide of this rising news, fanning the flames of fear shamelessly. Within days, Blackbeard had managed to convince hundreds of men to join an informal militia, waiting only for the word about what they might be able to do and where they needed to go.

The people were afraid. Despite the stories and the legends, most had believed the magicians were gone for good from their land. Which suited all of them just fine. They did not want magic in their lives; they wanted peace. The news that magicians were returning to the land meant only one thing: there might not be peace anymore. So some of the people had come to the dubious conclusion that they needed to do something now, before it was too late.

Laura, of course, knew none of this. She knew only the thrill of watching Tara and Kathryn learn from her, growing in knowledge and stature before her eyes. All her life, Laura had felt the universe had conspired against her, forced her into a weaker role she would never have chosen had she been given a choice in the matter. But now…

The three of them—Laura, Kathryn, and Tara, the newest magician in the land and the first ever of another race to cross over in this fashion—emerged from the ocean almost at the first sign of light in the western sky.

Tara had two enormous problems. The first, walking, was solved after several minutes of testing her new legs. Tara was such a quick learner; she had the hang of it in no time. The second problem, talking, was much, much more difficult. Laura helped Tara with a spell that gave her the ability to translate her thoughts into actual words and sentences. But it would be some time before Tara was entirely comfortable bridging the distance from her mind to the release of words into the air.

It felt strange to Laura to be able to talk again, using actual words she could form in her mouth, not her mind. He words sounded slow and slurred to her ear.

"That's not *too* bad." Laura stifled a laugh as Tara wobbled during her first couple of steps. Laura had grown accustomed to Tara's long dorsal fin. Now she'd have to acclimate herself to the mermaid's new, conjured pair of legs.

"Oh…be…quiet," Tara said with a great deal of trouble as she continued to take one very deliberate step after another. It was obviously quite a chore. The grimace on her face was proof enough of that, although Laura couldn't tell if it came from her attempt to walk or to talk.

"Bend your knees more," Kathryn offered, trying to be helpful.

"I…will…fall down." Tara had her knees locked firmly in place. She looked like she was walking on stilts.

"Trust me," Kathryn began to say but stopped short when Tara, legs still locked, wobbled too far to one side and teetered to the ground.

"All…right." Tara sighed from her position on the ground. "Maybe you're right."

Kathryn helped her up. "I know I'm right. I've been walking longer than you have."

Kathryn held her hand as the mermaid tried, bending her knees this time, to move across the ground more fluidly. Tara wasn't embarrassed in front of her two friends, but she desperately wanted to master the uncomfortable posture before she made her first public appearance.

What none of them knew was that an additional spectator, a silent observer, had been waiting patiently for their appearance that morning. The huge, black crow had perched in a solitary tree near the shore, carefully keeping hidden behind the foliage. But there would be no reason for any of the young women to notice this creature. And therein lay its ability to observe and record unmolested, a task it carried out with a skill honed and sharpened with practice.

As Tara slowly gained control of her legs, Laura decided to ask Kathryn something that had nagged at her for a long time, almost from the moment she'd first arrived in the land. "Why is this land so blighted?" she asked abruptly.

Kathryn gave her a strange look. "The drought, of course. It's ruined the crop seasons for the past several years."

"No, no, I don't mean that." Laura shook her head. "I mean the people. *They* seem blighted, unhappy, gloomy, depressed, afraid of their own shadows. They live as if they had nothing at all to celebrate or work for, other than to keep a roof over their heads and, as the saying goes, food on the table. Is there nothing more to life here?"

Kathryn let the question hover in the air between them before she answered. "Is there any more to life than that where you come from, in your own world?"

"Yes, of course," Laura said sharply. "The medical sciences are exploding in a thousand different directions. The computer has revolutionized our age. There are so many profound moral questions being asked, no one can possibly answer all of them to anyone's satisfaction."

"I can't say I understand any of that," Kathryn said, interrupting Laura's litany. "But are they happy with their lives? That's what I want to know. Are *you* happy?"

Laura looked into her eyes but couldn't hold the level, steady gaze Kathryn always seemed to manage with ease. Kathryn would look at anyone or anything without shame or embarrassment.

"Not all the time," Laura answered truthfully. "I can't really say I'm happy all the time. I have too many questions and not enough answers. And I would guess most people, at least those who think about it at all, are pretty much like me."

"Well, they're like that here, too," Kathryn murmured. "Only the questions don't seem as big or confusing. Because so much seems possible, at least according to our own history, people tend to shy away from the really big questions. They're afraid of what they might find."

A profound statement from someone so young. How often, Laura wondered, had Kathryn lay awake at night, alone in her bed, pondering the large, unanswered questions of life? "I'm sorry I asked the question the way I did," Laura apologized. "It's just that everything seems a little dreary to me here."

"Don't worry," Kathryn said with a luminous smile. "It seems dreary to me, too. But I'm going to change that. And you are, too. What do you think about that?"

Before Laura could answer, though, Tara suddenly squealed. They both looked over at the mermaid, who was staring at the ground with utter horror.

"Oh, I'm so sorry. I-I didn't mean to. I wasn't watching where I was going," Tara almost sobbed.

Laura glanced down at the mermaid's feet. Tara had inadvertently stepped on a starfish that had washed up on the beach. Laura stifled the urge to laugh, because the accident obviously troubled the mermaid a great deal.

"I don't think you hurt it." Kathryn knelt to inspect the small starfish. "You probably didn't put all your weight on it."

"I didn't," Tara said quickly. "I felt it under my..."

"Foot," Laura said for her.

"Yes, that, and then I got off of it as fast as I could," the mermaid said, her words continuing to emerge very slowly and deliberately. Laura was amazed she was able to speak at all, having never used her facial muscles to speak before now.

"Well, it's all right," Kathryn said.

"How do you know that?" Laura asked her.

Kathryn gazed at her with such pure, absolute delight that Laura blushed. "I used one of these spells you gave me. I used it to see if the animal had been harmed in any way and it hadn't."

Tara sighed in relief. "I'm so glad. I've never, ever harmed a creature of the sea."

"And you still haven't," Laura said with a smile. Then she changed the conversation. "Now I think we've got to find some way to get to the meeting hall. And quickly. Any suggestions?"

Tara coughed nervously. "Well, I would like to see the land. I've never seen it, you know."

"Okay," Laura said, assuming the mantle of leadership easily. "I think flying would accomplish that best and get us to the lodge quickly as well. We can't really conjure an airplane here, so…"

"A what?" Tara and Kathryn said in unison.

"An airplane is something like a boat with wings that can fly through the air." Laura laughed. "But never mind. It's too complicated to explain. What we need is something, an animal of some kind, that can carry all three of us as it flies."

"A dragon!" Kathryn exclaimed. "That would do it, and I've always wanted to see one."

"Are you out of your mind?" Laura shivered. "Dragons are horrible, terrible, evil creatures, aren't they? Every story I've ever read about them—"

"No!" Kathryn said emphatically. "Not all dragons are evil. Some, yes, but there are a few who aren't. Like the silver dragons, the ones who live near the very top of the mountains where the giants are supposed to have fled."

"Silver dragons?" Laura asked suspiciously.

"Yes," Tara said, "and she's right. I met a bronze dragon who was sunning himself at the edge of the ocean once, and he was quite nice."

"See?" Kathryn said eagerly. "And the silver dragons are also supposed to be really smart. I think it would help us an awful lot in our search."

"All right," Laura grumbled. "We'll call on one of these silver dragons. Let me think of the spell I need."

"I have it," Kathryn said quickly, her eyes blinking furiously when Laura turned a frosty glare in her direction.

"Is that so?" Laura asked her. "You have it handy, do you?"

"Well, yes, I got to thinking about it, and I guess I put the words of the spell together in my head."

"I see," Laura said in a clipped monotone. "And you're convinced the spell will work?"

"Pretty sure," Kathryn said, although she hardly appeared confident in the face of Laura's withering gaze.

"All right, then, give it a try."

Kathryn closed her eyes for a moment to make sure she had the words just right. It wouldn't do to make a mistake and call up one of those awful black dragons who live in swamps and marshes or deep, dark caves. No, that wouldn't do at all.

"*Seolfor derk gwa,*" Kathryn said slowly, making doubly sure the pronunciation was correct, at least according to the memory of it she could recall from Laura's own conception of the words.

"That's very good," Laura said evenly, masking her true feelings. "That's the way they should be spoken."

"Thank you." Kathryn flushed with embarrassment at the unexpected compliment.

The three stood anxiously awaiting the arrival of what, to Laura at least, was only a mythical creature. None of them knew just quite what to expect.

They heard the faint tingling of music first, heralding the dragon's arrival. It was a lovely, delicate sound, as if an orchestra of bells had been arranged to play a haunting refrain.

The dragon appeared on the horizon at the edge of the ocean, then approached them at an unimaginable speed. Laura had never seen anything living move so quickly. So fast was its speed, in fact, that it overshot the three of them and actually had to turn around in midair to come back. It hovered above them for a moment and then, graceful as a feather floating to the ground, drifted to the earth, its great sweeping wings kicking up a dust cloud beneath it that blinded the three women.

"Sorry about that," the dragon said. "I was in such a hurry to get here, I miscalculated my speed. And I'm still new at this anyway."

The three of them looked at the creature in amazement. "New?" Laura said, speaking for all three. "You're saying that you're a young dragon?" He, or she, appeared ancient to them.

"Why yes," the dragon said, surprised. "I'm less than a thousand years old. That's why I had to hurry here, before any of the others could stop me."

"The others?" Laura asked.

"My mentors," the dragon said. "They never let me go anywhere. Learn, learn, learn. That's all they talk about. This is my first adventure. No one's heard a magician's call since I was born, you see."

The three magicians glanced sidelong at each other. The dragon talked faster than anyone they'd ever heard. The words came out in a flood of syllables.

"What's your name?" Tara asked abruptly and then introduced herself and her companions.

"Sharpu," the dragon said, "but you can call me Shar. Most of my friends do…the other dragons, I mean. I don't really have any friends who aren't dragons. But you probably already knew that, didn't you?"

Laura sighed to herself. Who would have guessed that they'd conjure up a dragon who sounded an awful lot like a friend of hers in high school who once tried to give a two-minute, oral book review, took 20 minutes instead, then fled the room in tears because she never could get her main point across?

"Shar," Kathryn asked timidly, "are you…are you a he…or a she?"

The dragon chuckled. "Hard to tell, isn't it? I mean, we all look the same, now, don't we? Yes, well, I'm the male of the species, although that doesn't seem to matter much in the scheme of things, at least as far as dragons are concerned."

"I think it's time we were off," Laura said quickly, before Shar decided to give them the dragons' grand scheme.

"Off to where, may I ask? And if it isn't presumptuous, am I to assume that you have given me the honor of carrying you three magicians—you *are* all magicians, aren't you—to your destination?"

Laura couldn't mask an amused smile this time. "Yes, the honor is all yours. And as for our destination, none of us are quite sure how to get there. We need to find the ancient meeting hall, where the races once met in frequent council."

"Got it," Shar said, sounding faintly like a New York taxi driver Laura had known once. "I know the precise place. I've visited there twice, just to poke my nose around."

"Do you do that often?" Kathryn asked. "Poke your nose around, I mean?"

"Sure, why not?" Shar shrugged his massive, scaly shoulders in a colossal heave that might have frightened anyone who hadn't met the dragon first. "Who's to stop me?"

"Certainly not me," Laura said. "Now, can we climb aboard?"

"Be my guest." The dragon hunkered down on all fours to let the girls slip easily atop his scaly back. They scrambled on, situating themselves comfortably between Shar's two huge wings.

"And we're off," the dragon said, lifting easily off the ground despite the added load of passengers. "By the way, did I ever tell you about the time I tried to fly to the sun when I was little? Oh, I guess I couldn't have. We just met.…"

2

***

REUNION

They took a slight detour to return Nathaniel to his grandmother's farm, then resumed their trip to the great hall. Anna had been thrilled at the return of her grandson. But she warned Kathryn and Laura that the strange woman, Demeter, had been up to no good since they'd left. She'd been all across the countryside spreading vicious lies about them.

By the time they got to the hall, Laura knew more about dragons than she'd thought possible by the time they began the slow descent to the lodge an hour or so before sundown that night. She now knew every species of dragon, their likes and dislikes, and what Shar had spent the last thousand years or so doing.

The dragon obviously thought nothing of setting out on a jaunt that might take him a decade or two to finish. Apparently a few years to Shar were almost like a few days to her. So the trip from the edge of the ocean to the lodge, while a wearisome trip for her, must have seemed like nothing more than the blink of an eye to him.

The dragon settled on the weed-choked lawn out behind the lodge. The place looked like it hadn't been cared for in a long, long time, which was undoubtedly the case, Laura figured.

Because he was simply too large to enter the lodge, Shar reluctantly agreed to remain outside while the three went inside in search of the others—the priest and the warrior—the elders had spoken of.

Laura, had she been thinking instead of simply reacting to the events happening to her, would have guessed. Or at least considered the possibility.

"I don't believe it," Laura almost gasped when she was confronted by Jon just inside the hall, where he was in the process of polishing a huge oak table, of all things. "It's...it's *you*."

"What are *you* doing here?" Jon said, equally stunned, as he looked up from his work. Tara and Kathryn had joined her in the hall.

"I could ask you the same question," Laura said defiantly. Jon made her distinctly uneasy. He seemed rather self-absorbed. In fact, she'd disliked him from the moment she'd met him in the room, where those strange kids had been playing that game.

Jon shrugged. "Beats me. One minute I was reading that book..."

"And the next you were here," Laura interrupted. "Yes, I know. The same thing happened to me. I woke up on some farm, with people who had names like Demeter."

"Demeter?" Jon asked. "Zeus's wife?"

"Not that I could tell," Laura said. "She was just some old lady in a cloak."

Jon nodded. "So you're this great magician Mercury told us about." He'd never thought much of Laura. She'd seemed much too self-centered and aloof for his tastes during their first, brief encounter.

"Mercury?" Laura asked.

"The messenger god. He told us about you and another..."

"A mighty warrior, I know," Laura said. "I mean, you can't *possibly* be the fighter he was referring to. You must be the powerful cleric that Amphitrite..."

"Did you say Amphitrite?"

"Yes, when I was visiting the people of the sea. She seemed nice enough."

"Was her husband, Poseidon, with her?" Jon asked, still amazed that gods seemed to be everywhere in this world. "So you've managed to meet two of them already, Amphitrite and Demeter?"

"I honestly had no idea either was a god," Laura said thoughtfully. "That certainly explains some things, and why the elders paid Amphitrite such respect."

"Elders?" Jon asked. "Whose elders?"

"Mine," Tara said clearly. "I'm a mermaid."

"You are, huh? Where's your flipper?" Jon asked cynically.

"Look, you...," Laura began.

"Oh, calm down," Jon said quickly. "If she says she's a mermaid, all right, fine. I believe her. And, yes, I guess I'm this cleric you've heard about."

"Then that hulk, that wrestler, whatever his name was, is probably this magnificent fighter," Laura said, her mind finally clicking into overdrive. She vowed at that moment not to let her guard down again as she had almost from the instant she'd awakened in the land.

Jon frowned. "I guess. We'll know soon enough. He's supposed to come here as well."

"So have you figured a way back to our own world yet?" Laura asked hopefully.

"Nope," Jon said nonchalantly. "But there's a map of it upstairs, in one of the rooms on the third floor of this dive."

"Of what? Our own world?"

"Yes. They've carved the whole thing in one of the walls and even managed to get all the oceans in the right place."

"You're kidding?"

"Would I kid about something like that?"

Laura bolted out of the hall, completely unaware of the bizarre looks of the others, taking the stairs of the lodge two and three at a time until she'd reached the third floor. Frantically, she searched the rooms until she discovered the one with the map in it.

It wasn't hard to find. It took up nearly the entire wall. Numbly, she approached it. Jon had been right. They did have the oceans in all the right places. The United States looked a little too fat, Texas seemed to be too far east and Florida was much too close to the Caribbean, but it generally seemed to be accurate. The continents also seemed to be accurately drawn.

But what purpose had this thing served? Had someone from this world, or hers, drawn it? And why here, in this lodge?

She stood there, perusing every square inch of the intricately carved and detailed map for a long while before she finally spotted it, down near the coast of the Carolinas. It was a little mark, a tiny dot really, but it seemed just about where Durham, North Carolina, would be on a map. Perhaps even where that spooky old house had been built.

"Of course," she said out loud, her voice sounding strange in the empty room. "A portal to this world."

"You would think," Jon said aloud.

Laura whirled. Jon was leaning casually against the doorframe.

"How long have you been standing there, staring at me?" Laura demanded. "And why didn't you tell me you'd seen this mark on this map?"

"Not long, to answer the first," Jon said easily, "and you didn't ask, to answer the second."

"Are there others?"

"Yes, quite a few, in fact," Jon said.

Laura whirled around a second time and scanned the map. Now that she knew what she was looking for, it became crystal clear. She spotted several more, at various places around the world. "So what are they, do you think?"

"I think it's a pretty fair assumption, as you've already guessed, that those marks represent windows—portals of some sort—to or from our own world," Jon said. "It makes even more sense when you see where they are."

"Where?"

"All the ancient places—Stonehenge, Tiahuanaco, the site of the great Pyramids, the temples of Jerusalem. All places of some ancient significance," Jon explained. "Places where religion and magic had always collided, or coexisted peacefully, in some instances."

"And you know that because…?"

"Because it was my doctoral thesis, of all things." Jon laughed. "I pursued it because it made for an interesting game. Not because I believed any of it in the slightest. Until now."

"Really?" Laura asked, curious despite herself. "Surely that's not an accident?"

"No, not hardly. But it does make me wonder…"

"About why they chose us?"

"Yes, exactly. And what they hope we'll find—or accomplish."

Laura looked at Jon. "I've thought it odd that I don't really feel all that out of place here. Other than the fact that magic actually works here, of course."

"Me, too. All these gods we're familiar with, heroes from their past with names that we're all familiar with, almost as if…"

"We've heard echoes of this land as well in all of our myths and legends." Laura nodded. "I know. I've considered the same thing."

Jon scanned the room. "You know, there's really only one thing missing from this world—the one thing that is central to most of the myths about magic and religion from our own world. Virtually every myth says that a branch from the World Tree opens a portal to the Otherworld."

"World Tree? Otherworld?"

"Sure. The World Tree, the Center Tree, the One Tree. It's all the same. It's the way into the Otherworld. It's how King Arthur made it to the Otherworld in search of the magic cauldron. It's how the Celts made it here. The Druids believed a branch from a sacred oak could get you here."

"So you think that's what this is, that's where we are? This Otherworld place?"

Jon shrugged. "Sure, why not? It makes about as much sense as anything else. Except for the fact that there's no central One Tree anywhere to be found in this place."

"And that tree has something to do with the portals?"

"According to all the legends from our own Earth, a branch of the World Tree at the heart of the Otherworld opens a door, a portal. That World Tree is the spiritual source of all life and knowledge, the Celts believed. It was at the center of the King Arthur legends and stories. And this world is so very much like the Otherworld of those myths that it makes me wonder, where is that One Tree? I haven't seen it anywhere, or heard anything about it. Have you?"

"No, I haven't," Laura said.

"It's all mixed up, somehow, with the myths of our world, and what these people know as their own legends here." Jon turned to head back downstairs. "At any rate, we need to find our way back somehow, and I keep remembering some of what Eric told us, in that room."

194

* * *

Samson showed up the next morning at a full gallop on one of the most magnificent horses Jon had ever seen, a huge black stallion with a white tuft on its chest. Jon, outside strolling through the nearby woods, heard him approaching the hall and went to meet him.

From his tired, drawn look, Samson must have ridden all night to reach the lodge. There were dark circles under both eyes, his hair was a tangled mop, and his horse was fairly foaming at the mouth when he reined it in.

"We thought it might be you," Jon tried to tell him as he dismounted, but Samson simply shrugged it off. Either he didn't recognize Jon from their brief meeting or he simply chose to ignore it.

"No time for that," he said breathlessly. "Are you this priest I've heard about? The cleric?"

"That's me," Jon said cheerfully. He was definitely enjoying the warm, sunny day now that he'd grown accustomed to this world.

"Good, let's go, then," Samson ordered. "You can ride behind me."

"Hold on! What, exactly, are you talking about?"

"Someone…I know is about to die on me. The elves said you could cure him, heal him, or whatever. That's what clerics do, don't they?"

"Well, sure, that's one of the things we can do," Jon said uneasily. He didn't like the direction this encounter was taking. "But I don't feel like just galloping off into the sunset without—"

"Look." Samson grabbed Jon by his collar and almost lifted him off the ground with one hand. "We don't have much time. He's liable to die at any moment."

"Who is?"

"Regis. The king of the elves."

"Okay, I have that part. Now what's wrong with him?"

"He was gored by a stag, a deer, and the wound is infected. He's got all this yellow pus oozing out of it."

"Okay, okay, I get the picture," Jon said, trying not to think about it too much. "But we can't take this horse. It's about to drop."

"It's all I've got. It's all the elves could offer me." Samson still hadn't released Jon.

"If you let him down, I have a better idea," Laura said from behind him.

"And what's that?"

"I'm sure that Shar would be glad to take us wherever it is you need to go to find this king of yours."

"What's a Shar?" Samson asked.

"It's not a what, it's a who," Laura said with no small amount of disgust. Samson seemed like nothing more than a selfish, muscle-bound, mindless twit. "And he's a dragon."

"A dragon?" he asked stupidly.

"Are you deaf?" Laura asked. "That's what I said. And if you ask him nicely, I'm sure he'd be glad to take us."

"You ask him. And hurry," Samson demanded.

Laura almost turned away. She didn't like his tone or the way he treated people. But if someone was really dying and Jon could help him…

"All right, let's go." Laura sighed. "He's out back, behind the lodge talking to Peg."

"Is Peg a what or a who?" Samson asked Jon quietly as Laura hurried ahead of the two of them.

"Peg's a flying horse, if you can believe that," Jon said back.

Samson exhaled. "I'll believe anything here."

Shar was delighted. "Of course, of course," the dragon said, bubbling with excitement. "I haven't seen any of the elves in such a long time. It would be an honor and a pleasure. We'll be there in no time at all, a mere fraction of a moment."

"Can we leave now?" Samson asked the dragon impatiently.

"Certainly," Shar answered, not the least bit offended by Samson's rude tone. "Climb aboard."

Laura, however, wasn't about to take Samson's words quite so lightly. "Now that we're on our way, why don't you explain just who it is that anointed you king for a day and gave you the authority to act like such a jerk," she said when they were airborne. "If you'd just asked us nicely, reasonably, like a normal human being…"

"I'm sorry, okay?" Samson said plaintively. "I'm a little crazy right now. I don't want this king to die, that's all."

"Trust me, no one around here wants him to die," Laura assured him. "Just try to be a little more civil, why don't you?"

"I'll try," Samson grumbled.

* * *

Regis had fulfilled his pledge and come with Samson. Two of the king's closest advisors had hitched a makeshift litter behind two of their horses and followed in Samson's wake as quickly as they could. But Regis had worsened in the middle of the night, and Samson had gone on ahead to find help.

They found Regis in a glade, where he had spent a fitful night tossing and turning in a cold sweat. Laura hurried to his side and felt his forehead, then his pulse. The elf king was pallid, a deathly white. It was obvious to Laura that he was dying.

"All right, do your stuff," Samson demanded of Jon, who was waiting for Laura to come up with a diagnosis.

"Didn't I warn you about that?" Laura narrowed her eyes in Samson's direction.

"Will you do something, pretty please?" Samson asked in a syrupy-sweet tone. "And quickly, please, before he dies while we're standing here."

"I suppose that'll have to do," Laura said with an unhappy frown, turning to Jon. "Anyway, I don't think it's anything more than an infection, just in the area of the wound."

It was a simple healing spell, one that Jon had already put together in his mind on the trip there. *"Gwela,"* he said, gritting his teeth and laying his hands on the gaping wound.

As they gathered around the elf king, a warm light started to glow in and around the bloody wound. It looked, almost, as if the wound was on fire.

"That's strange," Laura mumbled.

"Part of the word I spoke, in its ancient form, means both 'bright' and 'cleanse,' " Jon said.

"How'd you remember it?" Samson asked him.

"It's hard to explain." Jon examined the elf king's ugly wound as he spoke. "But my mind links one thing with another until I can recall whatever it is I want. It's sort of a process I go through to remember things I've read."

"Makes sense," Samson said. Of course, it made absolutely no sense to him at all, but if it worked, it worked. He wasn't about to argue with success.

The bright light that pulsated in the wound had cleaned it within moments and then began to gently pull the torn and shredded skin back together. It wasn't long before the wound was only a memory. There wasn't even a scar.

Jon glanced over at Laura and was surprised to see that she was on the verge of crying. It seemed strange on such a cold, austere, forbidding face.

"Well, that's that," Jon said brightly. "Glad to be of service."

"Is that all you think there is to it?" Laura asked bitterly.

"To what?"

"Healing, of course. Do you think it's all that simple?"

"Don't be ridiculous," Jon answered, doing his best to match her acid tone. "I think I have a pretty fair idea of what it takes to practice medicine. It's just that this world is entirely different. And I happen to be the one with the healing hand, so just calm down."

"All right." Laura turned away. "Don't make a federal case out of it."

"Wait a minute. You were the one..."

197

But Jon stopped when the elf king opened his eyes and sat bolt upright on his litter. Almost in terror, his eyes searched the landscape until they settled on the two advisors who had accompanied him. He calmed down almost instantly.

"What's happened to me?" he demanded softly, unsure of his own voice.

"You had a terrible wound, my lord," said one of his advisors, Serena, whose short, clipped blond hair gave her a distinctly boyish appearance.

"But this cleric has healed it quite marvelously," said the other advisor, Gandy, a thin, almost gaunt, wisp of an elf who seemed to hover constantly in the background.

"Thank you," Regis said to Jon quite formally.

"No problem. It was his idea." Jon shrugged, glancing at Samson.

"Where is your friend?" Regis asked Samson. "Mark, the one who pulled me from the forest?"

"I sent him out to search for healing roots," Serena answered instead.

"When he returns, we must be on our way, then," Regis said with more authority than Samson would have thought possible, considering the fact that he'd been half-dead only moments before.

"You sure you're feeling all right?" said Jon, who obviously didn't trust his own healing powers.

"Haven't felt this good in years," Regis replied with a happy smile. "Now, are we going to this council meeting or not? If I am going to honor my word and our race is going to return to the land, let's be about it, shall we?"

3

* * *

THE GATHERING

They spent a day gathering at the edge of the forest under the cover of darkness. They were waiting for first light before charging the ancient hall.

The riders had come back with the news that there weren't many, but the magicians had arrived. They were at the ancient meeting place, the great lodge where the races had once held council.

Hundreds of men from the new militia gathered. Most had nothing more than large sticks as weapons. Some carried metal chains. A few had managed to bring crude bows and arrows.

The fear had taken hold of them, and would not let go—the fear that magicians had returned and would destroy their land and way of life. The fear was like a virus. It spread, unchecked, from home to home, until men felt compelled to do something about it.

They were there to hang the magicians, if they could, while they were few. Better to stop this now, if they could. That was what the hate-whisperers and gossip-mongers had said. Get them now. Burn them, hang them, drive a stake through their heart. Do whatever you can, before they grow in number and take us over again, as they once did.

Each and every one of these men was afraid. If the stories they'd heard were true—and magicians were, in fact, inside the lodge—what chance did they have against them?

But there was a frenzy among them, driven by years of despair and hopelessness in a barren land. They almost needed a conflagration such as this. They welcomed it. And who was there to tell them otherwise, lead them in a different direction?

Blackbeard had made the most of the opportunity presented him by Demeter and others. With the residents of the land convinced that they needed to act now, before the strength of the magicians grew too strong, Blackbeard had quickly seized the advantage and appointed himself as one of their first real leaders in years.

Now he paced nervously at the edge of the forest, waiting for first light. He'd already witnessed firsthand what Samson was capable of, when he felled the center tree in the Silver Forest and then vanished without a trace, like a witch. If the others with him were like that, or worse, it might not be easy.

"But there are so many of us now," the Weasel said reassuringly. "I mean, we'll just rush the place, take them, and be done with it. They can't resist so many of us."

"I don't know," Blackbeard considered. "What if they have more power than we think?"

"What can they do?" the Weasel asked. "They can't turn us *all* into toads. We'll get to them."

"Perhaps." Blackbeard returned to his pacing.

4

***

THREE NEW QUESTS

Laura, Tara, and Kathryn graciously provided candles throughout the Great Hall in the lodge to push back the darkness as they met deep into the evening. None knew what awaited them in the forest surrounding the lodge. They were all preoccupied—rightly so—with the meeting at hand.

It had been many centuries since such a meeting had been held. Three of the races were, as yet, not represented, but it hardly mattered to Lucas or Mark. They had dreamed of just such a moment almost from birth.

The two of them, by the way, had become almost immediate friends. And why not? They were from vastly different parts of the land, yes, but very much alike in many respects.

Both were dreamers, silent observers of a world they desperately wanted to change. Both had believed in the legends for as long as either could remember; both were confident in their own abilities. So it was only natural they should quickly come to respect each other.

The meeting took place at the round table. It was short, almost businesslike, thanks to both Regis and Maya. It lasted only long enough for the group to decide how best to approach the remaining three races.

For it was obvious that they needed to do so. They all knew it. The land was changing. It was time.

"It's obvious we need to split into three parties," Regis said when they were all seated around the ancient table. It was impossible to sit completely around the massive table, so they'd pulled up chairs only around one half of it.

"I agree," the fairy queen said with a pert nod of her tiny head. "No sense in wasting any time or effort."

"Good," Regis said. "And I think I can settle at least one of the parties. Although I'd dearly love to see my old friends, the centaurs, I think it's only logical that Samson and I undertake the perilous journey below ground to the dwarves' kingdom."

"And just why is that?" Laura demanded.

"Because, my fair lady, there is no easy route to the dwarves," Regis said easily. "It will require strength and stamina—and no small measure of luck, I might add—to reach them. I know you're a powerful magician, but with all due respect, you wouldn't make it."

Laura glared at the elf king. "All right, I'll agree to that," she said through clenched teeth. "You'll try to reach the dwarves. Besides Samson, who else will need to go with you?"

"I will accompany my king, of course," Serena said quickly.

"And I," Gandy said almost at the same moment.

"Are you *certain* one of the three magicians shouldn't accompany you?" Maya tried.

"There's no need," Regis said sharply, barely able to contain his disgust for the art of magic. "We can manage without a magician in our group, I think."

"Are you quite sure of that?" Maya asked him, barely able to contain *her* disgust for the elf king's arrogance.

"Very," Regis said firmly. "Now as for the other two parties, I think it would be logical to send one with the dragon, north to the mountains and the giants. The mountains are his home, after all."

"Then I'm going with Shar," Laura said without pause. She'd grown quite fond of the wordy dragon since he'd been summoned to their side. "And I don't really care if anyone else accompanies me there or not. I think I'm capable of presenting my case to the giants."

"I'm going with you," Kathryn told Laura.

"I will go with you as well," Tara added, "unless, of course, my services are needed elsewhere?"

"No, I don't think so," Maya said. "Jon and I should be fine. Especially with Peg along. He knows the lay of the land better than almost anyone I can think of, not to mention the fact that the centaurs almost consider him one of their own."

"It's settled, then." Regis stood up from the round table. "We'll set off at dawn."

"Wait a minute. What about us?" Mark asked plaintively.

Lucas, sitting right next to him, nodded in agreement.

Regis and Maya glanced at each other. Regis spoke first. "Neither of you joined this unusual group of your own volition. There's nothing to prevent either of you from returning home."

"Not on your life!" Lucas almost shouted. "We're not going back home, not now when everything is really starting to get interesting."

"That's right," Mark echoed. "I'm seeing this thing through, like the rest of you."

"As you wish." Maya tried not to smile at the exuberance of the two young boys, or men, rather. "Choose the party you would like to join, then."

"Well, we've already talked it over," Mark said slowly, "and, although we'd like to go together, we think it would be better if we separated."

"A wise decision for two so young." Regis smiled. "Have you settled on the two parties, then?"

"I'll join the magicians on their journey to the north and the giants," Mark said, his jaw set squarely. "I would only be in the way if I remained with Samson and Regis, I believe."

"And I will remain with Jon and Maya," Lucas said. "If that's all right with them, that is?"

Maya bowed her head. "Of course. It would be an honor."

Regis looked around the table. Everyone seemed to be in agreement. "Then let's get a good night's rest. We'll meet back here when our tasks are accomplished, however long it takes?"

"Yes, and then what?" Laura asked.

"We'll decide that when, or if, we come to that point," Regis said. "But I'm afraid there can only be one choice: to approach the magicians' city."

5

* * *

FIRST LIGHT

Jon saw them first. He hadn't been able to sleep much, not from the first day he'd arrived in the land. Dark circles were forming under his weary eyes.

He'd been up, pacing the room, as the first rays of sun made their appearance. The sight out the window had startled him—hundreds of men, all moving from the shadows at the edge of the forest. Toward them. Toward the lodge.

"Get up!" he yelled, running from his room. "Get up! They're outside. They're coming. I saw them."

"Who's that yelling?" Samson called from a nearby room.

"I am!" Jon yelled. "I need everybody out here, with me, right now! Hurry!"

All the members of the various parties gathered within moments. Tara and Kathryn were still rubbing sleep from their eyes. Laura was wide awake. She'd had a difficult time sleeping in this land, like Jon.

"What is it?" Samson demanded of Jon.

"Come, follow me," Jon implored. "You'll see."

Jon led them to the nearest window. The rest of the group peered over his shoulder and saw it, too. Hundreds of men approached the lodge from all directions. They would be there within a matter of minutes.

"What can that possibly be?" Regis asked.

"It looks like another lynching party," Samson said.

Mark saw his uncle before the others and could guess what was about to happen. "They're coming to get us," he told the others.

"Who is?" asked Laura.

• "I saw my uncle out there, leading the others. I'm sure they mean to attack us."

"But why?" Regis asked.

"That idiot doesn't need a reason," Samson said darkly.

Maya, though, knew. She looked over at Laura, then Kathryn, and finally Tara. "They're coming because of those three. The magicians."

"Well, I'm not waiting to find out. They'll need to get through me first." Samson headed down the stairs. Mark and then Lucas joined him. The rest trailed behind.

Samson opened the great door at the entrance to the vast hall. He walked out to the front steps and waited. Mark and Lucas joined him, on either side.

The sun was emerging above the top of the forest as the first of the men arrived. They assembled peaceably not more than 50 feet from where Samson, Mark, and Lucas stood.

"What do you want?" Samson called out loudly when most had gathered. "What business do you have here?"

"No business with you," Blackbeard answered, safely positioned behind a rather large group of men.

"Then who?" Samson demanded.

"With the witches, the magicians," the Weasel called out. "Hand them over, and we'll go away peaceably."

"Hand them over to a mob?" Samson yelled. "Are you all mad? What would make you think we would ever do such a thing?"

"Because there are so many of us, and so few of you," Blackbeard said.

"I like those odds," Samson retorted.

Blackbeard glared at Mark. "Boy, you're one of us. What need have you of witches and magic? Get down from there! Come, join us. We need no witches in our land. Hand them over, and you'll remain safe. I give you my word."

"Your word means nothing," Mark called out. "And they are not witches. They are women and deserve our protection. You have nothing to fear from them."

"They are magicians! They come from the city, and—"

There was a collective gasp as Laura appeared on the porch overlooking the still-gathering horde. She took a place to one side of Samson. "So you all are afraid of the likes of me?"

"And me?" asked Kathryn, swiftly joining Laura.

"And me?" said Tara.

The crowd of men buzzed angrily. A few of them edged forward. But many more took a step or two backwards. Blackbeard, sensing he needed to do something, started to push some of the men forward.

The Weasel started running along the line, urging the men forward as well. "Now, now! If we rush them, we can do this…"

Laura hoped she wouldn't have to do it. She hoped words alone could quell the mob. But there had never been a mob in history that, once gathered, would stand down from words alone. So she was ready, in case.

"We do not want your kind in the land!" Blackbeard called out. "We want no magicians! Give them to us now, or we will come and get them ourselves! This is your last chance!"

Laura glanced over at Tara and Kathryn. She could see they were scared. There were so many men, and they were so few. She needed to do something.

Laura whirled on the men. "I will tell you this. You are all mistaken, if you think the magicians are coming from the city. Kathryn is one of you, from a farm nearby." She glanced in Tara's direction. "And she has just come here on a long journey. She is one of the people of the sea."

A hushed silence fell across the crowd. They could not believe it. One of the people of the sea, here before them?

Blackbeard and the Weasel could see it. They had to rush them, now, or lose their advantage with the gathering.

"No more words! Now!" the Weasel yelled. "Go now!"

First a couple of the men pushed forward, then a few more, and finally there was a mad rush, as those from behind were afraid of being trampled from behind.

"Do something!" Tara said, turning to Laura. Her eyes were wide with fear.

Laura focused on the rushing mob. She was surprised at how calm she felt, considering that hundreds of angry men would arrive within seconds. It was as if the entire scene was somehow playing out in slow motion before her.

"*Mote*," she said simply, pointing to a spot just in front of the porch, between them and the mad, rushing horde.

There was a deep, cavernous rumble from far below the earth, followed immediately by an even louder, ear-splitting roar. The earth began to separate, all around the lodge. Within moments, the lodge was an isolated island as the earth parted all around it. The separation grew until there was a wide chasm on all sides of the lodge. The men would need bridges to get to the ancient meeting hall now, a task that would take weeks, if they had the heart.

"Nice trick," Samson whispered to Laura. "What was it?"

"A moat," Laura said, still grim-faced as she watched the crowd.

Many of the men had run away as the earth started to separate, but some were close enough to the edge to see for themselves what had happened. They were dumbstruck. None had believed until now that there truly were magicians in the land.

Mark saw them first. At least three men raised bows and aimed at the porch. But there was the sharp twang of a bow release from behind them. An instant later arrows struck all three bows in the crowd, knocking them from their shooters' hands before they could release their own arrows. He turned. Regis, Serena, and Gandy had joined them on the porch, and were fitting their own bows for a second round of shots if needed.

At that moment, Maya made her appearance on the porch. There was a collective gasp among the men still gathered near the edge. First, the magician, then the elves, and, now, a fairy!

"You need to disperse," Maya commanded as loudly as she was able. Only the first few rows could hear her, but the effect was enough. They had all heard a fairy speak in their land, for the first time in their lives.

"Your fight is not with us," Regis called out. "It is with those in the city. Not with us. That is why the races are considering a return to the land after all this time."

"We want the magicians!" the Weasel shouted.

"You will not have them." Regis pointed at the chasm that separated them. "And, as you can see from this, you do not want to test them again. So go in peace. Let us go about our business. Go back to your farms. There is no need to burn witches at the stake today."

And to finish the effect, Shar and Peg joined them, from opposite directions. They settled gracefully on either side of the porch.

The gathering had seen enough. Magicians, moats from nowhere, dragons, flying horses, fairies, and elves—all in one place, at the same time. Who cared about magicians! There would be no battles, no tests. Not today.

"We'll be back!" Blackbeard roared, shaking a fist at them. "We'll be ready for you next time!"

"You do that," Samson said quietly, so only the small group on the porch could hear. "And we'll be ready for you as well."

6

* * *

THE WAR OF THE ELVES
AND DWARVES

amson and the elves were the first to leave, once all were certain the gathering of men was dispersing. Some of the men hung around, but most wandered away as it became obvious nothing more was going to happen on this day.

Laura had provided them with a few items for their journey, including torches that stayed lit when they wanted them to, yet could be snuffed out and re-lit again.

Because they'd been forced to leave their horses behind, Shar graciously escorted Samson and the elves to the nearest dwarf hole Peg could remember. Samson couldn't understand what Laura saw in the dragon. He never shut up.

The four of them grimly set to their task without a word after the dragon had dropped them off in the southern foothills of the mountains, near where a rather large stream emptied into the central part of the land.

The dwarf hole began as a simple tunnel burrowed into the side of the foothill but quickly turned into a near rockslide. Samson had trouble sliding and skidding down the loose rocks. He lost his footing more than once and nearly trampled Serena during one particularly bad fall.

But, eventually, they managed to grind to a halt on a plateau of some sort. Though it was hard to tell because the light from their torches didn't carry far enough, it appeared the plateau overlooked a huge cavern. What was at the bottom they couldn't tell, but whatever it was made a monstrous, steady roar.

"Come on," Regis said, taking command immediately, "there's a path." The nimble elf set off at a quick pace down the path, followed closely by his two aides, equally as nimble. They almost looked like mountain goats the way they managed to prance down the path.

Samson, meanwhile, brought up the rear quite slowly. Which was fine by him. It meant the elves would stumble into anything strange or weird first. Not that he was a coward. No, that wasn't the case. But he liked to *see* what he was trying to throttle. It was more comfortable that way.

The elves waited for him at a fork in the road. Samson, breathing heavily, came upon them in the middle of their discussion.

"…isn't such a risk," Serena was saying. "Come on, you know both Gandy and I have trained as scouts. We should be the ones to go."

"No, I forbid it," Regis said firmly.

"Forbid what?" Samson asked, still laboring.

"Two of us need to check the paths—see if we can determine which is a better direction," Gandy said. "And Regis insists he take one of them. We insist he shouldn't. We're trained as scouts, and he isn't."

Samson shrugged. "I agree with them, Regis. If they're trained and you're not…"

"Oh, what does that matter?" Regis said grumpily. He didn't like challenges to his authority.

"It matters a great deal," Serena said calmly. "We might spot something that you'd miss."

"All right, then, get moving," Regis snapped. "But don't spend too long. I want you back in less than an hour. Understood?"

The two elves nodded and set off at once, vanishing from sight within seconds. Regis sat down with a heavy sigh to wait, and Samson quickly followed suit.

"Tell me something," Samson said after a while. "Why do you hate magic so much?"

"What makes you think that?" Regis said absently.

"Oh, come on. It's as plain as the nose on your face."

"Is it, now?"

"Yes, it is. You were awfully anxious to make sure none of those three girls, those magicians, came with us."

"We don't need them, that's all!"

"It would have been nice, though," Samson said wistfully. "We wouldn't have to worry about our supper, supplies, or water…"

"You know nothing about magicians," Regis murmured. "You know nothing of their ways, their thinking, their corruption, their *power*."

"No, I don't. But those girls seemed awfully harmless, almost nice, though I can't say I was especially attracted to any of them, even that—"

Regis cut Samson off mid-ramble. "Give them time. They'll learn how to abuse their newfound power. Trust me. It will happen."

"I don't understand. What makes you think so?"

"Because it's happened a thousand times before. Every time my people even look cross-eyed at those—"

Samson looked over quickly. The elf king had turned away, angry at himself for saying more than he'd intended.

"What have the magicians done to the elves in the past?" Samson asked as gently as his thick baritone would manage.

"Nothing. Nothing at all."

"No. I don't accept that answer. You started this. Now finish it."

Regis scowled in Samson's direction with such anger Samson almost winced. He'd seen that kind of anger. More than once. Every time he looked in the mirror each morning, in fact.

"All right, I'll tell you," Regis began, his voice edged with such bitterness Samson wondered how he managed to live with it. "A long time ago, before the magicians grew so powerful, the elves were, perhaps, the greatest of the races. We were respected everywhere in the land. Afraid of no one.

"Then the magicians extended their shadow further and further as they grew bored with their own power. There was almost no corner of the land left untouched. No stone was left unturned in their voracious appetite for new experiences and more grist for their games.

"Our people said nothing for a very long time. We minded our own business. We kept to ourselves. We heard stories, yes, that they were playing games, that they hunted the people of the sea like common animals just for sport, that they liked to hunt the centaurs as well and occasionally turn one or two into simple, ordinary horses.

"We also heard stories, terrible stories, that a few from each of the races—even the elves—were imprisoned within the city for some horrible deed. But no one knew the truth. They were just stories.

"It was widely rumored that they captured quite a few fairies and kept them caged, like birds, just for fun. There was, reportedly, something of a miniature fairy city set up within a cage in the magicians' city, though no one really knows for sure.

"The giants weren't even immune from their foul, evil touch. They turned some into stone statues and some of the larger ones into mountains.

"Only two races—the elves and the dwarves—weren't subjected to their horrible, wicked games. You see, we're immune to magic entirely, unlike the other races, which all have weaknesses of one kind or another that the magicians managed to discover and exploit.

"So they left us alone. For a time. Little did we know, or suspect, what they had in mind for us. Had we known how they hated us because their power could not touch us—harm us personally and individually, I mean—we would have fled the land long before we did. We never suspected their treachery. We simply played right into their hands. Like cattle led to the slaughter, we acted out roles exactly as they'd intended. A few of them, you see, assumed new identities. They shape-shifted, became elves or dwarves, then mingled with our two races.

210

"It took them very little time at all to foment rebellion, anger, hate, and fear between our two races, the dwarves and the elves. These magicians, as elves, whispered absolutely hateful things about the dwarves. As dwarves, they slandered and maligned us.

"And it grew worse. They revealed a terrible plan the dwarves supposedly had to attack and subdue the elves. And, of course, they revealed the same thing to the dwarves. It wasn't long before the elves were meeting in war councils to plan how they might repel the impending dwarf invasion. And the dwarves were similarly meeting in war councils.

"Whenever peace missions were formed to see if the two races could come to terms, one or two of the magicians managed to worm their way into the talks and sour them. Nearly all the missions erupted into terrible shouting matches, with neither side willing to give an inch.

"When the time was ripe, the magicians whispered in our ears and off to war we marched. In the bloodiest battle the land has ever known, we wiped out nearly two-thirds of the dwarfish race. And, likewise, they destroyed most of us. We would have destroyed ourselves entirely had the magicians not tipped their hand and revealed themselves and their foul plan to us. I assume they needed someone to appreciate it. It wouldn't have meant much had there been no one left to applaud their wickedness.

"Oh, how they taunted us, mocked us, laughed at our stupidity and our eagerness to fall into the trap they'd set for us. The greatest of the races! We were now the vilest. We had marched into war, goaded only by well-placed whispers. Our shame was greater than you can possibly imagine.

"It was then that the races, all of them, fled the land. After that battle. We, most of us anyway, realized that their power had allowed them to become as the gods. No, more than gods. Because it was about then that they seemed capable of binding the gods to this world.

"It wasn't long after that battle that they began to disappear from the land, from what I can tell. None of the races were aware of this, of course, because we'd all fled as far from the magicians' city as we could manage. It wasn't until centuries later that we learned the magicians had pulled their tentacles back to the magicians' city and seemingly vanished.

"No one has seen them since. Not even the gods, like Venus, who were almost as bad as the magicians themselves once upon a time, before they were restricted and bound to this world only."

Samson said nothing for a time. And when he did speak, it was with the knowledge of what had happened to his own people, according to the stories his parents had handed to him. It was knowledge that, in his own heart, bound him in a very special way to the elf.

"I can see now why you must hate the magicians so," Samson said slowly. "In a strange sort of way, my people suffered at the hands of another group of people. It is something I have lived with all my life."

"Can you taste revenge, see it, want it so badly that you'd almost consign yourself to eternal damnation for a chance at it?" the elf king asked viciously.

"Yes, I think I can." Samson's voice was quiet, but it still echoed in the cavern. "I've often thought about what form that revenge might take, but I've never managed to settle on anything."

"I haven't, either." Regis sighed. "I don't even know where the magicians are. And I can't take revenge on something that doesn't exist anymore."

"It's much the same thing with me," Samson admitted. "The world has changed a great deal since…since this horrible thing happened to my own people."

"But you'd still like it, wouldn't you?"

"Revenge?"

"Yes, the chance to do to them what they once did to you, or to your ancestors."

"Of course," Samson said quickly. "Without question."

"Then we are, indeed, brothers after a fashion," the elf king said formally. "Born and wed to a similar mission in life."

Samson paused. "But aren't you being just a little hard on those three girls, though? Like I said, they seem harmless."

"So were the magicians. Once." Regis's voice was rock-hard. "They were human, like you, once. They had emotions, like love and happiness, once. They lived in peace with the land and its people, once. But the power changed them, corrupted them. Forever."

Before Samson could say anything, Regis suddenly held a hand up, telling him to remain silent for a moment. Samson strained to hear what the elf king was listening to, but it was useless. He could hear nothing. It was obvious Regis' ears were much sharper than his.

"It's only Serena," he said with relief. "And, if my ears are correct, Gandy is also on his way back as well."

In fact, both arrived at almost the same time, winded from a hard run back up the path.

"It's a dead end to the left," Serena said first. "A rock slide has covered the path. It would take us a very long time to clear it away."

"Then it leaves us no choice," Regis said. "What did you discover, Gandy?"

His hopeless expression told most of the story.

Samson almost picked himself up and began to walk up the path, toward the dwarf hole opening in the side of the mountain foothill.

"We *could* get past it, I suppose," Gandy said with a frown.

"Get past what?" Regis asked. "Would you tell us what you found?"

Gandy sighed. "It's an orc city, I'm afraid."

"So close to the surface?" Regis said, incredulous. "It's absurd. Why would they build a city where almost anyone from the land could easily reach them?"

"Who knows?" Gandy shrugged. "It *has* been quite some time since anyone above ground challenged them. Perhaps they need to forage above ground for food now, or perhaps the dwarves have pushed them this far."

"Is there no way past at all, without our being seen, I mean?" Regis asked hopefully.

"Not that I could see," Gandy reported. "The path runs smack into the middle of their city."

"Well," Samson said, turning to begin the long trek back up the path, "I guess that's the ball game."

"No!" Regis hissed. "We're *not* turning back. We're going forward. I don't know how, yet, but we have no choice."

"You're serious?" Samson had no idea what one of these orcs looked like, but the sound of the creature alone made his stomach a little queasy.

"Deadly serious," the elf king said. "And there's no time to waste. Let's at least set up a temporary camp within sight of the city. That should let us know what our options are."

"There aren't any," Gandy said gloomily. "I'm telling you. There's no way past them."

"It's worth a look," Regis insisted. "I'd like to see for myself, at least, before I make my decision."

"You're the king, not me," Gandy said. "But it's hopeless."

"We'll see. Now let's move. And make it quiet."

7

***

THREE QUESTIONS

Shar was in high spirits, despite his early morning jaunt to the dwarf hole, as he flew north to the land of the giants with the three magicians and the young warrior perched securely on his back, between his sturdy wings.

His good humor was not without reason, for he hadn't seen the giants in ages. In fact, he'd never even spoken to one, although he'd longed to for some time now.

"Why not?" Tara asked him. "You live so close to them."

"Now there's the rub." The young silver dragon exhaled sadly. "Nearness has nothing to do with it. Not in the least. The giants might as well live at the other end of the land, for all the good it does me to know that they're just a hop, skip, and a bump away to the north."

"Shar," Laura said patiently, "what are you talking about? Exactly."

"It's quite simple, really," the dragon continued almost without taking a breath. "The mentors have made sure we—all the fledglings, I mean—were aware of the situation, of exactly where the imaginary line was, if you know what I mean, and we were all mortally afraid of going against the wishes of our mentors, of course…"

"Shar!" Laura said more emphatically. "What line? Why haven't you ever spoken to a giant?"

"Why, because the giants absolutely forbid it, that's why," the dragon explained, sounding surprised. "I thought I told you that already."

"No, you didn't," Laura noted crossly, "although I certainly wish you had. It might have been nice to know this little fact before we set off."

"But I thought *everyone* knew about the imaginary line, the mountain range we're strictly forbidden to cross over," the dragon almost whined.

"Oh, it's all right," Kathryn soothed. "It's not your fault we didn't know about this earlier."

"That's right," Tara added. "What's important is that we know about it now, so we can plan for it."

"Well, I'm not sure there's much we can plan for," Shar said even more sadly. "The giants don't take kindly to visitors, the mentors always told us, not kindly at all. When they tried to move themselves as far away from the magicians as they could manage, they erected a formidable barrier that they guard jealously."

"A barrier?" Laura asked. "You mean the mountain range you mentioned?"

"Yes, but it's not just *any* mountain range. The mountains are all next to each other, mostly because the giants pushed them all together, and the peaks are a good six or seven miles high."

"Six or seven miles!" Laura exclaimed. "You can't be serious?"

"I'm deadly serious," the dragon said. "The problem, as you'll quickly see, is that I'll be able to clear the peaks, sure, but it will take us the longest time to fly back down on the other side, into the giant's kingdom…"

"…and we'll be as conspicuous as rabbits in a fox den," Kathryn finished.

Laura frowned. "That won't do at all. Is there a way we could climb down the other side of those mountains?"

"Sure, if you have a few months," Shar said.

"And there's no mountain pass?"

"None that I know of and, believe me, I've traveled almost every inch of those mountains."

"Well, what about an underground passage?"

Shar, uncharacteristically, said nothing right away. "Yes, there is such a passage," the dragon acknowledged, the foreboding in his voice easy to detect, "but you don't want to take it."

"Why?" asked Mark, who'd said very little during the flight so far. "That sounds like our chance of working our way into the giants' land without their suspecting."

"It's not a good idea," Shar said. "There are fearsome things down there, horrible things, according to the legends, who followed in the giants' wake."

"Such as?" Mark persisted.

"Trolls, for one, who can make themselves invisible for short periods of time and who are immune to magic unless you know their names. And ogres, for another, who are likewise immune to magic."

"But what are our alternatives?" Laura asked Shar. "Can we reason with the giants directly?"

Shar appeared dubious. "Some of them, perhaps. Some are supposed to have intelligence, at least the legends say so. But their sentinels, the giants who guard the mountain barrier, are about as dumb as they come. They hardly know their own names."

"So we couldn't talk our way past them?"

"It's impossible, unthinkable," the dragon admitted. "The sentinels were chosen for their strength, not their ability to think. They'd turn us back at every turn. And I can't fly fast enough to avoid them. They take one step to about every hundred beats of my wings. They would crush us all like bugs before we could do anything. Even a magician like Laura could do nothing to stop it."

"So they wouldn't let us past simply to let us make our pitch to the other giants?"

"No, they'd simply swat at us like flies and ask questions later. And even then, they wouldn't be likely to listen to our answers," Shar said.

"What about magic?" Kathryn asked hopefully. "Perhaps we can charm them?"

"Not likely. Long, long ago, the ancient and powerful magicians discovered ways to use magic on the giants, but I sincerely doubt whether you have that key, whatever it is."

Laura shrugged. "I certainly have no idea what that might be. And if I don't know, then I don't think either Tara or Kathryn will know it either." The two girls shook their heads, confirming Laura's words.

"Then it doesn't seem we have much choice," Mark said confidently. "It looks like we'll have to take the underground passage. Or turn back in defeat."

Shar's remaining high spirits crashed to earth rapidly. "You can count me out, then. I can't fit in the passage, which is just too bad. I was hoping you might know of some way past the sentinels. I guess I should have known it wasn't possible."

"We'll call for you when we succeed in reaching them," Laura said, trying to cheer up the suddenly morose dragon. "You'll get to meet the giants, don't you worry."

"Sure, sure," the dragon grumbled. "You'll never get there, and I'll probably wait for all eternity, hoping that you did make it. I can just see it. They'll find me waiting patiently for you 100 years from now."

"Shar," Laura said softly, "give us seven days. If you haven't heard from us by then, you're free to go. We don't want you suspending your life just because you have no idea what happened to us."

"Oh, that's great," the dragon said, his gloom deepening with each passing moment. "I'll probably fly away and the day after you'll come for me, I won't be there...."

* * *

Two days later the dragon dropped them off at the entrance to the underground pass. He'd told them everything he knew about trolls and ogres, begged them not to go through with it, pleaded with them to turn around and come back later with either the elf king or the fairy queen, who might have a better chance of persuading the sentinels to let them pass.

But all to no avail. Mark, especially, was determined to press on. The young warrior was anxious—too anxious, perhaps—to prove himself. And the others, the two magicians, followed Laura's lead without question. And Laura was adamant that they press on as well.

The one thing the dragon couldn't help them with was where the passage eventually emerged on the other side of the towering mountains. Somewhere in the giants' land was all he could tell them. There was one account that it actually emerged in the giants' hall, but that was only a vague rumor, a whisper of a legend from a valiant warrior who made the perilous passage and returned to tell about it.

"Good luck," the dragon said almost tearfully as the four of them walked quickly into the shadows of the passage. "I'll be at the top, waiting for your call."

"It won't be long," Laura called out over her shoulder. "Don't you worry."

"Don't worry, don't worry," the dragon mumbled as it lifted its heavy heart off the ground and began the long ascent to the top of the mountain range. "And just how am I supposed to manage that?"

It was a gloomy, dank passage. But it had one thing in its favor, at least. It seemed to be straight and even, although how long that would last was anyone's guess. But, for now, the walking was easy. Some twists and turns, but mostly it was a simple matter of looking ahead to make sure you didn't trip.

Mark, by request, led the way. He was followed by Kathryn, then Tara, and Laura brought up the rear. They stayed close together, close enough so they could touch each other at any given moment.

The path slowly widened as they walked. It wasn't long, in fact, before the light from their torches barely reached to the sides of the tunnel.

After almost four hours of steady walking into the heart of the mountain, Laura called a halt. She gathered the other three around her before whispering the fear she'd carried silently for the better part of an hour. "Have any of you heard them?"

"Heard what?" Mark whispered back. "I've been concentrating on the path too hard to pay attention to the stray sounds."

"I have," Kathryn said quickly. "About an hour ago. That's when I first started to hear them."

Laura nodded. "Well, then they must be real."

"What?" Mark hissed.

"Footsteps," Laura said simply. "Someone, or something, has been following us. And if I'm not mistaken, there are more than one."

Mark gripped the broadsword Laura had provided him with tightly and pulled himself up to his full height. "I'll defend you," he said through gritted teeth. "Rest assured, they'll have to come through me first."

"I appreciate your bold words," Laura said acidly, "but what we really need right now are calm, cool heads, not someone about to march off half-cocked."

"He's just trying to protect us," Kathryn interjected. "What's wrong with that?"

"Nothing at all." Laura sighed. "But it won't do us much good in here, not if we're outnumbered."

"We need to think of a spell," Tara said reasonably, settling the argument before it had a chance to grow. "We need a shield of some sort."

"Exactly," Laura said. "That's what I had in mind myself. And I've already put the spell together in my head."

"Then go ahead," Mark whispered angrily. "Put up your stupid shield."

"Now, now, there's no need to get all huffy," Laura said smugly, unbelievably happy at the role reversal. It was nice, for a change, to be able to put a man in his place, even if it was only a kid like Mark who seemed nice enough.

"Go on," growled Mark, who was finding it very difficult indeed to keep from disliking Laura.

"All right. *Reg bheu skel*," she murmured. "There, that should do it."

Nothing tangible happened, but when Mark reached out his hand, a faint warmness surrounded the group.

"Wait a minute," Kathryn said. "I know what the first and last word mean, but what does—"

"Don't!" Laura cut the girl off. "Don't say the word aloud, not unless you mean it. The shield is up for good. We mustn't bring it down in here again, not for any reason."

"But I didn't have a picture in my mind of what I wanted," Kathryn protested. "I wasn't about to ask the word to accomplish anything."

"I know, but I want to be on the safe side. Okay?"

"Okay," Kathryn said morosely. "But what does the word mean, though?"

"It's a combination word, meaning the shield will protect us both physically and mentally," Laura said almost clinically. "It's the original root of the word *psychic*."

"It must be nice to have a memory like yours," Kathryn said.

"It is," Laura quipped. "Let's get moving again. But everyone needs to stay inside the shield. Once out, I'm afraid you may be forced to stay out. Permanently."

Although they were all, with the possible exception of Mark, mortally afraid of whatever was just behind them, they continued their trek with lighter hearts, secure now in the knowledge that their shield would likely protect them.

Gradually, as the minutes dragged into hours, even Mark was able to pick up the footsteps because they were growing louder. It was obvious, now, that they were being shadowed by quite a few of whatever they were.

"What I can't figure," Mark said over one shoulder to Kathryn, "is where they're coming from. I don't see any openings above us or in the walls of this tunnel, but there are definitely more of them now than there were before."

"Perhaps they're hiding as we pass them?" Kathryn suggested.

"No, that's not possible. I'm keeping a sharp eye out for anything like that. And I haven't seen a thing. I'm positive of that."

Yet even as he said this, Mark noticed a faint glow off in the distance. It was a funny light—mostly green and red, with just a little white. And it didn't appear that they had any choice, either. They'd have to march directly past the room.

Fortunately, the passage widened as they approached the eerie light. At Laura's command, the group moved over to the left side of the path, away from the light that appeared to originate from somewhere on the right side.

Unconsciously, they all slowed as they approached it. Not surprisingly, the footsteps behind them, seemingly just out of sight of their torchlight, also slowed.

Mark, the first to actually see into the room, gasped in wonder. "Who would have believed...?"

"But what is it?" Kathryn whispered at his side.

"If I don't miss my guess," Mark whispered back, "I'd say it's a troll horde. But I'd never thought such a thing was possible."

They found themselves looking into a huge vaulted room that literally overflowed with precious gems, gold and silver, exquisite tapestries, and ancient weapons. At least, that's what they could see from where they were standing. Who knew what else lay buried inside the room under that pile of treasure?

The light came from the brilliance of the gems, which shone by themselves—the green from emeralds, the red from rubies, and the soft white from the diamonds.

Mark took a faltering step forward to get a closer look at the treasure.

"Stop!" Laura hissed at him. "Don't take another step."

"But I just want to see..."

"Not another step, do you hear?" Laura said fiercely. "I don't want you stepping outside the shield. Once outside it, you won't be able to step back in. The shield would physically prevent it. And I'm not dropping the shield in here, not now."

"Oh, you're so dumb," Mark said, about to remind her of the dragon's words, that the trolls were immune to magic and that if this was, indeed, a troll's horde, then most likely there were trolls nearby. But he thought better of it. No sense in scaring them. "Anyway, there might be something in there we could use, so I think I'll have a look..."

"No!" Kathryn tried to restrain him.

But Mark simply shrugged her off, stepped outside the shield, and strode boldly across the passage toward the treasure.

"Oh, foolish human," a sepulchral voice said, filling the passage. It appeared to come from the vaulted room. "You should not have done that."

"Who are you?" Mark called loudly. "Where is your voice coming from?"

"Why, right before you, in front of this room where I have stood guard for countless centuries, of course." The voice chuckled. "Can't you see me?"

"No, I can't." Mark gripped his broadsword again. "And I'll ask you again. Who are you?"

"The guardian," the voice said simply. "And you should have heeded the three magicians who have accompanied you."

"How do you know they're magicians?"

"I know a great deal. Regretfully, though, very few pass this way and benefit from my great knowledge. Alas, such is the hardship of my eternal vigilance."

"What did you mean, earlier, when you said I should have listened to the magicians?" Mark demanded.

"Quite simple," the voice said. "You should have remained within the shield they offered you."

"But the trolls?" Mark asked. "They're immune to magic?"

"Yes, they are, to a certain point. Had you attempted to attack them or to seize anything from the room, you would not have been allowed to. But, likewise, they could not have penetrated your shield. They still can't. You'd have been safe behind it. But seeing as how you've stepped outside it and approached this room…"

Rough hands groped at Mark's side. It was all he could do to stifle a scream. He managed to wriggle free, though, and backed up a couple steps. Pulling the broadsword from its sheath, he held it out in front of him.

"Mark!" Laura called out to him. "What's happening?"

"Hands," Mark told her, his teeth clenched. "Something tried to grab me."

"Calm yourself," the silky voice said. "They were only trolls, to keep you from fleeing until I have finished with you."

"Finished with me?" Mark desperately attempted to keep the fear out of his voice. "What do you mean?"

"Why, until I've feasted on your soul, of course," the voice declared with obvious delight. "And by the looks of it, yours should be quite a tasty meal. A very tasty morsel. Delicious, in fact. I intend to savor it."

Kathryn screamed at the top of her lungs, nearly knocking Mark down with the force of it. Mark looked over at her, only to see the young girl collapse in a heap against the far wall and press both hands against her ears.

"Don't worry, Kathryn," Mark said bravely, not sure whether his words could reach her. "I don't intend to let this hyena feast on anything."

The voice gave a sinister chuckle. "Oh, there's no use in putting up a bold front. Courage and bravery won't help you now. I intend to devour your soul, and I doubt whether you have what it takes to stop me."

"Hold on." Laura's voice was firm and unwavering. She considered whether to risk dropping the shield to let Mark back in but quickly realized she couldn't risk it in the presence of this foul creature. "What can he do about it? It sounds to me like there's something you're not telling us."

"Yes." The voice sighed. "There is something."

"Well, what is it?" Laura snapped. "Be quick about it. We don't have all day."

"You're a feisty one, aren't you? You wouldn't care to step outside that shield, would you? No, I suppose not. Too bad, though. I haven't seen such an appetizing soul pass this way in quite some time, not since…"

"Get on with it!" Laura fought to keep the cold shivers out of her voice. "What can he do?"

"All right," the voice said, irritated now. "He has to answer three questions. If he answers them correctly, he can help himself to my riches. If he doesn't, then he won't be allowed to pass and I receive the honor of feasting on his courageous, fickle soul this fine day."

"Three questions?" Laura swallowed her repulsion. "That's about as corny as anything I've ever heard."

"I know," the voice said, "but there's nothing I can do about it. I have my orders, you know, straight from Beelzebub himself. It's pretty standard. We have to give you some chance. If it were up to me, I'd just end the farce right now and take the boy."

"Are we allowed to help him answer the three questions?" Laura asked.

"Oh, I suppose." The voice sounded tired and bored. "Not that it will help him in the least. You won't even be able to answer the first question, much less all three."

"Has anyone ever answered them right?" Tara asked timidly.

"A prince once came close to answering the first question, if I recall," the voice told Tara. "By the way, would you care to try your hand, little one? The last few souls have been rather rough on my digestive tract. Yours would certainly soothe my…"

"Be quiet!" Laura shouted. "Just ask the first question."

"As you wish," the voice rumbled. "Who are you?"

"Ego," Laura said without hesitation. "Go on to the second."

The voice paused for a very long time. And when it spoke again, it held a hint of anger. "Very good, indeed," it said. "Perhaps I underestimated you. I think I would like the boy to answer the remaining questions."

"Not on your life," Laura said firmly. "You said we could help him, and that's precisely what we intend to do."

"Only if I allow it," the voice said.

"You've already allowed it," Laura fired back. "Now ask the second question or we'll be on our way."

"You will *not* be on your way until I say so!" the voice roared, causing the very walls around them to shake. "Now, because I am such a nice fellow, I'll allow you to help him one more time. But, if by some miracle you answer this, he must defend himself on the third and final answer."

Laura crossed her arms. "I'll agree to no such thing."

"You have no choice in the matter!"

"Just ask the second question," Laura demanded.

"What is the original sin?" the voice bellowed.

Laura snorted. "I thought you said these were tough. It's pride, of course, or hubris. A cardinal sin you seem to be completely familiar with, I might add."

When the voice spoke again, a chill swept through the passage. "You are fortunate," it said, obviously speaking to Laura, "that someone has graced you with a mantle of protection in this world. I regret that you choose to cower behind that powerful cloak of magic. I would dearly love to challenge you openly, without any of these encumbrances."

Laura chose to ignore its challenge. "Are you going to ask the third question or not? We *really* don't have time to dally here, you know."

"Silence!" the voice said. "I will ask it in due time, but you may not answer it. Only the boy this time."

"Coward," Laura taunted. "You're afraid of me, aren't you? You're afraid I'll get it right."

"I fear nothing!" the voice rumbled. "But no one from your own world has ever passed this way before."

"You've grown fat and lazy, then," Laura said with no small amount of scorn. "Those questions might stump everyone in this world, but there are thousands who can answer it where I come from. You'd find slim pickings in my own world."

"Oh, I'm *quite* sure I could find several million ignorant souls to gnaw on, even in your own world," the voice said smoothly. "I doubt that most have the appetite for knowledge that you do."

"Quit stalling," Laura insisted, "and ask the last question."

"What two things do men hold most dear and around which their world revolves?" the voice asked without preamble. "And the boy alone must answer it."

"No, I refuse…," Laura began.

"The boy!" roared the voice. "Or else I begin the feast at this very minute."

"Let me try," said Mark, who had stood in awe while Laura challenged this ghastly creature.

"But I know the answer," Laura protested.

"The boy will speak for himself," the voice said.

Laura bit her lip, unable to decide whether it was worth the risk to call out the answer. Because she was *certain* she knew the answer. "Women are included in that question as well, you disgusting creature," she said finally. "Not just men."

"As you wish. I was referring to men in the whole sense of the word."

"I know exactly what you meant," Laura said coldly.

"I think I know the answer," Mark said quite suddenly. "It seems fairly obvious to me."

"Answer then," the voice whined. "I'm hungry."

"First, it seems to me you have to protect your own hide," Mark said uneasily.

"That's right, Mark," Laura said, surprised at Mark's intuition. "That's the second half of the libido—self-preservation. Now the first part should be quite easy for you, considering that you're a young man with natural urges…"

"Silence!" the voice roared.

But Mark had already picked up on Laura's hint. "Of course. It would have to be, you know, wanting to be with a girl, wanting to have a family and protect it and…"

"That's it!" Laura said happily. "Preservation of the species, the first half of the libido. Now, let's hit the road."

"Not so fast," the voice commanded.

But Laura was already hurrying the group along the path again. Mark quickly followed in their wake, his knees trembling horribly. Without Laura's help, he might, even now, be on his way down that creature's gullet.

"I didn't say you could leave!" the voice called out after them. "Come back here! Did I say just three questions? I really meant four! You haven't answered all my questions…."

But the three magicians had already vanished around a bend in the passageway and begun to run from the voice, holding hands, as fast as their legs could carry them. And Mark wasn't far behind.

8

* * *

DESCENT TO HELL

Jon discovered it was all but impossible to explain what cocaine was to Lucas and Maya. Peg, of course, knew precisely what it was. But he chose not to judge, as usual. Jon's business was his own and no one else's as far as the horse was concerned.

If anything, Peg was amused by Jon's own fantasy about the drug. He was especially tickled about Jon's fervent, almost religious, belief that he wasn't addicted to the white powder simply because it had no physical stranglehold on him.

"But I haven't suffered any real withdrawal since I've been here," Jon said, pleading his case. "Don't you see?"

"Is that so?" the horse said over his shoulder.

They were seated, again, with Maya perched near the horse's ear, Jon forward on his back, and Lucas behind him. They'd been the last to leave the council hall, for the simple fact that they had no idea where to find the centaurs, which roamed freely as a tribe throughout the Great Plains. They had spent the morning mapping out strategy based on where Peg thought the likeliest places to find them might be.

"Yes, that's so!" Jon snapped, irritated at himself because he couldn't make the horse understand that he simply was *not* addicted to cocaine.

"Your mind's as sharp as a hunting knife, is it?" the horse asked sarcastically. "Cool as ice? Clear as a mountain stream?"

"Yes, all of those and more," Jon growled. "My mental facilities are all in fine working order."

"You've recovered, then, from the somnambulant, almost catatonic, state I found you in at the spring of Hippocrene?"

"Of course. That was a fluke. I have no idea what happened to me there."

"And you're satisfied with the way you acquitted yourself before the fairies?"

"Yes!" Jon almost shouted. "Of course I'm satisfied. I managed to get myself off the hook, didn't I?"

"I suppose the fact that both Maya and Lucas came to your aid had nothing to do with—"

225

"What are you trying to say?" Jon interrupted hotly. The way the stupid horse dodged and skirted things was maddening.

"Nothing. Forget it. Let's just drop the entire matter," Peg said.

"We will not!" Jon insisted indignantly. "I get the feeling that you're trying to tell me something, and I don't think I like the message at all."

"You're the one with the superb mental faculties, not me," the horse protested. "I suffer under all sorts of delusions and pretenses, the least of which is that I'm a rational creature who knows what he sees when he sees it."

"There you go again!" Jon shouted. "For once, would you just say what you have on your mind?"

"Oh, it's not important," Peg said lightly, almost nonchalantly. "By the way, have you ever noticed that you tend to let others lead you around by the nose?"

Had they been anywhere but nearly a mile above the earth, Jon would have stomped off or, worse, stood his ground. But, fortunately for him, Maya stepped between the two of them.

"That will do, Peg," she whispered in the horse's ear. "There's no need to humiliate him. Let the boy choose what he wants to do with his life. It's no concern of yours."

"Oh, I suppose." Peg sighed loudly. "It's just that I hate fuzzy heads."

"Whose head is fuzzy?" Jon demanded.

"Oh, be *quiet*," Maya said, thoroughly exasperated with Jon by now. "Can we get on with this search? We are trying to find the centaurs, aren't we? If you want to numb your mind—you did say that white powder was an anesthetic, if I recall—then that's perfectly all right with us. It's your life."

"But…"

"No buts," Maya said sharply. "I'm deathly tired of the subject, and I don't want to hear another word about it. What I want are suggestions about what we can do in the event we don't find the centaurs right away."

* * *

As it turned out, their luck was absolutely rotten. After four days and nights, they finally arrived at the heart of the Plains. Jon was amazed at the vastness. The flat, barren earth seemed to stretch off into eternity. The enormity of their search began to overwhelm him.

They visited all of the centaurs' haunts known to Peg. They were simply not to be found. In fact, no one had seen the centaurs for quite some time, several decades even.

"That's odd," is all Peg had to say.

"Yes, I wonder where they could have gone to," Maya said.

"Didn't you tell me once that the centaurs were creatures of knowledge, that they would go to almost any lengths in search of new experiences to expand their cerebral horizons?" Jon asked.

Maya nodded. "Yes, that's true. But how does that help us?"

"It seems to me that if they've exhausted almost everything, we'll have to think of a place where they might have gone, a place where they would drop from sight and where they wouldn't be seen by anyone for years and years."

"Oh, no," Peg groaned.

"What's wrong?" Maya asked, worried.

"I think I know," Peg said. "Chiron used to tell me about it all the time."

"The Chiron who tutored Achilles, Hercules, and Asclepius?" Jon asked, amazed that the same ancient names from his own world, the Earth, kept coming up over and over in this place. Perhaps they had stumbled, after all, into the Otherworld of the King Arthur legends.

"The very same," Peg answered.

"Who's Asclepius?" Lucas asked.

"The god of medicine," Jon said quickly. "So what did Chiron tell you?"

"You *really* don't want to hear this," Peg said.

"Go on," Maya prompted.

"Hades," the winged horse said simply. "He never really took it seriously, but Chiron used to talk of trying to visit Pluto's palace just for the challenge."

"Come on." Jon snorted. "You can't be serious?"

"I'm afraid he's very serious," Maya said. "I don't think Peg would joke about something like that."

"So are you suggesting that we just drop in on Hell and wander around in search of the centaurs?" Jon's tone dripped with sarcasm. "Assuming such a place really exists, that is."

"Oh, it exists," Peg said. "I wouldn't fret about that too long."

"But it's sheer madness," Jon protested.

"Yes, it is that," Maya said thoughtfully, "but what will we do if we find we have no choice? If someone can tell us, in fact, that is where they've gone and where they've been for decades?"

"What is Pluto's palace?" Lucas asked suddenly. "And where is it?"

"Pluto, or Hades as he is sometimes called," Jon explained patiently, caught in his element, "is the god of the underworld. Somewhere in that nether region—probably in a wasteland along the River Styx, if I had to make a guess—is his home, known as Pluto's palace. It has quite a few gates, and it's supposed to have all sorts of guests.

Apparently, Pluto was quite a host. But no one from the land of the living has ever tried to visit there. For obvious reasons, I would think."

"Which is why Chiron always wanted to visit the palace," Peg noted. "The quintessential morgue of knowledge, he used to call it."

"But you can't be serious," Jon said to Peg. "We're not really considering a jaunt down the Styx to see if we can find Pluto's palace, are we?"

"You tell me. If that's where the centaurs have gone, what choice do we have?"

"Not much," Maya agreed, "unless we want to abandon our search and return to the land having failed our task."

"We don't even know if that's where they've gone," Jon argued.

"Oh, we can find that out quite easily," Peg said cheerfully.

"Would you mind telling me how?" Jon said, afraid his terror was all too evident to everyone else.

"The gatekeeper to Hades is an old acquaintance," Peg said casually. "He'll know whether the centaurs have passed through the gate on their way to the palace."

"Cerberus, the three-headed dog, is an old friend?" Jon asked incredulously.

"An acquaintance," Peg corrected him. "Not a friend."

"But no one who enters through the gate ever leaves again," Jon said, trying a new tack. "At least, no one living."

"Not true," Peg said easily. "That's an old wives' tale. I wouldn't say it's exactly *easy* to return, but Pluto runs the show down there and he can bring us back up if he feels like it. And, if I do say so myself, we are on speaking terms, although I wouldn't say Pluto's the cheeriest of the gods."

"Well, it's at least worth asking Cerberus whether the centaurs have passed his way," Maya said. "We can decide then what we want to do."

* * *

Cerberus, however, was in a foul mood. One of his heads had kept the other two up all night. In fact, it had been weeks since all three had gotten a good night's sleep.

The reason was simple. Even the underworld had heard of what was happening in the land. And the *last* time great doings were afoot in the world, Cerberus had been humiliated when Hercules had picked him up and carried him from Hades as his twelfth and final task.

"And now they say there's a new Hercules in the land, or someone very much like him," one of the dog's three heads growled miserably to Peg.

"Oh, it's all right, Cerb," Peg soothed. "He won't be coming this way. Don't worry about that at all."

"Easy for you to say," Cerberus snarled. "Anyway, what in Pluto's name do you want down here? Whatever it is, you can't have it."

"Now, now," Peg said, doing his best to mollify the creature, "it's a simple request. We'd like to visit your boss at his palace."

"No! You can't," Cerberus roared. "You know the living aren't supposed to come this way. I'm not about to change the rules just for you."

Jon, Lucas, and Maya cowered some distance away from the dog. Despite Peg's assurances that he really was pretty harmless unless you tried to pass by him without his permission, they chose to keep their distance from the famed hound of hell.

Hades, it turned out, had been easy to find. A wide path, paved with good intentions, had led right to it. But it was the gloomiest, nastiest, foulest place Jon had ever seen, a ghastly mixture of graying light, stale air, and strange sounds. It reminded him quite a bit of a Saturday night fraternity party.

"Would you like some cake, my friend?" Peg asked the dog with a sly smile.

The dog howled in agony. "Not that! How many times must I endure that absurd question? Ever since Virgil spread the notion far and wide that you could get past me by offering me a bit of cake."

"I was only kidding, friend," Peg said gently. "We're really here on another matter entirely."

"Well, why didn't you say so in the first place?" the hound sneered. "Name it and be on your way."

"Have the centaurs been this way recently, say, in the past several decades?"

"Yes, they have. Now, go back where you came from before I decide to dine on your scrawny carcass tonight."

"You let them through?" Peg persisted. "I thought you said the living weren't allowed to come this way?"

"I said they aren't allowed to, as a rule. But rules can be broken. And of course I let them pass. What choice did I have, with Pluto standing right here as they asked?"

"Pluto himself was with them?"

"Isn't that what I just said? Are you deaf as well as a cousin to the jackass?"

Peg ignored the insult. "So it's possible Pluto might have taken the centaurs to his palace?"

"Possible, yes."

Peg turned on his hooves and hurried back to the other three. "The centaurs have passed this way, with Pluto."

"Then it's obvious they managed to con Pluto into taking them to his palace." Maya shook her head. "They were always pretty resourceful."

"So what do we do?" Lucas asked, afraid of the answer. He didn't like this place, not at all.

Maya sighed. "I think we have no choice. We'll have to follow them or turn back. I think, under the circumstances, that anyone who wants to can remain behind. There is no dishonor in refusing to enter through the gates to Hades."

But no one took her up on her offer, though both Jon and Lucas were sorely tempted. Jon liked the place even less than Lucas. It seemed like the incarnation of some of his worst nightmares.

It was Lucas who asked the obvious question. "How do we get past that dog? He doesn't exactly look friendly."

"Oh, he's harmless enough," Peg said. "Just don't offer him any cake or mention Hercules."

"Perhaps we can bribe him?" Jon couldn't believe he was actually trying to enter a place he'd once snidely referred to as a figment of his imagination.

"What he really needs is a good night's rest," Peg hinted. "Offer him that, and I think he'll let us pass by."

"A good night's sleep?" Jon asked.

"Sure, why not? Anyone can lose sleep over a job, even the hound of hell. We all have our little problems we have to overcome."

"If you insist. After all, he is your friend," Jon said, putting the spell together in his head. "But has anyone ever told you that you run with a strange crowd?"

"I know," Peg agreed mournfully. "And, let me tell you, it's corrupted me terribly."

9

***

COURAGE OF A DIFFERENT SORT

The orc city seemed impenetrable to Samson. Gandy had been right. The path led right through the heart of it.

But Regis absolutely refused to give up the search. "What we need is a diversion," he whispered, "something to draw all of them away from the city so we can slip through quickly and out the other side."

The four of them were perched behind a huge boulder that had broken off and fallen to the ground from above, a vantage point that gave them an almost unobstructed view of the dismal, foul-smelling city. Orcs weren't known either for their social graces or their hygiene.

Their homes were mere caves crudely carved out of the sides of the rock that rose up on either side of the path. To pass through the city, they'd have to walk directly past the homes on either side of the path.

"Forget it," Samson said. "It's hopeless. Let's just turn around and try to find a more reasonable—"

"I have an idea," Serena murmured. The others glanced at her. The elven girl's eyes were looking directly above her. Dimly, they could see what she was looking at—a huge, sloping outcropping of rock that quickly became a ledge of sorts as it approached the orc city and disappeared from view.

It was from there that the boulder of rock they were now cowering behind had tumbled, for it appeared that there were quite a few loose boulders up there, just waiting to crash down on them.

"No," Regis said, quickly realizing what she was considering. "First, you won't be able to scale that. And, second, there's no guarantee it would draw everyone from their homes."

"Not true," Gandy corrected him. "We both know the orcs go everywhere as a group. They react like a herd of skittish cattle. They'd pile out of their caves to see a rock slide so fast we'll barely have enough time to react and slip though the city."

"But she'll be stranded up there," Regis said angrily. "And if they see her up there, she won't have a chance at all…"

"*We* won't have a chance," Samson corrected him.

"I don't see any other choice," Serena said quickly. "And I think it can work. As soon as I've started the rock slide, I can scamper along that ledge and drop down on the other side of the city. I'm the only one of us capable of doing this."

"You're assuming the ledge runs all the way to the other side," Regis argued.

"We'll have to take that risk," she said.

"It's madness. And as your king, I forbid it."

Serena didn't like the decision, but she wasn't about to question her king. Regis's word was final as far as she was concerned.

Which didn't sit too well with Samson. "So what's your bright idea?" he asked the elf king.

Regis slowly unsheathed a silver dagger and began to pull the oaken bow, slung across his shoulder, over his head. "If we can't slip past them, we'll take them on directly. There can't be more than a few dozen of them." He pulled an arrow from his quiver and notched it in his bow.

Samson and Gandy glanced at each other. Surely he wasn't serious? That was the unspoken thought that passed between them.

"I think we should let Serena try to scale the wall." Samson placed one hand on Regis's bow and the other on the arrow. "That's more sensible than what you have in mind."

"Well, who put you in charge?" Regis said with malice.

"No one, but there's no need to wage a war if we don't have to."

"I don't like orcs," Regis muttered darkly.

"Neither do I. So let's just leave them behind and be on our way," Samson said, wondering if he wasn't missing something here. Regis's personality had changed so abruptly it was almost frightening.

Serena had risen to her feet and placed a hand on the wall. It would just take a word from her king and she'd begin the climb. Regis looked from Samson, to Gandy, and then to Serena. It was obvious he was outnumbered three to one.

"I don't like her risking her neck like this," he said angrily. "I don't like it at all."

"You know she's the only one who can scale that wall." Gandy kept his eyes low.

"I know that!" the elf king shot back.

"So let me get it over with, Regis," she pleaded. "Please?"

Regis closed his eyes, in obvious pain. "All right, but I warn you. I'll kill every one of them with my bare hands if they so much as lay a hand on you."

But Serena was already on her way up the wall. Samson couldn't believe how quickly she managed it. She seemed to find the handholds with ease, almost without hesitation. In fact, it was only a matter of minutes before she'd disappeared over the ledge and scampered away from them, in the direction they'd just come.

"All right," Samson said, "we need to be ready to run when the orcs come streaming past us."

"I know that!" Regis viciously jerked the bow back over his head. "But I'm not running away like some coward. I'm keeping my eye on her."

"We know that," Gandy soothed. "You haven't placed her in danger because you were cowardly…"

"Oh, be quiet!" Regis snapped sullenly. "You talk too much."

It happened almost before they were ready, though, despite Samson's warning. Serena must have found the right place to loosen some of the boulders, because no sooner had one or two tumbled down than dozens piled down right after.

Regis kept his eyes riveted to the ledge, largely ignoring the supremely ugly, flapping, squawking creatures who started to stream past their hiding place.

His vigilance was rewarded. Serena's shadowy form suddenly appeared above them. She was working her way cautiously along the ledge. None of the orcs had seen her yet.

"Let's go." Samson took the elf king's arm. "She'll be fine. We can't help her by waiting here any longer."

Regis swiftly followed Samson's lead. Gandy was already well on his way along the path, moving like a gust of wind. In his own mind, Samson sounded like a diesel truck rambling down a highway compared to Gandy.

They were through the city in moments. It was smaller than they'd imagined, perhaps a couple dozen homes at best. Gandy had already found a new hiding place—a natural crack in the side of the right wall. Regis and Samson slipped in beside him without a word.

They waited anxiously. The orcs were screeching in anguish over the calamity just a short distance away. As yet, none had returned to their homes, but it would only be a matter of time.

Regis, meanwhile, stared intently at a point on the ledge almost directly over the orc city.

Samson tried to follow his gaze but couldn't spot a thing. "What do you see?" he finally whispered to Regis.

"There's a gap in the ledge," Regis said. "I don't think she can jump without falling."

"How wide?" Samson asked.

"I don't know. Ten feet, perhaps."

"She can jump it, then," Gandy assured. "You know she's won every leaping contest we've ever held…"

"It won't matter if the ledge won't hold her weight," Regis said quickly. "Or if it's too narrow and she can't land on the other side."

Serena's shadowy form appeared at the gap in the ledge just then. Samson could barely see her in the dim light afforded by the orc city.

"She's going to try it," Regis said tightly.

Serena leaped. And the ledge on the other side gave way. A shower of rocks crashed to the ground. Somehow, Serena managed to grab hold of the edge with one hand, but it was obvious she wasn't going to hang on very long.

Samson was already running as fast as he could back along the path. In fact, he'd been on his way the moment Serena had tried to cross the gap in the ledge.

He reached the spot just as her hand slipped from the ledge. Wordlessly, Serena fell the 50 feet or so down the side of the rock wall into Samson's waiting arms. The force of her fall knocked Samson down violently.

Regis and Gandy were at their side in an instant to help both of them up. The orcs, meanwhile, had also seen the fall and were even now wailing at the top of their lungs and high-tailing it back to their city. Serena, miraculously, appeared to be stunned but unhurt. She all but collapsed into Regis's arms.

"Get her out of here," Samson said fiercely to Gandy. "Now! Before they're on top of us…"

"But…"

"She's in no condition to fight." Samson forced the three elves to turn away from him. "They'll eat her for dinner, so get out of here."

Regis wasn't about to budge. "We are not cowards."

"There's no time for this!" Samson shouted. "I can hold them off. I can give you enough time to get well away from here. I'll join you later."

Gandy, realizing the logic in Samson's strategy, had already turned and begun to urge Serena along the path. Regis hesitated, torn between his duty to protect his own kind and his duty to stand by Samson's side.

Samson took the choice from his hands. With a roar that sounded more like a lion than a man, he pivoted and charged at the orcs. He was still bellowing at the top of his lungs when he crashed into the first wave of the creatures, knocking them over like bowling pins.

As Regis stood there in dismay, Samson picked up first one orc and then another and tossed them like sacks of grain up against one wall. Regis almost pulled out his bow. But he knew he was as likely to hit Samson as one of the orcs.

In the end, reluctantly, the elf king turned and hurried after his two advisors, who were now out of sight. There was nothing he could do to help the mighty warrior, he reasoned. Regis knew his own abilities were stealth and cunning, not brute strength in hand-to-hand combat.

Samson gave them more time than they needed to escape. The orcs were terrified of him. Although they swarmed over him like bees on a hive, Samson simply would not go down. Like a mountain refusing to yield in the face of a rushing stream cascading over and around it, Samson stood tall, shucking first one orc from his shoulders, then another.

When too many of them piled onto him, Samson would roar with rage and crash into the wall, knocking some of the creatures off and bruising a few others.

In a strange way, it reminded Samson of a game he'd played with his friends as a child. He'd always been big for his age. Much too big, in fact. So his friends had developed a game: see how many it took to bring Samson to his knees. It usually took five or six of them and it was all in good, clean fun.

But this was obviously no game. Orcs tend to play for real. Samson had just one thing in his favor. Because the landslide had taken them by surprise, they were weaponless.

Not for long, though. Out of the corner of his eye, Samson could see several of them straggling to their homes to find their broadswords. It was time for a new strategy.

With a new bellow of rage, Samson crashed against a wall one more time, shaking a couple orcs from his back, then managed to whirl around once or twice, shaking a few more off, and then capped it off with a forward roll that shook the remaining orcs free.

He turned and, running at full speed along the path in the direction the elves had gone, tried desperately to remember one of the spells he'd been able to peruse in that cursed book. He urgently needed one of the spells that created weapons.

He knew the weapon he needed here—a halberd, which was a particularly nasty weapon of the fifteenth and sixteenth centuries. It had both an axe-like blade and a durable steel blade mounted on the end of a long shaft. It was perfect. He could thrust the blade to keep the orcs at bay and swing the ax if any came in too close. And it was a *big* weapon, the kind that only someone like Samson could wield.

The word seemed to pop into his head and he repeated it without wondering where it had come from. "*Bharda*," he muttered, the thing sounding strange in his mouth.

But it was even stranger still when the weapon crystallized in his hand while he was running at full speed. The weight of it almost caused him to tumble forward, but he caught himself at the last minute and staggered on.

On the other side of the city, near the point where they'd waited for Serena, he swiveled abruptly to face the orcs. A few had seen the halberd magically appear in his hands and had stopped dead in their tracks. Gang-tackling the warrior was one thing. Rushing madly at him only to have their heads lopped off was quite another.

Samson, meanwhile, found himself wondering if he had the stomach to kill. It seemed different here. These creatures, though faintly human in appearance, hardly seemed real. With their big ears, wild tufts of hair, and leathery skins, they looked more like overgrown chimpanzees than anything else. But killing was killing in either world and Samson, in his heart, wanted no part of it.

"Leave me alone!" he yelled at them, knowing full well that the orcs, who were advancing on him cautiously now, had no idea what he was saying. "I don't want to harm you!"

They kept coming, the ones in front brandishing crude broadswords now. Samson could see the fear in their eyes. They seemed to know they were marching to their own death. Others behind them might finish the hulk of a human off, but they would most likely succumb to the bite of the huge ax-like thing he was now carrying.

Samson gripped the end of the halberd firmly with his left hand and placed his right hand higher up on the shaft, halfway to the axe blade. "Don't do it!" he pleaded one more time, knowing it was fruitless.

"Why not?" came a guttural croak.

The question startled Samson so much he wasn't able to answer right away. But still gripping his weapon, he answered, "Because I don't want to kill any of you."

"You are the one who will die, foul human," the voice said with a harsh laugh. It came from the advancing horde, but Samson couldn't see which orc it belonged to. They all looked alike to him.

"Maybe. But quite a few of you will, too."

"So be it. Prepare to die," the voice said.

"Wait!" Samson urged. "Show yourself first. And tell me why you speak my language."

One of the orcs stepped forward. He was similar to the others but different in one respect: he wore a necklace around his shoulders. And if Samson wasn't mistaken, on that necklace were scalps. Samson couldn't tell if they were dwarf or human scalps, but he wore them proudly, as the Indians in America had once.

"The dwarves held me prisoner for a while," the orc croaked. "I learned these foul, nasty words from them out of boredom."

"Why were you their prisoner?" Samson demanded, almost afraid to hope that he could keep the conversation going long enough to buy the time he still needed to avoid a fight with these creatures.

The orc raised his dark head and bayed like a hound, the sound that erupted from his throat that of a mortally wounded animal. "I am their sworn enemy, that's why. And they wanted to study me."

"Study you?"

"To see why I hate them so."

"And why do you?"

"Because we always have. And we always will."

236

"That's all? That's the reason?" Samson asked, still simply buying time more than anything else. He barely heard the orc's answers.

"It is enough," the orc snarled. "They have killed many thousands of my people for centuries. My own wife lost her head to one of their bloodthirsty swords."

"I'm sorry," Samson said.

"I have avenged it." The orc sneered, holding up the scalp necklace fondly with one hand.

Samson tried a new direction. "I have no quarrel with you. It's between your people and the dwarves, so just let me go on my way."

"*You* challenged us," the orc hissed. "You invaded our homes. You disrupted our lives and threatened us with death."

"We had no choice," Samson said intently. "And we only wanted to pass, not threaten you. But your city lies directly on the path."

"Enough!" the orc screamed, pulling his sword in front of him. "No more talk. Prepare to die, human. You will be our supper tonight."

But Samson had bought enough time. He'd stalled long enough, or so he hoped. "Not if you don't catch me," he said almost gleefully.

Samson took a couple lunges and sweeps at them with the halberd, forcing most to recoil in horror and fall over each other to get out of the way, and then turned.

His plan was simple. He sprinted down the path, perhaps 50 yards, and then turned again to face the orcs who'd chosen to follow in his wake. He was relieved to see that half, and perhaps more, had chosen to remain behind. It amazed Samson how a little distance allowed the more cowardly of the orcs to conveniently remain behind.

Samson brandished the halberd again. When the goblins were close enough, he lunged again and swept the weapon back and forth in front of him. No one was fool enough to challenge it. When enough had gathered to make a charge, Samson turned again and sprinted up the path.

Samson's plan soon became apparent even to the dim-witted orcs. Quite a few dropped out of the tiresome chase. What did they care if the idiotic, cowardly human had no taste for combat but chose to play these foolish games instead?

In fact, after a half dozen of these bloodless sorties or so, only a handful of the orcs remained in the hunt. And even they were grumbling loudly as they labored to keep up with Samson, who hardly seemed winded. All the running he'd done as a wrestler served him in good stead here.

"Curse you," the orc who'd first spoken to Samson said loudly at the end of one of these mad dashes. "Why won't you fight?"

"Because you aren't my enemy," Samson said through still-clenched teeth. "There's no reason for me to kill you."

The orc growled and charged. But Samson had turned again and the orc was left with but air to wave his broadsword at. Only three orcs followed this time.

"Give it up," Samson said as they met again. "Three of you? That isn't enough to risk against the weapon I hold."

"I don't care," the goblin said and charged again. But he should have known better by now. Samson had already turned again.

There was simply one when Samson came to a halt again. The other two orcs had finally stopped in their tracks. They'd had enough. All that remained was the one goblin, the one who couldn't seem to shake his thirst for blood.

"I don't want your life," Samson said. "There is no dishonor in giving up the fight now."

"Coward!" The orc rushed Samson still a third time. But this time, instead of turning as the orc expected, Samson stood his ground. And with a ferocious swing of the battle ax, Samson knocked the broadsword from the hands of the very surprised goblin. Samson reached down quickly to pick it up.

"Now will you give it up?" Samson asked him, holding both weapons before him.

The orc hesitated, considering whether it was worth it to him to make his point by committing suicide. Evidently, it wasn't. The orc was hot-headed and blinded by hatred but not stupid. "Another day," he croaked. "Because, fool, you must return this way to leave." Then he turned away before Samson changed his mind and decided to run him through with the wicked end of the halberd.

Samson almost chuckled, a lightness in his heart, as he watched the orc trot back to his comrades. *Not exactly the way heroic contests are supposed to end,* Samson thought. *But, then, heroic contests always seem to end in someone's death. And who does that serve? Who really benefits from that?*

Samson turned his sturdy back on the orcs for the last time, dropping the crude goblin broadsword at his feet, and began the long, slow trek to find the fleeing elves.

10

***

ORCUS

The footsteps were still there. There was no mistaking that. When Laura called a halt, the footsteps stopped. When the group continued, they did as well.

And it irked Laura. They should have dropped off as they ventured farther from that horrid, sepulchral vulture. But the shuffling continued and still sounded like there were a lot of them.

"I'm beat," she said finally. "We need to call it quits for a while, get some sleep."

Mark nodded. "Great idea." His ordeal had sapped a good deal of his strength along with a good bit of his courage.

It was a miserable break, though. None of them had any idea how long they'd been walking, although it seemed like hours and hours, whether it was night or day outside, or whether it was, in fact, time to sleep. They simply collapsed against a cold, hard wall and tried to shut out the dank, gloomy darkness.

Tara tried to think of a field of blue-green sea grass. Kathryn fondly recalled a summer day by the gentle river. Laura grimly considered how it was possible, strictly within the boundaries of science, to be mixed up in such an absurd predicament.

Mark collapsed near them. Once away from the ghastly voice, Laura had offered to risk dropping the shield and allow Mark inside. Mark had refused. He said it wasn't worth the risk. After some protests, Laura had acquiesced. Mark's troubled sleep was replete with nightmares about what it might feel like to have someone gnaw on your soul for supper.

It was Laura who forced them to press on a couple hours later, driving them with the same iron-willed determination she drove herself. As they walked, Laura did her best to work the stiffness out of her legs and the chill out of her bones. She never wanted to spend a night on a cold floor again as long as she lived. "What I wouldn't give for a nice, hot cup of coffee right now," she said to no one in particular.

"What is that? Coffee?" Mark asked.

Laura thought for a moment. "Hot water sifted through crushed beans. But it's more than that. It's a drink millions of people have first thing in the morning where I come from."

Mark thought it sounded, well, silly. "Why don't you conjure yourself up a cup?"

"I would if I knew the spell." She laughed. "But I don't think it was in the spell book. At least not the one I saw."

"What spell book?" Kathryn asked. "You didn't have anything with you when we found you on the shore, in the boat."

"It was back in the world I came from." Laura rubbed two hands across her temples, something she did out of habit whenever she was trying to recall something with her photographic mind. "You know, if I didn't see it in that book, then that must mean it didn't come from my world…"

"What?" Tara and Kathryn said at the same time, then giggled at each other.

"Oh, never mind. It's not important." But Laura's mind raced to put the pieces of the puzzle together. This new piece told her something….

"Hey, let go of me!" shouted Mark, who'd been serving unofficially as their vanguard, walking several yards in front of the magicians.

The two burly monsters who now had the struggling boy neatly pinned between their massive shoulders had appeared out of nowhere. They were gruesome, hideous creatures. Graying complexion, lifeless eyes, clammy skin, they were the embodiment of walking, warmed-over death. They brought fearsome nightmares to Laura's mind.

"Where are you taking me?" Mark demanded with an edge of panic.

The monsters said nothing.

"Can't you get free?" Laura called as the three girls hurried after the monsters.

"No. You wouldn't believe how strong they are," Mark called back. "And cold."

"What do you mean?" Laura asked.

"Their hands are ice-cold. So cold it hurts." He tried again to struggle free, but the monsters hardly shifted position. They just squeezed a little harder.

"Ouch!" Mark roared. "That hurts! You stupid, idiotic, moronic…"

"We are none of those," one of the walking nightmares rumbled, his voice more a cavernous boom than a product of wind forced through lungs. "We are servants."

Mark struggled again. "Whose servants? And where are you taking me?"

"Orcus," said the creature. "And we are taking you to him."

"Orcus?" Laura muttered. "Orcus? I know that name. I remember it from somewhere, some book I read once on the Roman Empire. He was…"

"He is the last one," one of the creatures said.

"The last one?" Mark's heart couldn't take another encounter like the one he'd survived only hours earlier. "What's that supposed to mean, anyway?"

Neither creature answered. Apparently, they felt they'd said enough. Or too much.

"I know!" Laura shouted triumphantly, remembering the exact page of the book she'd read. "Orcus is the Roman god of Death."

"Oh, great," Mark said despondently. "Just what I need to make my day complete."

Laura completely ignored Mark's mood. "That's where the term for *ogre* came from. The fable was handed down from generation to generation until it finally became a generic term for man-eating monsters…wait a minute," she said uneasily. "That would mean the two of you are ogres, wouldn't it?"

"Yes," one of the creatures said, "it would."

Mark cursed loudly. "That's it. I've had it with this quest. I don't think I like it at all. I should have stayed with Samson and the elves. Because this certainly was a big mistake…"

"Oh, quit sniveling," Laura commanded.

"I'm not sniveling," Mark fired back. "I'm just sick and tired of people deciding I'm the main course for the evening."

"We do not want you," one of the ogres said.

"You don't?" Mark said, relieved.

"No. We want the great magician," the ogre mumbled.

"Laura? You want her?" Mark asked. "Then why are you dragging me along against my will like a sack of grain?"

"Because she will follow," the ogre answered. "And we cannot touch her. Not yet."

Laura stopped in her tracks. "I'm not going a step further, then. Now that I know what your little game is…"

"Then he will have to do," the ogre said simply. The monsters continued to walk.

Now it was Laura's turn to curse. "All right." She set her jaw. "I'll go."

"Don't worry," Kathryn said confidently. "We'll stand by you."

"Yes," Tara added. "We won't let anything happen to you. They'll have to overcome the three of us."

"The *four* of us," Mark corrected her, calling out over his shoulder. It sounded a little ridiculous, though, considering the ease with which the two ogres were manhandling him.

Laura struggled with the unreasonable fear settling around her. *There is nothing to be afraid of,* she tried to tell herself. *None of this is real. It can't be real. I can master even this. I can control even this environment.*

But she knew her hold was slipping. It would only take a gentle push, a touch in the right direction, and her mind would careen over the edge, plummet into the abyss of confusion and chaos she'd always carefully avoided.

The path they'd been following emptied into a huge, cavernous hall. Although it was ringed by torches, it was still dimly lit. Its size was simply too immense to be adequately lit by measly torch lights.

"We are here," one of the ogres said.

"Why did you grab me," Mark protested, "if you knew we'd arrive here eventually?"

"I wanted to meet her on my terms, not hers," a booming voice, doubly as loud as the ogre's, called out from across the hall.

They peered through the gray light. Laura could barely see the hazy outline of a massive chair of some sort.

"A throne? In here?" Mark asked, dismayed, when he realized what it was.

"And why not? If I am to be consigned to this dreary world, can I not at least own a few creature comforts?" said the throne's occupant, clearly the prototype of the two ogres who unceremoniously dumped their prisoner at the foot of the throne.

"You're Orcus?" Laura asked.

"As far as I know."

"The god of Death?"

"The very same," he answered solemnly. "And please don't confuse me with Pluto or Hades, as so many of your ignorant kind have done. I simply harvest souls. I'm not their caretakers. I leave that disgusting duty to the lords of the underworld."

"So what are you doing here?" Laura demanded. Somehow, she'd imagined the god of Death would be more imposing, more like the very worst nightmare she'd ever had in her life. Not a gray, spiritless blob of a monster who oozed self-pity more than fearsomeness.

"I wish I knew." Orcus stood and moved down off the dais toward the three magicians. "That's what I intend to find out from you. That's why I've asked my two minions to bring you here."

"Me?" Laura asked, shocked. "You want *me* to tell you why you're here?"

"Precisely," Orcus said.

The ogre of ogres, the ancient god of Death once feared beyond any other in the world of men and women, had the same grayness as his sycophants, the same lingering feeling of lifelessness, the same resigned air of finality. The only difference, a slight one, was that Orcus seemed animated by a restlessness the others didn't possess. It seemed out of place.

"So what can I do for you?" Laura asked, not sure whether to shudder in his presence or laugh her fool head off.

"Tell me why it is that I'm stuck in this dreary place. No one interesting ever passes my way anymore. The minds in this world aren't sophisticated. Not like yours, not like others where you have come from."

"What are you talking about?" Laura snapped.

"Don't you know?" Orcus said. "We, the gods of your world, I mean, have been consigned to this terribly dull world."

"It isn't dull!" Mark roared.

"Not to you," Orcus said peaceably, "but you haven't been to myriad worlds, as I have. You haven't reaped and harvested the kinds of minds I have on their way to Hades. You haven't conversed with scholars and geniuses before their souls entered Pluto's domain."

"Are you trying to say that you could once move freely between worlds? And that now you're…?" Laura began.

"Forced to reside in this dreary place." Orcus sighed. "Yes. That's exactly the predicament I find myself in—harvesting dull, uninteresting souls and sending them on their way to Hades without so much as a word of conversation."

Laura couldn't exactly feel sorry for him. But his plight did pique her curiosity. "You have no idea why you've been consigned to this world alone?"

"No, I know who is responsible. What I don't know is why."

"So who's responsible?" Laura asked, though she was certain she already knew the answer.

"The magicians, of course. The men and women of this world who were dabbling here in the arcane, mystical, and spiritual powers of the universe long, long ago."

"Tell me, these magicians…do we all look the same? Are we alike?"

"At one time—a very, very long time ago—you were quite similar in appearance. But while in your own world it is your minds that have advanced in a short time, the magicians of this world took thousands of years to advance their spirits in conjunction with their minds. And that led, of course, to a point where they could change their physical appearance at will."

"What? What are you saying?" Laura asked. "That these magicians are a far superior race than we are, than I am? That although they were once human, they are now something…*different?*"

"That is a most appropriate description," Orcus said. "Your mind is skilled indeed. As I have been led to believe."

Laura ignored the compliment. "So then we could be like they are, if…?"

"No. You are most emphatically not as they are. Not now. You must remember. They have had a *very* long time to develop. A very long time indeed."

"So where do you figure into all of this?" Laura asked.

"It's quite simple," the god of Death said. "I and all the other gods I know of are now forced to reside in this world and this world alone. What none of us know is why."

"So I ask you again," Laura prompted slowly. "What can I do for you?"

"Get me out of here," Orcus said simply. "You have no idea how bored I am."

11

∗ ∗ ∗

REDECORATING

Jon's sleep spell worked quite nicely. With Cerberus snoring peacefully at the gate to Hades, Jon walked casually to the banks of the River Styx, picked up a flat pebble nearby, and tossed it out across the black water. It skipped three times and then sank, just as a stone should.

"So this is it?" he muttered to himself. "This is the infamous River of the unbreakable oath that all the gods swear by? Looks pretty ordinary, if you ask me."

"They have rivers like this in your world, so dark?" asked Lucas.

"No, not really, although there are a few on their way to this darkness."

Styx, however, wasn't just a muddy brown from pollution. It was pitch black, blacker than the dead of night.

Jon knelt on the bank and gazed into the calm waters. Not even a ripple disturbed its surface, which now reflected his image as black marble would. He couldn't see a thing beneath its surface. "You know, every story I've ever read about this river says it's a hateful, foul thing."

"Just hearsay," Peg answered, "from frightened people who've never been here before."

"So how do we get from here to Pluto's palace?" Jon asked abruptly.

"Charon will take us," Peg said casually.

"The ferryman?"

"That's him."

"But don't we need coins, the ones we're supposed to have come here with over our eyes?" Jon wanted to know.

"He'll take us. Don't worry."

"But I thought he only took the dead, not the living, in his boat."

"I think he'll make an exception in this case," Peg said breezily.

"But why? I don't..."

"So very many questions," Peg chided. "It's because of you, of course. One such as you has not come this way since we have been in this world."

"Someone like me? Since you've been in this world?"

"All in good time," the winged horse said mysteriously. "Pluto is better suited for these questions than I am."

"What questions? I don't have any questions."

"You will," Peg said, turning to join the others who gathered farther up shore, "when it begins to dawn on you why you're here, what you can do for this world and, perhaps, what you can do for your own."

A long, flat boat drifted toward Maya and Lucas from across the river. The ferryman poled the boat forward slowly and deliberately.

"That's Charon?" Jon asked, deciding to hold onto the questions that crowded his cluttered mind.

"Yes, and he's looking especially glum today," Peg said with a laugh.

"I heard that," the ferryman called out from the middle of the Styx. "And you'd be glum, too, if you were forced to spend eternity on this cursed boat, ferrying dolts and nincompoops along in a boat that doesn't go any faster than this one does."

"Maybe he'd like an outboard engine attached to the rear," Jon said wryly.

"That might do for a start," Peg replied, deadly serious.

Jon shot him a strange look.

"Can you take us to Pluto's palace?" Maya asked him hopefully.

"Oh, I suppose so." The ferryman sighed. "I don't have anything better to do."

Lucas's knees trembled as he stepped gingerly into the boat. He knew enough about this particular boat to fear it more than a little. He quickly took his place at the front of it without a word.

Jon was determined to enjoy himself, or at least resigned himself to the fact that it all seemed so bizarre and absurd that there couldn't be anything to really fear. Maya and Peg stepped in confidently, of course, knowing full well where they were headed.

"And we're off," Charon said gloomily, pushing off from the bank, the boat moving slowly out into the placid river. "Hardly at the speed of light, though. But we'll get there. Eventually."

As they drifted down the black river, gray mountains started to rise on either side.

"Who lives up there?" Jon still gazed at the barren stretches of rock that loomed above them.

"No one," the ferryman said.

Further down the river, the mountains gradually tapered off into a vast, rolling forest of withered and gnarled trees, none of which had any leaves or any sign of life. "So who lives in there?" Jon asked.

"No one, you idiot," Charon answered.

The forest gave way to a stretch of steaming, boiling hot springs. The gray mist from the springs curled up into the gray sky and melted into nothingness. "Does anyone live there?" Jon asked timidly.

"No!" the ferryman said more forcefully.

Jon leaned forward and whispered into Peg's ear, "What's wrong with him?"

"You're asking moronic questions," the horse whispered back.

"But I just wanted to know if anyone lived in those regions?"

"No one *lives* anywhere here. They're all dead. Everyone simply exists. You should have figured that out on your own."

Jon sighed and turned his attention back to the landscape, determined to keep his mouth shut for the remainder of the voyage.

Which didn't last much longer. The river began to flow into a vast wasteland. It was an abysmally depressing sight. Everywhere Jon looked, on both sides of the river, was a land that appeared to have been scorched by the sun. Black ashes, flecked with gray, were scattered in all directions.

"We're here." The ferryman stopped at a point along the river that didn't appear to be marked by any distinctive feature. The wasteland stretched off into the gray horizon in both directions.

"So where's here?" Jon broke his vow to keep his mouth shut.

"Pluto's palace is that way." The ferryman pointed off to his right and then poed away from the bank to begin the long trek back up the river.

"Wait a minute," Jon called out after him. "How do we get there?" The ferryman didn't look back. A shroud of oppressive silence settled on the group.

"Come on," Peg said confidently, "I know the way."

"You do?" Lucas asked.

"Sure," the horse answered. "It's in the meadow of asphodels."

"The what?" Jon asked.

"I thought you knew your history of the gods," Peg said. "At least, you've always professed an expertise in that area."

"I do," Jon said hotly. "But I don't know what a stupid asphodel is."

"It's a plant like the narcissus, with pale white flowers," Peg clarified. "And Pluto's palace is squarely in the middle of a meadow of these flowers."

"Why?"

Peg gave Jon a very queer look. "Don't you know? Are you really that ignorant?"

"Look, I've just about had it with your constant nagging," Jon almost shouted. "Would you simply tell me what's going on here or not?"

"Calm down, boy," Peg soothed. "It's merely that it's such an elementary fact of life for all of us here...or at least for most of us."

"Get to the point," Jon demanded.

"Haven't you noticed something about this world? Now that you've been here awhile?"

Jon thought a moment. "Well, I do seem to keep bumping into people—gods, actually—that I'd only read about."

"And?"

"And they seem to be pretty much like what I'd read about."

"But nothing more than that? Just as you'd heard, or read, about?"

"Well, yes."

"That's the point," Peg said with some finality. "We are as we were created. Nothing more and, in some cases, even less."

"What, exactly, does that have to do with asphodels?"

"It has everything to do with asphodels," Peg said reasonably. "Pluto's palace is supposed to be in the middle of a meadow of asphodels, as the stories were written. And so it must be."

"That makes no sense."

"Maybe not, but that's the reality."

"Well. I don't believe it." Jon shrugged. "It's an absurd notion."

"As you wish," Peg said simply. "Shall we go, then?"

"Yes, and if you know the way, why don't we fly? If it isn't too much trouble?"

"Not at all."

"Which raises another question," Jon added. "Why didn't we just fly there from the start? Why did we have to take that ridiculously slow ride down the Styx with that morose ferryman?"

"Someone else made the rules that govern this world. So, you tell me."

* * *

The trip across the wastelands to Pluto's palace was about as uneventful as anyone could possibly imagine. There was nothing but gloom and ashes as far as the eye could see.

But the wan and cold wasteland eventually did give way to a pale, ghostly field of flowers, just as Peg had said. And, sure enough, topping a small hill in the center of the dreary meadow was a palace.

And what a palace! It had more gates, entrances, and portals than Jon could manage to count, each with its own unique, distinctive, individual fashion. Some round, some square, some oblong, some rectangular. Some with magnificent porticos, some with ornate doors, some with intricate and twisting passages leading up to them, some with nothing more than a step or two.

Peg landed lightly at one with a rather large portico. They walked somberly up the walkway, passing by huge white pillars, toward a door with the largest knocker Jon had ever seen.

The door itself appeared to be crafted from solid gold. It was inlaid with a silver trim around its edges. Rich jewels were studded throughout as well.

"Should I?" Jon asked the group, afraid to even lay a hand on the door, which would be worth a king's ransom in his own world.

"Please do," Maya said with a strange smile.

Jon carefully pulled the knocker back and let it drop. There was a loud noise outside as it connected, but no corresponding sound within. At least none Jon could hear. "What happened? I didn't hear anything."

"Maybe it doesn't work," Lucas offered. "Maybe we should try another door."

"No, this door will do as well as any other," Peg said.

"I'll try it again," Jon offered. The effort produced the same result. It was, without a doubt, the strangest door knocker he had ever seen. "I don't understand. It almost sounds like there isn't anything inside."

"There isn't," Peg said quietly. "At least, nothing any of us can place in our minds."

"Here we go again," Jon muttered. "What in Hades' name is that supposed to mean?"

Peg looked squarely at Jon to make sure the foolish, young cleric didn't miss his meaning. "No one that I know of has ever described the *inside* of this palace before. All anyone knows is that such a place exists, has quite a few entrances, and that Pluto always entertains a multiplicity of guests within."

"There have been no creators, apparently, willing to set the laws inside this place," Maya added. "Just the outside."

Jon's head began to ache terribly. "And who, may I ask, is a creator?"

"Why, you are, of course," Peg answered.

"I am? So I can help shape the inside of this place? Just like that?"

"No, not just like that," Maya answered. "But you can certainly start, with some of those spells you've apparently mastered."

"At least tell me one thing." Jon's eyes were still closed as he tried to imagine what the lord of the underworld would furnish his palace with. "Are the centaurs in there?"

"Of course," Peg said. "We just don't know where or what they're doing. But they are in there, with the other guests, whoever they are."

"And the centaurs are real?"

"Certainly," Peg acknowledged. "And why wouldn't they be?"

"No reason," Jon said miserably. "You wouldn't have any idea how I can accomplish this little feat, would you?"

Maya waved a hand. "None at all. You're the one with the power to create. Not us."

Jon considered his options for a very long time. If this was, in fact, possible, then he meant to make the most of it. First, he wanted the inside to reflect not a stuffy, ornate palace interior but the famed Elysian Fields—the legendary fields the Greeks had always referred to as the fields of ideal happiness that the dead came to live in.

"*Ker Elusion*," he said, smiling at the irony of it. The word for the Elysian Fields, in ancient Greek, came from the root of illusion. Supreme bliss seemed to be a state of illusion to them.

A magnificent aroma wafted from the interior of the palace, a smell of spring flowers and new grass, of bushes and trees after a rain shower. "That's done," Jon said and turned his mind to what he wanted next.

He thought of the centaurs. A magnificent library, the best and largest he could imagine, would do nicely. "*Ker taberna*," he said.

There was a sudden roar of approval from within.

"Sounds like the centaurs are certainly pleased," Peg said with a raised eyebrow.

"They *should* be," Jon replied haughtily. Now for something to give the place some spice and spunk. A crystal clear spring, a crisply flowing river, and a bubbling waterfall would serve that end. "*Ker spergh*."

A rushing, roaring sound filled the air, obviously coming from the crashing of water on the rocks below.

Now to get rid of this oppressive gloom, the dreary foreboding of this horrid underworld. For that Jon would need light and sunshine, bright enough to cheer everybody up but not so much that it blinded everyone. "*Ker legwh*," he said boldly, feeling grandly like God must have felt on the first few days.

"Now don't get carried away," Peg warned him.

"I'm not," Jon lied.

Of course, everyone would need food to eat. *Orchards, that's what we need,* he thought, almost immediately forgetting Peg's admonition. *Those would have seeds. The fruit from the trees would constantly replenish the food supply.*

"*Ker gher*," he said quickly. Mixed with the sweet smell of spring from the Elysian Fields within came the new aroma of sweet fruit, delightful and tantalizing.

Jon tried to consider what else they might need within and came away empty. "That should do for now, anyway." He folded his arms, pleased with himself.

"But how big is it?" Maya asked him.

"Oh, I forgot that, didn't I?" Jon laughed. "Well, let's not think small. That wouldn't do at all, would it? *Ker aiw*."

"So how big is it?" asked Lucas, who had watched in rapture as Jon created.

"As big as it needs to be." Jon reached up to knock on the door for the third and final time.

12

* * *

MORTAL COMBAT

Samson heard the great bellows long before he actually saw them. He could hear the wheeze on the long intake of air and then the roar as it rushed out to forge who knew what.

He'd jogged quite a ways, yet still hadn't caught up with the elves. He had skirted another goblin city, one set well back from the path this time, however. He wondered fleetingly if perhaps the elves hadn't been captured as they, too, attempted to make their way around the city. But after listening for sounds of conquest from the city, he gave up on the idea. The place was as quiet as a church on a weekday.

So he continued his trek in search of the elves. It seemed strange that they wouldn't have waited for him, but thinking about it wouldn't accomplish a thing.

He stumbled on the Minotaur's lair quite by accident. Of course, never seeing a Minotaur before, Samson had no way of knowing whose lair it was. But he recognized bleached bones when he saw them. And there were plenty of those scattered around the entrance to the foul-smelling cave.

Samson wouldn't have come upon the cave if he hadn't been monstrously thirsty. He'd wandered off the path, thinking he'd heard the rushing of water. But the rushing had been nothing more than the Minotaur's loud snoring as it wheezed.

The Minotaur was huge, almost twice as large as Samson. Its muscular torso, similar to an ape's, was covered entirely by coarse fur. It had the head of a bull with vicious, cruel horns it used to spear its victims.

Samson almost stopped breathing when he came upon it slumbering peacefully at the entrance to its nasty cave. For trussed up neatly nearby was Gandy. The elf was held fast to a boulder, his arms pinned completely to his sides by coarse ropes of some kind. Samson was about to rush in wildly, take the Minotaur on with his halberd, when Gandy caught his eye. The elf shook his head violently and tried to say something silently, mouthing the words so as not to wake the sleeping monster.

It took Samson several attempts to understand his words, but he was finally able to decipher them. "Find Regis," Gandy was trying to tell him. Brave words from someone who was about to become another's supper.

ELOHIM

But his command was easier said than done. Find the elves? Well, where were Regis and Serena? Why weren't they trying to rescue Gandy? It made no sense.

Samson turned reluctantly. He would give it half an hour. If he couldn't find the elves in that time, he was coming back to free Gandy. Or die trying, which was the likelier option. It didn't appear the Minotaur was accustomed to losing.

He set off at a fast run down the path, covering new territory as rapidly as he dared while searching for some clue of what had happened to the other two elves.

He'd have run smack into the manticore if he hadn't heard him arguing with Regis before he'd turned the corner at the bend in the path.

"You're a coward, do you know that?" he heard Regis say loudly. "Let me go and fight me like a man."

"But I am not a man," Samson heard the creature say, "and I have no need to fight you. You are vanquished already. And I shall enjoy feasting on your meaty haunches with so little effort involved on my part."

Samson couldn't believe what he was hearing. Fortunately, he'd heard the elf king in the nick of time. Regis's voice had neatly covered the sound of Samson's mad dash. It had given him time to come to a halt and approach more slowly.

It was all Samson could do to stifle a gasp when he peered around an outcropping of rock for his first glance at the legendary creature. The manticore was hideous. It had a lion's tawny body, the wings of a bat and the head of a man.

And it had both Regis and Serena pinned neatly beneath a huge boulder. The creature had obviously been out stalking prey—with its wings it could roam far and wide in search of its supper—and it had come upon the two elves.

Samson quickly reasoned that the manticore must have plucked these two from the ground and carried them away to his temporary feasting ground. Probably it was too much of a burden to carry both his victims back to his own lair. Obviously he meant to eat one of them here and carry a second back with him.

Gandy, left behind, must have doubled back to find Samson, figuring that he was his only hope to save the others, and run into the Minotaur. Samson cursed silently to himself, gripping the halberd until his knuckles were white. He'd have liked to have been there. Oh, how he would have liked that.

But, now, this called for a plan. He had not just one, but two, creatures to contend with. One, the manticore, appeared intelligent. Or at least intelligent enough to carry on a conversation with one of its victims. The other appeared to be somewhere at the other end of the scale. Why else would it simply fall asleep, secure in the knowledge that it could eat when it suited its fancy?

Samson knew he could rush the manticore and take his chances. Perhaps he could vanquish it with only some difficulty and still manage to make it back to Gandy in time. Yet it seemed doubtful. Doubtful? It seemed impossible that he could even survive the manticore's deadly claws in combat, much less come out of it unscathed and still be able to return to take on the Minotaur.

The half-formed plan jumped out at him. Samson seized at it like a drowning man grasping at a piece of driftwood and acted immediately.

"Hey, knucklehead, you forgot one!" Samson called out loudly, stepping out to challenge the manticore. He managed to glance over at the two elves. Serena was still out cold. Regis was struggling vainly to free himself from the crushing boulder.

The manticore turned his head casually, to face Samson. "What do you want?"

"I want you," Samson answered.

"Be gone with you," the creature growled. "I have my meals for the day. So leave, before I grow angry."

"So big deal," Samson said boldly. "What happens when you grow angry?"

"I crush pipsqueaks like you, that's what." The manticore sneered.

Samson found it tough to ignore the blood-stained beard on the creature's ghastly face. "You and who else, pea brain?"

The manticore rose elegantly off its haunches, the muscled lion torso preparing to spring into action. "I'm warning you. Another word and I make you my first meal."

"Such an idle boast." Samson laughed uproariously but gripped his halberd firmly nevertheless. "You're a riot."

The manticore sprang without another word, bounding once, twice, and then leaping high to pounce on the human as he had done on so many occasions.

But he had never contended with one so strong, so quick, or so attuned to hand-to-hand combat. Samson, ready for the attack, swung the halberd with as much force as he could muster. The axe bit into the side of the creature, crushing one wing.

Samson quickly retreated around the bend in the path as the manticore roared with pain, glancing down at its damaged wing. *Good*, Samson thought viciously. *It can't come at me from the air. It has no choice but to follow me across the ground now.*

True to form, the manticore followed. It wasn't about to let this human go now. In fact, it meant to finish Samson off slowly and then savor each bite as it devoured him while he was still alive.

Samson had other ideas. When the manticore turned the corner, still in a blind rage, Samson clubbed him over the head with the flat of the axe. The manticore staggered under the blow but didn't collapse. Far from it. The blow only dazed it for an instant.

Samson retreated again, running full tilt back up the path, away from the two elves. He had no idea if the plan would work. But it was the only one he had now, and he meant to give it his best shot.

The manticore followed easily but more cautiously this time. It had developed a healthier respect for the human, though still tempered with its own supreme confidence in its own abilities. Bounding along, it overtook Samson.

Samson swiveled again to face it. When the manticore didn't pounce right away, Samson began to back up along the path.

"What? Afraid of me now?" The manticore laughed.

"I'm afraid of nothing, least of all you." Samson smirked.

"I will teach you to fear, then," the manticore said and pounced a second time.

Samson, thanks to the creature's boast, was prepared for the attack. He plunged the sword on the halberd at the creature's other, undamaged wing, and pulled with all his strength as soon as he'd seen the weapon reach its mark.

The manticore had managed to swipe at Samson with one paw when it felt its tender membranes being torn asunder in its wing. With a terrible cry, it folded the wing and collapsed to the ground.

Samson, meanwhile, didn't stick around to see how much damage he'd inflicted. He turned and sprinted again up the path as fast as his legs could carry him. He knew he didn't have much time. He would have to reach Gandy, now, before the manticore had recovered sufficiently.

The Minotaur, roused by the sounds of the battle, was pacing back and forth before its lair when Samson arrived. It snorted ferociously when it caught sight of Samson and rushed immediately. Almost caught off guard by the sudden attack, Samson was barely able to parry it and dive-roll to one side.

He leaped to his feet, however, and turned to face the dim-witted Minotaur's second, blind attack. Samson managed to club the creature once with his axe, stagger it, and then club it still a second time.

Samson moved across the ground to where Gandy was trussed up, quickly cut through the coarse vine-like ropes with one swift swing of the axe, and then sprinted back down the path before the Minotaur could recover from the staggering blow. Now, if only the creature would follow.

It did. Samson could hear its fierce, labored snorting as it rushed madly down the path. Samson began to pace the creature, keeping what he hoped was the right distance between the two of them as he continued to run away from it.

Samson increased his speed as he neared the manticore. *All right,* he thought, wildly considering the alternatives if the plan didn't end up as he hoped. *It's got to work. It has to because I've run out of ideas.*

Running at full speed, Samson came upon the manticore still nursing its badly damaged wing. He fervently hoped the timing was right. He'd tried to lead the Minotaur just right, allowing it to catch up to him slowly.

It worked better than Samson could have hoped. As he leaped through the air, vaulting over the manticore, the Minotaur followed a moment later and charged into the befuddled manticore. The two creatures, mortal enemies who staunchly avoided each other, had no choice. They locked in combat instantly, the Minotaur goring with its deadly horns and the manticore slashing with its powerful claws.

Samson didn't stick around for the outcome. He raced down the path to where Regis and Serena were still trapped. With a Herculean heave, he pushed the boulder off of the ground, enough for the elf king to struggle out and pull Serena after him.

Regis didn't say a word but tended instantly to Serena, who was still out cold. "Her leg is broken," he whispered. "It was crushed by the boulder. And I think it may have damaged her lungs as well. She took more of it than I did."

"What can we do about it?" Samson asked.

"We'll have to bind her legs together," Regis said. "That's the best splint we can offer her right now. And then one of us will have to carry her from this place."

"I will," Samson offered. "But let's hurry. We may not have much time."

Regis pulled the shirt from his back and ripped it into long strips. Mercilessly, he bound Serena's legs together. Samson tried not to grimace, knowing the elf girl didn't feel a thing. At least not at this very moment.

Gandy showed up as Regis was finishing his handiwork. "How did you manage that back there?" he asked breathlessly.

"Manage what?" Samson said absently, still absorbed in what Regis was doing.

"You know, freeing me and giving those two a taste of their own medicine."

"I was lucky," Samson replied simply, almost modestly.

"Well, whatever you did, it worked," Gandy said. "They were tangled up with each other so viciously they didn't even notice me as I slipped past them."

The relief on Gandy's face was so visible that Samson gripped his shoulder with a friendly squeeze. "I'm glad it worked."

Regis looked up at the two of them when he'd finished. "We've got to find a safe place to rest her," he told Gandy. "Can you find us such a place? Are you up to it?"

Gandy nodded grimly.

"Good," Regis continued, his face an impassive mask. "We'll have to leave someone behind to guard her. The other two will have to find the dwarves, then, and bring help. It's our only chance of saving her. And even that's a slim one."

Samson hoisted Serena easily to his shoulder, cradling her head as he would a baby, as Gandy set off to find a haven. The elf girl was limp, almost lifeless, in his arms, the only sign of life her ragged breathing through damaged lungs.

"I'm sorry," Samson said to Regis, who set off at a quick pace. "She's a real trooper."

"Yes, she is that." Regis gave a heavy, mournful sigh. "But she's more than that."

"How so?" Samson asked.

"She is to be my wife. The new queen of the elves," Regis said, refusing to look back as he forged ahead.

13

* * *

THE GIANTS' GRIEF

There was still one matter of unfinished business before Laura left Orcus and his minions behind. It was a business Laura preferred not to dwell on at any length, even though Orcus assured her it wasn't nearly as bad as she imagined.

You see, while Laura and Orcus had been discussing the sad state of affairs in which the famed gods of Olympus now found themselves, the vast hall had resounded with a chorus of foot-shuffling. They were the same sounds, only louder now, that had trailed them the entire way.

"What *is* that?" Laura finally asked. "It's followed us the length of the pass."

"The undead," Orcus answered.

Laura gave the god of Death one of her very best looks of skepticism. "That makes no sense. Something's either dead or it's alive. It can't be…"

"I beg to differ," Orcus said politely, "but these poor, drifting souls fall into neither category. Hence, the term *the undead*."

"Try it so I can understand," Laura demanded.

"Very well." Orcus sighed. "It's quite simple. I cannot send any of these poor unfortunate souls on their way to the underworld and, eventually, to their final destination…"

"Their final destination?"

"God. The Creator. Where there is meaning. For those who believe, that is their final destination. For the others, well, they go to the void," Orcus said.

"Void?"

"The absence of God. They have chosen that place themselves. But it is not…a nice place," Orcus said somberly.

"I've never thought much about what happens after you die," Laura admitted.

"But surely the fabric of your world hasn't changed so much that you've forgotten that there may be many gods such as me, but that there is but one God above all others?" Orcus said. "That all men and women must eventually look upon his terrible face? And that our feeble attempts to understand life and death are but a prelude to that moment?"

"Yes, of course, our religious beliefs are much the same in my world," Laura answered, though she had never been particularly religious.

"When I still remained in your world," Orcus continued, "my task—and Pluto's as well in the underworld—was to ease the transition, to comfort those who died before they journeyed to that final moment. I can only wonder what must happen now in your world."

"Can we change the subject?" Laura detested conversations of this sort. She preferred to leave them to others more suited for them. "You were explaining why this hall sounds like intermission during a concert at the Philharmonic?"

"The what?" Orcus asked.

"Never mind," Laura said irritably. "Who are these undead, as you call them?"

"Well, that's precisely it," Orcus said.

"What is?"

"I don't *know* who they are. I don't know their names, and I don't know the circumstances under which they died. I can't very well send them on their way if I don't know who they are, now can I?"

Tara, who knew the ancient legends almost as well as anyone, tried to explain. "Long ago, magicians and clerics would regularly watch over and heal the world and keep track of all who had died. It kept the order and gave everything a sense of history and permanence. There was an order to the community. But since they have vanished…"

"No one has kept track of those who died in battle and weren't buried but had their bones picked clean by vultures instead," Mark added.

"Or were raped and buried in a shallow grave," Kathryn said. "There is no record, no history. And no one will ever know, for no one remains in the world who is powerful enough to keep track of such things."

"Except you," Orcus said to Laura. "You are powerful enough. You have the ability to free these souls and send them on their way at last."

A shudder of fear passed through her. "What must I do?" she said with resolve, trying to keep the unnerving chill from her voice.

"You must hear their names," Orcus said, "and listen to their histories."

"Each and every one of them?"

"They all must have someone who marks their passing, who can serve as their intermediary between the land of the living and my realm," Orcus said.

"But that's an archaic notion," Laura said. "And it's absurd, besides."

"Nevertheless, it is the rite of passage your world once chose," Orcus said. "I am only serving in the fashion your ancestors believed in with all their hearts."

"But this could take years," Laura protested miserably. "There must be thousands and thousands of them."

"Yes, but it must be done. And I'm afraid you are the only candidate around. If you don't, they will be forced to wander aimlessly nearby for who knows how long."

Laura thought for a moment. She didn't like this, not at all. The notion repulsed her. But if it was a necessary thing, if she had no other choice in the matter....

Yet, perhaps there was another way. "I think," she said slowly, "that I will establish a new order here. I don't particularly like the old one."

"Don't do anything rash or foolish," Orcus warned.

"Oh, what do you know? You're only following orders anyway. We're the ones making the rules, aren't we? Didn't you just say that, in so many words?"

"Well, yes, but—"

"But nothing," Laura said firmly. "I'm changing the law. It's far too rigid, as are other parts of it. And because there apparently aren't any magicians around to contest it, I think it will stand."

"We may contest it now," Tara said very softly. "Kathryn and me, I mean."

Laura studied the mermaid. There was no defiance in her eyes, only a subtle curiosity. Kathryn's eyes held much of the same.

"Will you contest me?" Laura asked them. "Will you stop me?"

"You know we would never do that," Kathryn said, refusing to look away under Laura's intense scrutiny.

"But we would like you to know that, by virtue of your gift to us, we may shape the law, or shield it as well, just as you may," Tara said with a warm smile. "And for that privilege, we thank you."

"You're welcome, I think." Laura frowned. She wasn't quite sure what was happening here. They were trying to tell her something. But what it was she couldn't say. "Now if I may proceed?"

The two girls nodded humbly.

What she needed first was an ancient word to set the souls free. "That would be *pri*," Laura said aloud. Next she needed to keep that new law forever in the state of being—in effect, turning free into freedom. "*Dhe*," she said simply. And last, she needed to apply that freedom to these lost souls, or spirits. "*Spirare*," she murmured.

There was a sudden roar, as if a hurricane had decided at that very moment to sweep through the hall. Laura glanced at the dais where Orcus had been sitting. He was sitting no longer.

"Hold on, hold on, one at a time!" the god of Death was shouting at the top of his lungs. "I'll get to each of you. But, of course, now that you're able to go on your merry way, there's no need to accost me. You're all free to come and go as you choose now."

Laura, at first, thought that perhaps she'd made a mistake, that she'd overburdened and overwhelmed the poor god. But no, she quickly realized. Orcus had never looked happier than he did at this moment, fending off a rush of souls, some of whom had been lost for centuries and were now demanding to continue their trek toward the final moment Orcus had spoken of.

"Come on," Laura said to the others, tearing her eyes away from the dais, "let's get moving. We have a job to finish."

"On to the giants," Mark said, anxious to flee this hellish tunnel once and for all.

I wonder, though, Laura thought as they hurried from the hall and Orcus' shouts, *why didn't they choose to find heaven on their own and seek this Creator Orcus spoke of? Why did they think they had to go through all these steps and intermediaries?*

***

The legend had been right. The tunnel did, in fact, empty into the heart of the giants' kingdom, in their common room in the crudely fashioned palace. There was only one slight problem.

The giants had fallen asleep. A deep, sound sleep. Out of boredom, most likely, or perhaps after a good, rousing game of musical mountains. It was anyone's guess. Unfortunately, a giant's sleep could last for years. Because they didn't eat, or at least no one had ever told them they *had* to, and because they tended to slumber along at a pace as slow as they were big, they'd been known to snooze through entire generations.

None of them, least of all Laura, had the slightest idea what to do about their predicament.

"We can't use magic," Kathryn said, "because it doesn't work in their domain. At least, not unless they give us permission first."

"Which they aren't likely to do right now, are they?" Laura laughed.

The giants' common room was bigger than any structure Laura had seen. It was bigger than anything she'd imagined, actually. Pillars that seemed a mile high held the roof in place. Rimming the room were massive wooden benches, at least a few hundred yards off the ground.

One large wooden table sat squarely in the middle of the room. It was impossible to tell what might be on the table from the group's vantage point. That was like trying to figure out what might lie at the top of a mountain while looking up at it from a valley.

Several dozen of the giants lounged on the benches surrounding the room, snoring peacefully. And with each snore, the room rumbled slightly. It was all Laura could do to keep her footing as they strode across the floor in search of something that could help them wake the giants.

After a half hour's trek to the middle of the floor, they tried shouting. A pitiful attempt. Had the giants been awake, they might have acknowledged the shouts. But fast asleep, never.

"I don't think we have a choice," Mark said, his voice hoarse from shouting.

"What's the choice?" Laura asked him skeptically.

"One of us will have to climb up there and shout in one of their ears."

"But that could be dangerous," Kathryn protested. "What if the giant shakes his head, or stands up quickly, or swats at his ear because he's annoyed at the intrusion? You'd be killed."

"It's a chance I'll have to take." Mark shrugged.

"So who appointed you to this perilous undertaking?" Laura said warily.

"I'm volunteering," he said, refusing to give her the satisfaction by stating the obvious. None of the magicians could make the climb.

"Be my guest, then," Laura said, almost smiling.

They wandered for another half an hour or so before finding the easiest route to the top—a rough cloth curtain close enough to one of the benches that Mark could make the leap from one to the other. The curtain was porous enough, at least from Mark's perspective, that it would be like climbing a rope ladder.

The magicians fretted at the bottom as Mark made his way, hand over hand, up the curtain. Kathryn held her breath as he made the short leap without a hitch, landing squarely on the top of the bench. But they lost sight of him as he walked quickly but cautiously up the extended forearm of one of the slumbering giants. He almost lost his footing when the giant, perhaps sensing Mark, moved a little in his sleep. Fortunately, he didn't decide to roll over to his other side. Mark didn't waste any more time. He ran as fast as he could to the giant's shoulder.

The next part would be delicate. He wasn't sure how loud he needed to yell to wake the giant. Too loud and he risked a violent reaction. That obviously wouldn't do at all. As he pushed the coarse hair from the giant's ear and stuck his chin over the earlobe, Mark settled on a compromise. He started to hum, softly at first, and building up until he ran out of breath. Then he repeated the process, only a little louder this time.

The giant stirred the fourth time around. But before Mark could say anything, the giant suddenly blinked, turned his head to one side, and sat up.

Kathryn screamed.

Mark had the foresight to hang onto a couple strands of hair, though, and the giant's movements only swung him around behind his head while he hung on for dear life.

"Ho!" the giant said, his voice echoing through the common room like a sonic boom. "Someone is here."

"It's me," Mark yelled as he swung back toward the giant's ear.

"A spirit?" the giant asked, a logical mistake considering he could hear Mark but not see him.

"No, no, a human," Mark answered. "I'm speaking into your…left ear."

The giant reached a careful hand up to his ear. Mark stepped lightly into his palm. The giant brought it around to gaze at the intruder. "Well, so it is," he said with a hearty laugh. "It has been an age and then some since we've seen your kind. What can I do for you, little one?"

Mark struggled for words. "A great and powerful magician has something she wants to tell you. And the other giants."

"A cursed wizard here?" The giant scowled.

"No, she's nice. Not like those you knew long ago."

"All magicians have black hearts," the giant said, the scowl still locked in place.

"Trust me. This one is different."

The giant's visage suddenly brightened. "It has been a very long time. Perhaps the land has changed in our absence. So where is this great and powerful wizard?"

Mark pointed toward the floor. "Down there, but be careful where you step. She has others with her."

"More wizards?" the giant asked, scowling again.

Mark was growing weary of the giant's mood shifts. "They're harmless. They're just apprentice magicians. And they don't have black hearts, either."

"And what of you? What are you?"

To his own amazement, Mark found he couldn't answer that right away. Once upon a time, he would have answered without hesitation, "Heir to the Sanctuary's throne." But now that he had discovered very few who'd even heard of the Sanctuary, it seemed a frivolous claim. And, besides, he didn't much think of himself in that way anymore.

"I am an apprentice warrior," he said simply. "I have come with the magicians to shield them from danger."

"Since when do magicians need protection?" the giant asked with a raised eyebrow.

"As you said, the land has changed in your absence," Mark said, deciding it was futile to elaborate any further.

"Now what is it, again, that these magicians want?"

Giants are most emphatically not known for their quick wits, Mark realized. "One of them would like to speak to you and the rest of the giants. She has something of great importance to say."

"Very well." The giant sighed. "Where shall I set you?"

"On that table." He nodded toward the center of the room. "And my friends are at your feet."

The giant peered cautiously over the bench, only to find Laura and the others cowering just under it. "No need to be afraid of *me*," the giant rumbled. "I won't harm you."

The giant carefully laid his other hand, the empty one, palm up on the floor. Laura hesitated for a moment, then stepped in. Kathryn and Tara followed an instant later.

The three of them held hands as the giant lifted them up to eye level. Once there, Mark quickly hopped from one hand to the other.

The giant rose from the bench, keeping a very careful eye on his passengers to make sure none slipped from their perch. He walked slowly across the floor before setting them down gently on the table.

"Should I wake the others?" the giant asked.

Mark tried to keep from groaning. "Yes, please do, if it isn't too much trouble."

"Not at all," the giant said.

As the giant began to wake the others in his race, Mark huddled with the three magicians. "They aren't very bright," he told Laura. "Their memory span is very short. Except when it comes to magic. He seems to remember the old magicians quite well, so I wouldn't say much about that if I were you."

"All right, I'll just stick to the facts," she agreed.

"I told him that you had something of great importance to tell the giants. You do, don't you? I mean, I've just sort of assumed that you would speak for us...?"

"Don't worry," Laura said easily. "I'll manage somehow."

The giants—all rough, coarse males—were either groggily rising to their feet or at least rubbing the sleep from their eyes. To Mark, it looked like several dozen mountain peaks suddenly deciding to get up and wander around the earth.

The giants were a motley race, noted more for their uniformly large size than anything else. All wore beards, but that was where any similarity among them ended.

Their clothes were patchwork quilts of material. Their hair ran from almost white to black, all at different lengths. Some had huge noses, others had huge ears, while still others had jutting jaws or over bites.

As they gathered around the table, silently, Laura noticed a pervasive, overwhelming sadness in the room. Perhaps it was the fact they'd all just awakened from a deep sleep, but Laura could sense it was something more than that, something deeper.

She surveyed some of their faces carefully, trying to gaze into their eyes. There was a hollowness to them, a lifelessness. They moved listlessly across the room as they approached the table, their arms hanging aimlessly at their sides.

That's when Laura noticed how horribly unkempt the common room was. She hadn't seen it from the floor, but from the table it was obvious. These giants were slobs. Leftover plates and mugs were strewn about the room. Chairs that had been knocked over hadn't been put back upright.

A few of the giants wore such mournful, resigned expressions that Laura barely kept from bursting into tears. In fact, when she glanced over at Tara, she could detect a tear or two in her eyes. Kathryn, likewise, seemed to be on the verge. *What is going on here? What has happened to this race?* Something had obviously devastated them, taken the life from them. But what? What could have caused such sadness?

"What will you tell us, wizard?" asked the first giant, the one Mark had awakened, when the giants were all seated around the table, gazing intently at the newcomers.

"I have come with a request!" Laura shouted at the top of her lungs.

"No need to shout," the giant said quickly. "We can hear you just fine. Our ears are very sensitive. They're attuned to hear those smaller than ourselves."

"Oh, I'm sorry," Laura said humbly.

"Perfectly all right. You were saying?"

"I have come with a request," Laura said again. "But, first, I must tell you that one of the women who has accompanied me is, in fact, a mermaid."

Tara stepped forward and bowed slightly. There was almost no visual reaction around the table, which startled Laura. She'd expected something—a gasp, a puzzled look, anything but the blank, uncaring stares she now faced. "Doesn't that mean anything to you, that a mermaid now walks the land?" Laura demanded.

"Not especially," one of the giants said. "Why should we care?"

"No reason, I guess," Laura replied. "Well, I should tell you, also, that the people of the sea have agreed to return from their exile, to move their kingdom closer to the land, as it once was."

"That's nice," one giant said.

Laura was trying not to grow flustered. "The elves have agreed to return to the land as well. As have the fairies. In fact, the elf king, Regis, is on his way to see the dwarves at this very moment. And the fairy queen, Maya, is journeying to see the centaurs."

"All very interesting, but what does it have to do with us?" asked a giant with bright red hair, a bushy red beard, and the largest red nose Laura had ever seen.

Laura decided to risk it. "I've come here to ask you to return to the land as well."

"Why?" asked the red-bearded giant.

Mark, as puzzled by the giants' melancholy as the others, suddenly spoke. "Because the land faces grave peril. We have to act. There is even talk of storming the magicians' city. It is time the races unite against the magicians."

"Yes, but you still haven't told us why you've come to us," the red-bearded giant persisted.

"All the races must return to the land," Laura said firmly. "That is the strongest magic I can think of. According to your own legends, it is the only thing that has ever kept the magicians from completely despoiling the land. Your law…"

"The law has failed us," the first giant said simply. "We have kept the land safe but lost our own lives in the process."

"I don't understand." Laura's temper sparked. Now she was just about fed up with all these hang-dog looks around the table.

"The magicians vanquished us long, long ago," the red-bearded giant said. "We have nothing to live for any longer. Why do you think there are so few of us left?"

Laura hadn't considered that the sum total of the giants were now in this room. "Surely there are more of you? I was told the giants roamed the land far and wide long ago."

"Long ago, yes," said another giant with a tangled mop of black hair. "But not now. We are all waiting for our appointed time."

Before Laura could ask them what the "appointed time" was, Mark leaned over and whispered into her ear, "Giants turn to stone when they're overcome by grief or when they're mortally wounded. And by the looks of these giants, it won't be long."

Laura reached up to massage her temples, searching her own mind for why the giants seemed to be on the verge of extinction. It made no sense. Surely they had *some* reason to keep on living.

And then it dawned on her. She glanced around the room again, just to make sure. *That's it!* she thought wildly as every face in the room told the same story.

"You're sure there aren't any other giants?" Laura asked them. "Besides those in this room?"

"There are two sentinels," the red-bearded giant said.

"Where are your children?" Laura asked softly.

"We have none," the first giant said somberly.

"And your mates, your wives, the female giants?" Laura asked again.

"We have none," the red-bearded giant answered.

"But you did at one time, didn't you?" Laura kept her voice steady and her eyes level.

"Yes, long ago," the first giant said.

"It was the magicians? They're responsible, aren't they?"

The red-bearded giant cast a baleful eye in Laura's direction. "No, we are to blame, for we did not anticipate their treachery. Had we prepared, we could have stopped it in time. As it is, we were too late."

"What happened?" Tara asked suddenly.

"The magicians lured our children away with promises," the first giant said. "They told our children they would teach them the ways of magic. It was a lie, of course," he continued, a long dormant flicker of anger almost surfacing. "They never intended to teach them anything, but our children believed and they left us forever. We have never seen them since."

"And your mates?" Laura asked.

"Their hearts were so heavy, their burden so great, that it wasn't long before they'd all left us as well, before their appointed time," the red-bearded giant said.

Laura leaned over to Mark and asked him if it would be impolite to ask them where they were. Mark nodded that it would be fine, so Laura made her request.

The first giant offered his hand to them a second time. He carried them to a large window looking to the north. "Do you see that distant mountain range?" he told them. "That is where they have gone. We will join them soon."

Laura shook her head sadly at the injustice of it as they were returned to the table. It was obvious, now, why the giants would not return to the land, why they had no reason to do so, why there was simply no point, regardless of any real or imagined danger to the land. Their lives were over.

Kathryn glanced at Laura when they were safely returned to the table. Something was troubling her. "What is it?" Laura whispered.

"I'm not sure it's anything," Kathryn whispered back, "but I have a vague recollection of something in the back of my mind, something I learned from you about turning the giants to stone..."

"Of course!" Laura was barely able to contain her excitement. "I don't know why I didn't think of it before." She turned to the giants solemnly. "Tell me something. Has a giant ever returned?"

"From stone?" the red-bearded giant answered, slightly surprised by the question. Laura nodded. "No, not that I can think of."

"There is a distant legend," said the first giant, "of a powerful wizard, from another world, who performed such a feat on one of our ancestors thousands of years ago."

"But it is a very distant legend, one I don't think many in this room actually believe," the red-bearded giant said.

"You would admit, however, that it might be possible?" Laura asked.

"If a magician were willing to attempt it, yes," the first giant said. "Which isn't likely."

Laura nodded. It just might be possible. She had no real knowledge of what might happen, but it was worth the risk. She had no choice but to try. "If I can bring your mates back," she said slowly, making sure all eyes were on her, "and I promise to do what I can to find out what has happened to your children and return them to you if that is possible, will you, in return, promise to come back to the land with me?"

There was a murmur among the giants, the first actual sign of life in the room since the group had arrived. Their skepticism was obvious, their disbelief even more obvious. But there seemed little choice in the matter.

"For myself, I doubt that such a thing is possible," the first giant said finally, speaking for the entire race. "But no magician has ever, to my knowledge, made such a pledge. I am willing to strike such a bargain, as are the others."

"Wonderful." Laura clapped her hands with delight.

There was only one little problem, of course. The spell book had only instructed Laura how to turn the giants to stone, not how to bring them back to life.

14

* * *

PLUTO'S PALACE

Jon could not believe what his own mind had brought forth. He likewise couldn't believe the throng that greeted him at the door.

"Hail, priest, well met," said a towering man at the fore of the crowd that had gathered at the door to see who had transformed their palace from darkness to splendor. The man, whose face might as well have been chiseled from granite, wore a white, flowing tunic embroidered with precious metals and studded with diamonds. On his head, he wore a hat.

And Jon remembered. "Is that *the* hat?" he asked Pluto.

"You are indeed a perceptive young man," Pluto answered with a gracious, beguiling smile.

"What's so special about that hat?" Lucas asked nervously. Quite a few people, like none he'd ever seen before, had begun to gather around him.

"Pluto's helmet," Jon said, shaking his head in disbelief, "makes its wearer invisible."

"But he isn't invisible?" Lucas protested.

"He's a god, you oaf," Jon retorted. "Obviously, he chooses to be visible."

"In name and title only, it seems these days," said Pluto, the brother of Zeus and Poseidon, known far and wide in Earth's ancient literature as an unpitying, inexorable, but just god.

Unlike the other gods of Olympus, however, Pluto had never been known to leave his own dark realm much either to visit the other gods or the Earth. Now, looking at him in all his regal wealth and splendor, Jon could understand why.

The god of the underworld inspired terror. His towering presence probably contributed to it. But it was a terrible, otherworldly bearing he brought with him that weighed heavy in the balance. He seemed an incarnation of judgment itself. And no one wanted to be judged. Especially not Jon.

Maya, meanwhile, had begun to make herself at home in the palace. Indeed, the interior now matched what its exterior had promised—a vast, ornate hall decorated by superb sculptures, wondrous art, finely woven carpets, and plush furniture.

But a curious thing had happened. Jon had to smile. After all, he was responsible. "I'm sorry," he mumbled to Pluto. "I had no idea I was disrupting your palace so…"

"Oh, there's no need for an apology," Pluto said quickly, smiling for the first time since they'd arrived. Jon wondered if perhaps it wasn't the first time the stern god had *ever* smiled.

"Before you arrived," Pluto continued, "the place was gray. Just gray, everywhere. No colors, no light by which to see any of the paintings or the sculptures. Here, come with me."

Pluto led him through the mute crowd trailing in his wake toward an absolutely huge statue, a woman of heroic proportions clothed only from the waist down. It was a familiar figure, but Jon couldn't recall who it was.

"I'm sure you recognize this?" Pluto asked.

"Well, no, I'm not much of a connoisseur of art," Jon muttered.

"No matter. It's Venus of Milo—"

"Not the original?" Jon interrupted, remembering now that the Venus of Milo he'd seen was missing its arms.

"Of course, it's the original," Pluto said haughtily. "I would not accept cheap imitations in this palace."

"But…but what of the statue in my own world?"

"A perfect, flawless replica. No one will ever know the difference."

"But how did you manage it?"

"One of the tricks of the trade. The point, however, is that until you so graciously flooded our gray abode with light, no one could behold this statue in all its magnificence. That terribly sad state of affairs has now changed. And for that, I thank you."

Jon frowned. "That's crazy. Why didn't you just provide the light yourself?"

"You know the answer to that as well as I do, I think." Pluto gazed intently at him.

Jon turned away from those probing eyes. "Yes, I guess I do. You have been confined to this dreary place because someone's uninspired imagination consigned you to this drab fate."

"Unfortunately, yes."

Jon took in the rest of the palace, then, with less shame. He had completely disrupted the palace with his creations. Besides the bright light flooding the interior from sources Jon couldn't determine, a wide river now traversed the very center of the palace, cascading and tumbling along, oblivious to the opulence that surrounded it on both sides.

Dotted throughout the palace, in fertile soil, were dozens of fruit trees. These trees had not been selective in where they'd sprouted, either. One had intertwined its branches with a chandelier; another had come up through the center of a Persian carpet; still a third had hung a heavy bough over a wide staircase leading to the upper rooms of the palace.

But perhaps the strangest sight of all was off to Jon's right, in what once must have been a large, empty dance hall or perhaps an indoor patio. The hall was now filled with rows upon rows of books, stacks of them. At the center of that library, a tall oak had spread out. There were acorns scattered throughout the stacks of books.

And wandering excitedly up and down the rows were dozens of centaurs, randomly perusing as many books as they could get their hands on, occasionally exclaiming with pure delight. Jon noticed, however, that none of the centaurs ever actually read any of the books. They simply flipped through the pages, as a child would through a picture book, and then moved on to a new book.

"Curious," he said to himself. "It's almost as if..."

"They can't read, of course," Pluto explained. "Books are unheard of in the common parts of this world. Only the magicians, with their spell books, have employed the written word and they have done so only with great secrecy. Surely you'd realized that before now?"

"No, I hadn't, though I can't see how I would have overlooked that simple fact."

"Quite easy." Pluto shrugged. "With so much else going on for them here—magic, for instance—there isn't much need for a diversion like reading." Pluto gave him that gaze again. "And those who were responsible for so many of the legends in the first place didn't put much stock in writing. As you know."

Which was true, of course. The old Celts and Druids who were responsible for the World Tree and Otherworld legends believed only in oral history. They never wrote anything down.

As Jon watched the centaurs eagerly wander up and down the countless rows of books, a plan took shape in his mind. Perhaps it would work, perhaps it wouldn't, but it was worth a try. He would have gladly given the centaurs the opportunity to read regardless of the consequences.

As he approached the great library, one centaur abandoned his search and hurried to meet Jon. The clop-clop of his hoof beats echoing off the walls seemed strange in the palatial surroundings.

"Hail, cleric, and well met!" the centaur said with a sweeping bow, bending his forelegs until they almost touched the floor. He swept his powerful right arm grandly in front of him.

"How do you do?" Jon said, deciding that he didn't like these formal greetings. A firm handshake would do just fine as far as he was concerned.

"I am Cleo, king of the centaurs and a direct descendant of Chiron, the physician and scholar."

"Hi, I'm Jon."

"Pleased," Cleo said. "Your arrival has been long awaited and anticipated here."

"It has?"

"Certainly. Pluto informed us of it when you first arrived in our world."

"You knew when I arrived? And that I would wind up here?"

"There was never any question," Cleo stated with an air of supreme confidence. "You had no choice in the matter, really. We all knew you and the others who accompanied you to this world would attempt to bring the races back to the land and, perhaps, attempt to challenge the magicians in the city. That's what Pluto told us."

"Then you know why I'm here?" Jon said uncertainly.

"Of course they know why we're here," Maya added curtly over Jon's shoulder. "They're not stupid. Far from it. They're arguably the wisest creatures in the land."

"Well met, gracious fairy queen," Cleo said with another flourish and bow.

"The honor is entirely mine." Maya slightly inclined her tiny head.

"So will you join us?" Jon asked abruptly. "Will you lead your race from this realm to the land and help us?"

"Patience, lad," Cleo said. "Centaurs never hurry or rush decisions. We must weigh and measure the arguments in the balance of justice. We will see."

"But what is it you need to weigh and measure, as you put it?"

"Perhaps everything, perhaps nothing at all. But, first, would you be so kind as to explain these unusual things you have created in the midst of the palace?"

"The books?"

"If that is what you call them, yes."

A dozen or so of the centaurs, meanwhile, had abandoned their search through the library and now flanked their king. They looked eagerly at Jon.

Jon grappled for a suitable explanation. "They're stories that have been written down," he said finally.

"Written down?" Cleo asked.

"You know, our language transferred to paper." Jon frowned. It seemed awfully strange to have to explain writing to someone.

"Paper...?"

"It's a...a product of wood. Taken from the trees you are all familiar with. Clear enough to make impressions on it."

"The words I am speaking right now, they could be placed on a product of wood and you would be able to understand?"

"Yes, it's a way to transfer and store knowledge. A very simple way."

"I'm not sure I understand," Cleo said, accompanied by more than one nod of approval among the other centaurs.

"Here, I'll show you." Jon moved quickly to one of the rows, searched for a suitable book, and then pulled it from the shelf. By random chance—or perhaps not—it was Bunyan's *Pilgrim's Progress*.

"As I walked through the wilderness of this world," Jon intoned seriously, "I lighted on a certain place where there was a den and laid me down in that place to sleep. And as I slept, I dreamed a dream. I dreamed and, behold, I saw a man clothed with rags standing in a certain place, with his face from his own house, a book in his hand and a great burden upon his back…"

"You have found that story here, in that book?" Cleo asked.

"Yes, that's what I'm trying to tell you. I was reading you a story from this book."

"Reading?"

"Being able to understand the words and the language that have been placed here," Jon said, rapidly growing weary of explaining the process.

"I see. And what is the story about?" Cleo asked.

"Oh, it's about a man's spiritual progress from self-centered destruction to heaven and his knowledge of God's existence," Jon said casually. He'd read the book years ago and instantly dismissed it as the drivel he felt sure it was.

"Oh, how fascinating! I would dearly love to behold such a treasure. The story sounds marvelous."

"I hope to give you the opportunity. I would enjoy that a great deal."

Cleo looked closely at Jon. "You *are* serious, aren't you? You would open the path to this world for me?"

"And the other centaurs as well," Jon said with a careless shrug. "Then you can teach the rest of this ignorant world if you'd like."

"You can't know what this means to me," Cleo replied slowly. "Or to our race. All our lives we have dedicated ourselves to the quest for knowledge. And now, as if it is nothing more than a day's work, you offer us a world of knowledge none of us could have imagined in even our most fanciful dreams?"

"Forget it," Jon said beneficently. "It's nothing."

"It is hardly 'nothing.' The offer leaves me speechless."

"I sincerely doubt that anything would leave you thus," Maya said, unable to conceal a smile at the centaur king's forced humility.

"Well, perhaps you're right." Cleo laughed. "Speechless may be a bit too strong. But, nevertheless, the offer is one that I, at least, shall never forget. Nor any of my race."

"I think the priest has something else to say," Pluto suddenly interjected.

"He does? I mean, I do?" Jon said, confused.

"A bargain, of sorts?" the god prompted. "Your knowledge for their agreement to return to the land?"

"Oh, that," Jon mumbled in Pluto's direction. "But how did you know that's what I had in mind?"

"I know many things about you," the god said. "Some of which you yourself do not know."

"What is this bargain?" Cleo demanded, forcing Jon to look away from the god's terrible gaze.

"Oh, it's simple, really," Jon said quickly. "I'll promise to teach you how to read if you, or at least one of your representatives, agree to return to the land with me for a time."

"And then?"

"And then we confront the magicians," Jon stated nonchalantly.

"If all works out as we hope," Maya added, "the centaurs would return to the land permanently, with the other races, to live in harmony."

"It will never happen," Cleo said with a stern expression. "You know that, don't you?"

"But the centaurs have to return!" Jon protested.

"No, I don't mean that." Cleo shook his head. "Of course I will accompany you on this futile quest, in return for this gift of knowledge you have offered us. No, I only meant that confronting the magicians is a hopeless task in and of itself. They are far too powerful now. And as for the races living together in peace, well, that too is a lost cause."

"I don't think so," Jon said firmly.

"Nor do I," Maya said as well. "We must, at the very least, attempt it."

"At the very least." The centaur king sighed. "Yes, I suppose you're right. But it certainly will seem strange to gain one world, only to lose another just as quickly."

15

* * *

SAMSON AND
THE DWARF KING

G andy found a haven for Serena almost immediately. His outlook on the world may have been dour at best, but his instincts and his ability to find his way in the dark were nothing short of miraculous.

"It appears to be an old lair," Gandy reported. "There are still a few very old bones at the back of it, but it's long deserted. No question about it."

"Deserted or not, we don't have much choice," Regis said. "So lead the way."

The place reeked of death, even though it had obviously been quite some time since its occupant had fled to regions unknown. But Regis had been right. They had no choice.

Serena was slipping fast. Already her face was growing pale. If she didn't receive some attention soon, there was no question she would die from her wounds.

"One of us must remain behind with her, though I can't see what good it will do," Regis announced darkly.

"It will have to be me, I'm afraid." Gandy's face was more glum than usual. "It means you won't have a scout along, but I'm the logical choice."

"I agree." Regis gripped his advisor's arm affectionately. "The dwarves will only listen to the king of the elves, not one of his advisors. And Samson must come along as well."

"The enforcer." Samson grinned. "That's me."

"Right," Regis said grimly. He turned to face Gandy one more time. "We'll be back as swiftly as we can. I can't say how long because I have no idea how long it will take to reach the dwarves. But if we can't convince them or if we can't find them, leave this place after two days."

"But what of Serena?" Gandy protested.

"If we aren't back by then, it won't matter, will it?" Regis murmured.

"No, I guess not." Gandy sighed. "So hurry, then, all right? I don't intend to miss your wedding."

* * *

Regis and Samson settled into an easy, loping jog down the path. It was a relatively mild pace for both of them—Samson because he'd run a few miles a day since he was a young boy and Regis because he'd often hunted in this fashion.

They ran in silence at first. There was no mistaking how troubled Regis was, but he managed to hide it well. It came from being a king, Samson supposed.

As they wound their way further and further into the heart of the earth, the only light fitfully cast from the torches they still carried with them, the air likewise grew hot and acrid, as if they were descending into the basement of a burning house.

"It's the river," Regis said when he noticed Samson's obvious discomfort.

"The river?"

"The molten river, which the dwarves use to forge their weapons. It flows from the center of the earth, or so they say. I've never been this way before."

"It's not likely I'll spend my next vacation here." Samson was sweating profusely, his clothes soaked clear through.

"What's a vacation?" Regis asked.

"A break from work."

"I don't understand. Work is life. How can you have a break from life?"

"Oh, never mind." Samson added the conversation to the scrap heap of ideas and notions he was slowly accumulating in this world.

The river stopped them in their tracks. Or, rather, the sudden, intense wave of heat from it as they rounded a bend that forced them to pause for air.

They'd known they were approaching it for quite some time. An orange glow was creeping onto the walls surrounding them as they ran, faint at first but then stronger as they approached it.

But, even prepared, it was quite a shock to run flat into such a force of heat. It was enough to curl their hair. One minute they were running along in stifling air. The next they were bathed in an inferno of it.

"It's unreal," Samson said in shock. The river must have been a good 1,000 feet across. The molten lava, or whatever it was, glowed a dull or bright orange in most spots. But, in a few places, a blackened crust drifted slowly by as well. And the river bubbled, like a stew on the stove.

"It's very real," Regis said. "The lifeblood of the dwarves' kingdom."

"And we have to walk alongside this thing?"

Regis merely lifted a brow. "It appears so."

As much as they wanted to hurry on, they were forced to walk as they set off along the river's left side, keeping as far as possible from the fierce heat it radiated.

Running would have exhausted them within minutes. As it was, they found themselves tiring quickly even as they walked.

The river's only saving grace, if it can be called such, was that it cast off quite a bit of light, enough so that it would be difficult, if not impossible, for anything to sneak up on them as they walked along.

It was also doubtful that any living creature, save the dwarves, could stand this heat for very long. And even if they could, why would they?

Samson was certain they'd walked for hours and hours when they could finally make out the faint outlines of the dwarf city. Or at least one dwarf city, because who could say how many of them there were below the earth's surface?

"I don't believe," Samson said through a cracked, dry, parched throat, "that they actually do live down there beside this god-awful, horrible river. They must be mad."

"No, not mad, just ornery, unreasonable, and stubborn," Regis replied. "Their hides are as thick as hard leather. Thicker, even."

"I wonder what they do for fun. They certainly don't go swimming or boating."

"They never have any fun," Regis said seriously. "They are, by far, the grimmest race of the seven in the land. They work and toil night and day."

That didn't sound quite right, but Samson wasn't about to argue with the elf king right now. He was simply too tired. "Well, I can see how it might be tough to keep a sense of humor in this place."

"Sense of humor!" Regis snorted. "Their idea of humor is to club each other over the head until they knock each other out."

"Are they stupid?"

"As witless as they come."

"Isn't there anything about them you like?"

"The day they fled the land," Regis said sourly, "was a day I thoroughly enjoyed."

"Likewise, you skittish, cowardly, mindless twit," a gravelly voice growled above their heads.

Samson glanced up with a start, as did Regis. A grimy face, covered with smudge and soot, peered down at them from a hole in the rock ceiling. Absorbed as they approached the city, neither had noticed the path narrow.

"The day the elves ran from the land like frightened children was a day of great joy," the dwarf said. He worked his way through the hole and dropped to the floor, only a few feet in front of them.

The dwarf was half Samson's size but, from the looks of him, nearly as strong in his upper body. A massive head rested firmly on his broad shoulders. His squat, slightly bowed legs were firmly rooted to the earth. He wore a lightweight mail shirt over the grimiest undershirt Samson had ever seen. And at his side, dragging the ground, was a battle-axe with a handle worn smooth from years of use.

He didn't challenge Samson—he wasn't that foolish, not by himself—or the elf king, but merely placed two coarse, rugged hands on his hips and planted himself squarely between the city and them. "What possible business can a flower-tender have down here?" the dwarf demanded.

"Where did you come from?" asked a stupefied Samson.

"Surely you don't think this passageway you find yourself on is the only one in this entire, bloody mountain, do you? Or are you as witless as you appear?"

Samson held his temper. Barely. He was here to make friends, not to crush little upstart dwarves. "So there's a path above this one, I take it?" he managed in a sweet tone.

"Well, what do you know? For such a big, stupid-looking goon, you figured that out all by yourself?" the dwarf taunted.

"For such a runt of a creature, and an ugly one at that, you certainly do have a big mouth," Regis said quickly, before Samson's hair-trigger temper got the better of him.

"And for such a wan, pale, skinny little sprite of a creature, you obviously don't have an upstairs in your noggin," the dwarf shot back at Regis. "Why else would you be down here among sworn enemies?"

"Why I'm here is none of your business!" Regis said angrily. "I need to see your king. And quickly. It's of the utmost importance."

"The utmost importance!" The dwarf mimicked the elf's high-pitched voice as he shook his head sadly. "What really matters here is whether you intend to turn your frail, worthless bodies around and march back to wherever you came from."

"We need to see your king," Regis insisted. "Believe me, I wouldn't be here if it wasn't necessary."

"Look, mate, you have about as much chance of seeing the king as I do of soaring like a bird. Now either you two turn around or I intend to lop your heads off." The dwarf grasped the battle-axe firmly.

Samson, in kind, gripped his halberd. But perhaps they could still avoid a confrontation. "Look, we both know you can't take us, not two against one, so why don't you be reasonable about this?"

"Who says there's just the one on my side?" the dwarf said with a huge grin. Before Samson or Regis could react, a second dwarf dropped from the hole in the rock ceiling. He was followed in rapid succession by a third, fourth, fifth, and a sixth dwarf.

"Perhaps you'd like to reconsider my offer?" the first dwarf said, now flanked by five stout members of his own race.

"I don't think so," Samson replied, startled but not willing to give up. "Like Regis said, we need to see your king. It's important."

"Regis, you say?" One of the dwarfs peered closer at the elf king. "That's your name, truly?"

Regis nodded. "Truly."

"The king of the elves?"

"Of course that's who I am, you lump of mindless clay." Regis glowered.

"Well, why didn't you say so in the first place?" the dwarf said cheerfully. "That changes the picture entirely."

"It does?" Samson asked.

"Of course it does," the dwarf said. "The king will want the pleasure of lopping off your heads personally."

* * *

Samson had considered resisting, if only because he was sick and tired of being someone else's prisoner in this idiotic, backwards world. But Regis stopped him.

"We have to see the king," Regis hissed at him before the dwarves had surrounded them. "Even on these terms is better than no terms at all. It's our only hope of saving Serena's life."

So Samson had agreed and for the third time since he'd arrived in the land, he allowed himself to be trussed up like a turkey at Thanksgiving and taken prisoner. He was an old hand at it now. He knew precisely how his hands would feel, for instance, as the rope bit into wrists or how his legs would ache from walking without the use of his arms.

The dwarf city was disgustingly ugly from Samson's perspective. The homes were mostly a mixture of plain, dull metal and clay fired in a kiln—practical in this heat, but incredibly unappealing to Samson's more refined taste.

He was in for quite a shock, though. For inside the homes, which were so barren of art or decoration on the outside, were priceless and artful metal sculptures, fashioned metal hanging on the walls, and rich earth tone colors.

"Your homes are so much different on the inside," Samson murmured to one of his captors.

"You don't think we'd expose our best work to that withering heat out there, do you?" the dwarf answered. "What do you take us for, you oversized oaf?"

They were led to the rear of the city, through interconnected hallways that always managed to somehow keep the coolness of the earth in and the heat of the molten river out, where they were roughly pushed into a prison cell with a barred window overlooking a meeting hall of some kind.

Once they'd been left alone, Samson tested the strength of the metal bars. It would take hundreds of men straining at exactly the same time to yank one of the bars free, he finally concluded.

"Don't even bother," Regis said morosely. "The dwarves are superb builders as well as master craftsmen."

"I thought you didn't think much of them." Samson was surprised at the elf king's appraisal of his own mortal enemies.

"I don't like their kind, but I have respect for their ability. And they are good at what they do, though I would never actually say so in their presence."

"I see." Samson wondered if, in fact, the dwarves respected the elves' cunning and agility in similar fashion but would never acknowledge it.

Fortunately, for Regis's sanity, it wasn't long before they were granted an audience with the king of the dwarves. And in a rather unusual fashion.

Samson had been staring out the window at the courtyard below while Regis slumped in a corner of the cell, when the entire cell suddenly lurched, nearly tossing Samson to the floor.

Holding firmly to the bars on the window, Samson quickly saw what was happening. The cell was being lowered using pulleys to the courtyard. And as it was being lowered, it was also being rotated so that the open end of the cage would look out over the yard.

"See?" Regis managed a weak smile. "Didn't I tell you they knew how to build?"

"I'm a believer," Samson said.

The cell reached the ground floor with a bone-jarring crash, however, so they obviously hadn't worked out all the kinks. Or perhaps they had.

Samson found himself staring out at a procession of dwarves entering the courtyard in what, to them, must have been their finest attire. To Samson, the dress was garish at best and comical at worst—dull metal helmets perched on their heads, light mail armor with exaggerated shoulders, baggy trousers to hide their bowed legs and huge, ornate axes they could barely pull with them.

And at the end of the procession came the king, dressed in his own full battle attire, which included a huge broadsword as well as an axe. It was all Samson could do to keep himself from laughing at the absurdity of a man half his size wielding two weapons that he would barely hoist himself.

"I wouldn't find it *too* funny," Regis whispered, catching a fleeting smile on Samson's face as he watched the procession of dwarves. "They may look like fools with those weapons at their sides. But in their hands, they can be fierce and deadly with them. Trust me."

"If you say so." Samson shrugged. Perhaps the elf king was right. Their upper body strength did appear to be considerable.

The procession came to a halt in front of the cage. The dwarves formed a semi-circle around it, with the king furthest away from the two prisoners.

"So we meet at last under favorable circumstances, eh, Regis?" said the dwarf king, who had the largest nose Samson had ever seen and a huge pair of ears to match.

"These are hardly ideal circumstances, Gar," the elf king said bitterly. "For you, yes, but not for me."

"I trust you've enjoyed dancing among the flowers, carousing carelessly with the wood nymphs, and playing with rain dewdrops now that the dwarves are no longer around to slaughter you like cattle?" The dwarf king's smile was frozen in place.

"And I trust the dwarves have grown uglier, coarser, and more ignorant—if that's possible—down here in the slimy, disgusting bowels of the earth," Regis countered.

"Hold on you two," Samson said loudly, too loudly because the other dwarves glared at him angrily. "Can I assume you two know each other?"

"Is your friend as dumb as he looks?" the dwarf king asked Regis.

"Yes, we know *of* each other," Regis said to Samson, ignoring the dwarf's crass comment. "From the war I told you about."

"So you're the king of this place?" Samson asked, turning his attention back to the dwarves.

"Yes, I am Dvergar, or just Gar as my friends call me," he answered proudly, puffing out his chest, "king of the dwarves and a direct descendant of—"

"Oh, not again," Samson groaned loudly, cutting the dwarf king off before he could finish explaining how his father before him had been king, and his father before him, and…

"What's your problem, mate?" asked the dwarf who'd apprehended the prisoners. "Do you like to live dangerously?"

"I've had it with you people, do you hear me?" Samson roared. "I've had it with your lousy system, your kings and your queens and your childish wars and your ancient this and your ancient that. Understand? I don't want to hear about another ancient ancestor ever again. Not ever."

"What's wrong with him?" Gar asked Regis.

"He's a little edgy," Regis answered as if Samson weren't even there, "and he has a fierce temper. Plus he doesn't seem to like kings too much."

"Doesn't like kings?" Gar was incredulous. "Where's he from? Another world?"

"Yes, in fact, he is," Regis said simply.

"That's *exactly* where I'm from." Samson's voice reduced to a dull roar. "And where I come from, they killed all the kings and queens. Lopped their fool heads off."

"Then we'll be even now, won't we," Gar said maliciously. "Because that's precisely what we intend to do with yours for trespassing in our kingdom."

"Won't you at least give us a chance to explain?" Regis pleaded.

"You know the rules of the treaty as well as I do, Regis," the dwarf said, showing no sympathy at all. "After all, you signed it when you became king, as I did. And trespassing is punishable by death, no ifs or buts."

"I know," Regis added quickly, "but Serena, our future queen, is dying not too far from here. She was hurt by a manticore and needs medical attention right away."

"That's no skin off my nose," Gar said mercilessly. "We'll find her and lop off her head, too, while we're at it."

"Why, you slimy, rotten, ugly little toad!" Samson shouted, shaking the bars with all his strength. The dwarves cowered a little on the other side, despite the knowledge that the bars would hold an elephant, if need be.

"Now, now, mustn't get angry. It wouldn't do at all to lose your head before the actual beheading." Gar chuckled at his own pun.

"If I get my hands on you…," Samson growled.

"But you won't get that chance, will you?" Gar grinned.

"Wait a minute," Regis said firmly. "He isn't part of that treaty and you know it. You have no right to put him to death. None whatsoever."

"Perhaps," the dwarf king mused, stroking the handle of his axe lovingly. "But perhaps we can think of a suitable offense to charge him with."

"Come off it!" Regis said with scorn. "Since when did the mighty Gar, dwarf warrior, suddenly turn into such a coward? I never knew such a yellow streak ran down your back or that you'd be forced to hide behind your own men."

"I'm not hiding behind my men!" Gar almost shrieked.

"Ha! You are. And you're mortally afraid of this human here as well. Admit it. The man terrifies you. He makes your blood run cold. You know in your heart that you wouldn't stand a chance against him, not one on one, just the two of you in a fair fight."

"I'd chop him into little pieces." Gar sneered. "His life would be forfeit before he even knew what hit him."

"Brave words for such an ugly, cowardly, pathetic little creature." Regis's eyes blazed with intensity. "But you won't have to back them up, will you? You can spew that malarkey out in front of your men all you want, knowing full well it's a lie, that you won't have to—"

"Enough!" Gar shouted. "No more talk. The trial is over. The sentence is death, for both of you."

"What's my crime?" Samson asked.

"Spying for the elves," Gar said tersely.

Regis moved close to the bars and peered out intently at the dwarf king. "Listen to me for a moment, Gar. There's a reason we came here in search of you, to find the dwarves."

279

"And what could that be?" Gar asked warily.

"The other races are returning to the land. In fact, the rest have already returned. Yours is the only hold out. Only the dwarves have chosen not to return."

"Is that a fact?" Gar cocked an eyebrow. "I don't believe a word of it, but it's not a bad ploy."

"I'm telling you it's true," the elf king said. "Why else would I break the treaty, risk my neck, if not to find you and persuade you to return to the land with me? It's time we, all of us, challenged the magicians. We should have done it a long, long time ago."

"Maybe so, but today is today, and I doubt anything could persuade me to return to that cursed land. What I can't understand is why you have."

"Because I lost to this man." Regis nodded in Samson's direction. "In a contest more of my choosing than his, he bested me. He successfully tracked a stag, in my own kingdom, and carried it back, alive."

"Come on!" Gar laughed. "Him? He did that?"

"He could take you as well," Regis said quietly. "I'd stake my life on it."

"You have no life to stake. You forfeited it when you stepped into my kingdom."

"Nevertheless, I don't think you can handle him," Regis persisted. "Name the contest and he'll make mincemeat out of you."

Gar stared at the elf king for the longest time. Had his men not been there, had they not heard the challenge and heard his boast, Gar might have backed away from it. But he was in too deep and he knew it. If he shied away from the challenge, his men would never respect him. Not ever again. He would be their king, but in name only. Oh, the folly of waging a battle with words, for such a battle is usually followed by a very real war.

"I accept the challenge." Gar sighed. "Hand-to-hand combat, weapons of our own choosing."

"I've got all I need." Samson leaned casually on his halberd.

"Release the gate, then," Gar ordered one of the dwarves.

"I'll tell you what, king," Samson said lightheartedly as he stepped from the cage quickly, limbering up his cramped muscles. "I'll even offer you the same stakes I offered Regis. My life for your promise to return the dwarves to the land."

"Hardly much of a risk on your part," Gar said.

"It's the best I have to offer."

"Then it will have to do, although I do wish you'd brought something with you worth a little more than your life."

As they squared off against each other—Samson with his halberd, Gar with his battle-axe—dozens of swarthy dwarves streamed into the courtyard, forming a ragged circle around the two combatants. News of the challenge had spread quickly.

Gar waited patiently for Samson to make the first move. Samson took the offensive immediately. It made no difference to him whether he parried or made the first move.

It soon became apparent why the dwarf waited. He was lightning quick at responding to Samson's challenges. Samson found that it was all but impossible to get a blow even remotely close to the dwarf's stout frame without blatantly risking a counterattack against his own.

If Samson struck high and to the right, Gar easily met it. When Samson shifted quickly to a roundhouse, low and to the left, Gar's hefty ax was already there waiting for him. Regis had been on the mark. The dwarf's strength was more than enough to wield the heavy weapon with skill.

Which meant Samson had two choices. He could either wear him down, matching strength for strength, or try to use quickness and wits to reach the dwarf.

Samson believed he would prevail, eventually, in a contest of strength. But that was obviously the dwarf's intention as well, to wear his opponent down with his vast strength. And Gar was probably underestimating Samson's quickness, erroneously believing that one so large could not possibly shift his considerable bulk too quickly.

Samson chose to bide his time, to wait for just that moment when he could dart in for the crippling blow. Until then, he would give every appearance of a lumbering fighter simply trying to batter his opponent into submission.

They fought that way, Samson doing most of the attacking, Gar doing most of the defending, under a steady chorus of shouts, all of them pulling for Gar. Regis remained strangely silent, the serenity on his face out of place in the mob of dwarves cheering madly for their king.

After nearly ten minutes of fierce combat, Samson's chance came, as he'd known it would. After a particularly fierce blow had failed to land on Gar's head, Samson had seemed to drop his weapon wearily at his side.

Gar, seizing the opportunity, quickly and expertly leveled a vicious swing at Samson's midsection. The blow was delivered with enough force to almost cleave him in two. But it never landed. For, anticipating his attack, Samson had dropped to his knee and swung his considerable frame around to the dwarf's left side in order to grab hold of his left leg.

When Gar's swing failed to reach its mark, throwing him slightly off balance, Samson gave a violent tug on his leg. It sent the dwarf crashing to his back. Samson quickly followed up with a hammerlock to the dwarf's head. It was a wrestling move Samson could have performed in his sleep, but there was no way the dwarf king could have known this.

"You lose," he whispered into the dwarf's ear as he yanked Gar's weapon from his hand and tossed it a few feet away.

As Samson released the dwarf king and rose to his feet, a deafening silence filled the room. The dwarves were stunned that Samson had so easily manhandled Gar who was, as well as their king, their greatest warrior by virtue of his courage and intelligence. It was unthinkable that he should be defeated so easily.

"None of you could have done any better," Regis said to fill the silence, "so don't get any bright ideas."

Gar picked himself up and faced Samson. "You are truly magnificent. Your strength matches my own and your quickness is twice mine. I salute you."

Samson, startled by the gracious manner in which the dwarf had accepted defeat, simply nodded in acknowledgment.

"Now, I think, there is the matter of settling the wager," Regis said quickly. "You promised to return to the land with us?"

"Yes, I will go with you first." Gar spoke with a heavy heart. "The rest will follow later, when I've determined just why it is the other races have taken it into their fool heads to challenge the magicians after all these years."

"A medic," Samson added suddenly. "I know it wasn't part of the bargain we struck, but could a medic accompany us and tend to Serena's wounds? I'll go another round with you, if you'd like?"

The dwarf king waved irritably. "No, no, that won't be necessary. If we're going to risk our necks together against these magicians, then I suppose we can at least be civil about our relationship in other areas."

"Thank you," Regis said, somehow managing to keep the relief from showing in his face.

16

***

VALLEY OF
THE STONE GIANTS

The giants, every one of them, made the trek north with the magicians to the mountain range where they would rest until the Last Day. Even the two sentinels came along.

Which meant only one thing. If Laura failed, the giants would surely turn to stone from grief and disappear from the land forever. Forever. It was an awfully long time. Laura wasn't at all sure she wanted that kind of failure on her conscience.

She knew, in her heart, that it hardly mattered whether she failed. The giants, as sad as they were, would sooner or later make this trek individually. Her offer had only brought the appointed time closer, sooner than they'd anticipated.

The giants were silent, the sound of their footfalls echoing off the mountain range they were approaching. Mark rode with the first giant, the one he'd awakened, while the magicians had chosen to ride with the red-bearded giant.

Before leaving, Mark and the other magicians had learned the first giant's name. That, by the way, was a great courtesy. By telling Mark his name, the giant had given the young warrior and the magicians something none outside the giants' kingdom had ever possessed. For a giant's name says something about his or her character. And with that knowledge, a magician may be able to turn a giant to stone.

The giant had told them his full name and then added, "but you can just call me Nog. In the ancient tongue, it is a many-colored rock if you hold it up to the sun, but a gray stone in darkness."

"It sounds like an onyx," Laura had said thoughtfully. "In fact, I'm sure of it. It's a chalcedony."

"A what?" Mark had asked.

"A transparent quartz that can be milky or gray in dim light. An onyx, however, is a gemstone with bright colors when you hold it up to the light," she had said almost clinically.

"What is an onyx?" Nog had asked.

"Your name," Laura had said with a cheerful smile, "in my own tongue, in the world where I come from."

"Are there giants in your own world?" Nog had asked the magician.

"No, I don't think so," Laura had answered. "I'm afraid they have all turned to stone, for we have so many mountains there."

"Perhaps the magicians of your world are responsible, for a giant's life is very long before the appointed time," Nog had added gravely.

"Perhaps," Laura had said, not bothering to tell the friendly giant that she doubted there had ever been any of his race in the world she came from.

But Nog and the others refused to speak now as they approached the mountains looming above them. They marched with a purpose and determination that frightened Laura. When they reached the foothills and what seemed like an impenetrable wall of rock, they never hesitated, scaling the mountains with such practiced ease Mark found himself marveling at their ability instead of paying attention to what they would need to do if the giants indeed turned to stone, leaving them cut off on the other side.

The giants paused at the top. Kathryn and Tara gasped, almost as one, for far below them they were witnessing what none had ever witnessed: the final resting place of the giants. Spread out before them, in various states of repose and contemplation, were hundreds of stone giants in a valley enclosed on all sides by mountain peaks.

Mark's eyes drifted almost immediately to one giant caught in a pose of anguish, his arms thrust up to the heavens in anger, beseeching the gods for mercy.

"This is the giant who lost three children to the magicians," Nog said, breaking the giants' silence. "His grief was more than ours, for his wife was also the first to make the journey here."

Tara's eyes, however, had drifted first to a young female giant curled on the ground in a fetal position, forever caught in the position in which she'd reposed in her mother's womb.

Kathryn, meanwhile, was riveted by two giants, man and woman, standing and entwined in a loving embrace, their heads each resting on the other's shoulder.

Laura saw none of these. Her gaze flickered from one giant to the next, never resting for very long on any single one.

The giants solemnly started their descent into the valley, more slowly this time. Strangely, their pervading sadness had diminished some. Not a great deal, but enough so that the others had noticed.

Once in the valley, they wandered deliberately through the statues, gazing lovingly at old friends and pausing, occasionally, to give Mark or one of the magicians a brief description of the giant's life.

It was not, as Laura had expected, a bittersweet, melancholy reunion with the past. No, it was more like a fond remembrance of friendship and love, mixed with acceptance of the future.

For the giants, death was not a wrenching, painful end. It was a quiet passing, from one realm to another, as they waited for the Last Day to arrive.

"What is this Last Day you've spoken of?" Laura finally asked, embarrassed that she was the only one who seemed not to know what they were referring to.

"The day when the land passes into the greater Land," Nog said simply. "And we come face to face with the Creator, who gave life to the races and the land."

"And when will this day come?" Laura persisted.

"When the need is greatest, the legends say," Kathryn answered. "When we must give what we have learned here to others in the universe. The legends say that is the ultimate meaning of life—that we all learn so that we may become teachers to others, in the many parts of the Creator's universe."

"It is a very long time away, I think," Nog said. "At least, the giants have always thought so."

"And the people of the sea as well," Tara added.

"But how will you know when this Last Day is approaching?" Laura asked.

"No one knows," Mark shrugged. "It is only a legend, and a vague one at that. All we know is that it will come."

Laura kept her thoughts to herself. She doubted whether such a Creator existed, whether such a Last Day would ever come, whether, in fact, there was any rhyme or reason to this land. But there was no point in adding her own narrow beliefs to their simplistic religious views. Better to let them continue in their ignorance.

"I need you, each of you, to tell me where your mates have chosen to rest," Laura said gently to the giants. She looked directly at Nog. "But if it is all right with you, I'd like to try your wife first?"

Nod nodded slowly. He carried Laura and the others across the valley to a place where a female giant was resting easily on two knees, gazing intently at the ground.

"She used to tend the forests surrounding the mountains," Nog said with no trace of anger or bitterness. "This was her favorite position, the one she felt most comfortable with, when she tended to them."

Laura gathered Kathryn and Tara around her. "Have either of you come up with anything we can use here?" she said softly so the giants couldn't hear. "I know you realize, as I do, that we have no sure way of bringing them back to life."

Tara pursed her lips. "We need her name, I think, her real name."

Laura nodded fervently. "I agree. That's of the utmost importance."

"And I think a brief history of her life would help a great deal," Kathryn added. "You know, what she enjoyed the most, what brought her the greatest happiness."

"Right," Laura said, surprised at the way both of them had managed to plunge to the heart of what they needed here. Had they learned that from her? Or had they always possessed such intuition?

Laura turned to Nog. "We'll need her name, her real one, to begin with," she said, looking up at the giant's placid face.

"Of course," the giant replied without hesitation. "She had two names, really. We just called her by Wer."

"I understand. But what are her given names?"

"*Twer* and *Sme*." Nog gazed intently at the statue frozen on her knees as he did so.

Laura closed her eyes for a moment. "Of course," she said at last. "Quartz and mica, which would form granite. That's what they mean."

"Granite?" Kathryn asked. "What is that?"

"It's a hard, coarse rock used in buildings where I come from." Laura closed her eyes again, dredging the precise definition from her photographic memory. "Unyielding endurance and steadfastness. That's what granite also means."

Kathryn and Tara gazed at her in amazement. They would need spell books to remember something like that, whereas Laura simply remembered it. But, then, they didn't have total recall as she did.

"All right," Laura said with determination, focusing on Nog again. "Does that describe her? Steadfast? Unyielding endurance?"

"Why, yes, it does," Nog said, obviously surprised Laura had described his wife's best qualities without even having met her. "She was the strongest of us, the most faithful to her appointed task…"

"Which was?" Laura asked.

"To build," Nog said simply. "It was her appointed task to keep the mountains from crumbling and to keep other parts of the land from caving in as well."

"Makes sense," Laura mumbled to herself. "Granite. One of the strongest igneous rocks we know of. Of course she would build and strengthen."

"What's that?" Nog asked, curious.

"Oh, nothing," Laura said to him. "Just thinking out loud to myself. It's a habit I have. Now, is there anything else you can tell me about her, anything else that gave her the greatest joy?"

Nog was silent for a very long time. When he spoke again, it was with deliberation. "Two things only gave her fulfillment, if that is what you mean."

"And they are?"

"Her children and the forest land, which she tended so often, as I've already mentioned. She chose this position in her grief, I think, because her children had been taken from her."

Laura glanced again at the statue, kneeling as if planting a tulip bulb. But in Wer's case, she would be patting down the soil around a tree or perhaps trimming dead branches from the foliage of the tree. Laura turned to the other magicians. "Can you think of anything else we might need?"

"The names of her children?" Kathryn offered.

"That was my thought as well." Tara nodded.

"The boy was called *Smaragdite* and the girl *Reudh*," Nog said gently, overhearing the magicians' discussion.

"The roots of an emerald and a ruby," Laura muttered. "How interesting."

"You had just two children?" Kathryn asked the giant.

"Yes, just two. Before they left us."

"That should do it, then," Laura said. "I think we have everything we may need. Her name, the names of her children, and what she treasured most."

"What should we do now?" Kathryn asked nervously.

In a classroom, Laura would have immediately given her version of what she felt needed to be done, the precise description of what was needed to accomplish their stated objective. But here, for some reason, she chose to include the other two in the process. "I think we need a spell that somehow brings the breath of life to her as well as those things that meant so much to her."

"So you think we need the ancient words for breath and life?" Tara asked. Laura nodded. "I remember well the word for *breath* because it relates so well to my own kingdom," the mermaid said. "It's *bhreu*."

"And life is *leip*, I think," Kathryn added.

"Very good," Laura said. "And the ancient word for forest is *dwer*. Those should just about do it, I hope."

"What do you intend to do now?" Nog asked, confused by the magicians' banter.

"Wake her," Laura said simply.

"With what?" the giant asked.

"The power of language and knowledge, mixed with a little luck and insight, I hope," Laura answered with an easy smile. She was suddenly very confident it would work. It was, in a way, the same sort of confidence she had when she walked into a classroom for a test. Phrasing each carefully, Laura strung the words they'd collected together and directed them at the giantess—her name, the names of her children, her work and her joy in life, and the breath of life to recreate her.

A silence stretched into an eternity.

Her eyes opened first, fluttering briefly before they fell upon her husband. Then, as the magicians looked on in fascination at what their minds had wrought, the color returned to the giantess' limbs. Life stirred where only stone had been but a moment before.

"Is it the Last Day?" she asked her husband when she had fully recovered. "Will my children be returned to me?"

Nog looked at his wife with a sort of grim sadness, mixed with an aching joy at seeing the one he loved come miraculously back to life. "No, my love, it is not the Day, and your children have not returned."

"Then why have I been awakened?" she asked, closing her eyes again.

"Your children will be returned to you," Laura said in a very loud voice, "if it is the very last thing I do in life."

The giantess' eyes fluttered open a second time. "By what authority do you make such a promise?"

"She is a very powerful magician," Nog said.

"A magician?" Wer rumbled, anger flaring in her eyes. "One of those who stole my children?"

"No, a magician who intends to return them to you." Laura bit her lip. "At least, that's the plan."

17

***

OBERON, AUBREY,
AND CHIRON

The centaurs were, perhaps, the best students humankind would ever know. But eager scholars, of course, will always make bright, willing students.

Within a matter of days, the centaurs had learned the rudiments of reading and writing. Jon was convinced that it would not be long before the centaurs had spread his gift of knowledge far and wide in the land.

It was a strange feeling. Jon had never actually helped anyone in his life. Oh, he'd let someone borrow his notes from class, or let some poor, witless soul cry her eyes out on his shoulder while she was high, or knocked a few dollars off the price of an ounce of cocaine out of the goodness of his heart.

But those all seemed so petty compared to this. No, not petty, it was more than that. The centaurs were so genuinely excited, so utterly thrilled at the world of knowledge that lay open before them that they could hardly contain themselves.

Jon had taught them the alphabet first, of course, followed by a lesson on vowels and consonants. Then a few lessons on grammar—how to conjugate verbs, what a noun was, where adjectives were used. Because they were already well aware of the intricacies of language and were masters of an extensive vocabulary as well, they were able to read haltingly once they'd learned sentence structure.

Jon had always heard that someone with a firm grasp of the language could almost teach himself how to read, but here was living proof.

"It is truly a wonder," Cleo had said on more than one occasion during those days. "Here we have toiled all our lives, often roaming to the ends of the earth in search of knowledge, risking our necks to speak to the wisest who have secluded themselves as hermits from the rest of the world, and here is a storehouse of knowledge at our fingertips."

Jon had just shaken his head. If Cleo only knew how many libraries full of books there were in his own world, just how much knowledge was available to anyone who sought it, he would see what a pittance this tiny library in Pluto's palace actually was.

Lucas and Maya, meanwhile, had made some new friends. Or, rather, Peg had introduced them to quite a few of the guests in Pluto's palace.

Oberon, the fairy king, Chiron, the centaur king, and Aubrey, the first king of the elves were there, as well as a great many others—all heroes or heroines who had woven the fabric of the land's legends…and the Earth's legends.

It was a joyous time for Lucas. He found it harder and harder to remember his previous life as a simple shepherd boy in the mountains.

Chiron, especially, found it hard to believe that Lucas had ever been a shepherd. "You aren't a cleric, as the other is?" he'd asked Lucas, referring to Jon.

"No, I'm just accompanying him."

"Well, then, I don't think there's any question that you will, like him, be a great priest someday."

"No, I don't think so," Lucas had said quickly.

"Trust me. I speak from experience. I was there when the humans first began to learn the ways and power of magic. And there were those, just like you, who quickly ascended the rungs."

Lucas had blushed and mumbled his thanks, but he would never think of himself as anything more than a simple wayfarer, a person who was better at listening and watching than ministering to other's needs.

"But don't you see?" Oberon had said. "That is what a priest does best—listen and watch. If those are your best qualities, then you will be a boon to your race."

Lucas had thanked the ancient kings for their appraisal, promising to take their suggestions to heart. And he would. What he did not, or could not, know at the moment was whether they were accurate ones or simply idle chatter.

Maya learned some useful things too during those days in Pluto's palace. First, that among the humans who were guests there, not one had been inside the magicians' city. Second, no one had the slightest idea what had happened to the magicians, where they had gone, or even how they had come to learn the magic arts. And third, she learned from the three ancient kings how it was the races had come into existence.

"I believe we came from that world, that young priest's," Oberon had told her. "My memory is dim—that time was so very long ago—but I seem to recall that the races were created in his world first, before we came here."

"Jon's world?" Maya had asked. The idea seemed incredible. "That's where the origin of the races lies?"

"As far as we know," Aubrey had said. "We, those of us who made up the first council of the races, were born in the land. But our forefathers came from another world. Or so I was told when I was very young."

Chiron, who was older than the other two, had gone a step further. "There was a time, when the two worlds were not separated by all that much."

"How so?" Maya had asked.

"Well, as you know," the centaur king had said, "I was a tutor to the gods at one time. And the gods, then, lived in a place called Olympus, a place seemingly born of the imagination of men—or of the magicians—in the other world.

"But, back then, the gods could come and go between the two worlds with ease. They were free to meddle in the affairs of humankind in that other world, the one the young priest hails from.

"In fact, the gods terrorized humankind. It was only much later, after my time, that the gods were somehow confined to this world and the bridges and portals between the two worlds somehow vanished or closed forever."

"Not forever," Maya had corrected him.

"Quite right," Chiron had said. "But sealed to only a select few. It is a strange turn of events, indeed, that it is now the magicians, the humans, who wield power over the gods themselves. A very strange thing indeed."

But Maya had also learned more about a creature that she had always known and never questioned, a link to the past she'd always considered a friend and never a mentor.

"You realize, of course, that Pegasus is a god as well," the centaur king had said to Maya. "He is of Olympus stock. He was there when this world was created, I think, and here when the gods were confined to this world."

Peg, who never spoke unless spoken to, never acted unless called upon to act, had nodded solemnly at Maya. "I think the fairy queen is well aware of that fact."

And indeed Maya was. But history is often something we choose to forget rather than examine too closely, which may explain why Maya had never questioned the winged horse too closely about his origins. Their friendship, Maya's and Peg's, was based on a mutual trust in today, not yesterday. She wasn't about to break that with a bunch of silly questions about Peg's past, not unless it could help them in their quest.

"No, I don't think I can offer much there," Peg had said thoughtfully. "The magicians were a closed book to me, here in this world, long before the gods were imprisoned here. And as for those who created the land and the races who now dwell here, their names wouldn't be of much help, either."

"But there is one Creator, isn't there?" Lucas asked the winged horse.

Peg had simply shrugged. "Yes, Pluto claims there is and that those who are now guests in his realm will someday venture there. He speaks of a final destination, of sorts. I prefer to think of things as a journey."

They had also talked about the first Great Council in the land. The three ancient kings had been there, along with the others of that time.

It had been a magnificent time, a time of wonder and good will, they had said, when the races lived easily with one another. The problems arose much later, well after that first council.

And now it is time for the second Great Council, Maya had thought as she listened to the ancient kings regale her with stories of that era. *Only there is a difference now. This will be a council of war, not one of peace.*

The five of them—Jon, Lucas, Maya, Peg, and Cleo—left eventually. The other centaurs weren't far behind, carrying the books Jon had created with them in heavy saddlebags. Pluto had given them permission to borrow them for a time.

It was a bittersweet parting, but an inevitable one. As much as all of them might have liked to remain there, it was not their place. Not yet, at least. There was work to be done. So as they were ferried back up the Styx, each with his or her own memories of the place, they slowly turned their focus toward the land of the living, the council that must be called, the plans that must be laid and agreed to. And the magicians, of course.

Somewhere out there, the magicians and their mentors were waiting. There could be no question of that. The men and women, the scourges of the land who had wrapped themselves in cloaks of power, must be discovered again and confronted. There was simply no choice.

18

* * *

ON THE WAY

Shar got his wish. The dragon, perhaps sensing great things were afoot when the two sentinels left their post to join the others, had followed in their wake and joined the magicians in the valley of the stone giants.

Once many of the giants had awakened, Tara and Kathryn left for the sea and the southern reaches of the land, seated comfortably between Shar's leathery wings as the dragon easily covered the long distance from the giants' northern kingdom to the waters far to the south. The two young magicians had agreed, reluctantly, to set off for the sea without her because Laura had decided that she wanted as many different people, from every corner of the land, at the Great Council.

News of the council already swept across the land like a prairie fire raging out of control. Laura suspected that was probably the handiwork of a few of the more mischievous gods—Mercury, perhaps, who reveled in spreading gossip, or Mars, who delighted in carrying rumors of war to and fro.

But she was also certain Blackbeard and the others who had formed the militia to hunt the feared magicians would not go away so easily, either.

Laura's decision to include as many different factions of the land in the council was, to her way of thinking, a necessary one. And other decisions would have to be made later if the land was ever to live in peace. Of that she was certain.

If, indeed, it was the first council since the dwarves and elves nearly butchered each other, since the people of the sea fled to the depths of the ocean to avoid the magicians, since the giants turned to the north in their grief, since the fairies left for the second heaven to frolic their lives away, and the centaurs journeyed far to the west in search of knowledge after the land was all but deserted, then some things were going to have to change in the land. It was as simple as that.

So as Tara and Kathryn winged to the south to bring others to the council, Laura set off to the east with Mark, Nog the giant, and his wife, Wer. And as they went, they carried news of the Great Council to those who had not yet heard.

It seemed ironic to Laura that she hadn't really noticed the land until now. Oh, she'd appraised it, sized it up as she made her way across it, first from the southern reaches to the meeting hall and then later on her way to the giants in the north. But she'd never really taken time to study the land, to realize just how much it had been devastated as the magic drained from it. And without magic, the drought had taken its toll. There was no escaping that. The farms to the north and east were every bit as miserable and wretched as those to the south had been.

They visited as many farms and villages as Laura could manage and urged them to send representatives to the council meeting. So many had heard of the magicians' return to the land, they were afraid at first. But the presence of the gentle giants, once the initial shock had worn off, allowed many to agree to send a representative.

Laura also visited Nathaniel and his grandmother, assuring them Kathryn was alive and well. Laura discovered, much to her delight, that their farm was the talk and crown jewel of the land. People came from far and wide to gaze on the rich, irrigated fields. For the first time in a very long time, Laura felt useful. Needed.

Their last stop was the Sanctuary, to see Mark's grandfather and persuade him to come to the council, if only to observe. The Sanctuary, however, had changed in Mark's absence. And not altogether for the good.

Once they'd returned from their unsuccessful effort to seize the magicians at the hall, Blackbeard, the Weasel, and their followers had seized part of the Sanctuary, established their own little kingdom, and all but declared war on Mark's grandfather and those who had chosen to remain behind with him.

"Leave the Sanctuary to them," Laura urged Mark's grandfather after explaining what she hoped to accomplish at the council meeting.

"But it is our home. And the only haven from the magicians in the land."

"There is no need for the haven any longer," Laura said as gently as possible to the old man. "Leave this place—leave it to your youngest son who covets it so—and rejoin your cousins, the elves, in their vast forest land. It's time to reunite, not set brother against brother over small plots of land."

"Please, can we go see the elves?" Mark's little sister, Samantha, pleaded. "Please?"

"At least come with us to the council meeting," Laura said. "At the very least, do that and see what comes of it."

***

Samson, meanwhile, proceeded with all haste to the meeting hall. It was all he could do to keep Regis from Gar's throat during the long trek back to the lodge.

They were forced to leave Serena behind. The dwarves reluctantly agreed to tend to her broken leg and other assorted wounds. Gandy had also remained behind. There was no point in his going to the council meeting and *somebody* had to stay with Serena, he said.

The dwarf king took them by a completely different underground route that avoided manticores and Minotaurs alike as well as goblin outposts. And the route, which the dwarf king promised would lead almost to the lodge, was shorter to boot.

One thing still troubled Samson, besides the ceaseless quarreling between Regis and Gar, which he'd largely learned to ignore. He had wondered for some time—almost from the moment he'd come to in a daze under the oak tree in the Sanctuary—whether he would ever return to his home. Now he caught himself considering whether he wanted to return. That thought was, to say the least, unsettling.

* * *

Jon tried his best to avoid the gods on the way to the council meeting. He really and truly did. But it was inevitable that one or two should pop up along the way as they hurried across the land.

The first of them showed up on the second night out, a day after they'd left the Styx and Pluto's gloomy realm behind.

"Oh, no," Jon groaned when Diana the Huntress showed up just after dusk. "I thought I'd seen the last of you."

"Now, now," said Apollo's twin sister, one of the three maiden goddesses of Olympus also known as Artemis, "we have quite an interest in this little quest of yours. We need to keep track of your progress."

"You mean meddle in it, don't you? Can't you just leave me alone for a while?" Jon pleaded to the beautiful but fierce lady of Wild Things everywhere. "Please?"

"If you insist," Diana said, "but I wouldn't spurn our aid and comfort so quickly. The gods can do much for you."

"If I recall," Jon countered, "your aid usually comes with a pretty hefty price. Wasn't that you who kept a Greek fleet from sailing to Troy until they'd sacrificed a young maiden to you?"

Diana blushed. "Well, yes, the Greeks certainly did think highly of me. But, I swear to you in my father's honor, I never requested that of them."

"On Zeus's honor?" Jon laughed. "I never knew such a thing existed."

Diana's face became a troubled story. "Do not mock the gods," she warned sternly. "It will go hard for you."

"Come on." Jon frowned. "Admit it. The gods are as confused about all this as I am. You don't like your exile in this world any more than I do. So you can forget about the threats."

"Perhaps," Diane said before melting back into the night. "But the gods will not be reckoned with lightly. Remember that."

19

***

THE SECOND COUNCIL'S NEW LAW

They came from far and wide, the curious and the hopeless alike, those with everything to gain and nothing to lose, men and women weary of battling the elements in a land where the very essence of life had been drained from it. They wanted no part of an angry mob. They wanted something new. And they were not afraid of the new magicians or the return of the races.

Laura, the two giants, and Mark's family arrived first, before Jon or Samson and their entourage. And she immediately saw that she had been more successful than she could have hoped.

Not only had news of the council spread like a brush fire out of control, but news that magic and the other races had again returned to the land had spread with it.

The ancient lodge was crowded to overflowing. Families were camped within a mile of the hall in any direction. Thousands, literally, had shown up to see the emissaries of the various races as they arrived for the council meeting.

Most, but not all, of those who had come near to the hall fled from the giants in fear as they approached. A few brave souls cowered behind trees or bushes as the giants lumbered past with their passengers, however, and one or two even ventured out into the open to gawk without shame or prejudice.

As Samson, Regis, and Gar made their way through the crowded landscape, it reminded Samson of war stories he'd read or heard about, where families were uprooted and had stormed the capital of the nation for refuge—a city born overnight, one that would melt away again when the council had disbanded.

Neither Regis nor Gar was entirely prepared for the welcome they received. The people of the land were glad to see them. No, *glad* was too mild a word. They were almost ecstatic at the sight of the two leaders, who had abandoned their ceaseless bickering for the moment in the face of the reception they were receiving.

Cries of "Hail, elf!" or "Ho there, dwarf!" rang out from the multitude time and time again as the three of them made their way to the ancient hall. For Samson's part, he paused as often as he could to chat with families or give a few the chance to speak with Regis and Gar.

Samson had to laugh at both Regis's and Gar's obvious discomfort. This was hardly what they'd expected when they'd agreed to return to the land. They'd expected animosity and hostility, not a welcome embrace with open arms.

"If I'd known you people were so daft, I'd have stayed put," the dwarf king mumbled after one especially solicitous greeting from an old, grizzled, weather-beaten farmer.

"You can say that again," agreed Regis, who had patiently explained a dozen times already that the other elves were on their way and would arrive in the land shortly. "Your people have gone insane, Samson."

"They're not *my* people," Samson corrected. "You forget. I'm not of this world."

"Oh, they're your people all right." Gar rubbed the weariness of the journey from his eyes. "If not directly, then at least in spirit."

The strangest reception of all, however, awaited Jon and the three who had accompanied him. Not only had the people of the land never seen a centaur before, they likewise had never seen a fairy or a winged horse either.

And the arrival of all three at once created such a stir it was all Jon could do to keep them from storming the lodge and demanding an audience.

"Well, I never," Jon muttered to the fairy queen at one point as Cleo chatted amiably with a family that had traveled for nearly a week to reach the hall and Peg allowed first one small child after another to sit comfortably on his back or lightly touch his folded wings.

"Me, neither," sighed Maya, who was hiding on Jon's shoulder because most of the children had taken her for a delightfully animated doll rather than a living, breathing creature of the land. More than one had already tried to pluck a wing off.

"I hope you aren't angry about all this," Jon whispered anxiously, glancing over his shoulder at the fairy queen. "It takes time for people to get used to new things, and I don't think anyone has seen a fairy in quite some time."

"Oh, don't worry so much," Maya assured him. "I understand human nature better than you think. It's nothing more than idle curiosity, which will pass as soon as the novelty wears off."

"That's rather magnanimous of you," Jon said with a wry smile.

"It is, isn't it?" Maya laughed, leaping to the top of Jon's head as a little boy of perhaps five or six tried to sneak up on her from behind to pluck one of her tiny wings.

Laura deliberated for some time, but Jon and Samson eventually persuaded her that it would be fine to allow a bridge to span the moat. They could always remove it if necessary, they argued, but it was a nice, open gesture to those camped outside.

* * *

It was agreed, in the end, that the Great Council should have as many members as necessary. They tried to limit it to 12 members, as all the legends said. But after much arguing, Laura finally silenced everyone.

This was a time of new ways, new laws, she said. And the first new law was that the council would not be limited by ancient legends. The Great Council could have 12 members—or 14. "The council will be what it will be," Laura had insisted, and the others had agreed in the end. Whatever was required to work, that was the correct number. Numbers didn't matter. The council had to make the land work.

So the second Great Council included the respective leaders of the six races who had agreed to return to the land—Regis for the elves, Gar for the dwarves, Cleo for the centaurs, Nog for the giants, Maya for the fairies, and Tara for the people of the sea (chosen only the night before by her elders, nearly all of whom had made the journey to the hall).

It was also agreed upon that Mark, Lucas, and Kathryn would represent the human race, by virtue of their close association with the other races. Samson, Jon, and Laura would also sit on the council because they had brought the races back to the land. Peg agreed to be a member, after a great deal of discussion about the fairness of including one of the gods on the council. And the final member of the council, who was thoroughly delighted at the prospect, was Shar the silver dragon, who had agreed to represent the disenfranchised creatures of the land.

By the time the various races, family members, and assorted others had gathered, and the members seated around the round table again, the council chamber was standing room only. Strangely, there had been very little pushing, shoving, or elbowing from those shut out of the hall.

But that may have had something to do with the fact that Wer had situated herself right outside the two massive doors of the hall, serving as the sergeant-at-arms. Very few questioned her choices of who to let in and who to keep out.

"Before we consider anything else," Maya said when the hall had hushed still, "I think we'd better decide what to do about the magicians. Those from the city, I mean."

"What can we do about them?" Regis shrugged. "Either they're hidden away in the magicians' city or they're not."

"We need to know the truth, once and for all," Maya insisted. "And I think we have to decide whether we intend to defy them. Regardless of where they are."

"I agree." Nog's voice created a slight tremor in the vast hall even though he'd spoken softly.

"What courage does it take to defy something you can't see?" Gar insisted. "And what purpose does it serve?"

"I'll tell you what purpose it serves," Maya said quickly. "We must decide, right now, whether this land is ours. Or theirs."

"Perhaps it belongs to both," offered Shar.

"Maybe at one time," Maya replied, "but not any longer. They gave up that right when they used the land for their own purposes and we didn't stand up to them."

"But what purpose does it serve to defy the magicians now, when we have no idea if they exist any longer or where they might have gone?" Gar persisted.

"A very good purpose," Maya said with a smile. "For, if I don't miss my guess, magic is about to return to the land. To all the land, whether the magicians of the city like it or not."

A murmur spread quickly through the hall but died down when Tara stood. "As you know," the young mermaid said, "I have been graciously given the gift of magic by someone at this table. After discussing it with my elders before coming here, the people of the sea have decided to teach that magic to any and all who seek it in the land, using our ability to convey thoughts from one mind to another."

Laura stood, then, and laid several heavy volumes—almost encyclopedias, really—on the table in front of her. "These are spell books that I created last night. They include every magic spell I could possibly remember. And I have decided to turn these over to the people of the sea, who will in turn give that knowledge out freely to anyone who seeks it."

"Anyone?" Regis asked, incredulous. "Even the other races?"

"Especially the other races," Laura said firmly. "There must be no division in the land because one wields unearned power over another."

"I have something else to bring up." Jon's voice rose above the steady hum in the room that had begun as soon as Tara had made her announcement. He waited for the room to quiet down again.

"Go ahead, Jon, what is it?" said Maya.

"Just this. We must abolish the Law. It's that simple. It's the one thing this council must accomplish, above all others."

Maya couldn't suppress a smile, remembering Jon's futile effort to defend himself before the fairies when he'd first arrived in the land. He'd unwittingly broken the Law, setting in motion a chain of events that had led to this council. "I wondered when you'd get around to that," the fairy queen said. "So you don't think the Law is such a good idea, that each race has a sovereign duty to protect its domain in nature?"

"No, I think it's a lousy idea," Jon said miserably, as he, too, remembered the mental agony he'd suffered at the hands of Maya's subjects.

"And I agree," Laura said loudly. "It divides the land against itself."

"But it is all we have ever had to protect ourselves against the tyranny of the magicians," Regis protested.

"The *only* thing we've ever had," said Gar, who couldn't believe he was agreeing with the elf king. "And even that has done us precious little good."

"I think," Laura stated, "that your blind obedience to your domain made it nearly impossible to live in harmony with the other races. We *must* create a new Law, one that takes the best of the old but infuses it with the best of the new that we now understand."

"And what might that new Law be?" Cleo said.

"Simple," Jon replied. "Instead of vesting the power in one race or another, each with its own, separate domain, the power to protect the land—to keep it from being ravaged—will rest equally with all seven races."

"You can set up smaller tribunals across the land, made up of representatives from each of the races, to judge and decide on courses of action," Laura continued.

"And the final authority, of course, would rest here, with the highest council in the land, on any matter of great or urgent importance," Jon added eagerly.

"That way, you wouldn't set one race against another, or run the risk of alienating people because they don't like the way you're administering the Law," Laura said. "All would share equally in the fruits and sorrows."

"And how exactly do we set up all these tribunals, as you call them?" Regis asked suspiciously.

"Elections, of course," Samson said, delighted at the opportunity to punch a hole in what he felt was one of the land's most serious drawbacks. "I never have liked kings and queens running the show around here."

"No, no, each race would choose who it wants to sit on the various tribunals," Laura said swiftly, before the other leaders of the races reacted angrily to Samson's slur aimed at royalty and monarchy in general. "It would be your choice and yours alone as to who would sit on each of these tribunals. And it would be your choice as well about leadership among your own races."

Regis and Gar glanced at each other. A silent acknowledgment passed between them. As long as they could still lead, it would be all right with them.

"I will agree," the dwarf king said.

"I will as well," Regis said.

"Good." Laura inwardly sighed with relief that no one had been angered, either by the suggestion to abolish the Law or Samson's suggestion that kings and queens weren't exactly a good idea.

"All in favor of abolishing the Law and, instead, spreading the governing authority in the land throughout all seven races, say 'aye'," Laura added.

The vote was unanimous.

"This may sound stupid," Tara said after the vote, "but can we really do that? Abolish the Law that easily, I mean, and replace it with the one we just agreed to?"

Laura rose again. "Not right away. But when the magic has returned to the land, to all the races, the joint efforts of the majority of the people should be able to dispel the old Law, I would think."

"Does that mean my family can use the river to bring water to their crops?" Kathryn asked timidly. "And our neighbors as well?"

Laura smiled. "That's precisely what it means. Although I doubt you'll need to do that, now that you're a full-fledged magician."

Kathryn lowered her eyes. "I might be a magician, but I don't think I'll forget about the land just yet."

A slight cough shook the rafters. Those around the table looked up at Nog. "A promise was made to me," the giant said. "And to the others of my race as well..."

"I remember," Laura interjected, "and I intend to honor that pledge."

"What pledge?" Cleo asked.

"Yes, what pledge?" Regis and Gar asked almost in unison.

"To visit the magicians' city and find their children," Laura said. "And, perhaps, discover why they disappeared from the land long ago."

"You know, of course, that you've pledged the impossible." Cleo spoke for others around the round table. "No one, according to the careful history the centaurs have kept, has ever successfully entered the city. Save, perhaps, the gods."

"True," Laura reasoned, "but it's never been attempted by someone like me before, has it? I'll find a way in. I promise. And anyone who cares to follow me in is welcome to come along."

The rest of the Great Council was hardly the stuff of legend—deciding who should live where now that the races had agreed to return from their exile, who should keep the council chambers clean, whether dragons would be granted citizenship in the land, those sorts of things.

But it was all in writing somewhere nevertheless, in case anyone should ever care to examine just how it was that the council decided to turn the land upside down and shake it to its very foundations. Now that he knew how to write, you see, Cleo the centaur had taken careful notes.

20

***

BEGGAR GODS

It had taken quite a few blows from Thor's proverbial hammer to Jon's addled mind, but it was finally becoming clear to him. It had taken this world to help Jon understand his own.

There had been a time once on Earth when men and women foolishly walked around worshiping gods and goddesses, when magic had seemed awfully important to control the elemental forces of nature, when the mysteries of the universe seemed much too profound for ordinary humans to grasp and when the sons of God blatantly interfered in the lives of mortals.

But those days were long gone. The old wars of magic and religion were ended, and the gods of ancient Earth had been banished to this land, with little for them to do. And they were desperate.

A notion formed in Jon's mind, one that would have seemed incomprehensible to him not long ago. Shortly before the birth of Jesus, the Bible seemed to say, there had been a war in heaven. The archangel, Michael, had cast Satan and fallen angels to Earth. That, Jon was beginning to believe, seemed to be the time of banishment. Portals to magical worlds were closed, new covenants were formed on Earth, and a new path to redemption with God was formed through his son, Jesus. The old ways of magic became irrelevant, and the gods of ancient Earth became obsolete, consigned to the literary scrap heap of history and folklore.

Within several hundred years after the birth of Christ, the temples to the gods in the old world vanished, replaced by Christian churches. Kings and emperors became obsolete, replaced by governments of the people. The new had replaced the old.

And the sons of God? Satan and his fallen angels? The magicians of this land, who had learned the intricate ways of power and control over nature?

Jon didn't know. What he did know, however, was that the gods here—right now—were clearly driving him crazy.

Aphrodite, or Venus, showed up first, before the others were ready to set off for the magicians' city. The unfortunate thing, Jon soon learned, was that she was only the harbinger of the gods' harassment.

"So we meet at last," the goddess of love and beauty said softly as she slipped up on Jon late that night as he sat outside, stone-faced, staring at the dying embers of a huge fire someone had built to scare away the chill of the night.

Jon, bone tired from the long meeting, was still drawn to her seductive beauty. He knew who she was, or at least had an inkling that it might be Venus. The longer he stayed in the land, the easier he found it had become to recognize the fickle gods of ancient Earth—and their seemingly endless appetite for tricks and games with humans. Someone clearly needed to give them a new mission.

"Oh, just leave me alone, you witch," Jon said grumpily, barely glancing in her direction as she settled comfortably beside him. "I'm too tired to play any games right now."

"Too tired?" Venus caressed the nape of his neck. "Men would kill for the chance to let them touch me."

"Well, I'm not one of them, so why don't you simply tell me what you want?" Jon sighed, trying desperately to ward off the shivering sensation her light caress was producing in various parts of his body.

"Now, now, mustn't get so angry at me." The goddess laughed sweetly. "I am only here to serve and please. Remember, I led Samson from the wilderness…"

"For which we're all grateful. But I'm sure you had your own reasons for doing so."

"It was our hope—the hope and wishes of the gods—that you would all converge on the magicians' city," Venus said in a soothing voice. "We had faith in you."

"Hardly," Jon retorted. "You did everything you could to lead us here. Well, you have your wish, so leave me alone."

"But if you give me just a moment…"

Jon reached up, pulled her hand from his shoulder, and set it gently in her own lap. "Now stop that," he said firmly. "And I mean it. Just tell me what you want or leave. I don't much care which of those two it is."

"Oh, if you *insist*," Venus huffed. "It's only that I wanted to know if you have a plan yet, for the ancient city of the Magi tomorrow."

"The Magi?" Jon asked, his weariness suddenly dropping away. "Is that what you said?"

"Yes, that's what they were, you know," Aphrodite said with a sly smile. "The ancient magicians were the wisest men and women, able to recognize good and evil at the same time."

"Yes, I know what Magi are. But that's a term from my own world. Three Magi visited Jesus at his birth."

"Now isn't that strange?" Venus said sweetly. "I wonder why that could be?"

"What do you know about these magicians?" Jon asked the goddess crossly.

"All I know is what they were like. Once. I know it wasn't long before they ignored me completely. They would have nothing to do with me as they went on their merry way, doing whatever pleased them."

"Just tell me one thing," Jon said, almost afraid of the answer. "The three Magi who visited the baby Jesus in Bethlehem at his birth, were they from this world— Magi from this world?"

"We knew them, yes," the goddess admitted. "And that was just before we were exiled to this dreary world forever. We'd at least had hope until then—"

Jon interrupted. "Just who are these Magi anyway? And is there anything about them you can tell me that might help us when we try to enter their city tomorrow?"

"*What* they are is a better question. That, and who taught them. That's what we hope you can discover. Perhaps you'll need me along," Venus wheedled.

"No, I'm sorry." The last thing in the world he wanted was a meddling goddess at his side. "It's not possible. The others wouldn't allow it, I'm afraid."

"At least promise me one thing," she cooed. "Don't close every door to this world when you leave. Promise?"

Jon grumbled, "Oh, all right, I'll do my best. But I'm not promising anything yet."

Before the dying embers of the fire had even had a chance to cool, Vulcan reared his ugly head from the very midst of the orange, glowing embers, scattering fiery sparks in all directions.

Among the perfect and beautiful gods of Olympus, only Vulcan, the god of fire, was born ugly. And lame as well. Not surprisingly, he didn't last long on Olympus. Ancient legends say that either his father, Zeus, or his mother, Hera, kicked him out when they discovered his deformities.

Perhaps for this reason, only Vulcan appealed to Jon's innate sense of fair play. The god was later allowed to return to Olympus—probably because he was such a genius as a blacksmith and a kindly, peace-loving god as well—but it was hard to ignore his deformities.

"I have no requests to make," Vulcan said, his physical deformities only noticeably apparent as he spoke from within the narrow confines of his own element. "I come only with information you may be able to use."

"That's nice of you," Jon said dryly, wondering what the payment for that news might be. Gods, at least the ones he'd met so far, were perhaps the most selfish creatures he could have imagined. And arrogant to boot.

"The information is this," Vulcan said. "Do not use weapons or fire against the magicians' city, or the castle. They will turn against you. The magicians were taught those. They mastered the essence and meaning of those a long time ago. Your only hope is to change or alter, not fight or contest."

"What's that supposed to mean?" Jon asked sharply, not sure he understood the god's strange portent.

"Weapons and fire are of no use against the ancient magicians," Vulcan said placidly. "None at all. And within the confines of their own home, they turn against their users. It is a place of the basic elements of the land."

"Are you trying to say that if I try to break down a door with an axe, the weapon will turn against me?"

"At last, an intelligent human," the god quipped sarcastically.

Jon couldn't help but wonder: if the gods of this world thought so little of him and the others of his race, why were they now begging for their help? "You've tried to find the magicians and confront them, or at least follow them, and you've failed, haven't you?"

"The gods never fail," Vulcan said. "We have merely been delayed here."

"Delayed here?" Jon laughed. "More like imprisoned here, if you ask me, and you don't like it one little bit. The great gods of ancient Rome and Greece, who once inspired terror in half the world and thought of the other half as your own personal playground."

Jon now thought the whole thing, well, quite funny. There had been a time, even in the time of Jesus, where thousands of people wandered into temples worshiping this sad sack of a god and others. In fact, the Romans who conquered Palestine enforced worship of these gods, and people actually prayed to creatures like Vulcan and Venus, hoping fervently for their intercession.

How silly. Jon could see that so very clearly now. He almost felt pity for those poor souls from his own world who had thought, somehow, that they could receive any sort of blessing or help from gods such as these. If they had only known.

"Enough!" Vulcan bellowed. Even kind, placid gods can be driven to anger, apparently, when their own failings are thrown in their face. "I came here to help, not to be amused by a runt of a human."

Jon inclined his head ever so slightly. "And this runt of a human thanks the god of fire," he said politely. "Most gracious of you to drop by."

"Now, about the payment for the information," Vulcan said stiffly. "I would require that you take me along to your own world if, by some miracle, you succeed in your endeavors…"

"Get out of here!" Jon roared, trying to match Vulcan's earlier bellow of outrage both in volume and indignation. Any sympathy Jon might have still harbored for the god because of his deformities had disappeared in the face of his blatant self-interest.

"As you wish," Vulcan said, already beginning to melt back into the fire. "But it is not wise to anger the gods."

"I've heard that more than once," Jon muttered.

Venus and Vulcan, as it turned out, were not the only residents of Olympus who wanted to bend Jon's ear, however. Later that night, the gray-eyed, ruthless goddess of wisdom and reason, Pallas Athena, also paid a visit.

"Don't tell me," Jon said, opening one eye as he peered at the daughter of Zeus from the warm confines of a sleeping bag Laura had graciously provided for him next to the fire. "You'd like to come back to the Earth with us as well?"

"I am the protector, the battle-goddess," Athena said haughtily, her hand resting lightly on one of Zeus's thunderbolts. "I can help you with your quest, for I know the cities as no other."

"Okay, I'm game," Jon said, mildly curious.

"Enter by just one gate," intoned the goddess of the city, the protector of civilized life. "All others are deception and will doom you to wander forever in search of a way back."

"And how will we know that gate?" Jon nervously imagined wandering, lost, forever trying to find his way back.

"You'll know," Athena said. "Now as for payment for this information…"

Jon laughed. "You're too late. Venus and Vulcan have already been here, asking for much the same thing. And I turned both of them down."

"Venus was here before me?" she hissed. Jon nodded. "And you turned her away?" He nodded again. "Then I am defeated before I even begin." She disappeared into the night.

But no sooner had Jon begun to drift off to sleep than still another showed up. "Well, you must be Apollo," he said, wondering if he was ever going to get any sleep.

"Yes, that is so." The blond-haired, blue-eyed god of light and truth was Master musician, lord of the silver bow, the Healer, and more. He had once been the best-known and beloved of gods on Earth. His messengers, the crows, had inspired countless stories and myths.

"And you want a favor of me, like the others?"

"Not entirely. I come only with a message from the other gods," said Apollo, whose physique might have been chiseled from stone by Michelangelo himself.

"And that is?"

"To remember us as you uncover the trail of the Magi. We beg you. Do not leave us trapped in this world any longer."

"Tell me something." Jon abruptly changed the tiresome question. He sat up and faced the god, "Is it true that you can't tell a lie?"

"Yes, unfortunately, I have been burdened with that responsibility," Apollo admitted sadly. "The imagination of men left me very little room to grow."

"Then, tell me this," Jon said, knowing the answer before he even asked the question. "Those have been your black crows at every turn, every step of our paths since we've arrived? The messengers to the gods. Isn't that right?"

"Yes," Apollo answered reluctantly. "Zeus told me to keep track of you, and the others who came with you."

"And they have kept you, the gods, apprised of our every move?"

"Yes, they have."

"Allowing you to maneuver, connive, and meddle to make sure we would eventually do what we've done—bring the magic back to the land, reunite the races, and make our way to the magicians' city?"

Apollo sighed. "Yes, all correct."

Jon shook his head. "You do realize," he told the god, "that we would have done all those things regardless of your meddling?"

"I suppose," Apollo said, hanging his head, "but it is all we know."

Jon laughed. "Okay, fair enough. But can you tell me what *you* know about these Magi?"

"Only this." Apollo shrugged. "Their knowledge of the powers of nature, bequeathed to them by the masters, was unsurpassed. They knew, and mastered, the elemental forces of nature."

"The powers of nature?"

"To change their form at will, to shift as the seasons do, to harness the brutality of the hunt and the kill, to appreciate the infinite beauty of a flower in spring, to understand the towering strength of the mountains, and to evolve as the creatures of the Earth have over time," Apollo said.

"The stories about your oracle at Delphi were true, then, weren't they?" asked Jon, who hadn't understood much of what the god had said. "You're impossible to understand."

"I tell the Truth. I don't interpret it," the shining, brilliant god of the sun said before he, too, drifted into the shadows of night.

21

***

IN SEARCH
OF THE MAGICIANS

They assembled at the round table again that next morning, after the Great
Council had heralded the return of magic and the races had ushered in a new
law to replace the old one, delivering destiny into the hands of the people and
the races of the land, where it belonged.

It was a quiet morning. Most of the onlookers had drifted away from the lodge
now that the novelty had passed. If you'd seen one elf, you'd seen them all. Besides,
there was work to be done—local councils to form, news to spread, and those who
had witnessed the great event wanted to be first on the scene back home with the
news.

Only a few stray crows remained behind, right outside the doors to the hall,
picking idly at the garbage and food left behind by the vast horde that had descended
on the place so abruptly only to vanish almost as quickly. Jon had to laugh as he saw
them. So much for the vaunted dark messengers to the gods.

Laura was the first to arrive. A vague notion of what was occurring in the land,
and why, had finally grown in her considerable mind. She'd spent the night in the
map room, staring intensely at the crude design carved into the wall, wondering time
and again why someone had taken such pains to locate what must be portals between
the two worlds.

She had finally drawn several conclusions, but one seemed fairly certain. Samson
and Jon had been sent to this world with her because they were so *very* different from
her. But she felt secure in the knowledge that she had been the central figure in this
drama, for the simple reason she alone had served as the wellspring from which
magic had returned to this world. She wondered, vaguely, if she would ever learn just
how central she might be.

She was lost in thought at the table when Jon wandered in early that morning.
He looked terrible, as if he'd been up all night or had only grabbed brief moments of
sleep. The half-grown beard didn't do his appearance any favors, either.

"You're up early," Jon mumbled, rubbing the sleep from his eyes with the back of his hand as he sat down, hard, several seats away.

"I had a lot on my mind," she said.

Jon smiled to himself, remembering the parade of gods beseeching his help throughout the night. "I guess I do, too. But it wasn't of my own choosing."

"How so?"

"Oh, it doesn't matter." Jon shrugged. "Have you figured out yet how to make coffee in this place?"

"I think I could manage some bean curd water," she said, trying not to smile.

Jon grimaced. "No thanks. That sounds like a fate worse than death."

"By the way, have you ever heard anyone mention whether anyone besides the magicians have vanished from this world without a trace?"

Jon shook his head. "Nope. Not that I can think of. Why?"

"No special reason," Laura said easily. "Just thinking, that's all."

"You've been looking at that map upstairs, haven't you?" Jon smirked.

"I spent the night in that room," she said offhandedly.

"And you're wondering if maybe a few of the races in this world, besides these magicians everyone seems so mortally afraid of, somehow slipped into our own world through those portals, aren't you? Or, perhaps, whether they never made it back to this world?"

Laura studied Jon for a long while. Perhaps she hadn't given the guy enough credit. Perhaps there was more to him than met the eye. "It's a thought," she said at last. "It *would* make some sense out of all of this, you know."

"You're right, it would," Jon agreed. "And now that I've seen Apollo and Regis, all that blond hair and blue eyes, I'd say there's been some interesting cross-breeding in this world. Or, possibly, in ours. Hard to tell who's exactly responsible for the beginning and ending of things."

Laura nodded. "I've thought the same thing, too. The races came from somewhere. They have a common lineage, somewhere long ago."

Now Jon nodded. "Yes, I agree. And Araqiel…"

"Looks an awful lot like some of these gods we've run across in this world. Makes you wonder, doesn't it…?"

"If maybe there was a time when the magicians and gods could come here and then return to the Earth we know? But something must have happened. Something closed those portals for good…"

"…and someone chose us to open at least one of them again," Laura mused.

"I've been thinking. Magic is so predominant in this world. It's almost non-existent in ours. Religion is common. Science is common as well. But magic? It's gone."

Laura pursed her lips. "So who do you think Eric is? A magician?"

"Possibly, or someone who serves them. Or maybe even something else entirely. Remember, we don't really know what—or who—the magicians are yet."

"I've also been wondering about something else." She hesitated. "Why do you think we're here?"

"Well, someone—or something—is probably hoping we can reopen the portals, both coming and going. We got here. Can we get back?"

"And if we can achieve that?"

Jon shrugged. "I'm not sure I care. I've already been to Hades and back. I'm not sure anything else would faze me at this point."

*** *** ***

In the end, no one was excluded from the quest to end all others in the land.

Samson, at first, felt that only a few should make the perilous attempt to enter the city of the ancient magicians. The fewer lives risked, the better, he reasoned. He was quickly outvoted. None at the table wanted to be left behind, no matter the risk.

"But that means there may not be a Great Council if we fail," Samson protested. "That seems pretty foolish to create it only to risk every one of its members on a journey that will almost surely fail."

"But who among us is willing to be left behind?" Regis glanced around the table. When no one uttered a word, he said, "See? Your reasoning, while sound, has no place in reality."

Samson, obviously displeased, pushed his chair away from the table and began to pace nervously. "So we're all going, is that it? And what purpose will that serve?"

"It is the new Law," Maya said, speaking for the others. "No longer will we leave all the risks, and the rewards, to a few. It is all or none."

"All right," Samson growled, "then let's get the show on the road. I say we leave for the city this afternoon and make camp outside its gates by dusk. Agreed?"

It was agreed to unanimously. The council broke up again. Some of the group, those making their way there by foot, left for the city by late morning. Maya, who would travel with Peg, and Kathryn and Tara, who had developed a special fondness for the dragon, waited until mid-afternoon to leave.

They made their camp on the eastern side of the city, where there was still a remnant of light remaining for those journeying on foot. They made their fire there, in the growing shadow of the city as the sun set slowly in the east.

It would be a long night, longer than the one before, for none knew if it would be their last in this, or any other, world.

22

∗ ∗ ∗

THROUGH THE GATE

Lucas remembered. Not right away, mind you, but soon enough to keep them from picking one of the gates at random.

"I know which one!" he cried out, only minutes after Jon had described what the gods had told him so recently.

"You do?" Regis asked him.

"How could you know which gate is the right one?" Gar echoed.

"It's easy," Lucas said brightly. "There is a road that leads directly from the westernmost gate seemingly to the heart of the city, without all the twists and turns the other roads take."

"Is there such a gate, Peg?" Maya asked.

The winged horse nodded.

"That settles it, then. We'll have to take that one," Laura said.

Most of them involuntarily glanced at the imposing city, their eyes drawn to the castle at its very center, which rose majestically into the sky until it disappeared into the ever-present clouds that hung over the city.

"But what if I'm wrong and it isn't the right one?" Lucas asked, nervous now that the group had settled on the gate he'd chosen. "Maybe just a few of us should try it at first, see if it's the right one?"

"I'll go," Mark volunteered.

"I will as well," Samson said at almost the same time.

Regis and Gar glanced at each other. "Don't count us out," the elf king said, speaking for the both of them.

Laura started to laugh. "Hold on, now, or we'll all end up volunteering to go. But haven't you all forgotten something?"

"We don't even know if we can get in, regardless of which gate we choose," Jon finished.

"That's right," Laura acknowledged. "If I can't break their spell, we can forget about the entire expedition."

Thus chastened, they made their way around to the other part of the city while

Laura started to consider what she might need to break the spell that had kept all others, save the gods, from entering the city.

She still hadn't decided on anything by the time they'd reached the gate. It was rather plain-looking compared to the other ones, the stone crumbling a little at the top. The closed doors blocking the entrance appeared about to fall off their hinges from where the group cautiously gazed at them.

"Does anyone know the name of this city?" she asked suddenly, to no one in particular.

The blank looks all around gave her the answer.

Another thought occurred, one that probably should have come to mind long before now. "Is there even a name to this world, to this land?" she asked.

Maya glanced at the others. "It is the magicians' world. It has always been common knowledge that the name of it, of our world I mean, has belonged to them."

"You can't be serious!" Jon burst out.

"I'm perfectly serious," Maya answered with a straight face. "The land was named long, long ago, and no one has ever seized it from the magicians. It is theirs only to reveal now."

"But that's crazy!" Jon exclaimed. "Everything has to have a name."

"It has a name, Jon," Laura soothed. "They just don't know what it is. And if you think for a minute, you'll remember why."

"Because the name—undoubtedly an ancient word of power—must hold the key to something," Jon said after a brief pause. "You're right. I wasn't thinking clearly."

"The question," Laura concluded, "is whether we can discover the names, either one, on our own."

"Well, the name of Land is fairly obvious, considering all we've learned," Jon said confidently. "The old myths of our Earth have a name for a world such as this. Annwyn. The Otherworld. All it lacks is the One Tree at the center."

"I would agree." Laura nodded.

"And I also have an idea about this city," Jon added. "It reminds me an awful lot of one back in our own world. How many gates are there around this place, anyone know?"

"Twelve," Peg answered. "And you're right. It is constructed similarly to one in your own world."

"Why didn't you say so?" Samson fumed.

"No one asked before now," the winged horse said, nonplussed as always.

"Then I think I know what its name is," Jon said. "It's an ancient one from our own history. It was also, ironically, the name of a city where one of the more infamous witch hunts took place in our own world, where many people were killed because they were suspected of using magic in our world." Jon leaned close and whispered the name in Laura's ear.

"Makes sense," she said. "It's worth a try at least."

As Laura approached the gate to see if the word helped at all, Samson hurried over to stand beside Jon. "So what's your guess?" he asked Jon.

"This city is remarkably similar to Jerusalem, the most holy, religious center we have in our world," Jon said, keeping a careful eye on Laura, "and there are a couple of names for that city that hardly anyone in our own world has ever heard before."

"And that's what you think the name of this city is, because it's similar to Jerusalem?"

Jon nodded. "It would make sense. Magic and religion have intermingled since the dawn of time. And we know the two worlds were connected at one time."

Laura, standing boldly before the gate, commanded the gate to open and followed it by uttering the name Jon had given her. "*Upo Salem.*"

The two doors blocking the gate slowly creaked open at Laura's command.

"Well, I'll be," Gar said, incredulous. "It worked."

"So that's the name of this city? Salem?" Samson whispered to Jon.

"That's it." He beamed, following Laura into the city. "Hard to believe, isn't it?"

The ground suddenly shook as one of the giants stomped an angry foot. "We can't enter through that tiny gate," Nog grumbled.

"Well, break it then." Laura looked up at the giant. "Let us pass through and then walk right through it. The thing is crumbling already."

The others hurried through, not eager to remain behind when the giants crashed the gate. For all they knew, Salem might do something horrible to anyone who wantonly destroyed parts of it.

But Nog stepped on the decaying gate, showering splinters and stones, and passed through without a problem or a challenge. Wer followed, joining the rest of the group huddled 50 feet or so inside the city along the straight and narrow road.

"How strange," Maya said. "Every legend I know of claims the earth will practically swallow you up if you meddle with the magicians' city like that."

"Me, too," Mark acknowledged. "That's what I've always thought."

"And I as well," Regis muttered.

The others, equally surprised they'd passed through the gate so easily and that nothing had happened when it was torn asunder, nodded their agreement.

"No point in dwelling on the obvious," Samson stated loudly. "It looks like the magicians fooled all of you but good. If you ask me, this is just a normal city."

"Oh, I wouldn't say that," Jon said, a funny catch in his voice. "We have a visitor."

23

* * *

THE MAGICIANS' CITY

The enormous, fearsome lion came bounding down the road at them, covering 20 yards and more with each stride. It covered that distance easily, for it was aided by two gigantic wings that enabled it to soar as it bounded. And yet it wasn't a lion at all, for it had the face of a woman. A very ugly woman, with unkempt hair and a foul smell.

"Oh, I'm late, I'm late," they heard it muttering to itself as it bounded down the road at them. "They won't forgive me, no, they won't. Oh, this is just terrible, terrible..."

"Who won't forgive you?" Jon called out loudly as the horrible creature came to a surprisingly graceful halt, folding its wings easily beside its tawny hide. Most of the group, save Shar and the giants, cowered fearfully in the creature's presence.

"*Them,* of course," the creature said. "*They* won't like it at all, not at all. You've destroyed one of their gates, I see. Oh dear, *they* just won't like this. Not at all."

"What do you mean you're late?" Jon asked.

"I was to accost you on the other side of the gate, I was. Yes, I was," the creature bemoaned.

"Why didn't you then?" Jon demanded.

"I couldn't very well know that we were about to have visitors, could I? Not after all these hundreds of years without a single one."

"Do you mean to tell me that it's been centuries since anyone's passed through these gates?" Jon asked.

"Centuries? Yes, I suppose it has been that long. Yes, indeed."

"And you were to meet us on the other side of the gate?"

"Yes, yes, that was the plan. I have my orders, you know. Don't let a soul enter these gates until the riddle has been solved."

"What riddle?" Jon asked sharply.

"Why, the one I ask all wayfarers on these roads," the ghastly creature said, startled. "Surely you've heard of me? You've heard the riddle? You know that I devour all who can't answer it?"

314

Every member of the group grumbled to themselves, complaining that, no, of course none of them had heard of such an arrangement.

"I know who you are," Jon announced loudly, silencing the other members of the group almost immediately. "Ask your riddle, Sphinx."

"You *have* heard of me, then?" the Sphinx said, delighted. "Wonderful, wonderful. This is the best news I've had in, oh, hundreds of years. It's been so frightfully lonely inside this dreary city…"

"Just ask the question," Jon stated with a pained expression.

"Oh, if you insist," the Sphinx said, an equally pained, hurt look on its horrible face. "What creature goes on four feet in the morning, on two at noonday, and…"

"On three in the evening?" Jon finished the riddle for the Sphinx. "Is that all you can come up with? Nothing better than that old, miserable, worn-out riddle?"

"It's all I've been given," the hideous creature whined. "I have no other riddle, save that one."

"Well, the answer is man, so let us pass," Jon said brusquely, taking bold steps in the Sphinx's direction. When it became clear the creature intended to let them pass unmolested, the others quickly followed.

"You've been talking to that Oedipus fellow, haven't you?" the saddened Sphinx called out after Jon as they made their way up the road. "Haven't you? Admit it, now, Oedipus put you up to this."

"How in Zeus's name did you know the answer to that riddle?" Lucas demanded of Jon when they were out of earshot of the forlorn creature.

"Zeus has nothing whatsoever to do with it!" Jon growled. "And it's a stupid, outdated riddle. It's been around our world, the one I came from, for hundreds of years and it doesn't mean a thing anymore."

"But what *does* it mean?" Lucas persisted.

"It means that a man crawls on his four hands and feet as a baby, walks erect as a man and then hobbles around with a cane as an old man, that's all. It's an archaic riddle. Somebody should give that pitiful creature a new one."

"Why don't you do that, then?" Peg suggested wryly.

"Maybe I will," Jon said smugly.

"That certainly was a fearsome creature, wasn't it?" Kathryn shuddered. "I'd hate to think what might have happened if Jon hadn't been able to answer its riddle."

"I could have subdued the thing," Samson boasted. "No problem at all."

"I could have as well," Mark quipped.

"But there wasn't much need for that, was there?" Jon laughed. "So save your strength, you two. We may need it later."

The view from the narrow road leading up to the castle at a slight incline was equally depressing on both sides. What few houses there were, and which were still standing, were in serious disrepair and decay. A balcony had fallen in on the front porch of one, the living room wall had caved in on another, and the roof had collapsed on still a third. Grass, bushes, and brambles had almost totally enveloped most of the structures. One house in particular was nearly obscured beneath the wild, tangled undergrowth that had crept up around it.

"Doesn't appear anyone's lived here in a while," Regis said.

"*That's* a clever statement." Gar smirked.

"Perhaps you can do better," the elf king snarled.

"It doesn't appear anyone's lived here for a *very* long while." The dwarf king smiled.

"No, it doesn't." Samson stepped quickly between the two. "Now pay attention to what we're doing and keep your petty arguments to yourself."

"Or else?" Regis asked.

"Or else I'll feed you to that overgrown lion back there," Samson said.

Lucas had been right. The road led to the doors of the castle without so much as a twist or turn. Presently, they were standing outside a gigantic pair of doors, similar to those at the gate to the city, but with one difference. These doors appeared much sturdier.

In fact, as the group surveyed the outside of the castle, the place seemed to be an impenetrable fortress, made of some heavy, dull, silver metal—something the dwarves would have been proud to call their own. It had as solid a foundation as anything any of them had ever seen, curving off to either side in both directions.

There was an inscription on the doors, written in a strange language, and bizarre drawings of people writhing in torment and agony carved into the doors as well. As Samson stepped toward them to test their strength, Jon scanned the inscription.

"Can you tell what it is?" Lucas asked with a hint of anxiety.

"I think it's somebody's idea of a joke," Jon answered darkly.

Cleo suddenly cleared his throat. "I can read it," the startled centaur said.

"You can?" Regis and Gar said together, equally as startled as the centaur.

"Of course he can," Jon harrumphed. "Go ahead, Cleo, tell us what it says."

The centaur furrowed his brow to concentrate. "Well, it reads, 'Abandon all hope ye who enter here'…whatever that means."

"It means that someone is playing a joke on us, I'm afraid," Jon said. "This is about as remote from hell as anyplace I can imagine."

"Hell!" Gar exclaimed. "That's the *last* place I intend to enter of my own free will."

"Oh relax," Jon snipped. "This is hardly the place. I know. I've been there. Somebody's just trying to scare us, is all."

"Then you go first," the dwarf king said, "just as soon as we open these doors."

"All right, I will," Jon said.

Samson, who had been yanking on the doors with all his strength, suddenly cursed and turned back to his comrades. "They won't budge. Not an inch." But before the others could join him to help, Samson leaned up against them to rest his weary arms a bit. And the doors opened slowly inward, almost of their own free will.

"Well, I'll be." Samson recovered his balance in the nick of time as he stumbled through the open doors. "I tried pushing them once and it didn't work."

"Perhaps that's the trick," Mark offered. "Not doing anything at all?"

But Samson was already too lost in wonder to hear his words, gazing at the interior of the hall. It was absolutely huge, perhaps a thousand times the size of the Great Council room. It seemed to stretch on forever. The place was *so* huge, in fact, that it was impossible to see the other end of it from the doorway. The ceiling, likewise, was much too high up for any to see it.

Once upon a time, the room must have been beautiful, magnificent, splendid, awe-inspiring. Now it was merely a shambles of plush curtains fraying at the edges, glorious paintings that had almost faded from view, and hand-carved furniture coated in thick piles of dust. Curiously, the walls that receded in both directions appeared to be made of a solid, seamless, deep, dark wood.

The musky odor of dust filled the entire room. As Samson crossed the room, he left eddies of dust in his wake. When he reached up to peek behind a curtain, great clouds of dust showered down onto him.

They came upon the wide, stone stairs, leading downwards, almost immediately. Once, gates had blocked the way down, but decay and rust had opened the way. The gates had long ago fallen from their hinges. All but the giants, who could not fit through the doors to the castle, decided to make the descent.

They came to the abandoned forge and bellows first. Gar could see right off that, whatever their purpose at one time, it had likely been centuries since they'd been used.

They discovered the immense saws and empty metal vats in the next room. Regis could see what the vats had likely contained—the silver lifeblood from the trees revered by the elves, which in turn had been used in the forge clearly built by dwarves.

But the third and final room made no sense, for it contained doors to a catacomb beneath the castle. And in those catacombs were hundreds, perhaps thousands, of immense, dried-out roots, descending from the ceiling above them, ending in a deep, dark underground river flowing beneath the castle.

Jon realized, with a start, what they were seeing—and where they now found themselves. It had been right there, in front of him, the entire time they had sojourned in the land. "Follow me," Jon said, marching back up the stone staircase.

317

"What?" Laura asked, calling after him.

When they'd all retreated back to the entranceway, Jon examined the walls in both directions. It was all the same, of one piece. There were no cracks or seams to be found in any part of the wall. "Simply unbelievable."

"What?" Laura asked impatiently.

But Jon didn't answer. He walked silently through the twin doors to the outside. He looked up at the shape of the castle, again wondering why he hadn't seen it before. It was so obvious now. It had been there, all along, if he'd only had eyes to see.

Jon turned to the group then. "It's the World Tree. Yggdrasil. The only thing missing from this place. This castle is Caer Annwyn, from the myths on Earth. But it is also the One Tree at the center of this world—much like the tree of ultimate knowledge from Earth—with the water of life running beneath it."

"You're certain?" Laura asked.

"Yes, I'm certain. The magicians figured a way to imprison it, make it their own. They took the silver lifeblood from the other trees and used it to entomb the tree, turn it to their own purposes. It was how they gained the knowledge of good and evil in this place." He pointed toward the outside of the castle. "See how it's all metal on the outside? Yet, inside, it is all wood, of one piece, as far as the eye can see, in either direction. And the way it's shaped…"

Laura could see it now, too. "Shar! Can you take us up for a closer view?"

"Gladly, gladly, I'd love to do my part in this glorious quest," Shar said, practically falling over himself. "Just climb aboard."

An instant later, as Jon and Laura hovered away from the castle, up in the air, and viewed it from a distance, they could see they were right.

The entire structure of the castle looked remarkably like a tree of some sort. The balconies and porches were clearly part of the upper reaches of the tree, while dull, silver metal encased the massive trunk and foundation. It seemed impossible, but the magicians had found a way to enclose—capture—the entire World Tree at the center of this land.

Jon saw them, then, sitting peacefully on one of the more intricate and ornate balconies—an older, white-haired gentleman and an elderly woman with flowing, steel-gray hair. "Shar," he said quietly, pointing the way, "can you set us down over there for a moment or two?"

Shar landed gracefully on the balcony. Jon and Laura eased down from the back of the dragon.

"Well, it's about time," the older man said to them. "We were beginning to think you would never arrive, despite all our efforts to lure you here."

24

***

THE WORLD TREE

Jon had seen so many gods and goddesses by now that he was no longer surprised
when he came across them. But Zeus was no ordinary god, and his wife, Hera,
was no ordinary goddess.

Once, the world had held them in awe. The father of the gods, revered by
millions, Zeus had been held in higher esteem than the one, true God, the Creator.
Roman emperors staked their earthly claim to leadership at the feet of Zeus. But
those days were long, long ago. Magic had long ago been replaced by religion on
Earth, and the sons and daughters of the god, Zeus, were nothing more than literary
artifices.

A few black crows settled to either side of the balcony. Jon glanced at them and
then back to Zeus and Hera. "Yours?" Jon asked.

"Apollo's, actually," Zeus said. "But you knew that."

"Yes, I did. So you've been waiting here all this time? For us?"

"For an eternity, it seems," Zeus acknowledged. "We are prisoners, as much—or
more—than the tree you now sit atop comfortably."

"And you'd like us to do something about that?" Laura asked.

"Yes, please," Hera said graciously. "If you don't mind."

"Perhaps you can tell us, then," Laura said, posing one of the questions she'd
been hoping to ask someone for some time, "where are the magicians?"

Zeus turned back toward the castle. "Not here, of course," he said wistfully.
"They were here, once. But this place has served its purpose."

Laura asked the other question she'd wanted to ask. "Did you have anything to
do with bringing us here?"

"From your world? No." Zeus's voice was a deep rumble. Jon liked the effect.
"But once you were in this place, did we do everything we could to make sure you
arrived here with as much understanding as possible? Yes, we did. That is our
responsibility, as it is yours to free this tree from its imprisonment."

"You know that it is your only hope?" Hera interjected. "Your only way back to
your own world, now that the magicians are no longer here, in this land?"

319

"I think we can see that now," Laura said.

"And can you do this?" Hera asked Laura. "Deliver this tree from its horrible state and bring life back to this cursed land? None before you have been able, though any number has tried. And with the magicians gone, we are left with nothing."

Laura smiled knowingly. "I think I can."

* * *

Jon understood now. By imprisoning the One Tree at the center of this world, the magicians had tamed the elemental forces of nature, taken those powers to themselves, and deprived the land of its very life. Reversing that would be no easy feat. Jon could see why no one had been able to do so—until now.

The silver metal prison surrounding the tree was such a part of it, it would be a colossal undertaking to remove it. Impossible, in fact. You could not remove the silver metal that encased the tree, and the tree was simply not alive inside its dead prison. It must have been quite a feat, in its day. Something almost akin to alchemy, which had always been a poorly understood black art of equal measures of the elemental forces of air, earth, fire, and water.

But the world that Jon, Samson, and Laura inhabited was nothing like this Otherworld, the place known as Annwyn in King Arthur's day. In Laura's world, alchemy had given way to basic chemistry. The world Laura was comfortable in had begun to unravel the mysteries of nanotechnology, quantum physics, colossal magneto resistance, and a myriad other emerging chemical and biological wonders.

So Laura was a magician unlike any the land had ever seen—one with both feet squarely in both worlds, able to build a bridge from one to the other.

"I am going to fuse the two," Laura explained to Jon, Samson, and the others. "I will make the two as one—the silver and the wood. I am going to change the fundamental nature of this tree, giving it its own new covenant with the land."

"How?" Jon asked.

"By increasing the magnetic electron attraction between the two substances—the silver and the wood—until they have no choice but to become as one. Alive, inseparable. A silver world tree. The first of its kind," she explained.

"Is that possible?" Kathryn asked her.

"It is where I come from, in theory. And here, where I am able to use magic to change things such as the relative ratio of magnetism between electrons, then the theory becomes the reality. I believe it is possible, yes."

The giants, Shar, the elves, and the centaurs were not convinced. They retreated to a safe distance. The others remained, intent on watching the new magician's experiment.

As Laura put the elements together in her mind, it occurred to her that it was probably true: there were very few who might have been chosen for such a task, for good or ill. The basic, underlying principles of the elemental forces of nature and physics had only begun to emerge in the past two decades or so in her own world.

In a matter of moments, it was done. As the magic started to have its effect, Laura could not contain her own amazement. It really did work!

For the tree was changing even as they watched. The silver and the wood of the tree, no longer separated by elemental magnetic forces, were fusing and becoming a new substance, unique to this world.

When it was done, even the skeptics of the group could see for themselves. The tree had changed completely. It was different, stronger, unique, but very much alive. The One silver tree had taken its place again at the center of Annwyn. And its roots were freed from prison, now capable of extending themselves to other worlds and other places in the universe.

25

***

THE CHILDREN
OF THE GIANTS

Unfortunately, while the outer skin of the place had been changed for good, the inside was still as dreary, dusty, and barren as before, the lost grandeur and the sense of destruction and decay that had settled on the interior unchanged.

"I think we should go in three directions," Jon offered as soon as the group had reconvened inside. "Some to the left, keeping close to the wall; some to the right; and the rest of us directly across the center of it. We'll all meet at the other end and see who was able to find a way upwards, to the levels within the castle. All right?"

Seeing as how no one else could come up with a better plan, there was a general murmur of agreement. Most were still in awe at the transformation of the outside.

"A magician should accompany each of the three," Laura reasoned. "Just in case."

"I'll go to the right," Gar said.

"And I'll come with you." The elf king stepped sprightly to the elf's side.

Mark, likewise, joined the two kings, as did Kathryn. Tara, meanwhile, chose to go to the left, with Lucas, Cleo, Peg and Maya. The door was too narrow for the giants, so they chose to remain outside with Shar.

Which left Laura, the remaining magician, to explore the center of the seemingly endless room with Samson and Jon.

Regis and Gar were anxious to set off in search of the ancient magicians or, failing that, anything else of interest. There were no good-byes—only a few curt nods and grim smiles as each wished the other well until they should meet again at the other end of the enormous hall.

Only Peg remained behind to speak with Laura, Jon, and Samson as the other two groups departed to the left and right.

"I shall miss you," the winged horse said, looking directly at Jon. "For all your failings, you will make a fine priest some day. You have shown no fear at all of the gods, which is a good thing in this day and age."

"But we're not...," Jon started to protest.

"Hush." Peg stomped his foot as he had done when they first met, before Jon had bestowed the gift of speech on the winged horse. "The future holds what it will, and I have never been one to reveal it willingly, but I make an exception in this one case."

"But why?" Jon asked.

"To say good-bye and to ask a favor."

"What favor?"

"To promise that you will do your best to allow us to escape our own boundaries here, in this world," Peg said evenly. "We have been imprisoned by the petty, narrow, mean-spirited literary imaginations of your world for far too long. I have no interest in being worshiped. I would, however, like a few new things—and ideas—to try. Promise me you will do your best to change that."

"I promise," Jon said solemnly.

Peg inclined his head majestically toward Samson and Laura. "Farewell, warrior," he said first to Samson. "You have accomplished what I had always assumed was impossible, bringing the dwarves and the elves together again. This land is nothing without them, and it is now indebted to you."

Peg looked finally at Laura. "And farewell to you, magician. This land will thank you some day for leaving your trail of wisdom here for others to follow. As for restoring the One Tree, we shall see."

Before any of the three could say another word, the winged horse had already wheeled to follow the group that had gone to the left. They stood there, stunned and watching as the horse half-galloped, half-flew to catch up to the others.

"What do you think he meant by all that?" Samson said.

"Who knows?" Jon shrugged. "He's always been a little mysterious. He is a god, after all, though he never says much about it."

"Let's get going, then," Laura said, feeling a chilly draft in the musky, decaying room. "We may have farther to go than the others."

They came upon them almost immediately, within minutes after setting off across the floor of the immense room—the children of the giants, turned to stone and littered about in the room like toys left scattered after a day in the nursery.

Laura was strangely silent as she brought the first of them awake with a spell and whispered something in the young giant's ear that sent him scurrying across the floor toward the doorway and the two giants who'd chosen to remain outside. She brought the others back to life quickly and sent them on their way.

"Now the giants will have something to live for as well," she murmured.

They watched the last of the newly awakened children of the giants tumble across the floor toward the doorway, where faint rumbles of joy and delight could be heard.

"That was a nice thing to do," Jon said to the young magician.

"It was the least I could do for them," Laura answered.

As they resumed their trek across the room, they came to a solitary, wooden ladder, set firmly in the dust-covered floor and rising upwards beyond their sight.

"Shall we?" Jon sighed when they stood beside the ladder. Made of solid oak, it had somehow managed to survive the ravages of time that had wreaked havoc on the rest of the somber, dreary room. "Perhaps it takes us to the magicians' levels. We do need to find out, don't we?"

"Why not?" Laura shrugged.

"Let's get it over with." Samson stepped to the bottom rung to begin the ascent.

Laura went next and then Jon.

As they climbed, a dreadful weariness took hold of them, as if they'd been awake for a very long time and were only now being afforded the chance to rest from their burdens. It was all they could do to place one hand or foot over the other as they slowly climbed skyward.

After they'd been climbing for what seemed like hours to Jon, he looked down. "Look," he said to the others. "We can see the rest of the land from here."

And indeed they could—the mountains to the north and the great sea to the south, the sweeping plains to the west and the endless forest to the east, all converging in the very center. At this very ladder, in fact.

"It looks strange from here, doesn't it?" Samson said. "We're in the very center of the land."

"We are, and it's also fading from view," Laura noted.

After a few more steps up the ladder, the land simply vanished from sight far, far below them. The three champions of the realms of mind, body, and spirit continued their climb to the top, oblivious now to their surroundings. It was all they could do to reach the summit now.

"We're coming to it," Samson said eventually. "It won't be much longer now."

"I wonder," Jon mused, "if we'll be able to rest there first."

"I would think so," Laura said.

The ladder ended at one end of a sparse, rectangular room, which had but one other exit—a small, unobtrusive doorway. Samson stepped clear of the ladder and then moved to the side to allow Laura and Jon to enter.

At the other end of the room, seated comfortably in a solid-oak rocking chair before a roaring fire, was someone Jon had never actually believed in, though there were countless stories of him and others of his kind in many places on Earth. And, despite their best efforts and all they had learned in this world, the three found themselves cowering in fear at the magnificence of one of the sons of God.

"Fear not," he said, turning to face them. "My name is Michael, and I bring you great tidings."

26

* * *

MICHAEL

Jon knew the stories about angels. He had read those stories many times—the war between the angels in heaven, the banishment of the fallen angels to Earth, the end of the wars between magic and religion. But he had never actually believed. Not really. Angels did not seem real, or possible. Certainly an archangel such as Michael, who had fought Satan himself and had cast him to Earth, seemed nearly impossible to fathom. Yet, here he was, and he was not pleased.

"You do realize what you've done, don't you, by restoring the One Tree in this world?" Michael asked them. "Such a task was once impossible. But now, thanks to you, the impossible is now possible. And the way to other worlds has been brought back to life."

"We didn't mean to," Jon said.

"Not intentionally," Michael said somberly. It was hard to gaze at the archangel, so radiant was his being. "Nevertheless, it is done. And you three, alone, hold the keys on Earth, where the sons of God who rebelled have been imprisoned. You three, alone, must now do something about that. Do you know what you must do?"

None of them could speak. "No, we don't," Samson managed finally.

"We all realize you had no choice, of course. You had to find your way back. But you have now allowed the roots to extend into other worlds again, including Earth."

"What does it mean?" Laura asked, afraid of the answer.

"It means the time is short. You must close the portal on Earth, before it is too late," Michael said. "But I must ask you—why has it taken you so long to arrive here? You realize, of course, that you could have come here immediately. There was nothing and no one to stop you. Not in this world, at least."

"I think we know that now," Laura said, barely able to meet his gaze.

"And there was no real need for you to go wandering about the land as you did, either," Michael said, smiling for the first time.

"But there was," Jon said. "The land was so desolate, so barren. We wanted to give some life to it. Bringing the races back from their exile seemed like the best idea."

"And indeed it was," Michael said. "A noble gesture, though a belated one."

"What will become of the land now?" Laura asked. "The races? Kathryn, Mark, and Lucas?"

Michael smiled a second time. "The land will prosper, with its new covenant and your protégés at its helm. You chose them well."

"We didn't exactly choose them," Samson said uneasily, remembering how reluctant he'd been when Mark had persisted in tagging along.

"I know," Michael said. "But you chose not to turn them away, which is nearly the same thing. Nearly, but not quite."

"We tried," Jon said lamely.

Michael looked at them intently and nodded. "Yes, you did. Now, I will say this again. You *do* realize that you have opened a path again, by coming here willingly at the bidding of the *bene elohim*, by bringing magic and the races back to their full power in the land, and by restoring the center tree?"

"The *bene elohim*?" Jon asked.

"The sons of God," responded Michael. "Those who taught the first magicians, created the races and many worlds such as this one through the Tree of Knowledge of Good and Evil and, yet, were ultimately confined to just one."

Jon was horrified. "And we reopened a portal?"

"Giving them hope that they will soon be released from their long captivity, yes," Michael answered. "They have looked for three champions dedicated to this realm for a very long time. They were necessary to close the unholy circle and forge a path. All that is left is your choice—to help them and finish the task they set before you, or close the portal again, for good."

Laura and Jon both glanced over at the door. "But what of that doorway?" Laura asked.

"No need to fear that particular path," Michael said evenly. "No one comes through that door save those the Creator knows. No, it is the other portal you must now deal with, on Earth. The one you alone are now responsible for, because you have willingly chosen to make yourselves servants of the *bene elohim*."

EL

Book Three

***

PROLOGUE

All three of them could feel the urgency, though none could explain why. They could sense, however, that very powerful forces were about to crash down on them.

"But how will we know where to begin? Or whether we should do anything at all?" Samson asked.

"As for where to begin," Laura said slowly, "I have a feeling the magicians will come to us. Maybe not in person. But we'll hear from them, their emissaries, or even the *bene elohim*. They have no choice. A door has been reopened. And we hold the keys."

1

***

A NEW TASK

Thomas had been the first to discover them just sitting there in the gathering darkness of the room at the back of the old house on Druid Hills Road, near a second door in the room that always remained locked. He noticed right off that the three didn't seem much like college kids anymore. Something had happened to them. Something had changed the way they saw the world.

The most noticeable change was in the girl, the one with the stern demeanor and the eyes that pierced to your very soul. Thomas had known, before, what the girl had thought of him. A nothing, or worse. Yet now she smiled at him warmly when she looked at him. She actually regarded him with fondness, as if he were a puppy or some other creature worthy of attention.

But the other two were also different. The raging anger of the goliath, the hulk of a human specimen, had dissipated quite a bit. And the frail, soulless narcotic who pawned himself off as a priest had gained weight, added color to his cheeks, and found sparkle for his eyes…almost as if, heaven forbid, he'd found something to believe in.

It was strange with Eric gone. No, it was more than that. Without Eric, there was no game. Not really. For who would create the labyrinths and the challenges, if not him? Who would orchestrate the expeditions? Who would teach them? His disappearance had been almost as strange as the appearance again of the three misfits who didn't believe in the land or anything about it.

The true believers had trudged to the room every day for a week now, hoping Eric would make an appearance. He hadn't. They kept the flame alive, however, continuing to plot their new quest to the dwarf hole.

What a time for Eric to leave them! Dwarves had been spotted after all these years. And there were rumors that the other races had been sighted in the land as well. Some even said the races were returning to the land.

They'd all assumed the three had gone through the locked door on that day the three misfits had left the room so secretively. But no one had actually *seen* them leave through it. The three had just vanished, while they plotted at the other end. A

331

strangeness had settled in the room. They had all looked up at one point, and the three newcomers were gone. From that moment on, Eric had seemed distant, removed from the game.

Now the three were back, as mysteriously as they'd disappeared. Eric was gone. And there was no longer a game.

* * *

Laura, Jon, and Samson chose to take the long walk back to Duke's campus.

"The question," Laura said, "is what do we do now? We can't just continue on with our lives as if nothing happened, can we?"

Jon looked at Laura thoughtfully. "You don't think that maybe...?"

"Magic works here? No, I don't think so. At least not the simple magic we discovered in that world. There's more to it here, in a way we don't comprehend. *The Books of El* were meant for other worlds. It *has* to be that way, don't you think?"

Jon nodded numbly, still not entirely sure he believed everything he'd just been through. "That's basically the conclusion I've come to as well. The rules would have to be different here."

"Far different," Laura said eagerly. "Subtler. Deeper. Much, much harder to understand. The simple magic from those books doesn't work here. I've tried."

The room had been empty and dark when they'd come back to their own world, the Earth they knew. The game players, the kids Eric had used for his own purposes, showed up later to discover the three of them sitting silently in the darkness. That was when the three had learned that Eric had vanished not long after sending them to the magicians' world.

Coming back seemed strange. Leaving that room had been like walking through a mirror. There was simply no other way to describe it. What was ironic, looking back, was that it seemed the door had always been there. Only they hadn't been able to see it. They had no idea, of course, what new portal they had unwittingly opened for the *bene elohim*, or how they might serve as keys to that door. But they had given their word that they would find it—and close it. They needed to act quickly.

"We have to find Eric," Samson said forcefully. "If he doesn't know where the magicians are in this world, then no one will."

"I'm not sure Araqiel wishes to be found now," Laura mused.

"What about that portal to the magicians' world we've opened, the one we don't know anything about yet?" Jon said anxiously.

Laura's eyes shone fiercely. "We must deal with that, somehow. For better or worse, we are now the keys. Nothing can happen without us, but we must be very, very careful."

2

* * *

INQUISITION

The letter was waiting for him when he arrived back at his apartment. In fact, it appeared that someone had hand-delivered it to his mailbox, for there was no postmark on it. Jon knew before he'd even opened it what was inside. Oh, he didn't know precisely what it would say, but he had a pretty good idea of its nature.

It was a letter from his advisor, informing Jon he had to make a special appearance before his advisory panel to defend his doctoral thesis. It was a highly unusual move, but within the technical bounds. Some charges had been made and some questions raised about how seriously committed he was to the study of religion.

Jon sighed deeply as he held the letter in his hand. He knew it would be a futile effort. The house of cards he'd carefully constructed over the past three or four years was about to come tumbling down around his knees and there wasn't a thing he could do about it. What was worse, he wasn't altogether sure he cared anymore.

Jon gathered his research materials and the notes he'd taken over the past several months, dropped them into the frayed, worn backpack he'd lugged around campus for years, and began the long, slow trek to the Divinity School from the house he'd rented off campus.

He still hadn't adjusted to this world yet, even though he'd been back nearly two days. He hadn't seen Samson or Laura in that time. They'd agreed not to contact each other until something happened. *This letter certainly qualifies*, Jon thought ruefully.

What surprised him was what he'd done almost the moment he arrived at the basement apartment where he'd lived unobtrusively for more than two years, carrying on his lucrative trade. He'd destroyed his stash of cocaine. All of it. It was absurd, of course, and he'd obviously regret the rash move when his head cleared and he came to his senses. But he couldn't stomach the thought of drifting in that sea of confusion, not while he was still sorting through other realities. And the idea of peddling the stuff just for the sake of making money now nauseated him.

"I am a fool," he muttered to himself as he walked along, "and a mindless twit. I deserve whatever tortures surely await me."

Jon had no idea how he could possibly defend his thesis in his present state, but he had to smile at his choice of a thesis topic and the irony of it. Especially now. Like any good doctoral thesis worth its salt, he'd made the title long and convoluted: "Magic and Religion: the transfiguration of two disparate ideas throughout history, or the adversarial, yet symbiotic, relationship between two elemental forces of nature."

While the title was all but unintelligible, the idea was fairly simple and straightforward. Magic and religion had been at odds with each other for centuries, if not since the dawn of humankind. Both tried to control the elemental forces of nature but from virtually opposite directions. When Moses appeared before the Pharaoh and turned his rod into a serpent, for instance, he had confronted the magicians of the court who excelled in the "secret arts" that flourished in Egypt at that time. The ancient literature was replete with such instances.

Jon had a problem now, though. The old wars between magic and religion from the Old Testament times were harder to put in context in today's world. Yes, the magicians were undoubtedly foul creatures. But was that the result of their magical powers? Were the tools of magic themselves necessarily corrupt? Or was it something about the nature of magic that led to power, which ultimately seemed to corrupt?

What of religion as well, which had flourished on Earth as magic once had in the Otherworld? Had religion corrupted those who wielded it powerfully here? Was it possible to use religious beliefs to seize control of a world in much the same way the magicians had taken over the Otherworld?

Jon suddenly found that he couldn't answer those questions. Nothing was simple to him right now, least of all the meaning or purpose in his life. What once had seemed logical and rational now seemed alien and forbidding. What once seemed comforting now terrorized him.

He didn't want to confront either just now, magic or religion. He only wanted to find a comfortable chair somewhere, curl up in it, and ponder the fate of the universe. Or at least the fate of his particular corner of it.

There were three professors in the room when he arrived. They were seated casually around a large Formica conference table near the dean's office on the first floor of the Divinity School. All three were familiar faces, though he'd only taken classes with two of them. Yet he knew how each was likely to react to certain arguments.

Jeremiah Whitley was an Old Testament specialist. Jon had detested his class. The man had no sense of humor at all. He took his studies so seriously that there was never any life at all to his lectures and, consequently, no life in the material he presented. If a student didn't come into his class with a healthy respect for the old Law of the Bible, he wasn't likely to leave with one.

Jon remembered a few classes where Whitley would sit at his desk, his hands clasped before him, and simply stare out at the classroom as he droned on about one flood story or another that had shaped the Noah's Ark account, the myths about an antediluvian society, or the seed of monotheism in ancient Babylon.

Jon recalled, seeing Whitley, that he had once lectured on the extra-biblical myths of El, the "father of humanity" who'd introduced the dark arts of knowledge to the world and taken the fairest of the daughters of men as his companion to create a new race of beings on Earth, according to several obscure texts. But the research paper on El and Eloah—and the lecture it had been based on—had been so horribly dull that Jon had forgotten all about it. Until now.

Whitley's dull, brown eyes never flinched, his lightly graying hair was never mussed or out of place, and he never removed his tweed jacket even as summer approached. By all accounts, Whitley was a stern, austere man who afforded himself and his students few creature comforts. He was there to teach, and students were there to learn. Anything that interfered with that formula was anathema.

Charles Finch was another matter entirely. One of the finest, most gifted New Testament scholars of this or any century, he'd co-authored a volume presenting several of the lost works that bridged the gap between the Old and New Testaments of the Bible. His classes were brilliant, dynamic, fun, always entertaining. No one skipped one of Finch's classes. As if you had a choice. Class participation was roughly a third of your grade, so you either showed up and unburdened your soul, or you ran the risk of taking the class again.

As a religious scholar, Finch bordered on the heretical. In another time, in another age, most likely the church would have disowned him. That's why he was so beloved on the campus. For he taught that there was, in fact, an historical Jesus who could properly be placed within the framework of his own time and place through careful, scholarly research of source materials outside the New Testament. The Bible was fallible, Finch taught, and only a quiescent fool accepted everything at face value.

That wasn't to say, he always added as a postscript, that you shouldn't pay attention to what Jesus, the historical figure, had said. No, he taught his divinity students, his words held sway in the world and it was just and proper to pay them heed.

What you had to be careful of, Finch said, was placing too much importance on what Jesus had said about himself or the world around him. For that had been altered by his fanatical followers and the equally fanatical early Church, he said. Take everything with a heavy dose of salt, he taught.

His view of the historical Jesus and Christianity had slowly but surely taken hold among the upper echelons of the finest divinity schools across the country. The Ivy

League religion scholars and the rest of the intelligentsia in the field had been herded like cattle toward the world Finch espoused. Most, if not all, no longer believed that Jesus was the son of the Creator. Finch was something of a guru to many of them. At the conferences, he was always the center of attention, in demand. His services were always needed.

Jon had barely managed to snore his way through Whitley's awful lectures, but he'd thrived in Finch's class. Jon's gift for rhetoric had held him in good stead. It was apparent that Finch had quickly taken to him, for he called on Jon frequently and smiled beatifically at his answers.

The third professor in the room was something of a mystery to Jon. Almost a recluse, Harold Neuman taught just one course—a bizarre amalgam of arcane source material that seemed to point toward an imminent Apocalypse. Naturally, the Book of Revelation served as the course's centerpiece.

Neuman, unlike all his colleagues, never published anymore. He didn't need to, apparently, now that he had tenure. He never went out of his way to help students. If they came to him for help, well, fine, he would always sit patiently and go over the material. He would sit beside you, constantly adjusting his spectacles and fidgeting, until you mumbled a quick thanks and took your leave.

But he wasn't a Finch by any means. Whereas Finch pulled in scads of money for Duke's fine Divinity School and bolstered its reputation, Neuman pulled up the rear. How and why he'd managed tenure was beyond anyone's comprehension.

No one had ever seen his house. His office was always locked. He seemed to drift from place to place like a shadow. Students, pulling all-nighters, frequently found him buried deep within the stacks pouring over some ancient, dusty tome.

Neuman never met your gaze. And when he did, it was only for a flickering, intense moment. Then he looked away, leaving you with the feeling that you'd just taken a peek into something deep, dark, and forbidden.

Jon had nothing against the man. Far from it. The guy intrigued him, in a funny sort of way, even though he'd never had the heart to take his strange, little course. Neuman scared most of the students half out of their wits. But not Jon, who feared very little, least of all a reclusive scholar who had seemingly lost touch with the real world.

Not surprisingly, Jon had taken all of a few minutes settling on his advisor when he'd been accepted into the doctoral program. There had been no other choice, really. There was only one in the entire school he'd looked up to. And Finch had agreed the instant Jon had asked.

But Finch looked grave and very concerned just now. He barely glanced up as Jon took his seat opposite the three professors. "Well, Jon, how have you been? It's been some time," Finch boomed in that deep voice that seized command of a room so easily. Finch's wardrobe and appearance matched the intensity and depth of his presence. His hair was slightly gray at the temples. His suits were never rumpled. His ties always matched exactly. His shoes never appeared scuffed.

"I've been...preoccupied," Jon said hesitantly, trying his best to size up the situation. It wasn't easy. He didn't really know any of these men. Not enough to look for the clues he'd need.

"So I gather," Whitley said angrily.

"I've kept up with the requisite number of classes," Jon defended lamely.

"We know that, Jon," Finch said brightly. "No need to worry on that score."

"Then why have you called me here?" Jon demanded, suddenly deciding that he wasn't going down without a fight. There would not be a repeat of the disastrous trial before the fairies. Besides, Maya wasn't here to defend his worthless soul.

"Slow down there," Finch said easily, smiling. "This isn't an inquisition. We just have a few friendly questions and if, perchance, you answer them to our satisfaction, well, then, that will be an end to the matter."

Jon glanced away from his advisor to the other two. Whitley, in a blue tweed as usual, glowered at him. There was no mistaking his intention. He was out for blood, for whatever reason.

Neuman was another matter altogether. His face was a dark, clouded mask of uncertainty and introspection. A funny combination right now, it seemed to Jon. Neuman seemed to be searching the depths of his mind for something....

"You still haven't answered my question," Jon said in a somewhat calmer tone. "Why am I here?"

"Someone has raised a question or two about the authenticity of your academic search at this school," Finch began.

"Who has?" Jon asked sharply.

"That's of no consequence," Whitley retorted. "And it would not advance the progress here."

"I see." Jon nodded. He hadn't really expected an answer anyway. "So, let's get the show on the road. What's the first question?"

Whitley glanced at Finch quickly. *So,* Jon thought smugly, *those two, at least, have discussed the situation.*

"What, exactly, do you mean by magic, Jon?" Neuman asked, his voice cracking at the edges.

The question took Jon slightly by surprise, as much because Neuman had asked it as anything else. So he quickly fell back on a pat answer.

"It's an ancient art," Jon replied, shrugging, "that isn't practiced much today. Supposedly, magicians claim they can control natural events by invoking the supernatural."

"And do you believe magic is truly possible?" Neuman asked intently, refusing to look at Jon directly. "That it is, in fact, one of the two elemental forces in this world, as you have stated in the title of your thesis?"

Jon thought about his answer carefully, knowing that a foolish answer would consign his academic career to the graveyard. After weighing his options, he threw caution to the wind. As if anything he said here mattered. "I don't have any doubts anymore," he said, pausing to give his next words some weight. "I know it is possible."

Whitley's eyes almost popped out of his head. Finch just shook his head sadly. Only Neuman remained unaffected by Jon's answer.

"And how is it that you've reached such a conclusion?" Neuman persisted, this time hazarding a glance in Jon's direction.

Jon smiled to himself. *Because I've been to the magicians' world and seen the devastation they left in their wake. Because I've seen how a few simple, ancient words of power can invoke the forces behind the veil. Because nothing is ever as it seems and our own simplistic view of nature and reality ought to be adjusted somewhat.* "Because it's logical to assume there is a counterbalance in this world," Jon said instead.

"A what?" Whitley asked.

"An opposing force," Jon said simply.

Finch grimaced. "Jon, please. Surely you aren't about to tell us that where there is good, so, too, there must be evil."

"And why not?" Jon asked bluntly. "Isn't that the business of religion, after all? To believe that absolute good exists out there somewhere and that it is the sovereign duty of man to call upon that force? Well, isn't it?"

"In a somewhat circumspect manner, I suppose," Finch said easily.

"Well, then," Jon said, "what's to stop man from calling upon the absence of goodness, which is a very, very simple way of describing evil?"

"And magic does that?" Neuman asked.

"It can," Jon said. "Because the nature of magic is to control the elements, to control the forces, to take the basic elements of this world and use them to manipulate the supernatural…"

"To what purpose?" Neuman asked.

"I don't know," Jon answered truthfully. "All I know is that it works. Magic gives its users some measure of control over the natural environment."

"And what of religion, then?" Neuman asked, his eyes blazing with intensity now. "Does religion also give its user some measure of control over the natural environment?"

Jon sighed. He'd never really thought about any of this. It had only been a title anyway. The actual content of his thesis would have been mumbo-jumbo. "No," he said flatly. "Religion, as a counterbalance to magic, does not give anyone control over the land or the environment. It does not allow you to rule the world."

"Then what good is it?" Neuman asked.

"Religion gives you control over your own life," Jon said, surprised at his own answer. "Magic can give you control over the world."

"And which would you choose?" Neuman asked softly.

Jon thought for a moment before answering. "Well, religion, I suppose. If I had to choose between the two. Magic doesn't seem to be of much use, really. It's just a means to an end, a way to gain control of forces outside yourself. Religion is more of an end in itself."

"That makes no sense at all," Whitley said angrily. "None whatsoever. Magic doesn't exist. It's as simple as that."

"You can't be serious." Jon shook his head. "Of course magic exists. Or, at least, the principle exists, if nothing else. If you believe that there is a supernatural—that other worlds may possibly superimpose themselves upon the one we can see with our own, two eyes—then there must be a way to get at the supernatural."

"And you believe magic does that?" Finch asked, slightly incredulous.

"Sure, why not?" Jon shrugged. "All I'm really trying to say is that certain things seem to have an extraordinary amount of power in our own world. Language and words, for example, seem especially suited as a conduit for invoking supernatural forces. Religion, on the other hand, seems almost wholly outside language…"

Finch held up a hand. "Let me see if I'm clear on this. You're trying to tell us that, just by snapping your fingers and saying a few magic words, you can call on the supernatural and rule the world. Just like that?"

"Well, no, not just like that," Jon said lamely, although it certainly did seem to be that easy. There was something he wasn't quite seeing, though, something he was overlooking.

"And that religion, if it is to work at all, can't be discussed or conveyed?" Finch continued. "That words don't adequately describe it?"

"Something like that," Jon mumbled. "If you call on goodness, on God, and it takes root inside you, then it isn't the easiest thing in the world to talk about."

"Then what of the Bible, son? The Old and New Testaments?" Whitley asked sharply. "Do you not believe in those?"

"If God, the Creator, chooses to speak outside of man, that's his prerogative," Jon said, wondering how he'd reached that conclusion. "As for the goodness within a man, that simply cannot be adequately described…"

"So, in your estimation, priests are essentially worthless because they can't describe goodness," Whitley said sourly, "while someone gifted in the magic arts would flourish with rhetoric?"

"I guess," Jon said uneasily.

"You guess?" Finch asked. "You haven't researched all of this thoroughly?"

"Sure, I've researched it. But I didn't really believe any of it. Until now."

Finch and Whitley again glanced at each other. Neuman continued to gaze at some notes he'd brought with him.

"Jon," Finch said gently, "I'm not sure I understand what good it can do you, or anyone else, to pursue this line of reasoning. No one, at least to my knowledge, has ever proved the existence of magic. Religion, on the other hand, flourishes in the modern world. We have the evidence all around us. Millions of words have been written on the subject. Countless testimonies have been offered."

"Yes, and I'm not sure it would advance the cause of religious thought any to attempt to prove that the supernatural can be invoked—or controlled—simply by uttering a few words," Whitley added.

"To your way of thinking," Finch said, "there is no merit in religious discussion because God seems to be outside the boundaries of language."

"Not outside it," Jon defended himself. "It's just that the...the power of goodness can't be invoked. It can only be believed and then acted on. And in the absence of goodness, other forces can come into play."

Neuman, who had been strangely silent for the past few moments, appeared to have another question on his mind. He glanced first at Jon and then at Finch, though, and apparently decided to keep the thought to himself.

Finch held up a hand again. "Well, this is all well and good, but it has absolutely nothing to do with why we called you here," he said with a heavy sigh. "We could bat this subject back and forth endlessly and it would get us no further, I'm afraid."

"So why *have* I been called here, then?" Jon asked.

"It has come to our attention," Whitley said gravely, "that you seem to have a proclivity in a certain direction, in an area that is expressly forbidden by this university. More than just forbidden. Against the law, actually."

"What are you talking about?" Jon felt the mask beginning to slide from his face.

"You've been accused of using and selling cocaine," Finch said directly. "Now, this isn't a court of law and we aren't attorneys, so all you need to do is refute the charge and that will be that."

Whitley didn't seem to like this one bit because it obviously let Jon off the hook far too easily. But he simply glowered in Jon's direction and waited for an answer.

Finch regarded Jon with a blank expression, as if he expected Jon to laugh, shrug the question off, and be on his way. Apparently, he had complete faith in Jon.

Neuman, however, wore such a look of utter consternation that it was all Jon could do to keep from asking him why he was so worried. Neuman wasn't on trial here; Jon was. So why was he so intensely interested in the outcome of this event?

"Will you tell me who brought this to your attention?" Jon asked.

"No, we won't, Jon. I'm sorry," Finch said with a slight frown. "That really wouldn't be proper, I think. Or warranted."

The room grew silent as Jon considered his options. There were only two, of course. He could tell the truth and watch everything he'd worked for wither and die like a fig tree that's been uprooted and cast into the desert. Or he could lie and carry on with his life, with no repercussions and no pain. It seemed an easy choice.

"Yes, I've been using and selling cocaine," Jon said quietly, gazing intently at Neuman as he answered. The bizarre little professor smiled at the answer and then looked away.

"You *what?*" Whitley said, almost choking on the question.

"I've sold cocaine for years," Jon admitted. "I've quit, but I don't imagine you much care for that right now, do you?"

"No, I don't think so," Finch murmured. "You're sure that's the answer you'd like to give us, knowing what it's likely to mean to your academic and professional career?"

"I'm sure." Jon wondered sadly what he'd do for the rest of his life now that he had no career and no future.

"Well, then, I think that's all we need." Finch dismissed Jon. "We'll vote on the matter and get back to you."

"Why don't you have a seat outside?" Whitley said smugly. "We'll have that answer for you fairly shortly, I would think."

Jon rose and walked away from the table, his shoulders slumped in defeat. He could hear Whitley's whispering indictments echo in the room as he closed the door.

The verdict, as Whitley had predicted, was quick in arriving. By a two to one vote, Jon had been dismissed from the doctoral program. Just like that, he was out. They wouldn't tell him how the votes had been cast.

Jon wondered briefly who had supported him. It had to be Finch, of course, who had always been eager to offer a helping hand as his advisor. Too bad there weren't more Finches in the world, willing to entertain some radical thoughts and forgive mistakes along the way.

But Jon didn't regret what he had done. It was the decent thing, the proper thing. And, for the first time in his life, he felt good about himself. Too bad you couldn't put that on your résumé, or take it with you to a job interview.

3

* * *

THE SUMMONS

Laura had moped around her dorm room for two days after she'd gotten back. That was unlike her. She was used to going after what she wanted with a vengeance, heedless of the consequences and regardless of the obstacles.

But the problem now, of course, was that she didn't know what the obstacles were. She had no idea who the enemy was, or even if there was one. And she had no idea where to start her search, or even what her final goal was.

Michael had really only hinted at certain things. He hadn't given Laura, or any of them, much direction. Yet Laura felt certain that the magicians would find them, if they only had the patience to wait for them. There seemed no other choice. Laura, Samson, and Jon had reopened a path to the world the magicians had once ruled. And, according to Michael, they needed them now.

Laura had never really thought much about the meaning of life. Sure, she'd ached to understand the way the world worked, the mysteries of the human body. But that had only been a means to an end. She thirsted for knowledge of physical things so she could heal, not so she could learn more about herself. She almost didn't care whether a God existed. Perhaps if he could help her do what she wanted she might be more interested.

But now, she was forced to re-evaluate. She'd always known all life was precious. Every single life. There had never been any question about that. Yet now she had a greater sense of why that was important, and what that meant.

Creation—and creating—is boundless. It has endless variations. It probably exists on all sorts of different planes, in lots of different ways. Yet there has to be one constant, one central thread that runs through it all. She now had the faintest inkling of what that thread was, what held the universes together into one seamless, coherent piece.

What was that golden rule? Something about treating others as you would treat yourself? Was that even possible? It certainly made sense, Laura now felt. You had to look outside yourself, toward others. If all of your energies were directed toward yourself—which was only natural, it seemed—you would remain lost. You would never understand.

What Laura didn't know was whether she'd ever measure up to that rule. Could she put her own selfish interests aside long enough to be nice to others? She was so accustomed to doing what she wanted, whenever she wanted, there seemed little hope that she would change overnight.

Yet her sojourn in the magicians' world had taught her how people's lives were so intertwined that you had no real hope of acting in your own self-interest all the time.

Take Tara and Kathryn, for instance. In times past, Laura would have wandered through the magicians' world on her own, solving problems on her own, dealing with everything in her own way.

Yet both the young mermaid and the farmer's daughter had joined her as she traveled through that world. They had accompanied her, almost whether Laura liked it or not. In fact, Laura felt as if there was very little she could have done about it.

Was it like that here as well, in the world she was accustomed to? Was there no escaping the fact that every action you took had an impact on someone else in the world, and that you had to recognize that?

Do unto others as you would have them do unto you. How did you do that? How could you possibly manage to treat others as you would treat yourself? It seemed thoroughly impossible.

Laura was fairly certain of one thing, though. The magicians had violated that rule utterly and completely. They had plundered another world for selfish pleasures and vain reasons. They did unto others as they pleased, simply because it suited their fancy. They loved themselves. They acted in their own self-interest first and foremost, and swept aside all else.

Which meant Laura would ultimately have to confront them in this world, if only to undo the damage she'd already done. She was like them. She had their tendencies, their strengths, and, perhaps, their thirst for ultimate knowledge.

She fervently hoped that she would not *become* one of them. Perhaps once, before her travels through the wasted magicians' land, she'd been drifting down that path. But not now, she hoped. Still, she had no idea what to do next. That's what had caused Laura to mope around for days.

As she'd expected, the ancient words of magic were worthless on the Earth. She'd tried a few of them, just to see, and nothing had happened. Clearly, the rules of magic were different here.

Actually, Laura felt, the rules were likely to be totally different on Earth. If anything, magic was likely to be a black art in this world, a device that served the corrupted magicians.

Okay, she thought, *what would identify magicians in this world, if you were unable to invoke power simply by uttering a few ancient words, as she'd been able to do in the land?*

If people acted selfishly, in their own behalf, with no heed whatsoever for others, were they in service to the magicians? Probably not. More likely, they were just being selfish and vainglorious.

But, clearly, that had to be the key to understanding in this world. A magician would have to be someone who acted entirely in his or her own self-interest, no matter how torturous the path to that end.

That's how Laura would be able to recognize the magicians. If they were out there, they would surely have constructed things in such a fashion that everything ultimately funneled into their own self-interest. Even when they seemed to be in service to others, perhaps.

For instance, Laura knew of physicians who supposedly acted to heal others. That was what they said. But what they *did* was something entirely different. They were in medicine for both the money and the power over others' lives. Nothing more.

The magicians would be like that, only worse. For them, the only purpose in life would be to corrupt others and bend them toward serving their own very selfish needs. And that's how Laura would find and recognize them. She was certain of that. She would follow the path of wasted and trampled lives.

* * *

The letter arrived four days after Laura had come back home. Its return address was Duke's administration building. Her own address was typewritten. It looked very official. It was the kind of letter Laura had been expecting, so she almost smiled as she read it. *All right*, she thought. *The game begins, in this world.* They were coming toward her, cloaked in darkness, as she'd expected. *Well, let them come. I'm ready for the challenge.*

The letter was from the school's administrator, no less, summoning her to his office for a consultation. A charge, an anonymous one, had been leveled at her that she had abused her privilege as a student.

The accusation was that she'd somehow cheated in several of her classes, that she'd somehow been given "inside" information that allowed her to flourish in some of her pre-med classes.

"In fact," wrote the administrator, Mr. James Adams, "it now appears that there may be a network at work here allowing students to take advantage of the system to the detriment of others. The charge has been made that you are somehow integral to that system."

It was ludicrous, of course. There was no system Laura knew of that would allow her to do well in the pre-med courses. You either knew the stuff or you didn't. There was simply no way to skate by the process.

But, she was certain, something had been concocted. Somehow, they were setting in motion a series of fabrications to undo her in this world. *So be it,* Laura thought grimly. *I'm ready to take this on. I'm ready to take on whatever it is.*

The meeting at the administrator's office was in two days. That would give her time to do a little homework. And the first stop was Jon's house, because something had, indeed, happened and it was time to share that knowledge. Somehow Jon would help her find the key to understanding what was happening in this world.

4

***

A SHATTERED DREAM

For a reason he had not yet come to grips with, Samson had lost his passion for wrestling. The drive that had made him one of the best wrestlers in the collegiate world had waned enough that he now struggled to even make it through practice. Still, he was not about to give it up. Wrestling paid the bills. Without his full scholarship, he would not be able to attend such an expensive private school.

So he had no choice in the matter. He had to remain where he was, even though his heart and soul now seemed to be part of another world. For Samson had been captured by the magicians' world…by their passion for the Earth, their commitment to the simple things in life, the struggle just to exist.

It was so different than much of what he saw in this world. Here, everyone concerned themselves with personal pursuits—how to attain a position of power and influence, how to parlay good grades at the undergraduate levels into a medical or law degree.

Not so in the magicians' world. There, they were more concerned about how to make it through the day intact than anything else. And Samson liked that. He thought it was a good thing. He liked that kind of a struggle. He could relate to it.

He found himself sitting in classes daydreaming about what had happened to him in that world. He missed Regis and Gar…and their constant feuding. He also missed Mark. He wondered what had happened to the young warrior.

He had a funny feeling about Mark. Someday, probably before he was ready, Samson felt certain the various races would ask Mark to be their king, to take the position at the head of the round table in the great meeting hall, where the course of the land had recently been changed.

He always smiled at the thought. In the beginning, when Samson had first appeared in the land, he thought almost nothing of Mark. After all, he was just a boy. But in his travels with Samson, Mark had become a man. He had proved himself worthy of greater things. There was no question about it—not in Samson's mind and, he was sure, not in the minds of others who'd seen him in action and worked by his side during combat.

In the two days since Samson, Laura, and Jon had returned to the Earth, he'd seen no hint of the magicians. He'd looked for some clues as to their whereabouts, but everything appeared as normal as could be. He went to his classes and wrestling practice as if nothing had happened. Yet he couldn't help but believe that it wasn't over, that there was simply a lull before the storm broke over him.

On his first day back, his wrestling coach announced to the team that the school's president had informed the athletic director that random drug testing was to be instituted not only in football but in the school's other sports as well.

Fine, Samson thought as he listened to his coach tell the team about it before practice. *I have nothing to hide. Let them test me. I'm proud of my accomplishments. I've never taken a steroid. It isn't worth the risks.*

So, when he was selected for a drug test, Samson didn't even blink. There appeared to be nothing unusual about it. The school's president had sent along a directive to the athletic director, who had in turn relayed the message to the various sports' coaches. And Samson had been selected for a drug test at random.

Samson was a little startled when the wrestling coach, Bob Rust, asked him to stop by his office after practice the next day. *Maybe he wants to talk about the match this weekend,* he thought.

When Samson showed up at the office, his coach was sitting behind his desk, reading from a folder of some sort. "Sit down, sit down," the coach said warmly as Samson entered the room.

Samson settled into one of the two chairs facing the coach's desk. "What's up?" he asked easily.

The coach didn't look up right away. When he did, Samson could see that something was wrong. This wasn't about the next match. This was about something else entirely.

"Samson, this is hard for me…"

"What is, Coach?" Samson steeled himself.

The coach held up the folder. "I have the results of your drug test in this folder, son. I've been looking them over."

"Yeah? So?"

"And the lab results, well, they confirm there's some kind of a foreign substance in your bloodstream," the coach said, clearly ill at ease.

"A foreign substance?"

"They're not sure what it is." The coach frowned. "It appears to have all the chemical properties of a drug, but they haven't been able to nail it down."

"What, exactly, are you saying?" Samson almost growled.

"I'm saying the lab thinks they've found a drug of some sort in your system. They just don't know what it is, yet."

"I don't take drugs." Samson's voice was flat and emotionless. "Of any sort. I never have, and I never will."

"But the lab results?"

"I can't explain them." Samson shrugged.

In the back of his mind, Samson wondered if his recent sojourn didn't have something to do with this. Perhaps there was some residue lingering in his system that somehow mirrored the properties of a drug. But that wasn't something he could talk about here.

His coach looked directly at him. "Samson, there has to be some explanation for this."

"I'm sorry, I can't help you. I don't know what it could be."

"Are you taking some new kind of growth drug, something hot off the street? One of the new biotech drugs, maybe?"

Samson stiffened. It took all of his willpower to keep from bolting from the chair and throttling his coach. "I told you," he said slowly, his voice low and controlled, "I *don't* take drugs of any sort. I never have, and I never will. Everything I've achieved, I've done on my own."

"But there has to be an explanation for what the lab's chemists found in your bloodstream?"

Samson glared at his coach. "I'm gonna say this one more time. I can't help you. I don't know what they found. I can only tell you that I don't take drugs. My strength is my own. I've earned it, with hard work. It's all my own."

His coach looked away and sighed heavily. "I'd like to believe you, but..."

"Then why don't you? Why don't you believe me, and leave it at that?"

"I can't."

"Why not?"

"Because the athletic director has told me I have to act on it."

"The athletic director told you that? Why?"

"I don't know," the coach said. "He kind of hinted that he'd discussed the situation with the school's president."

Samson was stunned. People he'd never even met were controlling his fate, discussing his future and making decisions about his life? "You've gotta be kidding. The school president? What's he got to do with all of this?"

The coach tossed Samson's file on the desk in front of him. "Beats me. All I know is that I've been told I have to act on this. That's why I was hoping you could clear this all up for me, give me some idea what I'm looking at here."

"Sorry," Samson said coldly. "I can't."

"Well, I have no choice, really, as much as it pains me—"

"What do you mean, you have no choice?"

"I mean, the athletic director told me I had to take some kind of an action, set an example for the school and the rest of the athletes here." The coach refused to meet Samson's gaze.

"You're going to use me as an example, is that what you're saying?" Samson clenched his fists. "You're going to kick me off the wrestling team to set an example? Is that it?"

"Well, yes, I guess that's what I'm saying," the coach said grimly.

Samson stood. He felt strangely calm, which was unlike him. Perhaps it was because he had half-expected something like this. He placed both hands squarely on the front of the desk and leaned over toward the coach. "But I haven't done anything wrong," Samson told his coach in a clear voice. "And I think you know that."

"Samson, I'm sorry." His coach was barely able to meet Samson's steady gaze. "My hands are tied. I have no choice in the matter. I have to suspend you."

"And if you aren't able to determine what's in my system, if the lab fails to confirm anything? What then?"

"I think we'll have to presume you've taken some newfangled drug."

"You can't do that. It isn't right, and it isn't legal."

"It *is* legal, Samson. The statute says we have the right to suspend you if we find a foreign substance, even one we can't identify," his coach said firmly. "The athletic director said the school president would back him up on it. We would obtain legal counsel, if we have to."

"You may have to do just that," Samson warned.

"I hope we don't have to," his coach said, obviously perturbed. "I hope we can handle this quietly. I hope you don't choose to make an issue out of this."

Samson turned to leave. He was sure there was nothing more he could do here. It was obvious to him that someone was putting extraordinary pressure on his coach to take this action. "I can't promise anything," Samson said over his shoulder. "All I know is that this isn't right."

"Think it over, Samson," his coach called out to him. "Don't do anything rash."

Samson didn't answer. He walked away, his mind racing off in different directions. He hadn't seen either Jon or Laura since he'd gotten back. But he felt like he needed to see both of them.

It was time. The magicians were beginning to show their hand. He was sure of that. Now, it was simply a matter of finding them. And it wouldn't be easy.

5

***

THE ANCIENT WAR
OF MAGIC AND RELIGION

Jon had done a lot of reading since his appearance before the tribunal. An awful lot of reading. In fact, he'd probably done more reading at the Duke Divinity Library than at any time in the past few years, when he was supposedly slaving away at his doctoral thesis.

How strange, Jon thought. *How utterly ironic. Here I've lost my opportunity to earn my degree, and I'm more interested than ever in my thesis topic.*

For what Jon had been studying in the divinity school library was the roots of the war between magic and religion—or, at least, as much of it as he could glean from the meager writings on the subject. He also had a better understanding now of the *bene elohim* and their place in humankind's history.

He had also come across Araqiel's name, and others like it, in his reading. Jon couldn't help but wonder if it wasn't *the* Araqiel from his reading.

The first source material he had turned to, quite naturally, had been the Bible. The Old Testament had provided at least a partial, although very ancient, explanation of how the war between magic and religion had been waged at one point in humankind's history.

That war had been at the heart of the settlement of ancient Palestine. For centuries, magic had reigned supreme in the hills and valleys of what was now northern Israel.

But then the monotheistic followers of Moses and Joshua had invaded the land, bringing their sense of a relationship to one God with them. It was a brand- new way of living in the world, one that was foreign to the inhabitants of Palestine.

The people of Palestine were quite used to worshiping gods like Ba'al and Asherah, the mother goddess of fertility. They were accustomed to calling on magic to help them with their daily chores.

But the Israelites brought them a different message, one the simple, magic-believing people of Palestine were not ready to hear. "There is just one, true God," the Israelites told them. "He gives meaning to life. He is the reason we are alive. He has given the gift of life." The central message the Israelites tried, for centuries, to bring to the people of ancient Palestine was that the religion of the one, true God was more powerful than their magic, that it superseded their magic.

What made the war so difficult was that even the Israelites constantly slid backwards themselves. They would settle in a community that worshiped the gods of magic, and then proceed to fall into their ways and habits. They would begin calling on their gods of magic, as well. In fact, the lines became so blurred at times that the Israelites would refer to El and Eloah in much the same manner as the gods and goddesses of the region like Ba'al and Asherah. It took centuries, in fact, for the transition of El as a god among many to the established notion that there was one, all-powerful God above all others.

The Israelites themselves would slide back into the ways and practices of magic and many gods, time and again. And God, acting through a prophet or a king, would bring the Israelites back to the true path. This kind of battle was played out over and over, in place after place, in the Old Testament.

Yet, even before this war, there had been an earlier conflict between the sons of God on one side and the daughters of men and their offspring on the other, according to the ancient texts. That war, or rumors of that war, had almost certainly inspired the earthly tales handed down as Greek, Roman, and Norse mythology. It was in this much earlier war that one of the most powerful myths in the history of civilization—that a god-creator called El had chosen a companion called Eloah from the daughters of men and created a new race on Earth—had sprung forth and traveled across the earliest oral histories.

According to legends that had morphed into mythology, the *bene elohim* had left their own realm in order to cohabit with humankind, producing all manner of offspring, ruled above all by El and his female companion, Eloah. They had bequeathed their knowledge to neophyte humankind. The Great Flood had ended their days of influence on Earth, so the stories all said.

None of this should have been new to Jon, for he had put all of it into his thesis. Yet he'd only been going through the motions before. He'd plugged it into his thesis much as a mathematician plugs numbers into an equation. He hadn't paid attention to what it *meant*.

But he was paying attention now. He had no choice. For the war between magic and religion was still raging. The ancient gods Ba'al and Asherah—as well as the *bene elohim* and perhaps even El himself—appeared to be very much alive on Earth. And they were playing a deadly game, one that had now trapped and encircled Jon.

* * *

Laura showed up at Jon's apartment unannounced, in the middle of the day. It was clean as a whistle, in nearly every corner, and cozy and inviting. Books were placed in strategic places. She detected a hint of herbal tea in the air. Paintings and little knickknacks were tucked here and there.

"Come in, come in," Jon said warmly as Laura shed her jacket. Jon took it from her and hung it up in his closet as Laura perused the apartment. "So what brings you here?"

Laura didn't take a seat right away. She looked Jon directly in the eye. "Your apartment? It's so clean! It's different than I'd imagined it, somehow."

Jon flushed with embarrassment. "Hey, I know. One of the first things I did when we got back was junk half of what was in here. Then I spent an entire day cleaning the place. It was a real mess."

Laura shook her head in amazement. "Well, it's wonderful now. You've done a marvelous job."

"Thanks," Jon said proudly.

Something had clearly happened to Jon. Gone was the somnambulant mystic who just drifted through life in a cocaine haze. In its place was something else entirely. Laura found herself wondering what that was.

Laura gave Jon a curious look. "And the other problem? The one you were struggling with so much when we first got to the land?" She left the question hanging in the air between them.

Jon didn't even blink. "I didn't have much choice, really," he said forthrightly. "I was forced to kick cocaine cold turkey in the magicians' world. I went through that crummy nightmare while I was there, and it made it easier when I got back here."

"So you're off of it?"

Jon smiled broadly. "Yes, I'm off that nasty inspiration powder forever. It's horrible. It corrupts your mind and warps reality beyond belief. It forces you to walk around in a constant state of delusion. Right now, the straight and narrow looks interesting. But I'm sure that isn't why you've come. So, what's up?"

She took a seat. "Something has happened to me, and I'm not sure I know what to do next. So I was hoping, perhaps, that you'd found something…"

Jon took a seat, also. "Okay, but a lot has happened to me as well."

Laura regarded him quizzically. "Let me guess. You've had some problems with the school in some way? You've been challenged?"

Jon nodded. "Actually, it's even worse than that. Yes, some of the Divinity School professors challenged my thesis, which dealt with the war between magic and religion. But it got quite nasty after that."

"How?"

"Well," Jon said slowly, "they knew about my cocaine habit, and the fact that I'd sold cocaine around the campus. They challenged me with that."

Laura gasped. "And what did you do?"

Jon just shrugged. He'd already resigned himself to his fate. "I left the school, voluntarily."

"But all of your work toward your doctorate degree?"

"All down the drain," Jon said wanly. "The only thing left is the fact that I'd earned enough to become a pastor. I passed that milestone a year ago. I'll never be a professor at a university, though. Not now."

Laura looked down briefly. "Jon, I'm sorry. Really."

"Thanks," Jon said, his eyes a little moist.

"Something a little like that may be in store for me as well," Laura added after an awkward lull in the conversation.

"But you've never tried drugs, have you?"

"No, no, not like that," Laura said quickly. "I meant that I've been challenged by the school, too. And I'm sure they mean to harm me, perhaps even kick me out of school if they can manage that."

"What's happened?"

Laura explained about the note she'd gotten from the school administrator, with the veiled hint that she was somehow at the center of some conspiracy to share information with other students.

"But that's ludicrous!" Jon said. "Even I know how difficult it is to cheat in those pre-med classes. Either you know it, or you don't."

"Exactly," Laura stated grimly. "Yet I'm sure they've concocted something."

"You should fight it," Jon encouraged.

"Oh, I will. If I get a chance. That's why I came by, to see if maybe you've learned anything that might help."

"Not really. Or, at least, not yet. I've done a lot of reading in the past few days, and I've done quite a bit of research on what's happened over the centuries in the war between magic and religion."

"And?"

"And it seems that magic and religion always seem to square off against each other. They have ever since the Garden of Eden, it seems."

"The Garden of Eden?" Laura asked, confused. "What does *that* mean?"

"I'm not sure yet," Jon said mysteriously. "But I have this sneaking suspicion that what the serpent spoke to Eve about in the Garden is similar to the eternal life and ultimate knowledge the magicians sought."

"Ultimate knowledge? Eternal life?"

"There were two trees in the Garden of Eden—the tree of life, which gave you eternal life if you ate its fruit, and the tree of knowledge of good and evil, which gave you ultimate knowledge and wisdom if you ate its fruit," Jon explained. "It was the second tree from which Eve ate the fruit. And it wasn't an apple. That's just a myth. The Bible makes no reference to the type of fruit."

"So what is it with these two trees?"

"It's interesting. There was a type of tree, with a unique type of fruit, that once seemed to be at the heart of this ancient war between religion and magic."

"What was it?"

"The oak. Its fruit is the acorn, which most people don't even think of as a fruit," he answered. "Britain was once covered with an extensive oak forest, and tree worship is a major feature in the Celtic religion. Druids had their teaching centers in the middle of oak groves.

"The World Tree is an esoteric philosophy common to cultures and mythologies. The ancients saw the entire cosmos in the form of a tree whose roots grow deep in the ground, branches reaching high into the heavens.

"The Aztecs actually believed that there were celestial trees located at the four corners of the world, surrounding a great central tree connected to the kingdom of the fire god, the principle of life. These five trees are responsible for the organization of the entire Universe.

"The Mayans had a 'First Tree of the World,' which grew at the center of the Earth and spread its branches through various heavenly realms. Meanwhile, the early Egyptians had an image of a radiant tree in the middle of Paradise that furnished all living beings with food, protection, and immortality. And we've seen the One Tree at the center of the magicians' world…"

"You know," Laura interjected, "if I recall correctly, there seemed to be oak everywhere in the land."

Jon nodded. "There was. It was everywhere."

"Including that ladder leading to the top of the magicians' city. So the fruit from this second tree…"

"Apparently gives you the kind of ultimate knowledge that the magicians sought, I believe," Jon answered. "The knowledge of good and evil. The serpent told Eve that God had forbidden her to eat from the tree of the knowledge of good and evil because he didn't want her to obtain that knowledge. Eve believed the serpent and ate the fruit. The rest, as they say, is ancient history."

"And what of the tree of life?"

"God kicked both Adam and Eve out of the Garden of Eden so they wouldn't eat from the tree of life. They'd eaten the forbidden fruit from the other tree, but he also didn't want them eating from the tree of life."

Laura sat back in her chair. "And that has something to do with what's happening to us now?"

"Yes, I believe so. You see, that constant struggle has never really ended. To this day, we struggle with the question of whether we, as men and women, can control our own fate."

"You really believe it's that simple?" Laura tilted her head.

"Quite often, I believe, some of the most profound things are the simplest. I'm certain this is one of those instances. It's the difference between wisdom and understanding."

"Wisdom and understanding?"

"Someone who learns all the world has to offer is wise. Someone who learns some of what the world has to offer and discerns what that really means has understanding. Magic attempts to learn and control all the world has to offer. Religion attempts to learn some of what the world has to offer, and then seeks understanding from outside ourselves."

"A little esoteric, I think," Laura said wryly.

He grinned. "I know, I know. I'm always doing that. I like to drift off into the abstract like that. It's what makes learning fun, for me at least."

Laura rolled her eyes. "To each his or her own. Unfortunately, it doesn't help me much, in my own particular battle."

"Sorry. It's the best I can offer right now."

Laura stood to leave. "Well, it's a start. I'll let you know how things go at the administrator's office. I have this feeling that we've only begun to fight."

"I think you're right. But the rules are quite different in our own world."

"You're the one who understands them here." Laura gazed intently at Jon. "The simple magic we worked in that other place doesn't work here at all."

"I assumed that. Those who use magic here, on Earth, are probably on the wrong side. They're taking that knowledge and using it for their own selfish purposes."

"They've taken a bite out of Eve's apple." Laura smiled mischievously.

"Several bites of the apple, I believe," Jon said grimly. "Only it was never an apple. An acorn, perhaps, but never an apple."

6

* * *

TELLING TALES

The article was in Duke's daily newspaper the next day, on the front page, no less. Samson was taken completely by surprise.

"Top Wrestler Kicked off Squad for Substance Abuse," read the headline, which ran above a short story and a picture of Samson from one of his more recent matches.

> One of Duke's top wrestlers, Armand "Samson" Rothian, has been removed from the wrestling team following a recent, random drug abuse test. According to sources who asked to remain anonymous, the lab tests revealed foreign substances in Rothian's blood.
>
> Rothian has refused to identify those substances, but they are believed to be a new, black-market biotechnology growth hormone, perhaps imported from Japan or China, according to these sources.
>
> Rothian was undefeated so far this season and there was widespread speculation that he had a shot at a NCAA championship, perhaps even an Olympic gold medal someday. He was unavailable for comment.

"Unavailable!" Samson roared to no one in particular as he read the story, standing in the middle of the campus's main quad. "They never even tried to find me! They can't do this…"

"They can, and they have," a voice said nearby.

Samson turned. Standing behind him was Thomas, the pudgy game-player with a face full of pimples and mousy brown hair that hung around his ears carelessly. "So do you know where Eric is?" he asked Thomas.

Thomas shrugged. "Don't know. I was hoping *you* could tell me that."

"Beats me," Samson fairly growled. "I haven't seen hide nor hair of him since we got back."

Thomas's brow wrinkled. "Got back? From where?"

"From the land, of course," Samson said, more because he was curious how

Thomas would react to the news than anything else.

Thomas gasped. "The land. What do you know of the land?"

"We visited it, of course." Samson squinted one eye. "We went there that day, in that room."

"You *visited* the land?" Thomas said, incredulous.

"Yes, of course. But I thought you knew that? I figured Eric had told you."

Thomas shook his head. "Eric got up and left after the three of you left so quickly. You were gone for a couple of hours. And we haven't seen Eric since then."

Samson looked hard at Thomas, to make sure he wasn't lying. "A couple of hours, you say?"

Thomas nodded. "Then the three of you came back and left as well."

"But we were gone for days," Samson said, now thoroughly confused. "I personally visited both the elves and the dwarves. Laura and Jon brought the other four races back as well."

"You visited the dwarves and the elves? In the land?"

"Yes, I did." Samson frowned. "Or, at least, I *think* I did. But if you say I was gone for only a couple of hours, perhaps I just dreamed it all?"

"No, no, not necessarily," Thomas said quickly. "Time—Earth's time, I mean—wouldn't mean much if you traveled to another world, to another universe. That's what must have happened. It would be like being transported to heaven. Earth's time wouldn't mean much there, either."

Samson shrugged. "I guess. That makes some sense."

"So you really visited the land? You were there, you saw the races?" Thomas's eyes filled with longing for a world he'd only dreamed about.

"Yes, they've all returned to the land."

"Even the people of the sea?"

"Yes, even them. They've all come back. There is a new Law there as well, one that doesn't include the ancient magicians who ruined their lives."

"Wow! But what about the magicians? Where have they gone?"

"You tell me. Where *have* they gone? Are they here, on the Earth?"

"If they're not in the land anymore, then I would think they'd *have* to be here," Thomas said, his voice almost a whisper. "Where else would they have gone?"

"Then why won't they show themselves?" Samson growled.

Thomas almost started laughing. "But they have."

"What do you mean, they have?"

"They've shown themselves. The article, in the newspaper. The one about you."

"What about it?"

"Have you taken drugs—steroids, growth hormones, anything like that?" Thomas asked, glancing over Samson's shoulder at the story.

357

"No, I haven't," Samson said forcefully.

"Well, *someone* has accused you of that, someone who knows how to push all of the right buttons."

Samson thought back to his conversation with his coach. The order for drug tests had come from above, and the order to kick Samson off the team had come from there as well. *Maybe this kid's right. Maybe someone's pulling strings behind the scenes, where no one can see.* "I don't know," he said out loud. "It seems a little farfetched."

"More farfetched than the land you just came from?" Thomas laughed.

"True," Samson muttered.

"So what do we do now?"

"We?" Samson lifted a brow.

"Yeah, well, um, you know, you and me," Thomas stammered. "I just thought that maybe you might need some help now, sort of a sidekick."

Once upon a time, Samson would have laughed in this kid's face. He would have ridiculed the suggestion and sent him packing. But Samson had learned a little during his sojourn in the land. And he wasn't about to turn away allies now, not when he didn't even know who his enemies were.

"Sure, kid, come along for the ride. But I'll tell you, I have no idea what to do now. No idea at all."

"Well, I think the first thing we have to do is find Eric. If we can find him, I think maybe we can start to get some answers."

Samson scowled. "Where do we start? I don't even know Eric's last name."

"Neither do I. But if we call a meeting of the group, maybe we can come up with something."

"The group?"

"Back in the room at the old house," Thomas said quickly.

"Oh, there." Samson nodded. "But will that do any good? Are they any more likely to know something than you are?"

Thomas lifted a shoulder. "It can't hurt to try, can it?"

"I guess not. All right. Let's get this thing rolling. I'm ready for some action."

7

✳ ✳ ✳

THE SCHOOL'S ADMINISTRATOR

Laura didn't really know how to prepare for her meeting with the administrator. She had no idea, yet, what the charges were against her, so she didn't know what to review or even think about.

The administrator, James Adams, had a quirky reputation. He wasn't well known on Duke's campus—not like the school's president, a former college professor who'd become a United States senator and had eventually returned to his old alma mater as its president.

Adams' somewhat limited reputation was that he was tough but fair. He'd been involved in a couple of scrapes and had earned the grudging admiration of both the students and the faculty.

For instance, a former U.S. President who'd attended law school at Duke, but left the White House in some disgrace, had hoped to house the presidential library at Duke. Adams had objected strenuously, on the grounds that it would tarnish the school's image, and his arguments had carried the day with the faculty.

Laura, however, had never really met Adams. Before her meeting, she'd gone to the library and dug out a few school newspaper articles on him. They hadn't been much help. They shed some light on his public profile, but they didn't provide any clues as to how he would react in such a private meeting.

She arrived for her appointment 15 minutes early. The secretary kept her waiting in the outer lobby for most of those 15 minutes. And when she was finally ushered into the inner sanctum, she was forced to wait an additional 20 minutes because the administrator's previous meeting was running late.

Laura found it extraordinarily difficult to wait patiently. Patience had never been one of her strong suits. Yet she knew she had to go into this meeting with her mind clear and focused. There could be no muddling here.

The door to Adams' office opened slowly, and several middle-aged men emerged, laughing and joking with each other.

"*Capital* ideas, James! Brilliant," one of them shouted out through the doorway as he left.

"Yes, they'll do wonders for our school," said a second as he, too, left.

Laura stood to enter the office. The secretary glanced at her sternly. Laura stopped in her tracks, wondering what she'd done wrong.

"Mr. Adams will see you shortly, I'm sure," the secretary said shortly as she rose from her seat behind the desk. She walked over and closed the door to Adams' office and then returned to her seat.

Laura, confused, sat down again. *Now what?* A couple of minutes passed, and then there was a buzz on the telephone at the secretary's desk. She answered it, listened for a moment, and then glanced over at Laura.

Without a word, the secretary walked over to a large filing cabinet, pulled it open, and whisked a file from it. She disappeared quickly into Adams' office. The file was gone from her hand when she returned.

Laura continued to cool her heels, determined not to let any of the waiting deter her from her goal. She *had* to remain focused and aloof. There was no room for mistakes.

There was a second buzz on the secretary's desk. The secretary listened again and then looked over at Laura. She hung up the phone. "The administrator will see you, now," she said curtly before returning to her own work at her desk.

"Thank you," Laura answered just as curtly.

Laura marched into the room boldly. Adams was sitting behind his desk, reading from a file. Laura presumed it was her file, detailing whatever charges were being leveled at her. She walked across the spacious office and took a seat in front of the desk.

Adams looked up from the file, gazing at Laura over a pair of reading glasses that hung precariously at the tip of his nose. Adams was meticulous in his dress, his mannerisms, his entire appearance. Everything bespoke a man completely in charge of his surroundings.

"Well, Ms. Brisbane," Adams said slowly, "your academic record is quite impressive. *Quite* impressive, indeed."

"Thank you," Laura said with a nod.

"In fact," Adams said, laying down the file and removing his glasses, "it's one of the most impressive records I've ever seen, especially for a pre-med student here. Almost beyond belief."

Laura stiffened. She could sense a challenge when one was approaching, and it was fast approaching here. "I work very hard at my studies," she answered tersely. "I always have."

"Oh, I can see that," Adams acknowledged. "Your record in high school was equally impressive. No doubt about it. None whatsoever."

"I worked quite hard there as well."

"I have a question, though." Adams leaned forward in his chair and stared at Laura. "Your grade point in high school was flawless. You could have gone to any school in the country, including any school of your choosing in the Ivy League. Why here? Why did you choose to come to Duke?"

Laura shrugged. "There's no big mystery to it. Duke has a progressive undergrad program that lets you start medical school in your third year, if you make the grade."

"And you were sure you'd make it?"

"Yes, I am," Laura said firmly. "I have no doubt whatsoever that I will qualify for the program."

"But, Ms. Brisbane, every student has doubts about whether they will succeed at their studies and go on to greater things."

Laura stiffened. "I didn't. And I still don't."

"I see." Adams looked back down at the file laid out in front of him on the desktop. He studied the papers for a moment longer, and then looked up again. "So, I'll bet you're wondering what this is all about."

"It's crossed my mind."

Adams stood and walked around the desk. He motioned for Laura to join him over at one side of the desk near a huge stack of books, a sofa, two chairs, and a coffee table. Laura rose and seated herself primly in one of the chairs. Adams settled into one corner of the sofa.

"I'll tell you something, Ms. Brisbane," he said as he draped an arm casually over a corner of the sofa. "I don't have an easy job. I really don't. There are so many unpleasant tasks."

"Really?"

"Really." Adams nodded. "Take this meeting, for instance. You seem like a fine person, an outstanding student, someone with a first-rate mind. Yet, circumstances appear to have set us apart, forced us to become antagonists. How I wish it were not so."

Laura sighed ever so slightly. It was taking all of her will to remain patient. "Mr. Adams, I still don't understand why I'm here."

The administrator studied Laura, perhaps seeking some crack in the armor, some wavering of her resolve. Finding none, he went on. "Ms. Brisbane, you are here because your grades are simply too good. Your test scores are too perfect. No one could possibly have done as well as you appear to have done. It is categorically impossible."

"No, it isn't," Laura answered testily. "I've earned those grades."

"Perhaps. But the charge has been leveled against you that you have somehow been given the answers to many of the tests beforehand, that people are trafficking in such information and that you are somehow connected with this traffic."

"And who is making those charges?" Laura demanded.

Adams shook his head. "That isn't for me to reveal."

"But how can I answer them if I don't know where they've come from?"

"I think it's safe to assume they've come from professors you've studied under and the students who've obtained information from you. I cannot go beyond that."

Laura sat ramrod straight in her chair. She leaned forward. "Those are *lies*, Mr. Adams, and I think you know that. I've earned every single grade at this school. *Every single grade.*"

Adams sighed. "I'd *like* to believe you. Really, I would. But these charges must be dealt with somehow. After all, we have the school's reputation to think of."

"What about *my* reputation!"

Adams remained aloof. "The school remains above petty individual concerns. Institutions must be operated and maintained above and beyond such individual circumstances."

"That's absurd," Laura said stiffly.

"No, it isn't. It is the only way an institution such as this one can survive and prosper. The whole must be greater than the sum of its parts."

Laura could barely contain her anger. "Mr. Adams, unless you have proof of these charges, I think you'd better go somewhere else with your witch-hunt."

"Oh, we have proof," Adams said mysteriously.

"Where is it?" Laura demanded.

"Well, we were rather hoping it wouldn't come to that. We were hoping that you would choose to let this matter resolve itself quietly, and that you would choose to perhaps transfer to another fine institution of higher learning."

Laura persisted. "Who, exactly, are the others you're referring to?"

Adams simply shrugged. "We, the school."

"But who else, besides you, is interested in making sure I leave this place?"

Adams said nothing for a moment. Then, "Do you deny the charges?"

"Yes, I do."

"Then you leave us no choice," he said, rising as if to dismiss Laura. "We will have to bring this matter before the Board of Inquiry. There will be a public hearing. I regret that we must do this."

"Fine. I'd welcome such a hearing. Because I've done nothing wrong."

"I guess we'll both see about that, won't we?" His smile was grim.

Laura narrowed her eyes. "Yes, we will."

"Good day, Ms. Brisbane." Adams returned to his desk.

"When will this Board of Inquiry meet?"

"Don't worry, Ms. Brisbane, we'll be in touch. You can be certain of that."

8

* * *

THE OAK OF MOREH

s Jon walked across Duke's campus after dark, he was again struck by the beauty of the place. The architecture, fitfully illuminated here and there by the lights, was so extraordinary, so gothic. It really was an amazing place.

And how strange, he thought, *that I should only begin to notice such beauty now, when I'm about to leave it. Why did I never pay any attention to it before? Must we always lose something to appreciate it?*

Jon hadn't settled yet on a mission. He figured he'd just head over to Duke's Divinity School library and see where the Muses took him.

The Muses. Jon almost laughed aloud. The nine daughters of Zeus had almost cost him his life upon his arrival in the magicians' world. He had been so self-absorbed then, so completely unaware of his surroundings.

And now? Had he changed so much? Would the Muses lead him to his destruction now, were he to journey again to that world? Jon doubted it. He doubted it very much.

Jon couldn't put his finger on the exact moment he'd changed. So many elements had gone into that change. Being humiliated and humbled by the fairies had begun the process. Peg and his descent into Hades had been the forge that had forced the change.

And then here, in this world, where actions meant consequences, Jon had finally been forced to come to grips with who he was, what he'd done for the past few years. And, at that moment, he'd chosen the path he was now on.

Jon ducked into the Divinity School library, convinced that tonight would yield some special fruit, some special insight into the mystery of the ancient war between religion and magic.

He wasn't disappointed. On his very first cross-reference to magic and ancient Palestine, he came across something called the Oak of Moreh. Curious, he started to search the literature. A thread emerged.

Early on in the Bible's story of God's relationship with humankind, the Great Patriarch, Abraham, left his home at God's urging and began his trek toward the

363

promised land. This was in roughly the second millennium before Jesus. God promised Abraham that, if he broke his ties to land and kindred and served the one and true God, he would eventually lead him to another land and make his descendants a great nation. Abraham obeyed, and the long journey began.

"I will bless those who bless you, and him who curses you I will curse," God told Abraham. "And by you all the families of the earth shall bless themselves."

So Abraham, his wife, Sarai, and his brother's son, Lot, set out on their journey to the land of Canaan. At the very first place they came to once they'd reached Canaan was a place called Shechem. And at Shechem was something called the Oak of Moreh, the "oracle-giver."

Abraham built his first altar to God at Shechem, near the Oak of Moreh. This was no easy feat. The Oak of Moreh was the center of magic to the Canaanites. It was a sacred tree.

How amazing, Jon thought, *that Abraham should choose to build his first altar to God at such a place. Magic and religion, side by side.* The Creator had thrown the gauntlet down. He meant to challenge magic, right from the start.

The Canaanites were simple people. To them, magic seemed the easiest route to knowledge. They desperately wanted to control their surroundings, the world around them, so they sought to employ magic to do so.

Then along comes Abraham, and tells them there is a better way. Serve and obey the one, true God, and the land shall be yours for the asking. Jon chuckled. *That message probably went down like a lead balloon to the Canaanites.*

From that point on, Abraham and his descendants began a steady, consistent struggle with magic and the disciples of the Oak of Moreh. Curiously, Abraham and his descendants, as they became part of the land of Canaan, would find themselves worshiping the same Canaanite gods and practicing the same magic every so often. El and Eloah were, at times, both Canaanite gods and a concept of the one, true God above all others to the Israelites. God would bring them back to the narrow path, they would wander back to the ways of the Oak of Moreh and magic, and God would bring them back to the narrow path yet again. It was a never-ending struggle.

Shortly after Abraham left Shechem, he set up another altar to God, this time at the Oaks of Mamre, north of Hebron, which was yet another sacred ancient place. Abraham was squarely placing God in the center of the places of magic. No question about it.

Three men—most likely angels, or sons of God—representing the Lord, appeared to Abraham at the Oaks of Mamre. They granted his aging wife a son during that meeting. It was just one of many miracles for Abraham and his followers.

Jon couldn't help but wonder: three wise men, three angels, appearing at an ancient place of magic. Was there some connection he was missing? *Are there good angels and bad angels, who look similar in appearance but are quite different in intention and design? But how do you separate the two? How do you tell the two apart?*

Later on in the Book of Genesis, Jacob denounced magic by placing a number of "foreign gods" in his household—magical items—beneath the Oak of Moreh near Shechem. Even during Jacob's time, the allure of magic was strong. The struggle whether to serve God or call upon the gods of magic was still full-blown.

The principal foreign god worshiped at Shechem was a god called "Ba'al." Worship of Ba'al was rampant throughout Canaan, and it was centralized at Shechem and the Oak of Moreh. Jon found this fascinating. But what he found even more fascinating was that, when Joshua established a confederacy of the twelve tribes of Israel and a covenant with the Lord, he did so at Shechem.

"Put away the foreign gods which are among you, and incline your heart to the Lord, the God of Israel," Joshua told the confederacy gathered at Shechem shortly before his death. Joshua then made a covenant with the people at Shechem, as well as statutes and ordinances. Joshua clearly, and firmly, brought a new law to a new land.

So, Jon thought, *there had been two big changes in the law on Earth. First, the shift from belief that magic could control the world around you to belief in the one, true God who could help His people. And second, the change brought by Jesus—a path to a personal and infinite relationship with God.*

What had begun with an altar at Shechem by Abraham was later established as a vast confederacy of ancient Israel by Joshua. God had brought His nation along, set squarely against Ba'al and the foreign gods of magic.

What no one chronicled—not the Bible, not any of the ancient wisdom texts—was the fate of the loyalists, and teachers, of magic. Had they found a new land?

It was an interesting tale. It gave Jon quite a bit of insight into the lengths God had been forced to go to in order to combat magic and bring his people along the narrow path.

Unfortunately, it didn't seem to help Jon much in the present day. For, eventually, the magic at Shechem and the Oak of Moreh had faded from view. God had won at Shechem. Magic was very difficult to find these days.

Yet the Oak of Moreh held something. There was something there that Jon was not seeing, some thread to his recent adventure in the magicians' world that he wasn't quite latching onto. Oh, well. It would come in time. Jon was sure of that. He would find the link.

He would start by searching the literature for what had ever become of Ba'al, the god the Canaanites had preferred to worship at Shechem, as well as the *bene elohim*. And he would ask Laura and Samson about the Oak of Moreh. Perhaps they could find the link he'd been unable to discover.

9

***

A KNOCK
AT THE DOOR

S amson couldn't believe he was voluntarily going back to the room where that
silly fantasy game had first transported him to the land. But there seemed little
choice. He wanted to find Eric, and there appeared to be no other avenue.

Not that *this* particular avenue was likely to bear any fruit. In fact, Samson
doubted the visit would be helpful at all. More than likely, Eric had vanished to the
bowels of the Earth, as Jon suggested, never to be heard from again.

Who exactly is Eric? Samson thought as he and Thomas strolled through the
campus grounds on their way to the old, dilapidated house where the game room
was located. Eric seemed responsible for bringing them together in order to re-open a
portal to another world that had long been closed. So what did that make Eric, if
that was his role?

A sudden, not very pleasant, idea occurred to Samson. *You know, this portal
business goes both ways,* he thought grimly. Sure, Eric got them there. He brought
Jon, Laura, and Samson to the room, lured them into the game, and somehow
helped them step into that other world. *But does that mean Eric, and others, can enter
the land? Was that their goal all along?*

"Perhaps I'm a fool," Samson muttered under his breath.

"What was that?" Thomas peered up at the towering giant beside him.

"Oh, nothing," Samson growled. "Just thinking."

"Oh," Thomas mumbled, returning to the significant task of keeping up with
Samson, taking two steps for each of Samson's as they lumbered along.

They walked for a while longer without saying anything. Thomas had taken
them through the back of the campus, behind the science labs and the other outlying
buildings.

Samson had to admit he wasn't overly familiar with this part of the campus or
with *any* part other than the well-worn path between his dorm room and the school's
athletic facilities.

He'd never really thought about it much before, but he wasn't exactly a world traveler. He liked what he liked, and he tried to perform his tasks at hand with as much strength and energy as he could muster. And that didn't seem to include going from place to place to see the sights.

In fact, his sojourn in the land had been the most extensive trip of any kind he'd ever taken. He hadn't thought of it that way before, but it was true nevertheless.

Samson had never really had much of an imagination. There didn't seem to be any place in his own world for that. Imagination didn't produce results. Hard work produced results. Not much else did.

But perhaps he'd been wrong about that. Perhaps he'd been wrong about a lot of things. For instance, what good would his towering strength do for him, now that it appeared he'd been removed from the wrestling team, his lifelong dream suddenly and completely torn from his grasp?

What dream could he chase now? What could he follow? Who, or what, would his strength serve, now that his personal quest seemed to have ended? Was there something beyond his own vainglorious quest?

Samson wondered if Jon and Laura were having these kinds of self-doubts. Probably not. Laura, especially, appeared self-confident beyond reason. And Jon seemed rather caught up in himself as well. Samson felt sure neither was pressed by paralyzing, self-absorbed introspection. Samson almost envied the two. They seemed so sure of their place in the world, so sure of where they were going, where they wanted to be. Never mind that Samson didn't think much of their own particular holy grails. They had them. That seemed to be sufficient.

So what was Samson's holy grail, now that the one he'd pursued his entire life had been wrenched from his sight? Would there be a new one? Was such a thing even possible?

In the back of his mind, a flicker of an idea was growing, like the spark that catches the woodpile and fans to a roaring, blazing fire, fitfully pushing back the shadows.

Samson had this funny notion that he was learning how to grow beyond himself, how to serve others besides himself. He had no idea, yet, how to accomplish this. But it seemed like a worthy goal. Any goal now was better than none at all.

***

As if by a silent signal, all were gathered in the room again. Samson smiled to himself. Perhaps they never left this room. Perhaps they remained here on vigilant guard, 24 hours a day, waiting for a dwarf to show his face, or an elf to cross his bow.

Eight were sitting around the table somberly as Samson and Thomas arrived. Samson gazed at the motley group—so intense, so focused on the task at hand. They almost made Thomas seem normal by comparison. But he also knew that it wasn't his place to judge these misbegotten creatures. He was certain they had a place in all of this. What the role might be, Samson certainly couldn't say.

"Thomas, at last," one of them said, slightly exasperated.

"We thought the two of you would never arrive," added another.

"Yeah, when we got your summons, we came with all haste," a third muttered.

"We came as fast as we could," said Thomas, taking his place at the table. Samson took a seat beside him, saying nothing.

"So what now?" the first squeaked.

All eyes turned to Samson. They were eyes of blazing intensity. In Samson, these poor souls clearly saw a savior. Or, at least, they saw someone who could perhaps unlock a mystery that had consumed their lives.

For these nine, including Thomas, were devoted to the game. They had long ago pledged their fealty to the land. And now they waited to see if Samson could do the impossible—show them how to enter it and actually begin to master what had only previously existed in their imagination.

Samson took a deep breath. "Can any of you tell me where Eric has gone?"

Every head around the table wagged from side to side. "We haven't seen him since you came," one said sadly, speaking for the group.

"As I told you," Thomas murmured.

"And none of you have a clue where he might have gone?" Samson asked.

"No, we don't," Thomas said, after he'd appraised the group.

Samson thought for a moment. He'd expected this, but it was still disappointing. These kids seemed to be of so little help. "Tell me," he prompted, "how did all of you come to meet Eric? Where did you find him?"

"We didn't find him," Thomas answered with a curious look, as if Samson's question was somehow off-kilter. "He found us."

"What do you mean?" Samson did his best not to grow impatient.

"Eric found each of us and brought us here," Thomas replied, again speaking for the group.

"Each of you?" Samson asked, surprised. Had Eric truly sought each of them out and brought them here, individually, so they could form a group in search of answers to the land's problems?

"He met me in my chemistry lab," one offered.

"I bumped into him in the cafeteria," said a second.

"He was sitting next to me at one of the carrels in the library," a third said. "He came over to borrow a book, and we started to talk."

"He introduced himself to all of you like that?" Samson asked. "He sought each of you out individually?" They all nodded. "So, then, none of you know where he came from, where he might be found, now that he's vanished?"

"Yes, that's true." Thomas looked grim.

A deafening silence descended on the room. Clearly, the group was stymied, as they'd never been before. None of them knew where to turn to next for clues or answers. They had reached an impenetrable pass.

They all heard the knock, three times, at the same time. It was a resounding "boom, boom, boom!" It came from the second door in the room, the one that was always locked.

Samson knew they'd entered the land through another way. Not through that door. It had not been so simple with Eric. But Samson also knew what was on the other side of it, now.

His heart leaped. Unmistakable joy surged through him. He knew what that knock meant. But it was not for him. He'd been there once. He would not return. At least, not yet.

"So who's going to answer the door?" Samson said loudly with a funny half-smile.

Everyone glanced at everyone else. Finally, as Samson knew he would, Thomas rose from his chair. "I will."

As if walking to the gallows, Thomas crossed the room on wobbly legs. His hand was shaking badly as it reached for the doorknob. One turn and his life would be forever altered.

But Thomas was prepared. He'd waited his entire life for this moment. Now was not the time for a faint heart. It was the time for courage to seize the day.

10

***

THE BOARD OF INQUIRY

For the first time in her life, Laura was facing an important test that she simply could not study for. There were no books to pore over, no lecture notes to review endlessly, nothing to review, other than her entire academic life.

Laura didn't know what to expect at the Board of Inquiry. Would they bring out witnesses? Who would make charges against her? Would she be given an opportunity to cross-examine these witnesses, to shoot holes in their testimony?

She very much doubted that there would be much chance to do anything about the inquiry. Surely "they" would find a way to make sure she could do nothing to fight back.

But she was prepared, just in case. If there was even the tiniest sliver of a chance, she would move quickly. She would do her best to exploit whatever opening they offered her.

Laura arrived at the hearing half an hour early, so she could watch the board as it assembled. The hearing was in one of the psychology conference rooms, which was a couple of buildings away from Duke's hospital.

The gallery seats were empty when she entered. She hadn't expected an audience for this. She wasn't disappointed. This was between Laura and others, most of whom she had never met face to face.

James Adams was the first to arrive. He was accompanied by a very attractive woman Laura estimated to be in her early forties. The woman was immaculately dressed in business attire. Her face looked as if it had been sculpted from one of those cosmetic commercials Laura detested so much.

The two never acknowledged Laura's presence in the room. They took their seats at the table near the front of the room and continued their conversation as if she weren't even there. At one point, the woman glanced over briefly in Laura's direction, but it was her only attempt to make any contact.

Fine, Laura thought. *I won't be able to sway these people with the force of my personality anyway. Nothing but cold, hard facts will work here. If there are any facts to be found.*

Laura sat rock-still in her chair for the rest of the half hour as the remaining three board members arrived. Laura didn't recognize two of them—an older gentleman in a brown tweed jacket and a demure woman who was probably in her late twenties.

She faintly recognized the last board member. If she wasn't mistaken, he was a rather famous religion professor who'd written some arcane text on the lost books of the Bible, or something like that. She couldn't quite remember.

As James Adams cleared his throat to start the inquiry, Laura noticed out of the corner of one eye as a short, ugly, bearded man tried to slip unobtrusively into the room.

The man looked to be about four feet tall, with some rather twisted limbs. He took a seat at the back. He was wearing a dirty trench coat, which he didn't take off. He kept the hat he wore pulled down over his brow. He seemed to know someone in the room, though, because Laura distinctly saw him nod to someone on the panel.

Even as she walked toward the front of the room to begin the session, Laura couldn't help but feel sorry for the misbegotten creature who had slipped into the room to watch the festivities. *If only some doctor had paid attention early on in that poor man's life,* Laura thought, *they might have been able to help him.*

Of course, it was only recently that the pharmaceutical industry had developed the human growth hormone to help cure the problem the man suffered from. Still, there were other things that could have been done to help him.

"If we can begin?" James Adams announced loudly.

The other four board members came to attention and turned to look at Adams. The very attractive woman Adams came in with was staring at him as if he were the Messiah. *There's one vote I won't get,* Laura realized.

"You've all had a chance to read the background on this case?" Adams asked them. The four nodded somberly. "And did any of you have any questions?"

The professor in the brown jacket turned to look at Laura, who had taken a seat in front of the board's table. Laura straightened in her seat.

"Ms. Brisbane, my name is Curtis Wilkes," he said softly. "I am a professor of Chemistry. I've heard quite a lot about you." Laura nodded curtly, and Wilkes continued. "I had just one question. How did you prepare for your organic chemistry final last year?"

Laura almost smiled. The organic final had been one of her crowning achievements at Duke. One kid had literally snapped during the test. The pressure had been too intense. He'd fled the room, smashing his very expensive calculator on the way out.

"There was no magic to it," Laura said, quickly regretting her poor choice of words. "I read all of the texts that were on the curriculum at the beginning of the course…"

"At the *beginning* of the course?" Wilkes asked, incredulous.

"Yes, sir," Laura said briskly. "I always do that with extremely difficult and complex courses, such as that one. I read the texts before classes begin. That way my lecture notes are very organized and meaningful."

"That's almost like cheating." Wilkes smiled. "You know the material beforehand. You know what to look for."

"That's the whole point," Laura said coldly.

"The reason I asked that question, Ms. Brisbane, is that your organic professor indicated to us that you seemed unusually well prepared for his course. It was as if you knew what he would ask before he asked it. You always seemed to know the answers beforehand."

"I *did* know the answers beforehand," Laura concurred. "Organic chemistry is very well organized and structural. It rarely deviates from the texts."

"I want to be clear on this point," Wilkes said evenly. "The reason you seemed so well prepared, the reason you knew what to look for in that class, is that you read the texts before classes even began…"

"I just said that." Laura worked to control her temper. "Any fool can do it. The curriculum and the required reading never changes."

Wilkes nodded. "I know. I helped set it."

Laura shrugged. "It's a good curriculum. Easy to follow."

"Thank you," Wilkes said modestly.

"Can we please move on?" Adams urged brusquely.

Wilkes swiveled to face Adams. Something passed between the two of them, something remarkably like hatred. There was clearly no love lost between these two.

Laura wondered vaguely why Adams had allowed someone who so clearly disagreed with him to serve on the board. Perhaps he had no choice. Or perhaps he only wanted to stack the deck by majority. After all, he only needed two other votes—not four—to send her on her way.

"I brought this up," Wilkes pronounced, "because her organic final and the testimony from her professor in that course is central to this case. It is one of the foundations of the argument against her."

"I wouldn't say it's central," Adams said. "It's one element, certainly."

"Oh, I'd say it was central," Wilkes disagreed. "You used that course, and what the professor said about Ms. Brisbane seeming to know all the answers beforehand, as the central thesis of your somewhat circumstantial case against her."

"Circumstantial?" Adams glowered.

"Yes, circumstantial," Wilkes said firmly. "Hearsay testimony, a little conjecture, a few ill-placed words against Ms. Brisbane, and you've built a case for pre-knowledge. But, as Ms. Brisbane just explained, she knew the answers beforehand because she'd already read the texts. An admirable quality, I feel, and highly unusual."

"*Very* unusual," Adams spouted. "In all my years at this institution, I've never heard of a student who was so motivated that she read the texts before classes even began."

"I do that with a lot of my courses," Laura interjected. "That's the way I like to study. It gives me a chance to listen more closely in class. I can spend more time listening and less time taking notes."

"If you say so," Adams said in a pained voice.

Wilkes waded back in. "So, you see, Ms. Brisbane's study habits would explain a good deal of the rest of the testimony so neatly arrayed against her. If she's reading the texts before classes begin, she would clearly have plenty of foreknowledge, as the testimony suggests."

"We simply have Ms. Brisbane's word that she studies like that." Adams' voice was chilly. "We don't have any actual proof."

Wilkes bristled. "I thought it was our task to prove her guilty, not for this young girl to prove herself innocent. I thought this was a board of inquiry, not a rubber-stamp tribunal designed to run people out of school."

"Relax, Curtis," Adams soothed. "I'm only noting that we have no corroborating evidence to back up Ms. Brisbane's story."

"I don't think she needs such evidence," Wilkes insisted. "As far as I'm concerned, the fact that she studies beforehand sufficiently explains the thesis of this inquiry. It is by far the most logical explanation. It's the only one, in fact."

Adams looked at the other members. "Do the rest of you have any questions for Ms. Brisbane?" The two women glanced over at Laura and then shook their heads. The fifth, the religion professor, glanced up from some notes he'd been looking at and stared at Laura, hard. A deep, bone-wrenching chill careened through her.

"No, it's self-evident," the religion professor said. "It's clear to me who Ms. Brisbane is, and what she's done."

Laura and the religion professor locked eyes. His stare was so completely devoid of any warmth or good will that it took all of Laura's courage and fortitude just to keep from averting her gaze. Who was this man?

"Well, then," Adams said cheerfully, "that would wrap it up, then. You are dismissed, Ms. Brisbane. You will be notified of the outcome of this Board of Inquiry."

"That's it?" Laura asked, frustrated. "I won't be given a chance to respond to the allegations?"

"Oh, you may respond," Adams said. "By all means. What would you like to say on your own behalf?"

"But…but…I don't know the charges," Laura stammered, confused by this turn of events. "How can I respond?"

Adams glowered at Laura. "I laid them all out for you, in excruciating detail, at our last meeting, Ms. Brisbane. You've had ample opportunity to prepare for this inquiry. Now, if you'd like to respond to those charges, please do. We all have other, pressing business."

Laura's heart sank. There was no hope. "You never told me a thing at that meeting," she said quietly. "I *don't* know what the charges are."

"Are you calling me a liar?" Adams drew himself up brusquely.

"No, I'm saying I don't know what the charges are," Laura stated glumly. "It appears that you've interviewed some of my peers and some of my professors and that you found that, in some of my classes, I seem to know quite a lot going in."

"I explained all that to you at our last meeting." Adams frowned.

"No, you didn't," Laura said firmly. "But I can guess from what's happened here that this is what you've found. And I think I've just explained to Professor Wilkes why it would seem that way to the other students."

"Ms. Brisbane, with all due respect, *no one* studies beforehand. It just isn't normal. It isn't part of human nature."

"It's part of *my* human nature," Laura insisted.

"Very well." Adams sighed. "Your explanation is duly noted. Is there anything else?"

"No." Laura stared straight ahead, her eyes not flinching or moving. They could condemn her. But they could not force her to cower or tremble. They would not extract that from her.

"In that case, this inquiry is now closed. Ms. Brisbane, you will be informed of our decision in the next day or two."

Laura rose from her seat. The religion professor looked up from his notes again. He smiled at Laura. It was a terrible thing, that smile, like a scimitar of vengeance slashing its way to the core of Laura's being.

Laura had the strangest sensation of helplessness. The magicians had won, somehow, without ever making an appearance, it seemed. *This is so very strange. How can I ever fight what I can't see?* There seemed to be no hope whatsoever.

11

* * *

THE STORY OF BA'AL

Jon had passed by the desk so many times in his years at Duke's Divinity School library that he now gave it almost no thought. The desk was buried at the very bottom level of the stacks in the library, well out of the way of the library's normal traffic.

The only books down at that lowest level were old, dusty tomes that no one ever used as source material anymore, the kind of books that you needed to glance at only once and then footnote.

There was one desk on that level, though, that always had books piled high on it, disorganized and sticking out in all different locations. Jon had never really paid much attention to it. The desk had always been there. He didn't know who used it.

Tonight, Jon's mission carried him past that desk. Jon was searching the literature for clues to Ba'al, the mysterious god that the Canaanites and the other worshipers of magic had paid obeisance to in ancient times.

Jon wasn't quite sure what he was looking for—some key to unlock the mystery of what had happened to the magicians once they'd been defeated on Earth, some thread that would help him follow the trail that had now gone stone cold.

The literature on Ba'al—and other gods worshiped by the Mesopotamians, Egyptians, Canaanites, and other ancient peoples—were squirreled away on that lower level of the library. Jon couldn't help but smile at the symbolism of that.

In a funny way, it reminded Jon a little of his visit to Hades in the land. A dark passage through a dismal landscape. That's what the lower-level stacks were like. There were no windows to illuminate the place, only a few dim light bulbs placed strategically along the corridors.

Jon wandered up and down those aisles that evening, pulling reference books down and dropping them in the cart he'd brought along. Once he'd found the books he wanted, he'd find an empty carrel and study for a while, trying to connect all of the disparate dots that seemed scattered in every direction.

Jon was beginning to despair that he'd ever find any meaningful connections. There were so many threads, so many paths to follow, so many different ideas to explore. There wasn't enough time to do it all. He'd either have to get lucky, or get some timely help.

Once Jon had gathered the books he'd need for the evening, he wandered around the perimeter of the stacks, looking for an empty carrel. There weren't many carrels to begin with on this level, and many of the ones here were permanently assigned to someone.

He finally spotted the only available desk, roughly 20 feet away from the desk that always had the strange tomes piled high on it. Jon settled in and started to plow through the literature.

When the Israelites first came to the Promised Land, the ancient lands of Palestine, all the local residents seemed to worship this Ba'al character. It was pretty straightforward, it appeared to Jon. Ba'al was the local god of fertility—along with Asherah, the local mother goddess of fertility—and it was this local god who was supposed to keep the families growing in the region.

Over and over again, the Israelites would pull down one of Ba'al's altars, or one of Asherah's altars, and erect an altar to the one, true God in its place. This story was repeated over and over throughout the Old Testament, over a span of centuries.

One of the low points of that struggle between the Israelites and the worshipers of Ba'al came when one of the kings of Israel erected an altar to Ba'al at the urging of his wife, Jezebel. That set off quite a religious crisis in the land, a crisis that was not easily resolved.

In fact, it took quite a show of power from God to quell the dispute. In one of the most famous contests of the Old Testament, Elijah the prophet squared off against the followers of Ba'al and challenged them to a duel of sorts.

Elijah faced hundreds of the prophets of Ba'al and Asherah atop Mount Carmel. Then Elijah challenged the prophets of Ba'al and Asherah to urge their gods to set fire to their altar. When Ba'al failed to show up, God set fire to the altar Elijah built, thus proving who was supreme.

Jon couldn't help but wonder about this story. Clearly, there was no question who God was, and that he was supreme. But what of Ba'al and Asherah? Were there, in fact, such gods? Did they exist? And, if so, why had they not shown up to perform such simple magic? And what of the elusive sons of God, the *bene elohim*?

Jon was beginning to find the faint glimmering of an answer in that story about Elijah and the prophets of Ba'al. It seemed that the gods of magic were as mysterious on the Earth as they had been in the land. When called upon, they failed to show up. Yet their evil hand appeared to be in quite a few places nevertheless.

Shortly thereafter, Israel destroyed the house of Ba'al, and the mysterious god of fertility disappeared from the face of the land. But Jon couldn't help but wonder where Ba'al, and the other "gods" like him, had gone those thousands of years ago.

"Where *did* Ba'al, Asherah, and the *bene elohim* go to, after their defeat?" Jon mumbled out loud, leaning back in the hard chair at the carrel.

"Banished," said someone from behind him.

Jon almost jumped out of his seat. He pivoted and was startled to see Professor Harold Neuman standing behind him, a pile of books stacked high in both arms. Jon hadn't seen Professor Neuman since he'd played a part in ending Jon's graduate career.

"Wha...what are *you* doing here?" Jon asked in a tremulous voice.

It was difficult to see Neuman's face even in the glare of sunlight. Down here in the depths, it was almost impossible. "Studying, as I usually do late in the evening."

Jon glanced at his watch. It was nearly midnight. Duke's Divinity School library generally stayed open all night for those brave souls who were willing to study in the murky hours before dawn.

"Oh," Jon managed to mumble. "I see."

Neuman started to move away. "The answer to your question, by the way, is that they were banished from the promised land, and perhaps the face of the Earth, shortly after Elijah's victory at Mount Carmel. The Israelites sent them packing. Ba'al and the other gods of magic had to go somewhere else."

Neuman walked away, then, and dropped his stack of books at the carrel near Jon's. *So that cluttered desk all these years has belonged to the silent, mysterious Professor Neuman. What could he possibly be looking for in all those strange, dusty tomes?*

Jon sat at his carrel, slightly stunned by this unexpected encounter. He stared straight ahead, occasionally stealing glances at Neuman, who was buried in one of the books he'd brought with him.

Jon was still convinced that Neuman had been one of the two deciding votes against him when he was forced out of the Divinity School. For, surely, Jon's advisor—the magnificent New Testament scholar Charles Finch—had cast the lone vote in Jon's favor.

So if Neuman had voted against him, why was Jon suddenly so drawn to the dark, mysterious professor who taught one of the strangest religion courses in the land? Why did Jon have this almost overwhelming feeling that Neuman had answers to some of Jon's many questions?

Finally, his own curiosity practically immobilizing him, Jon worked up enough courage to get out of his chair and walk haltingly over to Neuman's carrel.

"What do you mean, banished?" Jon asked when he was still a few feet away.

"I mean, they were sent away, to some unknown destination," Neuman said without even looking up from whatever book he was studying intently.

"Where?" Jon asked, though he had this vague feeling that he was one of the few people on Earth who knew the answer to that question. But then there had been

Michael's war, and perhaps they'd been forced back to earth. After all, Jesus had once said he'd seen Satan cast down to earth like the lightning from the sky.

Neuman shrugged. "Who knows? Somewhere else, that's all I know. The one, true God won in Palestine, and the little gods had to go elsewhere."

Jon narrowed his eyes. "How do you know that?"

Neuman finally looked away from his book and pivoted to face Jon. "I know, because I study such things." He gazed intently at Jon now. "I have for years. I've chronicled the rise and fall of many such things. There have been others who have come and gone, just like Ba'al. History is replete with such encounters."

"It is?" Jon asked, eyes wide. He couldn't help himself. This professor, who had almost certainly cast the deciding vote that had ended Jon's career, frightened him a little.

"Yes," Neuman almost whispered. "Ba'al was just one of the more well-known gods of that age. There were others less known, who likewise sparred with God and lost. The battle has been engaged since the dawn of time."

Jon didn't move a muscle. "What battle?"

"Why, the battle between the sons of God, the *bene elohim*, and the daughters of men."

"Sons of God? You mean, like Jesus?"

"No, he always referred to himself as a son of man. The sons of God are angels. Beings of light. Pure energy. Beyond the reach of time. Able to change shape as they see fit."

Jon shook his head. "I'm confused."

"As are many people these days. But not the sons of God. They've never been confused. You've heard of the Nephilim?"

"Vaguely."

"One passage in Genesis," Neuman said curtly. "One of many ways the sons of God tried to win their war, corrupt mankind. They slept with daughters of men. It's where the myth of El and Eloah first began. Superhuman beings—the Nephilim— were the result. But I suppose that's what you might expect when humankind is seduced or corrupted by their ilk. Almost anything, any consequence, is possible."

"So how do you recognize one of these sons of God, or anything else like the Nephilim, for that matter?" Jon asked in a hushed tone. "How can you tell?"

"You can't. It's the nature of the beast. That's the problem, of course, these days—figuring out who's who. It isn't as easy as it once was."

"You know, this seems crazy," Jon managed to say, his voice raspy from fear.

"I suppose. It isn't something you think about every day. But I would think by now that you, of all people, would have grasped some of the elements of the battle."

"Why me?"

"Because you have explored some of the framework of that battle already in your thesis, of course," Neuman said, somewhat startled at Jon's naïve question.

"I have?"

"Certainly. You've established that magic and religion are constantly at odds on the Earth, with religion having won the day in Old Testament times. And with the coming of the founder of Christianity—the establishment of a religion that preached a clear path to God without the need for learned intermediaries—the landscape has now changed even more dramatically."

"I see," Jon said, though he did not.

Neuman leaned forward in his seat. "The pendulum has all but swung back in the other direction, however," he said in a quiet, conspiratorial tone.

"It has?"

"Yes, the gods of magic seem to have returned with a vengeance, invited here by those who have spurned and rejected the offers of religion. For hundreds of years, magic was consigned to the dark corners of the world, its practitioners forced to work elsewhere. But not now. The war has begun again. The ancient gods of magic seem to have returned."

"But how do you know all this?"

"Why, it's obvious. The unmistakable signs are all around. Magic is beginning to co-mingle with religion again, as it did thousands of years ago. That, alone, is a sure sign that the war has resumed and that we are headed into rough waters."

Jon couldn't help but wonder at the simplicity of magic in the land, where it had seemed so harmless. "But is magic so wrong?"

"No, probably not of its own. And that's where it becomes hard. Magic, of its own accord, is not evil. It is those who employ magic—and use it to control absolutely the natural world for their own purposes and design—who are evil. There is the distinction."

"I seriously doubt many would understand that distinction." Jon frowned.

"You're right. Many would not. But you do. Just as the ancient Israelites learned, in their day, you must serve others—your community—first and foremost, above all else. If you do so, there is no need for magic. Magic becomes obsolete, unnecessary."

Jon thought again about the land, the return of the races, the incessant fear of the power of magic there. *Perhaps Neuman is right. Perhaps it is better to look beyond yourself than to try to manipulate and control your own destiny.*

Jon turned back to Neuman. "Tell me," Jon said, surprised he had somehow found the courage to ask the question he was about to ask. "Why did you vote to condemn me? Can you tell me that?"

Neuman gazed at Jon with somber eyes. "What compels you to believe that I was one of the two votes cast against you?"

Jon was startled. "Why, it's obvious, I guess. There was only one vote for me, and that must surely have been Finch's. He's my advisor and I just assumed, then…"

"Perhaps you should not have assumed, then," Neuman said gravely. "Especially when it comes to Finch, I would not assume anything. Your brilliant, luminous advisor is, perhaps, not what he seems."

Jon caught his breath, not sure of what he was hearing. "Your vote?"

"My vote was an easy one," Neuman said almost casually. "Futile, but easy."

"Futile?"

"Yes, of course." Neuman shrugged. "Finch had already convinced Whitley of your guilt before I even entered the room. My vote in your favor was useless. I just felt it was the right thing to do. But you never stood a chance. Your fate was sealed before the inquiry."

12

***

ARIEL

Thomas struggled mightily with the door. It was as if his hands and arms had lost all their strength. Thomas could not seem to open it. At last, though, he managed to turn the knob and pull on the door. It swung open, inward, quite easily. Thomas stepped backwards, away from the door. It was obvious he was quite frightened.

Samson was expecting Michael. So he was mildly shocked when an absolutely beautiful woman with long, lustrous black hair walked through instead. The woman wore a white, flowing, embroidered robe. Either the robe, or the woman, shimmered slightly, as if the molecules in her body couldn't quite sit still for more than a moment or two.

"Be not afraid," the woman said in a clear, strange voice. She held Thomas firmly in her gaze and then scanned the rest of those in the room who sat transfixed, staring back at the wonder that had entered the room. "Be not afraid," the woman said again, "for the Creator has heard you. I have come to help lead you to the land you have dreamed of so often."

"Who…who are you?" Thomas found the courage to ask.

Samson almost cheered. *Good for you, Thomas. Good for you. You are facing it with courage.*

"You can call me Ariel," the woman said with a bright smile.

"But who are you?" persisted Thomas.

"I have been called many things." Ariel bowed slightly. "But perhaps you should think of me as the altar, or light, of God."

"I don't understand," Thomas said stubbornly.

Ariel gazed intently at Thomas. "I did not really expect you, of all people, to accept so readily."

"But what does that mean, the altar of God? The light of God?"

Ariel shimmered brightly for an instant. Samson caught his breath. The room filled with an intense, white light. There could be no shadows in the corners of the room when that Light was present. Darkness fled quickly in its presence.

"Oh," Thomas mumbled. "I see."

"But do not mistake me for the One whom I serve," Ariel said firmly. "I am merely a vessel, a temple, a window through which you may catch a glimpse."

Thomas, his chin trembling terribly, held his gaze. He did not look away from Ariel, as much as he wanted to. "Will…will we…?" he asked finally.

"When it is time," Ariel said mysteriously.

"But why are you here, then?"

Ariel turned back toward the door. "I think you know why. Are you all ready?"

Thomas looked over his shoulder at the others, who had remained silent as stones throughout the exchange. All eight nodded, almost in unison.

"Yes, we are ready," Thomas said loudly, his voice quavering.

"Then let us be on our way." Ariel turned then and looked at Samson. "And are you coming with us?"

Samson shook his head. "I've been there before," he said with an easy, knowing smile. "I'm not sure I'm needed on this quest."

"You are welcome to join us," Ariel told Samson.

"Thank you," Samson said with a slight nod. "But I think I'm needed here."

"Very well."

"I do have a question, though."

"Ask." Ariel inclined her head.

"I feel like I can go no further in this world, and I need help."

"Your question has been heard, and an answer is on its way."

"On its way?"

Ariel smiled. "An old friend has asked to visit this world. Between the two of you, the path should emerge from the shadows."

Samson wanted to press further, but this seemed sufficient. He would wait for this friend. He had a sneaking suspicion he knew already who it was.

Ariel, seeing Samson was satisfied with the answer, turned back to the eight adventurers. "Are we ready, then?"

The others gathered around the table rose from their chairs and shuffled toward the door. They lined up behind Thomas.

"Farewell," Thomas said to Samson as Ariel flowed back through the door.

"Until we meet again," Samson answered.

The room grew silent after they'd left. Samson didn't move a muscle. He remained in his seat, wondering vaguely what he ought to do next.

Another figure appeared in the doorway. Samson bolted from his chair and, in three long steps, was by his side. "My old friend." Samson quickly clasped his hand.

"You still don't know your own strength." Regis returned the handshake with as much strength as he could muster, which was considerable for an elf.

382

"I suspected it might be you." Samson's voice cracked slightly from the emotion that was close to overwhelming him.

"I *had* to come here," Regis said grimly.

"You had to? Why?"

"To protect our land."

"Protect it? What do you mean?"

Regis looked at his friend somberly. "The portal, this one, is sufficiently guarded by the likes of Ariel. But the roots from Annwyn's Silver Tree are opening portals to other worlds. Tara, Kathryn, and the others have begun to struggle with it, as has the Great Council. It is only a matter of time, I am afraid, until the magicians who called you are able to return to our land. It seems that this was their intent all along. They needed you—the three of you—for their own purposes. There may yet be some great contest or decision surrounding you, as yet undecided. We just don't know."

"So what can we do?" Samson asked.

"We need to find the magicians, here in your world. Before it is too late. And I have come to help you in that quest."

"How?"

"I believe," Regis explained, "that there are others of the races who have been trapped in your own world for a very long time. I have come to help you find them, so we may settle all accounts and end the magicians' ability to wreak havoc in our own world—or any others."

"Can we do that? Is it possible?"

"It is possible. It *must* be," Regis said firmly. "We have no other choice."

13

***

THE MISBEGOTTEN CREATURE

After the Board of Inquiry, Laura had the strongest desire to go back to her dorm room, curl up on her bed, and sleep for ages. The event had really sapped her strength. She felt helpless before the tribunal, unable to do anything to determine her own future.

Laura was now resigned to her fate. It was obvious that she would be forced out of school. The board was sure to vote that way. There was very little she could do about it.

For the first time in her life, Laura had no grand master plan. If she was forced to leave school, she wasn't sure what she should do next. Or, for that matter, what she *could* do next. Hopefully, she could transfer to another school. But she would lose time, and credits, by doing so. It would take her longer to go through medical school, assuming she got there. There would be no advanced quest for her medical degree, as she'd hoped for at Duke.

As Laura trudged slowly back to her dormitory, her spirits were as low as they'd been in years. She didn't even bother to look up as she walked along. She almost walked into several kids who were rushing somewhere, but Laura didn't care. Nothing seemed to matter much.

The low, guttural voice startled Laura. She'd been so absorbed in her own misery, she hadn't even noticed anyone shadowing her as she walked along.

"I know what it's like, Laura," the voice said just a few feet behind her.

Laura stopped and whirled in her tracks. "What?" she asked, facing the person following her. It was the short, ugly bearded man from the inquiry, and the happenstance meeting very much startled Laura.

"I said, I know what it's like," the man repeated.

"*What* are you talking about?" Laura asked sharply, not sure whether she should ignore this creature, turn and flee, or shout for the police. In the end, she decided to hear him out. She had nothing better to do, regardless.

"I'm talking about your state of mind," the man said, his eyes boring into Laura's.

"Who *are* you?"

"Ramiel. It's an uncommon name."

"And what do you know about my state of mind?"

"I know how you must feel right now. A little lost, a little helpless, a little angry at the injustice of it all. I feel that way most of the time."

"Some of that." Laura shrugged. "But why would you care about my well-being? And why were you at my hearing?"

"Oh, we all care a great deal about your well-being, where you're going, what you know," the man said mysteriously. He needed to tell Laura enough to see how much she knew and which direction she was going—but *not* enough to give her too much information. It was tricky business. "A great deal. In fact, it's critical to us..."

"We? Us?" Laura asked, confused.

Ramiel looked down at his shoes. "Actually, there isn't really an organized *group* of us or anything. Nothing like that. It's just that some of us have gotten to know each other over the years, sort of wondered if maybe there wasn't something else..."

Laura put her hands on her hips, a sign of agitation, and squared off against this strange, little man. "Could you be *slightly* more specific, please?" she said in that clipped monotone she reserved for times such as these.

Ramiel shuffled back and forth. "Well, it's sort of like this," he started to explain. "Over the years, some of us—"

"Some of whom?"

"Some of us who never grew to a full height, like me, of course," Ramiel said glumly.

"Oh, I see."

"Yeah, well, *some* of us began to talk to each other, to speculate on how dwarfism originated in the world..."

"Dwarfism is genetic," Laura said with a frown. "It's associated with several inherited disorders such as mongolism, Turners syndrome, and achondroplasia. It can also be acquired from chronic kidney disease, cystic fibrosis, and from a pituitary gland malfunction that can now be corrected somewhat with human growth hormone..."

Laura stopped herself. She was doing it again, sounding like a walking textbook. She just couldn't help herself. She hated mushy, sentimental explanations when there were hard, cold, scientific facts available to explain something.

"Oh, we know all *that*." Ramiel grimaced. "We've all read everything there is to read on dwarfism. We know all the possible causes and the possible cures. But, over the years, some of us have, well, fooled around with this notion that maybe there was more to it, that maybe, once upon a time, there was an ancient race of dwarves and somehow a few of their genes got mixed up with humankind's and, well..."

Laura stopped him. "I understand. And do you *really* believe that?"

"No, not really," he admitted. "It's just something we've sort of fooled around with, like I said. Until recently, that is."

They were passing by Duke's famous gardens. "Should we?" she asked, gesturing toward them. "They're glorious this time of year." She liked the gardens. But she was getting exasperated with Ramiel, and it would be nice to have a distraction.

"I didn't know these were here," Ramiel said, seemingly awed by the multitude of colors in the Gardens, and the variety of flowers beginning to bloom everywhere.

"Don't you live on the campus, or nearby?" Laura asked.

"Nearby, but I've never been this way before."

"Come on! You live here, and you've never been by this place?"

"I, um, stay indoors a lot." Ramiel looked down at his feet. "I don't get out much."

"Well, you ought to!" Laura snapped. "You miss places like this if you don't."

"I'll try to do better in the future," Ramiel mumbled with a strange half-smile.

They followed one of the twisting paths that meandered through the Gardens until they'd come to a stone bench situated nicely between woods on one side and flowers on the other. It was doubtful anyone could hear them here.

Ramiel half perched on the bench. He glanced off to one side or the other every few moments, as if expecting some kind of an invisible attack.

"Would you relax?" Laura settled on the bench.

"Sure." Ramiel clearly did not let his guard down, however.

"So you were fooling around with this notion, until recently?"

"What notion?"

"You *said* you, and perhaps some others, had entertained this fancy that you were somehow descended from an ancient race of dwarves?"

"Oh, yeah, that notion," Ramiel said absently. "What we really wanted to know is what *you* thought of that, what you've learned..."

"What I've learned?"

"Yeah, they all say you're maybe the smartest kid on campus. That was why I went to the hearing."

"Maybe you can explain," she said, trying to keep the exasperation out of her voice. She was beginning to wonder, however, why she'd consented to hear this person out.

"It's simple. Let's suppose it's true, that there are some of us descended from the race of dwarves. It would mean that there had once been dwarves in this world. And that, perhaps, dwarves still exist in this world. *Real* dwarves, I mean. Has that ever occurred to you?" He knew he was right at the edge of what he could safely reveal in an effort to find out just how much Laura had learned.

"Yes, I would suppose that would be true."

"If it's true, what would you do about it? What do you intend to do about it?"

"Me?"

"You, or anyone else with that knowledge…"

"Where are the dwarves?"

"Yes, where are they?" asked Ramiel.

"How should I know?"

"You mean you don't know?"

"Well, no, of course not. Why should I?"

"But…but I thought." Ramiel looked down at his shoes again. It was an odd habit. "Some of us were talking, like I said. We get together at my house, or at other houses, and talk about all of the possibilities. We make hot cocoa and stone-wheat muffins and—"

"Would you get to the point?".

"Yes, um, like I said, we were talking, and someone said they'd heard about you, and that you were really smart, and that maybe you might have learned about the dwarves…"

Laura got the gist. "That's it? That's all you know?"

"Yes, should there be more? Don't you know more, about where to look?"

Laura couldn't mask her disappointment. This seemed pointless. "Yes, there should be more. That doesn't help me a whole lot. There must be more to it than that."

Ramiel looked down for a third time. "I'm sorry," he mumbled. "I guess I've failed. I always fail. I've never gotten anything right. I can't hold a steady job, and I can't even get my fantasies right."

Laura softened a little. After all, it wasn't this man's fault she couldn't quite figure things out. She shouldn't have to rely on him at all, anyway. "It's okay."

Ramiel scrunched up his face, as if he were in pain. But he, and the others, simply had to know how much Laura knew, or might guess. And they still hoped that she was, in fact, the one they'd sought for the final part of a very long, intricate search. "You know, some people say that the legends are real…"

"The legends are real? What does that mean? About the races here on earth? Those legends? Atlantis, Avalon, those?"

A brief, knowing look crossed Ramiel's face. "So you do know about those, the myths about sanctuaries and havens…" But Ramiel suddenly stopped talking, as if he'd said too much.

Laura caught her breath. "Sanctuaries and havens?"

"No, I'm confused," he mumbled. "I only meant to ask you about the dwarves, about what you know…"

But Laura's mind was already spinning at a fantastic rate. A thought—a dazzling, wondrous thought—had just occurred to her. What if the legends were true, but slightly off-kilter? What if thoughts and whispers and rumors over the centuries had created legends about those mythical places? Pieces of the elaborate puzzle were finally starting to fall into place.

But now there was the much tougher question. What next? How in the world could she ever hope to find what others had failed to find for centuries?

Laura was, in fact, thinking so furiously that she had stopped looking at Ramiel altogether. Had she glanced in his direction, she might have caught a glimpse of something quite different than the dark mask of bumbling, incoherent confusion that had marked him from the beginning.

"I have to go now," Laura said abruptly.

"Okay," Ramiel answered.

"Thanks for all your help," Laura said, already dismissing the little man, her mind racing ahead toward the distant goal.

"Certainly," Ramiel said easily. "Happy to help."

"By the way, how will I find you again? If I have questions?" Laura asked as she rose to leave.

"Oh, don't worry about *that*. I'm pretty good at watching how things work out."

Laura nodded, turned, and strode away briskly.

Ramiel watched her go, and then turned quickly to go the other way, not entirely pleased at his progress or the direction Laura was inclined to go in. Perhaps she wasn't what they had anticipated.

14

* * *

PROFESSOR NEUMAN

"**Y**ou're serious, aren't you?" Jon asked, still too stunned at the news to actually believe it.

"Of course, I'm serious," Neuman said, eyes narrowed. "Why would I lie about something like that?"

"But what if you're one of *them*?" Jon half-whispered.

"Them?"

"Oh, never mind." Jon realized somewhat belatedly that his tales would sound inane, even to someone like Professor Neuman.

Jon was having a difficult time with all of this. His erstwhile advisor and mentor, Professor Charles Finch, had been someone Jon had admired and almost worshiped from the moment he entered Duke's Divinity School. Jon had placed complete trust and faith in Finch, as had hundreds of students and thousands of his followers around the country who'd heard his lectures or read his books. Finch's arguments about the true nature of Christianity and religion had affected millions of lives, directly or indirectly.

Finch was almost personally responsible, for instance, for the dramatic change in curriculum at most universities where a New Testament course was taught. Everyone now taught about the "historical Jesus," the search for Jesus' place in the long line of Great Teachers such as Buddha and Confucius. No one taught about Jesus as the son of man, the Messiah, anymore. Finch had, by and large, convinced them that it was just a myth.

Jon had seen this majestic power of thought and logic at work in Finch's class. He had believed it all. He had hung on every one of Finch's words, as had nearly all of the students in his course.

Oh, every so often, there would be some fool who would argue with him and try to puncture his logic. But Finch always paid special attention to such students and usually wore them down, or drove them to silence, by the end of the course. And, naturally, that student's grade suffered greatly as a result of his or her willingness to challenge Finch's thesis.

"So who *is* Professor Finch?" Jon whispered in the half-light of the basement of the library.

"Clearly not the person you thought, I'd say," Neuman answered.

The notion sent chills through Jon. He had believed one way for so long and now to suddenly change directions, to see that the world was not at all as he'd thought? It was hard. But he would manage. He would have to. There was no other choice.

"Yes, I can see that."

"I was just thinking," Neuman said, standing to leave, "it's late. Why don't we grab a cup of hot cocoa over at the coffee shop? I have a proposition for you."

"A proposition?"

"Yes, we can talk more there. It's just a thought, but I'd like to discuss something with you."

Jon shrugged. "Sure, I'm game. Let's go."

15

***

THE LOST RACES

"So where do we start?" Regis asked.

It was a natural question. Unfortunately, Samson had no answer, not even the beginning of one. "I don't know," he confessed.

Regis surveyed the room for the first time. His eyes grew wide in amazement. All around him were topographical maps, representations of the land from which he'd just come. He spotted his own forest land home off to the west.

"Fairhaven's in there somewhere?" he asked, pointing to the middle of the vast forest region outlined on the huge map.

"Yes, but it's not on there because these kids didn't know Fairhaven existed. They didn't know any of the places where the races lived even existed."

Regis was thoughtful for a moment. Something had clearly clicked in his mind. As a stranger, perhaps Regis could see what Samson could not.

"Where is a map of your own world?" Regis asked finally.

"A map of this world? Why?"

Regis looked a little startled by the question. "Why, I would imagine it would tell us where we need to go, where the races have gone in this world, of course."

Samson started laughing. It was a deep, guttural laugh. "That's funny, Regis."

"And why is that?" Regis scowled.

"Because there isn't a map in the world that will tell you where any of the races might or might not live here on Earth. As far as we're concerned, they don't exist. They're myths, fantasies, fairy tales. There are no such people, and they certainly don't have homes."

"Oh, I see," Regis said morosely. "So a map of this world wouldn't help?"

"Oh, maybe, maybe not. There *are* stories about the six races, shadowy stories about them that have popped up here and there."

"Can we find them, those stories, I mean?"

"Sure. We can go look them up in the library, though I'm not exactly a brilliant scholar."

"But you can find these stories there?"

"Yes, of course."

"Let's go, then," Regis urged. "I'm anxious to return to my own people. Fairhaven awaits."

***

As they walked along the sidewalk to Duke's library, Samson pressed his old friend for news of the magicians' world. Regis had, indeed, married Serena. They already had a child, a baby boy.

"How can you already have a child?" Samson asked, puzzled, as they continued to walk along.

"Why, it's been more than two years since you left us."

"Two years? You must be kidding me? I only returned a short time ago."

Regis frowned. "Time must be different between the two worlds. Quite different. Then I really must hurry."

Samson nodded. "If what you say is true, you have risked a lot by coming here."

"My young son will have grown to manhood if I tarry here too long. That seems clear enough."

"Then we must hurry. There is no time to lose."

The two of them spent nearly an hour wandering the stacks of the library, looking for reference material on elves, dwarves, centaurs, and the rest of the land's races. The pickings were slim. Not much had ever been written about the races, at least that Samson could find. He read everything he found aloud to Regis, who was growing rather despondent by the minute.

"This seems hopeless," he said at last, settling back in his chair in the reading section of the library.

They made quite a pair—Samson, who dwarfed others around him, and the diminutive Regis, whose dark-brown deerskin suit of clothes was clearly different from what most college kids wore. But Regis was unaware of the sideways glances he'd been receiving from people ever since they'd entered the library.

"I know." Samson exhaled in frustration.

Regis glanced down at one of the reference books they'd brought back from the stacks. "I mean, some of these have the elves all mixed up with the fairies! We have absolutely nothing in common whatsoever."

"Those are just stories," Samson explained.

"I understand. But they could at least get our size right. I know I'm not huge by any means, but I'm not a few inches high as some of these dolts seem to portray us. And what's this business about the dark elves, anyway? Who are these dark elves?"

"Just guesses and stories, I imagine."

"Well, *I've* never heard of anything such as a dark elf," Regis said dourly. "Elves can get angry, but that's hardly something to get all worked up about."

"Regis, I wouldn't worry about it. Not many on the Earth have ever seen an elf, so it's not fair, really, to expect an accurate description of what they're like."

Regis sighed deeply. "So, I ask again, where do we start? We have all of these rather vague stories about places where some of the races are reported to have lived."

"That's right. There's Avalon, the land of the fairies. And somewhere way off to the north is Jotunheim and Valhalla, the home of the giants."

Regis nodded. "There's a mention of Agarttha, an underground city of some sort that sounds like the dwarves."

"Don't forget Mount Pelion, in Greece, where the centaurs were supposed to have lived. Then there's Atlantis, which may be where we could find the people of the sea."

Regis closed his eyes. "But, with the exception of Mt. Pelion, you said none of those places are on a map anywhere? And you don't have a clue where the elves might be. No land seems to be firmly associated with their existence in this world."

"Except for Mt. Pelion, *none* of those places you mentioned exist here. They're all just stories and myths. They aren't supposed to be real."

"Then how will we ever find the lost races here? I have come in vain."

Regis looked so forlorn that Samson gave his friend an affectionate squeeze. "Don't worry, we'll find them. I promise. And we'll have you back before your son's out of diapers."

"Diapers?" Regis asked, confused. "What are those?"

Samson laughed. "Never mind. You don't want to know."

"If you say so. But what should we do next?"

Samson rose from his chair. "I think we need a war council of our own. I think it's about that time."

"A war council? With whom?"

"With Jon and Laura. Perhaps they can help shed some light on the subject."

"I'd forgotten about those two. I would imagine Laura is quite powerful here. Her magic is so strong."

Samson grunted. "I don't think it works that way. Magic doesn't seem to function real well here."

"Really?" Regis was stunned. "So Laura is not very powerful here?"

"No, not really."

"How very strange." Regis rose to leave as well. "So what does work here?"

"What you're born with. Muscles and a quick wit."

Regis grinned. "I think I would like it here. I think I would like it very much."

16

***

SANCTUARIES
AND HAVENS

As usual, Laura was three steps ahead of everybody else. Her discussion with Ramiel had lit a burning fire under her that was now roaring and blazing quite fully.

Unlike Samson, who was no scholar, Laura had managed to unearth a wealth of information. She had plumbed the depths of Duke's library and come up with every archaic reference to the races and where they might have sought haven in this world.

In fact, Laura was now quite certain that, just as Ramiel had mentioned, there *were* sanctuaries and havens for the races on Earth. The trick would be finding them.

Laura was not easily discouraged. She was not ready to give up on the fight just because it seemed almost hopeless. Never mind that no one but the legendary King Arthur had ever visited Avalon, the mythical home of the fairies. Laura would find a way. She was sure of it. The land had seemed impossible, but now it was very real. So the other places could be found as well.

Some of the references were easier to follow than others. Laura was convinced, for instance, that the Norse legends about the giants at Jotunheim and Valhalla were probably right on the mark. Old, but on the mark.

But where in the world was Valhalla? The legends said the hall leading into it was wide enough for 800 men to enter through it walking side by side. Surely, *someone* would have come across such a huge place by now. But no one had.

The rather oblique and vague references to a vast underground city called by various names, such as Agarttha, surely had to do with the dwarves' sanctuary on Earth. It appeared quite often in Tibetan literature. But why had no one ever stumbled across its entrance?

The Greek legends were filled with references to the centaurs and their home atop Mount Pelion. According to the legends, they'd waged a battle on Mount Pelion, and lost, and were now nowhere to be found. Where had they gone? Back to Mount Olympus, perhaps? And where might that be?

It seemed a sure bet to Laura that the people of the sea were responsible for the legends about Atlantis. Clearly, if there was a fabulous city beneath the sea, run by able magistrates, it would be the mermaids and the mermen.

The King Arthur legends, as well as others, clearly referenced the fairy kingdom of Avalon. But how did you come to Avalon? Where was it? Could it be found?

The references to the elves were the hardest to find, and the most obscure. The most conclusive appeared to be a reference to an island north of Germany in the Baltic Sea—the island of Rugen. Almost at the North Pole. There were stories associated with that island that raised some interesting possibilities, stories of primitive Germanic fertility practices associated with a goddess called Nerthus.

As Laura now knew, the elves shunned magic. They were both immune to it and utterly repulsed by it. So Laura wondered if, perhaps, the elves who had been stranded on the Earth had not waged some type of warfare with the magicians or *bene elohim* down through the ages, nipping in and out when the opportunities presented themselves.

The legends about the elves also confused them with other mythical creatures, such as fairies, and gave them no special place in the history of the world. That told Laura that the elves, of all the races, had managed to remain hidden in the shadows better than any of the others. It also told her they would be the most difficult to find.

Laura was fascinated with the legends of the blond-haired, blue-eyed warrior elves from the Nordic region that had spread across Germany and northern Europe. These legends—and those surrounding the sons of Seth and the *bene elohim*—had clearly had an impact on Adolph Hitler's sinister concept of a fierce, warrior-like Aryan master race.

Laura smiled to herself. If, in fact, the six races had managed to establish sanctuaries and havens for themselves on the Earth, they had done a marvelous job of masking their existence and covering any path to them with obscure myths and confusing legends.

One thing now seemed clear to Laura, though. They must close the portal they'd found, and it was time to bring the six races hidden within the bowels and mists of the Earth out into the open, and to send them back to the land from which they had quite obviously journeyed.

There would be a grave risk, of course. For that would bring the magicians out into the open as well. There would be confrontation, perhaps even a final one.

One of the most persistent Norse legends, which had trickled into legends of other cultures as well, was the story of Ragnarok. The "doom of the gods" spoke of the day in which the gods and the giants—or perhaps the *bene elohim* and their Nephilim—would finally meet in battle, resulting in massive destruction and a new Earth.

Stripped to its essence, Ragnarok would signal the end for the "gods" of the Earth. Clearly, then, the dawning of Ragnarok seemed to be something to be avoided at all costs by these "gods." Or, perhaps, an opportunity they had watched and waited for over the ages—a time when everything would at last align and free them.

Even as she was still working her way through the literature she'd dug up, Laura was already forming a plan. She knew where she wanted to go first. She felt relatively certain she could convince Jon and Samson to make an attempt to find two other places as well.

It was time to act, whatever the consequences. Laura could feel the certainty of that decision in every part of her. And if that meant the "doom of the gods," well, then, so be it.

17

***

FINCH

Jon was huddled over a heavy wooden table in the coffee shop, deep in conversation with Professor Neuman. They were discussing Neuman's "proposition," which, as it turned out, was an offer by Neuman to help Jon make the transition to a new life as a pastor.

Jon was mildly stunned at what he was hearing from Neuman. The man was a recluse, but not for the reasons Jon might have imagined. He wasn't crazy, or heretical, or mystical. No, Professor Neuman was simply a cautious, shy man who apparently loved learning above all else. There really was nothing more to it than that—stories, and nothing more. Neuman seemed to have a pretty basic view of the world. Serve others, walk the straight and narrow, and much of the rest is likely to fall into place.

"And that's it?" Jon asked him. "It's really as simple as that?"

"As simple as that." Neuman smiled. "And there's my proposition. Make your own life as simple as that as well. Work for others, not yourself. Follow the narrow path."

Jon shook his head. All his life, he had piled complication after complication upon himself. The more he read, the more complex the web had grown, to the point where he wasn't sure anything made any sense. Learning had become a burden, and a heavy one at that. He had come to the point where he no longer believed in anything. What Neuman offered was a way out of that entangling thicket.

"Just try it, Jon," Neuman said fervently. "You'll see for yourself."

Jon hesitated. "Okay, I will," he said finally, with some conviction. "I promise. I will."

"Good."

It was at that precise moment Jon's life lurched again. Even as he was nodding at Neuman, affirming the conviction to follow his advice, he caught sight of Professor Charles Finch walking down the aisle toward the two of them.

Jon watched in slightly fascinated horror as Finch approached. Neuman couldn't see him, but he clearly sensed the anxiety in Jon's eyes and turned to greet Finch.

"Good evening, Professor," Finch said in that loud, confident voice of his. "What brings you out at this late hour?"

Neuman scowled. "A bit of studying."

Finch smiled. "Studying, here in the coffee shop?"

"No, no, we've taken a break from our labors in the library."

"I see." Finch smirked. He swiveled to face Jon. "And are you studying as well, Jon?"

"No, not really." Jon tried his level best to keep his voice from trembling. He wasn't sure how successful he'd been.

"So what could you possibly be studying?" Finch prodded.

"Now that I've been kicked out of school, is that what you mean?" Jon's pitch rose a notch.

"Yes, something like that," Finch offered.

"This and that, really. Just for fun."

"For fun? Who would study for fun?"

"I would." Jon continued to meet Finch's unblinking gaze.

A shadow passed between them.

"Wouldn't it be better if you just moved on to something...*safer*, perhaps?"

There was no mistaking Finch's tone. Or the warning. There would be no misunderstanding. Finch was telling Jon not to meddle any further. And if he continued, what then?

Jon stiffened. "Oh, I think I have a few more things I'd like to explore."

"Such as?"

"Oh, this and that," Jon said vaguely, refusing to be drawn in.

"And you are *quite* certain that's a good idea, Jon? Have you really thought it through?"

"Yes, I have. And I have a pretty good idea where I want to go from here. It seems fairly clear."

Finch leaned closer. "Well, make sure you're careful about it, Jon. Next steps can be dangerous. Perilous."

"I can handle myself," Jon managed bravely.

"Oh, really? You can?" Finch asked breezily.

"Yes, I can. But thanks for the advice."

Finch's eyes flashed. "I hope you take it. For your sake."

Jon stood and moved close to his former advisor. What he said next was for Finch's ears only. "I know who, and *what*, you are," Jon said in a voice low enough so only Finch could hear him. "It may have taken me far too long to see behind the mask. But I see now. And I am not afraid—not of you, and not of *them*. You can threaten me as much as you'd like. I'm not going anywhere."

Finch stood very still, clearly torn about both his next words and actions. In the end, he chose not to acknowledge Jon's words, or its implications. "Good luck to you, Jon," he said loudly, whirled with a flourish, and continued on.

The encounter left Jon trembling, despite an effort to keep from being shaken. He looked at Neuman, who was watching him carefully. He took his seat again, slowly.

"You held up well," Neuman said quietly. "I know it wasn't easy, considering what you've learned."

Jon gazed off into the distance. "It *was* hard, seeing him that way. I've admired him for so long. I've liked his cold, rational view of the world. I was jealous of his ability to reduce Christianity to rubble."

"You were?" Neuman asked, clearly a little surprised.

"Oh, sure. Until now, I'd never believed in anything, so I guess I admired people like Finch, who could so artfully destroy something that was grounded in beliefs. I'd never really thought about it that way, before, but I can see it quite clearly now."

Neuman smiled. "You've come a long way. It's hard for me to imagine you making such a statement even a few months ago."

Jon was a little startled by that. "But you didn't know me a few months ago...."

"Oh, I've watched you, from a distance. I've watched your progress, or lack of it. Until recently, that is."

Jon continued to look off in the distance. "I think I ought to be going, get some sleep tonight," he said after a little while. "I have a feeling tomorrow is going to bring something new, something different. I have this funny notion that the grand Game is about to begin its final turn."

"Be careful, Jon. Okay? Promise me that?"

"I promise," Jon said somberly. "But if what you say is right, and I believe it is, then I'll really need help. The world may not be what it seems, but even the part I've seen now is frightening enough."

18

***

A WAR COUNCIL
(OF SORTS)

No one really knew who first called the meeting. Almost on cue, Jon, Samson, and Laura all left messages for each other, to meet somewhere and talk over what they each had learned since returning from the magicians' world.

They met at Jon's apartment, which was centrally located, under the cover of darkness. Jon had hot cocoa, coffee, and tea waiting for them as they arrived.

"Regis!" Jon exclaimed when Samson and the elf king arrived.

The two embraced warmly. "Jon, how are you?" Regis asked.

Jon looked over at Samson. "You never mentioned this."

Samson smiled. "I thought it might make a nice surprise."

Jon shook his head. "Then this must be serious, if the king of the elves would willingly journey to another world to risk a confrontation with the magicians."

Regis's face contorted slightly. "Since the three of you left to return to this world, it has gotten harder, and more complicated, for us in our own world."

"I'm sorry," Jon said.

"Oh, don't be sorry," Regis muttered. "It was inevitable, I guess. Once you've opened doors, all manner of things come in."

Jon was genuinely troubled. "But if we hadn't so foolishly—or selfishly—become accomplices in a plot to re-open the paths to and from your world…"

Regis waved a hand. "No, no, it isn't like that at all. If you hadn't come when you did, the land might have withered and died, regardless. No, there has to be a balance, between too much and not enough. You came at exactly the right time, for our own Land."

"Thanks." Jon sighed.

"But the three of you have still angered the gods of your own world. You have done their bidding, yes, but you have not acted since then as they would have you act. You have not returned and embraced them immediately, as I'm sure they would have hoped. And, for that, I am sure, there will be consequences."

"Perhaps you're right, Regis," Jon answered. "But I am still deeply sorry for any trouble we might have caused in your world. We had no intention of doing so."

Regis bowed. "We all know that, Jon. But thank you for your thoughtful consideration."

There was a second knock at the door, and then another warm embrace between Laura and Regis. "You have a son?" Laura asked when they were settled in Jon's living room with their mugs of hot liquid.

"Yes," Regis said proudly. "He looks more like Serena than me."

"Good." Samson laughed. "He'll be handsome, then."

Regis cast a dour glance in Samson's direction but then laughed. Fatherhood had clearly mellowed Regis a little.

"Okay, what do we do now?" Jon asked finally. "It seems patently obvious we have to do something."

"Yes, our own lives are being shattered, while we wait for something to happen. It seems obvious, as Jon said, that we must *make* something happen."

"We must bring the races out into the open here on Earth, and then make sure they are reunited with the races of their own world," Jon said. "And then, with some luck, we can close the portal to the land we are responsible for."

"Yes, that's it," Samson agreed.

"But there will clearly be risks, to ourselves, to the races," Laura warned.

"It's not like we have any choice. Not really," Jon said. "So, what's the plan?"

Samson and Laura glanced at each other and saw in each other's eyes that they'd reached the same conclusion.

"We must, each of us, try to find the havens of the races," Laura said.

"Like we did before," Samson added.

Jon frowned. "That's impossible. We have no idea where they might be found."

"Oh, I think we have some idea," Laura said.

"Yes, Regis and I found some mentions in the library," Samson concurred.

"I've done quite a bit of research myself," Laura explained, "and it seems clear that there are sanctuaries and havens. Some will be harder to find than others, I think. But I believe they *can* be found."

"And when we find them, what then?" Jon asked.

Laura looked out the window into the dark night. "From what I've read, there is a time in history when the gods of our world will meet their doom. There is a risk during this final confrontation, a grave risk that they will destroy the world in the process. But I think we have no choice. We must risk this Ragnarok."

"Ragnarok? From the Norse legends?" Jon asked.

"The same." Laura nodded. "Ragnarok, and other legends like it, speak of a time when the giants and other mythical creatures face the gods in battle. That time is upon us. I know it is."

"Me, too," Samson agreed. "I didn't know there was a name for it, but it is clearly time to do something."

"And how do we bring about this Ragnarok?" Jon asked.

Regis, who had said nothing so far, sat up in his chair. "I think that, if we find the others who have hidden themselves for so long in this world, the rest will take care of itself. We can only be messengers. Nothing more."

"So we find the races, here on Earth, and that's it?" Jon asked.

"Yes, I believe so," Regis said.

Laura and Samson nodded their assent.

Jon shrugged. "Okay, I'm in. It sounds reasonable to me, though I don't have a clue how we're going to find these races. If they've remained hidden for so long, what makes any of us hope that we can find them when others have failed?"

Laura smiled. "I have a feeling they'll try to meet us halfway, if they can."

Regis nodded. "They must surely know, by now, of what has happened. They will want to find the three of you as much as you will want to find them."

"And what of the magicians? Where are they? Do you think they will sit idly by as we try to find the races?" Jon asked.

"I don't think they've been sitting idly by," Laura murmured. "They've managed to destroy much of our personal lives since we've returned, without revealing themselves."

"That we know of," Jon noted.

"What's that?" Samson asked.

"I said, that we know of. For all we know, we *have* seen the magicians and just don't know it. They could easily have a human face. Shape-shifting, remember, is not out of the realm of possibility with them. It is their heart we cannot see."

Laura remembered the horrible Board of Inquiry, and her thoughts about some of its members. "Perhaps you're right," she mused. "But, nevertheless, I think we must press forward, no matter if they try to stop us. What more can they do to us, anyway? They've already done their best to shatter our hopes and dreams."

Jon laughed, remembering his own sordid brush with disaster at the hands of Professor Finch. "Yes, that's right. I'm not sure they can do much more to us."

"They can take our lives," Samson said softly.

There was a sudden silence. They were entering a part of the Grand Game where the consequences were very serious and, perhaps, quite final. The magicians would not give up their position without a fight of supreme magnitude.

"It is a risk I am willing to take," Regis said bravely. "For the sake of my own world, which I want my children to inhabit peacefully."

"I will take that risk as well," Samson said an instant later.

Laura and Jon glanced at each other and nodded. "Then we're all in agreement?" Jon asked. More nods of agreement sealed the decision. "Good. Then what's next?"

Laura opened the notebook she'd brought. "I have a plan, with some first assignments." She handed out photocopies. "We have to assume the races will meet us halfway, if we make a sincere, earnest effort to find them. What I've given you are instructions on how you might make an attempt to find the first haven."

Samson and Regis stared hard at their assignment. "You're sending us to Rugen, north of Germany?" Samson asked.

"Yes. Samson, because of your previous relationship with the elves, I thought you could go there to look for them. The fact Regis is now with you makes this choice all the more obvious."

"How will we get there?" Samson asked.

Laura laughed. "The way any normal person would. By plane, train, and then boat. I'll arrange to pay for the fares, out of my father's account."

Samson began to protest. "Oh, don't do that. I can—"

"Please, I insist." Laura held up her hand. "I am fortunate enough to have a trust in my father's name. I doubt any of you have such a resource?" Samson and Jon both shook their heads. "So it only makes sense that I shall pay for it. So it's settled."

"And what do I do when I get to…to this Rugen?" Samson asked.

"Find the elves, of course," Laura said matter-of-factly.

"Just like that? And then?" Samson persisted.

"And then, I think, events will unfold rather quickly. We'll just have to be prepared to move with them."

"And I'm going to Greece?" Jon asked.

"Yes," Laura answered. "To try and find the centaurs atop Mount Pelion."

"And if they've truly vanished, as the legends say?"

"Then you must pick up the trail again, no matter how cold."

"So where will you go, my lady?" Regis asked.

"I've arranged to take one of the small, observatory subs from Duke's marine biology lab on the coast of North Carolina. I plan to look for Atlantis."

Jon chuckled. This all seemed, well, preposterous. "And you think you have any hope of finding what none have ever found down through the ages?"

Laura was determined. "We'll see. It's at least worth a try."

"I guess." Jon shrugged. "Though it seems like an impossible task."

"No more impossible than the tasks you have," Laura countered.

"We, at least, have real places to go to. You only have an ancient myth to chase."

"I have to try. I do have a general direction I'd like to try."

Regis spoke up again. "So when do we start?"

Laura stood. "First thing in the morning. It is time to act."

19

***

THE SEARCH
FOR ATLANTIS

Duke was one of those rare universities that was able to maintain a marine biology laboratory outside of the campus, on the Outer Banks of North Carolina. It was located near one of the most famous sites in America—Kitty Hawk, site of the first airplane journey.

The lab was north of a well-known tourist trap, Nag's Head, and south of Kitty Hawk at a place called Kill Devil Hills. Laura couldn't help but wonder what someone had in mind when they named the place.

Not surprisingly, the marine lab at Kill Devil Hills was one of the most popular places within the university's curriculum. Students could study there for part of the day and enjoy the Outer Banks for the remainder. It was a great way to study.

But Laura had no intention of visiting Kitty Hawk, or Nag's Head, or any of the other places along the Outer Banks students visited during the school year.

Laura had already spent one semester at the lab, and she'd gotten to know one of the professors who spent the year on the site. In fact, Laura had enjoyed the course so much she'd almost been tempted into studying marine biology on a full-time basis.

She'd quickly discarded her notion, however, because it would only have distracted her from her eventual goal of becoming a physician. She'd toyed with the notion of getting a secondary degree in marine biology but had decided to stick to her narrow path and head straight to medical school.

As Laura drove east along route 64 toward the Outer Banks—chugging along in a rented red Subaru wagon—she couldn't help but smile now at how silly that choice had been. There was no reason she couldn't have chosen to study marine biology, taken all of the pre-med courses, and then gone on to medical school. No reason at all.

In fact, she'd be better off now if she'd done that. What did she have to show for her labors now? She hadn't taken courses she'd really enjoyed, and the possibility now existed that she wouldn't make it to medical school. So what had she gained?

Laura tried to put all of this out of her mind. She had a job to do. She needed to pay attention to what she was doing. For if she didn't, the results could be catastrophic.

The professor Laura had gotten to know had agreed to let her take one of the boats out by herself. The boat had a glass-encased observation sphere and a pressurized suit, both of which Laura knew how to use. It was unusual to go alone, but he trusted Laura.

Laura had told the professor she just wanted to run out and do some research for a project she was considering. The professor had been a little reluctant at first to let Laura go out alone but had consented in the end when Laura assured him she would be careful.

Laura had been out in the boats and used both the observation sphere and the pressurized suit dozens of times. She'd been fascinated by the ability to go down into the depths of the ocean and observe the marine life firsthand. During her semester there, she'd gone out every day, in the shallower waters.

What she hadn't told her professor, of course, was that she was planning to take the boat out a considerable distance east, to a place she'd decided on as the likely starting point for her effort to locate the entrance to Atlantis.

In all the research she'd done, Laura had settled on a point that was almost due east from Kill Devil Hills. There had been enough sightings of strange things there to make Laura think there must be something going on.

One of the most unusual aspects of the research Laura had uncovered was a thread that Jon had helped her trace all the way back to the Book of Job in the Old Testament.

Job had mentioned a sea monster, Leviathan, that is associated with chaos and some rather cataclysmic events. According to Job, the sea monster—variously called a serpent, or the dragon of the sea—could only be "roused" by magicians. Some of the legends of the day had God subduing Leviathan in order to create the watery portions of the world.

So, once again, Jon quickly pointed out, there were magicians of ancient times who were skilled at bringing up chaos where God wanted order. The same theme was always played out, time after time, through history.

The only difference, Laura thought, was that this was real. This wasn't history. This wasn't a textbook. She had deliberately set her sights on a part of the ocean where there had been reports of a huge sea monster over the centuries.

And, unlike her sojourn in the land, Laura had no magic to play with here. She was just one person against the elemental forces of nature.

She was so nervous by the time she'd arrived at the lab that she had to sit in the car for a time before she walked into the building to see her professor. If he saw how upset or nervous she was, he was certain to be suspicious and deny her the use of the boat. So, as she did before any test, Laura went through a series of steps to assure herself that she had everything under control. She steeled herself and then stepped out of the car.

She was almost disappointed to find a note, and an envelope, attached to the front door of the building. The lab was closed for the day, and the professor had gone down to Nag's Head, but he'd left the key to the boat. The suit and the sphere were on board.

So, this is it, Laura thought. *I'm really going to do it. I'm really setting off for the middle of the ocean, searching for chaos and an elusive myth.*

The warm breeze blowing in off the ocean felt good to Laura as she started up the boat's engine and set off to the east. It was a beautiful day—the breeze gentle, the sun not too hot. Laura kept a careful eye on the boat's instrument panel to make sure she continued to head in the right direction.

Laura had spent a good deal of time studying the geographical formations near the many sightings of this mythical sea monster. Though it was only a hypothesis, Laura was convinced that the ridge in that part of the ocean was unusual—that, perhaps, it was not as it seemed.

What it was, exactly, Laura couldn't say. A few of the big oil companies, noting the particular and unusual nature of the ridge, had explored the possibility that it was a huge oil reserve. But they'd come up dry, and some of their explorations had ended disastrously. There had also been reports of ships having trouble in those waters.

All of which led Laura to believe that *something* was going on above, near, or perhaps beneath that ridge. But could it be that easy? Could Atlantis be hidden somewhere nearby? Somehow, Laura doubted it was that simple. For if she could figure it out, then, perhaps, others could as well. Or should have. And others clearly had not, or the world would have heard about it.

As Laura guided the boat toward its destination, she tried desperately to quell the fear that threatened to overwhelm her. She had no real hope of finding what others had not found.

Other than the coordinates on her instrument panel, Laura had nothing to go by to tell her when she'd reached her destination. The ocean looked exactly the same as far as she could see in all directions.

As she shut the boat down and readied the exploration sphere, Laura was still, unsuccessfully, trying to dispel the uneasy foreboding that had descended on her. She knew her fear was irrational. More than likely, she would drift down into the depths of ocean, scare a few fish, and come back empty-handed.

Still, she couldn't help wonder what she'd do if she actually found something. Would she be brave enough to don her pressurized suit and go exploring? It would be suicidal to do so, alone, out here in the middle of the ocean. But Laura knew she would try it, if there seemed to be a reason to do so. It went against every part of her rational, orderly mind, but she still knew she would do it.

Laura placed the pressurized suit off to one side of the small cabin in the sphere, lowered the sphere down to the water level, and then climbed in the hatch at the top. She released it from the boat and began to drift downward, toward the ocean floor.

Gradually the light disappeared. For one terrifying instant, Laura thought she saw something coming at her off to one side, a huge shape of some sort, but it turned out to be a school of fish investigating the strange object entering their world.

Laura thought back to the land, when the boat had drifted down to the people of the sea of its own accord. *How different it is now, here in my own real world. There, I was powerful, the magic at my fingertips, but helpless to do anything. Here, I have no power at all, and I am choosing to go on this kamikaze mission.*

Murky shapes emerged on all sides of her. She had reached the top of what appeared to be a mountain range at the bottom of the ocean floor. More fish began to swim up to the sphere and then dart away. An especially nosy barracuda came up and stared at her through the window for a long time, then swam away lazily.

The sphere continued to drift downward. Laura didn't do much at the controls, other than to let the propeller blades whir softly during the descent, because she didn't have any particular destination in mind. She wasn't at all sure what she was looking for—a sign, an indication of something unusual or different.

Laura could remain down for several hours. She doubted, however, whether she'd be down that long. If she found nothing unusual, she'd go up and try another spot.

There was a gentle bump from behind. Laura jumped slightly and then turned around to see what it was. Her heart fluttered for an instant as she came face to face with a bottle-nose dolphin, which was gazing inside the sphere's cabin at Laura.

Laura breathed easier. "Hello, friend," she said, smiling. "What brings you here?"

The dolphin stared for a moment longer, then turned on a dime and sped away. Laura looked around for others but couldn't see any. *That's strange. They usually swim in schools. Where are its friends?*

Over the next half hour or so, Laura studied all the different sea creatures that ventured past. She moved the sphere around as much as she dared in order to survey some of the rock formations. It was all very interesting but not helpful in her quest.

There was nothing unusual down here. This part of the ocean floor was no different than other parts of the ocean floor she'd seen before. Nothing jumped out at her as strange or unusual.

She'd just made up her mind to ascend and try another place when she saw a movement, a flash of light, out of the corner of her eye, not more than a hundred yards off to the side. Laura quickly moved the sphere over in that direction.

As she moved closer, Laura couldn't believe what she was seeing. At first, she thought it was a huge monolith, half-buried in the side of the mountain. But on closer inspection, Laura could see that it was really a huge crystal, more than 100 feet in length. Part of it was buried in the mountain. It appeared to be octagonal, smooth, translucent, and part of the landscape.

Laura had never seen anything like it. She had no idea what it was. The flash she'd seen was probably a reflection from the spotlight on her sphere. The light must have caught one of the sides of the crystal and reflected back to her.

Was it possible that such a crystal would form naturally here? There seemed little likelihood of that, because the ocean currents would eventually grind an object like this into pulp. Nothing stood sharp-edged for long at the bottom of the ocean.

But this crystal had edges. It was clearly defying the steady, incessant pressure of the ocean. What was it made of? What purpose did it serve?

Laura remembered a little about crystals from her limited physics knowledge. Crystals, like topaz, formed naturally. They could be used as electronic devices. There was an electricity effect which, if she remembered correctly, was generated in crystals subjected to mechanical stress of some sort. Crystals could also have magnetic or semi-conductive properties.

Laura continued to stare at the crystal, seemingly stuck out here in the middle of the ocean. It was crazy, entirely unnatural. Something like this should not be where it was. But there it was. And that could only mean one thing. What if someone had placed this crystal here, for some purpose? She was getting closer. She could sense it.

Whatever power the crystal was generating, or absorbing, or carrying, it had to go *somewhere*. But how could she trace that back? How could she follow it?

The sphere moved slightly as an especially hard ocean current swept past her. It caused Laura to stumble a little. She glanced around her to see if anything had been jarred loose. Her eye caught the pressurized suit. *Well, do I have the courage to put that thing on and go exploring? Do I?*

Laura moved across the cabin and donned the suit. She refused to let herself think too hard. She just did it. She was outside the sphere within moments.

Moving her arms slowly, Laura eased her way toward the crystal. It was even more awesome up close. She reached out a gloved hand. A humming power surged through the crystal. *But that could simply be the crystal reacting to the ocean currents.*

Laura worked her way around and around the crystal for nearly a half hour, but found nothing else unusual about it. The crystal was buried deep within the side of the mountain. There were no caves or entrances at its base. What you saw was what you got.

Reluctantly, Laura finally returned to the safety of the sphere's cabin and removed the pressurized suit. She was hugely disappointed for some reason. She didn't know where to go from here. She was certain the crystal meant something, but what?

Laura saw it shortly after she'd stepped clear of the suit. Moving toward her at an unbelievably rapid rate was the largest mass Laura had ever seen. It was easily ten times the size of an elephant. At first glance, Laura thought it was a blue whale. The creature was monstrously huge. But as it sped into full view, Laura could see that it wasn't a blue whale. It had a long tail of some sort and a powerful, scaly body. It seemed to propel itself through the water with wings, and its head looked a little like a sea horse.

It was a sea dragon. Or *the* sea dragon, perhaps the Leviathan the Old Testament spoke of. And it was rushing straight at Laura.

The cry of terror died on Laura's lips. Before she could do a thing to stop it—not that there was much she could have done anyway—the dragon was upon her. It swung its mighty tail around and swatted the sphere. Laura was tossed violently to one side in the wake.

The sea dragon swung its tail a second time to finish the job. A microscopic crack appeared on the surface of the sphere and water rushed in a steady torrent into the cabin. After the initial panic as she realized she was about to drown, Laura felt a strange calm and peace. She said a silent prayer. She took one final breath before the water filled the entire cabin.

As she started to lose consciousness, Laura had the most unusual sensation—as if a team of horses had arrived at her side, picked her up, and begun to rush her at the speed of light toward some distant goal.

But then Laura slipped off into oblivion, that vast darkness that so terrorizes the sons and daughters of Adam and Eve.

20

***

MOUNT PELION

Jon couldn't sit still. He tried to read during the long flight from New York to Athens, but it was nearly impossible. He couldn't believe he was actually flying to Greece, not for a vacation on the islands there, but to wander around atop Mount Pelion looking for mythical centaurs. It all seemed so futile. How in the world could he find what others had not? He had no special powers, at least not here on Earth.

What's more, it wasn't as if Mount Pelion was some monster of a mountain that had largely gone unexplored for centuries. It wasn't even very tall, as far as mountains go. At 5,000-plus feet high, it was just a quarter the size of the largest mountain in North America, Mt. McKinley. And it wasn't even the tallest mountain in Greece. Ossa, for instance, in east-central Greece, was more than 1,000 feet taller.

Jon hadn't been able to find much about Mount Pelion, other than that the myths said the centaurs had roamed the plains around Pelion and were defeated in battle there. He'd found one myth describing how the Titans had piled Ossa on top of Mount Olympus, and then put Mount Pelion on top of Ossa in order to reach heaven. It hadn't worked.

But there wasn't much to go by. Which led Jon right back to why he was so certain his mission would end in failure. It seemed inconceivable that the centaurs had somehow escaped notice all these centuries. But he would look. He had to.

After he landed in Athens, Jon changed his currency and then booked a round-trip boat trip from Athens to Thessaloniki, in northeastern Greece, and back again. From Thessaloniki, Jon would take a bus to the foothills of Mount Pelion.

Greece's coastline from the boat was everything people said it was. While the mountains weren't fabulously tall, the view was still breathtaking. Jon stood at the railing, gazing inland, for most of the trip. He dozed some during the bus trip through some of the plains of northeastern Greece, however. He hadn't slept well during the flight across the Atlantic Ocean, and his fatigue was catching up to him.

It was dark by the time they arrived at one of the small towns near Mount Pelion. Jon wandered to the nearest inn, paid for the night, and was asleep almost as soon as his head hit the pillow.

The next day broke hot and clear. Jon's room was a little stuffy when he awoke, so he opened the windows and let in some fresh air. He was struck by how wonderful and clean the air smelled.

He had coffee and a bagel before setting off. His game plan was simple. Not having any idea where to begin, he figured he'd just start up one of the roads leading to the top of Mount Pelion, ask questions as he walked along, and hope he got lucky and stumbled across something. He'd be limited by not knowing the Greek language, though. He doubted the pocket dictionary he'd brought would be much help.

Jon stopped at every small store along the route as he walked. The first half dozen people he approached spoke no English at all, and most only shook their heads when Jon pointed out the word for *centaur* in his dictionary. One broke into peals of laughter when he pointed to it and then motioned him out of the store.

But Jon persevered. He trudged up the road, stopping at the stores, asking if anyone spoke English, and then continuing on when he received a blank stare, a curt shake of the head, or a wave of the hand.

About halfway up the side of the small mountain, Jon finally found someone who at least spoke halting English—an old, grizzled man who ran a ramshackle convenience store. Once through the door, Jon asked if the spoke English. Jon was half-turning away when he heard him answer.

"Yes, I talk English," the man answered in a gruff voice. "What I do for you?"

"Great!" Jon said enthusiastically. "I'm looking for information on the centaurs."

The old man narrowed his eyes. "You look center of what?"

Jon was a little confused. "The centaurs of Mount Pelion, I guess."

The old man shook his head and mumbled something. He looked down and pulled something from beneath his cash register. It was an old, worn map. He spread it out on the counter. "Mount Pelion," he declared, thrusting a gnarled finger into the center of the mountain.

Jon looked down at it. "Yes, I can see that. I'm looking for the centaurs."

"Here, center," the old man growled, clearly irritated at this obtuse young man who was asking such an inane question. He tapped his finger on the map again.

Jon looked down at the map, at where the old man was pointing. "The centaurs are located here?"

"Yes, center of Mount Pelion right here." The man nodded.

"Are you sure?"

"Yes, I sure."

Jon glanced again at where the old man was pointing. Something clearly wasn't right here. Jon pulled his dictionary from his pocket and thumbed through it until he came to the word for *centaur*. He held it out for the old man to gaze at.

The old man studied it hard, then broke out into cackling laughter. "Ah, ah, *kentauros!* You look those, not center?"

Jon finally grasped what was happening. "Yes, yes, kentauros. Not center."

The old man stopped chuckling and took a hard look at Jon. "Why you ask?" he said after a bit.

"I'd like to find them." He shrugged. "Perhaps I can help them."

"No kentauros. Not here."

"Are you sure?"

"Yes, I sure."

Jon was crestfallen. His hope was so slim to begin with, and he was tired of people simply laughing at him. "Has anyone ever heard of them, of the kentauros?"

"Yes, yes, we all hear."

"But they aren't here?"

The old man peered over his shoulder furtively. "We no talk about kentauros here," he whispered.

"What do you mean?" Jon caught his breath. "You can't talk, or you won't talk?"

"No talk about kentauros. No want to be crazy," he whispered again. "They not here."

Jon studied the old man. "*Something* is here, though, isn't that right? Maybe not the kentauros, but something?"

"Yes, something," the old man mumbled.

"What? What is it?"

The old man peeked behind him again. He was clearly looking for someone. He looked back, and reached out, gesturing for Jon's dictionary. Jon handed it over. The old man thumbed through the second half of the book, where it translated from Greek to English. He stopped when he'd found the word he was looking for and held it out for Jon to see.

"Horses?" Jon asked.

"Yes, yes," the old man whispered feverishly. He went back to the dictionary, looking for another word. He stopped when he found it and pointed a gnarled finger at it. It was the word for *wild.*

"Wild horses?" Jon asked him.

"Yes, that." The old man nodded. "They the kentauros."

"There are wild horses on Mount Pelion?"

"Yes." The old man jabbed a finger toward the top of the mountain. "There."

Jon looked out the window in the direction the old man was pointing. "Wild horses…"

There was a sudden commotion at the back of the convenience store. The old man fluttered and quickly stuffed the map back beneath his cash register.

A young man in sandals, a flowing robe, with tanned, olive skin and a full, black beard thrust a curtain aside and strode to the front of the store, casting a wary glance at Jon. He said something, in Greek, to the old man, who answered back softly.

"What do you want?" the young man asked Jon in nearly flawless English.

Jon was a little startled. "You speak English?"

"Yes, of course," the young man said brusquely. "I studied at Harvard. Now, what do you want from us?"

"You studied at Harvard?" Jon asked, incredulous.

"Is that so hard to believe?" asked the young man, who seemed to be in his early thirties.

"No, I guess not. It's just that, um, it seems so...out of place here."

"This is my father's store," the young man said. "I stop by here to help him every so often."

"So you don't really work here?"

The young man's eyes flashed. "Is it any business of yours?"

"No, of course not," Jon said, feeling slightly flushed. "I'm sorry."

"You ought to be. And not that you need to know, but I keep quite luxurious apartments in Athens, Geneva, Tokyo, and New York. I visit my father here every so often, just because I like to do so."

"I see," Jon answered, not sure whether he believed him.

"I am a venture capitalist," the young man declared. "I help finance the world's economic market."

"That's nice."

The young man studied Jon some more. "You are a student?"

"Yes, from Duke."

The young man stiffened suddenly, as if he'd been jolted with something. His neck muscles bulged slightly. "You're a student, from Duke?"

Jon sighed. "Yes, I just said that."

The young man turned to his father and snapped something at him in Greek. When the old man answered falteringly, using the word *kentauros* in the middle of the sentence, his son gave him a quick rap to the head. The old man winced.

"Hey!" Jon moved forward a step.

"Yes?" The young man bristled. "And this is your business?"

"Well, no, but..."

"Then stay out of it. And if you know what's good for you, you'll leave Mount Pelion as well."

"Leave Mount Pelion? Why?"

"We don't like strangers roaming around here." He gazed intently at Jon. "You'd be better off if you simply turned around and went back to where you came from."

Jon stared hard at this young man, wondering if something else wasn't going on here, something he hadn't anticipated.

"I thought I might pay a visit to the wild horses," he said bravely.

The young man laughed loudly. "You believe the old fish stories my father has told you?"

"What harm can it do?"

"You are a fool, then," the young man said angrily. "And you will never find them, regardless."

"I can try."

"Try, then, fool," the young man warned ominously. "But watch your step."

"Why?"

"We don't like strangers around here. *No one* does. We keep an eye on them."

Jon tried to still the fear. He now very much felt like a stranger in a foreign land. "Surely there can't be any harm in—"

"There is always harm, wherever you look. We don't like strangers nosing around."

Jon started to back away, nodding once at the old man who had tried to help. The old man did not acknowledge it, cowering behind the counter and his son.

"Well, um, thanks for your help," he said.

"Leave! Now!" the young man ordered. "If you know what's good for you."

Jon bolted through the door, his face flushed and his body racked with chills. He quelled an urge to run away as fast as his legs could carry him.

But it wouldn't do to show fear. Not at all. The sun felt good on Jon's neck as he continued his trek up the side of the mountain. It took him the better part of an hour to shake the numbness in his limbs. He tried to ignore the uneasy feeling he now had that people who passed by him were giving him malevolent looks.

The road started to turn wild as he neared the top. Jon walked blindly for another hour, wondering vaguely if he'd have to spend the night out in the darkness, hungry and alone. Then the road dipped into a canyon. It was a magnificent sight. As far as the eye could see, there were rolling hills at the top of the mountain. Jon could not glimpse a single house from this vantage point. It was pure, virgin forest.

Jon descended into the canyon. It had now been nearly an hour since a car had passed him. The road he was on had turned to dirt about a mile back, and it was starting to disappear entirely. Soon it would be nothing more than a goat path.

He heard the engine long before he actually saw it. It sounded so foreign out here in the middle of this canyon forest. The dark blue helicopter burst over the horizon an instant later, winging its way straight toward Jon.

It landed 20 feet in front of him, kicking up a huge dust storm. Jon shielded his eyes, but some of the dirt still managed to get in. He blinked a couple of times as the copter blades whirred to a stop. Two members of the local police emerged out of either side of the helicopter. Their guns were drawn. It took all of Jon's willpower to keep from turning and running in the opposite direction. Only the very clear thought that these two would shoot to kill kept him from doing so.

The two policemen flanked Jon. One grabbed his arm.

"Hey!" Jon yelled. "What do you think you're—"

The other policeman slugged Jon once, hard, in the stomach. Air whooshed out of him. He collapsed in a heap, gasping for air.

The first policeman knelt beside Jon and methodically searched through his pockets. He reached into Jon's empty coat pocket. His hand emerged and he held it high, triumphantly. There was a bag in it, with what looked to be 50 grams of white, powdery substance inside.

Even as he sucked in air, Jon panicked. He now knew what was going on. They would arrest him for possession of cocaine. There would be no witnesses, other than these two policemen. The trial would undoubtedly be quick, the sentence severe.

Jon closed his eyes and prayed. One of the policemen grabbed Jon's arm again, jerked him to his feet, and led him toward the helicopter.

Again, Jon heard the sounds first. It started as a slow rumble, then swiftly became the staccato thundering of many hooves. An instant later, dozens of wild horses charged down the goat path, neck to neck, side by side.

The policemen were so startled that they let go of Jon and turned their guns on the horses. But before they could fire, the first of the thundering horses were upon them. They careened past, some on one side of the helicopter, some on the other.

The two policemen were clearly too startled to react. There was nothing to fire at, nothing to aim at. They inched closer to their helicopter, hoping to stay out of harm's way. The horses continued to stampede past.

One of the horses—a dark gray stallion—stopped in its tracks directly in front of Jon. It reared up on its hind legs and then shook its head twice, three times, at Jon.

Jon reacted instantly. Despite his intense stomach pain, he rose to his feet and grabbed hold of the horse's neck with both arms. As soon as he'd pulled himself up and across the stallion's back, the horse bolted away.

Jon clung for all he was worth as the stallion raced away, rejoining the other wild horses. Shots were fired, but from farther away. None of them came close.

The stallion turned off the path and galloped his way through the forest. He slowed after a couple of minutes and allowed Jon to actually sit up on his back. Then he raced off again as the darkness fell.

21

* * *

THE ISLAND OF RUGEN

t was all Samson could do to restrain Regis during the flight to Berlin. Regis was absolutely certain he was going to die in the huge 747 that took them across the Atlantic Ocean.

Regis was sure the plane was guided by unseen demons. There seemed no other explanation to him. The notion that a huge, lumbering hunk of metal could be propelled through the air seemed so alien to him that he was sure there was a different kind of magic involved. Samson didn't even attempt to explain to Regis about the forged passport he'd used to leave the country, or that he likely wouldn't be able to come back into the U.S. with it because there was no record of Regis in any computer anywhere.

"Birds fly. We don't," Regis said grimly when Samson tried to explain the theory of flight, as he knew it, before they'd boarded. They were both standing inside the terminal, looking out a large plate glass window at the airplane they were about to board.

"But we *do* fly," Samson insisted. "And you've seen Peg and Shar."

"It isn't possible, not with these—things," Regis said flatly. "There must be some very deep magic involved here. There can be no other explanation."

"It's not magic. At least, not the kind of magic you mean. It's physics. Laura could explain it to you better than I can."

Regis narrowed his eyes. "See. There *is* magic involved, if Laura is the one who understands it so well."

Samson sighed. "Regis, I've told you. Laura's magic doesn't work here on Earth. She isn't a magician here. She doesn't understand how that stuff works here."

"But you said she understands how this…this airplane works?"

"Yes. It's science. Laura understands science very well."

"Okay, then, this 'science' is your magic here," Regis said confidently.

"No, no, you've got it all wrong. Science is all about understanding the way nature works, the way the world works."

"And then controlling it?"

416

Samson hesitated. "Yes, I guess."

"Then it is like magic. That is what the magicians did in our world. They used their magic to manipulate the natural order of things."

"That isn't what science does. Or, it isn't what it's meant to be."

"But it can be used that way?"

Samson shrugged. It was clearly hopeless. He wasn't going to change Regis's mind, at least not anytime soon. "Okay, I give up. Science is harmless. It's about understanding things, not about controlling or manipulating them.

Regis shook his head. "Anyone who can make *that* monster fly is manipulating the forces of nature. He is a magician," he said, pointing at the 747. "There can be no other explanation."

To his credit, once they'd leveled out over the Atlantic Ocean, Regis eventually calmed down. He was still certain the airplane would plummet any moment into the depths of the ocean, but he held his tongue. The two of them were even able to talk a little strategy.

Their game plan was to take a train from Berlin, north to the Baltic Sea and a coastal city, Stralsund, that served as a bridge between Germany's mainland and the island of Rugen. A ferry would take them to the island, and another train would get them to Bergen, a little town in the middle of the island.

"And after that?" Regis asked.

"Beats me," Samson admitted. "We ask some questions."

"What do we ask people? Where are the elves hiding?"

Samson laughed. "Sure, why not?"

"We can't ask people that."

"You're right. But what else can we do?"

Regis looked out the window, shuddered slightly, and looked back again. "We can visit the forest land there. It is possible I can learn something. The animals of the Earth's forests are nothing like those of my world. Here, they are deaf and dumb. But perhaps I can learn something of them anyway."

"Do you really think you could learn something that way?"

"No, I don't. But I don't know what else to do."

The rest of the flight to Berlin was uneventful. When they landed, Samson tried to explain the significance of Berlin, about the second world war, the way in which Berlin had been divided between east and west, how the city had been reunited when the two Germanys joined again.

"What was the war about?" Regis asked.

Samson thought for a moment. "A man who lived here in this country, in Germany, thought he could rule the world. Other nations went to war to stop him."

"And were they successful? Did they stop him?"

"Yes, they did," Samson said somberly.

"So who put this man up to it? Who convinced him he could win such a war?"

"What do you mean?" Samson asked, perplexed by the question.

Regis shrugged. "Surely, he didn't make such a decision on his own. No respectable ruler or king makes such a decision without consulting those who serve him. Or who he may be beholden to."

"I don't know. I wasn't alive then, and I don't know much about it."

Regis was equally awed by the physics of locomotive engines. In fact, he was almost more impressed by the fact that one engine could pull so many cars behind it, at such a rapid rate. "How does it work?" he asked Samson as they gazed out the window at the German countryside.

"The train?"

"Yes, how does it work?"

Samson scratched his head. "Um, there's an engine at the front of the train…"

"What's an engine?"

"It's a machine that…"

"What's a machine?"

Samson sighed. "You're not making this easy."

"Sorry. This is all so strange to me."

Samson tried to relate it to what Regis was familiar with. "You know the metal the dwarves forge in their bellows?" Regis nodded. "And you understand how the dwarves feed coal, from beneath the earth, into their bellows to make the fire roar?"

"Yes, I saw it with you, when we visited the dwarves and Gar."

"Right. Well, you hook some metal bars and rods together, so they can move back and forth in a complicated manner. Then you take some coal and build a fire to generate heat. That's turned into energy and is used to make the metal rods and bars move. The rods are attached to the wheels of the engine, which turn around and around and pull the rest of the train."

It was a lousy explanation, no question about it, but it was the best Samson was likely to come up with.

Regis seemed to grasp the concept. "I see. So, they are manipulating one of the elemental forces of nature—fire—to make something happen?"

"Yes, that's right." Samson sighed, relieved he'd managed to get past this line of questioning.

By the time they'd arrived at Bergen, Samson was worn out trying to answer all of Regis's questions. They never seemed to stop. The elf king was simply fascinated by what the Earth had to offer. It was beyond his wildest imagination.

"I can't believe you don't see the powerful magic that's at work in your world," Regis told Samson at one point in the never-ending conversation.

"There's no magic here," Samson said for the hundredth time.

"But there is," Regis insisted. "You just don't recognize it as such. There is clearly more deep magic at work in this world than you are seeing. The forces of nature have been severely and violently disrupted and manipulated."

"For the good of humankind."

"I guess. If you say so." But Regis appeared dubious. "Are people happier because of their new, wonderful…things?"

"Sure. The work is easier, and people have more time to enjoy life."

"I see." Regis cocked his head. "What gives *you* more pleasure? A walk in the woods or a ride on a train?"

"You can't compare the two," Samson said sourly.

"Why not?"

"Because you can't. They're totally different."

"Are they? You can do both in this world. Which would you rather do?"

Samson grimaced. "You're twisting things around. I'd rather take a walk in the woods, because I like to do things by myself. I don't like others doing my work for me. But you can't compare the two. People need trains to get from one place to another."

"In other words, people *have* to ride trains?"

"Yes, that's right."

"So they're slaves to…what do you call all this stuff?"

"Technology," Samson huffed. "And, no, they're not slaves to it."

"But you said…?"

"I said people use trains to get from one place to another. They can also use planes, and cars, and boats, and bicycles or their feet. It just depends on how fast you want to get there."

"Speed seems important in your world," Regis observed. "The ability to do things rapidly, without much thought, seems to be a valuable commodity."

"Would you just cut it out?" Samson almost roared. It was painful to listen to Regis's seemingly endless commentaries on the state of his own world. "You're driving me crazy with all of this."

Regis looked hurt. "I'm sorry. I didn't mean to offend you. I'm only observing all of this for the first time."

"Oh, you didn't offend me," Samson said gruffly. "It's just that you're making my world seem like complete, utter chaos without much rhyme or reason."

"I don't mean to. But it is so different from my own. No better or worse. Just different."

There were still a couple hours of daylight left when they arrived at the final destination, so they decided to walk around Bergen to see what was there. It was a very small town. A few shops, some houses, a couple of large buildings. It was clearly not a major center of commerce.

"Why would the elves come here?" Regis muttered at one point. "It makes no sense."

"I know," Samson agreed. "It doesn't make any sense."

The island of Rugen seemed so mundane, so normal. Why would the elves choose such a place as their home?

Regis's brow furrowed. "Perhaps they had no choice in the matter."

"No choice?"

"The thought has occurred to me more than once since I've been here that, perhaps, there is a reason why no one from your world has ever seen any of the races. Perhaps it has more to do with the magicians' wishes than those of the races."

Samson wondered why he'd never considered the concept before. "You mean they're prisoners?"

"Yes, prisoners. Is that what you call those who are captured in a war? Prisoners?"

"Yes, that's what we call them."

"And what do you do with prisoners?"

"You take them to camps, lock them up, keep them away from other people."

Regis nodded. "Perhaps something very much like that has happened here. Who knows?"

As Regis and Samson wandered around the town, asking an occasional question, they pieced together a local legend that all of the townspeople repeated. Nearly everyone had heard the legend in one form or another. They were all more than happy to repeat it.

The legend was a simple one. Across the Baltic Sea there was a land, or an island, upon which the race of elves lived. The island had no name. It was somewhere in the Baltic. In distant times, the elves, led by their king, would come to Rugen by boat and mingle with the people. Then they would leave, presumably to return to their own land again.

No one could say why the elves would visit Rugen. Or why they would leave again. All the townspeople knew was that they would arrive in a crude boat of some sort, stay for a little while, and then leave. That was the extent of the legend.

"It is most curious," Regis said as they wandered through a park on the outskirts of town. A huge flock of starlings, probably hundreds, swooped down out of the sky toward them, almost as one creature. They settled in the trees above them. Their jabbering and squawking was very loud.

Regis glanced up uneasily at the starlings. He looked up at the trees, silently, for the longest time. He was clearly listening to something, though what that might be in the midst of such a cacophony of squawks Samson couldn't imagine.

"Can you hear it?" he asked Samson after a while.

"Hear what?"

"What the starlings are saying."

"Birds don't talk," Samson growled.

"These do. But they aren't really talking. They're mimicking, repeating what they've heard others say."

Samson listened intently. His ears weren't nearly as acute as Regis's but, after a minute, he indeed could discern a word or two in the midst of the squawks.

"I can't believe it," Samson said in hushed fascination. "They really are talking."

"They're doing more than that." Regis wore a funny half-smile.

"What do you mean?"

"These starlings," Regis said slowly, "are not from this island. They've traveled here from someplace else."

"Where?"

"From the island of the elves. I know where they are now."

22
✳ ✳ ✳
ATLANTIS FOUND

I must be in heaven, Laura thought. *I've died and gone to heaven. That would explain it.*

"*No,*" answered the voice, the one that had called her back from the oblivion she'd descended into. "*You have reached your destination.*"

Laura struggled to open her eyes. They were so heavy. She was so tired. It was all she could do to press her eyelids open.

A funny memory rushed at her. She felt like the witch must have felt in *The Wizard of Oz* when Dorothy's house fell on her. Every part of Laura's body ached. She felt a weariness and tiredness like she'd never felt before. *Where am I?* Her eyes struggled to focus.

"*You are with us,*" came the soft voice. "*You are in the place your world calls Atlantis.*"

Laura blinked and looked. She saw one, then two, then several mermaids around her, their fins moving slowly back and forth through the water that surrounded her. Behind those were two strong men of the sea.

Laura was inside a translucent bubble of some sort. It looked to be made of the same material the crystal had been made of. She was lying on a bed of seaweed, raised on a pedestal of some sort. Her clothes were gone, replaced by a flowing, diaphanous robe.

Off to one side of her seaweed bed, Laura could also see several dolphin swimming around the people of the sea, who continued to gaze at her.

Did they...? she thought.

"*Yes,*" the soft voice answered. "*They brought you here after your ship was destroyed by Leviathan. You were nearly dead when you arrived.*"

Laura was surprised at how naturally it came to her, speaking with thoughts like this, as she had on the magicians' world.

Pleasant memories of the people of the sea from the land rushed at Laura. There were unspoken squeals of delight from the mermaids surrounding her.

"*You've met them?*" one of the mermaids asked Laura.

Yes, I've been there, to your world, Laura answered. *I've met your race. They are magnificent.*

The squeals of delight were quickly replaced by sheer, unabashed sadness. It was palpable, that sadness, like a mother would feel for a child she had lost.

"But we will never see them, never meet them," one of the mermaids said. *"We are forever trapped here, in this world, on Earth."*

Laura looked around her for the first time. She peered outside her translucent bubble at the world the mermaids lived in.

It reminded Laura very much of the city she'd come to beneath the sea on the magicians' world. She was at the bottom of a basin. Extraordinarily high mountains rose all around her. Dozens of caves were spread out in all directions. Glowing lights from crystals of some sort dotted the landscape.

There was little else beyond that, however. As on the magicians' world, the people of the sea lived simply here. They were clearly a community that thrived on the natural elements that surrounded them.

There was no elaborate system of buildings and edifices, as the legends hinted at when they spoke of Atlantis. There was no monstrous generating plant, no vast transportation system. Just the people of the sea, living in isolation here at the bottom of the ocean floor inside these mountains. Almost as if they were imprisoned.

"We are prisoners," one of the mermaids said. *"We have been for a very long time."*

Prisoners? Laura asked.

"Yes, we have been confined here since the portals of our own world closed so very long ago," she said sadly. *"We cannot travel far from here. They won't allow it."*

Laura felt the cold, white fury enter her heart again, as it had on the magicians' world. How dare they? *They have no right, none at all.*

"There is nothing we can do about it," one mermaid said. *"We are powerless against them. Occasionally we venture from here to help sailors or ships in trouble. But we must always return here. They have said they will destroy us utterly if we do not."*

And that creature, Leviathan? Laura asked.

"It serves the masters, the magicians," a voice said grimly. *"It is their weapon."*

Laura tried to move. Every muscle ached. Every bone felt like it had been crushed. She would be surprised if she had not broken any bones. *How am I able to breathe here?* she asked.

"We have managed to do a little during our imprisonment," one of the mermaids answered. *"We have learned how to generate electricity by using the crystals we collect and fusing them together. That has allowed us to generate a little of the oxygen you need to breathe. It allows some of the dolphins to rest here with us without having to return to the ocean surface for air."*

So that crystal I saw...? Laura asked.

"*It was one of ours that we have used to generate power. The magicians have, for some reason, allowed us that. They have not challenged our efforts to expand our city. They have refused to let us go much beyond its boundaries, however. We are trapped here, but we have been able to try different things to keep ourselves amused.*"

Laura stifled a shudder. This was so unspeakable, so monstrous…as great a wrong as she could conceive of. *Why?* she asked. *Why?*

There was a silence from the mermaids. There was an answer to the question, one they'd thought about for a very long time. But it was very hard to wrestle with.

"*They need us,*" one of the mermaids said finally. "*They need us here, to keep the peace, to maintain the natural order of things. The world as we know it would collapse without us. We're not sure how it would happen, but we are sure it would.*"

Keep the peace? Laura asked, confused.

"*We can sense from your memories of the land the way it is there,*" a mermaid said. "*There, our people have their own Law over the sea and the water. It is their domain. You may not violate that covenant with their part of the land. We believe it is the same here. We are the custodians of the Law of the Sea. Yet we are custodians without any power or authority. That has been stripped from us. We are rulers of the sea in title only. The magicians have taken the power unto themselves.*"

So you are like heirs to a throne, which you have never received? Laura said thoughtfully. *Without you, the forces of chaos would overwhelm your domain. Yet they have imprisoned you, kept you here, and usurped your natural authority?*

"*So we have guessed,*" the mermaid said. "*It has been this way for so very long none of us know for sure what would happen if it were any different from the way it is. The magicians now rule the Sea as they see fit. They are the principalities and powers, and we have no say over what they do to it.*"

If I am able, Laura vowed, *I will change this. But I am just one against many. I can't promise I will succeed.*

"*We understand,*" the mermaids said. "*We can't even ask you to try on our behalf. But we are all grateful.*" One of the mermaids moved closer. She laid a gentle hand on Laura. "*Will you be all right?*"

Yes, with your help, I think so, Laura answered.

The mermaid, who was younger than the others and, as a result, less shy, gazed intently into Laura's eyes. "*If you are unable to help us regain our authority in this world, do you think you can at least help us return to our own world? Can you do that?*"

Anger and determination coursed through Laura's body at the same time. *If I am able, yes, I will do so. I will do everything within my power to make it happen.*

The young mermaid smiled. "*Then it will happen. For we, all of us, can tell that you could be as they are, yet you have chosen not to. You have clearly chosen to follow another path, one of service and not one of self-knowledge and power.*"

Laura blushed. No one had ever put it quite so clearly to her. But, yes, they were right. She was not like the magicians, who sought to manipulate the forces of nature for their own personal glory and gratification. She sought harmony with the world, not domination.

I will do what I can, Laura said again. *I promise you that. In return for my life, which you have saved, I will do everything in my power to make sure you return to your rightful world.*

"*That is all we can ask of you,*" the young mermaid said. "*To try.*"

But what of the other races? Laura asked, suddenly remembering the rest of her quest.

Again, there was a palpable sadness around her. "*They are trapped as well,*" the young mermaid said. "*If you can, you must help them. They are, more or less, prisoners as we are.*"

Can I find some of them, from here?

Blurred visions of places and people rushed at Laura all at once. They clearly had some knowledge of certain things. They knew where one of the entrances to the dwarves' domain could be found. They knew, generally, where the giants and elves lived. But they had no idea where the centaurs could be found. They had lost track of them. And they knew the fairies lived at Avalon. But they didn't know where that was.

Laura sorted through the visions. Samson and Regis were moving in the right direction. They would likely find the elves. She could only hope Jon would find the centaurs. She couldn't visit Avalon from here. So it was a choice between the giants and the dwarves.

Can you take me to the dwarves' entrance? she asked, making her decision.

"*No, we can't,*" the young mermaid said. "*It is too far, and too dangerous, for us. But there is another who can. Orca can take you there. He can get you there before Leviathan can catch you.*"

Orca. Is that…a killer whale?

"*Yes, but he will not harm you. Not if we ask him not to.*"

Laura was very still for a moment. *If you say so, I will do it,* she said at last. *I trust you.*

"*Then, when you have recovered, we will help you on your way,*" the young mermaid said. "*Only promise that you will come back and help us return to our own land.*"

If I am able, I will, Laura vowed.

23

***

THE KENTAUROS
OF MOUNT PELION

By the time the dark gray stallion had caught up to the other horses, Jon had recovered only a little. He would clearly be in pain for several days. It was possible the blow from the policeman had broken a rib or two. It was hard for Jon to tell. The pain was too great right now.

The bareback ride wasn't helping matters. Each time the horse's hooves touched the ground as it galloped, a wave of pain jarred through Jon's body.

But he suffered that pain gladly right now. This horse had just saved his life. Jon had no doubts about that. Without them, he would now be on a one-way trip to somewhere in the dark bowels of a Greek prison.

After a half hour or so of steady galloping, the pack of wild horses slowed to a brisk trot. They worked their way through the forest land at that pace deep into the night. Jon had no idea where he was being taken. Not that he cared much. As long as it was away from those policemen, anywhere was just fine with him.

When the pack finally slowed, Jon was nearly out. The combination of pain and lack of sleep had sapped nearly all strength and willpower.

When the horses came to a stop, Jon didn't notice the sound of the waterfall nearby, or the smell of the flowers, or anything else for that matter. He slipped from the back of the dark gray stallion and collapsed in a heap on the ground. He was fast asleep within seconds.

***

The sun was shining brilliantly overhead when Jon awoke the next morning. It winked at him through the leaves of the tree spreading out over him as Jon tried to move his head. He moved his body slightly to one side and nearly cried out from the pain. The entire mid-section of his body was in acute trauma. It felt inflamed. He gingerly placed a finger on his chest. Even that hurt.

426

His head was resting on a bed of ferns. Although the hot sun was helping, his body was still slightly chilled from having spent the night sleeping outdoors in the cold, night air without a blanket or some other covering.

But all of that seemed of little consequence to him right now. He was so overjoyed at being rescued that any pain or discomfort he felt was almost something to be savored.

Jon saw some movement out of the corner of his eye. Carefully, to keep the pain at a minimum, he looked over. It was one of the wild horses. They peered at each other.

A second horse ambled into view. Soon several others arrived. They approached Jon cautiously, almost as if they were in awe of him. Or, perhaps, they were terrified of him.

They didn't much act like wild horses. They weren't skittish. They didn't prance back and forth. They weren't nervous or pawing the ground anxiously. No, if anything, they appeared calm, rational, almost regal. They appeared *intelligent.*

The pack of horses stopped moving when they were about ten feet or so from the spot where Jon had collapsed the previous night. The horses parted slightly, in order to let another horse through.

The dark gray stallion that had saved Jon's life walked through the narrow opening afforded him by the other horses and walked slowly toward Jon, his hooves making almost no sound on the dense forest floor.

The stallion lowered his head and gazed down at Jon. Jon met his gaze. The horse did not blink; neither did it look away. They looked at each other like that for nearly a minute.

This is no ordinary horse, Jon concluded in that minute. *No ordinary creature on earth could hold the gaze of a man like that. It just isn't possible.*

"Who are you?" Jon asked finally.

The stallion turned his head, glancing at the others. As if on cue, the horses spread out and flowed around Jon and the gray stallion. Within seconds, they'd surrounded them in a full circle. The horses settled to the ground, resting on their haunches. The stallion looked back at Jon.

"Is that your answer?" Jon asked. "That you are a family, or that you are all related somehow, or that you are good listeners?"

The stallion nodded violently.

"That last one, that you are good listeners?"

The horse nodded again.

Jon's mind raced. *Can it really be true? Are these, then, the kentauros of Mount Pelion, perhaps transformed by the magicians?* Jon addressed the dark gray stallion. "You can truly understand what I'm saying?"

The horse nodded.

"And the other horses, can they understand me as well?" Jon gestured around the circle of horses.

They all nodded solemnly.

"But to the people of Mount Pelion, you are just ordinary horses?"

The gray stallion didn't respond.

"So there are some on Mount Pelion who know your true nature, that you are not, in fact, ordinary horses?"

The stallion nodded.

"Are there magicians on Mount Pelion?" Jon asked after a moment.

The horse hesitated, then nodded.

"And why do they remain here? To watch over you? Are they keeping you prisoners here? Have they turned you into ordinary horses so they can more easily keep an eye on you?"

The gray stallion nodded once and then hung his head slowly, as if in shame. A deep sadness pervaded this spot. It was so real Jon felt as if he could reach out and touch it.

Jon rose painfully to a sitting position. He felt only slightly foolish addressing a pack of wild horses in this manner, but he knew he was right. These were no horses. These were the long-vanished centaurs of Mount Pelion described in the myths and legends. He was certain of that.

"I have been to your own world," Jon said loudly so all the horses could hear. "I have been to the world you came from. I have visited with the centaurs there. We have discussed many things. They, you, are a proud and noble race. And I give you this pledge. In return for saving my life last night, I will do everything in my power—limited as it is—to help you return there. And, once you are back, there are now people of the land who can return you to your normal state."

The horses stirred. A few rose to their feet anxiously. The dark gray stallion's ears perked up. He looked back at Jon and jerked his head once, twice. He wanted Jon to get up.

Then Jon heard the ominous rumble of a helicopter. They'd tracked him, found him again. They would have to make yet another run for it. Jon groaned but wearily climbed to his feet, pain shooting into every corner of his body.

The gray stallion knelt, making it easier for Jon to climb aboard his back. He clutched at the horse's full mane. Once Jon was secure, the horse rose. Almost as one, the pack sped off through the forest.

Jon leaned his head forward until his mouth was close by the stallion's ears. "I must find the other races, first, before I can help you return to the land you come from," Jon half-yelled. "Can you help me find them?"

EL

The stallion reared his head back once and then resumed his galloping stride. Jon took that as an affirmative answer and settled in for the long ride. He would ask more questions later, when they'd arrived at their next destination.

The horses raced through the deep forest with practiced ease, like water flowing over and around the rocks in a stream. It was magnificent to behold. These were truly regal creatures.

No, they are not creatures, Jon thought. *They are centaurs and likely quite intelligent. Even though the magicians have shamed and dishonored them, they are centaurs nevertheless.*

24

***

THE ELVES' ISLAND

Never in his wildest dreams would Samson have imagined that simple, common starlings might hold the key to finding the long-lost race of elves on the Earth.

In Samson's childhood, starlings had been a bane and a curse. They settled on the corn at home, destroying much of it. They were loud, raucous, vile, and filthy. They were common, like rats.

But, somewhere in the back of his mind, Samson now dredged up an old memory of a school lesson somewhere about starlings. In Europe, starlings were once quite something as birds go. They were valued—as parrots are now—for their ability to mimic human speech. In fact, the famous composer Mozart once owned a starling and wrote an elaborate funeral dirge for it when the bird died.

And now, today, it seemed, starlings were still at it, mimicking humans. For Samson could hear snatches of words if he listened carefully. Through the squawks and screeches, even Samson's dull ears could pick up enough of the words to reach the same conclusion Regis had.

"Can you hear it, from over there?" Regis pointed toward one of the trees to the north.

Samson listened. "Hunting words?"

"That's it. And over there?" Regis gestured toward another tree. "Building a fire?"

Samson nodded.

Regis pointed to a third tree. "And, from there, talk of homes at the tops of trees?"

Samson nodded. "There's only one place I know of where people build their homes at the tops of the trees."

Regis smiled wistfully. "Yes, and I miss my home very much. For all I know, my son is now walking and talking…"

"No, it has been only a day or so. Surely, he hasn't grown much, even with the difference in time?"

"We shall see," Regis said quietly. "At any rate, it is worth the sacrifice if I can find my own people and help them return."

"We will, if I have anything to do with it." Samson clenched his fists.

"Well, we won't if we stand here all day listening to these birds." Regis laughed. "We need a boat. And a guide who can tell us where we may find these islands these birds keep repeating over and over."

"What islands?"

Regis concentrated on the birds' chatter. "Bornholm, I think. That's what it sounds like to me."

"Never heard of it, but I wasn't very good at geography," Samson said.

They weren't about to find a guide right now, though. Night was descending rapidly. So they decided to stay at the only local inn they'd seen and set out first thing in the morning.

Samson decided to spend a little of the money Laura had graciously bestowed on them to buy dinner downstairs in the quaint old tavern. Regis ate cautiously, as if he was expecting something.

After dinner, a few of the guests gathered around the fire across the room, smoking pipes, drinking steins of beer, or simply snoring peacefully in the overstuffed chairs set nearby. Samson and Regis wandered over as well. They discussed what they intended to do the next day, quietly, between themselves.

"The fire's warm, cozy. Makes you sleepy, doesn't it?" a gruff voice said from behind them. Samson and Regis whirled together, almost as one.

"Yes, it is, friend," Regis answered.

"I wouldn't use the term so loosely," the author of the gruff voice said lightly. "Friends are hard to come by in this world."

Standing before them—or, rather, balancing before them on one leg and then the other—was a spry, young man with dirty blond hair. His face was rugged. There was a jagged scar above the right eye. It looked as if a corner of one ear had been lopped off. Regis thought he caught sight of a warrior's vest beneath his shirt.

"You're right." Regis nodded slowly. "I should be more careful with my language."

"Yes, you should," the young man answered. "And you should take more care as to who might overhear your conversations."

Samson frowned. "What do you mean?"

"I mean, there are some who would like dearly to hear what you two were discussing," the man answered.

Samson bristled. "And how is it that you heard what we were talking about? We were speaking softly."

"Not softly enough. For I heard enough to know that you should be more careful about the words you throw around. There are some who would kill you if they heard what you've been discussing."

"And why is that?" asked Regis.

The young man shrugged. "Because there is a bounty on your heads, that's why. Someone's offering quite a tidy pot of gold for the two of you, if you showed up in this part of the world."

Samson's jaw dropped in stunned surprise. "A bounty on *our* heads?"

"Actually, *for* your heads," the young man answered intently. "The word has gone out. There are others who've been watching with one eye cocked. I'm surprised you made it through the day alive."

Samson grimaced. "We never suspected a thing."

"I can see that." The young man held out his hand. "Name's Tristan Kennerbie."

"Pleased to meet you, Tristan." Regis shook his hand.

"And I will be your guide." Tristan wiggled a brow. "For a fair price. I know where Bornholm is. And, perhaps, the mystery island you seek as well."

Regis and Samson glanced at each other. "You do?" Samson asked.

Tristan grinned. "Like I said, I overheard your conversation."

Regis was staring extraordinarily hard at Tristan now. "Your ears are awfully sharp."

"Always have been," Tristan acknowledged.

"And your other name, Kennerbie, do you know what that means?" Regis asked.

Tristan shrugged. "Nope. It's my last name. Given to me at birth. I never knew my father, though."

"You never knew your father?" Samson asked.

"Gone soon after I was born," Tristan said angrily. "I don't know a thing about him, other than that he left me his name and nothing else."

Regis glanced at Samson. "So you don't know what Kennerbie means, then?"

"No, should I?" Tristan asked wearily.

"No reason," Regis said cautiously. "It's just that it's an old, old name for a brave elf warrior."

Tristan laughed heartily. "An *elf* warrior? What in blue blazes is an elf?"

Regis smiled. "A noble race, some say."

"Well, glad to hear it, glad to hear it." Tristan hopped onto another leg. He never seemed to settle in one position for very long. "So are we off, or do you plan to just sit here gabbing all night long?"

"You want to leave right now?" Samson asked.

"Better to approach the island near Bornholm under the cover of darkness," Tristan whispered.

"Why?" asked Samson.

"Trust me, would you? The island has no name. It never has any visitors. And those who try to reach it never return, or so they say."

"Really?"

Tristan nodded. "During the second world war, when the Germans put up a fierce battle on Bornholm after the surrender, some tried to flee to this island. They were swallowed up and never seen again."

"And this is the island you want to take us to?" Samson asked.

"It's the island you were speaking of, I'm certain. There can be no other."

"And why are you so eager to take us there, if no one ever returns from it?" Samson asked suspiciously.

Tristan smiled. "Because that's the way I am. I like adventure. I'll try anything once. And I suspect that the stuff about the island swallowing you up is just some story, to spook people away."

"You'd go, even if it might mean your life?" Regis asked.

"I've been in scrapes before," Tristan said proudly. "No one's gotten the best of me yet."

Samson and Regis looked at each other. A silent communication and an assent passed between them.

"Then let's go." Regis rose from the confines of the deep sofa chair.

"Great," Tristan said. "My boat's docked 200 yards from here. We can set sail immediately."

The three of them left as unobtrusively as they could. They'd already paid for the night's lodging, so Samson felt no qualms about leaving so abruptly.

As they slipped away from the sleepy inn, though, two dark, bearded men rose from their positions before the fire and left as well. And yet a third man—a pale, gaunt man in a flowing robe—rose and trailed in their wake. The dark night swallowed them all.

25

***

AGARTTHA

The entrance to the place the legends obliquely referred to as Agarttha lay halfway across the Atlantic Ocean, well to the north of where Laura was now.

Thanks to the mermaids' kind ministering, Laura had recovered rapidly from her encounter with Leviathan. She was back to full strength.

The people of the sea loaded her down with provisions—enough fresh water to make the trip north, for instance, as well as various food items they grew and harvested in the ocean.

They had also recovered her pressurized suit from the wreckage of the sphere. Remarkably, it looked intact. Laura should at least be able to wear it when Orca the killer whale rose from the murky depths to the surface of the ocean.

Laura couldn't hold back the tears as she prepared to leave. Twice now she had journeyed to the domain of the people of the sea, first in their world and now in her own. On both occasions, they had been kind and generous and more than willing to share their deepest sorrows.

So it saddened her to say good-bye once again. And, if she was successful in her efforts, she would likely be saying good-bye forever to them as they made their way back to their own world. Laura could visit them, of course, but she doubted she ever would. Some things simply pass on, forever.

As they had promised, a huge killer whale had shown up and was now waiting rather calmly just on the outskirts of Atlantis. Every so often it flashed its huge teeth, and Laura shuddered a little.

"*Don't worry,*" the mermaids said. "*We have told him what to do. He won't harm you. We promise you that.*"

I trust you, Laura answered. And she did. But she still couldn't quell the fear she felt whenever she glanced over at the menacing creature that could manhandle every creature in the sea.

The provisions securely strapped to her back with some tough seaweed rope, Laura donned the helmet to the suit and eased her way through the water surrounding the bed upon which she'd rested. Several dolphins swam around her playfully. Laura stroked them with a gentle hand as they passed by. *Farewell, for now, my new friends,* Laura told the people of the sea when she reached the outskirts of Atlantis. *I will be back, if I am able.*

"*We know,*" they answered collectively. "*Godspeed.*"

Laura turned and half-swam, half-floated toward the huge killer whale. She grabbed the rope that the people of the sea had slipped over its neck and pulled herself onto the whale's back. The whale waited patiently until Laura was secure. Then, with several powerful thrusts of its tail, it was off, racing toward the surface. It was all Laura could do to hang on.

She spotted Leviathan within seconds after leaving Atlantis. The sea dragon had been lying in wait for them. Laura could feel the muscles in Orca bunch, preparing for battle. Laura frantically tugged on the rope around its neck, urging it to move off in the opposite direction.

Reluctantly, the killer whale responded to Laura's prompting. Its natural instinct was to engage the enemy. Every nerve and muscle clearly ached for a confrontation with the huge sea creature. But the people of the sea had, somehow, managed to make it clear to Orca that its first and only duty was to take Laura to her destination.

So the killer whale turned and raced toward a mountain range perhaps a half mile away. They reached the range scant seconds before Leviathan caught them.

Orca clearly knew this part of the ocean as well, or better, than the sea dragon. It quickly sped into a dark cave—one that proved too small for Leviathan to enter—and, after a few scary moments and a couple of twists and turns, emerged out the other side of the mountain.

Leviathan, hovering near the top of the mountain, caught sight of them and gave chase again. But the killer whale had now put more than a mile between the two of them. They raced like that for nearly an hour and the end of Laura's oxygen supply in her suit, with the killer whale taking evasive action when it needed to and the sea dragon then forced to follow as best as it could.

Clearly, Leviathan had its own marching orders: to seek and destroy. Laura had no doubt about that. The magicians now felt sufficiently threatened by the direction Laura was headed and had clearly made the decision to remove her from the picture entirely.

Well, I think I am prepared, Laura told herself grimly. *I know what I have to do now to break their stranglehold on this world. I must free the races and help them return to their own rightful world. It will unleash the forces of chaos, but if that's what it takes, so be it.*

Obviously, the magicians knew this as well, hence their strong desire to end her quest as rapidly as possible. The apt student was not what they'd hoped, and a new plan was necessary.

Orca finally managed to lose the sea dragon completely when it sped into a huge crevice at one point, doubled back when it was out of sight, emerged more than a mile *behind* the sea dragon, worked its way around the other side of a mountain range and then fled several miles in the opposite direction.

It was quite a maneuver, and Laura applauded it. She thumped the killer whale on the back several times, not quite sure if the whale could even feel it or appreciate the sentiment.

Once it was sure it had left the sea dragon behind for good, Orca rose to the surface—where Laura would not have to rely on her oxygen tanks—and began to work its way due north. Laura took her cumbersome helmet off. They plowed straight ahead for hours. In all directions, as far as the eye could see, there was ocean. It never changed.

Laura soon found that she was able to doze fitfully as the whale sped along. Its powerful stroke propelled them through the water rapidly, leaving a large wake, but it was a relatively smooth ride. And the whale's back was broad enough that Laura could rest her head and sleep without too much fear of falling off. She lashed herself to the rope around the whale's neck, though, just to make sure.

After two days of traveling like this, an island, or a land mass, came into sight. Its perimeter was dotted by what appeared to be a vast mountain range. The peaks were snow-capped.

Orca slowed a little as it approached the land. When it was several hundred yards away from the shoreline, it came to a complete halt. It didn't move. It was clearly waiting for something.

"Oh, I get it," Laura said out loud, clapping her hands once she'd figured it out. "You want me to put my helmet back on." She quickly donned the helmet and turned the suit back on. The whale descended again, rapidly. It came to a halt again near the bottom of the ocean floor, next to a gaping hole.

Thousands and thousands of air bubbles rushed madly from the hole and rose again to the surface. Laura had absolutely no idea at all what this might be, but it was clearly where the whale had intended to bring her.

Laura let go of the rope and inched toward the hole. It wasn't easy. The current of bubbles rushing out at her was extraordinarily strong. It was hard to move forward against it.

The whale waited patiently until Laura had reached the edge of the hole. Once she was there, it raced off without looking back. It had fulfilled his duty. Now there was dinner to be caught and eaten.

As Laura's eyes adjusted to the murky darkness, she groped her way along the tunnel. Even through the gloves on her suit, Laura could feel a powerful thrumming on the tunnel walls. It was an ominous sound.

Laura moved forward. It was hard, hard going. The current of air bubbles grew stronger as she neared the source of the powerful thrumming. She literally had to put her head down and make each step count.

After almost half an hour of this, Laura was finally able to see what was both making the noise she felt through tunnel walls and what was causing the massive torrent of air bubbles. Directly in front of her was the largest fan she had ever seen. The propeller blades were easily 50 feet in length. The air it was pushing out must have been quite hot, because Laura could feel her suit warm, even though she was quite a distance from the monstrous fan.

It appeared to be an air duct. Very hot air was obviously being forced out through the duct, for whatever reason, which in turn caused all the air bubbles to go rushing along the tunnel.

Clearly, this was not the entrance to Agarttha. But, perhaps, there was *no* entrance to the place. Perhaps this was the only available option.

As Laura approached the duct, she could see no way past the propeller blades. They whirled furiously, with no room to squeeze by them without being cut to ribbons. Her suit, meanwhile, was rapidly becoming a pressure cooker. If she didn't make it past this duct soon, Laura felt certain her suit would either melt or explode. She had to do something.

The heat was nearly unbearable when she was right next to the duct. Curiously, the fiercest pressure from the air bubbles wasn't right up close to the duct; it was slightly away from it, where the bubbles formed. Up close, it was desperately hot, but Laura was more able to move freely.

Her mind now was almost paralyzed from the heat. The propeller blades deafened her. Laura examined the bottom of the duct. At the outer edge, there was only rock. No metal. And there were crevices in the rock. Not large enough to squeeze into, but perhaps...

Laura quickly turned away from the propeller and headed back the way she'd come. She had seen some large, loose boulders along the tunnel as she'd made her way. If she could push one of them forward, it just might do the trick.

She chose a boulder that was half as tall as she was. Above ground, Laura would not have been able to move such an object. But here, under water, she was able to propel it forward. When she'd gotten the boulder in position, right in front of one of the crevices at the edge of the duct, Laura took a deep breath and then inched the boulder forward. She wasn't quite certain what would happen next, but she had no other choice.

There was a terrible, shuddering crunch when one of the propellers struck the boulder. The boulder splintered, spraying shards in all directions. One of them ricocheted off of Laura's face plate.

With a colossal heave, the propeller blades came to a halt. The boulder held them in check. Laura didn't hesitate. Knowing it might hold for only seconds, she swiftly moved through an opening that had now appeared between the immobilized propeller blades.

Just as she reached the other side of the duct, a grinding crunch resounded from behind her. The boulder broke in half, and the propeller began to whirl again.

But Laura made it through safely. That was all that mattered. Yet, in the back of her mind, Laura wondered what signal she had just sent by stopping the massive blades, if only for a moment. Who now knew where she was and who would come for her? The dwarves, or the enemy?

26

* * *

ON THE WINGS
OF EAGLES

Jon thought he'd known pain before. He was wrong. Nothing he'd experienced could match the pain in every corner of his body as he slipped from the dark gray stallion's back in yet another part of the forest at the top of Mount Pelion.

The noonday sun was high in the sky. The horses had run for miles before stopping at the creek bed beneath a thick stand of trees.

Jon gratefully gulped water from the creek, along with all the horses. His stomach rumbled from hunger. He hadn't had a good meal since breakfast the day before, and his body protested loudly. He lay back in the tall grass around the creek and stared at the blue sky. There wasn't a cloud in sight. If he wasn't in such pain and there wasn't a contingent of police out looking for him, Jon would have been content to just lie where he was for the rest of the lazy afternoon. But he had no time to rest. He wouldn't be able to rest, in fact, until their quest was finished.

Jon wondered how the others were doing, if they'd had any luck. They really didn't have much of a master plan. They were so few, against so many. It seemed rather hopeless. But Jon didn't have much choice. He had to go on.

The gray stallion settled to the ground near him. He folded his legs under him and remained there that way, alert, listening for any approaching danger.

Jon closed his eyes for a moment. How he desperately wanted to sleep for an eternity. But that wasn't possible right now. When he opened his eyes, the rest of the horses were still milling around, taking occasional drinks from the creek bed.

Jon looked over at the gray stallion. "Tell me. Who do the animals serve on this world? Who are their masters?"

The stallion shook his head. Either they had none, or Jon was asking the wrong question.

Jon tried again. "Do they serve the magicians?"

The stallion shook his head, more slowly. So the answer was "no," but only barely so.

"But the magicians have quite a bit of control over them, is that it?"

The stallion nodded.

"I see," mused Jon. "So the animals serve no one. But doesn't humankind have dominion over the creatures of the Earth. Isn't that so?"

The stallion nodded once, but quite slowly.

Jon thought he knew the answer. "But the magicians have destroyed all that, or they've tried to. They've tried to usurp the relationship established between humankind and the creatures of the Earth, is that it?"

The gray stallion nodded vigorously. Jon was clearly on the right track now.

"To the magicians, wanton cruelty to animals and needless slaughtering is okay? Anything goes?"

The horse nodded again.

"Humankind isn't given the chance anymore to thoughtfully and carefully manage the creatures of the earth?"

Another nod.

"But why?" Jon asked, more to himself than to the stallion. "Why would they destroy? What purpose does it serve?"

But Jon knew the answer to that already. At least, he knew it in his heart. He would never truly know the grand nature or balance of good and evil. But he could see enough bits and pieces to understand that where one built and created and nurtured, the other destroyed and maimed and tortured.

Laura had once said there was an emerging new law of physics, something about a positive force in almost eternal conflict with a destructive force. You couldn't have matter without both. Jon didn't know about that. But he did know that when the destructive side of that equation began to tip, then chaos would surely follow in its wake.

Jon wondered often now whether he and the others had, in fact, been sent as destructive forces in the land. And then, by some unseen guiding hand or force, they had been given the chance to see their own self-interested folly in time. But in time for what? That was the question that nagged at Jon.

The stallion looked up at the trees. His eyes opened a little. Jon looked up as well. He was startled to see a rather large bird with a huge wingspan settle onto one of the branches above. It was an eagle.

"Are there eagles in Greece?" Jon asked.

The stallion shook his head and continued to stare skyward.

Jon gazed up high, off to one side of the sun. There were some dark specks up there, well up in the sky. As Jon continued to watch, the specks became bigger. There were dozens of them. They continued to grow larger.

Jon watched in fascination as the specks became large enough for him to discern what they were. His heart nearly stopped beating when he recognized them. It just didn't seem possible.

Dozens of eagles rushed straight at him, seemingly from the depths of heaven. They swooped straight down from above.

Jon knew that eagles were soloists. They rarely traveled together. So this made no sense, none whatsoever. Something truly extraordinary was going on here.

The horses gathered around Jon and stared skyward as well, watching as the eagles tore to the earth. When they finally arrived, they all settled into the trees surrounding Jon and the horses. They stood there on the branches, silent, unmoving sentries. They were clearly waiting for something.

And then Jon heard it—the loud whirring of propeller blades. A dark green helicopter appeared on the horizon. A second appeared, then a third. After that, perhaps a dozen more appeared.

They've sent half of the Greek military after me. I am doomed, now. There is no way out. This is the end.

Jon rose to his feet wearily to face his inevitable fate. There was no point in racing away again with the horses. They would only find him again.

The eagles stirred in the branches above him. One of them spread its wings and lifted off from the branch. More eagles lifted off and circled lazily over Jon.

When all the eagles were aloft and circling overhead, Jon began to think the impossible. *Are these creatures about to…?*

And then they did. As one, the eagles dropped down to the earth. Without fighting or clawing for space, as if they'd practiced this drill before, a dozen eagles descended on Jon and clutched at him. Their talons locked onto his clothing. A dozen more eagles joined the first wave once Jon was airborne.

There had been no time to say good-bye to the horses. "I'll be back," Jon called out to them as the eagles rose slowly toward the sky. "I promise."

The eagles who now carried Jon aloft were joined by still more eagles, who flew alongside them. Jon had no idea where they were taking him. But he didn't care. As long as it was away from those ominous helicopters, anywhere was fine.

27

* * *

BORNHOLM

The night was chilly, especially out on the Baltic Sea with the wind whipping around. Samson wished he'd thought to bring a heavier coat with him, or at least a blanket to keep him warm. He was huddling at the back of the boat, out of the wind. Regis was sitting beside him.

For some reason, Regis didn't seem to be as cold as Samson. Perhaps it was because he was still studying Tristan, who was standing, guiding the boat. Tristan had been the only smart one. He'd worn a heavy, wool coat.

Regis leaned over toward Samson. "I don't think he knows where he came from."

"Who...Tristan?"

"Yes, who else?" Regis glowered.

"Beats me. I can't always tell with you."

Regis frowned. "We have Kennerbies back in the land. Tristan's father is probably descended from them, I'll bet."

Samson nodded. "Most likely."

"And I don't think Tristan has the foggiest idea he's half-elf."

Samson looked over at Tristan and grinned. "You're right. He seems oblivious to that notion."

"So what do you think he was doing, Tristan's father?"

"Trying to escape, most likely." Samson shrugged. "They probably caught him and took him back."

"Escape? Why, escape?"

Samson shivered once as an especially nippy draft sped by. "No reason, other than the fact that this reminds me of what men locked up in jails act like when they've escaped. They run to the nearest town, have a good time, then they're captured and dragged back."

Regis was horrified. "So you think the elves are held prisoners on this island, against their will?"

"Sure, why not?"

"Because...because they're elves!" Regis stammered. "They wouldn't do that."

"What if they have no choice in the matter?"

"But they'd have to have a choice. They're immune to magic."

"They are immune to magic on your world," Samson cautioned. "Here, the rules are different. There are, most likely, other ways to keep the elves rounded up in one place."

Regis clenched his fists. "If what you say is true, this is monstrous. Never, in their darkest hours, did the magicians think of imprisoning my people. They did some pretty dastardly things to us, but they never threatened our freedom."

"Well, I hate to say it, but this is old hat on planet Earth. People get brutalized and locked up and even *exterminated* all the time."

"Exterminated?"

"Sure. Some government decides a whole race of people shouldn't be around and, presto, they're rounded up and gassed, shot, murdered, you name it."

"That really happens here?" Regis asked, horrified.

"Sure does." The burning knot in Samson's stomach tightened again as he thought of the fate of his own people, the Armenians, so long ago. So many of his own people had lost their lives in that bitter struggle. Needlessly.

"I'm not sure I like your world much, Samson. It is beautiful, yes, and has wonders. But it seems so violent, so wantonly cruel. There seems to be no respect for life."

"Oh, it isn't all that bad." But Samson defended his world half-heartedly.

Regis stood and stretched. "I don't know. It seems pretty awful to me."

"Where are you going?" Samson shivered.

"Nowhere. I just thought I'd limber up my limbs a little."

"Find a blanket for me, would you? I'm freezing."

Despite the chilly winds, the water was relatively calm. Tristan's boat made good time as it chugged through the water. There was enough wind that he was able to use the sails to complement the boat's small engine, so they seemed to be making excellent time. They would be at Bornholm before the sun rose.

Samson caught a few winks well into the night. Not many, but enough so that he wasn't totally groggy by the time they'd arrived. Regis had gotten some sleep too. Tristan had stood at the helm through the night. Samson was amazed at the man's stamina.

"Land ho," Tristan called out, jarring the two of them from their fitful sleep.

They both jumped to their feet. Samson rubbed his arms vigorously as he walked toward the helm. "I don't see anything," Samson said when he was standing by Tristan's side. It all still seemed pitch-black to him.

"It's out there, trust me," Tristan said confidently. "We'll beach in about five minutes, I'd guess."

"If you say so." Samson shrugged.

"The two of you had better arm yourself now, while you have the chance," Tristan warned.

"Arm ourselves?"

"I have no idea what we're walking into. Better to be prepared for the worst."

"You have weapons on board?"

Tristan cocked an eye in Samson's direction. "Are you witless, man? Didn't you hear what I just said?"

"I heard," Samson snapped. "It's just that my body is numb, I'm so cold. I guess I hadn't really thought that we'd have to fight or anything."

"So what *did* you think would happen when we got to this island?"

"I guess I hadn't thought about it."

"Well, think about it now," Tristan said forcefully, "and arm yourself. The weapons are in the hold."

"Weapons," Samson muttered as he walked back toward Regis. "Tristan said we should arm ourselves."

Regis nodded thoughtfully. "Probably a good idea."

They both dropped lightly through the opening. It was very dark, and it took a second for their eyes to adjust. Samson looked around him. The place was, indeed, chock full of weapons—cutlasses, broadswords, lances, knives, you name it. The man came prepared.

Samson took one of the broadswords. He turned it over in his hands, examining the handiwork. "This will do for me."

Regis had grabbed one of the lighter, pointed swords. "And this will do for me."

They glanced around again to make sure some weapon of choice hadn't escaped their gaze. Satisfied, they pulled themselves back up through the opening and joined Tristan at the helm. The dark outline of a coastline edged into view.

"There's your island," Tristan said proudly.

They all stared straight ahead, into the dark stillness. Tristan had turned off the engine and pulled it up. They were drifting toward shore in silence, using the sails.

Tristan whirled and disappeared into the hold. He emerged an instant later carrying a sword similar to the one Regis now carried.

There was a sliding, scraping sound from beneath the boat as the nose edged onto what must have been a sandy beach. A moment later, the boat shuddered to a stop as the bulk settled onto the shoreline.

Tristan quickly and expertly heaved an anchor over the side to secure the boat. He turned toward his passengers. "Are we ready?" he asked, brandishing his sword.

Regis and Samson nodded grimly. Tristan nodded back, threw a rope ladder over the side, and then clambered after it. Regis and Samson followed close behind.

The island was silent as a tomb. No bird calls or animal noises of any kind. It was as if the island was collectively holding its breath, waiting for something to happen.

The three of them started walking toward the tree line. They couldn't really see much. There was no moon to speak of. Dark clouds covered most of the sky.

Regis stopped in his tracks. "I heard something. Did you?"

Samson shook his head. "No, but your ears are better than mine. What did you hear?"

"A clinking, I think." He gestured to his right. "From the trees over there."

Samson and Tristan stood very still, listening. "I don't hear anything," Samson growled.

"I do," Tristan said quietly.

"I do as well," Regis agreed.

Tristan and Regis looked at each other. "I hear quite a few people in that forest." Tristan sighed.

"As do I," Regis said.

"I'd say we were badly outnumbered."

"It's too late to run now," Regis whispered. "We'll have to stand and fight."

Samson hadn't heard a thing, of course, but he trusted that Regis and Tristan had, indeed, heard something. He gripped the broadsword tightly. *So this is it. I've managed to avoid hand-to-hand combat ever since I heard of this confounded land, and now I probably have no choice. Can I take a human life? Can I?*

There was a blood-curdling yell from the forest, followed by a second, a third, and then too many to count. Instinctively, Samson, Regis, and Tristan quickly formed a triangle, their backs to each other.

Dark, savage men descended on them like a pack of wolves. Samson saw instantly that these were no elves. These were men of battle, scarred and combat-tested, much like Tristan. They were, most likely, paid mercenaries seeking the bounties on their heads.

The first few of them foolish enough to rush in paid dearly for their efforts. One ran away howling in pain as Tristan nearly lopped off his hand. Regis cut two others badly. Samson clubbed two more with the flat of his heavy blade.

"Go for the kill," Tristan yelled at Samson. "Use the edge, man."

Samson blanched and then rotated the blade a quarter turn in his hand. Tristan was right. He was fighting for his life now. There would be blood spilled.

The men circled more warily now. They didn't rush in headlong to certain death. There seemed to be a dozen or so, enough to overwhelm the three eventually.

"Lay down your arms," one of them called out.

"No," Tristan declared.

"Then you will all die," another said.

"So be it," Tristan flung back.

Two of them rushed at Tristan. He parried expertly. His blade flashed and cut another. The others scurried back.

Two others came at Regis, who also wielded his sword expertly. He parried both easily and drove them back.

Nearly half the group, though, rushed at Samson, attempting to overwhelm him and expose their backs. If they could break through one, they would achieve victory, and Samson seemed the likely candidate because he was forced to step forward a little in order to swing his broadsword.

But Samson stepped into battle, and his instincts took over. He found himself slipping into a savagery he'd only experienced on rare occasions. Samson's muscles bulged as he swung the sword back and forth, clanging through the swords thrust at him. The sword struck home once, twice, three times, cutting deeply, though not mortally. The men fell back. Samson pressed forward. The men fell back.

Samson realized an instant after it was too late that he'd been suckered. He'd pressed forward so far that his back was now exposed. In an instant, one of the men slipped behind him. Samson tried to whirl, but not in time.

A sword flashed through the dark night. The point pierced Samson's back, just beneath his left shoulder blade. The sword plunged deep, near his heart, and then came out his front. The man twisted the sword viciously and then pulled it free.

Samson collapsed in a heap. The sword had done major damage, perhaps even struck his heart. Blood gushed from the open wound in his chest. Samson knew he would die within moments. There wasn't even time to say farewell to Regis.

There was movement from the forest. Samson was able to turn his head slightly as he slipped into unconsciousness. Dozens of warriors raced toward him. As they neared, Samson could see they were wielding knives and cutlasses.

They were blond-haired, slight, and limber. They ran swiftly and joined the battle silently. The elves had arrived and were joining the battle against the mercenaries. Tristan cheered lustily.

But it was too late for Samson. He managed to smile weakly as the elves arrived, his grip on life fading rapidly.

The arrival of the elves proved to be the undoing of the mercenaries. They were routed within moments and ran back toward the cover of the forest. Many of the elves pursued them soundlessly.

Samson tried to say something, but his voice was too dry. No words were forthcoming. He began to have trouble seeing. His last memory was of firm hands lifting him onto something, and then he fell into the darkness, the last of his huge willpower failing him.

28

* * *

THE UNDERGROUND CITY

Laura quickly climbed out of the pressurized suit and tossed it against the wall, near the whirring, thrumming propeller blades. She was soaked with sweat. It was murderously hot here. *How in the world could anyone last down here?*

As she began to walk along the corridor, away from the blades, Laura looked around her. The walls of solid rock were easily 50 feet high before they reached the ceiling. The corridor was alive with an orange glow of some sort, which made it easier to see as she walked along.

It was quite difficult to breathe. The air was so heavy and blazing hot. It was like trying to breathe in a sauna, or a large furnace room. Laura was nearly gasping for air after only a half mile or so.

The corridor started to slope downward. The slope was slight at first, but as she walked, it grew steeper. After another half mile or so, it was all Laura could do to keep from running downward.

Laura was paying such close attention to what she was doing, she didn't notice the fork in the road or the smallish, hunched-over figure sitting patiently, his back against the wall near that fork, until she was right on him. The person hadn't said a word as Laura approached him. He'd waited, patiently.

"Well, it's about time," this person said when Laura was close.

Laura nearly jumped out of her skin. Every nerve bristled and jangled. But then she recognized him. It was Jon, a little bedraggled, but a welcome sight down here in the bowels of the earth. He looked different, somehow. A little gaunt, perhaps. He wouldn't meet Laura's gaze, which was unusual for Jon. But Laura was still glad to see a friendly face, at last.

"Wha…what are *you* doing down here?" she asked, amazed and so overwhelmed at seeing a friendly face that she nearly collapsed from relief.

"I've been waiting for you," Jon said with a warm smile.

"But how'd you know where to find me?" Laura asked.

"Oh, we thought you'd come this way, after you'd visited the creatures of the sea."

"We?"

"The king of the elves and I," Jon said quickly.

"Regis?"

"Yes, Regis and I."

"I found them, you know," Laura said excitedly. "The people of the sea and Atlantis…"

"We know," Jon said softly.

"They're trapped, prisoners down at the bottom of the sea. The magicians…"

"Can we be on our way?" Jon interrupted. "We have some distance to travel."

Laura's mouth snapped shut. Jon was awfully impatient. He seemed a little out of sorts, not the usual Jon. But, then, anyone was bound to be out of sorts in this place. "So how did you fare?" she asked him. "Did you find the centaurs? And where is Regis, anyway? I thought he was with Samson?"

"Samson and Regis are waiting for us, up ahead." Jon turned to walk down the slope to the left. He beckoned for Laura, urging her to follow. She never saw the path to the right. "They found the elves and joined up with me after I'd found the centaurs."

Laura hurried to catch up. "Were the elves where we thought?"

"More or less."

"And how are they? Did they tell you anything?"

"They told us nothing, and they are as arrogant as ever," Jon snarled.

Laura began to pant slightly as she tried to keep up with Jon's brisk pace. He was barely breathing hard. When Laura looked up at Jon quickly once, he almost seemed to moving more quickly than he actually was, which seemed strange. "And the centaurs, did you speak to them?"

"Yes, I spoke to them."

"Were they helpful?"

"Not particularly."

"Well, how did you find me, then?" Laura asked, slightly confused.

"The centaurs did tell me where you'd be, at least," Jon said, looking straight ahead.

"Well, that was something."

Jon didn't answer. He picked up his pace. Laura was nearly running now to keep up. "Would you slow down a little?" she pleaded finally.

"We must hurry."

"But why?"

"We have so little time, and such a long distance to go."

"Please," Laura begged, "I must rest. I'm nearly suffocating from the heat down here."

"No," Jon said sharply. "We have no time to rest."

"But I *have* to, Jon," Laura said, nearly in tears from exhaustion. The road before her was so wide, so huge, so long, forever sloping downward, Laura felt as if she might never reach her destination.

"Don't you know that in a race, all the runners compete, but only one receives the prize?" Jon called out to her. "Losing is such a disgrace. It's humiliating. So come on."

"I'm not a loser," Laura protested. "I just want to rest. And isn't that from the Bible, that running the race thing? I can't remember you doing that, quoting from the Bible to make a point…"

"Please hurry!" Jon almost yelled. "There is no time. We must keep moving."

Laura stopped in her tracks. She wasn't moving an inch further. "Are you sure about that winning and losing stuff?" she asked him. "I don't think you have that quite right. You've…you've gotten its meaning wrong, somehow."

"Oh, it's right," Jon promised. "It's the way I see it."

"Then you twisted it around a little, because I don't think it's a disgrace—or humiliating—to lose."

"Oh, and you're the expert?" Jon sneered.

"No, but I do have a pretty good memory." Fear fluttered in the pit of her stomach. "Or have you forgotten?"

"No, I haven't forgotten," Jon growled. "Can we be on our way, then? We'll go slower, I promise."

Laura took a deep breath. Despite the intense heat, the tips of her fingers were a little numb from the fear that crept into every part of her body. "Why are you in such a hurry?"

"Because we have to get there," Jon insisted.

"Get *where*?"

"To where we're going."

"And where is that?"

"Our destination, of course." Jon frowned. "Samson and Regis are waiting. We must get there, before more damage is done. We must…"

"How is it that you were able to free the centaurs?" Laura asked abruptly. "The people of the sea are still imprisoned. I couldn't change that."

"Oh, once we'd arrived, they realized they could leave anytime they wanted to. The chains were in their minds."

"Just like that?"

"Just like that," Jon said breezily. "Now, can we be on our way?"

"No," Laura said firmly. "I'm not going another inch."

Jon turned to face Laura. "What do you mean, you're not going any further?"

His eyes now blazed with a coldness Laura had never seen before.

"You heard me."

"But why? I've asked you to come with me. We *must* be on our way. Why won't you come with me?"

Laura took one tentative step backwards, then a second. "Because," she said softly, the word almost a whisper of defiance.

"STOP!" Jon bellowed at the top of his lungs. The word echoed in the corridor, reverberating back and forth.

Laura now stared at Jon in utter horror. Was it her imagination, or was Jon beginning to grow, change shape, his presence looming ever larger in the passageway? Without another word, Laura swiveled away from Jon, his command still echoing in her ears.

The precise instant she turned her back on Jon and sprinted back up the wide corridor, the landscape changed. In the blink of an eye, Laura found herself running madly along a straight, narrow path on a rock ledge that stretched out over a yawning abyss.

"*No one* turns away from Abaddon! Return to me!" the voice yelled.

The intensity of the command nearly caused Laura to lose her footing. She gasped but did not stop. She had this horrible feeling that, if she stopped, she would have to face whatever it was that was now behind her as well as what it had been leading her toward.

But the task in front of her was nearly as terrifying. For the path Laura now found herself on was anything but safe. It was straight and narrow, yes, but it was also a dizzying mile or so above a molten-red lake of some sort. Flames leaped high from the surface of the lake. It wouldn't do to fall from here.

Laura tried to quell her fear. Planting each foot securely in front of the other, she did her best not to stumble. Within moments, she was able to make out some blurry shapes in front of her. Soon she saw that it was a crowd of people. Little people. Dozens of dwarves waited for her.

But there was no time to hesitate, or wonder if they were friend or foe. Laura rushed forward, mindless of her safety now. She had only one goal in mind—to reach the other side safely, without plunging over the side into the lake of fire.

She fairly flew the last few steps along the narrow ledge. She took two steps onto a wide opening where the dwarves were gathered and then collapsed into their arms. Quickly, not wasting a moment, the dwarves picked Laura up and carried her away from the narrow ledge.

Laura closed her eyes. She didn't care what happened next. Nothing, she figured, could be worse than the shape-shifting nightmare she'd just escaped.

29

***

AVALON

The only time Samson had ever felt quite this peaceful was during his school days, on Saturday, when he could sleep until noon without having to worry about getting up and blindly stumbling out in the dark to where the bus always picked him up.

This reminded him of those glorious Saturdays. He slept, woke up, slept, and woke up. He never really opened his eyes to see what was going on around him. He didn't care. All he wanted to do was sleep. Nothing else seemed nearly as important.

While he slept, he had the strangest sensation of people poking, pulling, and prodding on various parts of him, mostly in his chest. But Samson didn't care. Nothing mattered much to him.

He also had the eerie feeling, at times, that there were hundreds, perhaps thousands, of eyes staring at him. They just stared, neither malevolently nor with mischievous intent.

Samson dreamt of many things as he slept. He remembered almost none of it. The dreams were pleasant and peaceful and soothing. That's all he knew or cared about.

He began to hear voices. Or, rather, the voices started to come at him, almost as if someone was standing directly outside his ear and whispering words of encouragement and inspiration to him. The words seemed to march directly from his ear canal to his brain.

They were kind and gentle words. Samson remembered none of them, of course, but he vaguely remembered their nature. They urged Samson to do something. He couldn't quite grasp what, but they incessantly urged him to do *something*.

He also had a vague memory of some great pain. He didn't remember much of it, but there was enough of it that it lodged somewhere near the back of his mind, away from the pleasant sensations of sleep, dreams, and soothing conversation.

Samson had tried, rather unsuccessfully, to move his arms. His left arm, especially, was completely immobile, almost as if someone had parked a Mack truck on top of it. But now he had some feeling back in his strong, right arm.

After planning and figuring how to do it for what seemed like hours, Samson finally managed to move his right arm toward the sky. The first raw sensation of pain coursed through his body. He bellowed loudly. There were a few squeaks, followed by three small thumps nearby. *It probably wasn't a good idea to move so quickly,* Samson thought briefly. *But at least I tried.* However, before he could file the pain in his weary brain, Samson instantly fell into another deep slumber.

His dreams were vivid. In one, Samson was defending himself and two others on a strange island. He was surrounded by dark, bearded, fierce men. They attacked relentlessly. He was stabbed and mortally wounded.

But then the dream changed, and Samson wondered why he felt no pain. *Surely, death must involve great pain.* He'd always thought so. But in his dream, at the moment of what seemed like sure death, there was no pain.

In fact, there was no memory of anything, neither pain nor regret. So it raised odd questions: *If, at our death, we cannot experience the pain, what does that mean? Was the pain only a function of our ability to remember it? And if we are unable to remember it, was there ever any pain to begin with? Was it a memory the world foisted on us all?*

Samson didn't ponder these questions long. They just sort of drifted in and out of his dream about the fierce warriors and his vain efforts to fend them off.

Finally, Samson had the strongest desire to scratch his knee. At first, it nagged at the edges of his consciousness. But, over time, it grew to an intense longing. Oh, how desperately he wanted to scratch his knee!

He plotted how he would do so. First, he would focus all his energies on one, big effort to move his good, right arm in that direction. Then he would give a Herculean heave and hope the hand landed somewhere nearby. And, assuming it did, he would quickly search for the spot on his knee that was causing him so much irritation and grapple with it.

All went as planned. His arm was ready, his mind focused. He felt the spot where he wanted his arm to descend. Ready, set, go, lift the arm, bringing it high, down onto the landing spot…

"Hey!" a small, muffled voice yelled at him.

Samson grunted. He'd been successful. His hand had found the mark. But there was something soft and pudgy, like a lump of a cookie dough, between his hand and the spot on his knee he was attempting to scratch.

"Get your big, galumphing hand *off* of me!" the little voice bellowed a second time. "And *warn* me next time you decide to do that!"

Samson's eyes fluttered once, twice, three times. He tried to open them. He was singularly unsuccessful.

"Oh, don't even bother to try to open your eyes," a second small voice said. "It won't work. You're still too weak. Give it some time. You'll get there eventually."

Samson obeyed. He fell asleep instantly, forgetting for the moment his grand success at moving his arm and the need to scratch his knee.

When he awoke again, the need to scratch his chest was nearly overpowering. There was a burning sensation across the left side of his chest, quite similar to the feeling he got as a youth when he'd laced his sneakers up too tight.

But, here, there were no laces to loosen. He'd just have to grow accustomed to the tightness and the burning he now felt in his chest. Samson practiced forgetting about the burning. It didn't work very well. The only way he could successfully forget about it was to go back to sleep, which he'd now grown quite proficient at doing.

There came a time, though, when Samson knew he could open his eyes, if only he tried hard enough. At first, he didn't have much desire to do so. He wanted to stay where he was. It was so calm, so peaceful. He just knew that, once he'd opened his eyes, everything would change. The world would change from light to dark, as it always did.

But he *really* did want to open his eyes, no matter what he might see when they were open. Dreaming and sleeping and hiding and avoiding were fine, up to a point. But Samson could feel himself growing restless, almost by the minute. He had to open his eyes.

His eyelids fluttered again. They blinked once. There was a commotion of movement all around him—whirrings and flutterings and small squeaks and thumps and all sorts of odd little sounds like that.

Samson didn't pay much attention to this. He was concentrating all his energies on attempting to keep his eyelids open for longer than a fraction of a second.

He felt more thumps all around him. He heard murmurings, like an army of small whispers. He paid more attention to them. They were helping him, somehow. Samson *wanted* to see what was going on around him.

He opened his eyes. They stayed open. He didn't fall back into his somnambulant stupor. And then the colors struck him—dazzling, blinding yellow and orange and deep blue and purple and pink. There were so many colors, all around him.

And then, as his eyes adjusted, he saw the others—dozens of tiny, plump, little people with constant whirring wings, all gazing intently up at him. They were perched all around him, on top of the colors, in the colors, behind the colors.

"So you're awake," one of the fairies said with an exasperated sigh. "It's about time! We were wondering if you'd *ever* wake up."

Samson didn't respond. He wasn't sure he could, even if he'd wanted to. It took everything he had just to keep his eyes focused on the sight before him.

After a bit, Samson was able to determine that the colors were actually part of the landscape. They looked to be like clouds. There wasn't much else in his "room." Only the clouds, colors, and the fairies.

"Go back to sleep," a third voice urged. "There will be time for explanations later."

Again, Samson didn't fight. He obeyed without thinking, closed his eyes, and drifted off to sleep. But the next time, he would keep his eyes open. And he would speak. There were things he wanted to know.

* * *

He was successful on the second attempt. Actually, it wasn't all that difficult. He had plenty of time to plan his strategy. He steeled himself for the attempt and then opened his eyes. The fairies were all still there, waiting.

"So, are you back for good this time?" asked a fairy, who was planted squarely on Samson's chest, looking up at him.

Samson opened his mouth to speak. Nothing emerged. He tried again. A croak came forth, and nothing else. He tried a third time. "I think so," came the guttural, almost inaudible, reply.

"Good," said the fairy on his chest. "We are, all of us, growing quite weary of caring for you. We are glad you will soon be able to care for yourself. We're worn to a frazzle."

"Who...who are you?" Samson managed.

The fairy pulled herself up to her full two inches. She tossed her full, dark head of hair back over her shoulders. "I am Brittany Morgana, direct descendant of Fata Morgana, queen of the fairies and the realm of Avalon, such as it is."

Samson winced once. "Avalon? Is that where I am?"

"One and the same," Brittany said regally. "Where King Arthur once recovered from a mortal wound quite similar to yours. Fata Morgana cared for him, much as we have looked after you. We've learned some since then, though, I might add."

"I'd hope so," Samson said wryly, managing a weak smile.

"And what's that supposed to mean?" Brittany glowered.

"Nothing." Samson closed his eyes again. "You've done a wonderful job. I owe you my life."

"Yes, you do. And, if you don't mind, we'd all like to ask for something in return."

"You would?"

"Yes, we would." Brittany took a step forward. "We've been trapped here, at Avalon, for so long I think all of us have forgotten what it's like someplace else."

Samson opened his eyes again and stared dully at Brittany. "Trapped?"

"Yes, of course." Brittany's wings buzzed impatiently. "Surely you, of all people, should know that?"

"How would I have known that?"

"Your quest, to seek the races held captive here, on Earth, of course. We've heard reports. Every so often, we risk our lives to make forays down to Earth—as we did to save you on the elves' island—and, during one, we heard reports of your progress."

"And what is our progress?" Samson asked wearily. There was a general murmuring in the room, as dozens of the fairies' wings began to hum. It reminded Samson of the sound you heard from inside a beehive.

"Your comrades have successfully found the other races, save one," Brittany said somberly. "But not without difficulty. The magicians have imprisoned us all on Earth and stolen our inheritance and natural rights. They will not give that up lightly or without a fight."

"What are you talking about?" Samson frowned.

"Why, the four elemental forces of nature, of course," Brittany snapped. "The magicians have imprisoned us, the guardians of those elements, and taken the authority and power over those unto themselves."

"What elemental forces?"

Brittany frowned. "You must be joking? You've been on this quest, and you don't understand something that basic?"

Some of Samson's old anger returned for a fleeting moment. "Look, would you just tell me? Before I start to get mad?"

Brittany sighed. "Air, earth, water, and fire. The four elements, building blocks of the universe. I thought everyone knew that?"

"I didn't," Samson almost growled.

"Well, you do now. And for each of those elements, one of the races has been its guardian, here as well as on our own world. And perhaps in other worlds as well. I can't say about those. All I know is that there is one Creator, who rules all worlds and all universes. And the magicians have tried to steal some of that for themselves."

"You're the guardians of the air?"

"Until we were imprisoned here, at Avalon, yes, we were the guardians of the air." Brittany lifted her chin regally.

"And the other elements?"

"The people of the sea were entrusted with the care of the water. The dwarves rule the fire. And the earth is the responsibility of the giants."

"What of the other two races?" Samson asked.

"The centaurs protect the wisdom of the ages. It is a difficult task, without much foundation to build on. But they've done it well."

"And the elves?"

Brittany gritted her teeth. "They are closer to the human race than any of the others, hence their arrogance. They are entrusted with the protection of the spiritual well-being of the worlds."

Samson laughed, remembering the fierceness he'd experienced firsthand among the elves. They were warriors, through and through. It was hard to reconcile that with the spiritual dimension. "I don't think of the elves as especially spiritual."

"Oh, they aren't," Brittany agreed. "That isn't what they're supposed to do. They aren't supposed to necessarily *be* spiritual. Their role is to preserve that dimension of the universe, to guarantee that it may flourish in the world without hindrance."

A faint glimmer of understanding crept in. "Like the soldiers guarding the fort, or warriors protecting the lives of the women and children?"

"Exactly like that."

"I see," Samson said heavily.

Brittany moved a step closer. "Your friends have contacted the other races, save for the giants. One is on the way to Valhalla, even as we speak. And I'm quite certain the elves will make sure the other arrives there, as well. So, as soon as you are able, you should go there, too."

"Valhalla?"

"The land of the giants," Brittany proclaimed.

"And when we all get there? What then?"

Brittany's gaze turned even more somber. "The world—as we know it—will end, I think. Either that, or you will fail, and we all will sink forever into the dark abyss, our lives and guardianship utterly destroyed."

30

* * *

GLACIER

Jon actually grew accustomed to the routine as the eagles flew along. About every 10 minutes or so, another eagle would grab a piece of clothing and one eagle would drop off. That way, there were always enough eagles carrying him aloft, yet each got to rest.

And they needed their rest. For Jon was being carried a very long way, so far to the north that he wondered if they hadn't arrived at the North Pole itself.

At first, Jon had watched with fascination as the landscape rolled by beneath him. But the eagles were flying relatively high and, after a while, the land below blurred.

He was fascinated at being able to observe Rome, Geneva, and London from the air. It was interesting to see how big the cities were, from above. They all stretched out quite a distance.

But Jon stopped looking down much when they'd flown north of England, toward the Arctic region. There wasn't much to see after that, and Jon was preoccupied with how cold and numb he was growing. He really wished he'd brought some warmer clothing with him to Greece.

On the eagles flew, until they'd reached a rather large chain of islands somewhere in the Arctic Ocean, Jon guessed. The islands were quite mountainous. They looked uninhabited, but who in their right mind would live here?

The eagles flew to what appeared to be the highest mountain in the group, on an island in the center of the archipelagos. They settled, finally, at an eyrie on the north side of the mountain, which looked down into a deep, deep valley ringed on all sides by 10,000-foot mountains.

The entire valley was covered by a glacier. As far as Jon could see, there was ice. Jon couldn't see much else besides the ice in the valley. It was uninhabited. Most likely, no human had set foot in this place for thousands of years.

The glacier seemed to come roughly a third of the way up the side of the mountains, which themselves were sparsely covered by evergreen stands and other assorted trees. Jon saw some movement across the way—it appeared to be a mountain goat, but he couldn't be sure—so there was animal life on these islands.

After the eagles lowered Jon onto the eyrie, they all rose again, as one, and settled onto another part of the crag, 20 feet or so away from him. They stood there then, silently, like sentries. It was quite strange, up so high. The wind whistled by. The air was still.

Jon was freezing. He looked around him, but there wasn't much to keep him warm. There were scraps of things piled into the eagle's nest in the eyrie, but nothing Jon could actually wear. So he just rubbed his arms and legs as vigorously as he could and tried to understand why in the world the eagles had brought him here.

Jon stared hard down into the valley. He stared at the perimeter of the glacier and at its center for the longest time, trying to discern something. There had to be a reason the eagles had brought him to such a barren place.

It had been late morning when the eagles had arrived. Now, as Jon continued to gaze down into the valley, the sun had reached its noon-time apex. It was a brilliant sun, though it didn't provide nearly the warmth that Jon hoped for. But it did scare away all the shadows in the valley that made it somewhat difficult to see what might be there, if anything.

The more Jon looked, the more he was convinced that there was something there. Jon looked at different parts of the glacier, over and over, and always came to the same conclusion. There appeared to be a dark mass beneath the surface of the glacier. It was rather large and filled up a good portion of the valley. Jon couldn't tell at all what it was. But it did appear to be something.

Yet so what? Even if there *was* something beneath the ice, why should Jon care? There was nothing he could do about it, regardless. So why had the eagles brought him here?

Then Jon saw it! There was someone down there! He was sure he saw someone looking up at him from the valley—the same someone who then swiftly ducked into a cave down in the valley.

But how could there be caves down there, in the glacier? Was that possible? And how could someone live in this godforsaken place? How was that possible, at all?

Jon decided he had to make the trip down the side of the mountain to look for himself. It would take him the rest of the afternoon, most likely, but he wasn't going to accomplish anything from this eyrie anyway.

With a silent thanks to the eagles for having delivered him safely from the clutches of the police on Greece, Jon began the long climb down into the valley of the glacier.

31

***

THE DWARVES' DOMAIN

Coarse, strong hands carried Laura away from the edge of the abyss—the lake of fire—she'd nearly fallen into. She shuddered at the unspeakable thought of how she'd nearly walked right into that abyss, the lake of fire, on her own accord.

How blind had she been? Why hadn't she questioned Jon more when she first saw him, asked him tougher questions about where he'd been and why he'd found her so easily down here beneath the earth?

It all made more sense to Laura now, of course. She wasn't sure who it was who had been leading her down that broad slope—other than in a general sense—but she was sure it *wasn't* Jon. *So what sort of creatures, exactly, are able to shape-shift here on earth?* she wondered.

Laura was finally able to open her eyes as the dwarves carried her along. She moved her muscles a little and was pleased to see that everything was all right.

"I can walk now, I think," Laura said finally.

The dwarves carrying her slowed and then lowered her to the ground. "Are you sure?" one of them asked.

"Yes, I'm sure," she said politely. "And thank you for rescuing me."

"Our pleasure," one of them answered. "You are the first, ever, to make it to us. We were beginning to think we would be trapped down here forever."

As she walked along the narrow path leading away from the abyss, Laura wondered again how she could not have seen it. The battle was an ancient one. So ancient, in fact, that it obscured what was at stake.

Jon had been right. The forces of fallen angels—whatever they were—versus humankind, some of the ancient texts said. That's where the battle was being waged, among the descendants of Adam and Eve.

Eve had been the first to succumb to the guile of the serpent, who had promised her that she would be as God if she ate from the tree of knowledge of good and evil. Eve had eaten from that tree and fallen from grace as a result.

Humankind now had the ability to know both the light and dark sides, both good and evil. Laura's only question, now, was the true nature of the magicians.

They could masquerade as anything, or anyone. They could appear as angels of light, or as friends in need. They could equally appear as authorities of power and might. Their shape-shifting depended on the need and the circumstances.

And their ultimate aim? The *bene elohim?* What did they seek?

Laura now stood between victory and defeat, somehow. She wasn't sure how, but she was certain she was squarely in the way. She, Jon, Samson, and all the other races. They were the enemies of the magicians and the forces of darkness. She had no clue, though, what she should do with this knowledge.

It had gone beyond control of the portal, well beyond.

32

* * *

CRYSTAL ICE CAVES

Jon managed to make his way down the side of the mountain toward the glacier. Sliding and slipping on the loose gravel, he was slightly bruised as he arrived at the edge of the glacier just as the sun started to fall below the horizon.

Jon estimated he had about an hour's light left. He'd have to find somewhere to camp for the night. Actually, it was less cold down here than on the eyrie. There wasn't much wind down in the valley, and the glacier wasn't as cold as Jon had imagined.

He made his way quickly across the face of the valley glacier, in the direction of the cave where he'd spotted someone. He had no idea what he was walking into. Most likely, it had been a giant goat or something.

Yet Jon felt compelled to find out. What choice did he have, anyway? It wasn't as if there was much of anything else to do here, regardless. He could keep moving and hope for the best, or do nothing and either die of starvation or freeze to death.

Jon had the strangest feeling, as if he were racing headlong toward some grand conclusion that had been foretold and discussed by others for a very long time.

But no one had bothered to fill Jon in on the script. He was an actor without lines. So he would have to improvise and hope the Author didn't object too much.

He spotted the opening to the crevice a few minutes later. It really wasn't a cave. It was more of a yawning crack in the glacier. Jon shuddered a little at the thought of actually descending into it.

He approached the edge cautiously once he was there and peered down. The drop was rather precipitous. If he tried to climb down the gradual slope, he might not be able to make his way back up, at least not without some climbing tools.

So how could he have seen someone enter this? He must have been dreaming. Perhaps it *had* been a mountain goat, who was equipped to climb back to this steep, icy slope.

Jon stared down for several minutes. He felt a powerful urge to just plunge forward, regardless of the consequences. Something was there.

Jon took a deep breath. "Oh well," he said out loud, to no one. "What do I have to lose? It's not as if there's anyone on this island who's going to come rescue me, anyway."

Feeling foolish nevertheless for dropping down into what would almost certainly be his death, Jon climbed over the edge. He tried valiantly to work his way down, finding little chinks in the ice to hold onto.

It was futile. Once Jon was a couple feet down, the slope became too much. Jon lost his grip in the ice. He careened down the steep slope, wildly flailing his arms. Fortunately, the crevice didn't end sharply but rather rounded out at the bottom. Jon rushed down the slope madly and then found himself pivoting horizontally. He felt like a three-year-old on his first trip down the giant slide in the playground.

He came to a skidding stop about a hundred feet later. He was deep inside the crevice now, but, with the noon sun, there was still enough light to see by.

Jon had landed in a honeycomb of ice crystal caves. It was a magnificent sight. Stalagmites shot upwards from the floor, to be met by stalactites reaching down. The network of caves seemed to go off away from him for quite a distance.

Jon rose to his feet carefully, checking to make sure nothing was too badly bruised from the fall. Except for a couple of bumps, he felt fine. He walked forward into the crystal cave. Thankfully, it was even warmer here than above ground. Jon felt sure he could spend the night here safely. What he would do tomorrow, of course, was a different question. But he would have to let tomorrow take care of itself.

The ice was dirty where he'd entered. Clearly, the water had mixed with mud to form the crevice he'd slid down. But as he walked into the crystal cave, the ice flow cleared. It was an awe-inspiring sight. He could actually see a few feet into the ice. Not that there was anything to see, except for some plants trapped by the glacier ice, but it was clearly extraordinary. Jon couldn't help but feel almost a sense of reverence in this old, old place. This glacier had probably been here for hundreds or thousands of years.

Jon turned the corner and saw it. He had to walk a hundred feet or so to get a closer look. The network of caves had broadened out. Jon now found himself in a rather large cave. Directly in front of him was a huge ice wall. And inside that ice wall, Jon could clearly make out something trapped forever inside that mass of ice.

Jon walked cautiously across the ice cave floor. He wasn't exactly sure what to expect, but what he found shocked him beyond belief.

Trapped inside the ice wall was a huge face—the face of a giant. Jon could make out the eyes, nose, and mouth of the poor, hapless soul.

The giant had clearly been buried alive in the ice, for Jon could see that his eyes were open. His face was a contorted mask of rage, which was unusual for the giants. They were normally so placid.

Jon's heart fell. It was a truly awful sight. Jon just stood there for several minutes, staring intently at the giant trapped in the ice.

That was the dark mass Jon had seen from the eyrie. Clearly, giants were trapped here. This, then, must be Valhalla, the great and ancient abode of the giants.

It wasn't much of an abode now. Jon wondered how long the giants had been buried under the ice. From the time before man's written history began, perhaps.

That would explain why no one had heard from them for quite some time. The centaurs were trapped on Mount Pelion as mere horses, and, here, the giants were caught like flies trapped in amber.

The faintest flicker of a thought crept in. He remembered how, back in the land, the giants had turned to stone. They hadn't actually died. What if much the same kind of thing had happened here? What if the giants could return?

But, as quickly as the thought came, it vanished. It was a hopeless task. For even if the poor giants could come back to life, how in the world could Jon—or anyone else, for that matter,—melt the glacier? It wasn't possible.

There was a sudden movement across the way from where Jon stood. As incredible as the idea seemed, someone was coming.

"Beautiful, yes?" the intruder said as he strode purposefully across the ice toward Jon.

Jon stared at the extraordinarily handsome man in his early thirties, with jet black hair, gray eyes, and a face that had been chiseled from polished stone. But Jon held his tongue. He continued to size the stranger up.

The man was decked out, from head to toe, in rich animal furs of some type. Quite a few creatures had died so this man could walk in comfort. A small pack was slung over his back and he carried climbing tools with him. Unlike Jon, he was clearly prepared for the elements here. No doubt he had provisions as well.

"I said, it's a beautiful sight, isn't it?" the man said again, gazing intently at Jon.

"Who are you?" Jon asked, trying to keep the tremble of fear from his voice. He wasn't entirely successful.

"Do names really matter?" the man asked.

Jon knew, instinctively, that this was no friend. Exactly what he was remained to be seen. "Who are you?" he asked a second time.

The man's eyes flashed. "I *said* that names do not matter. Not here. Not in this place, at this time."

"They do to me," Jon persisted.

"Then you aren't looking at it properly."

"Perhaps." Jon shrugged. "But I would like to know your name, nevertheless."

The man looked past Jon, ignoring the question. "It is a magnificent sight, the giant trapped in the ice, isn't it?"

"No, it isn't. It is awful, that he has been buried alive like that."

"But, surely, you must admire the exquisite beauty of it, almost like a statue carved by a gifted artist?"

"No, I don't admire it at all."

The man stared hard at Jon for several seconds. "You realize, of course, how futile all this is, don't you?"

"No, I don't. Tell me."

"There is no way you can possibly help the races here, on earth. We will prevail. It is hopeless, what you are trying to accomplish."

Jon stared back. "But *we* will try, nevertheless."

The two combatants gazed at each other, both waiting for the next move. As they waited, Jon heard the first crack. For a brief moment, consternation crossed the unblemished face of the stranger who now confronted Jon. But the tremor passed quickly, and the stranger's confident demeanor returned.

He smiled broadly. "This is all so foolish. There is so much we could offer you, if only you would take the time to listen. That was the plan, from the beginning."

"Offer me?"

"Sure. There is no reason why we, the two of us, can't be comrades-in-arms. I can offer you much."

Jon narrowed his eyes in suspicion. "Such as?"

"Well, for one," the man said slowly, "I'm quite sure a few of my friends could make sure you were reinstated in the doctoral program at Duke. It does seem rather unfair that you were removed from that program."

Jon tried to keep his composure. He tried not to stammer when he responded. "How do you know about that?"

"I know a great many things about you, Jon. We've marked your progress. You've done quite well. You've passed nearly all of the challenges we've set before you."

"The challenges *you* set?"

"Why, of course. Surely, you didn't think all of this occurred by happenstance? We knew you'd re-open the portal for us and make clear our path. And we *had* to make sure you were prepared to meet the other challenges. We don't accept just *anyone* into our ranks, you know."

"What are you talking about?" Jon demanded.

The stranger took a step forward. "Why, I'm talking about what we can now offer you, Jon. You've passed through the fires, so to speak. You've mastered the puzzles we threw in your path. You have proven yourself worthy to become an initiate master. There is just one final test, and acceptance by you and the other two that we've chosen."

Jon stared hard at the stranger. "Master of what?"

The man's smile broadened, if that was possible. He held his arms out wide. "Why, of the world, of course, of all you can see or conceive. We are the masters of this world, and others as well."

"And you want *me* to join with you?"

"Yes. You have proven yourself eminently worthy. You have navigated the many challenges and tests we've given you. We feel you would be a welcome addition to our select ranks."

"And what, exactly, would I gain if I become a full master?"

The man nodded. "A fair question. You would gain dominion over certain people, certain lands, certain possessions. There are principalities and powers who guarantee such dominion. There is almost nothing, in fact, that would *not* be yours for the asking."

"And what must I do in return for all of this?" Jon's eyes bored into the stranger's now.

The man shrugged carelessly. "Oh, nothing much, really. There is one master who has passed through every test, every challenge. He is the Supreme Master of all, the ruler of this world and lord of the earth. All of us who are in his service pay him homage. It is a simple thing, really. A mere pittance. Simply join him, in the ways of this world."

"So that's it, then? We must serve this Supreme Master, the god of this world?"

"Yes. It is not much to ask, when you compare it to everything we are given as a result."

"And who is this Supreme Master?"

"His name is not uttered," the stranger said. "Only those who directly serve him know him by name, and even they do not utter it in his presence."

"I see." Jon nodded. "So, tell me, I'm curious. I'd like to get some sense of what I might be inheriting if I were to take you up on your offer. What's your piece of the action? What do you happen to have dominion over?"

The stranger smiled again. A few more offers and Jon might be his. "My own particular specialty is the harem," the man said with a twinkle in his eye. "I am a delight to women the world over. I am able to provide women to any who care to procure my services. At any time."

"I see," Jon said thoughtfully. "You run an international prostitution ring?"

The stranger flinched. "Oh, that is a crude way to put it. Some of the most beautiful women in the world are at my beck and call. I pick and choose. It is a truly delightful existence. And what I do, you see, is share that delight with other men around the world. I offer them the chance to spend precious moments with these goddesses of beauty."

465

Jon nodded thoughtfully. He almost had his answer. He was almost there. "So you are, in effect, something of a god of the fertility rite. Something like that?"

The stranger gave Jon a quizzical look. A shadow briefly flitted across his face and then passed. "Why, yes, I guess you could almost put it that way. But fertility isn't really much a part of it anymore. We've progressed beyond that, you see—"

"Yes, I can see that," Jon interrupted. "And I think I know who you are, now. In fact, I'm almost certain of it."

The air grew suddenly still. The stranger tensed. Perhaps he had miscalculated, underestimated. Perhaps there was more work to do here. "What do you mean?" he asked tersely.

But Jon had his answer. He knew it to his core. "You are the god Ba'al. That is your name. The ancient bane and curse of Israel, the god of fertility who the sons and daughters of Abraham successfully removed from their land once upon a time."

The stranger's demeanor changed in an instant. Gone was the smile and the inviting twinkle in his eye. It was replaced by a raging inferno of anger. "You are guessing," he almost hissed.

"No, I don't think so," Jon said confidently. "Your name is Ba'al, and I will have no part of you, or your offer, or your own master. I have all I need. I don't want what you offer. So, be gone."

Every fiber in the stranger's body bristled with nearly unbridled fury. "Yes, I am Ba'al," he hissed. "But you have miscalculated this time, my friend. We will prevail. You are doomed on this island. You can go no further. You would have done well to take my offer when you had the chance."

"I am not your friend," Jon answered, holding his ground. "And we will see what happens from this moment forth."

As Jon uttered these last few words, the god Ba'al took a step backwards. "Yes, we will see," he growled. He vanished, literally, an instant later.

Once again, Jon was alone with the anguished, imprisoned giants in the crystal caves. Jon had no idea what to do next. But he felt certain that *something* was about to happen. He had no idea what it might be, though.

33

***

LAURA'S DECISION

The dwarves' domain on earth was a pale and wan shadow of its counterpart in the land. Here, on earth, Agarttha was a glum, colorless place, with clay huts and a few shaped-rock pieces of furniture and not much else to speak of.

The dwarves clearly lived the most meager of existences, in the most barren of locations. Their small community was gathered on a small plateau thousands of feet above the raging lake of fire. It was an island, really, with a small, narrow isthmus leading back to the road Laura had come in on.

But the dwarves rarely journeyed across that isthmus. Occasionally, as the need arose, one of them made the perilous crossing. But, generally speaking, the magicians didn't allow it. The dwarves were trapped here, their prisoners.

As with the people of the sea, the magicians had usurped the dwarves' natural authority over one of the four elements—fire—by enslaving them here. The dwarves were powerless to do anything about it.

And, until Laura, no one had ever voluntarily sought them or their counsel. The thought of journeying so close to the lake of fire beneath the earth surely struck pure terror into the hearts and minds of any reasonable soul. In hindsight, Laura wasn't at all sure why she'd so foolishly made the attempt. It seemed crazy, looking at it now. She was one against many. It seemed so hopeless.

"Do not despair. Please," one of the dwarves pleaded with Laura as they all sat around a large community table in the center of Agarttha.

"But what can I do?" Laura asked. "I'm not even sure I can get back, now."

"Oh, you can get back, we think," one of the dwarves said.

"But what then?"

"We don't know," a third dwarf said. "But you came this far. You must have extraordinary powers."

"It was dumb luck," Laura said glumly. "Not much else."

"What about the other two?" someone asked.

"Jon and Samson?" Laura perked up at the mention of her two fellow adventurers. "What do you know of them?"

The dwarves murmured among themselves. One of them finally spoke. "We get reports, when one of us goes out to get supplies. We have to do that, you know. The magicians certainly don't provide for us."

One of the dwarves—one of the more powerful figures in the group, with a face that appeared chiseled out of granite and a torso shaped in a forge—stepped forward. "I returned from the earth's surface not too long ago," he said. "And I heard tales."

"Of what?"

"Of a powerful warrior mortally wounded on the elves' island and carried off to Avalon."

Laura gasped. That was Samson, of course. "And how is he?"

"Didn't hear," the dwarf said brusquely. "I also heard a report of another who found the miserable centaurs—"

"The miserable centaurs?" Laura interrupted.

"Yes, the magicians have changed them into common horses, on Mount Pelion," another said. "That's where they now live, trapped as we are."

"I see." Laura's heart nearly burst with sadness for the hapless races who were so thoroughly enmeshed in the magicians' evil web. "And Jon, do you know where he is?"

"Eagles carried him to the ancient abode of Valhalla," said the first dwarf.

Shivers went up Laura's spine. "The land of the giants?"

"Yes, it is where they are buried."

"Buried?"

"In a mountain of ice," the dwarf said solemnly. "They have been like that for as long as anyone can remember."

"Do you mean a glacier?"

"Yes, the magicians could not physically dominate them, so they buried them, alive, in ice."

"So they might be revived?"

"Perhaps. Who's to say about something like that?"

It was possible, Laura thought. Giants were different from human beings. Their metabolism was likely to be far different. If they were frozen, and their hearts and circulation stopped, perhaps they *could* be revived. After all, they had come to life after being turned to stone, once, back in the land.

"What would it take to melt that ice?" Laura asked suddenly.

The dwarves looked at each other. "A volcano of fire would help," one said.

"Along with the sun, if it got hot enough," a second said.

"And a tidal wave to wash away the melting ice," a third said.

"Can you do it? Can you provide that volcano of fire?" Laura asked, almost afraid of the answer.

The dwarves murmured among themselves for several minutes. The first dwarf, the one who'd made the most recent journey to the earth's surface, spoke up. "There is a subterranean lava flow directly beneath Valhalla. It has always been there."

"And could we journey there, Mr., um…?" Laura asked.

"The name's Thorkin." The dwarf grunted. "And, yes, a few of us could probably make it. With a little work, we could probably create a fissure and direct it toward the surface. But…?"

"But what?" Laura asked.

"We couldn't be sure of what might happen after that. *Anything* could happen. We couldn't control it once it erupted. It could swallow the island up, as far as we know."

"It's a risk we have to take," she said finally. "There seems to be no other choice."

"Then it is done," Thorkin declared. "We will leave in a few hours, after we rest."

34

***

FLIGHT OF THE FAIRIES

In the end, all of Avalon chose to come with Samson. They voted on it and declared it was time to fight, or die. The fairies, who normally did not sustain a thought, much less an action, were sufficiently aware of what the choices were. They decided, together, to make one colossal attempt to break free of their horrible bonds.

Once Samson started to recover from his mortal wound, he healed quickly. *Very* quickly. It was nothing short of miraculous. The ministering of the fairies allowed him to move around quite freely within a matter of days.

They held a war council before they left. Samson had no idea what they were walking into, and he wasn't entirely sure he wanted to know. Perhaps he should just dive in, as he always did.

"The forces are all beginning to converge on Valhalla, even as we speak," Brittany said solemnly when they were all gathered.

Samson looked out over the sea of fairies who were gathered all around him in a full circle. "The forces?"

"The *bene elohim* and their students, the magicians, are coming out of their shadows, toward Valhalla," she said. "They can sense that the Great Battle is looming. Once, they had plotted for you and the other two to create a path for them. In fact, we had assumed that the woman was being groomed as El's queen consort, fulfilling the oldest prophecy from the dawn of time on earth."

"But they can't count on that now, can they?" Samson smiled.

"No," the fairy queen said, "and since you have moved away from them, they have tried to thwart your mission, turn it aside, corrupt you, push you away. And, having failed in that, they now must attempt to use brute force. Cunning has failed, and force is all that is left."

"And what do we have to combat that?" Samson caught his breath.

"Not much." Brittany shrugged. "But we, all of us, collectively, can muster what little authority we have over the elements."

"All of us?" Samson asked.

"The other races. Your friend, Laura, has found the people of the sea as well as the dwarves, as I understand it, and perhaps they can muster something during the battle."

Samson tensed. "Do you think there will be a real battle?"

"Who knows? Something is about to happen. We can all sense that. But none of us know exactly what it is."

"So what should be done next?"

"We go to Valhalla, and see," Brittany declared.

***

Whereas the sun always shone on Avalon, the land of the fairies, storm clouds gathered over Valhalla as the fairies winged their way toward the abode of the giants.

It took nearly a hundred of the fairies to carry Samson. They grumbled rather loudly under their burden, but they arrived at the island without mishap.

Samson couldn't see much as they descended into the valley of the glacier. There was ice everywhere. The place was barren. "Where are the giants?" he called out.

"Buried in the ice," one of the fairies close to his ear answered. "They've been there for ages."

Samson grimaced. "So it's hopeless, then. We've already lost."

"No, it isn't," Brittany insisted. "Not if we can free them from the ice."

"And how do we do that?" Samson asked. "Glaciers don't melt."

Brittany fluttered before him. "You're right, but I think we have to try."

Samson looked up at the darkened sky. "Perhaps you can help begin the process."

"What?" Brittany asked anxiously.

Samson continued to gaze upwards. "If you can push the clouds back, and then use what authority you have to bring the sun's heat beating down onto the glacier ice, perhaps we can begin the process."

"It will take much, much more than that to break the giants free of the ice," Brittany said.

"I know, but I just think we have to begin with something."

"Okay, we will do it," Bethany declared. "The heat will be intense for you on the island. Can you manage?"

Samson nodded grimly. "I will manage, somehow. I must."

Brittany turned to her lieutenants, gave them their orders, and then they, in turn, passed the word among the troops. A few minutes later, they lowered Samson to the ice.

"We will return," Brittany said.

An instant later, the fairies flew en masse toward the darkened heavens.

Samson watched the sky intently. The fairies rose to the clouds. Samson couldn't see them anymore. They were too high up. But he could see the results of their efforts.

A crack, a ray of sunlight, suddenly burst through the dark clouds. The crack widened. The fairies were pushing the clouds back! They were doing it!

Samson's eyes dropped to the ground. He looked around him at the barren ice. There was nothing, as far as the eye could see, but ice. And mountains, ringing him on all sides.

Samson's eye caught something near the top of one of the mountains. He looked intently in that direction. There *was* movement! He watched and spotted someone working his way down the side of the mountain. More people followed.

Over the next hour or so, Samson watched in fascination as two events unfolded—the fairies successfully managing to push the clouds back and the people, whoever they were, making their way down the mountainside.

Every so often, Samson thought he could see a flash or a glint from something the people were carrying. The sun began to beat harder. It was clearly growing warmer on the surface of the ice. Not enough to make it uncomfortable, but the temperature was definitely beginning to change.

One of the people made it to the bottom and sprinted across the ice toward Samson. Several minutes later, Samson was startled and overjoyed.

"Regis!" Samson called out, running to meet his old friends.

They embraced. "I thought you were dead," Regis said, holding his friend at arm's length.

"Me, too," Samson quipped. "And I would be, had the fairies not rescued me."

Others started to run across the ice as they reached the bottom of the mountain. They were soon by their side. Regis had brought the other elves with him. The small, lithe warriors silently flanked them on all sides. Samson acknowledged their presence with a solemn nod.

"So you've found your comrades here?" Samson asked Regis.

"Yes, they are not many, but they are willing to fight in this coming battle." Regis surveyed the dozens of elves who gathered. "We came here as rapidly as we could."

Samson spied Tristan among them. "And you too, my friend? You are willing to fight?"

"Why not?" Tristan said with a wry smile. "I had nothing better to do."

Regis pulled a sword from one of the two sheaths he wore. "Here, I brought this for you. I think you will need it."

Samson took the broadsword, gripped the hilt, and then let it fall to his side. "Thank you, but why do you say that?"

"Look." Regis pointed skyward.

Samson squinted toward the sky. He blanched at what now approached the island. "It can't be," he said in hushed awe.

"It can be, and it is," Regis declared.

The other elves glanced toward the sky nervously. They, likewise, blanched a little at the sight.

For approaching Valhalla, at a very rapid rate, was the largest dragon any of them could possibly imagine.

35

* * *

THE FIRE ERUPTS

Walking back across the straight, narrow path over the lake of fire was easier the second time, Laura found. She knew what she was up against, and that made all the difference.

Laura had slept for nearly eight hours before they'd left. The dwarves had let her sleep, for she clearly needed the rest.

When she awoke, the dwarves had taken a vote and decided that it was time they all took a stand. Every last one of them was coming with Laura, not just a few.

"But there's no need," Laura protested. "Your lives would be in jeopardy."

"We must come with you," said Thorkin, who now spoke for the group. "We have no choice. We have all been confined here against our wishes for too long. It is time we did something about it. We all believe that this is our one, best chance."

Laura understood. There came a time when you had to throw caution to the wind and take extraordinary risks. This seemed one of those times.

After they'd made it across the walkway safely, they hurried up the wide path that led down to the lake of fire. The dwarves couldn't run as fast as Laura, so she simply ambled quickly.

"Here it is!" Thorkin called out. He waited at a small crack in the wall on the right side. The crack was only a couple of feet across, just wide enough to allow the dwarves and Laura to slip through.

It didn't widen much when they were through, but there was enough room to walk. Every so often they had to walk sideways. Laura did her best to quell the feeling of claustrophobia.

"Will this open up a bit?" she called out at one point.

"Yes, eventually!" Thorkin answered from somewhere near the lead of the group, which was now strung out along the passageway.

They worked their way upwards, toward the earth's surface, after about a half mile. Within another mile the path started to widen.

Laura felt the heat before she actually saw the fires. Several minutes later, they emerged on a shelf plateau overlooking volcanic fires gurgling below them.

It was an incredible inferno. The heat was so intense, Laura found that she could only catch a glimpse of it by walking to the edge, peering over, and then returning to the back of the shelf where the heat was less intense.

Some of the dwarves were already disappearing into a second crack in the wall, away from the lava flow. Laura followed.

They journeyed like this, skirting the lava flow, in and out of fissures in the rock, for a very long time. The dwarves had brought enough provisions for the one-way trip. They had brought nothing for a return trip, which Laura thought curious. But she said nothing.

When they at last arrived at the place Thorkin had in mind, they camped and talked about their strategy.

"What we will need to do is move one of the tectonic plates, begin a chain reaction, and hope we can ride up to the surface in its wake," said one of the dwarves.

"Is that possible?" Laura gasped.

"Sure, why not?" The dwarf shrugged. "The heat will be nearly unbearable and it will be almost impossible to remain on one of the shifting plates once they start to move. But what choice do we have? It's either that or be swallowed by the erupting lava flow."

They surveyed the site. There was one quite large slab of rock that, if it were moved and fell in just the right direction, might hit one of the plates and start such a chain reaction.

"But how will we know which one to get to after the reaction starts?" Laura asked.

"We'll have to guess, most likely." Thorkin grimaced.

"No, not necessarily," said a second dwarf. "We'll have a few minutes to watch which way the plates are moving, *if* we're successful, and then we can make our choice."

"The lava will flow up to this shelf once it all begins. We'll probably have a minute or so to choose the one we want before the lava begins to flow over this shelf."

The dwarves talked among themselves for a little while, but their path seemed set. There was no need to wait any longer. And there was now no turning back. The day of Ragnarok seemed at hand.

"Let's go!" Thorkin rose to his feet and clapped his hands together. The other dwarves rose and cheered lustily.

They all moved over to the large stone slab and set to work. They rocked back and forth, alternately resting and pushing, resting and pushing, with a steady chorus of "Heave, ho! Yo, ho!" to accompany their extraordinary effort.

Laura stood off to the side and waited. There wasn't much she could do to contribute right now.

The slab inched forward. One end moved out over the edge. Laura held her breath as it moved out over the edge further. The dwarves pushed and strained without ceasing. The slab reached the halfway point. Several more shoves and the weight shifted. The slab teetered once, twice, and then fell over the edge.

Laura peered out over the edge as the slab fell. It struck one of the plates with a resounding smash, then disintegrated.

As they'd hoped, the plate the slab had struck shifted just enough to affect the surrounding plates. Within seconds, they'd all begun to shift. Grinding, cracking, smashing sounds came from all sides within a minute or so.

"It won't be long now," one of the dwarves said loudly above the growing din.

Laura watched in stunned fascination as the tectonic plates shifted and groaned under the enormous pressure of change thrust on them by the chain reaction.

Finally, one of the plates moved out of the way altogether and crashed into the lava flow. The chain reaction sped up immediately after that, with the plates rocking and crashing against each other continuously.

The lava rose steadily, as the dwarves predicted, once the plates containing it started to move out of the way. Several of the splintered plates slid onto the top of the lava flow. It was one of those the dwarves would need to ride to the surface.

Laura looked up uneasily. "Will this really create a fissure, or will we just be trapped here when the lava rises?"

"The moving plates will create enormous pressure," the dwarf nearest to her said. "There will be a fissure. The earth has no choice when something like this happens. There is only one escape valve, and that is upwards, toward the earth's surface."

Laura nodded and continued to watch the scene below. In just a few minutes, the lava would be at their level and they would need to move onto one of the splintered plates. "Which one?"

"The largest one, I think," one dwarf called out.

"Yes, the largest one," a second said.

Laura could hear the cracking, splitting sounds above her where the fissure was obviously beginning. She spotted the first sign of an opening way off to her left. Glancing down at the lava flow, she estimated the distance to the ceiling and decided they would need to choose one of the smaller plates at the furthest point left of their current position. She started to move in that direction.

"Where are you going?" Thorkin called. "The large plate is coming in this direction."

"I don't think we want that one." Laura pointed toward the ceiling where she thought she'd seen the fissure beginning. "The opening will occur over there."

Thorkin glanced up to the point where Laura was gesturing. "She's right!" he bellowed. "We need to move over to our left! Let's go!"

The dwarves followed instantly without any hesitation or grumbling. They reached the point directly beneath the place Laura had spotted and then stepped onto the plate as it reached their level. An instant later, the lava began to flow across the shelf where they'd been standing.

Laura's clothes were soaked through within seconds. The heat was nearly unbearable, as the dwarves had predicted. But she held her tongue. They had no other choice.

The cracking, groaning, splitting sounds above her were now deafening. The earth was moving, opening up to allow for the enormous pressure they'd created.

Rock shards showered down on them. Several big chunks of rock crashed down on all sides but didn't strike any of them. The lava moved inexorably upwards. The earth started to open up. They surged upwards.

Laura and the dwarves watched as the large plate they'd almost stepped onto was ground into dust against a part of the ceiling that did not crack. They had chosen the right plate, which was now rising through the opening earth crust.

And then, gloriously, a crack opened, widened, and they all saw the blue, blue sky! The first shaft of sunlight pierced the darkness like a flashing sword glinting in the throes of battle. It was a magnificent sight.

The earth opened even more. The lava pressed forward. Soon, Laura and the dwarves would know if they had truly succeeded.

36

***

THE GIANTS AWAKE

After Ba'al had vanished, Jon just stood there for a long time, rooted in place. So the magicians, or their masters, were finally showing themselves. They had no choice, really. They could only manipulate the landscape from behind the scenes for so long.

Jon now knew where the magicians derived their power. It was curious that it had taken him so long to come to grips with it. The magicians had learned from the *bene elohim*, the sons of God.

The oldest myth known to humankind was that a band of fallen angels, known as the Watchers, decided to leave heaven and journey to Earth. There were about 200 of these angels, the *bene elohim*, and they had more than a dozen leaders. Araqiel had been one of those leaders, as had been El.

They came to Earth to lie with the daughters of men and produced the Nephilim and other offspring. But they also taught humankind what it had not known before and created many new worlds for the magicians who served them.

But after Michael's war in heaven, when Jesus was born, the *bene elohim* were banished to earth. That was what Jesus had meant when he said he'd seen Satan fall to earth like lightning. Those who wished to learn from them on Earth could still find them, however, and Jon assumed that this is what had happened throughout the course of human history.

There were other fallen angels as well who also roamed the Earth and served the *bene elohim*. The little gods of the earth—like Ba'al—had deceived and seduced humankind for ages. It was a very old game, an ancient plot. Magic and religion had wrestled for a very long time, in many different ways.

Jon was certain that the new incarnation of the battle was even more complicated, with the magicians and the little gods mixing freely with the forces of religion. That seemed obvious. One sure way to deceive was to pretend you were one of the good guys.

But at least some portion of the Game seemed to be rushing toward a grand conclusion. Jon could sense it. Ba'al had shown up at this time, in this place, to attempt to turn Jon away from a path. There was a reason for this, Jon was sure. Something was happening.

After coming to the conclusion that he would not be able to climb back up the ice slope without an extraordinary amount of effort, Jon decided to explore the crystal caves. He just set off, at random.

He came across the faces of other giants trapped as he wandered through the honeycomb of crystal caves. They all looked anguished, as if they'd been trapped by surprise.

He found that the caves extended for quite a distance, in all directions. Most likely, he could spend days exploring if he felt like it.

But about an hour into his journey, Jon felt a second tremor, stronger this time. It lasted for nearly 30 seconds. Jon recognized the sound. He'd never actually heard anything like it, but he was sure he knew what it was.

It was the beginning of an earthquake. There seemed no other explanation. After the third tremor, Jon was certain of it. The earth was clearly beginning to move beneath his feet, and there was nothing he could do. If an earthquake did come to this place, Jon could only hope he wasn't swallowed up as the earth cracked and opened.

When the fourth tremor hit, it was violent and lasted for a very long time. Some of the ice around him began to crack. Big chunks of ice crashed on the floor around him. Many of the stalagmites broke free.

Jon quickly decided to seek haven in the largest of the ice caves he'd come across, a cave where he'd seen the faint outline of a large structure as well as the faces of two giants. He didn't want to be trapped in some narrow, confined space when the earthquake occurred.

He had just made it when the fifth tremor hit. The whole room shook violently. Jon was thrown to the floor from the force of it.

And then, just as suddenly, it stopped. Chunks of ice were strewn everywhere, but clearly the earthquake had not occurred here. Jon wondered what, if anything, was happening on the surface of the island. He could only guess.

He heard the hissing and steaming several minutes later. It was a very curious sound, one Jon could not immediately place. He rushed forward, through the ice caves, until he came face to face with where the sounds were coming from.

Jon stared in shock at the approaching lava flow, which was rolling inexorably through the corridors of the crystal caves, melting everything in its path. The seething, popping, boiling cauldron moved slowly. But it was clearly going to make its way through the entire network of caves.

Jon tried not to panic. But it was difficult. There would be nowhere to hide. He wasn't sure what he could do. There was no high ground in this place.

He turned and ran back to the big ice cave. He was scouring the landscape to see if there was anything he could do when he spied it! It was perhaps his only chance.

Enough of the ice had fallen away in the cave to reveal the tip of some giant structure. Jon was certain it was Valhalla, spoken of in the legends. It had to be. But the portion of the structure that was now exposed was dozens of feet above the cave's floor. He would need a long ladder to reach the top.

But perhaps I don't need a ladder, Jon thought. Littered across the floor were large chunks of ice. Jon began to push one chunk after another toward the exposed part of the structure against the wall.

Jon built a base of five flat chunks of ice first, and then piled the others on top of these in a pyramid fashion. If he did it right, he could build steps to the point where the structure was exposed.

But he didn't have much time. Even now, Jon could hear the hissing and steaming of the approaching lava entering this particular cave. He only had minutes now.

The first three levels were easy. After that, Jon had to climb back down and carry the next chunk up with him. It was hard labor. But Jon pressed forward mindlessly, paying no attention to the pain he felt in his overworked muscles.

The lava flow reached the base of his crude steps just as he'd placed the last chunk of ice on top. He clambered up and grabbed what appeared to be the top of a turret. Seconds later, the lava began to melt the base of his steps. They toppled shortly after that.

But Jon was safely on top of the structure. Now it was simply a question of whether the lava would destroy Valhalla as it melted the ice. Jon had no idea what the structure was made out of. He could only hope it was a type of rock that could survive the onslaught of the lava. But there was no way to know for certain.

Despite his growing fear, Jon couldn't help but stare in fascination as the lava melted everything in its path. The entire crystal cave network was collapsing around him. The sounds of the ice crashing were deafening.

Jon was in a slight bowl of what must be the very top of a turret. He might be able to weather the melting of the glacier from this point, but there was no certainty of that. None at all.

The lava continued to flow. It began to fill even the large cave Jon was now in. It must surely have completely filled the rest of the caves, melting all in its wake. The base of the walls on all sides melted away. The entire picture was changing rapidly.

After half an hour, Jon could see that the cave was vanishing. There were extraordinary cracks from above him. Even as the walls and the ice floor was melting under the crush of the river of lava, Jon was sure there was lava above him that would soon melt the top of the glacier as well.

There was nowhere to hide. Jon's one hope was that the ceiling would not melt evenly, that a portion would cave in first and that it would be somewhere away from where Jon now stood.

He watched anxiously, waiting for the first crack to appear in the ceiling. Several minutes later, a very large part of the ceiling collapsed. The ice vanished into the river of lava below. A new stream of lava flowed downward from the ceiling. The ceiling of ice above Jon crumbled rapidly after that.

Before his eyes, Valhalla was re-emerging from its prison of ice. It was standing firm against the lava. From Jon's limited vantage point, it appeared that the structure was remaining intact.

Finally, the lava reached Jon's side of the cave. As it poured down from the ceiling, it covered everything. Eventually it would fall on his head. There was no way to escape it.

And then Jon heard the bellow of rage. It was loud, deafening. It drowned out the hissing, crunching, crashing sounds all around.

The giants were waking up! The lava had freed them as well. Jon jerked his head around to his right. Thirty yards away, Jon saw one of the giants bleating loudly.

"Over here! Over here!" Jon shouted at the top of his lungs.

The newly awakened giant blinked once, twice, three times. Then he looked over at Jon bleary-eyed, clearly confused.

"You!" the giant bellowed. "MAGICIAN!"

"No!" Jon yelled back. "I am *not* a magician! I'm a friend!"

With one extraordinary effort, the giant thrust one of his arms free of the ice. His hand shot into the air and reached over toward Jon. The giant plucked Jon from the turret, nearly crushing him. "You did this to me, to Valhalla!" the giant bellowed in Jon's face. The giant began to close his fist around Jon's body. Jon would be a pulpy mass of flesh in a second if he didn't do something.

"I am not a magician!" he retorted. "We have come to free you from their grip! We have been to the land you came from, Annwyn, and we want to help you return there!"

"The land?" the giant queried. He relaxed his grip slightly. "You've been there? You've seen my brethren?"

Jon breathed more freely. "Yes, we've been there, and, yes, we've seen your brethren. They are well. They await your safe return."

"And *you* can help us return?" the giant asked suspiciously.

"Yes, if you don't crush me first," Jon promised.

"Then let us go," the giant said. He began to free his other arm.

The ice was now collapsing and melting around them in huge waves. Within minutes, the entire top half of Valhalla was loosened from its ice prison. Other giants were beginning to awaken. From somewhere above, Jon thought he saw something huge flying through the clouds.

Even as Jon marveled at how blue the sky seemed now that the ice ceiling had disappeared, he heard the new sound—a constant roaring off in the distance. For a second, he couldn't place it. Then it came to him.

"A tidal wave!" Jon warned.

"What?" the giant asked him.

"A tidal wave is coming," Jon said. "It sounds close. Tell your giant friends to brace themselves. It will rush through this place and sweep you away if you aren't holding onto Valhalla."

The giant looked down at Jon, then out across Valhalla. He hesitated only for a moment. "FRIENDS!" the giant yelled, his voice a deafening rumble. "Grab hold of Valhalla! The water is coming! Grab hold!"

The other giants reacted instantly and grabbed different parts of Valhalla. Moments later, the tidal wave crashed down over the mountain, sweeping away all of the remaining ice in its wake.

Jon found himself thrust into the front of the giant's heavy mail shirt. He held on for all he was worth, as the giant grabbed Valhalla and braced himself for the onslaught of the tidal wave.

It was brutal when it hit, but it lasted only for seconds. The giant held firm. The wave did not knock him free, and Jon was able to safely remain where he was.

The wave of water rolled back for a second time after hitting the opposite side of the mountain rim, but there was much less force to it. It swirled around the feet and torso of the giants. After a few minutes, it began to recede and fall back into the ocean.

Jon and the giants had survived. Valhalla was free at last, after centuries of imprisonment.

37

***

LOTAN

As the dragon lumbered toward Samson and the elves, there was very little time to prepare.

"How do you slay a dragon?" Samson asked Regis shortly before the creature landed.

"You don't," Regis said bluntly. "Its scales are impenetrable and the fire from its belly devastating."

"There must be something!" Samson protested.

Regis just shook his head sadly. "Truly, I know of nothing."

The rest of the elves didn't waste any time thinking or arguing about it, though. Even as the dragon approached, dozens of them quickly knelt to the ground, removed their bows, fitted arrows to them, and sent a shower of arrows winging toward the creature.

All of the arrows found their mark. None made even the slightest dent. The dragon continued to approach without slowing. The elves sent a second wave of arrows toward the dragon. Again, they reached their target, but did nothing.

"To the hills!" one of the elves yelled when it became clear they could do nothing to this dragon. The elves followed his command, turned, and ran back toward the mountain slopes.

Samson did not flee. Regis and Tristan held their ground as well, choosing to remain by his side.

The dragon landed an instant later, about 20 feet or so from them. But this was no ordinary dragon. No, this one had seven heads. One of its heads cast a baleful eye in their direction. Wisps of smoke slithered out of its nostrils.

"Flee, before it is too late," the seven-headed dragon said. The words that came forth sounded more like the roar of a bellows than the English language.

"You can speak," Samson said, unable to mask the complete surprise in his voice.

"Of course, you fools. What did you imagine? That the mighty Lotan was mute?"

"I-I don't know," Samson said, still too stunned at the thought of an intelligent, conversant dragon to think clearly.

Lotan suddenly let loose with a stream of fire. The flames burst forth toward the three of them, engulfing them briefly before fading. "Now, flee, like the others," Lotan commanded. "Leave this place, before I roast you."

Samson shuddered. The fire had been *very* hot. A few seconds of that and no amount of healing by the fairies would help. He glanced at Tristan and Regis. "Flank him," he muttered under his breath. "Occupy its two arms. Regis to the right, Tristan to the left. I'll charge right up the middle."

Tristan and Regis did not argue. They nodded once curtly and, without another word, sprinted off in opposite directions.

The dragon's seven heads followed their movements for a second or two and then fixed their full attention on Samson. "It is hopeless, you know," he hissed. "You cannot harm me."

"If you say so." Samson wasn't really listening to the dragon. He was staring very hard at the dragon's hide, searching for some sign of a chink in the beast's considerable armor.

Lotan's hide clearly seemed to be all of one piece. There did not appear to be a vulnerability or a weakness anywhere. It was all Samson could do to keep his heart from failing with fear.

"You know, we could offer you much, if only you would listen," the dragon said.

"What?" Samson asked, confused. "What's that?"

"We could offer you much, you and your other foolish friends."

"Laura and Jon?"

"Yes, them. There is no reason why the knowledge we've obtained cannot be yours as well. No reason at all. Lay down your arms, give up your quest, and it shall be yours."

"What knowledge?" Samson asked suspiciously, even as he kept one eye on the progress of Tristan and Regis, who were still working their way wide to the left and right.

"The knowledge of good and evil, of course, which is what you *must* learn to become a god," said one of Lotan's heads, its red eyes boring into Samson's. "We can offer you that."

"Why should I care?"

"I offer you life, and knowledge of the things the Creator has forbidden you to know, that's why!" the dragon roared.

Samson didn't answer right away. He almost started laughing, which wouldn't be wise just now. But this so reminded him of a story long ago.

"What is your *real* name?" Samson asked suddenly.

"Lotan, Yam, Tannin. Names do not matter. Answer me!" the dragon bellowed. "Which do you choose—life and the ultimate knowledge, or certain death?"

"And how will I attain this?"

"The Tree, the one from which all knowledge springs," the dragon hissed. "Eat its fruit, and you obtain all knowledge. You become god."

Samson did smile this time. "I know you, Lotan. You are like the serpent who first offered the fruit from this Tree in the Garden of Eden. You've probably offered that same knowledge to others as well, haven't you?"

"Those who accept my offer learn what the Creator has said they cannot know. It is a simple offer, with rich rewards."

Samson gripped the hilt of his sword. He glanced over to his right and left. Tristan and Regis were in position, ready.

"Your offer is a curse," Samson said. "I have no desire to eat the bitter fruit you offer."

"You will die, then!" the dragon roared, belching a stream of fire.

But Samson was two steps ahead of the dragon. He had bolted to his right to escape the stream of fire and then charged directly at the dragon.

"NOW!" Samson yelled.

Tristan and Regis burst toward the dragon as well. All three reached the dragon almost at the same time. The dragon swatted Tristan away almost casually with its right arm. Tristan went tumbling, head over heels.

Regis nimbly escaped the dragon's first swing. He thrust his sword forward. It crunched into the dragon's tough, scaly hide and bounced off. The dragon turned one of its massive heads to find Regis. Samson rushed forward.

The dragon loosed another volley of fire directly at Regis, burning him quite badly. Then the dragon reached down, pinched Regis's limp body between two claws, held him high, and began to heave him off to one side.

Samson saw his chance. He would only have one. If he missed, he, too, would soon be crushed. Gripping the sword as tightly as he could with both hands and holding it out in front of him, Samson launched himself at what appeared to be a soft spot just under the dragon's now-exposed left flank, just under its left arm.

Samson's broadsword found the spot. He plunged the sword deep, burying it up to its hilt in the dragon. With luck, he had found the dragon's black heart.

The beast roared with pain. It dropped Regis by its side and then doubled over. "YOU!" it bellowed at Samson.

The dragon sent a stream of fire after him. The fire enveloped Samson, who dove to the ground and rolled over and over in order to protect himself from the flames and the searing heat.

The flames stopped. Samson looked back. Lotan was doubled over in pain. The sword was still buried deep beneath the dragon's left arm. Samson could see its hilt glinting in the blazing sun.

The dragon turned one of its baleful eyes on Samson again. "Others will come!" it hissed. "I am only one. There are others. You think you have won, but the battle has only just begun."

The dragon tried to send its flames forth toward Samson one last time. The stream came out and then turned to thick, black smoke instead. An instant later, the dragon collapsed and fell to one side with a very loud thump.

Samson watched in utter disbelief as the dragon's body crumbled to dust in the blink of an eye. Only his sword remained, lying on the ground amidst the pile of dust.

From a distance, Samson could hear the dull roar of approval from the other elves, who'd run to the mountain foothills.

But there was no time to celebrate. For, even now, Samson could hear two different, distinct sounds. He'd never heard either, but he could guess. One was a deafening roar, coming at them from the sea. The second was a deep rumbling from the earth.

The earthquake came first. It shook the entire glacier. Samson saw one end of it open up, and the lava begin to flow across the face of the glacier. The roar from the approaching tidal wave grew louder.

"Tristan!" Samson yelled. "Help me carry Regis! A tidal wave is on its way, and we'll need to get to the foothills."

Tristan rushed to Samson's side and, together, they did their best to carry Regis to the mountains. They never even came close to making it, however. The tidal wave crashed down over the mountains on the other side of the glacier before they were even close to the foothills.

"We are coming!" a tiny voice called to them from above. Samson glanced up. The fairies had returned!

Hundreds of them descended on Samson, Regis, and Tristan. They picked them up and carried them high above the glacier just as the waters of the tidal wave swept across the glacier.

38

***

ANSWERS

A strange silence descended on Valhalla as the mighty waters receded and the lava flow either cooled or returned to its subterranean home. The powerful forces of nature had left a much-changed landscape in its wake. The giants were awake again, and the huge structure of Valhalla was again standing tall and proud.

It was everything the legends spoke of, and more. Its massive front gate did, indeed, appear to be able to accommodate hundreds of soldiers marching abreast.

Laura and the dwarves had barely been able to scramble up the mountain slopes as the tidal wave crashed over the top of the mountains across the way in front of them. There, the dwarves and the elves had been reunited. They had not seen each other in centuries. It was a warm reunion, even for races that often fought with each other.

Soon thereafter, the giants came to see them as well. Laura was surprised, and pleased, to see that Jon was with them.

She was even more surprised when the fairies descended from the sky carrying Samson and Regis. It was, indeed, a glorious reunion of old friends and comrades.

Laura couldn't help but marvel at how the races had combined their assault on Valhalla. The people of the sea, as she'd asked, had clearly summoned one final surge of authority over the waters to send the tidal wave to Valhalla. That, combined with the lava flow, had loosed Valhalla.

But now what? Laura wondered. *What would, or could, happen next?*

After visiting at length with Jon and Samson, Laura moved off to one side by herself and pondered the situation. Darkness was falling on Valhalla. They would all need to settle for the night and wait.

Jon joined her a little while later. They both sat there, side by side, and said nothing for the longest time as they watched the shadows lengthen over Valhalla.

They had been through much, both apart and together. They were bound to each other. And yet, they were not really friends or comrades. They had been thrown together by master planners. Their lives had been fused and joined, somehow, in a common cause.

"It is all very strange," Laura said at last, breaking the silence.

"Yes, it is," Jon responded evenly. "So much has happened, I haven't really had much chance to think about it."

They didn't say anything again for several minutes. But the silence was neither uncomfortable nor unpleasant.

"Why?" Laura asked eventually.

"I don't know," Jon said. "I think, at first, we were pawns. We did their bidding by reopening that portal. But, at some point, we found a different path. And others joined us."

Laura looked off into the distance. "You know, I met someone. We talked in the Duke Gardens."

"Who was that?"

"A very small man, a genetic dwarf. His name was Ramiel. I didn't think about it properly at the time...who he was, I mean. But it was Ramiel who first gave me the notion that maybe the races were alive and well on Earth, and that we could find them. But I think he told me that to see what I might already know..."

"Did you say Ramiel?" Jon asked.

"Yes, I believe that was his name."

Jon nodded, seeing it all even more clearly now. "Ramiel is one of the leaders of the *bene elohim,* the sons of God. There are legends and myths that refer to him as the 'god of thunder,' and that he has something to do with the race of dwarves.

"Araqiel was one of them as well. He taught men the signs of the earth. There are others, whose names are not widely known in the world—Semhazah, Baraqyal, Ezeqeel. Their supreme leader—the god of the Earth, the chief accuser—was Azazel, and also El. They each taught humankind of magic, and much else. And they needed us to set them free. But now..."

"We need to seal that door again, don't we?" Laura asked.

"If we can."

"But how? The races are free from their bonds here—or, at least, they have a chance to be. How do we get all of them back to the land? How can we manage that?"

Laura sighed. "I don't know. It wouldn't be practical to take them all back to Duke's campus and go through the portal there, would it?"

"No, it wouldn't. The giants, for one, wouldn't fit. Plus, it just doesn't *seem* like the right way."

Laura looked over at the rest of the group. She caught Samson's eye and motioned for him to join them. Samson begged off from the conversation he was engaged in and sauntered over to where Jon and Laura were sitting.

"What's up?" Samson asked when he'd settled down with them.

"We were just thinking about what we should do next," Laura offered.

"And we have to think big, because of the giants," Jon added.

"That's right." Laura nodded. "We need to find a place that is central, where the magicians would likely gather. For it will be in that place that we are most likely to end what we've begun."

Samson stared hard at his two comrades. "You know, I may have an idea. The dragon mentioned it."

"What is it?" Jon asked quickly.

"Well, when the dragon tried to offer me something, he spoke of a Tree, whose fruit gives you ultimate knowledge of good and evil."

"Yes, in the Garden of Eden," Jon said. "There are two Trees there, one of Knowledge and the other of Eternal Life. But after Adam and Eve ate from the Tree of Knowledge, God sent them away from the Garden of Eden and closed it off to humankind."

"But if the dragon was offering fruit from that tree, then it must now be open to humankind again?" Laura reasoned.

"Yes, it would have to be," Jon agreed. "And perhaps it is. It *would* make sense."

"And how could we possibly find *that*?" Laura asked.

Jon shook his head. "It would be nearly impossible to find. The second chapter of Genesis describes where Eden was, that a river flowed up from the ground—probably from a subterranean ocean—and divided into four rivers from that point. Those rivers were the Tigris, Euphrates, Pishon, and Gihon."

"I've never heard of those last two," Laura said.

"Neither have I," Jon acknowledged. "Pishon flowed around a land called Havilah. Gihon flowed around a land called Cush, which is a part of northeastern Africa that is now Ethiopia."

"And where was the Garden?" Samson asked.

"At the eastern end of Eden," Jon answered. "After God forced Adam and Eve to leave it, he placed the cherubim and a flaming sword which turned every way at the Eastern entrance to the garden to keep anyone from entering it."

"The cherubim?" Laura asked.

"Guardians of sacred places," Jon said. "They have four faces—a man, a lion, an ox, and an eagle."

"Four faces?" Samson asked.

"Yes, representing intelligence, strength, spirituality, and mobility," Jon said.

"What?" Laura asked sharply, knowing the answer to the question now that had nagged at her for some time. "Haven't you ever considered that there must be something that explains why the three of us were chosen for these tasks?"

"No, I can't say I've given it much thought," Jon said.

"Well, I have," Laura continued. "And now I know the answer. We, the three of us, embody the three elements of mankind—Samson, the physical realm; you, the spiritual; and me, the mind."

Jon stared at Laura. "I never thought of it like that. But you may be right."

"I know I am."

"What's this flaming sword east of the garden of Eden?" Samson asked, bringing them back to the task at hand. "And what do you mean that it 'turned every way'?"

"I don't know," Jon confessed. "Jeremiah talked about the sword of the Lord. It obviously cuts down those whom God wishes to destroy, for whatever reason."

"So how can we make it past such a sword?" Samson asked.

"I'm not sure we can," Jon admitted.

"And how can we possibly find this Garden?" Samson asked grimly.

"I think I know the way," Laura mused. "Jon, you said a river flowed from a subterranean ocean and then split to form four rivers?"

"It's only a guess that they flowed from a subterranean ocean, but, yes, that's what I said."

"Then we must go to the people of the sea. They could tell us where that ocean emerged. That would tell us where Eden can now be found."

"And what do we do when we're there?" Samson asked.

"Let's just get there first," Laura said. "We can worry about that when we've arrived, if we do."

"I agree," Jon added. "I have a feeling it will be obvious to us what we'll need to do at that point."

"And the races?" Laura asked.

"They'll need to wait for us, east of Eden, I would think," Jon concluded.

"Are we all agreed, then?" Laura asked. Jon and Samson nodded. "Then let's go tell the others about our plan."

39

* * *

ARAQIEL

Laura, alone, awoke from a troubled dream. Despite all she had learned, she was still uncertain about her choices. She wondered if she would struggle with them for the rest of her life. Araqiel stood beside her, waiting patiently.

"You...?" Laura said, startled. She felt alone, unguarded, in his presence. She could hardly believe her eyes. "We have searched so very long to find you."

"I know," Araqiel said. "And I am still your friend, as I once was."

Laura tried rubbing the sleep from her eyes. It didn't work very well. "You're my friend?"

"Yes, your friend. Nothing has changed. Won't you reconsider? Join us? There is so much we can do together."

Laura closed her eyes, for she knew she could not trust what she saw before her. "I understand, now. But I've chosen the path..."

"The world is not always as it seems," Araqiel interrupted. "You, of all people, should know that. Follow your instincts. Choose what is best for you."

"I am," Laura said. "Truly, I am."

"And you won't let me help you understand this...?"

Laura opened her eyes. "I think I know who you are, and what you offer."

"You do?" Araqiel said gently. "Are you sure?"

"I am a different person now. I am not the same person you met..."

"Are you so very certain of that, Laura?" Araqiel asked a second time.

"Yes, I am." Laura was so very tired. She wanted to rest. She closed her eyes again. "So, please, leave me be."

"As you wish," Araqiel said. "But my offer will remain, always. Nothing will ever change. There will always be an unbreakable bond between the daughters of Eve and the sons of God. You know that. And you, our Eloah, can be the most treasured of all throughout history."

But Laura was already fast asleep. Valhalla had been restored, and the doom of the gods approached. She had done—and heard—enough for one day.

491

40

***

THE GARDEN OF EDEN

It seemed so simple, Laura couldn't help but wonder why others hadn't discovered Eden before now. It was right there, for the whole world to see, in the middle of a handful of warring peoples of the Middle East.

The Garden had been there for centuries, peacefully waiting for those who could see and understand. But, of course, that was the problem. How many tried to see or understand something like that? *Not many,* Laura wagered.

The people of the sea knew right where to send them. They *had* heard of the four rivers Jon had spoken of, and they knew of the subterranean ocean as well. They knew where those four rivers emerged and told him where to find their headwaters.

And there, of course, they would find the Garden of Eden. As simple as that.

Most likely, the people of the sea estimated, the Garden of Eden was shielded by large mountains, for that is where the headwaters of the four rivers flowed down into the plains of the region and, eventually, into the other large bodies of water in the Middle East. The giants could take them there easily, now that Laura knew where to go.

The giants were willing to do almost anything for Jon, Laura, and Samson, who had freed them from their prison of ice. They agreed to take everyone—the dwarves, the elves, even the fairies, if they wanted. The fairies, however, said they would go to Mount Pelion and guide the horses there to the land east of Eden.

"Great!" Jon said excitedly. "Then let's roll."

Without any second thoughts, they all climbed aboard the giants' huge shoulders. The giants cast one longing look at Valhalla and then began the journey. They all felt the end—of something—was now at hand and were anxious to reach it, whatever the consequences.

No one said much during the journey to the mountains that surrounded the Garden of Eden. It wasn't a time for discussion. Everyone instinctively felt that.

Jon was amazed at the giants' ability to remember the route back to the mainland. They swam through the ocean from island to island, navigating by memory, even though it had probably been thousands of years since they'd been this way. The journey took three days and nights—two days to get through the ocean and one day to stride across the land to reach the place Laura directed them toward. They took an extra hour to drop Tristan off at his home and say a simple farewell.

On the mainland, people scattered right and left in terror as the giants strolled through the landscape. But who could blame them? It must have seemed as if gods had descended to earth and begun to walk among them.

In fact, Jon felt sure that it would only be a matter of days, perhaps hours, before several of the countries they walked through mobilized armies against them. That seemed logical. But, hopefully, they would have enough time to make it to Eden and finish their business before Armageddon erupted.

On the dawn of the fourth day, they arrived at the place where the people of the sea said the headwaters of the four rivers emerged from the underground ocean. There were, indeed, mountains rising up around it.

The mountains were not unique. There was nothing that set them apart from other mountains. The land was no different than the rest of the region. The river that cascaded down the side of the mountain they were now facing looked like a hundred other rivers on the Earth.

But no one lived anywhere near the place. The giants surveyed the landscape and there wasn't a house or hint of civilization anywhere near the spot. It was barren of any human activity and looked as if it had always been thus.

The fairies flew up to the clouds to take a closer look. Their report was favorable. There *was* a lush valley shielded on all sides by the tall mountains. There did seem to be fruit trees, of all kinds, growing throughout the valley.

A narrow pass led through two of the tallest mountains, into the valley. It was the only pass into it. All other routes led over the top of the mountains.

"Well?" Jon asked. "Shall we pay a visit to the birthplace of humankind?"

"Yes, if we can." Laura smiled.

The giants and the rest of the races chose to remain behind. This was not their place. This was the cradle of humankind. They would not be welcome.

One of the giants did, however, drop Jon, Samson, and Laura off where the pass between the two tallest mountains narrowed so they wouldn't have far to walk.

The giant offered to go over the top and deposit them in the Garden itself. But Laura said no, that they had to enter on their own. To do otherwise would almost be a sacrilege.

"Well, good luck, then," the giant said before turning to head back down the mountain slope.

Without another word, Laura, Jon, and Samson strode through the pass purposefully. They were all scared. None of them knew what to expect. Perhaps nothing. Perhaps everything.

Jon saw them first. At the point where the pass narrowed most, two outcroppings of rock hung over the pass. But they weren't outcroppings. They were stone statues, carved and jutted out from the rock face.

The two winged statues had four faces—a man, a lion, an ox, and an eagle. The statues of the cherubim were exactly as Ezekiel had described them.

They approached the statues cautiously. When they began to draw near, the statues came to life, as if summoned.

"Who approaches?" one of the cherubim asked, speaking through the man's face.

Jon glanced at Laura and Samson, who nodded. Jon answered. "Three weary travelers who would like to pass."

"No one enters here," the cherubim said, "except the anointed of God."

"Has *no one* ever passed this way since the days of Adam and Eve?" Jon asked.

"None of the sons and daughters of Adam and Eve have entered since God cast them out of this place," the cherubim answered. "Several have tried...and failed."

Jon frowned. There was something strange about that answer. "But others have entered here since then?" he asked finally.

"The *bene elohim* have," the other cherubim answered. "We may not deny them. They may eat of the two Trees. They have eaten of them already, so we cannot deny them."

"But no man or woman has entered this way, is that right?" Jon asked.

"Yes, that is right," the first cherubim answered.

"What must *we* do in order to pass by you and enter?" Jon asked.

"There is nothing you can do," the first cherubim said. "You may not enter. No one can."

"But I thought you said the anointed of God could enter here?" Jon asked.

"Yes, we did," the cherubim answered together.

"And how will you know who has been anointed?" Jon asked.

"Our Creator will tell us," the first cherubim said.

"Could you ask him, then?" Jon asked, his voice nearly a whisper. This was too much to hope for, really. But what choice did he have?

"Certainly," the cherubim said. An instant later, they were returned to stone.

"Should we try to run past them, while they are like this?" Samson asked.

"No!" Jon said firmly. "We will wait for their answer."

"But if they return and say no, what then?" Samson pleaded.

"We'll worry about that later," Jon responded. "We *must* wait for the answer. It's our only hope of passing through."

Samson sighed. "All right. I hope you're right."

The cherubim returned to life, then. "You may pass," the first said simply.

"That's it?" Jon asked, clearly surprised. "We can just walk right in?"

"Yes, you may," the second cherubim said.

Jon glanced at Laura, who shrugged. They began walking. The cherubim, meanwhile, returned to stone and their eternal vigilance.

They walked for what seemed an eternity before stopping again. A huge, menacing, flaming sword—seemingly suspended in midair—blocked their path.

"What now?" Laura asked. "If we try to pass, that thing will probably cut us to ribbons."

"Not necessarily," Jon mused. "The cherubim let us pass. Perhaps this will as well."

They walked forward cautiously. As they began to pass by the sword, the edged blade turned to follow their progress. All three of them kept a nervous eye on the blade as they continued to walk.

But, though it followed their progress, the blade did not fall or challenge them. The flaming sword let them pass. They had entered the Garden of Eden.

In all directions, the Garden was everything any of them had imagined it might look like. A babbling brook coursed through its center. There were fruit trees scattered throughout the valley. The sun shone brilliantly down into the valley. The birds' songs were light and melodious.

The whole place spoke of harmony with the land and nature. It was a truly marvelous place, where cares and sorrows never occurred. It was a place of idyllic peace and rest.

"There it is," Laura said after they had gazed at the lush valley for the longest time.

"What?" Jon asked.

"One of the Trees," she answered, pointing toward the center of the Garden.

Jon and Samson looked at where she was pointing. There was, indeed, a larger tree—taller than the others—in the center of the valley. Its twisted, curving branches literally spread out over the center of the valley. It was, perhaps, the largest, grandest tree they had ever seen on Earth—almost rivaling the One Tree.

"That would be the Tree of Knowledge of Good and Evil, in the center of the Garden. Shall we go?" Jon asked.

"Might as well," Laura answered. "But where is the Tree of Eternal Life?"

Jon shrugged. "It's here somewhere."

They started to walk toward the Tree, but Samson stopped suddenly. "Wait," he said. "I have an idea." Samson turned and walked back toward the entrance to the Garden.

"Where are you going?" Jon called out.

"To get the sword," Samson yelled back.

Jon almost called Samson back, but then thought better of it. Samson knew what he was doing. His instincts were nearly always right on the mark. So he would say nothing.

Samson approached the flaming sword without any hesitation. He walked up to it, grasped its hilt firmly, and walked away. The sword came with him, without protest or injury. The fire dimmed only slightly as he walked along, holding the sword out before him.

"Okay, now I'm ready," Samson said when he had returned.

"You're crazy, do you know that?" Jon said wryly.

"I know." Samson grinned. "But it works, doesn't it?"

"What are you going to do with that thing?" Laura asked.

"Beats me." Samson shrugged. "But it could sure come in handy, don't you think?"

They continued on into the valley, working their way toward the center of the Garden. It didn't take them long. The Garden really wasn't very big.

As they neared the center, they were all surprised to see that the tree was a huge oak, its boughs heavy with very large acorns.

Jon bent down and scooped up an acorn that had fallen to the ground. "You know, I would think these things would be tough to eat." He casually tossed it back to the earth.

The tree was horribly misshapen. A number of its limbs were missing, seemingly torn asunder or ripped off the trunk of the tree. Knobby stumps now grew where the limbs had once grown.

"How very strange," Jon mused.

"No, it isn't strange at all," Laura said. "If men cannot enter here, then the *bene elohim* must have carried the limbs outside the Garden, to the magicians. That's the only way they could have obtained their knowledge."

Jon nodded. "Yes, you must be right. That would make sense."

Laura suddenly turned her head back toward the tree. She stared hard at it for several long moments. Something was falling into place in her mind. Pieces of a very fragmented puzzle were starting to fit together.

Laura looked over at Samson, who still held the flaming sword out in front of him. "Samson," she said, "when you first entered the land, what was immediately near you? Do you remember?"

Samson squinted. "I was in a forest. I woke up under a tree. Then they found me and took me away."

"Was it an *oak* tree, like this one?" she asked.

Samson thought hard. "Yes, I believe it was, now that you mention it."

"And Jon," Laura said, turning to face him, "when you arrived, was there anything unusual nearby, do you remember?"

Jon nodded thoughtfully. "Now that you mention it, there *was* something, the remains of an old oak bucket that I cracked my head on when I awoke in the land."

Laura nodded firmly. "I thought so. I came to the land in a heavy oaken boat. That's the missing link, the key."

"What is?" Jon asked, not seeing the link.

"The oak tree," she answered excitedly. "A limb torn from this tree must have served as the magicians' talisman. In fact, I wouldn't be at all surprised if the land itself didn't spring forth from the limb. This tree—or some part of it—is the one path to and from the land, Annwyn. The roots from the Silver Tree we restored there…"

They all looked again at the knobby stumps on the tree. It certainly had a ring of truth to it.

"A truly astute guess, fair maiden," said a soft-spoken, fourth voice.

All three of them whirled as one to see its author, who was standing in front of a smallish tree less than 50 feet from where they now stood.

The tree itself was rather unimpressive, with leathery leaves, pretty yellow flowers, and oval fruit of some kind. But the creature who stood under it was another matter entirely. He was *very* impressive. He had a sleek, muscular torso, blond hair, a deep, rich tan, and eyes that gleamed like burnished diamonds. He wore only a garment of sewed-together fig leaves, wrapped around his waist. There was a luminous radiance to him, unlike anything the three of them had ever seen.

Jon glanced at Laura and Samson, unsure what to do next. Laura was blushing slightly, embarrassed by the man's near nakedness. Samson was gripping the flaming sword so tightly his knuckles were white.

"How did you enter the Garden?" Jon asked.

"Does it matter how?" the man answered in a smooth, intoxicating voice. "I am here. That is what is most important."

A thought occurred to Jon. "The cherubim said no one had ever entered here before?" he asked suspiciously.

"Until you, that is correct, none of the sons and daughters of Adam and Eve had entered here," the man acknowledged.

"But you are here," Jon challenged.

"I came here after you had entered successfully," the man said.

"Have you been here before?" Jon watched the man carefully as he answered.

The stranger smiled. It was a glorious, radiant smile. The Garden shimmered in its presence. Jon couldn't tell if the creature was the source or the reflection. "I have been many places, in many times," he answered.

Jon was about to ask him again but halted when Samson took a menacing step forward. "Who are you?" Samson growled.

"Easy, my impetuous young friend," the stranger soothed. "All in good time. We have much to discuss first."

"Tell us who you are," Samson said through gritted teeth. "We'll talk later."

The stranger stepped lightly away from the tree he'd been standing under. He reached up and plucked one of the fruit, tore it open, and took a bite. He ate in silence for a time, then finally answered, "I have many names. You might want to think of me as El…"

"The Father of Humanity?" Jon asked, incredulous.

The creature smiled again. "You might say that entire races owe, if not their allegiance and knowledge, then surely their lineage to me."

But Jon was not so easily duped. "Do they also call you the god of this world?"

"Yes, at times."

"Then I know you." Jon's voice quavered with fear. "You are Azazel, leader of the *bene elohim*."

"We have many leaders," Azazel said, feigning modesty.

"I don't think so." Jon blinked furiously. "You were singled out for your role in revealing the secret, hidden mysteries to humankind. The earth was nearly devastated by the works of your teachings. It's why the Great Flood was necessary…"

"An unjust accusation," Azazel said. "But one that was surely made by those who simply did not know any better."

Jon, Laura, and Samson all desperately tried to keep the fear from creeping into their hearts. It was not an easy task.

"You are all afraid of me," said the leader of the legendary *bene elohim*. "Why? What causes that fear? What have I ever done to you to deserve your fear?"

"I don't care what you know, or what you've done. Leave us alone." Jon's voice cracked.

"You *will* care." Azazel's eyes blazed. "I promise you that. You will serve me, for it is in your best interest to do so."

"We will never serve you," Samson said.

"Oh, but you will, when you see what I can offer you, when you see that the choice is between life and death, riches and poverty, glory and oblivion," Azazel said. "It is an easy choice."

Instinctively, Jon, Samson, and Laura moved closer to each other, forming a close triangle. Laura, especially, cowered behind Jon and Samson. For she was, by far, the most vulnerable—and clearly the focus of this creature before them. She was both utterly fascinated and repulsed by him.

"Laura, my lovely, come forward," Azazel said lightly. "Let me tell you something glorious—the promise of what can be with the two of us joined together in this world."

"No," Laura whispered.

"You have no need to fear *me*," Azazel said with a smile. "I won't harm you. My caress is light, my touch benign."

Laura shuddered. "Leave me alone."

He took a step closer. "Laura, Laura, you have so much to learn. Tell me, have you mastered all there is to learn in this world, or do you desire more? Can I help?"

"Stay away from me," Laura answered.

Azazel gestured toward the Tree of Knowledge of Good and Evil. "You know, my Eloah, if you eat of that Tree, you will come to understand what I have faced all of my days. Wisdom can be both good and evil."

"No!" Laura said. "I won't."

"But you have sought wisdom and knowledge all your life," Azazel enticed. "Now is your opportunity to attain the ultimate wisdom, to see and understand what no others before you have ever known. It is a reward so rich, how can you possibly pass it up?"

"Please, just go away and leave me alone," Laura pleaded.

"Take a bite of the fruit, my precious," Azazel encouraged. "You will be as God. I promise you that. Would God deny you that wisdom? Of course not. So take, eat. Your knowledge will know no bounds."

Laura clenched her fists. She *had* wanted this. All of her life. More desperately than she had ever cared to admit. It was probably this very quality that had led the magicians to choose her to forge a path to the land. But Laura had changed. She was different now. She did not serve her own needs as she once had. And that made all the difference in the world.

"No, I will not," Laura answered firmly.

Azazel did not hesitate. Even as Laura was answering him, his gaze had already fixed itself on Jon. "Do you know this tree, Jon? Do you recognize it?" he asked, looking over his shoulder at the small, unimpressive tree.

"No," Jon said dully, his mind partially numbed by the knowledge of what was before him.

"You do not recognize the symbol of all Israel?" Azazel's eyebrows raised in mock surprise.

Jon squinted. "Oh, an olive tree," he said finally.

"Yes, an olive tree it is." Azazel plucked a second fruit from its boughs. He tossed it carelessly in Jon's direction. It fell at Jon's feet.

Jon bent over and picked it up, cradling it in his hands. "What do I do with this?"

Azazel clasped his hands and held them up, as if praying. "Take a bite, my son," he said quietly. "You will be surprised."

"Why?" Jon asked suspiciously.

"For it is from the Tree that caused Adam and Eve to leave paradise," said Azazel, the faintest hint of a smile showing through his clasped hands.

Jon's eyes grew wide. "The Tree of Eternal Life?"

"Take a bite from the fruit, Jon," Azazel commanded, "and eternal life shall be yours. You will be as one of us. An immortal god. You will live forever."

Jon stared at the fruit he now held in his hands. *One bite, and he would live forever? Could it possibly be true?* "This is truly from the Tree of Life?"

"Yes, truly." Azazel laughed easily. "And it is all yours. Take a bite. You will see. You shall live forever."

Jon rolled the small fruit around in his hands. It was tempting to be sure, as tempting as anything he'd ever known. The urge to take a bite was nearly overpowering. But Jon, too, had changed. He had somehow managed to find his way clear of the path of self-destruction. He knew, in his heart, that there was no need to take a bite of this fruit. There was nothing to be gained, really, and everything to lose.

"No, thanks," he said simply. Jon tossed the fruit back toward Azazel. The fruit rolled past the fallen angel, the god of this world, and disappeared into the thick foliage behind the Tree of Life.

But Azazel did not see this. He had already shifted his terrible gaze toward Samson. "So, my turbulent young friend. You have journeyed far, seen much. Have you forgotten your roots, your heritage, so quickly? Say the word, and I will make you lord and conqueror of all you can imagine on earth."

"What are you talking about?" Samson demanded, still brandishing the flaming sword of the Lord before him.

"Revenge. Domination. Power beyond your wildest dreams," Azazel said simply. "Will you forget so easily? Can you just walk away from an opportunity to administer revenge on those who brought destruction on your people? And control any destiny—or land—of your choosing?"

Samson blinked. Angry memories stormed at him. It had been so long since he'd pondered the fate of his people. It had once driven him nearly insane, the wish for revenge. But so much *had* happened. He now had a different heart.

"That is my business," Samson said huskily.

"It can be mine as well," Azazel said firmly, his voice full of resolve. "Join me and I will exact terrible vengeance on your enemies. I will give you domination over lands and people—as much of the earth as you desire. I give you my pledge of honor. They will be yours. The *world* will be yours to control, as you wish."

Samson took a deep breath. There had been a time when he would have gladly sacrificed his own life for the chance at revenge. And the chance to be a lord, a king?

But Samson's heart had changed as well. There was no longer a place for such thoughts within it.

"No!" Samson nearly yelled. "I will not join you. Not now, or ever."

Azazel stepped away from the olive tree. "So none of you will join me?" he asked, his arms held wide. "You will not seek the wisdom that will make gods of you all? You will not eat of this simple fruit and live forever? You will not join the forces that make all humankind tremble with fear?"

Jon, Samson and Laura said nothing. They moved closer together, fearing what might happen.

"You have begun a path for us, the *bene elohim*, and now you will not finish that effort? NO!" Azazel clapped his hands once, hard. A thunderous bolt of lightning came hurtling from him, straight at the three of them.

Instinctively, Samson held the flaming sword before him. The lightning struck the sword and ricocheted off in another direction. The force of the blow nearly knocked Samson to his feet.

"You will be utterly destroyed," Azazel declared. "No one denies me. No one usurps my power. No one spurns my offers. And when you are gone, I will give to the world what the three of you have so foolishly refused. You so graciously opened a path to the land, as we all wished. And now, you have given these to humankind as well…"

"The Trees!" Jon exclaimed. "You will give them to the Earth?"

"Yes, I will!" Azazel said fiercely.

"But they are not yours to give," Jon protested.

"And who will stop me?" Azazel leered.

Without a moment's hesitation, Samson whirled, swinging the flaming sword before him. It was a ferocious swing. The blade struck the base of the Tree of Knowledge of Good and Evil. The force of the blow caused the sharp edge to cut through swiftly, felling it. An instant later, the oak tree crashed, showering acorns in all directions.

"YOU!" Azazel raged. "What have you done? That Tree is our key, to the path. Without it…"

"The portals will close again on you!" Jon shouted.

The world around them began to change. Colors drained or faded. Objects blurred. The world tilted sideways for a moment before righting itself and coming back into focus.

"There, it is done," Samson said. "For all time."

Meanwhile, even as Samson was wielding the sword, in the blink of an eye, Azazel had shape-shifted and transformed himself into a huge serpent. He slithered along the ground toward the three of them.

Samson thrust the sword into Jon's hands. "The second Tree," he whispered fiercely to Jon and then rushed forward to grapple with the serpent. The two were joined in battle instantly, the serpent beginning to coil itself around Samson, who held its ugly head at bay with his considerable strength.

Jon made a move toward the two combatants, as if to join in the battle.

"No, quickly, over to the other Tree!" Laura said insistently. "Before it's too late."

"But…," Jon protested.

"Hurry!" Laura nearly shouted.

Jon cast one longing glance at Samson, locked in mortal combat with the serpent, and then rushed around them toward the Tree of Life. He came to a stop before the diminutive olive tree and swung the blade toward its base, as Samson had done. The blade bit, but did not go through.

"Let me help," Laura offered. "Perhaps if we both try it."

Laura stood by Jon's side and grabbed the hilt. Their hands interlocked. They pulled the sword back and swung a second time.

This time, the blade went through cleanly, toppling the tree. It fell with a crash, showering yellow flowers on them and sending the oval fruit rolling off in all directions.

Laura released the sword into Jon's hands. Jon raced back to where Samson and the serpent still wrestled. Even with all his training, Samson was losing the fight. He had never tried to grapple with a serpent before. There was nothing to hold onto, and the serpent was beginning to wrap its coils around Samson, crushing him.

Jon raised the sword a third time and brought it crashing down on the serpent's tail. The end came off cleanly. No blood gushed out, though. The tail simply fell to one side, and a new tail began to grow back in its place.

It was enough, though, to force the serpent to loosen its grip for a moment and inspect the damage. That was all Samson needed. With one powerful thrust, he pushed himself up and out of the serpent's clutches and jumped to the ground.

Samson took the sword back from Jon. He stepped in front of Jon and Laura, brandishing the sword. The serpent coiled. Its tongue flicked in and out, in and out. But it did not strike. The serpent became the image of a man again.

"You have not won," Azazel said. "You may think you have, but the battle continues. I cannot be defeated so easily. We will find another path." He looked directly at Laura. "And another will gladly, freely, give herself to me as Eloah. We will start again, as it was meant to be."

"You will not find another path here, not through us," Laura said defiantly.

"We will always fight you," Samson added.

"It is hopeless." Azazel sneered.

"For you, perhaps." Jon peered out from behind Samson.

EL

The ancient, timeless leader of the *bene elohim*—who had taught the mysteries to the daughters of men and created the magicians, both old and new—stood there, glaring at the three of them for what seemed like an eternity.

"Until we meet again," Azazel said. He turned, then, and walked out of the Garden, his head held high, his bearing regal. A deadly stillness followed in his wake.

"What now?" Jon asked after a time.

"I think it is time for the races to go home, to the land, before the magic fades away," Laura answered. "If I'm not mistaken, their time on Earth is now over."

41

* * *

UNDER THE RAINBOW

Samson's sharp ears heard the sound of the approaching helicopters first. The troops were on their way, descending on the races who had gathered to the east of Eden.

Laura decided that they needed six boughs from the Tree of Knowledge of Good and Evil, now lying on its side. Samson quickly lopped off one of its limbs and chopped it into six boughs. Jon, Laura and Samson then carried two each with them back to the races.

They walked solemnly down the pass that led from the Garden of Eden. Samson carefully left the flaming sword of the Lord hanging in midair in the spot from which he'd taken it. They walked past the stone cherubim, who said nothing to them as they left.

All six of the races were gathered together, waiting for their three champions, at the bottom of the mountains. While they'd been in the Garden, the giants had brought the people of the sea to the river. The fairies, meanwhile, had guided the horses of Mount Pelion, along with the dwarves and elves.

Silently, without explanation, they handed the six boughs from the Tree of Knowledge to one member from each of the races. A dozen fairies had to accept their bough. One of the horses from Mount Pelion took the bough in his mouth.

Even as they were handing out the boughs, the sound of the approaching helicopters and advancing armies grew louder. It would only be a matter of time before the troops descended on this place.

"*Thank you, Laura,*" one of the mermaids said to her as she handed over the bough. "*We will never forget you.*"

Nor will I ever forget you, and what you have taught me, Laura answered.

"Thank you!" boomed the giants in chorus as Laura handed them their bough.

"You're welcome!" she yelled up at them with a smile.

"You may visit Avalon whenever you like," one fairy said to Jon as he handed over a bough. "It is your domain now, to rule over as you wish."

Jon bowed. "Thank you for the kind offer. I will take you up on it, if I am able."

As Jon handed the bough over to the horses, they pawed the ground to salute him. Jon nodded solemnly in return.

The dwarves gathered around Samson as he handed them their bough. "You are the greatest warrior the world has ever known," one of the dwarves said to him. "Thank you for fighting on our behalf."

"It was my pleasure to serve you," Samson beamed.

Samson turned to Regis, then. The two friends embraced. Both fought back the tears that would come shortly if they did not part soon.

"I will miss you, my friend," Regis said, his voice choking with the emotion of the moment.

"And I will miss you," Samson answered. "Rule well."

"I shall try," Regis pledged. "The elves will never forget what you have done for them. I can promise you that."

Samson stepped back and, with a slight nod, handed over the sixth and final bough to Regis and the elves. As the bough left Samson's hand and was transferred to the last of the races, the world tilted on its side yet again.

Immediately before them, spanning both sides of the river, a huge rainbow appeared. It was large enough that the giants could all walk through without stooping. They would carry the people of the sea with them.

And on the other side of the rainbow, Jon, Laura, and Samson could clearly see the world they'd journeyed to not so long ago. They could see that the land had changed already. Tara, Kathryn, Lucas, Mark, and the others had been busy.

"You must go, now, while you still have the chance," Laura insisted.

The horses turned and raced through the opening under the rainbow. As they entered the other side, they were transformed instantly into their true selves, the centaurs. They all turned and shouted their thanks with their newfound voices.

The giants gathered up the people of the sea, took two steps, and they were under. The fairies flew as one to the other side. The dwarves and the elves weren't far behind.

Only Regis lingered a little while longer. "I have to ask before I leave," he said quietly, gazing at all three of them, "what will you do, now that your long quest is over?"

They looked at each other. Jon shrugged, speaking for all of them. "Whatever is asked of us, I guess. Time will tell."

Regis smiled. "Fair enough. Now I must be on my way as well. Until we meet again." He turned and was gone. The rainbow began to dim as Regis crossed over to the other side.

Samson, Jon, and Laura watched their friends fade from view. Moments later, the portal they had opened to the magicians' world closed, forever.

ABOUT THE AUTHOR

Passion. Integrity. A Relentless Searcher for Truth. An Ever-Inquiring Mind.
A Dynamic Force for Change in Today's World.

Jeff Nesbit has written 20 inspirational and commercially successful novels for publishing houses, including his latest blockbusters, *Jude, Peace,* and *Oil,* for publishing houses such as David C. Cook, Tyndale, Zondervan, Thomas Nelson, Harold Shaw (now WaterBrook/Random House), Victor Books (now part of David C. Cook), Hodder & Stoughton, and Summerside/Guideposts.

Formerly VP Dan Quayle's communications director at the White House, Jeff was a national journalist with Knight-Ridder, ABC News' Satellite News Channels, and others, and director of public affairs for the National Science Foundation and the Food and Drug Administration. His public affairs consulting firm, Shiloh Media group, represented more than 100 national clients, such as the Discovery Channel networks, Yale University, the American Heart Association, the Robert Wood Johnson Foundation, and the American Red Cross. They helped create and launch three unique television networks for Discovery Communications, Encyclopedia Britannica, and Lockheed Martin, and developed programming and a new cable TV network concept for The Britannica Channel; global programming partnerships for the successful launch of the Discovery Health Channel, including a novel CME programming initiative and the Medical Honors live broadcast from Constitution Hall; and programming strategies for the creation of the first-ever IPTV network developed by Lockheed Martin. Jeff was the co-creator of the Science of the Winter Olympics and the Science of NFL Football video series with NBC Sports that won the 2010 Sports Emmy for best original sports programming, as well as the *Science of Speed,* a novel video series partnership with the NASCAR Media Group.

Jeff is Executive Director for Climate Nexus, Managing Director of OakTara (www.oaktara.com), Strategic Advisor and Cofounder of Thrive Sports/Thrive Entertainment Network, and writes a weekly science column for *U.S. News & World Report* called "At the Edge" (www.usnews.com/news/blogs/at-the-edge).

www.oaktara.com